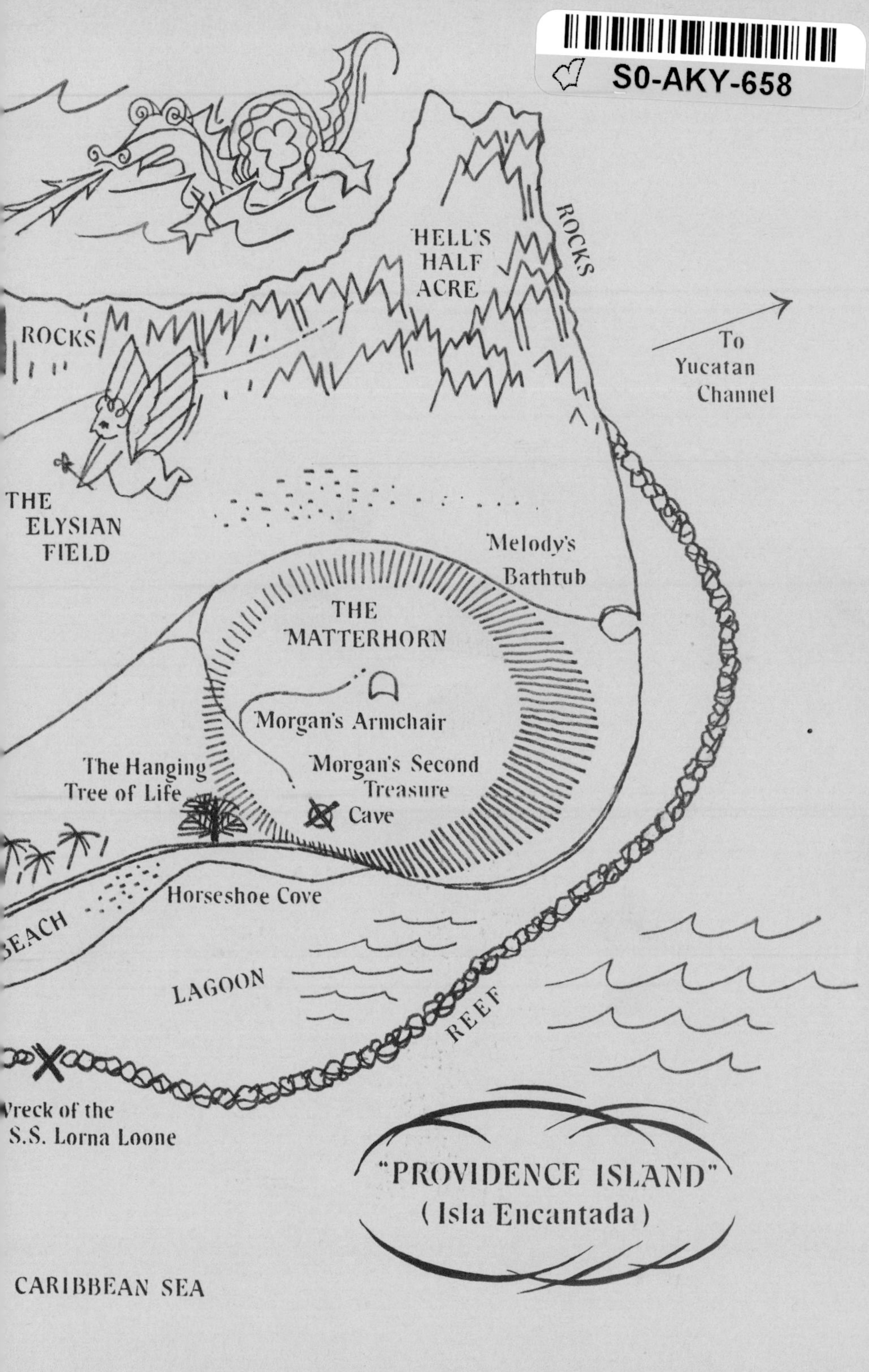
HELL'S
HALF
ACRE
ROCKS
ROCKS
To
Yucatan
Channel
THE
ELYSIAN
FIELD
Melody's
Bathtub
THE
MATTERHORN
Morgan's Armchair
The Hanging
Tree of Life
Morgan's Second
Treasure
Cave
Horseshoe Cove
EACH
LAGOON
REEF
Vreck of the
S.S. Lorna Loone
"PROVIDENCE ISLAND"
(Isla Encantada)
CARIBBEAN SEA

PROVIDENCE ISLAND

NOVELS BY CALDER WILLINGHAM

End as a Man **1947**
Geraldine Bradshaw **1950**
Reach to the Stars **1951**
Natural Child **1952**
To Eat a Peach **1955**
Eternal Fire **1963**
Providence Island **1969**

PROVIDENCE ISLAND

Calder Willingham

Author of "End as a Man,"
"Eternal Fire," etc.

The Vanguard Press, Inc.
New York

Published simultaneously in Canada by the
Copp Clark Company, Ltd., Toronto

Designer: Ernst Reichl

Manufactured in the United States of America

Library of Congress Catalogue Card Number: 68–8088

This book is for Jane

Hey Jude, don't make it bad,
take a sad song and make it better.
Remember to let her into your heart,
then you can start to make it better.

—John Lennon & Paul McCartney

CONTENTS

PART SIX ST. VALENTINE'S DAY

PART SEVEN MIDSUMMER NIGHT

PART EIGHT INDEPENDENCE DAY

PART NINE EASTER

PART ONE
Halloween

ONE

Wreckage

On a recent clear September morning, marred by only a trace of saffron haze suspended in the air over Manhattan Island, James Kittering sat at his desk in a large office and made a little paper airplane. As he worked on the airplane, he drank coffee, smoked cigarettes, and answered phone calls. Jim had always had the ability to do different things at the same time, such as patting his head and rubbing his stomach.

Shortly before eleven, Jim picked up the telephone and pressed a button to signal his secretary in the small private anteroom outside.

"Susan? Come in here, honey."

The airplane was finished. A few jokes would pass the time until Florence Carr and Al Ingerman arrived—a bit of sport, a little raillery, anything to ignore the wreckage; and "wreckage" was the word, although Jim was not quite ready to admit it.

On the face of it, Jim Kittering's situation hardly seemed desperate. Aside from the fact that he earned a great deal of money, fate had bestowed upon him precious blessings. He had a beautiful wife ten years his junior, two lovely children, and a poodle. At forty-two, he looked younger than his age and his health was good, despite certain distressing symptoms caused by too many cigarettes, too much alcohol, and too much stress. He had sound white teeth, all his own hair, and a naturally ingratiating smile, plus honest gray eyes in which there did not seem to be the slightest bit of meanness or deceit.

Furthermore, and this was very important to him, people liked him; both men and women found him charming and witty. In the opinion of his friends and acquaintances, the only defect in Jim Kittering was a certain moodiness that came upon him occasionally. "There's a funny quirk in Jim," they sometimes said.

But in the view of practically everyone acquainted with him, this moodiness was a minor foible, just as his excessive love for his wife and daughters was a foible. He worshiped his wife and doted ridiculously on his two girls and this was peculiar. No one, however, doubted Jim Kittering. He was a brilliant success in the prime of life and he had it all.

"Good God," said Jim aloud. "Where's that girl, anyhow?"

Making herself pretty for the boss, beyond a doubt, although by now she seemed close to writing him off as a bad bet. Apparently, the only thing that kept her in there was her profound conviction that any man clever enough to earn a hundred thousand dollars a year could not be all bad.

"Hell," said Jim, reaching for the phone. As he did so, the door to the small anteroom opened. Hawk-nosed Susan stood there, fresh whitish lipstick on her mouth and shoulders back to emphasize her sole good feature: full, widely spaced, uptilted breasts.

"Yes?"

"Take a look if you want to see something beautiful."

"Is that what you called me in here for?"

"Yes."

"That's all you wanted?"

"Isn't it enough?" asked Jim. "Look, Susan. It's based on a new and superior aeronautical design. This thing could soar practically all the way down the corridor to the elevators."

"It's a great paper airplane," Susan said, and turned and walked across the shaggy white rug toward the anteroom door.

"Wait a minute, Susan. I have a confession to make."

Slowly, the girl turned around, put her hands on her hips, and walked back to the desk. "Okay, what is it?"

"I really called you in here to ask you to hold my hand so I won't jump out the window and fall thirty-four floors to my death. We have a terrible litterbug problem in New York, Susan. Do you realize this town is filthier than Calcutta?"

"I know it's pretty filthy."

"Besides, think of the poor street cleaners, vomiting and fainting and everything."

"Uh-huh."

"But I guess it's too much to ask, isn't it?"

"Oh, I don't know. Anything to save a life."

Jim smiled. "You're making a mistake not to admire this airplane," he said, "but I appreciate the fellow feeling behind your offer to hold my hand."

The situation was out of control already. How had he gotten into such a supercilious conversation so fast? The girl's hands were still insolently on her hips and now an angry glitter was in her eyes. Her mouth was twisted with a resentment out of all proportion, he felt, to his mild joking around. But Jim had forgotten something. An unpleasant shock ran through him as the girl, with a tiny but perceptible movement, thrust her pelvis forward and said in a tone of heavy irony: "I seem to remember holding your hand already. Or was I dreaming maybe?"

The thing he had forgotten was that a week before he had taken off her pants and had intimate relations with her on the couch. Even so, it was a piece of outrageous impudence. What was the matter with the fool girl? Jim smiled wistfully and replied, "All of life is a dream, Susan."

"Yeah, I guess so. Ha ha. I was dreaming."

"This is no joking matter, Susan. The dividing line between dream and reality is as subtle and elusive as a cherub's fart. It is *there* and yet it is *not* there. A little stinky wisp of purity, if you know what I mean."

"That's a new one. I thought I'd heard all your gags, but *that* is a new one."

A fool thing to do, thought Jim. Philosophical speculation had been his undoing. He had wanted to know if those full, widely spaced, uptilted breasts were real. Unfortunately, they were, and so was the rest of her. Jim smiled and said, "I have many gags of which you know not, Susan."

"Uh-huh. Well, to me, that's insulting. Is that what you called me in here for, to insult me?"

"Holy Hannah. Should I cut my throat now or later? Far from calling you in here to insult you, Susan, I called you in here to *con*sult you."

"Look, I don't have to take insults from you or anyone else. I'm free, white, and twenty-one."

"Really?" asked Jim. "Are you implying that I'm a slave, black, and forty-two?"

The girl blinked as the tip of her pink tongue came out and moistened the pale lipstick on her upper lip. Now a look of worry was in her eyes; it was plain she felt she had gone too far. Solemnly she said, "I'm not implying anything, Mr. Kittering. I'm just saying what I think straight from the shoulder."

"Mr. Kittering? What's this Mr. Kittering stuff? You've been calling me Jim for a month."

"Well, this is a serious conversation. And I'm *not* implying anything, I'm just saying what I think, honestly, because it's the only way I know how to be."

"And an admirable trait it is," he said. "Actually, you're two-thirds correct. I'm a slave and I'm forty-two, but I'm *not* black, Susan. You just *think* I am."

In bewilderment, the girl peered at him from beneath lowered lashes, as if considering the possibility he might have Negro blood despite gray eyes, fair skin, and light brown hair. "I never thought any such thing," she answered. "And . . . and I must say, some of my best friends are colored, including girls in this very building."

"In this very building?"

"Yes."

"Um-hmm, convenient they're not on the next block. You'd have to walk a ways to rub butts with them."

The girl's pink tongue came out again and moistened the whitish lipstick as she thought it over. He was sure she would object to "that kind of talk," but she took another tack. "You can think what you want, Mr. Kittering. But to me, prejudice is un-American."

"A splendid sentiment, Susan, but you're not being logical. How can I be a prejudiced un-American bigot and a black nigger simultaneously?"

"What?"

"First you imply I am black, by ostentatiously calling my attention to your own whiteness. Then, when I deny I am black, you insinuate I am anti-Negro by piously declaring that some of your best friends are colored and prejudice is un-American. The two don't go together, honey. I might be a beefy sheriff with the Confederate flag wrapped around my ass, or I might be a misfortunate nigger with a slice of watermelon in my lap and a rope around my neck, but I can't be *both*."

Briefly, Jim felt sorry for her. She was even more dim-witted than he had believed. The mixture of confusion, hostility, and fear on her face was ludicrous. Fear predominated. Susan, who was not as yet a permanent employee, liked her job; she considered it very glamorous and exciting. The celebrities who came to the office awed her to the core. And now she had called the boss a slave, a nigger, a bigot, and a lot else, or at least he thought she had. Somehow she had gone too far and the ax would soon fall. As Jim stared at the girl and read her transparent thoughts, a sadistic impulse took hold of him. It was not enough to taunt and tease and frighten her. He wanted blood.

"Look, Mr. Kittering. I . . . I don't know what I said, but all I meant, all I really wanted was a little politeness. I think I deserve that much, especially since what happened the other afternoon."

"Um-hmm," said Jim.

"I don't know what kind of girl you think I am, but I don't *do* that sort of thing. I mean, very seldom."

"Listen, Susan," said Jim gently. "You've misunderstood me and I think I'd better stop joking around. Maybe I carried the teasing too far. The reason I actually called you in here was to tell you I've sent a memo to Personnel recommending that you be given permanent-employee status and a ten-dollar raise. You've done a good job for me since you've been here, and I appreciate it."

Perfect. With satisfaction, Jim observed the flustered look in the girl's eyes and the slow spread of a blush in her cheeks. Finally she pulled herself together. "Thank you. Thank you very much."

Jim smiled. "And let me say, if my jokes offended you, I'm sorry. I guess I *was* a little crude there."

"Oh, no, no," she answered, "not really. I . . . I was a little crude myself."

So far, so good—but then it was Jim's turn to be surprised. The girl suddenly smiled with a naturalness, warmth, and feminine appeal he never would have dreamed possible. The change in her was so remarkable it was like an hallucination. A bleak black-and-white view of the Kalahari Desert at midnight had been swiftly replaced by a color transparency of the Alps at dawn. It was impossible. The nasty, superficial, heartless little creature did not have it in her to smile like that.

But her smile, jolting though it was, was not the most astonishing thing. To his amazement, he saw a pinkish film of tears start in her eyes. Impossibility compounded! What could make her smile in such a way and show such emotion? An awful thought, an awful suspicion came into his mind. Was it possible Susan was not a cold-blooded and calculating little bitch at all, but a naive girl foolishly in love with the boss? Could she have told the truth when she said she didn't "do that sort of thing," except "very seldom"? Could this account for her hostility, her injured brooding, and perhaps in some measure for her dim-witted confusion? Jim lowered his eyes in embarrassment. As he studied the blotter on his desk, he heard a meek whisper: "Anyhow . . . thank you again."

"Not at all," said Jim. He did not quite dare look up as she tiptoed out; she might see his astonishment and his disgust with himself. The girl had fooled him completely. Of course she had a crush on him; that was why she had believed him and swallowed whole his cruel lie. The promotion and raise were only incidental to her. He had liked her: that was the meaning of her smile and her tears. Susan was no cold-blooded slut, but another struggling and suffering human being exactly like himself.

A grating noise filled the room, a kind of *cr-r-runge*, as Jim turned in his chair, inclined his head, and ground his teeth together. It was a bad habit. The dentist had warned him that if he did not stop it he would wear away the enamel and also get periodontal trouble, but he ground his teeth even when loaded with barbiturates and it drove his wife crazy in the dark night to listen to him. Probably he would soon have to wear to bed a prosthesis, a corrective contraption of leather and stainless steel strapped around his head and stuck in his mouth. Either that or change his way of living.

Jim Kittering shook his head, as if pestered by a swarm of gnats. "To hell with it," he said aloud. It was all garbage, and he was damned if he would be robbed after all that effort. A sick weakness came in his knees as he opened a drawer, took out a sheet of paper, and inserted it into the I.B.M. electric on its stand by the desk. Briefly, he collected his thoughts, then with swift sure skill typed out the memo.

September 11

TO: Personnel
FROM: James Kittering
RE: Miss Susan La Chance

It is my recommendation that Miss La Chance be dismissed immediately.

During the seven weeks she has been in my employ I have found her surly, fresh, lazy, and incompetent. On a number of occasions she has been rude on the telephone to important callers. On an even greater number of occasions she has been abrupt, negative, and unhelpful, if not openly rude.

Aside from her poor handling of her telephone responsibility, the girl makes a bad personal impression. She is not unkempt and is reasonably attractive, but her choice of clothing is tasteless, vulgar, and provocative. A more serious shortcoming is the sullen manner with which she greets people who come to the office, unless she recognizes them either as attractive males or "celebrities," in which cases she is either aggressively flirtatious or embarrassingly gushy.

Repeatedly, despite friendly but firm orders to the contrary, she has asked for autographs, and twice she has demanded signed photographs. But the aggressive flirtation is worse. Although the girl is young and inexperienced, her moral attitude seems to leave something to be desired. Messenger boys linger as flies linger in the vicinity of sugar; and conversation with them is so absorbing that the phone goes unanswered and letters go untyped. Unfortunately, she does not confine her flirtation to messenger boys—any good-looking or important male visitor between twenty and sixty is subject to hoydenish posturing and "come hither" smiles, again despite friendly but firm admonitions to cease and desist. One tires of being a cautionary Daddy to a sullen child, especially a sullen child who cannot or will not keep her mind on her work.

In view of the extreme difficulty these days of obtaining suitable help, I am reluctant to write this memo and thus add another small problem to the many problems of Personnel. For that reason, I have taken the pains to express my views fully, clearly, and unmistakably. Since Miss La Chance's probationary period expires soon, and since I do not feel this young lady at her present level of maturity has anything positive to contribute to the organization, it is my considered responsibility at this time to recommend her dismissal.

JAMES KITTERING

Carefully, Jim read through the memo. The girl herself, of course, would never see it; but she would know, oh yes, she would know, and that was the beauty of the whole thing. When she came in tearful consternation with the slip from Personnel, he would smile sadly and say, "I'm sorry, Susan, I tried. But I guess they just don't rate you very highly down at Personnel. If you ask me, they're a bunch of jerks."

Personnel, of course, would not fire her against his wishes and she would know it. The sad smile would throw her off long enough to get her out of the office and down the corridor. In the elevator what had really happened would dawn on her. A great little trick. Jim had picked it up from his boss, a man known to one and all as "the Goblin," but he had never actually used it before. She would be demolished. There would be nothing left of the little bitch but bits of wreckage.

TWO

Garbage

The word "garbage" had a special place of honor in the vocabulary of James Kittering. He used it to describe the love life of the Goblin, the burgeoning product of the American economy, the statements of political figures, both local and national, the dialogue written for feature motion pictures and for television drama, the flowers of Mother's Day and the toys of Santa Claus, the moral prohibitions based on Judeo-Christian ethics, the efforts of philosophers and artists to grapple with truth and beauty, and many, many other things. He loved the word, relied on it, and played games with it.

Jim Kittering often played games with words and he often played games with himself, most of them silly and without apparent point. Certain games he played, however, fell into a different category; they were serious and dangerous. "Kidding Along Linda" was a dangerous game and "Tailing the Goblin" was another dangerous game. Although he was worried sick about his wife Linda and although he feared the Goblin as he feared death itself, these games had a fascination for him and he could not stop playing them. So far, he had had some hair-raising close calls but had never yet lost either "Kidding Along Linda" or "Tailing the Goblin."

On this clear morning marred by mere traces of murk suspended above the towers of Gotham, he had a premonition, an awful foreknowledge that he soon would lose *both* these games, which would be a catastrophic and shattering double disaster.

In the first place, he could not afford to lose his job. For some years he had spent, or otherwise disposed of, twenty to twenty-five thousand dollars more than he earned, thus he was monstrously in debt. The big money he made had no meaning; he was so encumbered and entangled with mortgages, loans, and debts that his actual financial condition was worse than that of a pauper.

He owed money to the private school attended by his daughters. He owed money to department stores, to his art dealer, and to the newsboy who delivered the *Times* to his home in New Jersey. Finally, he owed a small fortune to Linda's grandmother, a wealthy and crotchety woman who had declared she would not lend him another penny even if he crawled on broken glass seven miles to ask for it.

His financial situation had become a screaming nightmare. To be fired by the Goblin was unthinkable. Jim, however, had no illusions it could not happen; he knew very well the power-crazed, whimsical, and fiendishly sadistic man for whom he worked. To provoke the Goblin, to be caught tailing him, would mean the loss of his job and total financial ruination.

In the second place, if to be fired by the Goblin was unthinkable, then the loss of his wife was both unthinkable and unendurable. This had been brought home to him with an especial poignance that very morning, as he listened to her weeping in the bathroom at five A.M. To lose his job meant financial ruination, but the loss of his wife meant the end of everything. If Linda left him, he would get dead drunk and blow out his brains.

But he kept on playing the games anyhow. It was a mystery to him why he behaved toward his wife as he did, but he felt he understood his compulsion to pin a forked tail on John Terrence Hobson. It was simple—the man was a horrible son of a bitch, that was why. Jim liked to say of the Goblin: "Everything he touches turns into garbage. The revolting swine has a perverted Midas touch." Besides which, the awful bastard tormented those in his power, made his own wife participate in disgusting orgies, and did all kinds of dreadful, nasty things. What else could one do but hate such a monster and pin a forked tail on him in various subtle ways?

"Eccc-ch!" said Jim, as a rattlesnake buzz interrupted his second perusal of the memo to Personnel. The thing had an aesthetic glow and he was reluctant to tear himself away from it, just as an admirer of oriental architecture would be reluctant to stop staring at the Taj Mahal after a long hot trip through the dust and heat of India. The nicest part was that, although none of the comments on Susan was wholly untrue, the memo considered in totality was an absolute and monstrous lie. It was a solid job of demolition; not so elegant, perhaps, as the Goblin would have done, but one could hardly hope to equal the inspired art of the Goblin himself, one could only hate and emulate it.

Again the phone on the desk buzzed like a rattlesnake. Jim sealed the memo in an envelope and dropped it in the out box with a slight shudder, convinced he had committed an act of satanic destruction. But in reality he had done no such thing. Jim was merely playing a game. He would later take the envelope from the out box, tear it into tiny pieces, and flush the pieces down the toilet of his private bathroom; then he would write another memo praising Susan as convincingly as he had damned her. That was the trouble with him; unlike the Goblin, he had chickenshit in his blood and always shrank back at the last moment. Susan would get her promotion to permanent-employee status and a ten-dollar raise exactly as promised.

To all appearances, a silly and pointless game, indeed. Jim tried, he really and truly tried, but something always stopped him, something he could not put his finger on except in terms of disappointed invective.

Once again the telephone buzzed, but Jim continued to sit staring with haunted absorption at the memo in the out box. For all his glibness, which was immense, there had always been a streak of honesty in him; and for all his cynicism, which was profound, there had always been in him an odd quixotic concern for elemental questions of right and wrong. Such a man was bound, sooner or later, to get into serious trouble. Time and the contradictions of his own character had caught up with James Kittering.

The anteroom door opened and Susan looked in. "Oh," she said. "I thought maybe you were in the bathroom. Is anything wrong?"

"What?"

"I'm sorry, you didn't answer. There's a call for you."

"I know. Who is it?"

"It's your wife."

"Oh, Christ," said Jim. "Tell her I'm in a meeting."

"Well . . . it's the third time she's called."

"I know it's the third time she's called, honey. Tell her I'm in a meeting."

"All right . . . I'll tell her." Still agitated by the genuine-phony-genuine promotion, which she had naively but correctly taken to be genuine in the first place, Susan backed out of the room, blushing. A moment later she returned, blushing more. "Oh, I'm sorry, I forgot. The Goblin called too. But . . . ah-h, when I pushed the on button to tell him you must be in the bathroom, there was nobody on the wire."

Jim clenched his jaw. *Il silenzio* again. It was the second time in two days. "Are you sure it was Hob?"

Of course, it was not so bad to have it done to one's secretary. The worst thing was to receive *il silenzio* direct, to listen to the hum of wire static and the faint soughing of his breath.

"I ought to know that nasty whisper of his by now," she answered. "It was the Goblin all right."

"Listen, Susan. The name is *Mister* Hobson. Please don't refer to him again as the Goblin in my presence, if you don't mind."

"Well, . . . I'm sorry . . ."

"I know, I know," said Jim. "Everybody in the building calls him that. But do me a favor; please don't call him that in front of me, okay?"

"Sure, of course. I . . . I'll tell your wife you're in a meeting."

"Yes, please do," said Jim. For the moment, under the strain of realizing the Goblin was still after him, he had forgotten Linda. A sudden image flashed into his mind, a nightmare vision of trousers dropped to gartered calves and an evening gown bunched high above bare breasts. He'd wondered in a daze where her bra might be until it dawned on him she hadn't even worn one, and no panties or girdle either. Not many women had such a figure after two children. Of course she was only thirty-two and stress had had the peculiar effect of making her even more beautiful. Before, like many rich girls, she had had a doll-like prettiness, but no more; she now had the sad beauty of a woman in pain, a woman who sobbed in a towel in the bathroom in the gray hours of dawn. Jim shook his head and quickly picked up the little paper airplane he had made earlier that morning. It was a thing he would not think about. He flinched as the phone buzzed again.

"Yes, Susan?"

"That writer is here, and her agent."

Disconcerted, Jim sat forward. "*What* writer?" he asked.

"That Carr woman."

Jim winced. "For God's sake, Susan. Don't refer to her as 'that Carr woman' to her face, honey. I need this person, I need her desperately—"

"Oh, she isn't here. The front receptionist called in. But I think I hear them now coming down the hall."

"Thank God. Now, let me explain, Susan. This woman thinks she's famous. She isn't, but she thinks she is."

"They're here now. They just walked in."

"Don't refer to them as 'they,' honey. Would you refer to Charles de Gaulle and his Minister of Finance as 'they'? And De Gaulle's a piker compared to her, as she sees it. He's a mere politician, but she's an artist and a genius—much more important."

"They're here. I mean . . . ah-h . . ."

"Listen, and you'll learn. The thing to say is, breathlessly, '*Florence Carr* is here!' Like the *Angel Gabriel* is here. Understand?"

"Yes, I think so. Ah-h . . . Florence Carr is *here*."

"Oh, God," groaned Jim. "I didn't mean *now*, I meant *next* time. And holy Hannah, what a delivery. But never mind, don't get flustered. Bring her in, Susan. Bring her in with a toothy smile."

Jim hung up the phone and took the last cigarette from a pack he had started when he first sat at his desk that morning. As he held his lighter to the cigarette, he glanced at a photograph of his wife in a silver frame by his desk calendar. He liked square touches of this kind, and besides, he was proud of Linda's beauty. People often thought it was a picture of a movie actress and would ask, "Who's that?" The golden hair, wide blue eyes, and serene smile were flawless, perfect. But of course she didn't look like that any more. No. The hair and eyes were the same, but the serene smile had got lost somewhere.

Jim shook his head and scrounged out the cigarette, which tasted a bit like a rat's ass, or as he imagined a rat's ass might taste if one should taste it. And such a thing was not totally impossible. In effect, it was what had happened the night before. Disgusting. He'd never liked that idiot Herb in the first place. The man's lechery was coarse and nauseating and his puerile vanity about his prowess made it a hundred times worse. He was a lewd rat and a fool besides, without even enough brains to lock a door. That was the most imbecilic thing of all; the door had had a lock.

Jim put the palm of his hand on his forehead, which was damp with perspiration. There was no point in denying the truth. It had been a very unfortunate little accident; nothing cosmic, nothing to get hysterical about, the world was still turning on its axis—but it was unfortunate. The night before at a party he had looked for Linda and could not find her, and since he was tired and half drunk and knew she could get a ride, he decided to go on home without her. He'd gone to the bedroom where they had the coats and he had not noticed—he really and truly hadn't—a chair ineffectually stuck under the knob of the door. And so he found Linda. She was there on the bed among the hats and coats, her evening gown up above her breasts and the host of the party on top of her, trousers around his ankles and going great guns. Jim could not have intruded at a more indelicate moment. They were in the very throes of orgasm; she had glared furiously at him over Herb's shoulder and made a choking sound, unable to speak.

He was speechless himself, for that matter. Jim prided himself on being calm and mature on questions involving the human sexual drive and never would have expected to react as he did. The thing hit him with the impact of a bull whip. He had known his wife went to bed with other men, just as she knew he himself went to bed with other women, but such abstract knowledge was a feeble thing in comparison to the raw reality before him. His reaction was totally emotional and irrational. Linda, of all people! Linda, his wife, the mother of his children! Linda, who'd been an innocent and naive virgin when she married him! And look at her now, stockinged heels locked over Herb's calves, her small hands gripped like pale claws on his hairy behind, her body heaving in a frenzy to meet and receive his billy-goat thrusts—it was ghastly, appalling, unspeakable. Was this what it meant to be realistic and sensible about sex, was this the consequence of a mature understanding between a man and his wife not to smother each other with Victorian possessiveness? Undoubtedly, yes—and there should not be anything so horrible about it, either. But there *was* something horrible about it, something utterly horrible, something unreckoned by sensible maturity. As he gazed in shock at the relentless, monomaniacal double-backed animal on the bed, Jim feared he might faint. It had taken him at least five seconds to back out of there and shut the door.

Jim looked up as Florence Carr and her agent entered the office, led by a smiling Susan. Briefly, he could not collect himself—who was this freckle-faced, bucktoothed woman with the sleek little man in the raw silk suit? Jim stared at them empty-eyed. That was the trouble the night before; the thing had stunned him and he could not collect himself. First he had sulked in a corner, resisting a childish impulse to punch Herb in the nose; and then, worse, much worse, in the car going home he had tried to joke about it. "Well, Herb was pretty cool," he said. "As far as I could see, he didn't even lose stroke." Linda, who was staring straight ahead in somber silence, did not answer. Early that morning, around five A.M., he heard her crying in the bathroom. It was sad. For all her sexiness, liberation was not for Linda. If she had married a different kind of man, a man who would have insisted on fidelity instead of giving her freedom, she would have controlled her sexiness and been a faithful and happy wife. Sex was her weakness, as it was the weakness of countless women in a barbaric civilization consecrated and dedicated to power.

But Linda herself was not a weak person and she was not a fool; she would have mastered herself and there would have been a certain beauty in her control. It was a square idea, no doubt, but what was more beautiful than the faithful love of a truly passionate woman? He had denied them both an opportunity to achieve something above and beyond the gluck of materiality in which they drowned. And for what? What had they gained for the thing they had lost? A ragtail and bobtail of empty passing pleasure that made life a miasmic swamp without a path. That was all. He had robbed himself and corrupted his wife for nothing.

And "corrupt" was the word. As things stood, Linda had no incentive and no chance. The combination of desire, alcohol, and a permissive husband overwhelmed her. What did she have to lose, why attempt to control herself, why not go to parties without her panties and have a little fun and excitement? But it didn't work, it couldn't work. Liberation was not for Linda. Invariably, her underlying shame and misery erupted into hysterical despair and forced him to pacify her with the Let's Reform discussion, the basic ploy of "Kidding Along Linda." But it could not continue much longer. She had become harder and harder to cope with as one Herb followed another. It was sad. The more emancipated she became, the more wretched and guilt-stricken was Linda.

And Jim was not so happy himself. As he lay there at five in the morning and listened to the sound of his wife's sobs muffled by a bath towel, an ache came in his throat and he had to fight an impulse to get up, go into the bathroom, and ask her to forgive him for the hideous thing he had said to her in the car. How could he have said such a thing to her, when he knew it would shame and humiliate her beyond all endurance? Herb didn't even lose stroke. God in heaven! It was too much, too much to bear. He should go in there and throw himself at her feet and beg her to forgive him for being such a rotten and empty man. Jim had stared at the dark ceiling through a blur of tears and fought it. The whole thing was true and the punishment fit the crime. But he was damned if he would go in there and play a *mea culpa* scene with her out of Dostoevski by way of Hollywood. To hell with such garbage and to hell with her. She had acted like a promiscuous little bitch and in the last analysis that was exactly what she was. He hadn't ruined and corrupted her, she had ruined and corrupted herself. Let the little bitch cry, let her sob, to hell with her.

Time and the contradictions of his own character had indeed caught up with James Kittering, who knew the difference between garbage and gold.

THREE

Gluck

When Jim returned from the dark realm of garbage to the bright world of Vice-President and Program Director of American International Television and Radio, Incorporated, he saw standing before him Al Ingerman and a very homely woman. He hardly looked at the woman except to note she was unattractive; his attention was on smiling Al, and the thought that came in his mind was, "Oh, God. Here we go with the gluck."

Gluck was another word that had considerable significance for Jim Kittering. If garbage was his favorite of all, gluck was the runner-up. This was a word he had invented himself and he was proud of it. It had a specific meaning, but the beauty of the term lay in its rich connotations. It suggested, he felt, other such words as glue, gloom, glib, glut, pluck, buck, fuck, muck, uck, and guck.

"Hey-y, come out of it, Jimmy, wake up. You look like a waif baby with nobody to take you to lunch."

It was Al Ingerman and the new writer for "Tramp Steamer." The sight and sound of Alvin was emetic; Jim could not stand the tone of that voice or the cut of those clothes. Anything was better than Alvin, even the ugly woman with him. Jim glanced at her again and felt a small shock. She had a look of honesty and genuineness that did not belong in the murky world through which Al Ingerman swam and wriggled like a lamprey.

For some reason beyond his comprehension, Jim took an immediate liking to the freckle-faced woman writer, Florence Carr. He liked her at once and hated the idea of going through the usual routine with her. Something about the woman gave him an urge to be honest. Under the circumstances, of course, honesty would be swiftly fatal, but he was tempted from the start to reveal to her the Law of Audience and the Law of Gluck, those two theoretical pillars upon which the medium rested.

"Al! Come in, come in."

Jim rose and stood behind his desk, shoulders slightly humped and head a trifle forward—a posture he had picked up from the Goblin; it gave an impression of great intensity. He did not smile as Al Ingerman, a supposedly independent agent but in reality a stooge of the Goblin, led into the office an incredibly freckled woman with buck teeth and nervous blue eyes. In addition to these defects, she had no detectable trace of a feminine figure. She wore a tweedy hairy suit, large scuffed walking shoes, and a semi-mannish haircut. The woman was undoubtedly a Lesbian and a tough one, but there was something likable about her.

"Jimmy, I want you to meet one of the most *talented* girls I've ever had the privilege of bringing to your office. And you better believe it. Florence Carr, Jimmy."

"Florence, you don't know what this means to me. I can't tell you how terrifically excited I am that you've decided to bring your gifts to bear on the challenge of this medium."

"Well . . . thanks very much. You're very kind."

"I mean every word of it," said Jim. "You have a great talent and you and I are going to do great things together."

"I think I might be of some use," she answered. "But if you believe all that, you've got a shock coming. I'm not really a good writer. I can't tell a story and I overwrite something terrible."

"I'll have to dispute you on that emphatically," said Jim.

"I'll have to dispute you there, too, Florence," said Al Ingerman. "You're being modest to a fault, honey."

"You're both full of horseshit to a fault," said the freckled Florence. "And I wish you'd cut it out. I'd much rather start this thing off on an honest basis."

"So would I," said Jim, "so would I."

"There *are* certain things I can do and it seems to me that's what we ought to work from. I can write pretty good dialogue and I have a feeling for wild crazy characters."

"You write very good dialogue indeed," said Jim, "and with construction, that is all you need for the dramatic media."

Until recently, Jim had never heard of Florence Carr. He had happened to read a short story she had published in one of the quality magazines. The story was rather amusing and since he was always on the lookout for writers, he had read one of her novels and had been strangely impressed by it, although the book presented difficulties for the general reader.

He had been much impressed by the novel. Immediately, he'd written the woman care of her publisher, but got no answer. In the meantime he'd given the short story to Hob and had "talked her up." Another letter was sent to Miss Carr, but still no answer. Jim finally got her on the phone by the simple expedient of looking up the number in the Manhattan book; the jacket of her novel said she lived in New York. He had then managed after much difficulty to convince her she wanted to be rich. Since, incredibly, she had no agent, Al Ingerman had been assigned to her.

Her book—and the personality of the woman herself as it came through over the telephone—had made a strong impact on Jim Kittering. The book showed great ability, he felt, although it did not have an especially dramatic narrative. The story was about an extremely sensitive and not too attractive young woman who wandered like a wraith amongst the breast-shaped dunes of Cape Cod, weeping over dead sea gulls and gazing out at the gray slate sea, while carrying on a weird relationship with a horribly ugly Portuguese fisherman who seemed to be a representation of a kindly Satan. Jim got exasperated with the book because he could not figure out precisely the meaning of the relationship between the fisherman and the wraith-girl. And yet there was something haunting and real about it. The image of the girl wandering sadly among breastlike dunes and weeping over sea birds stayed in his mind.

Jim also had liked the short story. It was in a different vein altogether and dealt with daffodils, a young girl and her nanny in the park, a wild-eyed Jewish policeman, a nauseated Alaskan bear, a Negro heavyweight champion reduced to peanut vending, a dying swan, and other such curiosa. The story didn't have much of a narrative either, but it was written in a clearer manner and the mad dialogue between the nanny, the policeman, the bear, and the fighter was very funny. Jim had laughed aloud several times at the weary, doleful comments of the sick bear, who seemed to be the hero of it. The woman might not be able to tell a story, but she had a weird, dry humor. If a little moisture could be added to that humor and the weirdness taken out of it, she had possibilities. Wet humor could coat gluck and make it glisten like diamonds.

But whatever the ability or limitations of Florence Carr, she was of desperate importance to Jim Kittering. In the first place, the supply of writers had gotten worse and worse, instead of better. There were no writers around, none at all. To find even a halfway plausible writer nowadays was almost impossible, and that was strange, considering all the money they could make. Again and again he had thought he had his hands at last on a real writer, but every time when the bum sat down at a typewriter it came out gluck.

However, the peculiar shortage of writers, serious though it was, was not the factor that made Florence Carr of such desperate importance to Jim at this time. The memory of the Goblin was short—that is, short insofar as gratitude was concerned; he never, of course, forgot a grudge—and the Goblin himself had said it: "You're in trouble, Jim, creatively. You're not coming through at all and that disturbs me, Jim. It puzzles me."

It puzzled Jim himself, too. In recent months, after several truly brilliant years during which time the children of his brain had, as he put it, squawked and yowled and made pooh-pooh on the rugs of seventy million living rooms, Jim Kittering had suddenly lost the touch. Overnight, he had unaccountably lost it all. The most vapid ideas occurred to him, ideas that seemed superb until he enthusiastically proposed them, at which point they sounded to his own ears like the babblings of a Mongoloid idiot—worse than that, a Mongoloid idiot making peculiar mocking noises, strange and unnatural snutters and giggles.

It was harrowing. He had not long ago jumped up at a top-level meeting, smacked his fist in his palm, and suggested in dead earnest a series that would deal in a satirical way with the wife-swapping proclivities of Greenland Eskimos. "But warmhearted! Respect for primitive culture, no derision, just gentle satire, a soft smile. And I see a hunter, yes. Kayuk. A clown, yes, but brave, good. And suspense?—my God, out on the floes, polar bears, killer whales, wolves! Brave, yes, and good—and a different woman on every trip, what a guest-star proposition! This baby will fly. It will soar. Kayuk and His Wives, a great title. I can see it tearing down the runway already with jets blasting. The true beauty of it is *moral titillation.* Umm, well, no . . . different moral standards, *that* is the key. I mean, it isn't a sin with them, it has . . . charm and . . . innocence, tranquillity, a lightheartedness with just a *soupçon* of *post coitum triste* to wet it up a little and make it glisten. It's much more than a cheap gag about wife-swapping, much more. You know, *autres temps autres mœurs,* or to put it differently, *tout comprendre c'est tout pardonner.* Of course, I haven't worked it out in any detail, or the exact balance of it tastewise. Actually, I'm just spit-balling. What do you think? Does it stick on the wall?"

The Goblin, needless to say, did not pay Jim Kittering two thousand dollars a week for odd, mocking whimsy that was un-American in essence. "That is a fascist idea, Jim," he had said. "I don't know what's gotten into you lately. You seem to have begun to lose your respect for the medium, and that worries me a great deal, Jim, a very great deal." It could not have been put more plainly, but to be sure that his message was received, the Goblin since then had called Jim several times and subjected him to *il silenzio.*

Florence Carr was of vital significance to Jim Kittering. The Goblin was wildly enthusiastic about her, beside himself with joy and wonder, so much so he had pulled the Jiminy crickets trick not once but twice. "Gee whiz, Jim. It . . . it *moves* me. Gosh, that girl can write up a storm. Jiminy crickets, she can *really* write." Florence Carr was perfect for the new comedy-adventure series, "Tramp Steamer," which the Goblin himself had dreamed up, since no one else around there had any ideas any more. He had seen it one day at lunch over a plate of sweetbreads—a tramp steamer chugging through blue water. A tanned, bearded, handsome captain at the wheel, a thin wisp of smoke coming from its stack . . . electrical! It was the greatest idea he had ever had and he had had some great ideas. The Goblin's pet, that's what it was. Florence Carr had to be handled like eggs—delicate, perfect. It was no time to tail the Goblin, not with Greenland Eskimos or anything else.

"Well, Florence," said Jim, "you wait, this is an historic occasion. We're going to make history, you and me. But let's don't just stand here; sit down, Florence, and make yourself comfortable. Would you like some coffee?"

"Not right now, thanks."

Florence Carr's voice was not deep or masculine and it did not go along with the tweedy suit and mannish haircut. But she had to be a Lesbian and considering how homely she was it was probably a good idea. Jim smiled and asked, "A drink, maybe?"

"Not this early, thanks."

"It is kind of early, isn't it," said Jim. "I think I'll have coffee myself. How about you, Al?"

Al Ingerman glanced up from straightening the seams of his raw silk trousers. For the hundredth time at least, the thought occurred to Jim that Alvin Ingerman had the sleek look of a small but very well-fed rat. Already he seemed doubtful of Jim's handling of the interview. "Yeah, Jimmy, sure. I guess so." Sleek was right, and well-fed, too. The man was not only a stooge for the Goblin but his pimp as well, and that job was lucrative. The Goblin liked six or seven girls at one time; he ran with an erect penis from one to the other, giggling and splashing himself with Wesson oil.

"I shouldn't drink more coffee, I guzzle the doggone stuff all the time," said Jim. "One of these days I'm going to turn into a coffee cup. But gee whiz, I don't know, you get kind of . . . well, *addicted* to it, sort of."

Jim's melting smile had gradually faded. A look of deep meditation had replaced it, a meditation that could only gain additional profundity in contrast to the deliberate gee-whiz triviality of the chitchat. It was the Goblin's Jiminy crickets trick, an elementary form of psychological judo—the basic ploy was to combine some strong emotion with an unpretentious hokey-pokey banality as honest as all outdoors. The Goblin usually did it with tears in his eyes, pale, trembling: "Gosh, Danny, that's a *beautiful* idea. It . . . it *moves* me. It's electrical. Jiminy crickets, Danny."

At least, thought Jim, he could convince Al he was doing his best, even if the woman had insisted on denigrating herself. Jim fixed his gaze on a bowl of flowers on the coffee table and stepped on a button in the rug to call Susan. He couldn't bring himself to cry like the Goblin and had to substitute something weaker, but he could do the hokey-pokey banality pretty good. As they waited for Susan to come in and make fresh coffee, Jim said:

"Gee whiz, look at those flowers. They're . . . they're *beautiful.* The colors, and the hues, and all. Jiminy crickets, they're pretty."

Jim stared for a full two counts longer at the flowers, then turned rather abruptly to one side, squinted his eyes tightly shut, and ground his teeth together hard. A loud grating noise filled the large office as Jim continued to grind his teeth back and forth, eyes closed to slits and head tilted to the side. It flabbergasted some people, this trick; the impression of mysterious inner tension and sensitivity was awesome. Jim opened his eyes, stared reverently at the flowers for several seconds, then glanced over innocently at Florence Carr to see how she was taking it. Not too well—her brows were ironically lifted and a gleam of amusement was in her eyes. The Jiminy crickets trick hadn't impressed her. Hmmph, thought Jim. Of course the trick didn't flabbergast *every*body and it *wasn't* awesome when it didn't work. But if the Goblin had done it, she would have been impressed.

"Ahem," said Jim. "Susan, coffee for me and Al, please. Well, now . . . where shall we start, Florence?"

"You're the boss."

"All right, let's start with a crude question concerning money. Has Al told you what you can make from a successful series?"

"He said it would be a lot."

"I thought I'd let you picture all that to her, Jimmy."

"I'm glad you did, Al."

"We discussed an initial guarantee, that's about it. And as I told Florence, I'm sure there's no problem in that area."

"Oh, I'm sure there isn't."

"The main thing, of course, is degree of ownership."

"Of course, always."

"Hob, I know, wants her to have an appealing, attractive deal. He's very keen for you, Florence, he has a tremendous respect for your ability."

It came out automatically a moment later, before Jim Kittering had a chance to think what he was saying. The name "Hob" meant nothing to Florence and she asked, "Who is this you're talking about?"

"The Goblin," answered Jim.

"The what?" asked Florence.

Cold-eyed, Al Ingerman stared across the marble coffee table. Jim grinned sheepishly, spread his hands, and shrugged. He hadn't meant to say it, he really hadn't, it had just slipped out.

"What did you say?" asked Florence. "Did you say the Goblin?"

"No, not really," said Jim.

"I thought I heard you say the Goblin. In fact, you *did* say the Goblin."

"Forget it. It's just an in-joke we have around here, a little gag we have in the organization."

"And a tasteless gag, too, I must say, Jimmy," said Al Ingerman. "Very tasteless."

At that moment the phone on the desk ludicrously began to buzz. Jim clenched his jaw and ground his teeth together, but this time he was not putting on a show and was not even aware he did it. He was suddenly, furiously angry. The desire to get up and grab Al Ingerman by the scruff of the neck was so strong it made him dizzy. "All right, Al," he said. "It was a Freudian slip. Don't you ever make a Freudian slip yourself? How about it, Al? Huh?"

"I just said it was a tasteless gag. And it is."

"All right, Al. Fine. You have made your point."

"Excuse me," said Florence. "Your phone is buzzing."

"What?"

"Your phone, it's buzzing."

"Oh, yes, so it is." Again Jim ground his teeth, in such a rage he barely could contain himself. Someday, somehow, he would get revenge on Al Ingerman. And he would get revenge on that stupid Susan, too; he had told her explicitly to put through no calls. How could she be so dumb? Suddenly the truth dawned on him, as a silly memory popped into his mind, a recollection of his barber saying to him, "You are getting a little more gray hair around your temples than looks good. I know you don't want to touch it up, but if this keeps on we're going to have to do it, irregardlessly." The truth was Susan *wasn't* that dumb. One call was always put through, irregardlessly. In some strange and mysterious telepathic fashion. Hob already knew of the crime. Jim did not doubt it, could not doubt it. The man's powers were eldritch, eerie, beyond belief. And if there was one thing the Goblin did not like, it was to be called the Goblin. He would whisper over the phone: "You are through, Jim."

"Well," said Florence, "I can't sit and listen to the telephone ring. Some people can do it but I can't, I always answer."

Jim smiled. "The gluck is endless," he said, and picked up the phone.

FOUR

Kidding Along Linda

"Yes, Susan?"

"It's your wife again."

"Goddamn it! I *told* you no calls!"

"I know, I know—but she's crying!"

"I don't care if she is! That is no reason to interrupt an important meeting, Susan!"

"Yes, but that isn't all! She's crying and says if you don't talk to her, she'll kill herself!"

Jim sat like a gargoyle in his chair. Finally he managed to turn to Florence Carr and Al Ingerman. "I'm terribly sorry," he said, "but I'll have to take this call. It'll only be a moment."

"Go ahead, I'll have some coffee," said Florence.

"Wonderful," said Jim. He turned in his big black swivel chair away from the picture windows of the sitting area, pressed a button on the phone, and said calmly, "Good morning, Linda."

"It isn't a good morning. How can you call it a good morning? It's a filthy, horrible morning, Jim, and you know it."

Jim smiled thinly. Linda's idea of invective was pretty primitive. When she lost emotional control, she lapsed into the rhetoric of an hysterical teen-ager. It was funny—funny peculiar, of course, not funny amusing—to listen to an honor graduate of one of the best women's schools in the world talk in such a way. Pushed by her domineering grandmother, Linda had graduated *summa cum laude* at nineteen. She was not only beautiful, but extremely intelligent. However, she did not have certain of his gifts. "I'm sorry," he said. "I've been in meetings all morning and I'm in one now."

"How could you have done it, Jim? That's what I want to know, how could you have done it? You hypocrite, you liar!"

"Linda, it was unintentional."

"Don't lie to me! You did it deliberately, completely deliberately!"

Jim hesitated. Probably he should take this call in the anteroom. Florence and Al were silent at the coffee table and obviously were listening to him. "Now, now," he said, "it isn't serious. I'm sure Debbie will be all right."

"*What?* What do you mean, *Debbie?* It has nothing to do with Debbie, or Sandy either! It has to do with *you* and *me*, you hateful hypocrite!"

"Well, I have people in the office," smiled Jim. "I'm in the middle of an extremely important meeting. Can we talk about it later, honey?"

"If you hang up that phone, I will kill myself. Instantly! I have a bottle of one hundred aspirin in my hand, Jim."

She was lying. Linda had no aspirin in her hand and no intention of killing herself, but he had better talk to her anyhow. "All right," he said calmly, "if you're really anxious about it, although I'm sure Debbie will be just fine."

"This has *nothing* to do with Debbie!"

"Hold for five seconds, honey." Jim pressed the hold button on the telephone and turned with an apologetic smile to Florence and Al. "I'm sorry. My wife is upset, one of the girls is in trouble at school. I'll have to try and calm her. But . . . don't go away." Jim shook an admonishing finger at the freckled Florence, smiled, and quickly walked from the office to the anteroom. "Susan, go clean up the coffee cups or something. Linda's having a goddamned fit."

"I know," said Susan, "she sure is, and I thought—"

"Close the door," said Jim. It was *too much.* Twenty seconds, that was all she would get. As the door to the office closed, Jim sat in the small stenographer's chair and picked up the phone. "All right," he said, "Linda, will you calm down? What happened was an accident and you know it."

"Debbie and Sandra, thank God, have nothing to do with it! It's our own filthy mess and *my* children are *not* involved, thank God for that!"

"Oh, for Christ's sake! Will you stop being stupidly hysterical? I had people in the office and I couldn't talk about it!"

"Isn't that nice. *You* can't *talk* about it, and *I* can't *think* about it!"

"Look, Linda, will you stop it, please? It was an unintentional accident and you know it."

"You did it deliberately, you hypocrite! All your talk of freedom, of being sensible, and you do a sneaky thing like that! Oh, God, how I felt! I could have died, died!"

Despite his anxiety to get back to Florence Carr, a sick dismay was on Jim Kittering's face. The raw reality of his wife's wretchedness was overwhelming. Maybe she did have a bottle of aspirin in her hand.

"Now listen," he said. "You are mistaken, honey. I didn't know where you were and I wanted my coat so I could go home, that's all."

"You're a liar. You knew I was in there with Herb and you went in there deliberately."

"I did not know you were with Herb. The last time I looked around you were with Billy."

"Oh, God!"

Jim shut his eyes as his wife began to weep aloud over the phone. It really was distressing. To hear an adult sobbing like a child was a thing that shouldn't happen to a clever man. How had he gotten into this position, anyhow? "Oh, come on, Linda," he said. "Will you stop it, please?"

"Oh-oh-oh-oh-oh!" she said. "Oh, God! God!"

"Look, Linda, what *difference* does it make? So I walked in on you. I got out, didn't I?"

"Oh, God! I can't stand it!"

"Linda, please! Can't you control yourself?"

"No, no, no, I can't!"

Well, he had known when he heard her crying in the bathroom at five o'clock that the scene when it came would be a dilly. But he had not reckoned on anything like this. She was having an upside-down flying fit and it really was beginning to wear him down. A tic jumped in Jim's cheek as he listened to her carry on.

"I can't stand it! I can't endure it any more! I can't, I can't, I can't!"

"Then for God's sake don't do it any more. If you can't be calm about it, then be sensible and cut it out."

"Oh, sure! And where would *that* get me?"

"Look, stop blaming *me*, Linda. I never forced you to do anything, and I didn't force you to do anything last night either."

The sound of weeping abruptly ceased. Silence. It was *il silenzio*, domestic variety, but not calculated and not contrived, a thing far more frightening than any trick of the Goblin. Jim's knees began to tremble beneath Susan's small desk as an interminable faint hum of nothingness came over the phone.

"Linda? Isn't it true? Correct me if I'm wrong."

"I despise you," she answered in a toneless voice. "And I despise myself. I despise everything in this filthy world and I wish I were dead. I wish I were dead and in my grave and maybe I will be soon."

Another tic jumped in Jim's cheek, not only in reaction to her threat but also in anticipation of the crash of the receiver in his ear. But no, Linda was still there. She hadn't hung up, she was waiting for him to give her an answer. Well, he had an answer, although it had gotten a bit shopworn. Gently, he said, "I'm *sorry*, Linda. I know how you feel, and sometimes I feel the same way myself. It just . . . doesn't seem worthwhile, especially not for you."

"Oh, Jim!" said his wife, weeping again but quietly now. The Let's Reform discussion had a calming and mesmeric effect upon her. She never tired of it and never saw that it went on forever and ever like the Morton salt girl. But that was what it was: a girl on a salt box holding a salt box with a girl on a salt box holding a salt box and on and on into senseless infinity.

"I guess it's one of those things that sounds great in theory but doesn't work so well in actual practice. Like anarchy. A great theory but it doesn't work."

"Oh, Jim! If you knew how I felt, if you only knew!"

"I do know," he answered. "I know, honey, and it's no good. Not for you it isn't. It's no good at all, and maybe I *am* to blame. I encouraged you, led you on—"

"No, it was me too. I'm as bad as you are—worse, even worse!"

"I doubt that, honey. I doubt that very seriously." The conversation had fallen comfortably into a familiar pattern and Jim put an elbow on Susan's desk and reached into the breast pocket of his jacket for a cigarette. "No, I can't buy that. You have always been a child of the Judeo-Christian ethic, but I myself seem pretty much apart from it. I don't know how or why, but that's the way it is."

"Oh, Jim, that isn't true! I never realized it before, but you're just as unhappy as I am, maybe even more so."

"Well . . . yes," said Jim uncomfortably. She was hardly playing fair—*that* wasn't in the script of the Let's Reform discussion; *she* was the one who was supposed to be miserable, not he. This was a new and dangerous ploy that could be strategically fatal. To admit he really and truly was miserable was tantamount to a salt box with no girl on it; the Let's Reform discussion would come to an abrupt end and the game of "Kidding Along Linda" would be lost. The correct formula, of course, was an agreement that Linda, because of her nature and moral attitude, would henceforth be faithful to him; but he himself, because of his nature and moral attitude, would make no comparable sacrifice and would not blame her if she should fail. Jim knew the speech backwards and forwards: "I agree it doesn't work for you, Linda, not at all. But I am not the type of man who can be totally faithful to one person, I'm just not, that's all. And it would be pretty selfish and unfair of me to insist that someone else do what I can't do myself. I think you should be faithful for your *own* sake, but I just want you to know that if you fail, honey, I won't reproach you." The game could not be won without that speech, and how could he make the speech if he himself were as miserable as she? It was a dangerous ploy, indeed, and Jim could not think of a counter. He frowned at his cigarette as she rammed the point home.

"It's true, Jim. It took the shock of last night to make me understand it, to make me see how you really feel. It made you sick, what you saw. How in the world did we ever get in this mess in the first place and now that we're in it why do we *stay* in it? Why? Why, Jim? For what?"

Fumbling, Jim answered, "Well, I don't know if it's on a rational level, Linda."

"It certainly *isn't* on a rational level. I ask you again—why, Jim? Why do we have to go on like this when it makes us both completely miserable? Why can't we change, change our whole way of life? Don't we have minds and wills of our own? Are we animals or human beings?"

It was staggering. Linda no longer sounded like an hysterical teenager asking empty rhetorical questions, but rather like a horribly articulate woman of thirty-two asking questions that hit dead bull's-eye center. Still fumbling, he replied, "Well, Linda, we've talked about this many times. Now, I *want* to talk about it, I feel we *should* talk about it. But the point is that any change has got to be realistic."

"Realistic! Oh, God, how I hate that word! How can you say *realistic* to me after last night? Wasn't that realistic enough for you?"

Jim shook his head and answered, "I don't understand your point."

"Yes you do. And I want to know what has to happen before you stop talking like that and pretending you believe such things."

Speechless, Jim again sat hunched at the desk like a gargoyle, lips apart and an empty insensibility in his eyes. He hadn't the faintest notion of what to say and it was a thing that had never really happened to him before in his adult life. Open-mouthed, horrified, he sat there at Susan's desk and stared vacantly at the coils of smoke that rose from his cigarette. At that moment the door to the office opened and Al Ingerman entered the anteroom.

"Just a moment," said Jim into the phone, and then to Al, "Be with you in a minute, Al."

"Excuse me," said Al. "Bathroom."

"You can use my private one."

"That's all right, no trouble."

Jim watched Al walk through the anteroom door. The thought occurred to him it was peculiar Al would go all the way down the corridor when there was a bathroom right next to the office. Where was Al going and what was he up to?

"I'm sorry, Linda, there're people here. This is interrupting a very important meeting."

"Nothing could be more important than the question I just asked you. What is to become of us, Jim? Are we animals or human beings?"

"We're human beings," he replied. "And I don't *know* what's going to become of us. I guess I've wrecked our lives. Sure I have. That's exactly what I've done." With a part of his mind, Jim believed it certainly; but with another part of his mind he did not believe it; thus it was a legitimate counter in the game of "Kidding Along Linda." He could not help but half smile at the solemn tone of his own voice. Maybe the bullshit by which he lived was thinning out, but it was not all gone yet and he had not lost this game either. The answer to her ploy was to demand fidelity of her and conceal his own philandering for a while, but not conceal it forever or totally. A little subtle evidence in a month or two, a bit of strange perfume on his neck or a trace of lipstick on his collar would let her know. Nothing really would be changed and in a few months they would be back where they had started. She would merely appear for a while to have won the game. "I didn't mean to do it," he said. "But without understanding how or why, that's exactly what I've done. I've wrecked everything, Linda. Everything."

"We've both done it," she answered. "It's true you never forced me to do anything. I've been very foolish and very weak. But it isn't too late if we really want to change. We can change, Jim. We can, we can change if we try."

"I agree," he answered solemnly. "We can change, Linda, and we will. Life isn't worth living like this."

"Oh, God! Think of Debbie and Sandy! If you don't care anything about my life or your own, then don't you care about your children? Don't you have even the slightest bit of pity for them? Is their love too much of a burden for you too?"

She didn't believe him. Again Jim stared into space like a gargoyle, a rather good-looking gargoyle with handsome gray eyes in which there seemed to be no trace of guile. It was unfair. She had no right to see he was lying—his remarks had been so honest, so genuine, so humble. Jim said in an injured tone, "I meant that sincerely, Linda."

"You don't mean *any*thing sincerely. You've become a complete and total liar—to yourself, to me, and to everyone else. And that's one difference between us. I may be a bitch but I'm not a liar."

"All right, Linda. Let's just say I was under the illusion I meant what I said."

"You were under no illusion and I've had enough. I told you I can't stand it any more and I meant it. Last night was the end."

"And what does that mean?"

"You don't want my love, Jim. You love *me*, but you don't want my love in return; it's a burden you can't endure and that's why you let me go with other men, painful as it was for us both. You're a child, Jim, a bewildered child for all your cleverness. I don't want a child for a husband, I want a man. And do you know something? I love you, I really do, I always have and I guess I always will, but I am *not* going to kill myself over you. No, I'm not, Jim. I'm going to live."

"All right," he answered, "good for you! And now will you listen to *me* for a moment? I have never heard a more self-righteous and egocentric speech in my life, Linda. Never. You have interrupted, distracted, and upset me in the midst of a meeting that could mean the difference between survival and disaster for me, you, Deborah, and Sandra. Did you hear me? Linda, I owe almost two hundred thousand dollars! I'm in desperate trouble, on the verge of being fired, and you pick *this* time to call me up and dump seven thousand tons of Victorian guilt and hypocritical prudery on my head, throwing in for good measure a cowardly threat of suicide that you now bravely rise above in order to put me down all the more. Now let me tell you something. For an intelligent, modern, well-educated woman, you are acting like an hysterical Baptist virgin in Alabama. Linda, this is not nineteen oh three and we do not have a horse and buggy in the garage. Queen Victoria is not on the throne, times have changed, a moral revolution has occurred and is occurring, intelligent men and women no longer tremble with fear before an imaginary ogre of sex. You know better, Linda, what's the *matter* with you? Where is your sense, your intelligence, your poise and self-control? Am I going to have to pay twenty-five thousand dollars to have you psychoanalyzed? What the hell *difference* does it make if you went to bed with that man, a thing you damn well knew you were going to do in the first place and the only trouble is I caught you at it? Isn't it true you went to that party without your panties, and without even your goddamn bra? Isn't it also true that you *are* promiscuous, Linda, that any number of men attract you enormously? Now I know I'm being very cruel and crude, but isn't it also a fact you were in the middle of a very uninhibited orgasm when I opened that door? Did your love for me prevent you from screwing Herb's ears off? Who are you kidding, anyhow, me or yourself?"

Silence. Or near silence, anyhow. He could hear her breathing and an occasional sniffle.

"Now, I will tell you something else. Aside from the fact that for some years now I have spent considerably more than I have earned in order to buy *you* mink coats, swimming pools, fuchsia T-Birds, a palatial modern home in the gentle farmland of New Jersey, trips to Vegas and Colorado Springs, perfume for your pussy, and God knows what the hell all else, *I* have got problems of *my own!* I have a racking cough induced by the three to four packages of cigarettes I smoke every day of my life in an effort to endure the pressures brought on by my struggle to support you, Debbie, and Sandy in the manner to which you have become accustomed—and don't say you don't like that mink coat or that fucking swimming pool or I'll call you a liar. I can't get out of bed in the morning and drive to the office without amphetamines to push me and I can't go to bed at night without barbiturates to knock me over the head and put me to sleep! The pressure under which I live is inhuman and unbearable, and what does it all mean to you, what significance does it have for you? Are you even aware of it at all? I don't ask *gratitude* of you, God no, all I ask is a *dim* awareness of what I endure every day for you and the children. And now you call me a total liar and dump seven thousand tons of philosophical garbage on my head because I don't beat you up for being unfaithful to me. You're a nincompoop bitch, Linda, that's what you are! An immoral, oversexed, nincompoop bitch—and don't tell me *I* wanted you to go to bed with other men, because I didn't! The very idea is revolting and disgusting—you, a mother and a wife who supposedly loves her husband, yowling like an alley cat at every flea-bitten tom that comes along. I said we should be sensible about sex because I knew damned well you were going to be unfaithful to me anyhow. In fact, now that the truth is finally coming out, I will make a little bet with you—I will bet *my life* against a bottle of Replique you already had been unfaithful to me many times before we ever discussed being realistic about sex. Isn't it true, you little non-liar? And there's something *else* you don't think I know—that I've worked myself half dead and half crazy for a spoiled child-woman. That's what you really are, Linda, and you have the fantastic, incredible gall to tell me *I* am a child! But need we go on with this? Let's sum it up, let's wrap it up in a pearly ribbon like Saks Fifth Avenue, your favorite store and you never give a thought to the monstrous bills you run up there—I am fed up, Linda, fed up! Fed up with you and everything else! Go to hell! Take your little perfumed nincompoop pussy and go to hell!"

Jim banged down the phone. That would teach her, that would do it. It would wrap it up in a pearly ribbon. His position was as solid as the dikes of Holland, because the thing he *really* had wanted had finally occurred. Old-fashioned morality, whipped by intolerable degradation, had reared its hoary head and roared. Linda, deafened by that elemental and mighty roar, would behave herself for the rest of her life, barring accidents such as temptation or a perfectly human thing like forgetting to put on her pants.

Of course, Queen Victoria would never have understood it, and there *were* a few leaks in the dike hither and yon. It would take a thumb or two to keep out the North Atlantic. One of the more horrible of the leaks was the basic inconsistency of his tirade in the first place; the final posture of moral outrage ("You, a mother and a wife!") did not fit at all with his earlier hip declaration that this was not nineteen oh three ("Where is your sense, your intelligence?") and it made no difference about her going to bed with Herb. That little inconsistency, no doubt, would have confused Queen Victoria. It would not confuse Linda. But the most horrible leak of all was his vulgar and coarse charge that she had been unfaithful before he suggested they be sensible about sex. It had sounded beautifully convincing, he had almost believed it himself as he said it, but it simply wasn't so. There had been no unfaithfulness on Linda's part before the realistic discussions of sex and human nature. Quite a leak. Big enough to cover all the tulips of Holland with six inches of salt. It was not exactly probable she would accept that charge as valid.

But even if he had not been carried away by panic, the roar of old-fashioned and/or new-fangled morality would not have deafened Linda for long. There was truth in his tirade, just as there was truth in his memo on Susan, but this truth would avail him nothing. The coarse language and vulgar fury could have only one result. The game of "Kidding Along Linda" was lost.

FIVE

Tailing the Goblin

Al Ingerman walked in from the corridor, smiled, and asked, "Finish your call?"

"Yes, I did. Finish yours?"

"What, Jimmy?"

"Your call of nature, Al. The call that sent you all the way down the corridor past Hob's office to the men's room. What other call could I have meant?"

"What are you, crazy or something?"

"I could talk to you all day, Al. Your conversation has all the sparkle of sediment at the bottom of the Philippine Trench."

"Boy, you *really* got up on the wrong side of the bed this morning."

"Beautifully expressed, fresh as whaleshit—but shall we go?"

"Sure, but first—I got to talk to you like a Dutch uncle, Jimmy. And the word is, calm down. This pilot is very important to a lot of people and I am talking serious to you now, all jokes aside. I didn't tell Hob about any such silly thing as you calling him the Goblin, that is beneath my dignity, but whether you can understand it I owe a lot to that guy and I'm loyal to him. And you might not know it, but Hob is in a little trouble himself with the Chairman of the Board. All those unfounded rumors about wild parties and that name the Goblin. But worse, we've had some bad shows. I am telling you in front, this pilot is *important* and you better handle Florence careful. I'm with Hob on that a hundred percent and not just because of my commission either. I am *proud* of the work I do—I take *pride* in giving the public not only Shakespeare and a lot of horseshit but what it wants, and I tell my wife that. So *calm down,* Jimmy."

Despite himself, Jim was impressed. The pressure must be enormous. The orgies of the Goblin, it was true, had gotten into the columns, and the man's sadism was a legend in the industry. After all, there was a limit on how many times a man could semipublicly put his tongue up the behinds of shuddering beauty queens without getting into at least some difficulty. Besides, the ratings had gone down. Could the Goblin be in real trouble? Jim could not believe it, but a thrill ran through him. If the Goblin's position was threatened, it should be possible *to pin a tail on him nine miles long.* "Tailing the Goblin" would have a breadth, scope, and grandeur hitherto unknown. It would also be fantastically dangerous. The Goblin cornered was a fearful thing to contemplate. Jim smiled to himself. It was, of course, an idle dream. The Goblin was far too smart ever to be cornered. Tailing him was out of the question.

"Al, darling," said Jim, "to mint a little language fresh and shiny, I am calm as a cucumber. I know which side my bread is buttered on. I'm with you, Dad."

In the office, Jim sent Susan back to her post, apologized to Florence for the delay, and took up the conversation where it had been interrupted.

"The answer to my crude question concerning money, Florence, is that the writer of a successful series stands to make a fortune. And I do mean a fortune."

"Well, what I want," said Florence, "is enough money to buy a cottage on the Cape somewhere near the ocean, a place to go in the summer. I've always wanted that."

"Give us what we need and you can buy fifty cottages."

Florence laughed. "I know I sound greedy, but that's because I *am* greedy. How much would I really make?"

"You'd make what I said, enough to buy fifty cottages—assuming each cottage costs, say, twenty thousand dollars."

"You're joking. That's a million dollars."

Jim suppressed a bored sigh. Inflaming the cupidity of writers—in order, of course, to make them more pliable—usually amused him; but he hated to do it to this woman. He had an urge to tell her that although it was true some series did earn a fortune, most scripts for pilots were not produced, most pilots did not go on the air, and most shows did not run. The writers, as a rule, wound up with ulcers, nervous breakdowns, and a few hard-earned dollars.

"I'm not joking, Florence," said Jim. "A truly successful series can earn considerably more than a million dollars for a writer. In a couple of years, with reruns and everything, you'll be pulling down twelve, fourteen, sixteen thousand dollars a week or more."

Even Florence's freckles seemed to have gone pale. "I don't need that kind of money," she said, "and I'm not even sure I want it."

Jim smiled. "Everybody wants money, including Aunt Maggie. You'd find things to do with it."

"Sixteen thousand dollars a week—that's obscene. I can hardly make that in a *year* writing books."

"Who reads books, Florence? Only a tiny fraction of the audience this medium commands. You've been on the periphery of our culture. Now you're at its center. You're in the main arena."

"How much does the President make? But never mind—I'd rather not think about it."

"You shouldn't. That was my point in bringing it up. Give us what we need and you will have no money problems. You should concentrate completely on the creative challenge."

"Well, that's what I want to do."

"All right, let's go to the job. Now, in this business we start with an idea, a concept, which in this case is a comedy-adventure series entitled 'Tramp Steamer,' basic locale probably the South Pacific, although we can go anywhere we like and that is one of the assets of the show. It has a travelogue dimension, and with color becoming—"

"Just a minute," said Florence. "I'm sorry, but there's one thing that's bothered me from the beginning and I think we ought to talk about it."

"Why, absolutely," said Jim. "What's bothering you, Florence?"

At that moment an odd little interruption occurred. Susan, slightly pale, opened the anteroom door and said, "There's an electrician here."

Jim was so annoyed he felt like throwing the pot of flowers at her. An *electrician* on top of everything else! "Have you taken leave of your senses, Susan? What are you talking about?"

Ludicrously, a loud grinding WHIR-WHIR-WHIR drowned out Susan's stammered reply. Bits of plaster fell from the wall above the door and a three-quarter-inch drill slowly wriggled into the room. It stopped and Susan became audible. "I kn-kn-know! I told him you were busy but he says it's his orders!"

Jim could see through the open anteroom door a blue-overalled electrician standing on a small stepladder, a leather belt filled with tools around his waist and a thick cable in his hands. "This is utterly ridiculous," he said. "Tell that electrician to get the hell out of here!"

"I did, I did!"

The heavy cable began to snake into the room, falling in a coil down to the floor from its hole near the ceiling. "Good God almighty!" said Jim. He threw his cigarette into an ashtray, got up, walked to the door, and into the anteroom. "We're having an important meeting. What do you think you're doing?"

The electrician, a scrawny man with glasses, looked over his shoulder and squinted at Jim as he continued to shove the cable through the hole. "I'm doin' my job," he said.

"Oh, you are, are you?"

"That's right. I got orders from the Chief Electrician hisself."

"Look, get the hell off that ladder and get out of here!"

"Well, I got strict orders to put it in this morning. It's for the intercom."

The intercom, in Jim's opinion, was another mad pretentious notion of the Goblin, on a par with his decision some months before to put three identical color television sets in the offices of all major executives for the sake of simultaneous viewing of the various networks. The three color TVs stood in a corner like blind soldiers. And now a goddamned intercom, an absurd whim that was costing tens of thousands of dollars. It was actually a closed-circuit television system; the monitor and other equipment were already there, ugly on a shelf near the ceiling. The point was to enable the Goblin never to leave his locked, sealed, darkened office; he could communicate with his various executives without the necessity to breathe the same air they breathed. The inner sanctum of his office would become a total and inviolable Goblin's den. It was a megalomaniacal idea, but he had sold the Chairman of the Board on it. The Directors' Room would be a part of the system. Perhaps there might be some convenience for the Directors to question and get reports from various executives who would not have to be physically present during board meetings, but in Jim's opinion the idea was not worth a tenth of its cost.

"Now listen," said Jim, "we are having an important meeting in that room, and *I* am giving you *strict orders* now to get out of here and leave us alone. You might work for the Chief Electrician, but I assure you I outrank him and if you don't get off that ladder and out of here and stop bothering us with this nonsense, I guarantee you you'll be sorry."

"All right," said the man, "if that's how you feel."

Jim went back into the office, shut the door, shoved the dangling loops of cable out of his way, and walked toward the sitting area. "What can you do?" he asked. "This kind of madness goes on around here all the time."

"What's it for?" asked Florence.

"It's for nothing," said Jim. "Now, you were saying, Florence, something is bothering you?"

"Yes. It sure is. It seems to me no matter what medium it is, a writer must know what he's writing about. I don't know *anything* about tramp steamers. How can I write about a tramp steamer when I never saw one? I don't even know the difference between poop and starboard."

Al Ingerman sat forward. "You can fill that in with research, Florence."

"How do I go about filling it in with research?"

"Why, research it, that's all," said Al. "Look into it. There must be piles of stuff on them down at the library."

"Look, I don't know a thing about tramp steamers, and I think we ought to do the series on something else."

"Oh, no, no, no," said Jim. "The . . . my boss, the genius who runs this show . . . he *loves* the idea."

"Well, I think he ought to get a writer who knows something about tramp steamers."

"Oh, no, no, he loves *you* for it, Florence, he loves you for it specifically. He's mad for you."

"That is true, Florence," said Al. "He really *loves* you."

"If he loves me so much, why doesn't he let me write about something else?"

"You don't understand," said Jim. "He loves you and tramp steamers *together*. He sees you as an entity, a synergism greater than its parts. We can't possibly go to him and say, 'Look, Hob, forget it about tramp steamers, she wants to write about a cuckoo family that raises dachshunds in Vermont.' It would be a personal injury and he'd never forget it. Believe me, *never*. Thirty years later you'd be sleeping in a tent in Afghanistan and a dacoit would lift the flap at four A.M., cut your throat, whip out a short-wave set, and whisper into it, 'I got her, boss'—and I am not exaggerating."

"Umm," said Florence.

"Heh heh, I think you *are* exaggerating slightly, Jimmy," said Al Ingerman. "Hob is really a deeply sentimental guy underneath. But this series *does* mean a lot to him, he has his heart set on it. That's what Jimmy means."

"Well . . . I don't want to ruin everything," said Florence nervously.

"And you won't," declared Al. "There is no danger of that."

"Of course you won't, Florence," said Jim, who had gotten a bit carried away by the dacoit story; a thing like that could and would get back to the Goblin. "You don't realize what it means to have a *determined* man like John Terrence Hobson behind you. People are deceived by his short stature, they think he's . . . ah-h, chubby, ineffectual, but he's actually quite muscular, he's a good handball player—but what I am trying to *say* is that plenty of writers would sell their grandmother for the chance you've got. Hob's interest guarantees not only that the pilot will be made but that the series will run, almost certainly."

"Very true, Florence. Hob has a *lot* of influence."

"He sure as hell does," said Jim with a solemn enthusiasm. "You don't realize it, but we are practically airborne already. Our seat belts are buckled and the jets are rumbling on the runway—and all because a tremendously determined and, yes, deeply sentimental guy named *John Terrence Hobson* is up there in the cockpit."

"I enjoy flying," said Florence. "But don't we need wings?"

"Wings?"

"I mean, even with John Terrence Hobson at the controls,

wouldn't we look kind of silly, tearing madly down the runway without any wings?"

"My dear girl, we've got all *kinds* of wings. You wait. We haven't even begun to work on this yet. Great ideas will occur to you."

"The only idea that has occurred to me so far is . . . oh, never mind, it isn't any good."

"Go ahead," said Jim, "spit-ball."

"Well, since it's a comedy-adventure series, I thought for the comedy part a diabolical midget cabin boy that causes trouble might be funny."

"That's not bad," said Jim. "Except he should be pesky, not diabolical. I think you've latched onto something—I can see him, a snaggle-toothed, freckle-faced, all-American boy, a pesky l'il devil and loaded with vitality, a kind of cleaned-up Huck Finn off having grand adventures all over the world with the tanned, bearded captain whom he idolizes, worships, adores. He fights with the Chinese cook, Yim-Yee, and the dour first mate, Hulk Svenson. Yes. Terrific! It adds a whole new dimension. Get the kiddie trade and the mommie trade, we already got Pop and Junior with the barracudas and blood. You have made a great contribution already, Florence. Wait till Hob hears about it, he'll lap it up on his hands and knees. He'll collapse all over himself. This freckle-faced, pesky, all-American kid is a touch of sheer genius."

"Are you kidding?" asked Florence. "What I had in mind was a horrible midget who wades through the ship's bilge catching rats and cutting off their tails."

"We could have that too. 'Rat-Catcher,' an eccentric, a weirdo, a Barbudian helper to Yim-Yee, hates rats, sets traps for them all the time and sings calypso, 'Lemon Tree, Lemon Tree'—has one eye maybe, tells ghost stories, a charming eccentric weirdo, protects the pesky kid from hot-tempered but lovable Yim-Yee—'Rat-Catcher,' a great character! You've done it again, Florence. We're a team already. Hit me with something else."

"How about a crocodile in the boiler?"

"Mmm," said Jim, "can't do much with that. But we can get a crocodile on board somewhere, charging back and forth and knocking over bales of jute, treeing Yim-Yee up the mast—a trick of the pesky cabin boy somehow. Nothing basic, but it's a show. Hit me again, Florence, I'm hot."

"This is crazy," said Florence. "Who's supposed to write this, anyhow, me or you?"

"I'm a creative producer, honey," said Jim. "Wait a minute, wait a minute, I've got something basic. The crocodile, that's going too far, it's a dangerous prank, poor old Yim-Yee could've been seriously hurt. I see a basic scene—runs right through the whole series like a strand. The captain calls snaggle-toothed Pesky Boy in the chart room, sits him down all solemn, fixes a beady stare on him, and says, 'Snag, it's time for you and me to have *a captain to cabin boy talk.*' How's that? Get the echo from Andy Hardy and the Judge? What do you think? Does it stick on the wall?"

"Does it what?"

"Do you *like* it, Florence—the tender man-boy thing as a basic scene?" The phone on the coffee table buzzed before Florence could answer. Jim put a hand on his forehead. "Jesus in heaven above, what now?" he asked, and picked up the phone. "Yes, Susan?"

"I . . . I'm sorry . . ."

"What *is* it, Susan?"

"Well . . . it's the Chief Electrician. He's here and he says he's absolutely got to speak to you."

"All right," said Jim. "An example of what happens when an organization makes more money than it knows what to do with. This kind of madness goes on around here all the time." Jim got up, walked to the anteroom door, opened it, and stared flatly at the chief electrician, a gray-haired man who could not quite meet his eye.

"Look, Mr. Kittering, I hate to bother you, but I got orders from Mr. McAllister personally to hook up the intercom this morning without fail. There's a meeting of the Board of Directors this afternoon at three and he wants to demonstrate it."

The chief electrician seemed a bit nervous and edgy, as well he might be. Wallace McAllister was the big boy of them all, Chairman of the Board of American International Television & Radio, Incorporated, the Goblin's boss, a stuffy and starchy man worth many millions of dollars. "Well," asked Jim, "why didn't you tell your man to say so in the first place?"

"I'm sorry, but it'll only take a minute, I can do it myself."

"Go ahead," said Jim.

As the chief electrician quickly stripped wires buried in the thick cable and connected them to the ugly electronic equipment on the shelf above the door to Jim's private bathroom, the conversation continued as if he were not there.

"All right, Florence," said Jim, "what I was asking you is, do you like the tender man-boy thing as a basic scene?"

"To be completely honest," said Florence, "I'm not crazy about it. I didn't like Andy Hardy a hell of a lot the first time around."

"Well . . . it's solid stuff, Florence. Don't turn your nose up at it till you've smelled it twice."

"You're making me dizzy. And I *still* don't know anything about tramp steamers. Let's go back for a second. I know you were kidding, but I kind of *liked* that idea about a cuckoo family that raises dachshunds in Vermont."

"Florence, there's nothing in Vermont but sugarbushes and stretchpants."

Al Ingerman said, "I think Jimmy is right, Florence. There've been too many families lately, and the locale isn't any good."

"Sorry to have bothered you folks," said the chief electrician. "This is a hectic day. We got sixteen of these to hook up before three o'clock—"

"Thank you," said Jim. "You can go out, just close the door."

"Sorry again to have bothered you."

As the door closed, the phone buzzed. "This place is a madhouse! How can I work under these conditions? I'll slaughter that girl!" Jim grabbed the phone. "Susan, I said no calls!"

"It's *him!* The Goblin! I mean, I'm sorry—Mr. *Hob*son!"

Paralyzed, Jim stared at the extension phone on the coffee table. With an effort, he pressed a button. "Yes, Hob?"

Silence. Jim gripped the phone and maintained a calm composure despite little dancing spots before his eyes.

"Hello, Hob? Are you there?"

He had expected it. He could not call the Goblin the Goblin and get away with it. Anything said in front of Al Ingerman might as well be said to Hob himself. Of course Al had reported the incident and this was the punishment.

"Hob?"

Il silenzio. It was an old and favored trick; even back in the heady days before millions were made and power was consolidated, the Goblin had loved to call people up and lurk on the phone like a monstrous silent spider. It was one of countless tricks he had to inspire nameless dread, and the amazing thing was the blood-curdling effectiveness of it. What was the Goblin *thinking?* What did it *mean?* Was it an innocent thing, had he put down the phone for a moment to light his pipe? No, he was there, eyes gleaming beneath half-shut lids, pipe in mouth, short athletic figure erect at his desk in the gloomy, locked office no one dared enter without a specific invitation seldom given. He was there, all right, shoulders squared and pudgy jaw set firm against a stubborn universe that foolishly resisted his demands. Oh, yes, that faint soughing was his breath, and what was one to do? To hang up was unthinkable, but what else? How long could a man endure the absolute reproach of total noncommunication?

"Hob—are you there or not?"

Little clicks on the wire. *Il silenzio* had been administered. Jim forced himself to face Al Ingerman, the loathsome rat who had caused it all. "Must have been cut off," he said casually. "Where were we?"

"We were talking about the problem of my ignorance of tramp steamers," said Florence. "At least that's what *I* was talking about. *You* were talking about Andy Hardy and the Judge and a whole flock of lovable characters named Rat-Catcher, Hulk Svenson, Yim-Yee, and Snag."

Jim Kittering stared off abstractedly into space. The son of a bitch had punished him with *il silenzio* at the very moment when he was coming up with one brilliant idea after the other. A tail should be put on him for that. Once again the thought crossed Jim's mind that perhaps the Goblin was in trouble. Perhaps he was putting on the pressure of *il silenzio* not out of playful sadism but out of desperation. It was certainly possible. A stuffy and dignified man like McAllister, who attended all the big charity balls and even went for dinner at the White House, would be appalled by the Goblin's orgies. And those falling ratings. But Jim could not believe it. The Goblin had seemed to be cornered many times before and he always came out of it stronger than ever. "Mmm, yes," said Jim. "Andy Hardy and the Judge. Well, art is derivative, Florence. We all borrow a cup of sugar once in a while in the creative sphere. Beethoven's Seventh Symphony is based on a folk tune, or a movement of it anyhow."

The phone buzzed again and Jim quickly picked it up. This was a real call. Now the Goblin would talk—or, rather, whisper.

"Yes, Susan?"

"It's *him* again."

Jim pressed the lighted button. "Yes, Hob?"

"Hello, Jim," said a voice as if from far away, although in fact the Goblin's locked and sealed office was right down the corridor. "Hello? Jim, are you there?"

"Yes, Hob, I'm here."

"Good," whispered the Goblin. Jim pressed the receiver tightly against his head and put a palm over his other ear. It was one of the most maddening of the Goblin's tricks—that barely audible whisper somehow contained an immeasurable egomania. "I called you before but we were cut off. How is mmum muzz blutuh muh?"

"I'm sorry, Hob, I can't hear you."

"I said, how is everything going with the mutuh bizz bluh mum bum?"

"Hob, maybe I am getting deaf, but I simply *cannot* hear you."

"Oh. I will speak louder. How . . . is . . . everything going . . . with Florence Carr?"

"It's going fine," said Jim.

"Nuh muh tuh?"

"*What*, Hob?"

"I said, no problems?"

"Not any serious problems."

"Oh. What problems do you have?"

"Not any, really."

"Jim. *Jim*. I asked a question. Won't you answer?"

"Well, Florence feels she doesn't know anything about tramp steamers, Hob, that's all."

"Muh tuh guh nugga mum?"

"What, Hob?"

"I said, Jim, I can't understand you."

"I can't understand you either, Hob. I've got to get a hearing aid, I'm getting deaf as a post."

Watch out, thought Jim, *danger*. The Goblin had no sense of humor and he did not like jokes about his tricks. But the whisper when it came showed no anger: "Excuse me, Jim, I'll try to speak louder. What I said was, I don't understand why you consider that a problem."

"Hob, she feels a writer should know something about his subject matter."

"Jim, the subject matter of a writer is humanity. That is the only subject matter any writer ever wrote about. And there is only one theme, Jim, one single theme in all of literature and all of dramatic art. It is the only theme any writer worth his salt has ever written about, Jim, you know that you know that. The rights of the individual in conflict with the rights of other individuals singly and collectively, the struggle of the individual to live with his fellow man, yes. Man struggling to live with himself in war, in love, and in peace. But most especially, Jim, in the area of *love,* because *love* is at the core of human existence and survival, thus it dominates both war and peace, wholly so. There, Jim, is the great theme: *love* between man and woman, father and son, mother and child, friend and friend. But most of all, man and woman, yes, man and woman, because there lies the *future,* not the past, not the present, the *future* and the hope of us all. What happens between *man and woman* determines with a logarithmic exactitude the nature, quality, and essence of civilization itself. Can you hear me clearly now?"

"Yes, I can hear you clearly."

"The theme of 'Tramp Steamer' is this universal single theme, isn't it?"

"I suppose it is, Hob."

"Then I don't see how you can say there's any problem with Florence Carr."

"I said it wasn't serious, Hob."

"But I don't see how there's any problem at all, Jim."

"Well . . . perhaps it's . . . perhaps there isn't."

"Of course there isn't. Life on a wandering merchant ship is life *any*where. The human equation is constant, the terms of our deal with God do not alter and do not change. Artists—or I should say, great artists—perceive this, and with an unfaltering inspiration confirm it anew, as the sun confirms anew each day of our lives. That is the purpose of the artist, Jim, to remind us of our deal with God, to awaken within us a consciousness of our unending challenge to live with one another in *love,* despite all the pressures of growth the destiny of the species inflicts upon us. Why, now, Jim, there is no true originality in art, you know that you know that. The artist reaffirms and reinterprets the truth of our condition in terms of our changing experience. It is a simple thing, yes, but a profound thing, too, a thing that requires great independence of spirit and a defiant moral courage that goes far beyond the human norm. I have always *loved* the story of the prisoner at the bar who was sternly read his fate by the judge: 'I condemn you to be hanged by the neck until you are dead, dead, dead. Do you have anything to say?' And the man replied: 'Yes, I do. You can kiss my ass until it's red, red, red.' Don't you just *love* that story? What a story, gosh. It . . . it *moves* me. How I admire the gumption of that fella. Jiminy crickets, what courage."

For a moment the Goblin was too overcome by emotion to continue. Jim could hear the rustle of a handkerchief, then an abrupt snorting sound as the Goblin blew his nose. Jim, of course, had heard the man-woman love speech and the dead-dead-dead, red-red-red tale many times before. To listen to it was maddening. The whisper resumed, cold and calm:

"That, Jim, is the mark of the artist, an intransigeance beyond the norm, a spirit able to rise above the herd instinct that governs and numbs the sensibilities of most men. And that is the spirit I have detected in Florence Carr. Let me repeat. Life on a wandering merchant ship is life anywhere. The circumstances and surroundings in which the drama of love unfolds do not matter." The Goblin paused for such a long time Jim began to think he was through, then suddenly the cold whisper turned warm and friendly. Jim braced himself. He knew from experience that when the Goblin became warm and friendly, all hell was about to break loose. "How can you fail to understand that, Jim? It worries me. I seem to observe an unexpected and hurtful thing, a thing hurtful to me personally, Jim, and it disturbs me oh it disturbs me. It disturbs me a great deal, more than I would care to say. I refer, Jim, to *growing traces of cynicism in you lately*."

The son of a bitch was unendurable. The Goblin might or might not be in trouble, but he *had* to tail him! Not a big one, a little one about five feet long with a fork on it. "Hob, I know you're a great authority on *love*, especially the man-woman aspect of it. But we *do* have a practical problem here and Florence is right to be apprehensive. She might not need to know *much* about tramp steamers, but for crying out loud she's got to know *some*thing. Frankly, I think she ought to take a trip on a merchant ship."

Silence. The adrenalin was pumping. Jim leaned forward and said: "I like that story about the prisoner, too, Hob. And if I didn't have at least *some* of that quality in me, would I be much use to you or anyone else? Presumably, you don't pay me for kissing your ass, but for having it in me, if necessary, to suggest you kiss my own." Jim paused, and a final spurt of adrenalin put him over the top. "And that's *exactly* what I'm suggesting, Hob. You detect traces of cynicism in me, huh? That's like the Great Dismal Swamp calling Walden Pond a bog. Hob, you can kiss my ass until it's red, red, red."

"Hee-hee-hee-hee!"

The adrenalin was gone and a wash of fear flowed through Jim Kittering. What madness had possessed him? The Goblin would never forgive him. Jim moistened his lips and swallowed, taking care to make no audible gulp. "Well . . . that's what I think, anyhow. And I don't see anything so amusing about it. If we're planning to spend eight hundred thousand on this pilot, why shouldn't Florence take a five-hundred-dollar cruise on a merchant ship?"

"Jim. Jim. Don't you know me better than that? You have misunderstood me completely. I'm not laughing because your suggestion is stupid, I'm laughing because *neither* of us thought of it before. Of course, I expected the writer to do research but it hadn't occurred to me to send her off on a journey. I am grateful to you, Jim, and it's quite true I don't pay you for muz guh ubble um bum bum. When you are through with your conference—please don't rush—would you kindly nuh guh uffuh hum bum?"

"I didn't quite get that last part, Hob."

"When you're through with your conference, please stop by the office. I'll tell Cecily you're expected. But please don't rush. When you're all done, stop by."

"You mean with Florence?"

"Oh, yes. *Both* of you. Ha, ha, ha, ha. You have surprised me, Jim, and now I shall suh muh um-bum bugger-ugger."

"What, Hob?"

Click. The Goblin was gone, off on a broomstick over the rooftops and up to God-knows-what-kind of mischief. That last inaudible mumble had sounded like a threat. But Jim Kittering did not care. Let the Goblin fire him, let ruination come—it was a *real* tailing, it would go down in legend! Oh, the beauty of it! If there was one thing sacred to the Goblin, it was that hateful speech of his about love being the theme of all literature and dramatic art. And not only that, he had thrown the red-red-red thing right back at him! The Goblin for years had used the story to remind his victims what pusillanimous wretches they were. Beauty! Truth! Jim could almost have cried with joy.

Al Ingerman was gray. "What . . . what happened?" he asked.

"We are summoned to the throne," said Jim with a smile. "Or should I say *den?*"

"You mean . . . Hob wants to see us?"

"Yes, he does. We'll stroll around there in forty-five minutes or so and have a little chat with him. The gypsy in me tells me you're going on an ocean voyage, Florence."

Florence nodded. "I think that's a good idea. Damned good. In fact, I feel encouraged. If we could just get away from Andy Hardy and the Judge, I think we might make some headway."

Jim's exhilaration was ebbing. He had a feeling something was wrong. A peculiar damp sweat had come on his forehead. Perhaps it was a malfunction in the air conditioning. The ducts were making an odd soughing noise, a kind of slow *whew, whew, whew.* For all the money they spent around there, nothing worked. "Well," said Jim, "we might be able to give it a little ironic edge, not play the man-boy thing completely straight. That might help."

"I don't think it would," said Florence. "But actually some of your other ideas weren't bad. Rat-Catcher and all the rest of them were kind of cute. My only complaint is they're all *lovable.* You can't have a story with all the characters being lovable. There's no drama to it, no conflict, no meaning, nothing."

"Umm," said Jim. "You don't understand this medium." The phone buzzed again. Jim was too limp to react with annoyance. He shrugged and picked it up. "Yes, Susan?"

"It's him *again.* But wait—he wants to speak to Mr. Ingerman."

"Oh?" said Jim. He turned to Al. "It's for you. Hob."

"*Me?* He wants to speak to *me?*"

"Yes, Al, you."

Al reached over and took the phone. "Hello, Hob. Yes. Yes, Hob. Well . . . sure, I suppose so. You mean tonight?" Jim took out a cigarette and lighted it, eyes fixed on the sweating Al. What was all of this? What was the Goblin up to? Again Jim had a feeling something was wrong somewhere. "No, I don't think so, Hob. Not after last week. Well, I know, I like her too. I know, Hob, I know. But some of them are hopeless. No, Hob, a coat wouldn't help. She's hysterical, forget her. What? I can't hear you, Hob. Betty? Yes, definitely. And

Joyce, sure." Jim listened in amazement. The horrible toad was arranging an orgy with Al on the phone, indifferent to the fact that he and Florence Carr could hear half the conversation and probably understand it. Al Ingerman was perspiring like a pig and kept glancing around with nervous guilt at him and Florence. "Oh, yes. Tina is fine. What? What, Hob? Oh, that one. Well, I don't know about her. She *is* ambitious. Maybe, I could try. But Hob, we're in a meeting, it's kind of hard to go into it on the phone. What? What, Hob?" Al suddenly sighed with relief. "Yes, good. I'll come right down and we'll . . . discuss this casting problem. Right." Al hung up and turned with a slightly sick smile to Jim and Florence. "Hob wants me to come to his office and discuss a casting problem for an important pilot. Do you need me?"

"Of course we need you, Al," said Jim gently. "But if Hob has a casting problem, we'll struggle along without you."

Al's smile became even sicker. Incredible as it was, the wretch was embarrassed. "Well, these things come up," he said.

As Jim watched Al slink out of the office, he suddenly realized what was wrong. The air conditioning was not working right, the ducts were still making that soughing noise, but this was not the reason Jim had damp perspiration on his forehead. The truth was he had tailed the Goblin and gotten away with it. The Goblin was not going to fire him and this call to Al was proof of it.

First, the Goblin had taken his anger out on Al, by deliberately exposing him as a pimp in front of them both. Therefore it was plain he could not and did not intend to take his anger out on Jim. Second, Jim knew from long observation that whenever the Goblin was frustrated, when McAllister or some important star would not do what he wanted, there was always an orgy. The Goblin was in trouble and he had no choice but to take the tailing.

Somehow Jim was disappointed, let down. He had given the Goblin the worst tailing imaginable and gotten away with it. Thus, in a sense, it was not a real tailing at all. If the Goblin would accept it, if it was to his own best interest to let Jim get away with it, then no tailing had occurred. The game of "Tailing the Goblin" depended on doing something intolerable to him. Jim frowned as he listened to the soughing air conditioner. What could he do that would be intolerable to the Goblin?

Jim smiled at Florence. "Well, now we're rid of that loathsome rat,

I can be honest with you," he said. "Your so-called agent, Florence, is a stooge of the Goblin, and the Goblin, as you may have guessed, is my boss, the mad genius who runs this place."

"Yes, I guessed that," said Florence.

"Now, you objected a moment ago to Andy Hardy and the Judge."

"And to all the characters being lovable."

"Precisely. Now Florence, I want to outline for you, as succinctly as possible, the principles by which this medium operates. Let's talk about money again, but this time without any effort to bamboozle you. Money is what interests us here, Florence. It might not interest you, but it interests us, it's the *only* thing that interests us, because money is the measure of the success with which we move our product and sustain this medium. We are neither artists ourselves nor are we patrons of art like the Medici. Far from it. We are salesmen. We sell a specific product on which we make a very great profit. Our profit is so gigantic, it's a scandal. I refer, of course, not to myself when I speak of profit, I am merely an employee here. I refer to the stockholders and to the medium itself."

"Sure, I understand you. Go on, this is very interesting."

"You haven't heard anything. Let me ask you, Florence—do you know what our product is?"

"Entertainment, I suppose?"

"Oh, no. I am sorry, Florence, we have no interest in entertainment. That is not our product."

"Okay. What is it, then?"

"There are *two* products: an intermediary product and a final product. Let us start at the end and go backward. Our final product is *audience*. Here we have the *Law of Audience*. Eyes and ears. This is generally recognized by those familiar with the medium and it has been described by several theoreticians as the *sole* product of the medium. Eyes and ears. Ten million pairs of eyes and ears are worth x dollars on the market. Fifty million pairs of eyes and ears are worth, however, considerably more than five times x dollars, because the progression tends to be geometric, which accounts for the ruthless premium on success, success, success. It also explains the merciless death administered to 'failures' that would be triumphs in any previous era of human culture. The medium is *a new thing,* hitherto unknown. Do you follow me?"

"I follow you," said Florence.

"The theory of the Law of Audience holds, as I said, that we are interested *solely* in eyes and ears, that audience is our only concern. Thus, we hire people like yourself to beat a drum to gather an audience, then we sell the audience to a pitchman who in turn sells snake oil. Understand?"

"Exactly," said Florence.

"I knew you would. Now, this theory holds water and is true as far as it goes. Our final product *is* audience. However, a second theory, which I modestly claim for my own, takes us a step farther to the truth. The problem, you see, is how we attract audience in the first place, because if we do not attract it we cannot sell it. The answer is we must manufacture an *intermediary* product in order to obtain our *final* product. Therefore, let me ask you what is the intermediary product by means of which we attract and sell audience?"

"Well," said Florence, "back to my first answer. Entertainment."

"No, our intermediary product is *gluck*. Pure gluck."

"Mmmm, gluck."

"Yes, gluck. Think about it logically for a moment, Florence. The overall purpose of the medium is to sell audience to those who in turn sell garbage to that audience. Billions and billions of dollars' worth of garbage. Thus, the purpose of the medium has nothing whatever to do with art, truth, beauty, or the struggle of the human spirit. No, the purpose of the medium is simply to assist in the distribution of garbage, the greatest amount of garbage known in the history of the world, a vast mountain of garbage. What else would barbarous pinheads use computerized mass production *for*, Florence, than to turn out an annual Mount Everest of garbage? The garbage is *there*, like Mount Everest, but no one would want to climb it, therefore it must be gobbled up every year. We help people gobble garbage, Florence. That is our job."

Florence Carr seemed fascinated by the discourse. "You know," she said, "you have really surprised me."

"I'm glad, but let me conclude, Florence. The key question is: Who will buy garbage, who will gobble it? Let us be generous and say ten percent of the people in this country are immune to the lure of garbage, they won't buy it, they won't gobble. But ninety percent will buy, they will gobble. We don't *care* about that ten percent because such fastidious people are useless. Our target is the ninety percent. And my final question is—how would you attract people who like garbage? Logically, how would you do it?"

"Give them gluck?"

"Right! And that's what we give them. Gluck. Andy Hardy and the Judge. Lovable characters. You see, Florence, the thing about gluck is it *exists in a vacuum.* We have learned from bitter experience gluck contains nothing disturbing, controversial, exceptional, depressing, exciting, true, or beautiful. Art contains such elements invariably and necessarily, gluck does not. It tells us of lovable eccentrics who catch rats and sing 'Lemon Tree, Lemon Tree' while protecting a pesky, snaggle-toothed, all-American boy from a lovable cook who wouldn't hurt him in the first place. There is nothing of the sweat and grime or the beauty and glory of life in gluck, Florence. It exists in a vacuum."

"I can see what you mean, and it's an interesting theory. But I wonder if you're completely right. Do you really believe the public is so dumb? I mean, that empty?"

"I *know* it, Florence. The fact is confirmed in millions of living rooms every day, as endless gluck pours out on the living room rugs. Ninety percent of the people like gluck. They love gluck, they relish it. They eat it off the living room rug with a spoon and go yum-yum-yum."

Florence seemed gloomy. "Maybe you're right. Maybe it's the ten percent that wants truth and beauty and so forth."

"Certainly," said Jim. "Great art requires a great audience. To respond to a great painting, for example, one must have qualities of high sensibility and perception. The vast majority of people simply do not have such qualities. Therefore, we manufacture gluck."

For some time now, the slow soughing of the air conditioner had seemed to be louder. Several times Florence had glanced around in a puzzled manner and now she asked, "What *is* that noise?"

"It's the air conditioning," said Jim.

"No, it's a kind of funny *huuuh, huuuh, huuuh* noise, almost like somebody breathing. Besides, it isn't coming from the air-conditioning ducts. It's coming from that equipment up over the bathroom door."

Jim looked up quickly at the small TV monitor and the other electronic gadgets hooked to the cable above the bathroom door. In a flash, in an insant, he saw the trap. It was not McAllister who had ordered the chief electrician to hook up the cable, there was no board meeting that afternoon at three, and Al Ingerman had not been withdrawn from the room to plan an orgy but to give James Kittering rope to hang himself. The Goblin was not in trouble, the Goblin was in command.

"Well, Hob?" asked Jim. "Have you enjoyed the conversation?"

The tube of the TV monitor began to blink and specks of light raced back and forth across the face of it until it came into focus to show a small but clear picture of the Goblin at his desk. His voice came loud and clear into the room from twin speakers on either side of the monitor.

"I have found it interesting, Jim."

"You can see me clearly?"

"Oh, yes. And the young lady beside you as well—Miss Carr, I presume?" Florence stared open-mouthed. "My name is John Hobson. I hope you'll forgive me for eavesdropping on you like this."

"Oh . . . ahh, sure," said Florence.

"How long have you been watching and listening?" asked Jim.

"Since the Chief Electrician hooked up the cable, Jim."

"You mean you were looking into the monitor during our phone conversation?"

"Oh, yes. Sneaky of me, wasn't it?"

"Strange," said Jim. "I think subconsciously I knew it the whole time. The Chief Electrician couldn't look me in the eye and it occurred to me he was lying about something. And I think I knew deep inside that soughing noise wasn't the air-conditioning. We could hear you breathing, Hob."

"Yes, I know. An oversight on my part. I should have turned off the speakers in your office as well as the monitor. Of course this wouldn't have affected my own speakers or picture. I won't make the mistake again."

"You're going to do this again, Hob? Watch and listen to people without their knowledge?"

"Why, certainly, Jim. That's the whole point of the intercom—to enable me to know what is going on at all times."

"Kind of like Big Brother, huh?"

"Oh, I don't think so. Of course, in private life such snooping would pose an ethical problem, but this is a business. As the Chief Executive of this organization, don't you think I'm entitled to know what's going on? Besides, why should my executives want to conceal anything from me? Aren't we a team here, and am I not the coach?"

"I think you'll get a few resignations."

"I doubt it. However, let's come to the point, Jim. I found your theory of audience and gluck interesting. It reveals to me a cynicism so profound I could not credit my ears. I don't mind telling you—and Al, who is here, will confirm this—I wept while I listened to you, I wept. As a father would weep over a son."

"Oh, for Christ's sake, go on and fire me and get it over with!"

"Fire you? I'm not going to fire you, Jim."

Jim leaned back in his chair as he gazed up at the small glowing monitor over the bathroom door. "You're not going to fire me?"

"No, I'm going to *save* you."

"Oh, I see," said Jim. What diabolical thing was the Goblin going to do to him? "How are you going to go about saving me, Hob?"

"Don't worry, Jim. I will save you, despite the terrible harm your remarks surely have done to Miss Carr. But first I want to speak to her briefly. Florence, don't judge Jim harshly. He didn't mean those things he said and of course none of them were true. We want the best you have got. In fact, we demand the best you have got. Nothing is too good for the people of this great country, but we will talk about this in greater detail when you come to my office. Let me ask you if you are free at once to take a cruise on a merchant ship?"

"Yes, I suppose so," said Florence.

"Wonderful. Now, since Jim made that suggestion, I have had three secretaries busily consulting with travel agents. It's very difficult to do these things on the spur of the moment, but we've managed it. I have a reservation for you on a ship sailing from Savannah, Georgia, tomorrow at midnight for Bluefields, Nicaragua, and other ports in Central and South America. You will leave tonight by jet from Kennedy, fly to Atlanta, change to a flight for Savannah, and board the *S.S. Lorna Loone* tomorrow at your convenience. How does that sound?"

"Exciting," said Florence.

"The *S.S. Lorna Loone,* I'm afraid, is not one of the most modern or luxurious merchant ships in the world. It—or I should say, *she*—isn't very large and I understand the air conditioning is broken. You might find it a little uncomfortable in the tropics without air conditioning, and I imagine the food won't be quite on a par with that of La Caravelle. The ship *is* seaworthy, I am told. The captain—I spoke to him briefly long distance—doesn't have a lot of English. He seems to be a Norwegian or something. I believe he was drinking. I wouldn't say 'exciting' is quite the word to describe the *S.S. Lorna Loone*, Florence. But of course this isn't a pleasure trip."

"No, of course not," said Florence.

"I assure you it was the best we could do on such short notice and I hope you aren't too uncomfortable. As a solace, I am having the accounting department draw you up a check for ten thousand dollars. This is an advance against your guarantee, which will be larger, to do this pilot. We will work out a deal with Al when you come to the office, if that's agreeable with you."

"Sure," said Florence.

"Wonderful. Now, back to Jim. Let me say, Jim, I know what is wrong with you, I understand the cause of cynicism. It is caused by isolation, Jim, isolation from the hurly-burly of life. Ivory-towerism causes cynicism, Jim, therefore we are going to take you out of your ivory tower and that is how I am going to save you."

"Can you be a little more specific about how this salvation is going to work, Hob?"

"Yes, I can. You are going with Florence, Jim."

"I'm going with Florence?"

"That is correct. It will not only remove you from your ivory tower and put you back into the hurly-burly of life, it will also provide opportunity for you to work closely over a period of time with Florence. This cruise of the *S.S. Lorna Loone* will last twenty-three days, Jim. You and Florence should be able to do an enormous amount of research."

How like the Goblin it was. To fire him outright was too clean. Instead, he would send him off on a horrible cruise for twenty-three days on a horrible boat with a homely Lesbian for company, then calmly fire him when he got back. Jim hadn't a doubt of it. That was precisely what the Goblin would do. But the diabolical part was Jim could not be *absolutely* sure. He had no choice but to go to Bluefields, Nicaragua.

"You're very kind, Hob."

"It's because I think of you as a son, Jim, even though there's not much difference between our ages. You're a child, an erring child. But don't worry. Go with Florence, help her with her research, guide her in developing 'Tramp Steamer,' and go back into life and get over this attack of ivory-tower cynicism—and I guarantee you, Jim, your job will be waiting for you when you return. And I don't know if you can see it on this small monitor, but I say that with tears in my eyes."

It was impossible to tail the Goblin in the first place, just as it was fundamentally impossible to kid along Linda. Jim Kittering, in one sweet short morning, had lost both wife and job in exchange for a trip to Bluefields, Nicaragua, and other ports in Central and South America. The game of "Tailing the Goblin" was lost.

PART TWO
New Year's Eve

SIX

Goodbye, My Lover

As he drove over the George Washington bridge in a blowing rain, Jim Kittering thought of a sweet little song his mother used to sing to him to comfort him when he was a very small child. Even years thereafter, the words of the song—"Steamboat coming 'round the bend, goodbye, my lover, goodbye"—would occur to him when the terrors of life seemed too much to endure.

Well, it was a fitting theme song for him; he had said goodbye to quite a few lovers in his day. Something in his nature appealed strongly to girls and women and he had often wondered what it was. Desire? Need? They frequently said they wanted to "mother" him. And they also said: "You wanted me so much." Whatever the answer, something in his personality or outlook appealed strongly to women. None about whom he cared had ever said "Goodbye, my lover" to him and meant it. Not yet.

Jim could not get the melody out of his head and to escape it he turned on the car radio as he reached the Jersey shore. By a small coincidence—he soon would hear again the identical record—the mournful dream of holes in Blackburn, Lancashire, greeted his ears. A far cry from his mother's little song, and yet not really such a far cry at all. The Beatles were fearless, yes, and critical of the insane world in which they found themselves, but like all truly brave men they were tender. "I read the news today oh boy . . ." Jim flinched and shut off the radio. Better a steamboat vanishing 'round the bend than four thousand empty holes in Blackburn.

It had begun to drizzle shortly before four o'clock and by the time

Jim turned into the driveway of his home in Cherry Dale an early autumn downpour made it difficult for him to see far enough ahead to stay on the asphalt. Silvery trees leaned dimly right and left in sheets of rain and the windshield wiper went ka-puh-*click*, ka-puh-*click* with an idiot insistence that was futile and depressing. The weather could not have turned gloomier, but the rain would wash the sky and tomorrow would be clear and beautiful. He'd be gone by then, however, to Nicaragua and points south.

Linda was packing when Jim walked into the kitchen from the garage breezeway. He could see her through the serving counter as she walked back and forth in the living room with bits of clothing and toys of the girls. Hands on hips, he stood and watched her, unobserved. She seemed calm. A cigarette was between her lips and a lock of blonde hair hung over one eye. She wore a conservative beige suit and a white shirt with a pair of his own cufflinks. As always, she looked beautiful. The lights were dimmed and the dark day outside did not show her expression clearly, but she seemed in complete control of herself as she neatly folded children's shirts and sweaters and put them in a suitcase.

The record was playing somewhere in the house, undoubtedly in Deborah's bedroom. Jim winced as he heard the joyous twang-twang-twang of an electric guitar and recognized the Beatles' reprise of "Sergeant Pepper's Lonely Hearts Club Band." He winced again as the song was followed by the haunting melancholy of "A Day in the Life." The music conveyed to him such a sense of loss he could not bring himself immediately to go into the living room.

To the incredulous surprise of his older daughter Debbie, Jim liked the Beatles very much. At first Debbie had not believed he meant it; this was some kind of adult sarcasm, a nasty put-on meant to mock her. How could he admire such a song as "Help!", to say nothing of the later, more subtle Beatle works? Deborah, although still a baby, was a highly intelligent and precocious child just as her mother had been; she had gazed at him with a remote anger when he first told her he thought the Beatles were great. "Oh, they're all right," she said.

Jim reached into his pocket for a cigarette as he stood in the dark kitchen and watched his wife spread sweaters in a suitcase. It had been a lovely moment when Debbie realized he meant it. She had looked at him not only with the beautiful transparent emotion of a child but with a new respect.

It was Deborah playing the phonograph. She was precocious in some ways, surprisingly childish in others. Linda must have told her what was happening and, confronted by the loss of her father, she had turned to common ground between them, Sergeant Pepper and his one and only Lonely Hearts Club Band, her favorite of all the Beatle albums and the one he himself liked best. Lucy in the Sky With Diamonds, Mr. Kite and Henry the Horse, Lovely Rita Meter Maid, and those four thousand sad and mournful holes in Blackburn, Lancashire.

And they had to count them all. Jim shook his head with something not unakin to envy. Those crazy boys were poets afraid of nothing. Unaffrighted youth was the thing they had and it was wonderful. He himself had once been like that, but he had lost it completely. How could such a loss have occurred? It could not be an inevitable process of growing older, because it did not happen to all people who grew older. But it had happened to him. Four thousand holes in Cherry Dale were all that was left, four thousand sad and mournful holes that might fill Radio City Music Hall but never had and never could fill the void inside himself.

Jim pushed open the kitchen door and walked through the dining room and on into the living area. "Hello, Linda," he said.

"Oh, hello," she answered.

A peculiar smell was in the air, an acrid reek of something burned. Jim clasped his hands behind him, rocked on his heels, and sniffed. "What's the funny smell?" he asked.

Linda nodded toward the fireplace. "That," she answered.

"Oh?" said Jim. He could see a large gray-black pile of ashes in the center of the fireplace. "What is it? Or rather, what was it?"

"My mink coat," said Linda.

"You burned it up, huh?"

"Yes, I burned it up."

"Looks like it burned pretty good."

"It wouldn't at first. I couldn't get it started, it would just singe a little and go out."

"I guess it is a little hard to burn a mink coat at that. What did you use, charcoal lighter fluid?"

"No, there was some gasoline in the garage for the lawn mower. I used that."

At this moment a pale and weeping child of eleven came into the living room with an armful of clothing. "Hello, Debbie," said Jim. "I heard you playing the record."

Deborah, who was a blue-eyed blonde like her mother and just as beautiful, turned a tearful gaze upon him but did not reply. Jim noticed, mingled in the midst of the clothes, a large and battered Raggedy Ann doll he had not seen for years. Precocious as she was, she was still a baby. Under pressure, Deborah wept and clutched her doll.

"We can't take all that, Debbie," said Linda.

"Most of it isn't even mine! The dresses are Sandy's, not even mine!"

"Stop crying, Debbie, it isn't doing any good. Where's Sandy?"

"She . . . she's locked herself in the bathroom."

"Well, take Raggedy Ann and half this stuff back, and tell her I said come out."

"Oh, Mother . . ."

"Go and do what I said."

As Jim watched his older daughter walk weeping across the living room with children's clothing and a rag doll in her arms, he felt faint and sat on the arm of the big living room sofa upon which Linda had placed four suitcases. Three of them were already packed and closed. Tiny oblong blood cells floated before his eyes as he lighted the cigarette he had been holding in his hand for the past five minutes. "The girls are upset?" he asked.

"Yes, they're upset," said Linda. Calmly, she folded another child's shirt and placed it in the last remaining suitcase.

Jim glanced again at the gray-black pile of ashes in the fireplace. "It's funny," he said. "That mink coat was just about the only thing in this house that's paid for. When did you burn it, right after our phone conversation?"

"About an hour after. It was pretty silly, I suppose, but I don't think I've ever done anything in my life that was more satisfying. What was it they said at Watts—burn, baby, burn? I'm sure I don't know what it's like to be a Negro in an obvious ghetto, but I've lived in a ghetto of my own and that's exactly how I felt."

"Debbie and Sandy must have thought you were crazy."

"They didn't witness the cremation. I hadn't brought them home from school yet."

"Well, that's good. No point in upsetting them unnecessarily."

"Give me one of those cigarettes," said Linda. "I've run out."

"Sure." Jim held out the pack for her and lighted her cigarette. Briefly, her blue eyes lifted and stared into his. "So you're leaving me, huh?" he asked.

"Yes. I'm leaving you."

"Well, it looks like the Goblin is firing me too. This has been one of my bad days, to coin a phrase. All I need now is to vomit blood."

"It *looks* like he's firing you? Is he or isn't he?"

"With the Goblin, you never know."

"I hope he does fire you. It would be the best thing that could ever happen to you to get away from that horrible man."

"I think your hope will be realized. I'd say the probability is about ninety-nine point nine. Do you know what the fiend is doing to me? He is sending me off to Bluefields, Nicaragua."

"To where?"

"It's an awful little port in Central America and don't ask me why it's called Bluefields because I don't know. It has bananas, tarantulas, that sort of stuff."

"What on earth is he sending you there for?"

"It isn't just Bluefields, that's only the first stop. I'm also going to Colón, Cartagena, Barranquilla, and finally Caracas, where, if I'm still alive, I'll catch a jet back to New York."

"I don't get it. Why is he sending you to those places?"

"To punish me, really. Ostensibly it's for research on 'Tramp Steamer.' Three weeks without air conditioning on a broken-down merchant ship. With a Lesbian to keep me company. He'll fire me when I get back sure as God put worms in crab apples."

"Don't go, then."

"I can't do that. You can't predict him, it's impossible to predict him. There's a remote chance he might *not* fire me. He might even promote me. In fact, if I quit, it will turn out that's *exactly* what he intended to do, promote me and give me a big bonus, a juicy stock option or something, maybe even a piece of the show."

"Well, don't quit, then, if you really want the job."

"You don't understand him, Linda. If I *don't* quit, he will fire me. You can't outguess him. It's impossible."

"It sounds to me like if you quit, he will just *pretend* he meant to give you a stock option in order to make you feel bad. So why play his game? Why not just quit?"

"You still don't understand the Goblin. He wouldn't just *pretend* he meant to give me a stock option, he would *actually* have meant to. The man has second sight, Linda. He can read minds and predict the future."

"Oh, nonsense. That's the worst nonsense I ever heard of."

"No, it's true. The Goblin has supernatural powers."

"He hasn't got any power you don't give him."

"I don't give the Goblin anything, he takes it. The power to fire is greater than you know, Linda."

"Maybe. But there's something to be said for the power to quit."

"Sure, I could quit. And I would immediately lose everything I have, including first of all this house."

"That's all right with me. I don't want to ever see this house again."

For the second time, tiny oblong blood cells swam before Jim's eyes. "Are you going to divorce me?" he asked.

"I don't know."

"You don't know, Linda?"

"I probably will, but I don't know."

"I see. You probably will."

"Yes."

Jim nodded and blinked at the blood cells. "Where are you going—to your grandmother's, I suppose?"

Linda said, "Yes, to Gram's," and turned to look over her shoulder. A child, probably the younger Sandy, could be heard crying somewhere in the house. "Sandy?" she called. "You and Debbie get your coats and come here. We've got to go."

"I'm surprised your grandmother would take you in," said Jim.

"She didn't want to at first, but I told her what happened last night and she said for us to come."

"Good God, Linda. You told your *grandmother* what happened last night? You mean about Herb at the party last night, you told her that?"

"Yes, I told her. I didn't want to, but I had to. You know Gram. She told me flatly I couldn't come live with her, the children were too much for her nerves. I had to tell her. I even had to tell her about our pact so she wouldn't think it was an isolated incident."

"Pact? We've never had any pact, Linda, what are you talking about?"

Linda glanced up from the last suitcase, which now was ready to be closed. "Have it your way," she answered. "Believe whatever you want."

"Excuse me for saying so, but I think it was slightly unwise to tell your grandmother such a thing. She'd never understand it in a million years. I can't imagine how she'd react to such a piece of information."

"Do you want me to tell you?"

"I'm not sure I do," said Jim.

"First she said, 'Linda, you're a fool.' Then there was a long pause and she said, 'My poor darling,' and began to cry."

Jim squinted half in pain and half in disbelief. "Your *grandmother* began to cry?"

"I was amazed too. I never heard her cry before in my life, but she did. Then she said for me to leave at once and bring the children."

"Good God, she must despise me."

"That is putting it mildly," answered Linda. "But she doesn't think too highly of me either, if that's any comfort to you. Before she was through, she was calling me all kinds of names and threatening to lock me up in the bedroom."

"She'll do it too," said Jim.

"That's fine with me. It's what I want, a good sound lock with the key in Gram's pocket. And locks on the windows too."

Jim shook his head. "You can't stay locked up the rest of your life, Linda."

"No, but I can stay locked up for a while, at least until I decide what kind of job I'm going to get."

"Job? What are you talking about?"

"I'm going to get a job and pay my board."

Jim smiled. "That's the funniest thing I've heard all day. Your grandmother's worth three million dollars, Linda."

"I don't care if she's worth thirty million. I'm going to get a job and pay my board."

Jim did not believe it. Linda would forget this idea. "Well," he said, "one thing is definite. You've made it impossible for me to have any further relationship with your grandmother."

"Maybe, but I doubt it," said Linda. "She pities you. That's what she said, and she never lies."

"Uh-huh. Well, that *is* comforting. Gram pities me. Maybe she'll pay for my funeral."

"I'm sure she will," said Linda, "and your tombstone, too. But of course you understand—nothing elaborate, just decent."

Jim grinned. "You're really tough, aren't you, Linda? The little blonde I married has become pretty hard-boiled."

"I'm not hard-boiled, Jim," she answered. "That's the whole trouble with me and I don't think I can change it. But Gram was right to call me a fool and that's something I *can* change. I'm not going to be a fool any longer if I can help it."

"A fool, you mean, by staying with me?"

"Yes, a fool by staying with you."

"You're not going to let up for a second, are you? Well, I'm glad you can joke about the modest decent tombstone your grandmother will buy me. That humor might come in handy."

Again her eyes lifted and stared into his own. The dim lamps in the living room and the light of gray day from the window wall did not give enough illumination for him to tell if she'd been crying or not. "Who's threatening cowardly suicide now?" she asked quietly. "It's your life, Jim. There's nothing I can do."

Jim stood on shaky knees and turned on a floor lamp behind the sofa as rain blew against the insulated glass that separated the huge living area from the flagstone veranda and the swimming pool. Linda's face was brightly lighted. She'd been crying, all right. Her eyelids were red and swollen and the whites of her eyes were pinkish. She'd cried all day long while packing and making arrangements to leave, and she was on the verge of tears at this moment. Her control was not nearly so perfect as it had seemed and a tiny hope stirred in Jim Kittering. He said: "Suppose I quit, Linda, and get another job. The house and all this ridiculous furniture would go, everything would go. I'd have to declare personal bankruptcy and start all over with nothing. I'd probably earn a third of what I make now, maybe less. What do you think?"

"I think it would be the best thing you could possibly do, Jim. I hope you do it."

"All right, don't answer me then."

"I answered you. I said I hope you do it." Linda brushed the lock of blonde hair from her eyes and pushed down on the suitcase. "Would you help me close this?"

Jim shoved down on the suitcase, but could not close it. "You'll have to take out some of these things."

"No, the girls need it all. I'll push too. It'll close."

As they pushed the suitcase shut, Jim's arm touched Linda's side and a nervous shock ran through him. A sudden longing to put his arms around her came upon him with such strength he felt sick, feeble, unable to control himself. "There," she said, "it's fixed." Linda's voice was trembly. She had felt the same thing. Jim reached for her and she stepped quickly back. "*No*," she said. Her hands were raised to push him away.

"Linda . . ."

"*No*. I mean it."

Jim tried to smile. "Aren't you going to kiss me goodbye, at least?"

"No, I certainly am not."

"All right, but may I offer a suggestion? This is probably the most important decision you've ever made, Linda, next to marrying me in the first place. Won't you at least take twenty-four hours to think it over?"

"No, I won't," she answered. "I've thought it over for three years and that's long enough."

"Three years?"

"Yes, three years. I was unfaithful to you for the first time on Labor Day weekend three years ago. If you think for a moment, you'll remember the man and the motel we stayed at and my opinion of his love-making, because you know all about it."

"Of course I know about it, you told me about it. But you haven't been thinking of leaving me for three years, Linda."

"I have thought of it again and again and again."

"All right, you've thought of it for three years. I'm asking you to think of it for twenty-four more hours, Linda. Will you do that?"

"No, I won't, Jim. I won't and I can't."

"Linda, I swear to God I won't lay a hand on you. I'll sleep in another room, I'll sleep in here on the sofa. I'll sleep in the swimming pool on an inner tube."

"I'm sorry," she replied. "It's too bad you came home early. I'd planned to be gone before you got here."

"Well, I'm being sent to Nicaragua by the Goblin. I had to come home to pack a suitcase. He's making me take a plane from Kennedy tonight for Atlanta with this Lesbian writer. But if you'll stay, if you'll think it over for just twenty-four hours, I'll quit my job." Was there, or was there not, a trace of irresolution in Linda's eyes? "I'll phone

Hob this minute and resign. Just stay for twenty-four hours, that's all I ask. You can still go to your grandmother's tomorrow if that's your decision."

Linda stared palely at him. For many, many months she had wanted him to quit his job, to "get away from that horrible man." It was her belief Hob had a sinister influence upon him. In fact, Jim's hatred for his boss did not even begin to match Linda's loathing of him. From the beginning, she had despised John Hobson with such intensity she could not control herself in his presence. Five years before at an office cocktail party, she had thrown a lighted cigarette at him. The Goblin giggled in reaction and this infuriated her so much she would have thrown an ashtray at him if Jim had not stopped her. Hob made her ill, literally ill. On those occasions when it was impossible for her to avoid the Goblin's company, she almost invariably wound up vomiting in the bathroom. Again and again she had declared she would rather be dead than to work for such a man. There was hope, definitely hope in Linda's pale face.

"I mean it, Linda, I'll do it, I'm not bluffing. I'll call him up right now and resign if you'll just stay tonight. And I promise I won't touch you, I'll sleep in here or in the swimming pool or wherever you say."

"You wouldn't sleep in the swimming pool," said Linda, "you'd sleep in my arms. It would be a torture for us both and I'm not going to do it."

"Linda, *twenty-four hours*—is that asking too much?"

"Besides, it wouldn't mean anything for you to quit that way. He'd hire you back tomorrow morning. You have to make up your mind independently of me, Jim. If you want to spend your life working for that man, then go ahead and do it." Linda turned to the side and called the girls. "Deborah! Sandy! Will you come now?"

It was all over. There'd been no chance in the first place, not even remotely. In silence Jim carried the suitcases out to the station wagon, then kissed his two weeping children goodbye and turned to Linda. The rain was still coming down and water had run into the breezeway.

"Here's the key," he said. "Drive carefully. The roads will be very slippery and dangerous."

"I just hope I get there before dark," answered Linda.

"You will, it's only about an hour. But I'd take the Connecticut Turnpike, not the Merritt Parkway, in this weather."

"Well, it's a little farther, but I think you're right."

Jim resisted a terrible impulse to grab her by the hand and pull her back as she opened the station-wagon door and slipped into the driver's seat. His knees trembled as he shut the door after her. He smiled and said: "Linda, this reminds me of a song my mother used to sing to me when I was about four years old. 'Steamboat coming 'round the bend, goodbye, my lover, goodbye.' That's about it, I guess. Take care of yourself. . . ." Jim had not meant to put on an emotional exhibition, he had been determined at all costs not to do so, but the thing was beyond his control. At the end of his little farewell speech, which he had intended to have a light philosophical irony, Jim's voice broke and his eyes filled with tears. He could not see Linda clearly. Her pale face and blonde hair were a blur. But he could hear her and he knew from the sound of her voice that she too was crying. At last he had moved her. Now she would get out of the car and he would carry the suitcases back into the house. "Take care of yourself too, darling," she said. "Goodbye, Jim."

"Goodbye, honey," he replied.

It could not be happening. Stunned, Jim stood there in the breezeway as Linda started the station wagon, shifted from park, and drove off slowly down the driveway. For several seconds he continued to stand there, rain blowing in on his face and hair. The station wagon was halfway down the winding drive when Jim suddenly ran out into the pouring rain down the driveway between the leaning silvery tree trunks. He was soaked from head to foot before he'd gone fifty feet and twice stumbled and almost fell, but somehow he caught the station wagon at the entrance gate just as it was about to turn onto the highway.

"Linda, wait!" he cried. He could not see her very well in the gloom through the closed window and for a moment he thought she was not going to lower it, but then she did. Out of breath, Jim put his hands on the open window and said, "Linda—don't leave me! Please don't leave me!"

"Oh, Jim," she said, "don't you understand? There's nothing else I can do."

"Linda, I love you! Don't leave me!"

"I've got to," she answered. "Please go back to the house, Jim. Please."

The girls were silent now, staring at him in awe from the back seat, their little mouths open and their eyes wide, but whatever shame or pride Jim Kittering had felt was all gone now. "Linda, I can't *live* without you! Don't leave me!"

"Please move your hands," she said. "I'm going to close the window."

"Linda! No matter what I've done or failed to do, don't you see how much I love you? Doesn't that mean anything at all?"

Silence. The rain poured down on Jim Kittering's head. Surely, no matter what his crimes or mistakes, she could not be so pitiless as to desert him when he loved her so much and needed her so terribly. It had been a near thing, but she would not really do it. She loved him and would not abandon him. Jim was certain of it. Once again, however, he had underestimated Linda. "All right," she said, "I'll promise you this much. I won't do anything for a year. I told Gram I would file for divorce, but I won't. I'll wait for a year. Now move your hands because I'm going to close the window."

"The children, the children!" he said. "When can I see them?"

"You can arrange through Gram's lawyer to visit them, but you won't see me. Not for a year—I'll meet you then and we'll see what's what." Linda pressed a button and the window began to rise under his fingers. "Goodbye, Jim."

Jim had to snatch his hands back in order to prevent his fingers being pinned to the top of the door by the glass. Darkness surrounded him as the station wagon turned onto the highway and the red taillight receded into the rain and was gone.

So much for all of that, thought Jim as he walked slowly back through the rain toward the house to pack his bag for Nicaragua. There wasn't much else he could do, except blow out his brains and to his surprise he had no such impulse. Now that Linda was gone, he felt relieved. Heartbroken, of course, and in utter despair, but also relieved. It was a reaction he could not even begin to understand. Bewildered as a child, Jim walked up the driveway in blowing rain past silvery trees toward his empty home.

SEVEN

The Blue Unresting Sea

As he waited for the hour to depart for points south and the blue sea, Jim Kittering sat alone in the brightly lighted living room with a bottle of Scotch between his knees and passed the time with sexy dreams of the future and sexy recollections of the past. While exploring these byways along the road of the future and the past, Jim struggled with an increasing desperation to understand the mystery of his own character.

He took a swallow direct from the bottle of Scotch. He did not really feel so bad and the idea of jumping in the swimming pool and drowning himself was just a notion, but the emptiness of the house was too depressing to endure sober. Besides, why not get drunk? During the time he had spent packing his bag, changing from his wet clothes to a tropical suit and then picking indifferently at burned scrambled eggs, Jim had polished off half a fifth of Johnny Walker. He had quite a capacity for whisky but the Scotch on an empty stomach had gotten next to him and he was slightly drunk. In order to see more clearly and diminish somehow the awful emptiness around him, he had turned on every light in the house. He had even turned on the lights of the swimming pool and could see through the window wall a glow of green water in the continuing rain.

"Lovely Linda meter maid," he sighed. "What will I do without you?" It was bewildering to the point of torment. There seemed to be no consistency whatever in his reactions. His initial relief at Linda's departure had been relentlessly displaced by an unbearable despair worse than anything he had felt during the final scene with her and the children. It had come home to him with an undercurrent of horrible surprise that he'd been telling the absolute truth in the rain. In a sense it was true he could not live without Linda; he did love her, he adored and worshiped her, and he was determined to win her back even if it would take a miracle for him to do so.

Queen Victoria, however, would have been as puzzled by his approach to winning back Linda as she would have been puzzled by his tirade on the telephone that morning. As he sat there on the sofa and stared at the remains of his wife's burned mink coat in the fireplace, Jim wrestled with a subtle philosophical question. What, he wondered, had been the sexiest experience of his life? All jokes aside, no kidding, no tomfoolery now, a serious question—what was it, the very sexiest experience, the peak, the Mount Everest of erotica? Which was it, where was it located, what woman or girl? Was it possible at all to pin down this elusive butterfly—or, to stay with the mountain metaphor, could any man of fairly wide experience hope to draw near that distant tower of ambrosia fields and sparkling nectar waterfalls?

"Mmm," said Jim as he rubbed his jaw and narrowed his eyes in cogitation. Linda herself, maybe? That would be nice and . . . well, in a way, perhaps so. Sex with Linda, before all this trouble and even during it, had had a tenderness and a low-key power not to be gainsaid. At times the power was quite a bit more than low-key. He had a very good relationship with his wife in this area, despite all the difficulties between them. Besides, Linda was wonderful, beautiful, he loved her.

But the *sexiest* experience of his life had to be an encounter with another woman; or, rather, a girl, Linda's own nineteen-year-old cousin—nineteen, that is, at the time it happened, but now considerably older, with a dull husband, two orange-haired children, and quite a few more pounds. Jim was pretty sure this was *it* . . . the summit, the peak in the clouds circled by singing cherubs. Maybe Linda's red-haired cousin was not Mount Everest, but she was at least Annapurna. Although he had known more beautiful women than this one, it had been a fantastically sexy experience and an awful thing as well that could have caused catastrophic difficulty.

Catastrophic difficulty was a wan understatement. It had been one of the most cuckoo things he had ever done in his life, but the recollection was helpful at this point. After all, his wife had abandoned him and other women might do the same. It was an irrational fear but he could not quite put out of mind the image of hordes of women fleeing from him in every direction, giving little cries of disgust. It was comforting in this hour of rejection to recall the triumphs of yesteryear. Furthermore, such recollection might throw light on the mystery of his character and the problems that confronted him. For example, *why* had the experience with Linda's cousin been so sexy?

Jim shifted uneasily on the sofa. The future was what counted, not the past. Why bother with a depressing examination of ancient history when a much more powerful experience lay just ahead of him?

A little earlier in the evening, as he stared through the window wall at the rain pocking the emerald surface of the swimming pool, an eerie *déjà vu* had taken possession of Jim Kittering. He would soon see water very much like this but far more beautiful—indeed, on some strange plane of experience *he had seen it already,* and not the familiar ocean of Nassau and St. Thomas but the unknown blue sea of the far-west Caribbean. He had been there already and had known in those blue waters a lovely woman.

The premonition, or illusion, or whatever it was, was so strong Jim could not dismiss it, although he had never claimed psychic powers for himself and did not really believe in such things. But he knew beyond the slightest doubt that the trip before him would be something more than an absurd and pointless punishment. Somehow, in some way, his journey to the blue sea would be a tremendously significant event in his life.

In some incomprehensible way, although he had never been to the west Caribbean, he had previously experienced this trip and had met a woman with whom he shared a love that had changed—or *would* change; the tenses of the thing were a bit murky—his entire point of view toward life itself.

Thus, his subjection to his ogre of a boss, his compulsive pursuit of girls and women, his self-destructive contempt for the work he did, his equally self-destructive financial irresponsibility, and above all else his dreadful emotional conflict with his wife—all of that would be changed as a direct result of his experience with this astounding woman. He would be free at last, free to feel again the joy and beauty of life.

He was not done for and finished after all. The future could and would offer him experience that would enable him to solve all his problems. It was only necessary for him to accept that experience, to welcome it, to learn from it. Change could not come wholly from within, it had also to come from without.

Jim could not doubt the essential reality and truth of his dream, if dream it was. The woman herself was as real to him as his own pale, strained face in the mirror above the mantle. She was there, a beautiful and mysterious woman aboard the *S.S. Lorna Loone,* an olive-skinned South American aristocrat with liquid dark eyes, red lips, and a slender, graceful figure. It was not a matter of conjecture, it had already happened; he had stood with her hand in hand at dawn after a night of love and gazed languidly at a wake of white foam in blue water.

The vision was vivid and rich in specific detail. She wore the bottom half of a brief bikini and one of his own shirts. The shirt was unbuttoned and hung open and the sleeves were rolled above her elbows. Her breasts were conical-shaped and uptilted, with girlish nipples and areolae of coral pink. A small mole was located three inches below and one inch to the left of her navel, which was a rather unusual button type on a smooth stomach of golden tan. As they stood there, a magic scent of musk blended with the smell of the sea, dolphins played, flying fishes flew. Cotton puffs of fair-weather cloud floated overhead.

A smile, gentle pressure on his hand, a whispered word. And then a sigh, opened arms, pale olive breasts lovely and naked in the sun, a heart beating against his own with eagerness to return to the couch of Venus and while away the hours in blissful abandon, so close, so tender, as the air conditioning thrummed approvingly and little Cupids wept with joy at the beauty of it all. How could a vision so vivid be mere wishful thinking? He even knew her name—*Maria,* plus a number of other Spanish names, among them *Concepción.* And no religious connotation there, it was a common given name in lands of the True Faith. . . .

"Damned fool psychiatrist," said Jim aloud. A psychiatrist once had told him he was too "reverent" toward women and had fears of homosexuality. What a crock. If anything in this world affected him less than the sex appeal of men, he could not think what it might be. A drunk doodlebug maybe, or a hairy caterpillar. Of course the man had not said he was a suppressed homosexual, he had put a different light on it than that, but to hell with it. Why had it popped into his head, anyhow? Better to reflect on Maria Concepción. Such thoughts made her shimmer and waver, obscured the specificity of her charms, caused him to wonder if her navel really was a button rather than a dimpled dent.

"Lay down bread for a crazier pad," said Jim aloud. "Build thee more stately mansions, O my soul. Rise from choppin' cotton to Memphis town." That was just about the size of it. The thing was simple as an early Beatle song, comparable perhaps to "Strawberry Fields Forever," or even "I Want to Hold Your Hand." Or maybe it was on the order of "Dedicated to the One I Love," by the Mamas and the Papas. It was a new stage, that was all, a new plot point on the continuum of growth that was life, and what could be simpler than that? If the Beatles could do it and the Mamas and the Papas could do it, then so could he too do it. Like the chambered nautilus, he must leave the low-vaulted past and build a new temple nobler than the last.

"Idiot psychiatrist," said Jim. What was it the fool had said about reverence being at the opposite pole from love? That had seemed a fairly sensible observation, but the rest of it was jargon. The way the nitwit had rattled on with one psychiatric cliché after the other was beyond belief. Jim rolled his eyes heavenward and shrugged. If he had any "fears of homosexuality," he was certainly oblivious of them. Besides, the proposition was ridiculous on the basis of internal contradiction. The man had said he was *not* a suppressed homosexual, therefore how could he have fears of such a thing? Nitwit!

Frowning with vexation at the psychiatrist, Jim uncorked the bottle and took another swallow of Scotch. The man had batted him about the head with psychiatric clichés like a clown belaboring an innocent person with a pig bladder. What a neat little trick it was. "You secretly want to eat feces." "Why, I certainly do not!" "Ha ha, that proves you do." Damnable nitwit.

Maria Concepción temporarily out of mind, Jim Kittering lit a cigarette and shifted on the sofa, unable to find a comfortable position and suddenly depressed. As had happened repeatedly during the evening, the thought had come to him once more, like the recurring pang of a terrible truth, that Linda was gone, really and truly gone, and almost certainly gone forever. He could not deceive himself on that point. She had said she would not divorce him for a year, but it would indeed take a miracle to win her back. It would take a basic change in his own character, nothing less, and he could never mislead her about it either. He would have to change himself or she simply would not come back to him, and at his age how was such a thing possible? Linda herself had no real hope. She had agreed to wait a year because she loved him and because of the children, but she expected, perhaps even knew, the year would be wasted. He was neither a flexible Beatle nor a flexible Papa, but a man of forty-two set and fixed in his ways. A real change in his character would be like the murder of his old self and he could not do it.

"Build thee more stately mansions, O my soul," said Jim with a wry smile. "Till thou at last art free, leaving thine outgrown shell by life's unresting sea."

It was an odd little quirk of the mind he would now recall with perfect precision a memory gem that had not entered his consciousness since seventh grade. He could not have had the slightest idea what the poem meant when he'd learned it, but the subconscious had kept a record of it and now drew it from the files. What a truckload of nineteenth-century foolishness it was, and in such hoity-toity language, too. The notion of the inevitability of growth and progress had suffered a few setbacks lately. A man could go backward as well as forward; instead of growing he could decay, degenerate, go to hell. And the same applied to civilization on the whole. How naive the Victorians really were—O my soul, and all of that.

But despite the stilted poesy and contrived resolution, the verses had a kind of power. As he smiled at the ingenuous thought expressed, Jim felt a tingle down his backbone. "The Chambered Nautilus" might not be a great poem, but it had a certain inspiration, a certain relevance and significance, a certain fundamental truth. Why else would he have thought of it after so many years, and why else would the line "Build thee more stately mansions" cause his hair to stand slightly on end? The poem was saying something to him and the thing it was saying was very important.

Again Jim shifted in discomfort on the sofa and rubbed perspiration from his eyes. The trouble was he did not have the least inkling how to begin to change himself, even if he should find the courage to attempt it. What were his most serious faults and weaknesses, what was the fundamental cause of his difficulties? Was it one thing, or a number of things? He did not have the remotest idea where to start and could not quite subdue the belief he really was a pretty nice guy and not wholly to blame for the mess he was in.

But no. If he himself was not responsible, there was no hope at all. Such a view made him a puppet pulled first by one string and then another. It was his own mess; he had made it and he would have to get out of it. But how? Where to begin? What could he do? At the edge of panic, Jim again rubbed perspiration from his forehead and struggled to find a clue somewhere. He had to get an insight into himself or go out of his mind and that was all there was to it. What *was* it, what awful thing had made him drive away the wife he loved?

Utterly bewildered, Jim Kittering shook his head as he stared at what was left of the mink coat in the fireplace. He could never in this world understand why he had behaved in such a way toward Linda. Never. It was true he had pushed her toward other men, painful and awful as it was for them both. Why had he done such a thing as that? Again Jim shook his head. He could not understand it. But Linda herself had seemed to understand it perfectly. Was it possible she knew something he himself did not know, and if so, what was it?

Jim sat forward and reached into his shirt pocket for a cigarette, his forehead wrinkled and corrugated with the intensity of his effort to think. What did Linda know? Well, for one thing, at a critical point in their conversation on the telephone, she had called him a child and she had seemed to attach a great deal of significance to that particular epithet. Furthermore, it was clear from the position she had taken that she disagreed with his moral attitude. Linda considered him a sex-obsessed child. Could it be she was correct?

Jim folded his arms and stared at the luminous green water of the swimming pool and wondered about it. All men and women, in a sense, were children insofar as basic emotions were concerned, and if he was sex-obsessed, then so were many, many others. That did not rid him of his "problem," perhaps, but he surely had company and plenty of it. Something in the character of modern life, specifically in the urban West, forced many people to find in personal and private experience the satisfaction of basic human needs. Perhaps this was a bad thing, perhaps it was an unwise thing, but good or bad, wise or foolish, it was incontestable. The underlying attitudes, if not the overt behavior of most people did not differ from his own.

Nonetheless, in Jim's conviction, most people were hypocritical about the matter, even in this so-called age of emancipation. This, he felt, was particularly true of girls and women. Of course there were frigid girls and women, but most of them were not so at all. How many times had some girl or woman piously upbraided him, even half seriously called him such things as a satyr and a sex fiend, only to turn around and display a sensuality more than equal to his own?

It had happened again and again, an aloof self-righteous piety followed by a moaning refusal to let him out of their arms. They were total little hypocrites. Women, in his belief, for the most part had stronger sexual desires than men, who tended to be more preoccupied with the outside world; thus the hypocrisy of women was accordingly greater. But men were not much better; they lied about it too. Society on the whole lied about it, lied smugly and idiotically, and who could even begin to estimate the pain and confusion caused by such fundamental dishonesty?

Some people, it was true, out of fear or lack of opportunity, or as a result of plain nasty hostility toward the opposite sex, tied themselves in knots and concentrated their thoughts on tomato juice. And many others, no doubt, wearied of the struggle, tired of the effort demanded by any close relationship with another person, gave up on sex as not worth the aggravation and bother, withdrew into a disappointed neuterland of other pleasures surely more gross than sex itself—stuffing their faces with food, for example, or alcoholism, or the vulgar acquisition of expensive possessions.

Such weak sisters naturally would scorn those not similarly defeated, they would howl furiously about "morals," hurl self-righteous imprecations and glare malevolently at those with the courage to love a man or a woman rather than a huge slice of roast beef swimming in gravy followed by two pieces of chocolate layer cake. Who was moral and who immoral? How was a gluttonous pig superior to a man or woman whose joy and delight in life was derived from the love of another person? All normal, unfrightened, and undefeated human beings were just as "obsessed" with sex as he was, particularly in the Western world, and perhaps this was not a "failure" of the urban West but a jewel in its crown. What greater happiness was possible in life than that which could be felt by a man and woman in love, and what fundamental expression could that love take but sexual? "Sex-obsessed," indeed! Far from being obsessed with sex in any reprehensible way, he was merely an honest man in a world of liars.

"Mmm," said Jim with a nod of satisfaction. He would have to remember all of this and use it sometime. An argument like this would knock a pig or a hypocrite right off his pins. But somehow Jim was a bit let down. He had felt he was on the verge of getting somewhere, then he had wandered off on the pigs and hypocrites and lost it. All of that was true enough but it was beside the point. What was it that had nudged him several times from the back of his brain, what truth above and beyond the dishonesty of most people toward sex?

Jim again rubbed perspiration from his forehead. Nothing. No such half-formed thoughts had nudged him. Of course it was true his *behavior* was slightly different from that of most people. He admitted that. Undeniably, he did waste a vast amount of time chasing girls and women and got in frequent trouble because of it. Very frequent. In fact, he was in pretty serious trouble at the moment, even if he was not really tempted by that green water pocked in the rain, that rectangle of emerald oblivion beyond the window wall.

"Well," said Jim, "it's true."

Yes, it was true. His behavior was different from that of most people and a man had to be judged by what he did, not by what he thought or felt or said. Perhaps others were as interested in sex as he was, but he did something about it. He did plenty. Restraint was not a word in his vocabulary. He would go after the most *inappropriate*, the most *wrong*, the most *ineligible* women conceivable, and to his unending delight and horror he often got them.

An especially insane example was the thing that had occurred, gruesomely enough, only one day before his marriage at Linda's grandmother's summer place in Maine. That was a piece of sheer madness. Although he loved Linda and wanted very much to marry her, he had made a horribly crazy pass at her freckled nineteen-year-old cousin who appeared as a bridesmaid at the wedding. The girl was so upset she almost collapsed and he himself was trembling with terror. Linda, thank God, never learned about it.

Jim shook his head and smiled with a pained fondness at the memory. How had such a mad thing happened, anyhow? He could remember being nervous from all the hooraw of the wedding, very nervous, and weary of the skeptical glares of Linda's beetle-browed grandmother. The old tyrant had later come to like him better and even halfway accept him, but at that time her hostility was unvarnished and unnerving, too. So was the wedding itself, with the banks and piles of flowers everywhere, the limousines, the dining room stacked high with expensive gifts, the huge tent in the garden for the reception, the case upon case of vintage champagne, and all the rest of it. Jim's own family was financially comfortable, if not so rich as Linda's grandmother, and he had seen such things before, but not from the center of it, not with himself there in the middle stuck like a fly on a pin. He'd decided to take a walk to the lake and get away from it all for a while. A kind of compulsion had come upon him when he saw the girl down by the boathouse.

Later, his reaction puzzled him for more than one reason. In the first place, the bridesmaid cousin was certainly attractive but her figure was of a type he did not as a rule greatly admire. He liked slender, elegant women, but this girl had almost a Gay Nineties figure, with shockingly large breasts and wide hips with big rounded buttocks. The bathing suit was not her own and it was much too small for her. Her breasts swelled over the bra part and the lower half cut diagonally across the cheeks of her behind. At the house she had worn modest Peck & Peck clothes and he had no idea she had such a figure. Her body was so voluptuous it was not far from being gross, although the girl herself was sweet and rather shy, with blue eyes and a freckled smile. Her best feature, in Jim's opinion, was her dark auburn hair, which was very long and hung down below her shoulders. Her figure, however, was too much of a muchness and he did not care for the typical buttermilk redhead skin and the sprinkle of freckles on her arms, shoulders, and face. She even had freckles on her knees.

The plain truth was the girl was not all that attractive, but an insanity possessed him when he saw her standing there with a hand on her hip gazing out at the lake, her magnificent buttocks half exposed and her breasts swelling over the top of her bathing suit. It seemed to him he had never before in his life beheld such a sexy woman. A madness took hold of him, an utter madness, right there in the boathouse with other bridesmaids and ushers and house guests wandering all over the place—what more likely thing for some guest to do than explore the boathouse and take a look at Gram's boat? There were detectives crawling all over everywhere to protect the wedding presents, to say nothing of extra servants on cots at the beach pavilion not two hundred feet away. He was out of his mind. But the impulse came upon him so suddenly he had no time to consider and resist it. And anyhow, who would have thought the girl would acquiesce?

Jim put a hand over his eyes, a blush of embarrassment on his face and his smile of pained fondness turned into a wince. A nut, that was what he was. But he really hadn't dreamed anything would come of it and in a way it wasn't his fault. All he had done was pat her on her behind after a friendly smile, a joke or two, and a brief gaze into her blue eyes.

He had, it was true, said one "dirtily arousing" thing to her, but he'd said it merely to be devilish and because it came into his head. Who would have expected a well-bred girl from social Philadelphia to become lustful simply because a man patted her on the fanny and said: "You have a beautiful ass, honey. A *lovely* behind. And very, *very* sexy."?

No man in his right mind could have anticipated she would respond to such crudity as that, although it was true a certain type of woman from a certain type of background often was titillated by just such language. In Jim's experience, if the first shock did not drive them away, prospects were excellent. But even if he had had a subconscious hunch such talk might affect her, who would have dreamed she would allow herself any leeway in such a terrifically dangerous situation?

Jim flinched; even after years, the memory still had the power to make him shudder. If someone had caught them, which easily could have happened, the girl would have been disgraced and his marriage to Linda would have ended before it began. Gram, no doubt, would have nodded her head with grim satisfaction, her worst suspicions proved only too true. Until Linda defied her and threatened to elope, she had bitterly opposed the marriage on the ground that Jim's character obviously was unformed and he was plainly unworthy of a first-class person such as Linda. Maybe old Gram had a point there. She actually called him a donkey, which infuriated Linda so much she threw a vase at the wall and threatened to leave home that instant. "Linda! You *don't* mate Citation to a donkey, no matter how charming or agreeable the donkey may be." Jim grinned. He could not help but like the nasty old buzzard even now. Besides, she was right. What other conclusion could be drawn than that he *was* a donkey?

Jim shook his head, uncorked the bottle of Scotch, and took another swallow. He was not a donkey any more than Gram herself was a buzzard. The old lady had weakened her case by saying such a thing. Until that donkey remark, Linda had been almost willing to agree to wait six months. The truth was he was not an animal but a human being lacking in self-control and good sense; if the old woman had put it that way, calmly and judiciously, Linda might have listened. Probably not, however. She was madly in love with him and very young. No one could have convinced her he had any faults at all.

He did, however. Yes, a few here and there. But the incident with Linda's red-haired cousin happened so suddenly and in such a way he could not altogether blame himself for it. It was, of course, an insanely reckless and foolish thing to do and God knows he hadn't intended to do it, but what else could he do when the girl didn't object to the pat on her behind but pat her again, and again? And since it was clear she was willing to play, how could he then resist the temptation to place both his hands on her half-naked buttocks, pull her toward him, and kiss her? And having kissed her once, how could he help but kiss her again, and then once more? A foolish thing to do, no doubt, but with a magnificently voluptuous girl practically naked in his arms, what else could his kisses be than increasingly passionate? And when she still did not make any complaint but, on the contrary, ground her pubic bone hard against him and breathed fast with obvious excitement, what else could he do but lower the straps of her bathing suit and expose her tremendous breasts, hold them in his palms, kiss her again and again, then drag her by the hand into Gram's boat, lay her down on a dusty bunk, tug off the tight lower half of the bathing suit, kneel above her, and push her freckled knees apart—what else, indeed? Was he then supposed to say: "Sorry, I'm marrying your cousin and we'd better not do this. Put your bathing suit back on and we'll take a little cooling dip in the lake."?

Jim shifted on the sofa and reached for a cigarette, aroused by his own reflections. This was Annapurna all right. Perhaps there were weird creatures in the world who, if suddenly transported into the situation, would have made the let's-take-a-dip-in-the-lake speech to her. That would have been the sensible thing to do and for a brief moment an awareness of terrible risk did flash through his mind. It had not affected him in the least.

Yes, it was a terrifically sexy experience and, horrible though it was, it had a kind of beauty. He made love to the girl almost continuously for over an hour. When it finally ended, they were both groaning for breath in the stifling cabin and drenched with perspiration. The girl's dark red hair was plastered on her head and hung in coiled strands as if she'd been in a shower bath. He had never seen then, and he had never seen since, a woman express a more abandoned and delirious sexuality than Linda's red-haired cousin. Her response was fantastic. She had had, or certainly had seemed to have, at least six or seven orgasms, all of them powerful, especially the last, which caused her to groan so loudly, heave her body so hard, and clench her arms around him with such strength it almost blocked his own final agonized discharge. "In a minute!" he cried, but the girl continued to heave, groan, and squeeze the breath out of him. It was like riding a wild bucking bronco, but he finally managed to take away her leverage and stop the heaving by grabbing her under the knees and tilting her backward. He also managed at this angle to penetrate her more deeply, which caused her to give such a yowl it seemed impossible no one would hear her and investigate what kind of murder was going on in the boathouse. It was then she "dirty-worded" him in turn, crying out advice to him in language seldom heard in Sunday school or at polite Philadelphia lawn parties. The main gist of her thought was he should keep right on doing what he was doing, except more so, even though he was killing her and she couldn't stand it. Jim, at that point, felt he couldn't stand it either. They both, however, managed to endure it. Annapurna, in due course, was climbed.

"Hmmph," said Jim as he uncorked the bottle and took another drink. He was aroused by his cogitations. But he was more disturbed and puzzled than aroused. Why had the experience been so immensely sexy? How could such an insane thing have occurred in the first place? Assuming, if only for the purposes of argument, that neither he nor the girl were depraved subhumans, how could they have done such a crazy stunt? Jim did not know. The very wickedness and foolishness of it had seemed to grip them both with a kind of brainless insanity. To do such a naughty, awful, dangerous thing was terrifically exciting, and yet there had to be more of an answer to it than that.

Afterward, as the girl lay panting for breath, rubbing sweat from her eyes with his shirt, and trying nervously to puff on a cigarette, she said she was not really promiscuous and had never before in her life done such a bitchy thing. "You surprised me," she said. "I'm no virgin obviously . . . but I . . . I'm not really promiscuous . . . and I . . ." The girl was so out of breath and rapidly becoming so flustered she could hardly talk. "And I . . I've never done anything in my life . . . never anything as bitchy as *this*. Never! Nothing like this. I lost my head, I just lost my head." The real shock did not hit her until she was halfway through the cigarette, at which point she became so appalled, horrified, and frightened Jim had thought she would faint. "Oh!" she said. "This is awful! Awful! We've got to get out of here, somebody will catch us! Where are my trunks? Oh! Oh, Jesus! Oh, why did I do it, I could die . . . oh, oh . . ."

That wasn't the end of it for the girl either. Later, Jim had been so afraid she would faint at the wedding, he could hardly listen to the minister. "What? Oh, yes—yes, I do." The girl stood there swaying in her bridesmaid gown, an emptiness in her eyes. It was always a wonder to him no one noticed how upset and guilt-stricken she was, but then, most people, to be sure, would not dream of what had happened in the boathouse.

Then Jim remembered. Six months after the wedding he had found and read a rather pathetic letter the girl had written accepting the invitation to be a bridesmaid. "Darling Linda," she wrote, "I'm so happy for you. Is he nice, Jim, wonderful and handsome and strong? I'm sure he must be and I'm so happy for you I could cry. Ever since that summer on the lake, when you were so sweet to me and me with braces and fat and all and you so beautiful, I've always loved you. Why, you're my ideal! I do love you so much. Nothing could make me happier than to be a bridesmaid and I'm *dying* to meet Jim, I know he must be wonderful. . . ."

In acute discomfort, Jim shifted on the sofa and half shut his eyes. Of course he didn't know it at the time, but he had shot a trout in a barrel insofar as Linda's red-haired cousin was concerned. The girl was utterly vulnerable to him, it was pathetic. But he hadn't known—or hadn't he? He had seen her at the house, he had watched the way she behaved toward Linda. Sure he had known. Maybe the knowledge was not wholly conscious, but he had known the girl worshiped Linda and he had known she would be very vulnerable to him. He had known, all right, and he had taken a ruthless advantage of his knowledge.

Of course, the girl had been very foolish and was to blame for her conduct, but then, so was Linda foolish and to blame for her various infidelities. It would seem he had a knack for taking advantage of the weaknesses of women.

The truth might as well be faced. His seduction—and that was what it was, a rare case of true seduction—of Linda's cousin was absolutely dreadful and absolutely immoral. The girl's entire life could have been ruined by the advantage he had taken of her. And that was not all. He and the girl were not alone in that cabin, Linda also was there. Not literally, but Linda was there—her heart, her pride, her love for him, the strongest emotions she had were exposed to destruction in the cabin of that boat. His own strongest emotions, his love for Linda, his heart, his pride were equally exposed to destruction.

"Pretty rough," said Jim aloud in a voice that did not sound like his own. "Pretty goddamn rough."

And for what? It had not even been an act of love, but an act of lustful copulation. He barely knew the girl; all he'd known about her was she had a crush on Linda and was vulnerable. And there was no doubt he knew that. He now could remember watching the girl fling her arms around Linda and kiss her and cry when she arrived. He could remember experimentally touching her leg with his knee under the bridge table, and he could remember the blush in her cheeks and the solemn expression in her eyes. A kind of compulsion had come upon him when he saw her at the boathouse because he knew he could get her.

And this was Annapurna, the sexiest experience of his life. In that fact something was sad, something was pitiful, above and beyond the immorality of his behavior. Annapurna, in reality, was a little molehill about four inches high. That was the summit he had reached in his years of compulsive pursuit of girls and women.

Jim took a badly needed swallow from the bottle, then stared groggily once again at his wife's burned coat in the fireplace. It seemed to have a hypnotic fascination for him. The gray-black outlines were no longer too clear, he was getting quite drunk now, but that was not important; the important thing was where to begin, where to start, what to do. The only thing he'd learned from his reflections was that he was an even worse son of a bitch than he'd dreamed. What could he do?

"She burned her coat," said Jim aloud. "Linda burned her coat." In a total absorption, Jim stared at the remains of his wife's coat in the fireplace. To burn her coat was not an act of mere petulance on Linda's part, but a brave thing for her to do. Linda had loved that coat, just as he said to her in his harangue on the telephone. It took moral courage for her to burn her coat and moral courage for her to leave him, too. If Linda could be brave, then could he himself not show at least a little bit of courage?

"I am afraid not," said Jim aloud. "The cookie-jar type doesn't have that."

What was it the man had said, the psychiatrist he had consulted once or twice during a brief period of impotence after Linda's first infidelity?

"Love to you is a cookie jar rather than an experience to be shared with the humanity of another person, because you are too strongly female-oriented. Now, female-orientation is a good thing within reasonable bounds; it helps men understand women, love them, be kind to them, protect them and their young. But when it gets out of hand we find compulsion rather than impulsion, reverence rather than love, and all kinds of erratic and trouble-making behavior. Reverence, you see, is at the opposite pole of love. A man cannot love that which he reveres, because love is an acceptance of humanity with all its strengths and weaknesses. It's plain the opinion women have of you is important to you out of all proportion. You are too reverent toward them. They are only weak creatures like yourself, why are you so afraid of them, why do you care so much what they think? Do you have a single good male friend? I'm sure you don't, and may I ask why not?"

The man had gone on with a lot of nonsense on the subject of fears of homosexuality, the "male image," the "phony stud hero of the twentieth century," and a lot of other such drivel. Jim had insisted he could not be less interested, but the glib scoundrel would not accept it. "It's possible," he said, "to be afraid of homosexuality—that is, to be afraid one is not a complete man—without being a homosexual. It's also possible to be overly dependent on women. I never saw a Don Juan who wasn't, and impotence is the other side of that coin. I suggest you join a golf club, or an athletic club, or play poker with the boys, and get your mind out of the gutter."

The man was so infuriating Jim had felt like grabbing him by the beard and throwing him out of the window down onto Park Avenue. But the comment of the man had stuck in his mind and he often thereafter had furtively wondered about it.

Groggy in his drunkenness, he wondered about it straight and direct in the brightly lighted living room after forty-two years of not wholly successful existence in this world. He also wondered if it might not be a good idea to get up and go jump in the swimming pool and put himself out of his misery. The thought had a frightening appeal. Why not? It would solve everything, all his problems would be gone forever—emerald oblivion was just outside the window wall.

Drunk, very drunk, Jim clenched his fists and stared into the fireplace as tears filled his eyes. Linda was gone, brave and beautiful Linda who had burned her coat. If Linda could be brave, so could he, even though it all was impossible and he still had no idea where to begin. But he would not drown himself in the swimming pool like a rat. No, he would try, he would struggle on in the hope a miracle might occur on the shores of the blue unresting sea.

PART THREE

Christmas

EIGHT

A Golden Thread

Ludicrously and yet reasonably enough, it was still summertime in Savannah. Heat wigglies wavered over the broken asphalt and the sun was a blinding yellow ball above shacks and Nehi signs of rusted tin. The outskirts of the city had a squalor beyond belief. Even the live oaks seemed stunted. The dirt, the mess, the lack of all beauty was enough to make a man feel like hanging himself. Jim said so to Florence, but she kept talking about the squares of Savannah. Meanwhile, the cabdriver, a pixy-faced man, kept intruding in the conversation.

"Insanity and absurdity," said Jim half to himself.

"What?" asked Florence.

"Nothing," answered Jim. "Just thinking about the texture of our nights and days. These moods come over me once in a while."

Jim Kittering had majored in philosophy at Princeton and considered himself an American pragmatist, but at times he toyed with the notion that the insanity of the world and the absurdity of human life rendered effort not only futile but laughable. His view was closer to Stoic gloom than Existentialism. Jim was not much of an Existentialist.

To be sure, the world was insane and life was absurd, but all men of perception know this and do not need to have it pointed out to them. The problem presented to the man of wisdom was not to perceive insanity and absurdity, but to discover in the warp and woof of just such insanity and absurdity a golden thread, exactly as it was the task of the artist not to sneer at folly but to penetrate past moral contradiction to the unexpected truth.

No, Jim was not much of an Existentialist, and not much of a Stoic or American pragmatist either. As a ski instructor once had told him: "There is no name for that turn." Jim hacked it. He was, in a sense, uneducable and the ski instructor finally gave up on him as hopeless. "Smooze! Smooze, make the turn smooze! Acch! Forget it." It was not very graceful, but Jim did get down the mountain in his transcendentalist fashion.

It was summertime in Savannah and the sun was blinding bright. Although Jim had such a hangover he could hardly see and Florence was so excited by the trip she could hardly see either, they caught a glimpse of the *S.S. Lorna Loone* when the taxi crossed the high bridge over the Savannah River. The ship looked like an ugly little toy. It was a dismal white color streaked with brown and the deck was littered with disorderly piles of tiny boxes.

"Well, from here it is not a terrifically impressive vessel," said Florence, "and I can't imagine what would possess Maria Concepción Diaz to get aboard it with her nineteen pieces of luggage and those little hairless Mexican dogs she uses for hot-water bottles."

"*Maria Concepción Diaz?*" asked Jim wonderingly. "How do you know about *her?*"

"I heard about her last night all the way from New York to Atlanta."

"Oh," said Jim.

"Oh is right. I got slightly weary of those pale olive breasts and those hairless hot-water-bottle dogs."

"The dogs are new to me," said Jim.

"She travels with three of them. They are almost totally hairless and run a normal temperature of a hundred and five. She rests her lily-white feet on them and they lick her toes. What's more, she has a silly *button* for a navel and her pale olive breasts are crested with *pink* nipples. You said that several times."

"Oh, Christ," said Jim, "did I?"

"You sure did. But from the looks of it I don't think she and her superheated dogs are going to show up on the *S.S. Lorna Loone.* In fact, from the looks of it I wonder if I myself am going to show up on it. That boss of yours might just possibly be trying to drown us."

"Gray-et Godd," said the cabdriver. "I never heard of such doggs. Is they ectually hot like thot?"

"Hob won't drown us while he needs a new hit series," said Jim. "I assure you he wouldn't let a murderous impulse jeopardize his own best interests. And yes, driver, the dogs are hot. They run a high normal temperature and are used by Mexican aristocrats as hot-water bottles."

"Gray-et Godd, isn't that somethin'?"

"The Mexicans also eat them."

"Gray-et Godd!"

"A funny accent you've got there, driver," said Jim. "Does everyone in Savannah talk like you?"

"No-o," said the cabdriver. "Mostly, no-o. Aside from the foct I spent thrrree yearrrs in Scootland and Irrreland durrring the warrr, I'm bawn an' raised in Chaa'ston."

"You are giving me a swimming in the head," said Florence. "And I still don't like the looks of that ship."

"All merchant ships look awful," said Jim. "It'll be better aboard. The staterooms and lounge are probably fine. I just hope the air conditioning is repaired."

"It isn't," said the cabdriver. "I happen to know all about thot ship. Lucky you high-yahhed my cab."

"We high-yahhed your cab for transportation, not conversation," said Florence. "No offense intended."

"Of course not, Mo'm."

"Relax, Florence," said Jim. "That story in the paper has disturbed you unnecessarily. Modern merchant ships are overengineered for safety."

"Not the *Lorna Loone*," said the cabdriver, "no, sirrr."

"Well," said Florence, "I'm glad it doesn't leave till late afternoon. That'll give me a chance to investigate a little. There must be a Merchant Marine office or a first-rate travel agent or somebody in this town who really knows about that ship. What time is it, anyhow?"

"Ay-et past eleven," said the cabdriver, "and podden me for interruptin', but I happen to know *all* about the *Lorna Loone*, the ship to which you refer in the river theah—"

"Wait a second," said Florence, "I don't want rumors and gossip, I want facts."

Florence's pale blue eyes were popped with anxiety. Although she was very excited by the trip and loved every second of it, she was not, as she herself admitted, a good traveler. By a stroke of ill luck, during the flight from Atlanta to Savannah she had glanced through a newspaper and stumbled on a feature story about the large number of merchant ships that disappear every year on the high seas, vessels that vanish into thin air and deep dark water without a radio distress call or the slightest hint of what happened to them. She was agitated to begin with and the article had unnerved her totally. The glimpse of the *S.S. Lorna Loone* had not reassured her and neither had the remarks of the cabdriver.

As the cab turned onto a wide boulevard lined with live oaks, Jim lay back on the seat and shut his eyes. He had not quite managed to neutralize the prodigious amount of alcohol he had drunk and he was not sober even now, for which fact he was grateful. A hangover such as this faced in total sobriety would require hospitalization. Jim never before in one night had had so much to drink; the trip to Kennedy in a taxi, the wait in the airport, the flight from Kennedy to Atlanta, the long delay and change-over in Atlanta were mostly a dim drunken dream.

Very dim. Jim had no recollection at all of whole stretches of it. He remembered seeing Florence in the airline lounge at Kennedy with a camera around her neck and her lap full of tourist pamphlets and Chamber of Commerce throwaways. And he remembered his shock at the sight of her. It was jolting. Even as he'd dreamed of Maria Concepción (he discovered in the cab going out to Kennedy that her last name was Diaz, but he could not remember his psychic vision of the three hairless hot-water-bottle dogs), Jim had been secretly holding Florence in reserve as a desperate substitute to throw into the game if he got down to his one-yard line with his back to the goal posts. Three celibate weeks on the high seas were unthinkable and Florence *could not* be as homely as she had looked at the office. She was, after all, human. Somewhere under that horrible tweedy suit Florence was a woman.

As for his impression she was a Lesbian—well, that was a hasty judgment based on no evidence. More likely the poor thing had never had any love, no man had ever wanted her. She would probably leap at the chance and cry and sob with gratitude. And even if she was a trifle Lesbic, he had jumped greater hurdles than that in his day. He could woo and arouse the slumbering Aphrodite within her and this would be a profound experience and a moral thing to do besides. What could be a nicer, more gentlemanly deed than to save poor Florence for heterosexuality?

"Oh, God," groaned Jim to himself when he saw her. The woman was hopeless. Florence was a likable person and probably a very nice human being, but she simply had no sex appeal whatsoever. It was impossible for Jim to imagine making love to her, and he was a man who considered himself capable of making love to almost any woman.

But Jim did not abandon all hope at once. He could scarcely afford to do so. Maria Concepción might be delayed; her rich diplomat husband in Washington might have one of his fiendish jealous fits and make her miss connections with the *S.S. Lorna Loone*. Three celibate weeks at sea were too ghastly to contemplate; the very thought made Jim feel like whimpering. Florence might be *the only woman aboard*.

Horrific. Awful. But if he became desperate enough on that ship, if he got down to his one-inch line with his back right to the goal posts . . . well, he could not imagine it really, but . . . well . . . in the dark the freckles wouldn't show . . . he could put a pillow over her head. Or perhaps it wouldn't be as impossible as it seemed. Was not the human element infinitely more important than mere prettiness? In time he might even come to admire and be attracted to Florence. What of the good-looking, successful man who had married a one-legged, one-eyed girl with a withered left arm, false teeth, and a flat chest—and adored her? Somewhere he had heard of such a mysterious case.

The hope was dim and it did not last for long. There was a pretty little honey-haired stewardess on the plane who looked a bit like Linda, and Jim caught Florence turning her head to stare after the girl as she walked down the aisle. Unlike Linda, who always dressed modestly, the girl's skirt was tight and the outline of her rounded buttocks was visible, a fact of which she seemed quite aware; she was wagging the whole thing with a gentle vengeance as she trod down the aisle. The girl was very pretty, very attractive, but Jim was more interested in Florence's stare after her. It was the way a man would look at her, eyes furtively slewed, an eyebrow casually raised with a bland unconvincing affectation of disinterest. "Not bad, huh?" he said when Florence faced front. For a moment, but only for a moment, Florence pretended she did not understand him, then she shrugged and grinned.

So ended the dim hope. Florence was a Lesbian all right, and who could blame her? She was really a man in a woman's body and could not help herself. Nature had made a mix-up, that was all. But for some reason Jim had pried into it. "You could go for that, huh?" he asked. Florence glanced at him, picked up a magazine, and began to turn the pages. It was a gross question. But Jim could not leave it alone. "Look," he said, "we're going to be traveling together and we might as well be frank. You *are* a Lesbian, Florence, aren't you?"

Silence. Jim thought she would ignore him again, but she finally looked up from the magazine and said: "I don't know why you need to know any such thing even if we are traveling together. Let's just say I'm a thirty-eight-year-old virgin and intend to remain one."

Jim's first thought was that it was an odd little remark, but a plain warning to him to stay away. Well, he would certainly do so. He was relieved; now he could be friends with Florence, he could joke around with her and be pals with her instead of becoming entangled with her. She was too homely in the first place, and a confirmed Lesbian in the second place, and that was that. Almost, but not quite. The tone was wrong. It was as if she'd said: "I have leukemia and I do not expect to recover."

"Open your eyes and behold truth and beauty," said Florence. "Look beneath the surface of the drab and ugly city and see what wonders God hath wrought."

Jim blinked at her. "What are you talking about?" he asked.

"I'm talking about the squares of Savannah, you hungover Doubting Thomas, what do you think I'm talking about? We're approaching one right now. There it is. Look."

Jim shut his eyes again. "I don't want to look," he said. "I want a drink."

"I am trying to correct your misapprehension that Savannah is just an ugly and dirty little seaport on the coast of Georgia," said Florence. "Isn't that what you said while we were driving from the airport toward the bridge?"

"We wouldn't have gone over the bridge if you hadn't insisted we go out of our way."

"But didn't you say that?"

"Well, I'm not even sure that's part of Savannah."

"Stop quibbling. Did you say it?"

"Yes, I guess I did."

"Sure you did and you're wrong. Savannah is one of the most beautiful small cities in America and the squares make it so. Open your eyes. Come on."

Jim opened his eyes. He saw in the bright sunshine a small and rather attractive park surrounded on four sides by old homes. Huge live oaks and many flowers grew in the little park. Streamers of silvery gray Spanish moss hung from the oaks. "It's a silly little park," he said.

"It is not a silly little park."

"It *is* a silly little park, and I want lunch and a drink."

"You're a barbarian! No wonder your wife left you. You haven't got any sense."

Jim blinked again. Florence actually was angry. "Don't bring my wife into this," he said. "I'm suffering enough already with this hang-over."

"*That* is not a silly little park, *that* is a beautiful little park."

"To you it's beautiful," said Jim. "To me it's silly."

"You bastard!" said Florence. "Here we come into this grimy city, with the shacks and the billboards and the ruts in the sidewalks, and we find in the midst of all that ugliness a little park like *this*, and you say it's *silly!*"

Hmmph, thought Jim. Well, there was a mean streak in Florence but she was quite an esthete. All that lengthy description in her book of the dunes of Cape Cod and the lonely girl wandering everywhere and weeping over sea birds in an effort to love an ugly fisherman—he had forgotten that side of Florence. "Of course it isn't silly," he said. "Actually, it's nice."

"It's nice?"

"Yes, it's nice." Florence was so angry and upset her hands were trembling on her knees and Jim thought he could detect a trace of tears in her eyes. "What else can I say, Florence? It's nice."

"To hell with it," she answered. "You're a maddening fool and I'm tired of talking to you. Driver, take us to a good restaurant. I want a drink and something to eat, then I'm going to find out about that ship."

How had he hurt her? What had he said? In consternation, Jim stared at the tears now plainly visible in Florence's eyes, then, on an impulse, put four fingers on her freckled hand. "I'm sorry," he said, "please forgive me. It's a beautiful little park." Once in a while, like a blind weaver, Jim Kittering could recognize by feeling if not by sight the presence of a golden thread.

NINE

He Shall Give His Angels

Blackbeard's Haunt had murals of pirates on the walls and grisly buccaneer decorations hither and yon. It also had a bar. While waiting for Florence to return from the Spratt & Bowser Travel Agency, which by a stroke of luck was located next door, Jim consumed two double Gibsons and wondered once again if by some miracle Maria Concepción would be aboard the *S.S. Lorna Loone*.

"Excuse me, I'm Muriel Page. Are you Tyrone Power?"

"What?" asked Jim.

"I said, are you Tyrone Power? If you are, I want your autograph."

Jim rubbed his jaw and squinted his eyes. In the dim light of the restaurant he could see a plumpish, smiling, white-haired lady peering around another plumpish, smiling, white-haired lady at the table next to him. "Tyrone Power is dead," said Jim, "and besides, I don't look like him."

"Oh, yes you do. You look just like him. Are you sure he's dead?"

"I'm positive he's dead. He's been dead for a long time."

"I didn't know that. You really aren't Tyrone Power?"

"No, I'm not."

"Well, thank you very much. The autograph wasn't for me anyhow, it was for my little grandniece."

"Well, you can have my autograph if you want it, but I'm not Tyrone Power."

"Oh, no, I wouldn't want yours if you're not him. But thank you anyhow."

"Not at all."

"Sorry to have bothered you."

"No bother," said Jim.

The plumpish, white-haired ladies were still smiling intently at him and in order to get away from them Jim pulled his reading glasses out of his breast pocket and unfolded the newspaper clipping Florence had given him. The ladies must be blind or drunk. In his opinion, he did not bear the vaguest resemblance to Tyrone Power. First a leprechaun cab driver and now these two ladies who thought he looked like Tyrone Power. Savannah was getting more and more cuckoo all the time.

"Do you want duck soup?"

Jim flinched and stared over his glasses at a small blue-eyed waitress in a pirate outfit. "Do I want *what?*" he asked.

"Duck soup," she answered. "It's on the main-you."

"No, I don't want duck soup," said Jim. "But I do want another double Gibson."

"*Another* double Gibson?"

"Yes, another double Gibson."

"You're not eating lunch?"

"I am waiting for a lady," said Jim.

"Oh," said the waitress. "Then you'll have the soup later?"

"I don't know," said Jim. "I'll think about it. Now, bring me a double Gibson."

"Yes, sir."

Jim lowered his eyes to the newspaper clipping and rubbed again at his jaw, which felt a bit sandpapery. He needed a shave and his suit was badly rumpled from sleeping on the plane and in the lounge at the Atlanta airport. Could it be that he did look like Tyrone Power? No one else had ever thought so. A girl had once told him he looked a little bit like a young Humphrey Bogart. It was a remark he had treasured for years, but this comparison to Tyrone Power was even more flattering. Tyrone Power had been an extremely handsome man. If women still thought he looked like that after a horrible night of little sleep and much drinking, there was still play in the position. Jim turned and smiled at the two old ladies, but their heads were bowed over their plates and they did not see him. Well, they were eating their duck soup and God bless them, a word like that cheered a man along life's road.

"BEAUTIFUL BUT TERRIBLE, SEA TAKES HIGH TOLL," said the headline of the clipping Florence had torn from the paper. What was keeping her, anyhow? She'd had more than enough time to ask Spratt & Bowser about the S.S. *Lorna Loone.* Jim adjusted his reading glasses on his nose and glanced through the clipping.

"*Many men who go down to the sea in ships vanish without leaving a clue as to how they met their doom. The U.S. Coast Guard says that an average of more than one big cargo vessel a month mysteriously disappears, to say nothing of many more smaller boats.*"

"Good grief," muttered Jim under his breath. It was no wonder the story had unnerved Florence. How could a merchant ship disappear in such a way? Jim frowned skeptically and read on:

"The general public hears remarkably little about most of these disappearances. Yet each year some 600 crewmen vanish into limbo. The Coast Guard boils down the causes of such baffling tragedies to a relatively few:

"Not all large steamship companies require their ships' masters to radio their positions every day; navigation equipment and communications practices can frequently stand improvement; the abruptness with which certain conditions may cause a ship to founder; the failure of some skippers to let authorities know where they are heading, what course they are following, and when they expect to arrive."

"Here's your double Gibson."

"Thank you. Put it there."

"You want it on the table?"

"No, put it on the floor."

"What?"

"Where *else* can you *put* it but on the table?"

"Well, that's what I said—you want it on the table?"

"Um-m-m-m," sighed Jim, "*yes.*" Savannah was getting more and more cuckoo, and where was Florence, anyhow? Had Spratt & Bowser shanghaied her? Jim took a reassuring glance at the frosty double Gibson and returned his attention to the newspaper story.

"The Spanish steamer, Castillo Montjuich, *for instance, was due to arrive home in La Coruna with a load of grain on July 20. On the 14th, she radioed her position about 400 miles northwest of the Azores. Then silence—until the Coast Guard got word she was considered missing on the 27th, a full week after the ship was due. No distress call from the vessel was ever heard; no flare or signal sighted. Without a trace went the ship and her 37 good men."*

"Ridiculous," muttered Jim to himself. How could such a thing happen? He glanced again at the frosty double Gibson, then read another paragraph.

"According to the Coast Guard, a vessel like the Castillo Montjuich *is liable to sink in virtually the wink of an eye. Carrying grain, a lightninglike emergency may strike if, for example, the cargo has been improperly stored and suddenly shifts its tremendous weight in rough weather. Should there be a leak, grain may swell with such power as to burst the ship's hull open like a broken balloon."*

There was quite a bit more of the newspaper story, but Jim crumpled it up and dropped it under the table. It was certainly not a thing for a high-strung, nervous person like Florence to read just before getting aboard a merchant ship for a three-week cruise in hurricane season. And they were, were they not, going directly into the hurricane area, the very breeding ground of horrible tropical storms that could blow a ship right out of the sea? Again Jim rubbed thoughtfully at his unshaven, sandpapery jaw. Could it be the Goblin really *was* trying to drown them? Could he have insured them heavily and sent them off in the hope they would wind up in Davy Jones's locker? It was possible. This would give him an excuse for the already considerable delay in getting the series off the ground. He could say: "A tragedy. I wept. Brilliantly creative, both of them, a terrible, terrible loss. But thank God I had the foresight to insure these key people and as a result we have an extra five hundred thousand to play around with." Holy Hannah! That was *exactly* what the Goblin had in mind! Jim almost believed it.

"Are you *sure* you're not Tyrone Power?"

"Well, I'm not completely sure, no," said Jim.

"Ha ha ha ha ha!" said the old lady, fluttering her eyelashes in a kittenish manner. "Well, you *cert*ainly do look like him!"

"I'm not really him, though," said Jim. "However, there comes Katharine Hepburn."

"Oh, *that's* not Katharine Hepburn! You're a naughty, naughty man to tease me like this!"

Florence looked elated as she walked toward the table. Several travel folders were clutched in her hand and she was smiling broadly.

"Katharine," said Jim, "I'd like you to meet Mrs.—excuse me?"

"Muriel Page."

"How do you do," said Florence.

"Just fine. And this is Olivia Chandler."

"How do you do, Mrs. Chandler."

"Oh, fine, thank you. Just fine and dandy."

"We're having us a grand old time!"

"Oh, yes!"

"Your friend looks so much like Tyrone Power I could just die!"

"He certainly does!"

"But you don't look like Katharine Hepburn. I mean, not much."

"No, not much. A little."

"Mm," said Florence. "Well, nice to have met you ladies."

"The pleasure was *all* ours."

"It *sure* was."

Florence sat down at the table across from Jim and lifted an eyebrow at him. "What's this Katharine Hepburn stuff?" she asked.

"The old ladies are drunk. They think I look like Tyrone Power."

"They're drunk, all right."

"Well, actually I think I *do* kind of look like Tyrone Power."

"There isn't the faintest resemblance," said Florence. "Those old ladies are tipsy and flirty, that's all, and you ought to be ashamed of yourself for stirring them up."

"Is it my fault I'm sexy?" asked Jim. "What took you so long?"

Florence smiled triumphantly. "I have great news," she said. "The *S.S. Lorna Loone* is perfectly safe. That cabdriver was babbling just as I thought. He was sent to spook us, I honestly believe it, and all I can say is thank God I didn't let that little pixy spoil my trip. Believe me, no good ever comes from a talking cabdriver and that's why I tell them, 'Would you mind not talking? I'm engaged in silent prayer.' Or else I tell them they sound exactly like a man who attacked me when I was fourteen and if they don't stop talking I might scream at the top of my lungs. Or if they're real dumb I use even worse methods on them. I can't *stand* a talking cabdriver!"

"Calm down for a moment and tell me about the ship," said Jim. "What did you find out?"

"I've found out everything," said Florence excitedly. "Bowser knows all about it and so does Spratt, and what's more, I've cheated on you a little, I've been aboard it! Jack just took me there, Jack Bowser—Spratt, the other one, he was busy, but he confirmed what Jack said and let me tell you the staterooms are simply beautiful! I saw my own stateroom! Do you know this is the most exciting thing that's ever happened to me? I've never been *any*where, I've never had the money to go anywhere, the farthest south I've ever been is Washington, D.C.—oh, Jim, I'm telling you, I couldn't be happier. The lounge is a little small, but it's all right and the staterooms are beautiful. And we have a little deck we can sit on. It's wonderful!"

"Hmm," said Jim. "I was beginning to think maybe you were right about the Goblin being out to drown us, but it sounds fine."

"It's great."

"What cargo is the *Lorna Loone* carrying?"

"Cargo?"

"Yes, what cargo is aboard?"

"Oh, I don't know. Medium transformers, I think. Yes, medium transformers to Bluefields and . . . some secondhand electric typewriters. They recondition them in South America, Caracas, I think. I also saw a whole pile of cases of Dinty Moore beef stew. God knows where that's going. But the main thing is the ship is safe, safe as the *Queen Mary*."

"Well, if Bowser and Spratt say it's safe, I guess it is," answered Jim. "With names like that, they couldn't be liars."

"They all have crazy names in the South," said Florence. "The other passenger has a crazy name too."

Jim's eyebrows lifted. "Other passenger?" he asked.

"Yes, there're only three of us aboard, although the *Lorna Loone* has four staterooms and can carry as many as eight. It's off-season, that's no reflection on the ship, it's completely safe. Both Jack and Paul say so. It was in drydock only last year and has new pumps and everything. That's to control the bilge—you've heard of bilge? All ships have it."

"Yes, I know," said Jim. "Who's the other passenger?"

"And what's more, the air conditioning is all repaired and they've hired a new cook, a *master* chef. They have frozen Western steaks aboard and imported caviar and everything! Why, these merchant ships are luxurious!"

"Yes, but who's the other passenger?"

"I'm coming to that. As for the captain, he's held master's papers for over ten years and has never been involved in an accident of any kind. He's a Hollander and that's about the only truthful thing that pixy cabdriver said. He was trying deliberately to spook us!"

"Excuse me," said the waitress, "are you ready for your duck soup now?"

"No, go away," said Jim. "I mean, not yet."

"*Duck* soup?" asked Florence.

Jim shrugged. "I know, but that's what they have here."

"I've never been in a place in my life that had *duck* soup," said Florence, "although I don't know why not. You hear about duck soup, but there never is any. I think I'm going to try it."

"Now?" asked the waitress.

"No, first bring me a Scotch and soda."

"Who's the other passenger? Is it a woman?"

"*Wait* a second, will you? I'm trying to tell you the captain is very reliable. The other ship's officers are Scandinavians mostly, and they're the best seamen in the world. The crew are Jamaicans and other Caribbean islanders and a few South Americans and they're all competent too. The ship is Panamanian registry and it's owned by an extremely rich Brazilian who spends most of his time in the south of France. There's a picture of him in the lounge."

"Well, good," said Jim. The double Gibsons on his totally empty stomach had hit him like a sledge hammer and he felt woozy. "Is the other passenger a *man*?"

"No, a woman," said Florence. "But I'm afraid she isn't your friend Maria Concepción. She's not a South American aristocrat, she's an American."

Jim sighed with relief. At least the other passenger was of the correct sex. "What does she look like," he asked, "how old is she?"

"I didn't see her, but she's already aboard. She was in her stateroom. Jack was going to knock and let me introduce myself but I told him not to."

"I wish to hell you hadn't."

"Well, I was taking up his lunch hour. He was *very* nice. For nothing at all, he told me all about the ship and took me there in his own car. The Savannahians are incredible—can you imagine anybody doing a thing like that in New York? Actually, I think he and Paul are a couple of fags but they're very nice. I seem to fascinate fags somehow. Maybe they feel at ease with me because I'm so ugly."

"Oh, you're not ugly, Florence."

"The hell I'm not, I'm gruesome."

"Well, I agree with you anybody named Jack Bowser and Paul Spratt have got to be fags."

"They were terribly sweet to me and I shouldn't call them fags, but I think they are."

Jim suddenly felt discouraged. If the woman aboard was not a South American aristocrat, probably none of his *déjà vu* dream had any truth to it. "Do you suppose she was taking a *nap*?"

"Who?"

"Why, the other passenger, the woman in her stateroom. Do you think she was taking a nap?"

"I don't know. The little Norwegian steward said she was in there, that's all I know."

"If she's taking a nap, she's probably *old*," said Jim gloomily. "And that must be what she's doing."

"Not necessarily, she could be unpacking. Or reading. Or taking a shower, writing a letter, lots of things."

"Well, that's true," said Jim. "The part that really worries me is that she's an American."

Florence looked around at the cutlasses tied to the fish nets hanging from the walls and took a sip of her Scotch and soda. "This is a nice place. I really love Savannah. Sometime I'm going to come back here and stay a while. You should see the live oaks down on Bay Street. But according to Jack we have *got* to go out to see Bonaventure Cemetery. He says it's the most beautiful cemetery in the world."

"Thanks just the same."

"Why not? We've got plenty of time, the ship doesn't leave for hours."

"About that woman," said Jim. "How do you *know* she's an American if you didn't see her?"

"Well, her *name* is American for one thing—"

"What's her name?"

"I don't remember. It's a funny name, worse than Jack Bowser, and it's definitely American."

"Well, she could have married an American—if she's married at all."

"I think she is."

"Okay, she might not be American by birth. She could be a Venezuelan or a Colombian or anything."

"No, it listed her nationality on the passenger list. She's American."

"Passenger list? You saw the passenger list?"

"Sure, Jack got me a copy of it, and the ports of call too. I have it in my purse."

"Good Christ! Why didn't you say so? Let me see it."

Florence opened her pocketbook and began to burrow in it. "I'm sure it says 'nationality: American.' And I'm sure she's American by birth too. She's got a Southern name, one of those funny double names, Malarkey Betty-Lou or something like that, I didn't pay much attention—"

"Malarkey Betty-Lou? Give me that!"

"Wait a second, will you?"

Anxiously Jim leaned forward over the table as Florence took a folded sheet of paper from her purse. "What is it? What's her name?"

Florence spread out the paper, looked at it, then laughed. "Oh, God," she said. "Was I ever right. It *is* worse than Jack Bowser."

"What is her *name*?" asked Jim.

"Meh-lo-dee Caro-loo-cee *Dubbs,*" said Florence.

"What?"

"You heard me. Melody Carolucy Dubbs. And she's married. There's a Mrs. before it."

"Give me that!" said Jim. Angrily, he snatched the sheet of paper from Florence. "Nobody could have a name like that."

"She must be a Southerner," said Florence. "The name Melody's not that unusual in the South, I knew a girl in school from Kentucky whose name was Melody. She was a very sweet little girl and after a while we got used to the name, it was kind of cute. But I don't know about 'Carolucy,' that seems to be going a bit far."

"God!" said Jim. But it was true; there it was, typed out on the passenger list: *"Dubbs, Mrs. Melody Carolucy—nationality* U.S.A." Of course a rose by any other name would smell as sweet, but how could a woman capable of shipboard romance have such a name as this? It was a matter requiring a moment of thought and a certain amount of adjustment. In order to be sure he was making no error, Jim put on his reading glasses and looked again, then said: "Well, I agree with you the 'Melody' is . . . not too bad. And as for the 'Carolucy,' it must be a typo, that's got to be two words."

"You mean like, Carol *Ucy?*" asked Florence.

"No," said Jim coldly. "I mean like, *Carol Lucy.*"

Florence was laughing. "Cheer up. People have all kinds of funny names in this world. The president of my senior class in high school was a girl named Sally Sleet. I swear to God. And I once knew a man whose name was Max Banana. Really and truly. That was his legal name, Max Banana. Oh ho ho ho, God! Ridiculous."

Jim put his reading glasses back in his breast pocket and gave Florence an aloof stare. "Well, frankly, *I* think Jack *Bowser* is a *far* more absurd name than . . . than hers."

"I don't know about *that,*" said Florence.

"What's wrong with her name? It's kind of . . . musical."

"*Dubbs* is musical?"

"Well, that's her husband's name. She can't be blamed for that."

"Oh, ho ho ho ho, you're a howl!"

"All right, the initials are the same," said Jim solemnly. "How about *that?*"

"What do you mean, the initials are the same?"

"I mean precisely what I said. Maria Concepción Diaz and . . . ah-ah-h, Melody Carolucy Dubbs. Em, See, Dee. The initials of both names are identical, and don't you think that's . . . *a slightly strange coincidence?*"

"Oh, Christ!" said Florence, a hand against her side. "Stop it, you're killing me, I'm getting a stitch!"

"Well, it *is* a funny coincidence," said Jim sulkily. "Psychically, I was . . . well, probing for it."

"Oh, no! Probing, he says! Stop, you're killing me."

"Okay, I don't care if you laugh. Go ahead and laugh, goddamn it, just go right ahead and laugh. It doesn't bother me a *bit*, Florence. This happens to be vitally important to me, but go right ahead and laugh your damn fool head off and see if I care."

"Sorry," she answered. "I don't mean to be a beast. I didn't know you were quite so serious about it."

"I am *not* serious about it. On the other hand, I don't have a closed mind either. To have a closed mind is *very* stupid, Florence."

"That's true."

"I say *déjà vu* is not nonsense, there's something to it. I had a real psychic experience and you just wait. I don't care what her name is or even if she's not terribly beautiful, but this woman is going to be very unusual and very interesting. And unless I miss my bet, I think she *is* going to be beautiful, or at least *very* attractive."

Florence had dabbed the tears of amusement out of her eyes with a napkin and was now staring at him gravely. "Well, your theory is very interesting of itself," she said. "Do you know what I'm beginning to suspect? That if Maria Concepción doesn't exist, she will have to be invented."

"Now, *that* is a stupid remark. How could I invent her? And why should I? Tell me that—why should I?"

"Who knows?" asked Florence. "There are many mysteries locked in the human heart and soul. Why should the squares of Savannah make me want to cry? And by the way, I'll always love you for taking it back about them being silly. That really was very sweet of you."

"I was just humoring you," said Jim, a bit mollified. For a moment he had been so angry at Florence he'd felt like kicking her on the shin under the table. "And I don't see any comparison at all. You really were kind of nutty about those squares, Florence, but *I* admit I could be wrong, wholly wrong. This might just be a silly daydream. If that's all it is and the woman's impossible, then I assure you I will be philosophical about it. Completely so."

"Will you?"

Jim hesitated, wondering if he did or did not see a mischievous half smile in Florence's eyes. "Yes, I will," he answered, "what do you think I am, a simple-minded nut or something?"

"No," said Florence. "I don't think you're a simple-minded nut, I think you're a very complex man. You've surprised me many times already since I've known you, and I don't think the surprises are over yet."

"Uh-huh," said Jim. "I didn't say she was going to be absolutely beautiful. All I said was I *think* she's going to be very attractive."

"For your sake I hope she is. And I hope you have a nice shipboard romance, too, to take your mind off your troubles."

"It is more than that," replied Jim with dignity. "I don't want merely . . . a pointless adventure. What I want is . . . something more."

"Good luck," said Florence.

At three-thirty that afternoon, numbed by four double Gibsons and half blinded by the brilliant yellow sunshine, Jim Kittering stood on the cobblestones by the Savannah River and got a look at the *S.S. Lorna Loone*. He also got a look at Mrs. Charles Arthur Dubbs, nee Melody Carolucy Warfield. The lady was behind the railing of the deck and staring down directly at him through her steel-rimmed spectacles. A little black umbrella was lifted above her head to shield her from the sun, but at this moment it was tilted to the side and the sunshine glinted on her spectacles in such a way that she resembled a large, plump, glowing-eyed insect from Mars. The impression of a strange big insect or bird from Mars was increased by the grim line of her mouth and by the peering, downward thrust of her head. She looked about fifty years of age and wore a pale gray shapeless dress. The sight of her was as cruel a blow to Jim Kittering as a cat-o'-nine-tails upon his naked back. He literally groaned aloud as if a whip had struck him.

"I'm sorry," said Florence quietly. "I'm really sorry."

"Yeah," said Jim in a defeated voice.

Well, deep inside he had known it all along and that was why Florence's skepticism had infuriated him so much. Of course the *déjà vu* illusion was just that, an illusion—and also a childish daydream, a transparent piece of wishful thinking. He had known it really and had almost admitted it to Florence under the spell of Bonaventure Cemetery. At least he *had* said to Florence: "The thing I really want is not a crazy sex adventure with a beautiful South American aristocrat. The thing I really want is to love my wife. That's what I really want, Florence, more than anything else in this world—to learn how to love Linda."

In the light of his confession, the *déjà vu* dream seemed not only absurd but insane as well. Where was the ludicrous reasonableness in this dream? How could an affair with another woman teach him to love his own wife? It was ridiculous and so was his so-called psychic experience. Such phenomena could only be the creation of his unconscious—and strange mother-of-pearl indeed for this new and nobler temple of his soul. But even as he flinched at the irony of his approach toward winning back Linda, the *déjà vu* dream held him in thrall.

One thing was certain beyond doubt: if there ever was a place in Christendom that could provoke psychic phenomena, it was Bonaventure Cemetery. Jim had gone there under bitter protest; he was eager to get to the ship and did not want to see, as he said, "a goddamn boneyard" in the first place. But Florence was adamant; she had insisted they hire another cab and drive out there. Very disgruntled and three-fourths drunk, Jim had rested his head on the back of the seat and shut his eyes. He refused to open them to admire the stately palmettos and azaleas of Victory Drive and was half asleep and had half forgotten where he was when the cab turned a corner and he heard Florence suddenly catch her breath. Startled, he opened his eyes. An incredible, weirdly luminous area was before him, overhung with gigantic trees laden and covered with brown-gray Spanish moss, backlighted and shining in eerie grandeur. "Good God," he said, "what the hell *is* it?"

"It's Bonaventure Cemetery," said Florence in an awed whisper.

A clammy unidentified *thing* crept toward Jim Kittering. This was no bright and cheerful square of Savannah, but a nether region by a misty river. The unearthly beauty of the place was staggering. Huge limbs of live oaks thrust out almost at right angles in such a way as to form a tremendous canopy over the entire area. Spanish moss hung in fantastic profusion everywhere, great streamers and coils glowing and shining with the light of the hidden sun. Underneath the trees he could see ancient tombstones and grave markers in the light that filtered through the moss.

The *thing* crept closer as Jim stared at the great arms of the live oaks spread out above the jumbled phalanx of tombstones stained with age. And then it was there. Beyond pity, it raised its shaggy, rotten head and grinned at him. Beneath that ground lay the bones of men and women who once had lived, breathed, laughed, and thought they never would die. But they had fallen and were gone, and in the wink of an eye he himself, his wife, his children, and everyone he knew or cared about would be as lost to this world as the bones beneath that moss. The *thing* slowly nodded its horrible head and smiled.

Cold fear seized Jim Kittering and held him. He would die, fall into a pit of nothingness, cease to exist—and the time when it would happen was not far away at all. It was true, life was short. He had never believed it as a young man, he had thought the old-time prophets were merely talking, but they were telling the absolute and horrible truth—an empty eternity waited just around the corner for him and for all living human beings. Why, in the light of such a fundamental fact, had he made such a miserable mess of the brief hours given to him?

The fear of death that gripped Jim Kittering was so overwhelming he barely could see the tombstones in the light filtered through the hanging moss. He would fall into a pit of nothingness all alone, without the love of his wife or his children or anyone else; he would die alone because he had lived alone. In a panic he barely could control, Jim shut his eyes to exclude the moss and the tombstones. Such a solitary descent into eternity was unendurable. Something would have to be done about it and done at once, before time ran out forever.

But again the unanswerable question came to him: What could he do? The problem itself now lay before him with an ultimate clarity; but the answer, if there was one, had become even more elusive than before. "Love thy neighbor, maybe," thought Jim with a bitter inner smile. What a measureless insanity was contained in that piece of absurd advice. "Love thy neighbor"—fine, wonderful, but *how* love thy goddamned neighbor? That was the difficulty. How could any man of perception "love" the lying, thieving, and dangerous scoundrel next door? The Sermon on the Mount was the greatest practical joke in all of human history. Was it possible Jesus Christ was a conscious put-on artist, a comic genius laughing hysterically to himself for two thousand years at the result of his great gag? "Dad, that bullshit I threw at 'em on the mountain—they *went* for it! Funniest thing since the Flood, Dad!"

But no, not really. Who took Christ seriously, anyhow? Certainly not the Christians. It was an historical fact that Christians were the most ferocious pack of wolves ever to roam the surface of the earth. Even the "best" of them did not follow Christ's advice. The thing they really practiced was: "Love thy neighbor—but keep thy gun loaded and ready and when he comes after you shoot him in the ass." Christ was not a put-on artist because his joke had failed. No one believed him.

Jim frowned unhappily at the tombstones beneath the hanging moss. He had gotten nowhere. The fact remained that the only way not to die alone was not to live alone. The Sermon on the Mount was a total absurdity, but was it nevertheless the only possible answer? Well, it was true, Christ had not died alone on his cross.

"Let's get out of here," said Jim. "In a minute I'm going to start getting religion."

"So am I," said Florence. "It's fantastic. I never saw such a place in my life. It is *literally* out of this world—there's no other way to put it."

"I'll tell you this. I have a severe case of the creeps. Let's get out of here."

"I want to take some pictures first. But there's something I want to tell you. You asked about the cargo on the *S.S. Lorna Loone*—remember?"

"Yes," said Jim.

"Did you read that clipping I gave you?"

"I read part of it."

"You read about the *Castillo Montjuich,* the ship that was loaded with grain and disappeared?"

"Yes."

"I said the *S.S. Lorna Loone* is carrying medium transformers and secondhand electric typewriters, and it is. But I think you ought to know it's carrying something else too."

"What?" asked Jim.

"*Wheat,*" said Florence.

"Oh, for Christ's sake, Florence! What are you trying to do, make me dig up one of these graves and crawl into it? Ships carry wheat all the time. You're as nervous as a cat with seven lost kittens."

"Well, I lied about it and I thought you ought to know."

It was shortly thereafter that Jim made his own confession and on the way back to the ship he felt better because of it. He had decided he was right about Jesus Christ in the first place, that "Love thy neighbor" was carrying absurdity one step too far; but he had conceded one thing to the Nazarene by saying to Florence: "The thing I really want is to love my wife. That's what I really want, Florence, more than anything in this world—to learn how to love Linda." Somehow it helped. As the cab rolled down Victory Drive, the eerie graves of Bonaventure became less frightening and the *déjà vu* dream returned full force.

The dream returned in all its hope and beauty, then the dream was gone. On polished cobblestones that made him feel unsure on his feet, Jim stared up at the lady with the shining spectacles beneath the small black umbrella. Drunk as he was and half blinded by the sun, Jim could not see her clearly, but he could see her clearly enough and she was impossible. "There's still about one chance in a thousand," he said. "Maybe that isn't her."

"Maybe you'd better stop kidding yourself," said Florence.

"Yeah," said Jim.

Florence, of course, was right. The lady on the deck was the other passenger, Mrs. Melody Carolucy Dubbs. There was no Maria Concepción with a button navel and there was no Santa Claus with a beard either. As Florence paid for the taxi, Jim stared sadly at the rust-streaked *S.S. Lorna Loone* and at the woman on deck. She was up above him by the railing at the gangplank entrance and the sun was behind her. The umbrella was raised above her head and her face was partly in shadow, but he could see old-fashioned steel-rimmed spectacles and a grim-lipped mouth upon which there was not a trace of lipstick.

She was impossible but Jim continued to stare at her. After all, there was nothing better to do. The woman was of indeterminate middle age; she looked about fifty, but could be forty or forty-five. Actually, her posture was good and she might be somewhat younger. She wore a long-sleeved cotton dress of pale gray and it came down well below her knees. She was a big woman and had a bosom of the type the French called "*le balcon*," although the dress was shapeless and it was hard to tell what her figure really was like. Of course she was so old and unattractive it was an academic question. The woman was also full of hostility. She was returning his stare and in fact glaring at him with indignation, and Jim idly wondered why. Maybe she had seen him staggering when he got out of the cab and was disgusted by his drunkenness.

"Let's get aboard," said Florence. "Can you carry your bag or do you want me to carry it?"

"Hell, I'll carry it," said Jim. "I'm all right."

Halfway up the gangplank Florence cried: "Watch out!"

"Okay, okay," said Jim unworried, though he was teetering half over the rope railing. Down below he could see garbage and strips of toilet paper floating in oily water. A jet was spurting out of the brownish white side of the ship and Jim could smell sewage. He also could smell the heavy, funguslike odor of wheat and could see wheat dust floating above the freight deck. Florence had gotten a bit carried away; the *Lorna Loone* was disappointingly small and looked like hell and smelled worse. The staterooms were probably better and thank God he soon would be in one. Staggering, suitcase in one hand and briefcase in the other, Jim went up the gangplank with lilting steps in the singing sunshine. A lightheadedness had come upon him; he could hardly feel his feet and the bright sunshine was making music in his ears.

"Hoomph!" said a voice.

Melody Carolucy Dubbs, hitherto known as Maria Concepción Diaz, stood before him. It took Jim Kittering about ten seconds to reduce her age by twenty years and transform her from a plump Martian insect into Hera, the ancient Greek queen of heaven. Jim saw nothing miraculous in his feat, which in all truth was based on fairly accurate observation of her outer appearance and a reasonable guess at her inner qualities. However, his ten-second burst of mental activity was quite a performance indeed, a kind of supernova of the mind beyond the limitations of matter and energy. Florence later was so astonished she gazed at him empty-eyed in wonder.

"Hoomph!" said the voice again.

The woman was four feet away, umbrella firmly raised to shield her grim pale face from the burning sun. But the face was not really grim and there were far fewer lines of age than Jim had expected. She was younger than he'd thought, perhaps thirty-five or forty, maybe even a bit younger, and on closer inspection she did not bear any resemblance to a plump insect or bird from Mars. Her features were even and not wholly unattractive. In fact, she could almost be considered a handsome woman, despite the black mole on her temple and quite a few too many pounds, plus the handicap of no make-up, the ridiculous steel-rimmed spectacles, an unbecoming dress, and an old-fashioned arrangement of her hair. The hair, which had real possibilities, was combed straight back from her forehead and fixed at the rear of her head in a big braided 1890-style bun. Judging from the size of the bun, she had hair three feet long and the color was very attractive, a dark silky brown without a trace of gray. She was much younger than he'd thought, probably not more than thirty, if that. He had gotten an inaccurate impression of her from the cobblestones down below. Of course, he had not been able to see her very well with the sun in his eyes and he had been thrown off by the glasses and her clothes. She did carry a few extra pounds, but she was not plump. She was a big woman, at least five feet ten inches tall, but she was not really plump. And besides, most cultures of the world greatly admired a real woman such as this and would scorn as sexless the fashion models of Fifth Avenue. Although the mole on her temple was not too attractive, it served as a kind of beauty spot to accent the perfect whiteness of her complexion, which in turn accented the deep blue of her eyes. Her complexion, her eyes, and the dark walnut-brown hair were all attractive features, and even her mouth, now grimly compressed with indignation, had sensitivity and well-shaped lips of the kind always called "sensual" in romantic novels. Furthermore, that was no "*le balcon*" bosom; she was full-breasted, that was all. Her figure was actually that of Hera, the ancient Greek queen of heaven and the goddess of women and marriage, the broad-hipped and big-breasted personification of womanhood and indeed of the mother earth from which all life is born. Finally, she was not hostile either, her anger was a sham. The blue eyes behind the steel-rimmed spectacles had a gentle and lovely expression even as she attempted to stare at him in stern disapproval. Jim Kittering had arrived at the truth but, stunned by the power of his mental explosion, he did not yet realize it. He dropped his suitcase on the deck, put a hand on his hip, smiled at her, and said: "Hi, there. Did you say 'Hoomph' at me?"

"Drunk as you can be," said the woman softly. "You ought to be ashamed of yourself. Don't you realize God sees you plain and clear?"

"Yeah," said Jim. Dizzy from the furnace-like sunshine, the double Gibsons, and his own thoughts, he stood there in the gangplank entrance as Florence edged by him with her suitcase. The lady was some kind of religious nut but Jim did not care. The sound of her voice had charmed him tremendously. It was the voice of a much younger woman than he'd thought and the tone with which she spoke had an indescribable femininity and loveliness. Melody Carolucy was barely thirty years old and she was not "almost" a handsome woman, she *was* a handsome woman.

"Are you Mrs. Dubbs?" asked Florence.

"Yes . . . yes, I am."

Better and better—it was incredible. She had a small white hand with slender, delicate fingers. She was a big woman but her hand was small and feminine. She was also shy. A blush showed in her cheeks and a timid look came in her eyes as she shook hands with Florence. Jim smiled, delighted. The small hand, the blush, and the shyness were beautiful.

"My name is Florence Carr."

"I . . . I'm very happy to meet you, Florence."

"This is Jim Kittering. You'll have to excuse him, he's slightly under the weather."

"Call me John Barleycorn," said Jim.

"I wouldn't call you such a thing," said the woman as she held out her hand. "You're one of God's children even if you are drunk."

Dizzy in the singing sunshine, Jim took her hand. It was fantastic. Her small hand fit into his own as if it belonged there and a strange current not unakin to electricity flowed from it to his own. He was sure the current also flowed from his hand to hers—she too seemed startled. Jim could not let the hand go. She pulled once, then pulled again before he released her. "Well," he said, "one of God's illegitimate children, maybe."

"God has no illegitimate children," she answered.

Jim smiled. "I guess I'm the Devil's child then, because I'm sure not one of God's children."

"Of course you are," she replied, "and it's a pity. How can you do it, Mr. Kittering? You don't look like a weak or wicked man to me, how can you do such a thing to yourself? Don't you know God didn't put you in his beautiful world to pour filth and poison into the temple of your soul?"

"Temple?" asked Jim as a faintness came upon him. "You say . . . temple of my soul?"

"Yes, your soul. Rise above fear and whisky, Mr. Kittering. Put your faith in God. 'There shall no evil befall thee, neither shall any plague come nigh thy dwelling. For he shall give his angels charge over thee, to keep thee in all thy ways.' Psalm ninety-one, Verses ten and eleven."

The sunshine was singing louder in Jim's ears and a velvety blackness was beginning to spread at the periphery of his vision. He could not possibly have been more mistaken on those cobblestones. A plump fifty-year-old insect from Mars? Melody Carolucy was not a day over twenty-five and not merely a handsome woman but a beautiful woman. But the most astounding thing was the remark she had made. Had he not sat in his living room by emerald oblivion and been saved by the hope that he could find a way to build a new temple for his soul? Of course religious people talked like that, but how could the woman possibly use the very same word? "You mean a temple like in the poem?" asked Jim. "A new temple nobler than the last, and all of that? Is that what you mean?"

"I mean the body is the temple of the soul," she answered. "And *yours* is full of *liquor*."

"No, no, no, no—I mean like in the O'Neill play and the poem. You know, the chambered nautilus, that goddamn seashell thing, it's a squid, I think, with a house that's too small."

"Squid? I will talk to you tomorrow, Mr. Kittering, when you are sober."

"No, no, wait! You don't understand me. I mean Oliver Wendell Holmes's poem. Forget O'Neill's bullshit, I don't care about that, I'm interested in the growth aspect of it, the original idea."

"Oh!" she exclaimed, the blue eyes opening wide and the well-shaped lips forming a brief circle of pious horror. "What a thing to say! You ought to be ashamed of yourself, thoroughly and completely ashamed! Why, you can hardly even talk or make any sense—look at you, you can hardly even stand up!"

"Oh, fuck, I'm not getting across," said Jim. "You really don't understand me. *Hey!* Where are you going?"

"*I . . .* am going *. . . to my stateroom!*"

"When will I see you again?" See her again he must. The light of the supernova had reached Jim Kittering, he had seen the splendor of its beacon in the sky. Even in her pretended anger, there was not a trace of anything but love and gentleness in her voice, her eyes, her heart, and her soul. She was not angry at him *per*sonally, she was merely full of wrath at Beefeater's gin. The poor darling thought there was something *bad* about Beefeater's gin, but she did not think there was anything bad about *him*, James Kittering, phony double of Tyrone Power, Princeton graduate of no-such-turn philosophy, woman-spoiler and right-hand man of the Goblin. It was too much. The singing sunshine in Jim's ears became louder and the velvety blackness spread, but he could still see her as she walked away with perfect posture and feminine grace from the abomination of Beefeater's gin. Silly of her to have a thing like that about gin, he would have to be firm and get her over it. He called after her:

"When will I see you? Cocktail hour in the lounge? I want very much to talk to you."

For a moment she turned and looked back and in the magic flick of an eyelid the gray dress was whisked off her. It was doubtless an illusion and Jim knew it, but the illusion was very powerful. She stood on the deck magnificently and beautifully naked without the slightest shame, her full breasts glorious and lovely, the Hera triangle of silk between her thighs as distant from carnality as wildflowers in a Himalayan meadow, and the small, rather unusual button-type navel on her womanly stomach a perfect symbol and reminder of her fundamental humanity and need. The gray dress whisked back upon her as she turned and opened a door, but it was a great illusion while it lasted. Jim had no doubt it was exactly the way she looked without her clothes—and to hold that beautiful body in his arms would be paradise enow.

It was much too much. The sunshine became louder and the blackness complete. He knew what was happening. On one of his visits to the Coast, perhaps to discuss with one of the California boys a "cute meet" or a casting problem for some Special, he had stopped off in Arizona to view the Grand Canyon and like the typical tourist had leaned out too far over the mule. Jim had abruptly shifted backward in the saddle, dropped his handicapping briefcase, grabbed blindly at the reins, winced at sharp pressure on his hip, and felt himself begin to fall into the Grand Canyon toward the Colorado River far below.

Jim did not land in the Colorado, however, but in a smaller stream. As Florence cried out in exasperation, tried frantically to grab his hand, then screamed, he toppled over the rope of the gangplank into the Savannah River and landed with a great splash in the oily water among the garbage and the toilet paper. The shock revived him immediately. Spluttering and choking, he treaded water and attempted to brush a strip of clinging toilet tissue from his forehead as Negro workmen laughed gutturally and lowered a big hook to fish him out. It was preposterous and he was furious. "Christ almighty!" yelled Jim.

"Don't stick that fucking hook in my suit, I paid a hundred and eighty-five dollars for it at J. Press!"

However, absurd as life might be, it had its compensations. As he brushed at toilet paper, treaded oily water, and avoided a cotton-bale hook, Jim caught a glimpse far above of a pale frightened face and a black umbrella against the deep blue sky. The loss of his dignity did not matter at all. She had come back. She was worried about him. She loved him already, as he loved her. "He shall give his angels charge over thee"—Melody Carolucy, in all her beauty, was aboard the *S.S. Lorna Loone.*

PART FOUR
May Day

TEN

Himself Surprised

As Jim frequently pointed out to Florence to her extreme annoyance, leprechaun cabdrivers are sometimes right. By the same token, fairies of this world such as Jack Bowser and Paul Spratt are often wrong and had best not be listened to but rather left in peace unto themselves to do their funny little thing. "Oh, shut up, stop pestering me!" Florence would say. "You're as surprised as I am!"

Surprised? He was not surprised, not at all, not by that silly ship and certainly not by Melody. She was the one who was surprised, not he. His seduction of her was a masterpiece and a miracle of love to boot, even though it had not yet quite occurred.

After numerous misadventures and considerable sacred-and-profane conflict between Jim and Melody, the *Loony Goony* ran into the fringes of Hurricane Beulah somewhere in the vicinity of the Yucatan Channel, a wide stretch of sea between the Mexican mainland and the far western tip of Cuba. On that same day, which was the fifth at sea, the Norwegian steward, a cross-eyed boy named Odd, lost "sissty-two" *Playboys* to a big bad wave and the captain got drunk and set fire to the radio shack.

However, Jim Kittering was not concerned with the fate of the S.S. *Lorna Loone*, but with the sacred-and-profane conflict that wholly absorbed the hours of his nights and days. He literally could think of nothing else. He brooded, he fretted, he agonized—he wondered constantly with an increasing suspense when the stubborn creature would succumb.

As Hurricane Beulah drew nearer and the cargo of wheat began to grumble below decks, Jim sat at a table in the ship's lounge and amused himself with a fantasy announcement of a great Special the Goblin would have loved and eaten with a spoon:

"Ladieeeees and gentlemennnnn! We are proud to bring you at this hour a thrilling engagement direct from the waters of the blue Caribbean! In this corner, the Challenger, Jim Kittering, armed with Cupid's fragile but insidious arrows; and in that corner, the Champion, Melody Dubbs, armed with God's heavy thunderbolts of spiritual love. Florence Carr, referee. It's the fight of the century, folks! A rrrrreal scrrrrrap, and may the better participant emerge victorious!"

It was maddening. She was out on her feet, why didn't she throw in the towel? Look at her, sitting there smiling and talking and playing a silly game of checkers with Florence, as if he had not won a great round the night before. He had lost some rounds, true enough; she was a great counterpuncher and had the basic advantage of not knowing when she was licked. But he had won that round the night before even though this morning she had bounced back and was ostentatiously ignoring him. The stubborn creature had icily addressed him at breakfast as "Mr. Kittering"—what a nerve!

And what an injury. It was not as if he had forever. She was not going on to Barranquilla, Willemstad, and Caracas, but was leaving the ship at Cartagena to catch a plane to Bogotá and another to San José del Guaviare, where her husband Charles awaited her with a stack of Bibles. Cartagena was only two ports of call and five short days away.

But the situation was by no means hopeless. The fight had gone his way from the beginning. Jim stared broodingly out of the porthole at the cerise sky and roughening sea. She would fall soon. Let her smile and play checkers with Florence and pretend he was not in the room. She might not know it, but she was out on her feet and had been so almost from the start.

As big, froth-topped, bottle-green waves rose in slow motion like huge elephant backs outside the lounge portholes and an ominous creaking groan sounded from the innards of the *S.S. Lorna Loone*, Jim recalled the first round, which he had won decisively by extreme speed afoot and three or four powerful blows delivered under her guard.

Jim remembered very well—indeed, he could never forget—that first wondrous morning at sea when he awakened early and went out to explore the *S.S. Lorna Loone*. It was only quarter past six and he did not expect to find anyone else up and about. But Melody had lived on a farm as a child and was accustomed to early rising; she also was up and exploring the ship. Jim found her at the rail of the stern deck, her hair partly down and blowing in the wind as she gazed at a thin line of land that was undoubtedly the coast of Florida.

After his ridiculous fall into the Savannah River, Jim had not had the nerve to show up for dinner the night before. And besides, he was quite drunk by then. It was clear she disapproved of drinking and rather than stagger into the dining room and risk seriously alienating her, he had taken four Alka-Seltzers in two glasses of water, lain down on the bed in his underwear, and slept like the dead for twelve hours.

When he awakened, surprisingly enough he had no hangover and felt better than he had felt for months. A light breeze was blowing through the open porthole and he could smell the fresh salt odor of the sea. Blue ocean was outside the porthole, ocean of incredible deep cobalt blue, with small white waves and a distant purple horizon blending with the sky. The blueness of the southern sea, although he had seen it before a number of times, always came as a pleasant shock. Jim smiled as he stared out of the porthole at the distant horizon. It was a beautiful day. The faint vibration of diesel engines and the gentle rolling motion beneath his feet meant the *S.S. Lorna Loone* was on the high seas bound for Bluefields and points beyond.

The stateroom, as Florence had said, was comfortable and pleasant, if not so luxurious as she had implied. It contained twin beds, a private bath with a shower of ceramic tile, wall-to-wall carpeting, and a desk and other furniture of blond mahogany. As Jim put on a pair of tropical slacks, a white golf shirt, and socks and leather sandals, he felt something of the romance and exhilaration of travel that had gripped Florence in Blackbeard's Haunt, the Savannah restaurant with the murals of bloodthirsty pirates on the walls.

They would be going directly into old pirate territory, the blue waters of the Spanish Main itself, where all kinds of amazing and marvelous adventures had occurred. Amazing and marvelous adventures still occurred every day, and who could tell if such an adventure might not occur on this very trip? They might get stranded in a revolution in Bluefields or something. Who knew? He'd been right about Melody Carolucy being aboard and maybe he was right about this too.

Jim smiled to himself and shook his head. It was too much to get involved in another *déjà vu* dream, even though in an unexpected way the dream had come true. If anything happened on the trip, it would be blind accident. Or maybe . . . good luck. A revolution in Nicaragua could give him more time with Melody Carolucy. Maybe they would be held hostages in some hotel and they would escape into the mountains and be saved and hidden by an elderly, civilized English tea planter who would shrewdly conceal them in a secret room with a large double bed.

Jim smiled to himself again as he fastened the straps of his sandals. The romance of travel had seized him, all right. So far as he could recall, it was Guatemala, not Nicaragua, that had mountains. All the same, a revolution that could delay them in Nicaragua would certainly come in handy. Jim grinned again as it occurred to him that in any event Hob was foiled—the horrible bastard had actually done him a favor by sending him on this wild-goose chase.

Ironically enough, it was the first "vacation" he had had in almost six years. The Goblin always found some emergency that kept him in New York or sent him off to cuckoo conferences on the Coast. The only way he and Linda had ever gone anywhere was to combine business somehow, which meant whispered long-distance calls and constant botheration. If there was one thing the Goblin hated, it was for anyone in his power to have any fun. But the son of a bitch could not get him on the phone and whisper at him now—and whoopee for that, it was like being out of jail.

Jim ran a comb through his hair, which still, thank God, did not show very much gray except a little around the temples. He actually *was* a rather handsome man. There was a pleasing honesty in his eyes, no matter what kind of liar he might be. Furthermore, there was no blubber on his stomach, or at least very little. For all the Martinis he had drunk and the strain he had endured, he looked ten years younger than his age.

And he'd been thinking he was all washed up! Well, it would do him good to get away from the whole thing for a while, far removed from the life he had known—the stomach-burning Martinis at expensive lunches, the countless phone calls and cigarettes and coffee, the meetings, the script conferences devoted to grave discussion of bullshit stories about bullshit people, and the grinding anxiety and fear of Hob and all the rest of it, including the saffron pollution and spiritual madness that floated over New York, the bad air and bad manners and the frenetic rush, rush, rush to nowhere. It would even be, yes, a good idea for him to get away awhile from Linda and from things that reminded him of her.

Jim's mood of exhilaration was only slightly dampened by the grim corridor outside his stateroom. A maze of pipes ran along the ceiling and rust showed through the gray paint on the iron walls. It was ugly but that didn't matter. Full of curiosity, Jim walked down the passageway, saw a door of heavy blond plywood with the stenciled word "LOUNGE" on it, opened the door, and glanced inside.

He saw a disappointingly small room with several oilcloth-covered tables, chromium-plated tube furniture, and a small built-in bar in one corner. The bar did have a mirror and various bottles of rum, whisky, and gin. Foolishly enough, a gatefold from *Playboy* was stuck to the bar mirror with Scotch tape. The "Playmate of the Month" was a thin little girl with huge eyes and gigantic breasts out of all balance to her arms and legs and wasplike waist; she was gazing poutily across the room at him with narcissistic complacency, as if to say:

"Look what a figure I've got, isn't it great? Aren't my breasts fabulous? You like? Well, if you aren't just another clown but can do something important for me, then maybe . . . just maybe I might find myself terribly attracted to you, and that's why I have this little lewd glitter in my eyes. . . ."

Jim, who liked *Playboy* and found it an entertaining and intelligent magazine, did not as a rule buy the innocence of "Miss Playmate." A few looked like the girl next door, but most of them looked like the naive whore next door. All were pretty and some were beautiful, but he was sick unto death of the type. He had seen a million of them around the office, poking out their cute behinds and thrusting forth their overdeveloped chests like weird, starved pouter pigeons.

And most of them ready and willing to "do anything, just anything" for a chance at that golden career and that wonderful fame. As a beautiful brunette had said to him only a week before, with a "naive" smile and a breathless Marilyn Monroe voice: "Mr. Kittering, I realize I have to be cooperative in every way toward those who can help my career. I am so willing to learn, really I am."

Willing to learn. Her career. What a laugh. Jim was sick unto death of the little bitches; they were worth just about as much as they cost, and that was nothing at all. How many times had he held one of those pathetic girls in his arms and wondered what he was doing it for? And they *were* pathetic. That was the worst part, the thing they did to themselves, their real femininity and human feelings.

But in a way the girls were victims and not to blame. It was a pity and a horror, but the world in which they lived regarded female beauty as a commodity just like soap. If they had valuable merchandise, who could call them illogical for selling it, especially since they themselves did not have enough sense or judgment to understand its real value? The sad part was that the men who bought and used them went right on with their stomach-burning Martinis and expensive lunches, while the girls lost their womanhood and went to hell.

Such were Jim Kittering's not-exactly-swinging reflections as he stared across the lounge of the S.S. *Lorna Loone* at "Miss Playmate." As he shut the door of the lounge and walked down the passageway, the thought occurred to him that a different kind of woman was aboard the S.S. *Lorna Loone* and this fact no doubt was a considerable part of his early-morning euphoria. At the same time, he felt a floating anxiety in the area.

There were difficulties. He had been very drunk when he came aboard the ship and had made a complete ass of himself by falling into the river. And not only that, his recollection of the brief conversation with her was not reassuring. She had not known what he meant by his reference to "The Chambered Nautilus" and he seemed to remember using in his excitement a Madison Avenue term here or there, one of those routine expletives that meant nothing at all in script conferences but might shock such a person as she, a harmless word like "bullshit," for example. She just possibly might not dig the word and he seemed to remember using it and perhaps one or two others.

But if Jim was vague about his own choice of language, he was not vague about the rest of it. He remembered with the vividness of total recall his impression of her and the thoughts he had had about her. He could not have been mistaken in his evaluation, that was impossible, but he had a certain anxiety nevertheless. Surely she *did* look like Hera and there *was* a wonderful gentleness in her eyes? Jim was sure of it but he was anxious. He was also anxious about the impression he would make on her. The first meeting with her—that is, the first calm and sober meeting—would be of tremendous importance, of such importance it might even determine the outcome of everything.

As he opened the heavy door of the corridor and walked out on the small passenger deck, a pleasant sea breeze blew Jim's hair back from his forehead. The golden-yellow sunshine of early morning slanted across the scrubbed and bleached deck and a limitless expanse of blue ocean lay beyond the white rail with its row of life preservers. Jim took a deep breath of the clean sea air and resisted an impulse to reach into his pocket for a cigarette.

The deck itself was small and not very attractive. There were four or five deck chairs and a metal table with a blue and orange striped umbrella. Brown rust was eating through the painted side of the ship and the wooden deck was bleached almost white. Hands on hips, Jim surveyed the scene, which had an abandoned feeling in the early light, then turned and walked slowly in the direction of the bow and the freight deck. When he got there he discovered there was nothing to see, except more rust and the large sealed lids over the cargo holes.

It was not the most beautiful ship in the world. In fact, it still looked to him like an ugly little toy. He was surprised a ship of this size could contain four staterooms or carry enough cargo to amount to anything, but there probably was more room below those lids than he supposed. At any rate, it was a dismal little tub and seemed abandoned and bereft in the morning light; there were no crew members or ship's officers to be seen anywhere.

Idly, Jim spat down on the freight deck, which was about fifteen feet below him. That seemed to accomplish nothing. He had a creepy impression the ship had no crew or officers on it and somehow or other ran itself like the *Flying Dutchman.* It was a feeling he would have again; the passengers seldom saw the crew and had little contact with the ship's officers, who either spoke bad English or were surly and antisocial.

The bow section had no interest. Jim shrugged and glanced around behind him up at the bridge of the ship and caught a glimpse of a bearded figure in a black, gold-braided cap. One of the ship's officers, the captain or first mate, probably. The man was not staring at him, but gloomily straight ahead.

Hands clasped behind him, Jim walked back in the other direction past the door to the staterooms and on across the small passenger deck. He paused for a moment to examine a shacklike structure with a large radio antenna on the roof, then walked around it and there, down on the lower stern deck, he saw her.

Jim recognized her immediately even though her hair was partly down and blowing in the wind as she stared in a direction away from him at a thin line of land on the western horizon. Or at least it seemed she was staring at the line of land; he later learned in actuality she was not. Jim shaded his eyes and held his breath as he gazed down at her.

She wore a modest dress similar to the one she had had on the day before, but it was not long-sleeved and was made of a lighter material. As the wind blew the dress against her, the form of the body beneath it was revealed and Jim sighed with joy and relief. He had not been wrong the day before—if anything, he had underestimated her. The blowing wind revealed an excellent and youthful figure.

It was true she was no fashion model. She was broad-hipped and full-breasted, but she was a tall woman and her figure actually was in perfect proportion. Again he noted that her posture was superb. She stood with her shoulders back straight and graceful, and with her long blowing hair she really did resemble Hera. Drunk as he had been, his first observation of her had been quite accurate. At the least, she was a very handsome woman.

And soon he would see her closer, he would look in her blue eyes and determine if she was as beautiful as he had thought. He had not considered her to be merely "a very handsome woman," but a beautiful woman. Was he wrong? Jim stood frozen by the ladder steps to the stern deck. She had not seen him and for a moment he was tempted to flee back to his stateroom, not because he doubted her beauty but because he did not know what he could say to her. He had blown his alcoholic breath on her and used gross language and then fallen into the river like an idiot—what could he say to her? Jim was tempted to take to his heels and at least think of some verbal approach. However, no good ever came from too much thinking about such matters, and as the poet said, faint heart ne'er won fair lady; it might as well be now as later.

Jim went down the ladder steps and walked across the small, semicircular stern deck. His sandals made no sound and she did not turn toward him until he stood beside her at the railing. Then a thing happened he never would have expected. Blankly, without a sign of recognition, she gazed at him with a quizzical expression. She did not have the vaguest idea who he was. How could she have forgotten him? Jim's bewilderment was made all the more painful by the fact that she not only looked beautiful, but more beautiful than when he had first seen her by the gangplank. Her even features, perfect complexion, and deep blue eyes looked different, somehow. Again, as on the day before, her eyes had an indescribable gentleness and loveliness, but it wasn't just the wonderful expression in her eyes —her whole face looked more beautiful.

"Yes?" she asked.

She did not know him! Shattered, Jim attempted to smile and said: "Good morning."

At once a blush came in her cheeks and a startled look in her blue eyes. The moment he saw the blush Jim understood it; he understood it even before she reached her hand toward the pocket of her dress. A part, but certainly not all, of the wonderful expression in her eyes came from the fact that she was so nearsighted she could not recognize him without her glasses, which she now took from her pocket and put on.

"Oh," she said, "it's you, Mr. Kittering. I'm sorry, I . . . I really can't see without my glasses. I was just . . . well, just listening to the wind and the sea."

Shy. Very, very shy. It took an effort of will for her to speak to him, but her blush had a meaning beyond her shyness and so did the slight tremor of her hand as she put on the glasses. She had recognized his voice even though he'd spoken only a handful of sentences to her, and the recognition of that voice brought an instant blush to her cheeks, a blush she had not been impelled to bestow upon the stranger she had thought him until that moment. He was right about everything. A current akin to electricity *had* passed between their hands and she had felt it too.

"That sounds like a nice thing to do," he said, "to listen to the wind and the sea." Jim paused, his eyes upon her in a kind of hypnotized wonder. "It's beautiful to look at, too."

Another blush; he was not looking at the sea, and she knew the thought in his mind or sensed it. And she didn't quite like it; it disturbed her. Her lips pressed briefly together and she asked softly, in a manner that was probably intended to be ironic but was not: "And how do you feel this morning, Mr. Kittering?"

Fantastic—everything about her was wonderful. The soft, slightly Southern intonation of her voice made Jim feel such a tender love for her it seemed perfectly reasonable to suggest they not waste precious time with foolish maneuvering but fall into each other's arms at once. She might not know him yet quite as well as he knew her, however, and besides, to win a woman's love always involved, perhaps sadly enough, a certain amount of spadework, such as tension-reducing humor, the physical dent, and even at times the cold-turkey shock.

"My name is Jim," he answered, "and yours is Melody Carolucy. Right?"

"Yes . . . yes, that's my name."

"To answer your question, I feel a *lot* better than I did yesterday afternoon. In fact, I feel wonderful this morning, better than I've felt in a long time. How do you feel?"

"I'm glad you're feeling better this morning than you did yesterday afternoon," she answered with a smile. "And to tell the truth, I feel wonderful this morning too." It was the first time he had seen her smile. Her teeth were even and white and the smile removed forever any doubt in Jim's mind that she was a beautiful woman. He stared at her as she turned her head toward the thin line of land on the horizon. "Yes, I do feel wonderful," she said. "I've waited for this trip a long time. It's been the dream of my life, and my husband's, too. All the years studying medicine and nursing, we've dreamed of this trip."

The hideous sound of the word "husband" disrupted Jim's daze of bliss. A sickening fear ran through him—was it possible the husband, by some awful mischance, was aboard? "Your husband?"

"Yes. We'd always planned to go by ship, but I'm afraid it wasn't practical for him. It isn't for me either, really, but it's cheaper than by plane and I couldn't resist."

The husband, thank God, wasn't aboard. "Too bad he couldn't come along," said Jim.

"Oh, he left three months ago, by plane because it's quicker and easier. But we'd always dreamed of going together by ship. I love the ocean and so does Charles."

This conversation about Charles would *not* do. "I wonder what that line of land is," said Jim.

"I don't know. Maybe it's Cumberland Island. That's a fairly big island off the southern coast of Georgia."

"Oh, we must have come farther than that. I should think it would be the coast of Florida."

"I have no sense of distance or direction either," she answered with another smile. "I lived in Knoxville five years and got lost there fifty times. But whatever the land is, we're on the way."

Jim returned her smile and said, "We sure are. We're on our way on the blue sea with white clouds overhead."

"That's nice. It's simple but that's just what it is. We're on our way on the blue sea with white clouds overhead."

"I don't always talk like a truck driver," said Jim, "assuming truck drivers talk the way I talked yesterday, and I don't really think they do." He paused for a moment, then added: "I'm afraid I owe you an apology for being in such sad condition when I came aboard. I hope nothing I said embarrassed you."

"No," she replied. "No, you didn't embarrass me. But I thought maybe it wasn't . . . well, the best possible time to talk to you."

"Actually, I was very interested in what you said to me. I'd had too much to drink, but I remember it extremely well. I remember every word you said, every expression on your face, every tone of your voice."

A faint blush again was on her cheeks. "I'm surprised you would remember it so well."

"It was one of the most important experiences of my life."

The blush deepened and a tiny frown appeared on her forehead. "In what way?" she asked.

"I understand part of it," said Jim, "but when all is said and done I couldn't begin to tell you. Who can know about such things? The way you looked at me, the things you said. It made a tremendous impression on me. Didn't you know that at the time?"

"Well . . . I don't know . . . "

"I had the feeling you did."

She was blushing badly now and having difficulty meeting his gaze. "Yes . . . at first I thought you understood me. Yes, I did think so. But then you were so . . . drunk. . . ."

"I was drunk but I understood you perfectly. The trouble was, you didn't understand me. You mentioned the temple of the soul to me, remember?"

"Yes."

"And I mentioned a poem called 'The Chambered Nautilus.' The theme of the poem is growth—or, if you like, spiritual growth. Now, I'll tell you something and it might surprise you a little but I'm not trying to be forward or fresh; the only reason I'm telling you this is so you'll understand why I reacted to you as I did. Do you mind?"

"Oh, no, I don't mind, not at all."

She was keenly interested, extremely interested. Jim had had no idea what he would say and still didn't, really. He plunged on: "A couple of days ago I examined my whole life and it seemed to me such a mess I wondered if it was worth living at all. I don't suppose I would really have done it, but I had an urge to drown myself in the swimming pool. Then a strange dream came to me that I would meet on this ship a beautiful woman who would change my life and change it forever. I also remembered that poem, which has a line that goes: 'Build thee more stately mansions, O my soul.' Do you know the poem?"

"Yes, I know it now," she answered. The blush was gone and her face now seemed to Jim a trifle pale. She was staring intently at him.

"The poem goes on: 'Leave thy low-vaulted past. Let each new temple, nobler than the last, Shut thee from heaven with a dome more vast, Till thou at length art free, Leaving thine outgrown shell by life's unresting sea.' That was the poem I remembered when I was dreaming about the beautiful woman who would be on this ship, and when you spoke to me about the 'temple' of my soul I thought you were that woman, and then when you said, 'He shall give his angels charge over thee,' I was sure of it . . ." Jim paused, so moved by the memory of the moment that his voice briefly failed him. "And when I look at you now, I know it's true. You are that woman. You are the beautiful woman of my dream."

True, every word of it! So true, Jim's vision was blurred by emotion. He blinked in anxiety at her—what impression had he made on her? Apparently none whatever. In silence, she stood there and gazed at him, then he noticed a slight tremble in her lip, and another tremble. "But," she said, "but . . . I'm sorry . . . I'm married."

Joy ran through Jim. She had not been silent because he had failed to move her. She was sorry she was married, and the words meant what they said and were as true as his own words to her.

"It doesn't matter to me whether you're married or not," said Jim. "You're the beautiful woman I dreamed would be on this ship."

She smiled and asked softly, "Beautiful? Do you think I'm beautiful?"

"I sure do," said Jim.

"You're wrong. I'm not beautiful." Jim did not reply and after a moment she smiled again and gave a little shrug. "I'm not. You must be blind if you think so. I'm not even a girl any more. I'm twenty-eight years old and plain as can be."

Jim looked at her in silence for several seconds, then turned, put his hands on the stern deck railing, stared out at sea, and said: "To me you are beautiful. And I'm not blind either, I'm not even nearsighted. I can see perfectly well and you're beautiful."

"No one ever accused me of it before." Jim could tell from the sound of her voice she was still smiling. "Except Charles, my husband, he thinks I'm beautiful, but of course he's not objective at all. He loves me."

The husband again. To hell with him. "So do I," said Jim with a little smile to take the edge off it. The time was not ripe for him to tell her he loved her and say it straight, although God knows he felt it.

She returned his smile, at ease with him now despite a certain underlying tension about which something would have to be done very soon. "You couldn't possibly love me. Why, you don't even know me."

Jim paused for a moment to think. Thus far everything he had said to her had been not only true but uncalculated. However, in his view of feminine nature, the man who wanted a woman's body in his arms could not always base his approach on spontaneity and strict truth. An unnatural Platonic "love" ensued thereby, love that was not love at all but an abomination to the man and an equal abomination to the woman.

The time had come to make what Jim called "the physical dent." Making the physical dent, in his belief, was of utmost importance in the wooing of a woman. Unlike men, women did not operate visually or intellectually, but sensually and emotionally. The physical dent had to be made at an early stage and it had to be made with sufficient force so they could not get it out of their minds. When they looked at him they had to think: "He kissed me. He put his hand on my leg. His arm was around my waist."

However, in this particular case there was a serious difficulty. In his anxiety to make Melody realize how enormously important she was to him, he had set up dangerous inhibitions based on the very knowledge he wanted her to have. If he touched her now after the things he had said, she would draw back in shock and that was not a physical dent but merely a disturbing jolt.

But it had to be done all the more now; the knowledge he had given her made an early dent an imperative necessity, because as time went by the inhibition based on that knowledge would not lessen. The barrier that existed between nearly all men and women had to be shattered at once, especially since he had given the barrier conscious reinforcement.

And yet if he touched her she would recoil in alarm. In effect, he had to do it without her knowing he was doing it, a fairly subtle thing but not as subtle as it seemed. There were ways, and fortunately it wouldn't take a great deal to make a physical dent on this woman.

Thus, after a moment or two of reflection, Jim put strict truth and spontaneity aside. He did not consider his approach cunning or unfair, but rather a reasonable effort to help her toward a mutually desired goal.

"Important authorities disagree with you," said Jim solemnly. "You are outnumbered four to one."

"Four to one?"

"Sure. You say I couldn't fall in love with you at first sight, but the Beatles say they're sure it happens all the time. There're four Beatles but there's only one of you. How about that?"

"The Beatles?" she asked with a smile. "You mean the Beatles that sing?"

"I certainly don't mean beetles in the woods. *They* don't know anything about the mystery of love, they just know about bark and old leaves and mushrooms and things."

"But the Beatles that sing *do* know about love?"

"They know *all* about it," said Jim. "And in their song, 'A Little Help From My Friends,' they say they're sure love at first sight happens all the time. Maybe I *am* crazy, though. But love itself is crazy, when you think about it. Why should two people love each other, anyhow?"

"Nothing in the world is more natural," she answered, "assuming the two people are free to love each other."

Uh-uh, honey, thought Jim, forget Charles, put him out of your head. "Maybe it is natural," he replied, "but all the same, people fall in love for the most ridiculous reasons imaginable. I once knew a girl who fell madly in love with a man because she liked the way his reading glasses fit on his temples. Do you believe that?"

"I believe that may be why she *thought* she loved him, but there must have been some other things she liked about him too."

"Oh, no, she didn't like anything else, just the reading glasses," said

Jim. "She adored those glasses and made a home and had two children for them." Melody smiled again, far more amused than his mild little joke warranted. A look of delight was in her eyes.

The tension was down and the time had come for the physical dent. Her hand for a starter. How to get at it? "That isn't the worst," said Jim. "Did you know the Duke of Windsor gave up a throne because the Duchess had small feminine hands like yours?" Jim reached for her right hand—not the left, that had a gold wedding band—as if it were a cucumber or a tomato on a supermarket shelf. "Hmp, you *do* have small hands," he said as he gently but firmly held her fingers in his own. "Very small, for a person of your height. What's this, a class ring?"

It was not dangerous at all. He had known she would be too startled to snatch the hand away and would not be so ill-mannered, especially since he was only examining it like a tomato and comparing it to the hand of the Duchess of Windsor, about whose hands Jim had no information and did not want any. "What?" she asked. "Oh . . . yes. Yes, that's my class ring."

"It's an unusual type," said Jim as he fiddled with the ring and turned it on her small finger as if he were interested in it. "I never saw one like it before. What school is it?"

"Tom Armour University," she replied.

"It's pretty. I like it."

"Well . . . thank you."

Her voice was getting nervous and in a moment she would pull the hand away. Jim released her before she could do so, folded his arms, and swiftly reflected on "Tom Armour University," of which by chance he had heard. This was bad news. An actress he'd known some years before, a wild little girl from North Carolina, had gone there briefly. The girl sat naked on the bed and drank straight bourbon and told him hilarious stories about an insane, unbelievable so-called "university" where the students prayed morning, noon, and night and boys were expelled for saying "damn" and girls were expelled for holding a boy's hand.

"Jesus Christ was all over that place like you wouldn't believe it," the actress had said. "I'm telling you, such nuts you never saw. If they caught you fucking God knows *what* they'd do. Hell, they expelled *me* because my skirt was too tight and showed my ass just a little. Doll, that place you wouldn't believe."

Bad news. Melody Carolucy had graduated from a fantastic mad institution devoted to "good old-time religion," an incredible anachronism flourishing somewhere down South with thousands of students and all kinds of money. The actress had said it was a going concern.

"Where's Tom Armour University?" asked Jim. "I've heard of it, I think, but where's it located?"

"It's in Tennessee."

"Are you from Tennessee?"

"No, Arkansas and Pennsylvania, but I went to school there and studied nursing at a hospital in Knoxville."

Jim paused to estimate progress. The blue eyes were fairly solemn behind the glasses and her voice seemed a trifle shaky. A physical dent of sorts had been made, perhaps even a moderately strong one on this graduate of Tom Armour University, where girls were expelled for holding a boy's hand. For him to hold her hand and examine her ring in such a manner probably seemed to her a pretty intimate contact. But Jim wanted the dent to be stronger if possible and he acted on a sudden inspiration that came to him. He looked out at sea with an expression of startled wonder, then took her by the arm just above the elbow, exerted pressure to turn her around, pointed with his other hand, and said: "Look, a porpoise!"

"Where?" she asked.

Jim kept his hand on her arm, which had a warm and very pleasant feeling, as he leaned forward over the rail beside her and shaded his eyes with his free hand. "It was right out there," he said, "about a hundred yards from the ship!"

"Are you sure it was a porpoise?"

"I'm positive." Jim leaned forward a bit to his left, simultaneously raising his hand from her arm and casually putting it on her shoulder as if to support himself in his keen effort to peer out at the porpoise and spot the elusive creature. "There!" he said. "Isn't that a fin?"

"*Where?*" she asked in frustration. "Oh, I wish I could see it! Where exactly?"

"Right over *there*," said Jim, pointing and leaning to the side and shifting his hand to her left shoulder, thus lightly half-embracing her with his arm in an innocent manner; he was, of course, absorbed in the porpoise and not even thinking about her. Not much. The curve of her back under his arm and her own soft arm and shoulder against his side affected him so strongly he was tempted to make his half-embrace something more than light and casual.

Why not? She might catch on he was interested in something more than the porpoise, but she couldn't be sure of it, especially if the porpoise would obligingly jump out of the water at the very same moment. And why shouldn't the animal do that—was not the porpoise a friend of man? Risky. How well did her glasses correct her vision? Risky! But as the poet said, faint heart ne'er won fair lady. Jim squeezed his hand on her shoulder, tightened his arm around her, leaned against her, and exclaimed: "*There!* It just jumped out of the water *again!* I saw it plain as day—and there's a fin! To the left, over there!"

She was practically in his arms. His hand was on her shoulder, his arm firmly across her back, his chest touching her arm and side, and his leg against the soft Hera curve of her right hip. The contact with her body—whatever she herself felt about the contact with *his* body—made Jim so dizzy he could not have seen the porpoise even if there'd been one. But he could still hear and he heard a tiny little gulping noise at his left ear as she swallowed. He was making a dent on her now, and a real one.

"Oh," she said in a small voice, "I can't see it. I can't see anything except waves. But I . . . I don't see too well at long distances . . . even with my glasses."

Jim heard another tiny little gulping noise at his ear and her body seemed to soften and melt against his own. It was a magnificent dent. Surely by now, porpoise or no porpoise, she knew what he was doing. The thing was getting dangerous; a dent should be a dent, not a pass. "Gee, it was a pretty one too," said Jim. "Black, with a white stomach like snow." Reluctantly he lifted his hand from her shoulder and took his arm from around her. "Maybe it'll come back after a while."

"I hope it does. I never saw one . . . I mean in real life, a wild one. I've seen tame . . ." Another little gulp. ". . . tame ones on TV."

She was badly flustered and the poor thing really believed he had seen a porpoise. His womanizing tricks, obviously enough, were not in her realm of experience. She did not seem to think his arm around her was anything other than an innocent gesture, and blamed only herself for her reaction. Jim almost felt sorry for her, but all was fair in love and war and there was simply no other way to win a woman's love than this. And he had certainly made a dent on her, a dent indeed. She was looking at him in a totally different way than before. A mixture of stirring fright and solemn, absorbed interest was in her eyes.

Furthermore, as an added dividend, he'd discovered a thing he'd suspected anyhow but that was important to know—whatever her beliefs and attitudes, she was a passionate woman. Not all women had the physical and emotional endowment for real passion, but this one had it. The fright and solemnity in her eyes was a thing Jim Kittering could read like a book. The attraction she had felt toward him had been powerful and it had disturbed her. In a moment this would be confirmed by some reference to her husband.

"I guess it's gone," said Jim. "We'll probably see some more on the trip before we're through. I wonder when they serve breakfast? I haven't really eaten for two days and I'm starved."

"It ought to be soon," she answered. "Actually, I'm hungry too. I've been up for a couple of hours. . . ."

"That long, really?"

"As a girl I lived on a farm. In Arkansas. We moved to Scranton when I was nine. That's where I met Charles, he lived next door."

"Childhood sweethearts," said Jim with a nod. There was no getting out of it; the husband had to come into this thing, even if only briefly.

"Yes, that's what it was, childhood sweethearts." Silence. Jim turned toward her. She was frowning worriedly. "You know, I was . . . touched by what you said about your dream. And of course . . . naturally, very flattered you would think I'm . . . attractive, even with my glasses and these old-fashioned clothes. I know they're old-fashioned. Charles likes me to wear such things. He's old-fashioned himself in some ways, maybe too old-fashioned, but . . . well, he's a wonderful man and . . . and he's my husband."

"I do think you could find more becoming clothes," said Jim. "A long-sleeved dress like the one you had on yesterday not only hides your figure, it makes you look much older."

"I know. I hate that dress. No. No, I don't really *hate* it because it doesn't matter. There's no need for me to look attractive, I'm already married."

"Mmm," said Jim.

"I don't quite know how to say this, but . . . well, you understand I couldn't possibly be that woman you dreamed about even if such things could happen . . . because, as I told you originally . . . I'm already married."

Very naive, very sweet. Hadn't she ever heard of adultery? In a way, no. It wouldn't occur to her as a possible alternative and that of itself was a bit of a problem. "So am I," said Jim.

Her eyes opened with surprise. "Are you?"

"Yes, or at least I was. My wife left me a couple of days ago."

"She did?"

"She sure did."

"I'm sorry. But I think I understand now a little better. A couple of days ago—that's when you felt your life wasn't worth living and you thought of the poem and everything?"

"Yes."

"I'm very sorry. I understand you much, much better, the liquor and everything else. Do you have children?"

"Yes, two girls."

"That's awful. Terrible. Girls need a father more than nearly anything. Do they love you very much?"

"I guess they love me," said Jim.

"*Awful.* For them and for you. I've never had children, we can't and I've always wanted them so much. I'm sure a real father must feel a million times more so about his own living children. Do you think she might come back to you, your wife?"

"She might," said Jim. "At the moment she doesn't intend to, but if I change, she might."

"Of course . . . . that's why the poem. You want her back."

Jim nodded. It was an uncomfortable area, a kind of built-in irony intrinsic to the entire situation, but it could not be avoided. He could not lie to Melody about this. "Yes," he said. "I want her back."

"That proves you love her."

"Maybe not well and maybe not wisely," said Jim with a pained smile, "but yes, I love her. However, I won't see her for at least a year. In the meanwhile I've got to live. And I'm not the kind of man who can live alone."

She seemed puzzled; not antagonistically or disputatiously puzzled, but puzzled puzzled. "Of course you can't live alone. No one can."

It was incredible, but she really did not understand his thought at all. "I mean," said Jim, "I can't live without . . . . another woman."

"*Another* woman? You mean . . . ." The blue eyes opened wide.

"Oh, no. Oh, *no*. That would be the worst thing you could possibly do. You must be faithful to her now more than ever."

Jim clasped his hands behind him and rocked on his heels; he knew that beetling his brow in a boyishly baffled manner often had a helpful effect on women—to see a confused man who just could not get the point when some cruel denying thing had been said to him sometimes made them take it back and sigh helplessly and go into the next room to "slip into something more comfortable." But could it be she *really meant that?* Faithful for a year? Was she crazy? "That would probably be . . . a lovely gesture," said Jim. "But I don't know as I'm up to it."

"You *must* be—it seems to me the only way you can ever win her back. To be faithful to her and prove how much you love her."

Jim resisted the impulse to reply: "Linda would think I've lost my mind." Instead, he said: "I'm sure for some men that would be . . . *the answer*. But I'm kind of an unusual man. I have a . . . well, very affectionate nature. I need a woman's love in order to live really. I'd waste away and die in a year all alone."

"Now, that's a mistake. What about when you were a boy before you were married? You lived many years then without . . . a woman's love, didn't you?"

Could she possibly be *that* innocent and naive? Good grief, she was a grown woman and married and had studied nursing in a hospital in Knoxville. But she had also graduated from Tom Armour University, the motto of which was: "Arm yourself at Armour to do battle for Christ!" That was what the little actress had said, and she'd also said: "Jesus Christ was all over the place like you wouldn't believe it." The lamentable truth was *yes*, Melody was that innocent and naive.

The cold-turkey shock was the only answer. This was a woman who would never get the point in a million years otherwise. Her liking for him and attraction to him would make her refuse to believe him capable of misbehaving. She never *had* heard of adultery! She'd heard of it in an abstract sense, yes, but it had no reality for her. The cold-turkey shock was an absolute necessity, although as a technique Jim did not like it, he found it aesthetically unpleasing. The equivalent, in a sense, was necessary for most women, but a brief intense stare, a lifted eyebrow, an oblique word could hardly be called a cold-turkey shock. The cold-turkey shock by its very nature was crude, direct, undisguised.

It was also dangerous. The crude bluntness of it could drive a woman away forever if her defenses were not down already. On the other hand, if her defenses were down, the cold-turkey shock could deliver a powerful blow to a vulnerable area of the feminine anatomy. It was amazing what an effect the cold-turkey shock could have on certain women. The sure knowledge that a man, given the opportunity, would not discuss the stock market or how to breed orange canaries but would take off their clothes and make passionate love to them drove some women cuckoo with relief, gratitude, and sheer opportunism. They sometimes capitulated at once in a smiling daze. Jim had learned that many women suffered from chronic, vexing anxiety that men would not *do* anything even if given the chance. Or else they could not conceive of it as possible, as in the present case.

The cold-turkey shock could work wonders with such retarded or unfortunate types. As a rule, it operated a bit like a depth bomb; they would gasp with horror, fuss at him, bawl him out, upbraid him for moral idiocy, yammer hysterically about the husband or boy friend and all in all shudder with wet-hen indignation, then they would go off and think about it, and think about it some more, and some more, and then a phone call, a meeting, and BA-LOOM!—"This is crazy. Wait a second, I don't want to wrinkle my dress, I'll take it off." If, of course, they were strongly attracted to begin with. Not aesthetically pleasing, no. But a necessity in this case. Melody Carolucy would never get the point otherwise.

"Listen," said Jim in a gentle tone. "I know you're married and I don't want to hurt or affect your marriage in any way, but I'm extremely attracted to you and I have been since I first set eyes on you and I might as well tell you I want very, very much to make love to you."

"You want what?" she asked.

"I want to go to bed with you," said Jim.

"But I . . . I'm married. And even if I weren't, what kind of thing is that to say?"

"A crude thing, I suppose, but it's exactly the way I feel and I might as well be honest."

"You call that *honest?* Why, it's nothing but a bald and vulgar proposition! How dare you say such a thing to me? What kind of man are you?"

"Passionate," said Jim with a grin, "and very attracted to *you.*"

Melody was frowning and pale with agitation; her small hands were nervously twisting and retwisting a tiny handkerchief. Her eyes were fixed upon him as if she were attempting to peer deeply into his incomprehensible mind and heart to see what was there. Jim felt hopeful. Thus far her reaction was almost classic in its purity. Now if she would really get steamed up at his immorality and lambast him with the husband, the situation would have real play in it. The thing to fear, of course, was not anger or indignation, but for the woman to laugh and walk off.

"This is amazing," she said. "Have you no moral sense at all? Don't you realize you have no right to say such a thing to me? Let me repeat it again: I am *married*."

"I know," said Jim, "but whether you're married or not, I can't help it. I'm tremendously attracted to you and I had to tell you."

"All right, let me tell you this," she replied. "Whatever strange kind of values you live by or think you live by, they're not mine. I love my husband and I'd rather die than be disloyal to him and break his heart. I don't wonder your wife left you and if you get her back I'll be surprised. The *nerve* you've got, to talk nice and kind to me, then say such a thing! Wicked and sinful, that's what you are! I'd never *dream* of being unfaithful to my husband, even if I were separated from him for a year, or for two years, or three—and *not* because I'm a pious goody-goody, either! I'm a normal woman with normal feelings but I am *not* a beast or an animal that knows no better, and my answer to you is—thank you just the same. And having given you that answer, I will ask you not to speak to me again in such a familiar and disgusting manner while we're on this ship."

"I fell in love with you the minute I saw you," said Jim quietly, "and I want you. Is that a crime?"

A frown almost like a flinch came on her forehead, then her lips pressed angrily together. "Under the circumstances, yes! And this morning you don't even have the excuse you're drunk! As far as I'm concerned you have no character at all and you can fall in that ocean and I wouldn't even bother to pull you out!"

"I bet you would too," said Jim.

"Good morning, Mr. Kittering," she replied, and turned and walked across the deck to the ladder steps, her shoulders back with Hera pride. She was wonderful, marvelous, the ancient queen of heaven come back to earth again, and an angel of God as well. Jim watched her mount the steps with a Hera grace as the wind blew her dress against her.

There was no doubt about it. He had won the first round decisively by speed afoot and three or four powerful blows delivered under her guard. Thus, on the fifth day at sea, as he gazed unheedingly at the big, froth-topped, bottle-green waves that rose and descended like elephant backs beneath a threatening cerise sky, Jim Kittering considered his Goblin prize fight. She would fall soon, she was out on her feet.

Yes, truly enough, the Champion was in trouble, she could hardly defend herself at all. It had taken longer than he expected for her to recover from the cold-turkey shock, but the delayed reaction BA-LOOM was violent. She would not speak to him at breakfast and was extremely distant at lunch. She nodded half politely during a stroll on deck at midafternoon, then broke down and smiled during tea. A delight returned to her eyes as she listened to his jokes and laughed at the funny things he said, a delight replaced by solemn inner absorption as she pretended she did not know his knee was touching hers under the table. And at dinner—talk, talk, talk, Florence ignored as if she were not there, heads so close together he could feel her breath on his face. And her smile, again and again her smile, beautiful and wonderful with lovelight in her eyes. "You just need to be *better*," she said. "I understand you. You aren't a wicked man at all, you just need to be better. God's love, that's what you need."

For five days, from early morning until late at night, it had gone on. They were together all the time; talking in the lounge, sitting in the deck chairs, strolling on the deck at all hours hand in hand. He had persuaded her, with a little joke about her not still being at Tom Armour University, that it was perfectly all right for her to hold his hand. They were shipmates and fond of each other and no one would think anything about it. At first not wholly convinced, she now reached for his hand herself and held it constantly; she seemed to derive an endless pleasure from it.

Although Melody did not dream Florence suspected a thing, it was obvious both to Florence and to Jim that she was as crazily in love with him as he was with her. A thousand electric moments had occurred between them: countless blushes, solemn intent stares, words that meant more than they said, fleeting but powerful contact of hand or knee under the dinner table, similarly "accidental" bumping of elbow and side in the corridor, more blushes, more solemn stares, and much dry-mouthed swallowing by them both.

When would the stubborn creature succumb? It would be soon. He had finally, thank God, made a real breakthrough the night before, kissing her and putting his hand in her dressing gown on her breast. The kiss was passionate and she fully returned it, to say the least, her hand gently touching the side of his face with a beautiful caress. And the naked breast under his palm—he had felt her heart thumping and pounding away before she came to her senses with a horrified gasp and pushed him off and made him leave her stateroom. Thus, for the moment he had lost, but she was crying and trembling in near-hysteria and it would be soon.

Perhaps he needed God's love, but it was not God's love she wanted to give him, but her own. At times he felt that on a purely physical level she was even more attracted than he was, although it was difficult for him to imagine how this could be possible. But it was Melody who was weeping and trembling in near-hysteria, clutching at his fingers with one hand even as she pushed him in the chest with the other to get him out of her stateroom.

Perhaps her moral conflict was greater than his—Jim did not consider he himself *had* any moral conflict. But her physical attraction to him plainly was a terrible problem for her and she simply could not resist for much longer, even though at the moment she was blithely playing checkers with Florence as if nothing had happened the night before.

"Now that was dumb of you, Florence," Jim heard her say, with a satisfaction that seemed to him slightly unchristian. "Don't you see I can now jump all three of your kings on my next move after this, and there's nothing you can do to stop me? Ha ha, I've beat you again."

"Oh, fooey," said Florence.

In Jim's opinion, Florence loathed checkers but liked Melody and played with her to please her. Jim stared sourly at them, injured by the memory of how Florence had crawled all over him that morning. Her referee rulings lately made him feel as if he were fighting both of them. Florence knew he had kissed Melody, although Melody herself was not aware of Florence's referee role and did not dream she suspected anything at all.

And thank God for that—even Jim's love-deadened conscience quailed at the thought of the humiliation it would cause Melody if her feelings were known. The wife of a man of God, engaged in mission work herself, consecrated to God's love and God's laws, hater of *Playboy* and all things of the flesh—a pure and virtuous woman such as herself, tempted by adultery, that most horrible of sins?

Florence, of course, knew exactly what the situation was and Jim had told her about the great breakthrough. He had expected a compliment, an acknowledgment from the referee that he had won a spectacular round, but to his surprise Florence bawled hell out of him. Some referee. When Melody left the lounge to get the checker set from her stateroom he'd accused Florence of unfairly hampering his fight and she'd exploded all over him.

"All *right*, Florence," he said. "So I kissed her! What do you *expect* me to do, read the Bible with her?"

"Okay," said Florence, "you love her. I admit that, I believe it. I didn't at first, but I do now. You really love Melody and I understand why. I still don't know how on earth you figured her out just by looking at her on the deck, but you were right. However, you are not objective or sensible about her any more than she is about you. I don't love her but I like her very much and I am sensible about her. And I say you're being unfair and taking advantage of her—looking at her the way you do, saying the things you do to her, touching her every time you get the chance, and now *kissing* her! Don't you understand her at all? Don't you know the worst thing that could happen to her would be for her to be unfaithful to her husband? She loves you because of the *better* side of your nature, you son of a bitch—don't you have any respect for that? You're nauseating, Jim, you really are! If you love her, why don't you have a little pity on her and leave her alone? *You make me sick!* And I am rooting for *her*, not for you! You might get her, I know that, you've gotten her so involved with you she doesn't know what she's doing—but I hope to hell you don't, I hope she comes out of this and gets up off the floor and knocks you on your ass!"

So much for his appeal to the referee. Jim was bitter. Melody could hit in the clinches, sure. Dear sweet Melody could do anything she wanted to and that was fine, it was just good clean fighting when she kept talking about Linda and the children and how she would give anything on earth to have a child of her own, but let him try to throw a punch and the referee was all over him. And this was the most horrible ruling of all—it practically outlawed boxing!

The very idea, it would hurt Melody for him to go to bed with her—what bunk! Why, it wouldn't hurt her a bit, or Charles either if she'd keep her mouth shut about it, and he'd have to advise her strongly not to make any crazy confessions. It would not "hurt" Melody, it would do her good, teach her more about life, make her a more complete woman. There was nothing "wrong" about the love between himself and her, it was true and real and beautiful and *had* to take a physical expression. Didn't she want it as much as he did? Of course she did. Far from being cruel to make love to her, it would be cruel not to. So Jim told himself.

Florence's remarks, however, had depressed and bothered him no small amount. Was a crowd in his mind roaring for murder: "Hit her in the belly! Knock her head off!" It was a thing that had worried Jim from the beginning more than he cared to admit—what would it do to Melody if he knocked her out?

Florence was wrong and so was his own simile. Of course the sin of adultery would be a burden to her, but in reality there was no crowd in his mind and this was not a Goblin fight at all. Perhaps at the start, yes, a crowd had roared, and for that very reason he had not moved as fast as he could have done. He could have kissed her long before; there'd been many opportunities during those strolls on deck at night—he could have probably gotten her in bed by now, but had not done so out of fear of hurting her.

"Well, that's very clever of you," said Florence as Melody smilingly jumped the three kings, "but my stomach is upset from that boiled tongue last night and this storm worries me. I can't concentrate in this awful weather."

"No, I can just beat you at checkers," said Melody, "because I think and you don't, Florence. Do you want to play another game? I'll give you a checker and first move to encourage you a little."

"Oh, all right," said Florence, "but first I've got to go to the john. That damn tongue had me up all night."

"Well," said Melody in a lower tone, "I'm glad I didn't eat it. It looked funny and smelled tainted and I guess it was."

Such candor as "go to the john" always shocked her. They did not go to the john at Tom Armour University but withdrew to the washroom. Jim half smiled as he watched her set up the checkers for another game. At least she had on a dress this morning that was not quite so modest. In fact, for her it was downright bold. Unbelievably enough, the dress was not only short-sleeved but low-cut. He could actually catch a glimpse of the cleavage between her breasts. An odd thing—why had she worn the most daring dress she owned after the scene that had occurred in her stateroom the night before?

A sudden chill ran down Jim's spine. But of course. She had worn the dress *because* of the scene the night before. Why had he not realized it at once? The icy "Mr. Kittering" at breakfast was a feeble and pathetic effort to ward off what she herself knew was inevitable. Her choice of this dress told the whole story. To return to his prize-fight simile, her defenses were totally down. She was helpless and she knew it.

"Melody," he said, "you've got a nerve calling me Mr. Kittering like that."

As she glanced at him, the color left her cheeks. "I'd rather not talk to you after the way you acted last night," she answered in a trembling voice, then lowered her head over the checkerboard.

Jim stood up as the bottle-green waves rose and fell outside the lounge portholes. Melody did not move or turn her head to look at him as he walked over and stood behind her. For several seconds he stared down at the coiled braids on the top of her head, then he put his hands on her shoulders, kept them there for a moment, stepped closer to her, and moved his hands down over her dress and on her breasts.

"Oh, please," she whispered, "don't."

Jim's hands were on the outside of the dress. He pulled them back and slid them into the dress and down into her brassiere, which was tight and offered resistance to his fingers. He got his fingers into it, however, and on her breasts.

"Oh, please," she said. "Jim, please don't."

Her breasts were very full and more than filled his hands. Gently, taking care not to hurt her, Jim squeezed them in such a way that he could feel the mass of veins or gristle or whatever it was deep inside them, the part he supposed produced milk when a woman had a baby. Melody never had had a baby. Charles was not impotent but he was sterile. And that was a pity because the thing Melody wanted more than anything in the world was a baby of her own.

"Oh, please!" she said. "Jim, will you take your hands away?"

"In a minute," he replied.

"Please. Somebody might come in and see us."

Jim bent down and put his lips on the light, silky hair at the nape of her neck and kissed her. The breasts swelled under his hands as she leaned her head back with a gasping inhalation, then raised her hands, put them over his own, and pulled his hands against her so hard her fingers paled. It was a gesture of such erotic power Jim's knees began to shake. Again he could feel the mass inside the soft breasts.

"Ohhhh!" she sighed. "Ohhh, God! Ohhh, *please!*"

Jim took his hands out of her brassiere and out of her dress, then pulled up a chair and sat beside her. Pale and trembling, she stared into his eyes. "It's got to happen," he said, "and you know it as well as I do. I'm coming to your stateroom tonight at ten."

"No, don't," she whispered.

"I want you to put on your nightgown and go to bed and leave the door unlocked."

"No . . . no, I can't."

Jim put one hand on her wrist and the other on her shoulder, stared into her eyes, and said, "I love you, Melody, and I want you so much I am almost out of my mind. This can't go on and you know it, because you feel the same way I do. Isn't that true?"

"Yes, but feelings aren't all . . ."

"Now listen to me," said Jim quietly. "I want you to do what I say. Go to your stateroom around nine-thirty and take off your clothes and put on your nightgown and go to bed. Leave the door unlocked. Will you do that?"

"I can't . . . I really can't, I might get pregnant."

"You probably won't."

"But I might."

"When was your last period?"

Melody moistened her lips, swallowed, and said, "Two weeks ago. It's the time when I might get pregnant."

"We'll have to take that chance," said Jim. "We'll just have to, that's all." She was silent and he asked, "You're willing to take that chance, aren't you?"

"I suppose I might," she replied.

"All right, then do what I said. Leave the lounge early, go to your stateroom, and go to bed. Leave the door unlocked. Do you understand?"

Slowly, she nodded and replied, "Yes. All right. I will."

"Good," said Jim. "I'll see you tonight. And don't be afraid of me. I love you very, very much and the last thing on earth I'd ever want to do is hurt you."

"I know," she answered.

Jim stood up, gave her a pat on the shoulder, and walked back toward his own table as Florence shoved at the door of the lounge, then shoved at it again and entered. "Filthy door sticks," she said. "I guess it must be the humidity from this weather."

"Yeah," said Jim, "they ought to fix it. If you shut it all the way you can hardly open it."

"I know. I got caught in here last night while you and Melody were on deck and I couldn't get out till Odd and the first mate rescued me. All three of us could barely force it open and it seems to be getting worse every day. They ought to fix the thing. Melody, are you ready to beat me again?"

"Oh, I don't feel much like playing now," said Melody in a voice that astonished Jim by its calm. "I think I'll go to my stateroom and write a letter or read for a while."

"I'll play if you want to."

Melody stood up, amazingly calm and self-possessed. She had just made a firm date to commit adultery and she was acting as if it were an appointment to play tiddlywinks. "No, I think that's enough. Thanks anyhow, Florence. Maybe we'll play a game this afternoon." With an amiable nod at Jim, she walked toward the lounge door. "See you at lunch."

Incredible. She was calm as a blue-skied day in June and she was not backing out of it, either. Jim had no doubt she would go to her stateroom early and be there in bed in her nightgown and the door would be unlocked.

Who, Jim wondered, could figure out a woman? He had been afraid she would be semihysterical to the point of revealing everything to Florence, but not a bit. Apparently, now that she had made her decision, she was no longer anxious or nervous. The thing was going to happen and that was that; in the meanwhile she would write a letter or read and she would see them at lunch. Jim shook his head in wonder as he watched her walk with her usual queenlike posture out of the lounge.

"What have you done to her *now?*" asked Florence.

"Nothing," said Jim. "Mind your own business."

"Huh," said Florence. "You've got a funny look in your eye—what did you do, kiss her again or something?"

"I didn't do a thing to her," said Jim, "and I just want to tell you, Florence, I think your blow-up at me was a piece of dim-witted Puritanism and you were absolutely dead wrong. I *do* love Melody, and my going to bed with her won't hurt her, it will help her."

"Maybe so," said Florence with a shrug. "I might have gotten a little carried away. I was thinking about it on the john. If she loves you that much, there must be a reason for it, something wrong in her relationship to her husband. She seems to love him, but maybe . . . well, maybe he doesn't play her like a violin or something."

"I am sure it could not be anything as simple and stupid as that," said Jim aloofly. "Charles' love-making, primitive though it may be, is probably quite adequate for Melody. After all, she doesn't know a thing. It excites her for me to hold her hand."

"All right, how do you explain it then?" asked Florence.

With an even more aloof dignity, Jim replied, "I'm sure it would never occur to you, Florence, since you're so down on me, but it *could* be I might have *some* qualities Charles does not possess."

"Boy, you sure are full of yourself," said Florence. "*Something* must have happened while I was in there squatting on that toilet."

Jim frowned. "I wish you wouldn't talk about yourself like that, Florence. You know you've really got a complex. Of course you hate and despise *me* for wanting Melody—as if any man worth two cents wouldn't want her just as I do. But *I* don't hate and despise *you*—I like you, Florence, I like you very much and I always have. It's neurotic of you, all this talk about squatting on a toilet and being so ugly and everything. You aren't all that ugly; I've gotten used to you and you're really kind of cute."

Florence smiled. "Seduce me, then," she said, "and leave Melody alone."

Jim smiled back at her. "I would," he said, "if you really wanted me to."

Florence smiled again and took out a cigarette. "You know, for such an awful son of a bitch, you are sometimes kind of a nice guy? I almost think you *would* seduce me as a kind of humane favor."

"Sure I would," said Jim. "But you know as well as I do if I even looked at you with a glint in my eye, you'd run ninety miles an hour in the other direction."

Florence sadly lighted the cigarette, with an overemphatic strike of the match. "I probably would," she said. "In fact, I'm sure I would." She took a deep drag at the cigarette and blew out smoke with a sigh. "Anyhow, at the moment you've got another woman on your hands, I'd say. Are you about to fuck her?"

Jim hesitated. He really did like Florence. However rough she might be and whatever emotional problems she might have, there was something solid about her. To return briefly to the prize-ring simile, Florence was a good referee and would call the fight as she saw it. "Now listen," said Jim, "have you got your score card in your hand again? Or are you still rubbing rosin in my eyes and hitting me yourself?"

"I've got the score card," said Florence with a sad smile. "Are you about to fuck her?"

"That's a disgusting word to apply to her and I wish you wouldn't keep *saying* it," answered Jim.

"Well, that's what it is, isn't it?"

"No, it *isn't*. The connotation of the word implies an experience totally different from what it would be like to make love to Melody, and if you say it again I'll kick you."

"All right, are you going to make love to her, maybe like tonight? Is that it? Has she thrown in the towel?"

"Furthermore, that simile doesn't apply either. You were insulting and unfair, Florence, to bawl me out the way you did. You couldn't have been more wrong in what you said. I love this woman and I'd rather go through hell than hurt a hair of her head. In a way, I love her as much as I do Linda."

"All right," sighed Florence. "I have to admit as far as I can see you do love her. I can't blame you, I kind of love Melody myself, and believe me, not in any unnatural way. There's a kind of purity about her no matter what she says or does. Maybe I was wrong. Maybe she knows what she's doing as far as you're concerned. I don't believe that woman could do a really evil thing if she worked at it."

"No, she couldn't do anything evil," said Jim. "But she's human even as you and I. The answer to your question is yes. I'm going to her stateroom tonight and she'll be waiting for me."

Florence nodded with a slow melancholy. "That's it, then. I knew something had happened to her. It was as if a burden had fallen from her shoulders."

"Of course, with a woman you never know. She has almost twelve hours to think it over. She might change her mind."

"No, she's given up," said Florence. "I could tell from the look on her face. She can't fight it any more. You've got her."

Jim stared at a swirl of spilled salt on the oilcloth table. A depression had come upon him. He had expected to be elated, but he was not. "You make it sound as if I've got a deer in the sights of a high-powered rifle and I'm about to pull the trigger and shoot it through the heart."

"You said it," answered Florence. "The referee didn't make that ruling, Jim. *You* did."

Jim resisted an urge to groan aloud. "Oh, come on, Florence, for God's sake. What are you trying to do to me?"

"I'm sorry. But you did say it."

"I know I said it. But she's not really a deer and this isn't a fight. I love her and she loves me and you know that."

"I guess I do," said Florence with a smile, but the sadness did not leave her eyes. "I've had to watch the damn thing five whole days morning, noon, and night and I never saw anything like it. Do you realize what a pair you are? A missionary's wife and a Madison Avenue television executive giving competition to Romeo and Juliet? You're both out of your minds—do you realize that?"

"Florence, you don't know the half of it," said Jim. "While you were in the bathroom I touched her, I put my hands on her, and I swear to God it was like the atom bomb going off."

"Yeah," said Florence. "Well, it can't be helped. It's going to happen and I guess the only thing all three of us can do is grin and bear it. And in a way, I'm happy for you both. That kind of feeling is rare, most people never know it. I'm sure it will be . . . an experience, and I'm not using any four-letter words either, I mean something . . . something beautiful. That's what she feels and you do too, and that's why neither of you can help yourselves. It's got to happen, husband or no husband. It's just got to, that's all."

On an impulse, Jim took Florence's freckled hand and squeezed it. "You know," he said, "you can be pretty nice. And a pretty good referee too."

"Yes, but I was going to say . . ." Florence paused, a look of hesitation and the beginning of tears in her eyes. "Oh, it's no use. It's hopeless."

"What were you going to say?"

"It's no use."

"What was it?"

"Well . . . I know it's impossible for you, but surprise me again!" Florence squeezed Jim's fingers so hard it hurt him. "You've surprised me every time so far, surprise me just *once* more. Let her go, Jim. Don't shoot the deer, be a real man and let her go."

Jim was silent for several seconds, then folded his arms across his chest and said, "Florence, you are *no* goddamn referee. You are no goddamn referee *at all.*"

"I guess not," said Florence. She picked up a paper napkin and dabbed at the tears in her eyes. "You two are driving me nuts. Here I am making sentimental appeals like an idiot just because you and that woman are going to bed. What came over me, anyhow?"

"You love Melody yourself."

"Maybe I do. But not the way you think."

"You love her," said Jim, "in an absolutely pure way, Florence, I'm sure. But you really and truly don't understand her as well as I do. Of course it's impossible for me to walk away from Melody, but even if it wasn't impossible it wouldn't be the right thing to do. It would be one of the cruelest things I've ever done. Don't you know what this decision means to her, a woman like *Melody?* She's giving me her *love,* Florence, despite her husband, despite Jesus, despite everything. If I spurned her now out of some misbegotten Puritan insanity, it would break her heart."

"Maybe so," said Florence, her head bowed.

That afternoon at five o'clock, Odd, the Norwegian steward who was mentally retarded and forgetful, finally remembered to pull out of his pocket and deliver a radiogram to Melody. The radiogram had actually arrived around noon, shortly before the captain drunkenly set fire to his own cabin and the radio shack adjacent to it, thereby destroying the ship's communications equipment and preventing a May Day call on the following day when Hurricane Beulah struck the *S.S. Lorna Loone* full force. The radiogram was from the American Embassy in Bogotá and it contained distressing news concerning Melody's husband.

However, although the radiogram would have handicapped the ten-o'clock assignation, a surprising thing had already happened before it arrived. The thing began around four-thirty. Melody and Florence were sitting in the lounge having tea; Jim, who was not hungry, was sitting on the lounge sofa thumbing through a limp, out-of-date copy of *Time.* It seemed to him the day would never end. The prospect of making love to Melody had kept him in a state of arousal all day long. He could think of nothing else. It was driving him crazy and a restless fidgetiness had come upon him.

Melody herself was quite calm. There had not been the slightest hint or suggestion she would not keep that ten-o'clock date. On the contrary, it was clear from the way her eyes met his she would be waiting for him in her nightgown. Florence was right: Melody would not change her mind.

Jim moistened his lips nervously, looked up from the limp copy of *Time* in his lap, and said: "Here's another picture of Arpeth La Rue and her latest husband. I wonder how long *he'll* last. Or those children she adopted, either, for that matter. Do you suppose she'll throw away the children too when she gets tired of them?"

Melody turned around in her chair and looked across the lounge into Jim's eyes. "What?" she asked.

"Arpeth La Rue," said Jim casually. "You know, the actress, you've heard of her."

"Yes," said Melody.

"Picture of her here with her latest husband and a bunch of children and dogs. She travels with a lot of pets." Jim was puzzled with himself. There was no picture of Arpeth La Rue and her latest husband in the limp copy of *Time*. For some strange reason he had made it up.

"Yes, I've read about that," said Melody. "She travels with two or three big dogs and cats and birds and all sorts of things. Plus of course the children she's adopted. She can have children of her own, I wonder why she adopted them."

"Oh, I don't think that makes much difference," said Jim as he idly turned another page of the limp copy of *Time*. "A woman can love an adopted child just as much as she can one of her own. I'll give La Rue credit for the adopted children."

Melody smiled, a puzzled expression in her eyes. "You've changed your mind, then, since day before yesterday?"

"Day before yesterday? What do you mean?"

"Don't you remember our discussion on deck when we saw the outskirts of the storm, those pearly clouds in the sunset? You said you thought every woman needed to have her own child, it was a deep biological drive and need. We were talking about my not ever having had children and the whole question of adoption, which Charles and I have considered many times. Don't you remember that?"

Jim frowned, annoyed with himself. He should never have gotten onto this subject with her. It was the first time she'd mentioned Charles all day. Her hands in her lap were fidgeting with the material of her dress and she was looking at him with a trace of doubt in her eyes. He should *never* have mentioned Arpeth La Rue or the question of adoption. It was a high-radiation area and no good could come from entering it. "Well," said Jim, "yes, I think it's a biological need for a woman to have a child of her own, but I'm sure a woman can love an adopted child. Don't you think so?"

She was staring at him coldly as if vexed with him. "Not as much as one of her own, no. I agreed with what you said the other day. A woman has a deep need to have a baby of her own, it's part of a woman's . . . sex instinct. I've often felt that myself. It's been one of the biggest problems for Charles and me in our marriage that I've had no children."

"I . . . I think I'll go to the bathroom," said Florence in a low tone. "Should I go to the bathroom, Jim?"

"Good God, how do *I* know whether you should go to the bathroom?"

Melody laughed. "That *is* a funny question, Florence. How should Jim know?"

"Well," said Florence in confusion, "my tongue got twisted up. Forget it. Where's Odd? He hasn't been in here all day, I want a drink."

"I'll ring for him," said Jim.

"Maybe it's selfish of me to want my own child," said Melody. "Under the circumstances, I guess it *is* pretty selfish. And I know it hurts my husband, this feeling I have. He said so once, that it made him feel as if he wasn't a real man. But of course he *is* a real man, and a very fine man. And the child would be adopted as far as *he's* concerned, even if I . . . you know that artificial thing they do like women were cattle or something?"

"Artificial insemination," said Jim.

"Yes, that. We're opposed to it on religious grounds. Or at least Charles is, I'm not sure myself."

"Well," said Jim, "from what you've told me, I'd say you were more . . . 'liberal' than Charles."

"Not really," said Melody in a tone not filled with Christian warmth. "I agree with my husband on everything that's important."

Mmm, thought Jim, it had been a well-intended but cretinous blunder, a product of the fidgetiness and strain he was under. He now knew what he had done: he'd been anxious about that calm of hers, afraid that behind it she was brooding and thinking and might change her mind; so he had hit on Arpeth La Rue in an effort to remind her of sex and adventure, make her think of the excitement of the night to come, the moment when, even like Arpeth La Rue with her various titillating loves, she would hold him in her arms—but it had backfired because he had stupidly included mention of those goddamn adopted children. Otherwise Arpeth La Rue would have aroused her.

So Jim told himself, wholly unaware of the thing he really was doing. Arpeth La Rue's adulterous adventures would arouse Melody and so would the oblique reminder that she did not have the right to ask her husband to raise and love another man's child. A ludicrously reasonable proposition, indeed.

At this moment a shove came at the door, and another shove, and a blond scarecrow in a rumpled black uniform stumbled into the lounge. Jim shut his eyes with a groan. Odd was his nemesis, the only person he knew who did not have the intelligence to mix a Scotch and soda. But the worst thing about the Norwegian steward was his moronic lechery. The "Miss Playmate" taped to the bar mirror had been his, until Melody took her down and threw her in the ocean. She loathed *Playboy* and all its works, although she never read the magazine and knew nothing about it.

Odd had a fascination for Jim; he abhorred the simpleton so much he enjoyed it. The boy was about eighteen or nineteen, spoke English with a ridiculous accent, was ugly as an albino mule, had a cast in one eye and blackheads and pimples all over his face. He was forever regaling Jim with stories of his "conquests" of feminine passengers, lewd accounts of how they "couldn't get enough of it" and how they went ga-ga when he "let 'em have it" and other nasty fantasies of his dim little brain. Odd was mentally retarded, an imbecile. The thing about him that disgusted Jim the most was the way he ogled Melody, leering at her and following her with his crossed eyes. It embarrassed her to the point of tears, even though she was sorry for the boy and kind to him.

"Ycsus, Yesus!" cried Odd. "A terrible ting!"

"Oh, Odd, please!" said Melody with an angry frown. "Do you have to come bursting in here like that and startle us half to death?"

Unlike her, thought Jim. She was upset. But the deal was still on, that was plain enough from the expression in her eyes and her manner, too. A little tension-reducing humor would calm her down and make her forget Charles and any moral conflict that might inadvertently have been dredged up in her. Melody *loved* his jokes, it was one of the things about him that charmed her most. Jim had a hunch that Odd, bless his cuckoo cross-eyed heart, would provide the basis for a few real good tension-reducing gags.

"Yah, I know!" said the tow-haired boy, who seemed to be in quite a dither, at least for the moment. "But dis is a terrible ting!"

"All right, what is it?" asked Melody.

"Val, I tal you," said the boy in a tone suddenly casual, as he put a finger in his nose and began to pick it. "Cook got appendicitis. He might not expect to live."

"God save us from the fury of the Northmen," said Florence. "This is the end. We'll starve and the man will die."

"I agree," said Jim. "Let us prepare to meet Yesus."

Melody glanced coolly at him and Jim quailed inside. That was a boo-boo. She did not like jokes about Jesus. "I'm sure it's just indigestion, Odd," said Melody. "That tongue last night was spoiled. Is anyone else sick?"

"Yah, dey all sick," said Odd dreamily. "De captain, de first mate, engineer, radioman . . . dey all pukin' an' runnin' to de bat'room. But not sick like de cook. He groanin', he all green."

"Wonderful!" said Jim. "Just what you'd expect of the *Loony Goony*—the damned scoundrel shitting purple on his own cooking."

Another boo-boo. Melody was frowning at him. She liked filthy language even less than she liked jokes about Jesus.

"Oh, yah, I forgot," said Odd. "De radioman say someting. For you Miz Dubbs. He tal me someting. Vat? Huh? I dunno. I ask him, I ask him sometimes."

"But what was it?"

"Nudding important. By de vay, de captain dronk."

"*What?*" asked Melody. "The *cap*tain?"

"Yah-h-h, he vorried about de storm so he dronk."

"That's reasonable," said Florence, "in a *Loony Goony* kind of way. Best thing a captain can do in a hurricane is get drunk and forget it."

"Jesus Christ on the cross!" said Jim. "On *that* note, I think I might get drunk myself! Captain, oh captain, you're up there at the wheel drunk as a skunk. Except I thought the crazy bastard was pukin' an' runnin' to de bat'room."

"Oh, he vas dis mornin,' but he dronk now. De storm comin' straight toward us, *yah-h-h*. . . ."

"I thought the storm was supposed to be going *away* from us," said Florence.

"Val, may be?" said Odd with a philosophical shrug. "But *I* don't *tink* so." Suddenly the boy gave a violent start. "Oh, yah!" he said. "Now I remember about dot terrible ting! A big vave bust de porthole and vash all my *Playboys* off de shelf! How about dot? Sissty-two *Playboys* all *rooned!*"

"Oh, God, what a tragedy," said Jim. "All that lovely quiff soaked in salty brine. Makes me want to cry."

"Huh!" said Odd. "Maybe *you* like to lose all dem *Playboys?* I get a lotta money for dem *Playboys* in my l'il hometown in Norvay." Odd was making Melody wince. He alone, with his lewdness, would turn her off if a little tension-reducing humor was not introduced into the situation soon, but Jim was having trouble striking the right note. "And my gul fren back in Norvay, Anne-Marie, she look *yust* like dem guls in *Playboy*. Ack like 'em, too, huh-huh-huh-huh. Except she ain't got nudding but her baby teet', de big uns ne'er come down in her l'il old mouf cause her Gramma won't give her no potato ven she come to de back do' . . . an' . . . an' . . . val, I'll tal you . . . she a liddle pop-eyed."

"But Anne-Marie is really *stacked*, huh?" asked Jim.

"Val, naw-w-w," said Odd sadly. "A liddle skeeny. But she can't resast *me*, huh-huh-huh-huh. Only she like to kill herself vunst, sad ting."

"Odd," said Florence. "there's no soda here—get some, will you?"

As Odd walked out of the lounge picking his nose and thinking of Anne-*neh*-Marie-*eh*, Jim said to Melody, "Tragic about those *Playboys*. Sad loss."

"So much filth gone from the world," she answered.

"Oh, come on, Melody, don't be such a prude. *Playboy's* an intelligent, well-edited, beautifully illustrated mag with a modern point of view."

"Is that so! *You* might believe that, but *I'd* like to send Beulah up to Chicago and blow that magazine right into Lake Michigan, and that man's mansion, too. I read all about it—those practically naked *ponies* or whatever he calls them, those poor little girls he catches and lures into living there! Why, the orgies and *things* that go on there must be simply horrible!"

"Oh, orgies aren't so bad, Melody, once you get in the spirit and lose your inhibitions."

"Is that so?" asked Melody. She was angry. His jokes were not going over very well. "I suppose you mean by your sarcasm they *don't* have orgies in that man's mansion, it's all innocent and he just wants to give those poor little girls a home. All right, perhaps they don't have orgies, I've never been there and I don't know. But I do know this. The philosophy of that man is nothing but childish hedonism—live for yourself, do what you want, have fun no matter whom it hurts or what it costs. Pleasure is all that counts in life, your own pleasure. Real love, sacrifice, denying yourself something for the sake of others—that's prudery. Except it isn't. You can make fun if you want, but it's God's love, Jim, and in your heart you know it."

"God's love, huh?"

"Yes, God's love, the most powerful love there is in the world and the only kind that really counts."

"God's love is fine for those who like to exercise their tonsils over a hymn book," said Jim. "But me, I'd rather curl up with a cigarette and a drink of whisky and read *Playboy*."

"I don't believe it. I don't believe it for a second. You are no hedonist, not in your heart. I know you better than that."

"Maybe I'm not a hedonist," said Jim, "but I think the *Playboy* philosophy is quite interesting."

"Why, it's dreadful," said Melody. "And it has a terrible effect on young people too. One of the young nurses at the hospital was reading that thing and acting on it."

"Horrors," said Jim. "What was she doing?"

"She was kissing practically every doctor in that place!"

"I feel faint," said Jim. Actually, it was no joke; he did feel faint—he was losing Melody with every word he said and he could not stop himself.

"All right, you can be sarcastic, but some of the doctors were married and it didn't matter to her, she still kissed them. It was fun to kiss them so she kissed them."

"I feel giddy," said Jim. "If you keep piling up horrors like this, I'm going to collapse."

"Oh, I'm sorry, I forgot," said Melody, "you agree with that man, you think it's all right for a girl to kiss married men. And you also think it's all right for a man to kiss married women."

The situation was desperate. By an incredible series of blunders he was on the verge of losing her and if he did not check her and check her at once, she was gone. There was only one recourse. She had to be intimidated. He would bring it all out into the open with a good strong "hint" to Florence and this would knock Melody off her pins.

"Melody," he said, "I don't want to shock you or anything, but I myself have heard of married women kissing married men, and kissing them passionately too. Haven't you?" Jim paused with an empty sinking despair and said: "I've even heard of a married woman making a date to go to bed with a married man. You never heard of that?"

The color was so gone from her face Jim feared she would faint. What had he done to his darling, a hair of whose head he never would want to hurt, the beautiful angel who loved him for his funny little jokes, his desperate need, and his better side—and for compelling reasons of her own, which, he was sure, he had only dimly discerned? What had he done to her and to himself?

A funny noise came from Florence, who had turned her head away and was picking foolishly at cigarette butts in the ashtray, but Melody did not seem to notice or see her at all. Slowly, her eyes fixed on Jim, she rose from her chair. "Yes," she said, "I've heard of such things, and I think they are pitiful and weak and wicked."

Loss overwhelmed Jim as Melody turned and walked from the room and was gone. He would never hold her beautiful body in his arms and the pain was too much to bear. Jim turned his head aside and bit his lip in an effort to control himself. What a "ladies' man" he had proved to be! He had driven her away like a clown.

"Okay, Florence," he said, "go ahead and laugh, I'm sure it amuses you to see me fall on my ass like this."

"Amuses me?"

Florence's voice sounded so strange Jim turned to look at her. To his amazement, she raised her hands to his shoulders, leaned toward him, put her cheek against his, and whispered: "Oh, Jim, I'll always love you for that! I'll never be afraid of men again after seeing the beautiful thing you just did."

Jim put his hands on Florence's shoulders and pushed back from her. "What are you talking about? I screwed it up, that's all. I got nervous. This is the worst day of my life."

"The hell it is. It's the best day you ever had. When you suddenly threw that Arpeth La Rue thing at her, I swear to God my hair stood on end. I'll always love you for the way you love Melody."

"You're out of your head." Jim lighted a cigarette and decided he would get very drunk very soon. "I messed it up by stupidity and pusillanimous nervousness. I never was really good with women, anyhow. I'm too sentimental with them. You have to be firm with women, like training a dog or closing an overpacked suitcase."

"You surprise me even now," said Florence with a grin, "and I really do love you in my Dragon way."

"Well, I like you too," said Jim, "and you'd better stop inviting me to seduce you or you'll hear a tap-tap at your door."

Florence laughed. "Give me a year to get used to the idea, then choke me a little, chloroform me, and penetrate those thirty-eight-year-old cobwebs while I'm mercifully unconscious."

Jim smiled wanly. "I guess that's the only way I could get a woman, with chloroform."

In a different tone Florence said, "Give yourself a little credit, Jim. You know what you did for Melody. You had her and you let her go."

"Did I?" asked Jim.

"Of course you did. You said the wrong things on purpose. You turned her off like a light and I never saw anything like it."

Jim had to smile, miserable as he was. Despite his feeling of frustration and loss, he was profoundly relieved. It was true. He had said the wrong things on purpose even though he hadn't realized it at the time. He had let Melody go and it was amazing. If Florence was surprised, then God in heaven knows he was himself surprised.

ELEVEN

Herself Astonished

As Melody explained to Florence, the blinders of sin had fallen. "I finally see him as he is," she said. "Why, *he* isn't a poor, unfortunate man entangled in sex and empty hedonism, he's evil and wicked to the core! Florence, you won't believe this, but *he tried to seduce me!* And I was almost tempted. That devil has the cunning of a fox and the appeal of an innocent child, to say nothing of being so charming and everything. He's *a real devil,* Florence!"

It was the biggest shock of her life, those awful things he said before he got up and stalked off in fuming drunkenness to sit at the bar by himself and brood wickedly.

"Stop talking to me about 'God's love,' you naive little creature. I have information for you—there is no monkey on the moon."

And when she said, sweetly and gently in an effort to help him: "No, Jim, there is not any monkey on the moon, but there's a God in heaven and he's watching you right now!" he had given her the unspeakable reply: "I know, he's watching you too. It's all he's good for, watching. Watching the Chinese die, watching the Russians die, watching the Americans die, watching the pretty mushroom clouds and cackling in his long white beard! The old fucker makes me sick—why doesn't he *do* something, instead of just watching all the time?"

It really almost made her burst into tears with shock, such dreadful blasphemy, but she had said bravely: "Jim, you ought to be ashamed in your very soul to say such an awful thing! You ought to get down on your knees this very instant and pray for forgiveness to your Creator!"

And he had answered: "Oh, fuck off. Stop bothering me."

He did not care about the blasphemous stain on his soul—he was evil and wicked to the core! And besides, he had hurt her terribly in a personal way. After all, she had been very . . . well, fond of him and had thought he was fond of her too, but now it was plain he despised her.

"Florence, I can't get over it. You think you know a person, then something like *this!* I thought he liked me—why, I thought he loved me, as a friend. And I . . . I really am very upset. I mean, after all, I loved him too, as a friend."

"I know," said Florence. "Maybe you better go to bed."

"But how can he *say* such awful things to me? Especially since I'm leaving the ship tomorrow and won't ever see him again!"

"Melody, Jim isn't evil, he's just drunk. And he doesn't hate you. He loves you as a friend, believe me."

"Then how can he *talk* to me like that?"

"I told you, he's drunk and he's not himself. If I were you, I'd go on to bed. It's eleven o'clock and you're very tired—why don't you?"

"Well, I can't go off and leave him in a condition like this. Look at him—he can hardly stand up at the bar!"

"I'll take care of him. Why don't you go on to bed?"

"But I can't get over his saying such things to me. Why, just this morning—oh, Florence, he was so nice! Of course . . . he was only trying to seduce me but . . . I don't understand it, I . . . I . . ."

"Now look, don't start crying. Please, Melody, this situation is bad enough as it is."

"You don't understand. I'm very . . . fond of him and sympathetic to him in his trouble with his wife. He wants her back so much, Florence—and I *don't* think he really is a devil. Except he is. You don't know the tricks he has."

As he stared at himself in the bar mirror with a slightly Mephistophelean drunken smile, Jim listened to the little bitches talking and jabbering about him. They thought he was too drunk to hear them or understand what they were saying. An inspiration came to him as he heard Florence say, "I'll put Jim to bed." Why not subject Melody to a *real* test? A hint that Florence was wise to it all, maybe. A little pressure-cooker treatment for Melody, yes. This "innocent" thing did not ring wholly true—what was her character really like? Slowly, with a dignity he felt worthy of Robert E. Lee at Appomattox, Jim turned around and said: "I'll put *myself* to bed, Florence."

"Good grief, he's listening to us," said Florence.

"Too much chickenshit in my blood to put anybody *else* to bed, maybe, but I can sure as hell put *myself!*"

"All right, Jim, now you shut up."

"Go frig thyself," said Jim with what he considered an aloof, princely poise. "I haven't said one little old word too much, Florence baby, and I ain't gonna, aware as I am that the better participant has emerged victorious. Grant, you have my sword. Take it and stick it up your ass!"

In a low tone, eyes on Jim, Melody said to Florence, "He's *very* drunk. But what did he mean by that? And why is he angry at himself?"

"Now listen," said Florence. "I'm giving you good advice. Will you go to bed, Melody? I mean, like right now?"

Jim turned a slightly wobbling head toward Melody to see her reaction. She was staring at Florence in consternation. Briefly, she glanced in his direction, then looked back at Florence and asked in a small voice: "Have you been talking to Jim about me? Why did he say he wouldn't say a word too much? What did he mean by that and why are you trying to protect me? What's going on here? Will you answer me, Florence?"

"I can't answer you," said Florence coolly, her eyebrows raised with a bland innocence, "because I don't know what on earth you're talking about."

"You know about tonight," said Melody in a shaky voice. "He told you about it, didn't he?"

"I don't know anything about tonight; all I know is that it's eleven o'clock and you're dead tired and worried about a sick husband and you've got a long day tomorrow with all kinds of airplanes to catch and a long way to go."

Melody turned and stared at Jim, who smiled wanly back at her. Her eyes were remote as distant Siberia. "So that's the kind of man you are. On top of everything else, you humiliate me by bragging to Florence, you take my wicked weakness and my heart itself and throw it out on this table for her to see?"

"That is not true, Melody," said Florence. "Jim didn't brag about anything to me."

Helplessly, his wan smile gone, Jim attempted to return Melody's glacial stare. "I won't live long enough to forgive you for that," she said. "I'm not a good enough Christian. God will have to forgive you for what you've done and tried to do, not me."

Florence flinched, opened her mouth as if to speak, then shut it. "Well," said Jim with a little shrug, "I didn't exactly tell Florence anything, she knew it already."

In icy disdain, Melody turned to Florence and said quietly: "I don't suppose it really matters if you know. I know myself and nothing could be more awful than that. But I don't regret this experience. It has taught me something very valuable—how frail I really am. I will be on my guard in the future, and you can believe that."

"This is a thing between you and Jim," said Florence, "but there's one thing I can tell you. Jim did *not* brag to me about *any*thing, Melody. He didn't need to, even if he was that kind of man, and he isn't. I knew you were in love with him. Nothing could be more obvious."

"All right, I'll tell you something else that's obvious. He *is* a devil and a complete one. From the very beginning he used every trick and wile he could on me. I knew he was doing it but I wouldn't let myself admit it because he had already planted wickedness in my heart by telling me I was beautiful and an angel." Again she turned an icy gaze on Jim. "You didn't see a porpoise. You pretended to see one in order to have an excuse to put your arm around me. Does it surprise you I know that?"

"A little, yes," said Jim.

"I knew what you were doing but I wouldn't let myself admit it, because I *liked* having your arm around me, it excited me and filled my mind with thoughts of sin. It takes two for such a thing as this and I am just as guilty as you are." Melody turned back to Florence. "But there's a difference. I wasn't aware of what I was doing and he *was*. The worst thing he did to me was to use his *own* wife to win my sympathy and touch my feelings. He's a devil, a complete devil, and I pity him." Again her eyes turned on Jim. "Yes, I was attracted to you, naive creature that I am. But I'll tell you this. It's all over now, baby blue."

Jim blinked. Where could she have heard that Bobby Dylan song? Surely not at Tom Armour University. But her insight was even more startling than her knowledge of "baby blue." For the first time, it occurred to him that Melody must have been quite a misfit at Tom Armour, just as she must be something of a misfit as a missionary's wife.

And he had certainly not been wrong that morning on deck when he concluded she had the emotional and physical endowment to be capable of real passion. She had it and she had it abundantly. What would it have been like to have made love to her? Good God in heaven, she would have been beautiful in bed—Jim felt like groaning and jumping in the ocean in disgust with himself.

"When I was small," said Jim, "my mother liked me. She even loved me, poor misguided soul."

Melody's eyes flashed. "I thought I was through with you, but I'll tell you one more thing. Your mother might have liked you and loved you, but your mother *had* to like you and love you and I *don't* and neither does your wife! If the wife you use to seduce other women ever comes back to you, she ought to have her head examined!"

"*I* like him," said Florence, "and I'll say this, even if Jim doesn't approve. You are right, Melody, but you are also wrong. You have never been more wrong in your life."

"Forget it, Florence," said Jim, "there's no point."

The certainty was not shattered, but it was cracked. It was not quite all over yet, baby blue. Confusion again was in Melody's eyes. This peculiar exchange between Jim and Florence clearly did not make any sense to her at all. Why was Florence so certain she was wrong, in the face of overwhelming evidence of Jim's perfidy and wickedness? What could support such absolute conviction in Florence, and why had Jim told Florence in a resigned and hopeless tone to forget it, there was no point? Could it be that the devil who was not a devil but really *was* a devil was once again not quite a devil after all? Jim felt he could read all these thoughts plain as newsprint in her bewildered blue eyes.

Melody pushed back her chair and rose to her feet. "Right or wrong, I'm going to bed. I *am* tired and I *am* worried about my husband. I agree with you about that, anyhow. Good night, Florence."

"Good night, Melody."

In the doorway of the lounge, Melody looked back at Jim. "Maybe I am wrong," she said, "maybe there's something I don't understand." She hesitated, uncertainty in her eyes, then gave a little helpless shrug. "I do know I can't hate you. I hope for your sake you will repent of your blasphemy."

She turned to go. Jim had not expected to say anything to her, but he could not quite leave it at that. "Good night and sweet dreams," he said, with a little ironic smile, "and may an angel guard your rest and keep you from harm in all your ways."

For at least ten seconds, which seemed to be a full minute or more, Melody stood in the doorway of the lounge and stared at him as if paralyzed. When Jim saw tears begin to come in her eyes he was sure she knew what had happened, even if she could not comprehend how it could be so.

"Oh, I don't, I can't understand you!" cried Melody half in anger and half in despair. Biting her lip and shaking her head in annoyance at her tears, she turned and went out.

"Well," said Jim to Florence, "you'll have to admit that was a nice bit of poesy about the angel guarding her."

"An angel *is* guarding her," said Florence. "I wouldn't call it poesy."

"Bullshit," said Jim wearily. For a few minutes, amazingly enough in view of the whisky he had consumed that night, he had damn near sobered up, but now he felt very, very drunk and very, very tired. "What a goddamned fool I am. She loves me. That woman really loves me. I could have gotten her even after the radiogram if I'd just kept my idiot mouth shut in the first place. What a horrible, horrible fool I was. Arpeth La Rue and *Playboy*. What a fool, what a fool!"

Florence got up and walked across the lounge to Jim and put her arm around his shoulders. "Come on, I'll help you to bed."

Jim felt very drunk and it was too much for him. Florence, who was terrified of men and always avoided physical contact with him unless moved by some strong emotion, had put her arm around him. It was an amazing thing for her to do; he could actually feel a small soft mass against his right elbow and realized with a shock it was her breast—he hadn't even known Florence *had* any breasts, but apparently she had little Lesbian ones under her shirt somewhere. "I've lost her, Florence, she's gone. She loves me but she won't unlock that door now. I could bang on it all night long and she wouldn't open it. Why was I such an absolute puritanical idiot? It wouldn't have hurt her a *bit* if I'd made love to her, *goddamn* it! What madness! Why did I talk myself right out of her arms? Why?"

"You're a blabbermouth," said Florence. "Come on, I'll help you to bed."

"Yeah," said Jim, "okay, kid."

Jim needed help. His brief near-sobriety under the stress of Melody's rejection was gone. He was so drunk he barely could walk and so disgusted with himself he really did feel like jumping into the blue Caribbean.

He'd wrecked his chances forever with that horrible Arpeth La Rue-*Playboy* gambit and he bitterly regretted it. Good God almighty, what puritanical folly—the Pussy & Pecker Soap Co., Inc. was fully justified in being outraged to have had its dearly bought hour of prime time thus snatched away from it by the Pure Bluebird & Buttercup Seed Company or the God's Love Marching Society or whatever unfair competitor it was that had sneaked in there and pulled the Goblin Special off the air. Jim was so disgusted with himself he kicked the desk of his stateroom and damn near broke his toe. Florence had to help him limping and cursing over to the bed, upon which he collapsed in a fury.

The moment when Florence had cried and he had felt he had given something of himself to Melody had not lasted for long—it had soon floated off on a little pink cloud to heaven, as the smoke of sinful brimstone rose curling from the floor.

At five o'clock that afternoon, Melody had returned to the lounge, distaught and in tears with a yellow slip of paper in her hand. Dim-witted Odd had finally remembered to give her the radiogram, but Jim at first did not know this and he had a brief irrational idea she had come back to say she had changed her mind again, that if he thought she would allow him to inflict that kind of denying puritanism on her he was badly mistaken, there was nothing wrong with a little adultery once in a while and the deal was still on!

But no such filthy luck. Melody had returned to inform them she had received a very distressing radiogram from the American Embassy in Bogotá. Her husband Charles had fallen ill and although his condition was not critical he was being flown back to the States for treatment at the medical center of Duke University. The plan to establish a mission at the far western headwaters of the monstrous Amazon and do battle for Jesus among Colombian Indians who knew not God had been jeopardized and perhaps ruined permanently.

And thank God for *that*, anyhow. It was a relief to Jim to know Melody would not be going into some hideous Colombian jungle to have blowdarts shot at her by Jesus-hating savages and he hoped it *would* "break Charles' heart with disappointment."

However, the blade of the guillotine was that Melody was leaving the ship. She would not go on to Cartagena and Bogotá and San José del Guaviare and points beyond, but would leave the *S.S. Lorna Loone* at Bluefields, then proceed at once by local plane and jet to Managua, Jamaica, Miami, and Durham.

It was the final catastrophe—the ship would dock at Bluefields in twenty hours. Although the "affair" with her had been sent spiraling wingless to earth by him before the radiogram was received, Jim could not help but feel a sense of utter disaster when he learned she would be leaving the ship on the following day. It made him recall a terrible tape recording he had heard, a recording of the voice of an airline pilot whose jet plane had just had its wing sheared off in a midair collision with another plane; the jet was falling to earth and the pilot was shouting into the radio, "May Day! May Day!"

May Day. "It's all over now, baby blue." With a sick husband on her mind and only one night remaining on the *S.S. Lorna Loone*, the probability of a reversal of the situation was flat-out zero. It was impossible to correct his mistake and he hadn't even tried; he had gotten blooped with whisky and pointlessly hurt her feelings with obscene sacrilege and a despairing hostility she could never understand. Perhaps he had salvaged a little something at the very end when he bade her good night and sweet dreams, just as the pilot who shouted May Day had done. "This is it," said the pilot calmly. "We're going down." Jim sank into an anaesthetized unconsciousness, wondering how he could bear the disaster he himself had brought about.

In his preoccupation with Melody, Jim had paid scant attention to the giant storm that had shifted its course and was now bearing down directly on the Yucatan Channel and the *S.S. Lorna Loone*. Florence had spoken of the storm on a number of occasions and Jim had half listened to her. It did sound like a hell of a thing. According to weather reports received while the ship's radio was still functioning, Hurricane Beulah was one of the most violent and dangerous tropical storms in many years. It contained winds of one hundred and eighty miles per hour and had raised tremendous seas and beyond doubt would spread all kinds of devastation in its path before finally blowing inland God knows where to bring dreadful tides and floods and spawn dozens of tornadoes and waste itself at last on unsustaining land. An awesome phenomenon, the greatest display of the raw power of nature that could be known—except, perhaps, an exploding volcano and certain other raw powers of nature.

Jim was not concerned by Florence's worried comments. The radio reports had indicated the storm was going away from the ship. It was difficult to understand the radioman, a thin balding Norwegian who spoke reluctant singsong English and never looked anyone in the eye; Jim had understood the man to say the eye of the storm was located three hundred nautical miles southeast of the Isle of Pines and was headed on a course that would cause it to strike the central section of Cuba between Cienfuegos and Camaguey, after which it would pass on in the direction of Key West and the Florida peninsula, well away from the *S.S. Lorna Loone*. They would reach Bluefields without seeing anything more than the outer fringes of the huge cyclonic disturbance with its weird central shaft of windless weather, blue sky, and sunshine, the ten-mile-wide "eye" surrounded by raging fury. Jim had pretty much dismissed the storm from his mind despite the increasingly bad weather on the fifth day at sea, and also despite the fact that Odd had reported the hurricane had shifted course and was coming at them and the captain was "dronk" because of it. Odd had never been right yet about a single thing and Jim did not believe him.

Besides, he was preoccupied by other matters more important than a mere hurricane. Thus and therefore, drugged by whisky and emotional exhaustion, Jim slept very late on the morning of the sixth day at sea, even though on several occasions he was almost thrown out of bed onto the floor by a strange thing that seemed to be happening to the laws of gravity. The foot of the bed would go down, down, down and the head of the bed would go up, up, up, then the whole thing would give a violent shudder and abruptly commence tilting steeply to one side or the other.

Something definitely had gone wrong with gravity, or with the bed or with something. Jim muttered and grumbled in annoyance and clutched the pillow more tightly, hoping it would go away. But it didn't, and another strange thing bothered him as well: the football game. He could hear them roaring and screaming and whistling. Apparently they were making one touchdown after the other in this game; he had never heard such cheering in his life. The entire stadium was creaking and groaning as the crowd jumped up and down. But how could a football stadium possibly tilt back and forth in this way? Jim finally opened one eye and a moment later was thrown half out of bed. As he stared out of the porthole with one knee on the floor and the sheet twisted around him, he saw above him a mountain of water and heard the roar of Hurricane Beulah.

"Good God almighty!" said Jim aloud as another violent pitching roll of the ship almost threw him across the stateroom; he had to grab the wooden frame of the bed to stand. He stared in awe out of the porthole, then glanced at his watch. It was ten-thirty. How could he have slept through *this*? He stared again in open-mouthed disbelief at the rising and falling mountains of roiling water beyond the porthole.

Jim knew a little bit about the storms that could occur on the open sea. He had made the crossing to Europe by boat a number of times and had gone through a full gale on the North Atlantic; it had been a rough enough proposition to empty the dining room of everyone but himself and a handful of other seasick immunes. It was before the days of dramamine, he was a boy then and had thought he saw wild weather on that voyage, but it was nothing like this. He had not conceived it possible for waves to be quite so high; he was literally looking up at water, the waves were above his own stateroom porthole on the passenger deck. And the wind was almost as fearful to behold; it was blowing with such power as to shear off the tops of the waves like a giant knife. "Jesus Christ in heaven," said Jim aloud as he scrambled to his feet and grabbed for his clothes. He was afraid the ship would go down before he could even get dressed.

The door of his stateroom was stuck tight and Jim shoved angrily at it, gripped by an unpleasant feeling of claustrophobia. All the passenger section doors were of new plywood; they had been put on during the recent overhaul in dry dock, and put on stupidly and improperly. No allowance had been made for tropical humidity, some idiot carpenter had fitted them like winter storm doors in New England. But the doors were no exception; nothing on the goofy ship worked properly—the food was of good quality but awful, the air conditioning had been repaired but blew sickly damp air, the toilets were nice and new but went *gobble-gobble-gobble* and would not flush, and so forth and so on. The pixy cabdriver in Savannah had been dead right about the ship and Florence admitted she had made an error there. It was she who had dubbed the ship the *Loony Goony* the second day at sea.

Jim shoved angrily at the stateroom door. It was almost as bad as the one in the lounge, which now would not close at all and had to be tied shut with a silly little piece of string. "Goddamn it!" said Jim as he drew back and rammed at the door with his shoulder and somehow got it open. He almost collided in the passageway with a whey-faced, staring-eyed, bearded man in streaming yellow oilcloth slickers. The man reared back at him and scuttled on by like a hunched crab.

"Hey!" cried Jim. "Hey, wait a second!"

"Okay!" cried the man. "All okay! Possengers to lounge!"

"Wait a minute, will you!"

But the man scuttled on, shoulders twisted to the side and head craned as if he had a crick in his neck. It was Captain Yönkel, master of the *S.S. Lorna Loone*, a dour and melancholy soul who almost never said a word and often would not even nod his head at the passengers. Jim had asked him the first day at sea if they were passing Cape Kennedy and he had shown a little enthusiasm even though his reply was incomprehensible. "Yuh-h," he had said, "Kuh-nu-duh. Dull-us, *Tack*-sus. Sodd. Sodd. Goodbye."

Well, thought Jim, at least the man had seemed sober this morning. He had also seemed panicky and small wonder. Bracing himself with his hands first on one wall and then on the other, Jim walked down the careening and wet corridor toward the lounge; water somehow had seeped in everywhere and ran in little rivulets down the walls and all over the floor. "Holy cow," said Jim aloud as the door of Florence's stateroom tilted up higher and higher in the wall opposite him. How could the ship take such rolls as this without tilting all the way over upside down, and what would such extreme inclinations do to the cargo of wheat? A nasty chill ran through him as he remembered the fate of the *Castillo Montjuich*, the ship loaded with grain that had vanished without trace somewhere in the vicinity of the Canary Islands. The door to Florence's stateroom slowly righted itself and Jim knocked on it twice but got no answer.

Florence and Melody were up and had been up for quite a while, as Jim discovered when he stumbled into the lounge. They were there eating breakfast and seemed amazingly calm.

"Good morning, Jim," said Florence. "How do you like this weather?"

"I don't like it hardly worth a damn," he answered. "You two seem pretty calm, I must say."

"Well, it's *really* going away from us now," said Florence. "We'll be all right, the captain says. He actually came in here and made us a little speech. I couldn't understand half he said, but I did gather the storm is now headed due east toward Jamaica. The wheat, by the way, he says is properly stored and won't budge. They were careful about that because it's hurricane season. We'll really be all right, he says. But about four hours late getting to Bluefields."

"That's good news," said Jim. Melody thus far had kept her eyes on her coffee cup, but now she glanced up coolly at him and Jim smiled at her. "Good morning, Melody."

She stared expressionlessly at him for several seconds and Jim thought she would not even greet him, but then she turned her head in another direction and said coldly, "Good morning."

Huh, thought Jim—icebergsville. To be expected. He stood there with a pained smile, rubbing his hands together.

"It's too rough for the cook to fix a real breakfast," said Florence, "but we finally got some toast and coffee out of Odd. Would you care to join us?"

Jim sat down at the table, one hand on his aching forehead. Luckily, he had remembered to grab a tin of aspirin before he left the stateroom. "Slight hangover," he said with a grin at Florence, then took out three aspirin and poured himself water from the duck-shaped carafe on the table. He saw evidence of spilled coffee on the oilcloth. It was too rough for regular breakfast, all right; the lounge was slowly tilting back and forth at what seemed to Jim dangerous degrees of inclination. But at least it was quieter in the lounge, which seemed to have been better built than the rest of the ship and apparently had been soundproofed. The wind was audible, to say the least, a continuous roar and whine with eerie intermingled whistles and screams rather similar to a huge crowd at a football game, but it was not so loud as to make conversation impossible.

"Nobody seasick?" asked Jim.

"We're both full of dramamine," said Florence, "and Melody says she never gets seasick anyhow."

"Neither do I," said Jim.

"I feel okay so far," said Florence. "Be glad to get out of this though."

"Yes, I'll be glad too," said Melody.

Jim wondered if the women had believed Captain Yönkel. He himself did not. If the captain said Hurricane Beulah was going toward Jamaica, then it really was roaring up the Yucatan Channel headed for Texas.

"There's one comfort," said Florence. "Drowning, they say, is an easy death."

"Florence, *please*," said Melody. "Don't talk to me about it. I've always had a morbid fear of drowning. Awful, it frightens me to death, and that's funny because I'm a very good swimmer."

No, the women did not believe Captain Yönkel. On closer examination, Jim saw that both of them were ashen with fear. Florence's freckles stood out on her face in mottled relief against an underlying bloodless pallor and Melody was so colorless that her lips, which normally were a natural pink despite the fact she never wore make-up, seemed almost gray. They were both terrified. The giant waves, the roaring wind, and the violent rolling and pitching of the ship had frightened them as much as it had himself.

"If you're a good swimmer, Melody," said Florence, "then maybe if this thing sinks you could swim to land."

"I couldn't swim in those waves," said Melody, "no one could. Besides, I'm afraid this is open sea. We're at least a hundred and fifty miles off the coast of Honduras, and there're no islands at all in this part of the Caribbean."

"None at all?" asked Florence.

"No, it's empty sea, and I'm afraid I can't swim a hundred and fifty miles to the coast of Central America, especially not in that water."

"There was an old antique map on the wall by the door," said Florence. "Where'd it go?"

"The wire broke and it fell off," said Melody. "Odd put it in the lifeboat closet, I think."

"Good. I want to take a look at that lifeboat, anyhow," said Florence as she rose from her chair.

"It isn't a life*boat*, ladies," said Jim, "it's a life *raft*. The life*boats* are out on deck."

"Well, I want to look at it anyhow, and I'm curious about that map," said Florence as she walked across the lounge toward the life-raft closet to the left of the bar, bracing herself against the tilting of the ship by holding onto the bolted-down furniture. Jim turned to Melody and said, "Seems funny there'd be no islands at all in this area. Are you sure there're none, Melody?"

Again he thought she would not reply to him, but she finally glanced at him and asked in an icy tone: "Did you ever hear of any in the far west Caribbean?"

"Yes," said Jim, "there's Cozumel near the Yucatan peninsula and there's the Isle of Pines off the coast of Cuba, and the Cayman Islands are in there somewhere."

"*That* is a 'naive' answer," said Melody. "Those islands are hundreds of miles from where we are. There is nothing anywhere near us, nothing at all."

During this slightly frigid exchange between Jim and Melody, Florence was poking around in the life-raft closet, a six-by-ten-foot windowless room used to store a life raft, extra life preservers, and deck furniture. It contained an emergency exit to the passenger deck and had a gloomy low ceiling with a hanging electric light bulb. "Ha ha!" said Florence. "Every time you are thoroughly positive about something you are wrong, Melody, including calling Jim a devil last night and being so snooty to him this morning. Here's a little speck right here."

"A little *what*, Florence?"

"A little speck on the map. It isn't much of a speck and the map's only an antique, but there must be such an island or they wouldn't have it on here. It's called Isla Providencia."

Melody looked up, startled. "Isla Providencia? That's strange . . . I wonder. Could it be Providence Island, the one settled by the Puritans hundreds of years ago?"

"It must be," said Florence as she picked her way back to the table, holding onto furniture. "Isla Providencia, that's got to be Spanish for Providence Island."

"I was wrong and I apologize," said Melody, "about the island."

"Mmf," said Jim in what he hoped was a comic way, but all he got out of her was another cold glance. It was icebergsville in spades. If she'd felt any conflict the night before, she felt it no longer. He was an evil, wicked, and disgusting devil and to hell with him. Jim rubbed at his aching forehead; the aspirin had not helped his headache very much. "What a hangover I have this morning," he said. "Maybe I need mercy killing." *That* would get a rise out of her, a human reaction of some kind—he had once talked with her about euthanasia and capital punishment; she was violently opposed to both and she would turn to him now and say something to him.

"I thought Providence Island was down nearer Panama, Florence. Where is it exactly on the map?"

Again Jim Kittering heard in his mind's ear the doomed pilot cry: "May Day! May Day!" She had not even glanced at him. This was no mere game of icebergsville or anything like it. The truth was plain: she hated him. She hated and despised him and there was not even a vestige of conflict in her about it. Sick at heart, Jim stared down into his coffee cup.

"Just guessing from that old map," said Florence, "I'd say it's about fifty miles off the coast of Nicaragua."

"I wasn't wrong at all, then," answered Melody. "That's *much* farther south than we are. I thought so. It's closer to Panama because of Morgan and his treasure."

"Morgan and his treasure?"

"We are up even with Honduras, *much* farther north than Providence Island, Florence. There are no islands where we are, *none* at all. I wasn't wrong."

"Okay, you weren't wrong. Let's get back to Morgan and his treasure."

"Yes. It just happens I have read *two* books about Providence Island and I know a little about it. I'm wrong every time I'm positive about something, however, so perhaps you'd rather not hear about it."

"Oh, fooey," said Florence.

"Why do you say 'fooey' to me? Don't you dare say 'fooey' to me, Florence, or I might get angry with you!"

As he saw the fire flash in Melody's gentle blue eyes, Jim could hardly believe it. She hated Florence too, merely because Florence had stuck up for him. He hadn't known or understood Melody Carolucy at all! Underneath that Christian veneer she was a mean and hateful bitch. Now he understood what had actually happened—Melody had not been "in love" with him at all; she had merely felt a strong physical attraction toward him, but her superego had conquered that attraction and the energy of it had turned into a tigress-like hatred of him. She had never loved him at all. In a way, she had hated him from the very beginning. Jim sat back in his chair, sick in his soul. The wingless airliner had crashed in flames.

"Look, Melody," said Florence in a gentle tone, "we're all nervous and frightened because of this awful storm. If I said anything to offend you, I'm sorry. Please forgive me."

"It's none of your business about *me* and *him*, Florence. It's none of your business at all."

Jim shut his eyes, ill. The violence of her hatred was appalling. He'd been right about one thing—she was a passionate woman, all right, but in a way he had not expected. Underneath that sweet exterior she was meaner than hell. Even Florence, a pretty tough egg herself, seemed to shrink back from her, as if confronted by a violence too formidable to challenge.

"You're right," said Florence. "It's none of my business at all, and I'm sorry. Tell us about Providence Island, Melody."

"Very well, if you want to know about it. I'm perfectly willing to be polite, Florence. I don't want to fight with you."

"I don't want to fight either, Melody. Tell us about the island."

Melody flinched in fear as the *S.S. Lorna Loone* shuddered down into a trough and spindrift simultaneously rattled like buckshot against the portholes of the lounge. "All right," she said, "maybe it'll take our minds off the storm. Let's see . . . first, I studied about Providence Island in 'Religious History of Protestant America' at Tom Armour University. Most people don't know it, but the Puritans founded *two* colonies in the New World. They know about the one that succeeded but they don't know about the one that failed. The Puritans founded a colony on a tiny island in the far west Caribbean long, long ago, an island they called 'Providence.' The colony failed. The Puritans made rum and became buccaneers."

"Hmmm," said Florence, "that *is* an interesting story."

"There's more. Morgan's treasure, very possibly, is somewhere on that island. But first about the Puritans. The main trouble was, all they could grow there was sugar cane and coconuts. English crops failed in the climate. Another trouble was the island was much too small."

"Is it as small as it looks on the map?" asked Florence.

"Oh, it's tiny, very tiny. They stressed that in class and in the book—it was much too small for the colony ever to have had any chance to survive. They were raped and killed completely."

"Raped and killed *completely*? Sounds awful."

"It *was* awful. As I told you, they turned from God to rum, sin, and piracy. They were preying on the Spanish treasure ships, which used to go right by there on the way to Spain. The galleons would load gold and silver and all kinds of treasures at Cartegena and the Puritan pirates would attack them when they went by the island."

"Puritan pirates is a great contradiction in terms, I really love it," said Jim, who was a trifle encouraged by the fact she had not directed an icy hate-filled glance at him for several minutes now. Maybe she would answer this and talk to him, explain to him they weren't bona-fide Puritans any more, or something.

"Well, Florence, the Spaniards got tired of it and sent an expedition and wiped them out completely. I remember reading about it. They destroyed everything on the island, killed all the men, and took off the women and children and left it deserted. I don't think anybody else settled there again, it's such a tiny island. I know the Puritans never did. It was the wrong place for them to begin with."

"Mix a bottle of rum and a Puritan and you get a pirate," said Jim.

"If it was ever resettled, it would have to be fairly recently. I read this other book about it, an account of a man and his wife shipwrecked there back in 1850 or some such time, and there wasn't a sign of life on the island except for a few wild pigs. There wasn't even a trace the Puritans had ever been there. They found part of Morgan's treasure there, this couple. Not much of it, but enough to make them rich."

"That sounds pretty romantic," said Jim, who was determined to make her talk to him. There they were, in the middle of a hurricane, and she hated him and wouldn't even speak to him. It was unbearable.

"Yes, Melody, that does sound romantic," said Florence. "I'm a little surprised you'd be interested in such things as pirate treasure." It was nice of Florence; she was trying to help him out and involve him in the conversation. Florence, Jim was sure, was no more interested in Morgan's treasure than he was. "I think that's what Jim feels—surprise that you'd be interested."

"Treasure is my hobby, Florence. Listen to this. When I was eight years old I was digging a hole at the farm in Arkansas to bury my pet chicken that had died, and I found an old rotten box that contained *three hundred dollars* in gold coins. Ever since then I have been fascinated by buried treasure. I've read *everything* about it, and Providence Island is one of the great treasure islands in the world, maybe the greatest."

"That's interesting," said Jim.

"Very possibly the greatest treasure island in all of human history, because Morgan's treasure is almost certainly buried there."

"What exactly *is* Morgan's treasure?" asked Jim.

"Morgan's treasure is famous to those who know a little bit about history. It's the greatest pirate treasure of all, by far. No one has ever found it, except that stranded couple who are believed to have stumbled on a tiny fraction of it. Morgan's treasure is from the sacking of Panama. He didn't deliver all of what he took from Panama back to England. He hid a large part of it somewhere and it has never been found."

"What's it worth?" asked Jim.

"There's no estimating," said Melody. "Ten million dollars, twenty million dollars, thirty million, a *hundred* million—who knows? Probably closer to a hundred million than to ten. It's the greatest pirate treasure of all. Gold ingots, hundreds and hundreds of them, and basket upon basket of ceremonial gold Indian jewelry not melted down yet—and the jewelry today would be priceless, they were master goldsmiths and their work now is in museums. I read all about it in this book about the couple stranded on Providence Island. They found a little bit of Morgan's treasure there, about half a million dollars' worth in today's money, and this would seem to indicate the rest of it is somewhere on that island. Why hide it on *two* islands? I am sure the rest of Morgan's treasure is somewhere on Providence Island."

"You do surprise me, Melody, even if you did find a box of gold coins when you were a child," said Jim. "All this talk about treasure and gold ingots and everything. I didn't know you were that interested in money."

"Is that so?" said Melody as she turned toward him with a cold stare. "Think what *Charles* and I could do at San José del Guaviare or for the Indians of New Mexico with twenty million dollars or more."

Jim gritted his teeth. She was absolutely unrelenting. She hated him, that was all. It was useless to try to talk to her. "Okay," he said. As Jim spoke, a giant wave crashed down on the passenger deck, completely covering the lounge portholes and causing the entire ship to give a lurching shudder. It was the first time this had happened. The storm was getting worse, not better.

"Good God!" said Florence. "I don't like this, I don't like it at all. If this keeps up, those medium transformers in the hold are going to break loose and when they do that wheat will shift too, and this thing will roll over like a dead duck. I don't like it."

"I don't like it either," said Melody, "but it's not going to do us any good to talk about it."

To hell with her, thought Jim. "Are there really medium transformers aboard, Florence?" he asked.

"Yes, and they weigh about four tons each. I saw them. Odd took me down in the hold. There're six of them and they didn't look to me as if they were lashed down any too well. If one breaks loose it'll knock the others loose. They'll slide back and forth and break through the bulkheads and the wheat will shift and goodbye, Charlie."

"I don't want to talk about it," said Melody. "Besides, I wasn't through with what I was saying. I was saying something to *him*."

"Excuse me for living," said Florence.

Melody turned coldly toward Jim. "What I was saying is, I don't think you understand the meaning of money any better than you do the meaning of other things, such as decent love between human beings. It's not *money* that's evil, it's what you *do* with it. Just as *sex* is not evil. It's what you do with it, that is the evil part."

"Oh, Melody, for crying out loud," said Florence. "I know it's none of my business about you and Jim, but here we are in the middle of a terrible storm, scared out of our wits and in danger of losing our lives. Whatever happened between you and Jim, it's all over. Under these conditions, can't we at least be human with one another?"

Melody flinched in fear as another giant wave crashed down on the passenger deck. Florence and Jim also flinched in fear. How much more punishment of this kind could the ship take? "I'm being human," said Melody. "I'm talking to him, aren't I?" She glanced at him, her lips bitten together.

"Mmm," he said.

"Why do you say 'Mmm'? Isn't it true? Aren't I talking to you?"

Jim stared at her with a wistful sadness. The ship was not going to survive this storm, they were doomed to drown and die, and even if she was mean as gunpowder and hated him, he still loved her. "Yes, you're talking," said Jim with a rueful smile. "By the way, how did you sleep last night, Melody? Did that angel watch over you?"

Dynamite! It was not a ten-second pause this time, but it was a long one. A cold fury, not confusion, was in her eyes. Finally she said, "I'm sorry, but I'm afraid your sarcastic good night didn't help my rest." Jim was silent. He could not say it *was* sarcastic and he could not say it was *not*. "Well?" asked Melody. "I don't hear you denying it. It was a sarcastic good night, isn't that true?"

"Oh, I don't know," said Jim casually.

"You do know," said Melody. "And it *was* sarcasm. You don't believe in angels of any kind, and *I* know where that remark came from. It was one of the first things I ever said to you, a quotation from the 91st Psalm. 'He shall give his angels charge over thee, to keep thee in all thy ways.' You said to me last night, 'May an angel guard your rest and keep you from harm in all your ways.' The words are a little different, but it's the exact same thought as the quotation from the 91st Psalm. And that quotation means faith in God, faith in love, faith in the infinite power of God's love, and *you* don't believe in the existence of that power. It was a sarcastic remark, and in view of your pretense that you had been deeply moved by that quotation when you first heard it, that in *fact* it caused you to fall 'in love' with me, I think the remark was something more than mere sarcasm. I'd say it was a brutal and nasty and sneering reminder to me of how 'naive' I was to believe for a moment you cared two cents about me. It was a cheap, sarcastic, and vicious remark, and if you can convince me otherwise, I'll be very surprised."

For a moment Jim was stunned. His attempt the night before to pull himself together and make a graceful gesture toward her had detonated in his face with fury. There were, indeed, unplumbed depths in Melody Carolucy. The power of her mind seemed to him almost to match the power of her emotions. On the basis of what she knew and understood, her analysis was accurate and there was no possible answer he could give her except one: the truth.

"All right!" said Jim. "I've had enough of this bullshit from you, Melody, and I'm going to accept that challenge. Florence, I hate to ask this, but could you go to the bathroom or something for a few minutes?"

"No!" said Melody. "I don't want to listen to his profanity—you stay here, Florence!"

"Sorry, but as you pointed out, this is none of my business," said Florence.

As Florence got up and picked her way to the lounge door, undid the little silly string that held it shut and went out into the corridor, Melody shifted nervously in her chair and said: "I don't want to listen to you. There's nothing you can say that I want to hear."

"Okay, Melody, there's nothing I can say that you want to hear, but you'll agree with *this*. I'm cunning as a fox, I'm a real devil, and I have all kinds of wiles and tricks to seduce a woman. Right?"

"Yes, that's right."

"All right, if I know how to talk a woman *into* bed, then I'd know how to talk her *out* of bed too, wouldn't I? It'd be a simple thing for a fox like me. I'd know what to say to make her change her mind, and that's what happened yesterday afternoon. The fact that I talked to you in a vulgar way about Arpeth La Rue and *Playboy* was no accident, Melody, although I didn't realize it myself at the time."

"I don't understand that at all," she said. "What do you mean?"

"I mean what I said. I didn't know at the time I was doing it, and I didn't even know it later till I saw Florence's reaction after you'd left the room. I was amazed, but it's true, I let you go. I *un*seduced you, Melody, I said things I knew would make you change your mind and lock your door. I wanted more than anything in this world to go to your stateroom, but I couldn't do it. My remark to you last night was not sarcastic and I think you knew it wasn't. 'He shall give his angels charge over thee'—I had the right to say that to you. What's more, even if there was no porpoise, I only put my arm around you because I love you."

"I see," she answered in a toneless voice, "you don't believe in God's love but you practice it just the same. If you don't know it yourself, how am I supposed to know it?"

She did not believe him! "Melody," he said, "it's true! Every word I've told you is true!"

Melody lifted her hand and put it on Jim's shoulder. There was no expression on her face and he could not understand her gesture until she said, "I know that," and raised her other arm and put it around his neck and leaned her cheek against his. "What a relief," she whispered, "what a relief! I thought you hated me. . . ."

The emptiness of her eyes had come not from doubt but from astonishment. It was the last comprehensible remark she made for quite a while.

TWELVE

Themselves Discovered

Shaken by the beauty of the show put on by that great organization, the God's Love Marching Society, and shaken also by the raw power of nature now fully aroused by the basic interaction of the golden yellow sun and the deep blue sea, Jim and Melody braced themselves against each other as best as possible while the S.S. *Lorna Loone* pitched and rolled in a roaring wind. It was difficult to keep their balance in such a storm and they clutched at each other in an effort to avoid ruining a tender moment of perfect love by falling indecorously off those bolted-down chairs on their behinds.

"Oh, Melody, my darling!" cried Jim.

"Oh, Jim, darling, darling!" cried Melody.

Neither at this moment was aware of the wind that howled and screamed around the *Lorna Loone,* and neither was aware that greater winds than Beulah doth blow, as a consequence of another and a subtler interaction of the golden yellow sun and the deep blue sea.

"What a lot of mix-ups there are in this world," said Jim. "You thought *I* hated *you,* and I was absolutely convinced *you* hated *me.*"

"*Hate* you? How could I? I *love* you!"

"I also thought you didn't believe me when I told you I unseduced you."

"Oh, no! I knew it was true when you said you didn't know you were doing it yourself—I knew it that very instant."

She was still weeping almost hysterically, her arms around his waist and her head on his chest. It was difficult to quiet her. He could not move his chair closer to hers and she could not move her chair closer to his, because both the chairs were bolted down. The position was awkward and twice they were nearly thrown to the floor, but she would not take her arms from around him and she would not or could not stop crying. Jim did not mind; he was in no hurry for this moment to end.

The God's Love Marching Society had put on a hell of a show. There *was* such a thing as pure and perfect love and he felt it now as he held Melody in his arms. To Jim's astonishment, although he felt a tremendous tender love for her, he had no desire at all to take off her clothes, unfasten her bra, pull down her underpants, or any such wicked things as that. For the first time in his life he was able to hold in his arms a woman to whom he was enormously attracted and nevertheless feel no desire at all to do anything sexual to her. Her breasts against his chest were merely part of *her*, that was all. He loved her breasts, but no more than her hand or her finger or any other part of her body. He loved Melody herself and his love was pure.

It was a truly great sensation and the God's Love Marching Society had a thing going that wouldn't stop. He understood it all now. The poor angel had been hateful because her heart was broken, she had been in despair at the loss of his love just as he had been in despair at the loss of hers. It had cost her something to give him up too, which, after all, she had done. He had helped her, but she had done it on her own. "Thy words are tinsel, thy tears are gold"—was that from the Bible, or some Irish poet, or had he thought of it himself? "Those who can't cry, must die." That had to be Blake. No, not Blake—himself, or some obscure writer he could not recall.

Jim smiled ruefully as he held weeping Melody in his arms. There was a kind of poet in him somewhere and he had often thought he could write better shows than the ones he produced, but he had never had the time to try. Or maybe the nerve—a man could look pretty silly, like an idiot even. And yet he felt he had at least a speck of talent and could do something good. Probably the answer was to be willing to look like an idiot. One of these days he would have to try it, maybe in collaboration with a real writer such as Florence.

At that moment Florence came back—Jim saw her as she peeked in the door, lifted her eyebrows in mock surprise, grinned, and withdrew. A real pal, Florence, and a clever and talented woman. Maybe he *could* write something with her, get a better idea than that horrible, phony "Tramp Steamer" thing—what the hell, shows did not *have* to be bad, the Law of Gluck was a lot of nonsense. Such were Jim's thoughts as he held weeping Melody in his arms.

He had indeed met an angel on that ship and she had changed his life. It was incredible, the effect a good woman could have on a man. Jim was certain he would never again be quite so compulsive about chasing girls and women. He might lapse occasionally, but it would not be as it was before. And his attitude toward his work had changed too. There he was, thinking of scuttling "Tramp Steamer" and doing something really good. Melody had had a tremendous influence on him. To hell with the Goblin, he was not the only man in the industry, he and Florence would go elsewhere—a *good* show, why not? Maybe that family raising dachshunds in Vermont was not such a bad idea after all—Florence wouldn't write it cliché, she'd make the family wild and woolly.

Jim smiled as he patted Melody on the shoulder in an effort to calm her down. Florence was a real pal, and *she'd* had quite an influence on him too. Quite an influence, indeed—she was a truly honest referee and had made some great rulings. And the greatest ruling she had made was the one outlawing boxing, the ruling that had yanked the horrible Goblin prize fight off the air.

A truly great ruling, that one. Why, the Goblin Special was no better than the meretricious, conniving, ruthless organization that wanted to sponsor it, the Pussy & Pecker Soap Company—ecccch! the very thought of the crummy bunch was revolting. They were a loathsome group, an organization that cynically appealed to the lowest common denominator in an effort to sell their worthless soap, which ironically enough wouldn't wash anything anyhow. Why, that horrible Goblin Special wasn't worth the tape it was recorded on! Give the public something *really* good, like this great Spectacular by the God's Love Marching Society, and they would sit enthralled, grateful for a little truth and beauty in this grim, lonely world. Such were Jim's thoughts as he held in his arms his weeping true love, and the thoughts were indeed quite a contrast to the thoughts he had had on that recent clear September morning when he had surveyed the wreckage of his life with an increasing despair and dismay.

It was clear that Jim was Melody's true love too. When she finally calmed down enough to talk, her words made this plain. "Oh, Jim!" she cried. "I've never loved anyone the way I do you. I don't love Charles like this, I don't, I admit it. I love him, but not like this. I fell in love with you the minute I saw you and that's the truth. Not when you were down on the cobblestones by the taxi, then I thought you were just a drunk man, but when you came on the deck and looked at me. Those Beatles are right, they know more than the ones in the woods, people do fall in love at first sight—you and I did! Oh, Jim! I've never been happier than I am at this moment, and I don't care if this ship sinks and I drown! You love me, that's all I care about! Nothing else matters to me!"

Jim finally managed to calm her. It amused him to recall he had thought her mental powers matched the power of her emotions, a thing he did not consider healthy in a woman—or in a man either, for that matter. Intellectual geniuses with cretinous emotions were worth very little either to the world or themselves; they could invent new mathematics, maybe, but probably not even that; true genius, in his belief, came from emotion and desire, not from mind. There was nothing to worry about on this score insofar as Melody was concerned. She had a mind and a good one, but her emotions outweighed her mentality a thousand times.

"Now, honey," he said, "I feel the same way you do, the exact same way. I don't care even if this stupid ship sinks. But honey, you sit back in your chair because I can't hold you up any more, my leg and arm both have gone to sleep. You sit back and we'll talk, okay?"

Melody sat back in her chair, adjusted her dress, smiled, and delivered herself of a little speech with which Jim found himself in one-hundred-percent agreement. "That's right," she said. "I don't have to put my arms around you or any of that. The most wonderful thing is you've shown me *sex* doesn't matter at all. Real love is so far beyond it, you don't even need *sex* any more. Do you realize that's the most wonderful thing?"

"Yes, I do, and it's amazing you would say that. I was thinking the exact same thing myself. *Sex* is the most ridiculously overrated thing in the world and it's not necessary. I was holding you in my arms and it had no effect on me like that at all."

"Me either," she answered. "Not a bit. I loved it, but it had no effect on me like that at all."

"It's incredible," said Jim, "simply incredible. I never dreamed the day would come when I could feel this way about a woman."

"I never dreamed I could feel this way either, if you want to know the truth. Oh, I've always *said* sex doesn't really matter, and I thought I believed it, but I really didn't. I used to tell myself and say to Charles it didn't matter, but deep inside it bothered me. You see, it's always been a defect in my character."

"It's always been a defect in *mine* too," said Jim, "believe me."

With a smile, Melody leaned forward, her elbows on the table. "Kiss me once," she said. "Not . . . passionate, but just nice."

Jim smiled back at her. "Okay," he said. Jim put his own elbows on the table, leaned toward her, and kissed her lightly on the lips.

"Mmm," said Melody, smiling. "That was too quick to be any test. A little more."

Jim raised his hand to her chin, put his lips on hers, and kissed her again, this time more lingeringly. The kiss was about three seconds old when Jim felt his knees lose their strength. Her lips were very, very sweet. Somehow he managed to end the kiss and draw back from her.

"Mmm," said Jim, with a solemn and slightly worried expression on his face.

"Well, yes," said Melody, with an expression similar to his own. She was silent for a moment, then said, "We passed the test. I can kiss you without going crazy, that's what I wanted to prove."

"So did I," said Jim. "But . . . I think we're still attracted."

"Yes."

"My knees, I'm afraid, are a little shaky."

"I know what you mean," she answered.

"Honey, we're human. And sex might not amount to much of itself, but it *is* a basic drive."

"Too basic with me," said Melody. "I've always had a weakness that way."

"So have I, except a thousand times worse."

"You don't know how bad I can be," said Melody. "The worst thing is the misery I've caused Charles. He's never been strong, physically strong, that's why it probably was a mistake for us to try to go to Colombia—he's not *sickly* or anything, but his nature is different from mine. I'm more . . . I don't know how to put it . . ."

"You're more strongly sexed than Charles," said Jim.

Melody slowly nodded her head. "Yes, I am," she said. "Much more. And I don't feel ashamed to say that to you either, you'd forgive me for anything."

"Forgive you? That's nothing to be ashamed of, Melody; it shows you have feeling, imagination, sensitivity, a loving nature, and other wonderful qualities. You shouldn't be ashamed of that."

"I should be if I can't control it—and you saw how I acted yesterday. I would have been in that bed waiting for you and trembling in my nightgown if you hadn't made me see what I was doing to myself and my husband. I was even willing to get pregnant! I couldn't control it, Jim, I really couldn't. When you put your hands on my breasts yesterday I thought I'd faint. I couldn't control myself, but I *can* now because you've taught me it doesn't really matter. I don't think I will ever have a problem like that again . . . although, of course, I can't let myself get in a situation like *that*."

"Neither can I," said Jim as he remembered the overwhelming moment when he had put his hands on her breasts and she had raised her own hands and pulled his hands against her. "But I understand exactly what you mean, because I myself have a problem and a half in this area. You talk about what you've done to Charles, but I've done worse things to Linda, infinitely worse."

"I doubt that," said Melody. "You don't know how demoralized Charles has been these last three years, since we learned we can't ever have children. It's gotten so he doesn't feel like a man at all. He was *glad* to go ahead of me down to San José del Guaviare. He wanted to get away from me. I was making him utterly miserable—you wouldn't dream how awful I can be, Jim, you wouldn't dream it. The things I said to him, the little remarks . . . it's terrible."

"You wouldn't dream how awful *I* can be," he answered, "and it's funny you would say three years. Linda had several miscarriages and didn't want more children, so she had her tubes tied and our troubles started soon after that, almost exactly three years ago. She wanted the operation very much, but it demoralized her just the same and I'm afraid I've done worse things to her than just make little remarks."

"*I've* done worse things too," said Melody, "not even counting the way I've acted on this ship. I can tell you something, I can tell you anything, because you love me and you'll understand. But that nurse at the hospital who was kissing all the doctors . . . *she* wasn't the only one who kissed a doctor. *I* kissed a doctor too, and I didn't even love him. I kissed him more than once and let him touch my breast, then ran home and told Charles. How about *that* for complete and total wickedness?"

Jim had to smile. The conversation was beginning to remind him of a meeting of Alcoholics Anonymous. He had attended one of their meetings with an ex-drunkard friend and had been very amused by the way the reformed alcoholics would jump up and try to outdo each other in their descriptions of how awful they'd been. But poor Melody hadn't been much of an alcoholic with a couple of stolen kisses and a hand on her breast. In effect she was saying: "Why, about once a month I would *have a cocktail before dinner!* How about *that* for complete and total drunkenness?"

"Melody," he said, "you have no idea what sin and wickedness really are like. Why, I couldn't keep my hands off women, I was *awful!* Little secretaries who'd come work for me, the wives of my friends, even my own wife's cousin. I've never been able to leave women alone, but do you know something? I think I can now. In fact, I know I can. If I can control myself with you, I can easily resist some girl or woman I don't even really want. The compulsion is gone, Melody."

"It is with me too," she answered with a smile. "We've both learned something and it's really changed both our lives. I'll be much happier with Charles now and you'll get your wife back too."

"I'm sure you'll be happier with Charles. But I don't know about Linda. I really don't know. Linda and I have gone through some awful things."

"She'll see the difference in you. I'm sure you'll get her back, if she's the kind of woman you say she is."

"She's human and she's made mistakes, but basically she's wonderful."

"So is Charles," said Melody, "a fine and wonderful man."

Jim smiled. "I used to feel jealous of Charles, I kind of hated him, but I don't any more."

Melody returned his smile. "I kind of hated your wife too. But I don't now. I just hope you and Linda are happy."

"I just hope you and Charles are too. That's all I want, is for you to be happy."

"That's all I want too, is for you to be."

This hour of God's love triumphant, this sweet and tender time of unselfish devotion, which beyond doubt would have endured to Bluefields but for the intervention of a providential breeze called Beulah, was interrupted by the arrival of the biggest wave yet to hit the S.S. *Lorna Loone,* and interrupted also by a preliminary blast of the wind that doth blow, a blast that heralded the approach of an even greater storm.

Although the wind was roaring so loudly now that conversation was becoming difficult even in the soundproofed lounge, Jim and Melody had ignored Hurricane Beulah, just as they had ignored the prolonged and rather odd absence of Florence. But Hurricane Beulah had not gone away. On the contrary, Hurricane Beulah was coming closer all the time, headed up the Yucatan Channel toward Texas just as Jim jokingly had said.

Jim saw the wave through the lounge portholes and was too petrified to warn Melody. A horrible mountain of frothing and raging water was up far, far above the ship and coming down. It was not a credible wave on the blue sea but an unbelievable gray-green white-foaming monster beyond imagining. Jim instinctively grabbed the arms of his chair as tons upon tons of water crashed down upon the passenger deck and the top of the ship as if to drive it to the bottom of the sea.

As Jim later learned from Florence—three of whose ribs were broken by thc wave, although in her fear she did not discover it till long afterward—the wave almost *did* drive the ship to the bottom of the sea. Under the terrific impact, the S.S. *Lorna Loone* sank shuddering deep down in the water and lurched far over on its side as the lights in the lounge flickered and went out and coffee cups and other crockery flew from the table and Melody herself was thrown from her chair and down to the floor and across Jim's lap and knees. If he had not caught at her shoulder and half stopped her, she would have gone all the way over the chair upon which Florence had been sitting and would have hit her face and head against the heavy plywood door. From somewhere in the innards of the *Lorna Loone*, Jim heard an ominous crashing and splintering sound—it dimly occurred to him this boded no good, but at the moment he was more concerned with Melody, who seemed half stunned.

"Melody!" he cried. "Are you hurt? Are you all right?"

She was sprawled across his knees and lap with her arms half on the seat of the chair in which Florence had been sitting. Her dress was in sad disarray and one of her deck sandals had come off. Slowly, she propped an elbow on Florence's chair and felt gingerly of her face and forehead. "Well, my head," she said, "I hit it on your knee or something. And my nose seems to be bleeding."

"Don't try to get up right away or you might faint," said Jim. He had felt the blow on his knee and she'd hit him hard, but he did not believe she was seriously injured; the main thing he was concerned about was that she would panic with fear and become hysterical. It was obvious the S.S. *Lorna Loone* could not possibly survive such a storm as this. Very few ships of any kind could live through this god-awful Beulah—it sure as hell *did* have winds of a hundred and eighty miles per hour and it sure as hell had raised a tremendous sea. That wave had been unbelievable—the thing had looked at least a hundred feet high. Jim put his hand on Melody's back and patted her to reassure her, although at this moment he needed reassurance as badly as she did. In a shaky voice he said, "It'll be all right, don't be afraid, honey." The lights flickered feebly, flickered again, and came back on. "See, the lights are on. That was a bad one but the ship's all right."

Melody put her arm on the seat of Florence's chair and lay her face down on it with a sigh. Jim could see bright red blood on her mouth and nose. She'd hit his knee harder than he'd thought and probably *would* faint if she raised her head immediately. In an almost casual tone she said, "We're not going to get to Bluefields. You don't have to fool me, Jim."

"No, I think it'll be all right."

"I can face it, I'm not afraid. The truth is, we're going to drown and die."

Jim hesitated. She was no child and she knew they were in extreme danger. "I suppose we might, honey. That was quite a wave."

"I thought the ship turned over," said Melody as she shifted her hips to lie in a more comfortable position across his lap rather than his knees. Jim looked down at her body. She was lying like a child about to be spanked and the outline of her buttocks was plainly revealed by the stretched rayon material of her dress, which was twisted up far above her knees. Beautiful, thought Jim. Melody, in his opinion, had a lovely behind. There was a day when he would not have considered it so, he would foolishly have thought there was too much of it—but that was back in the dark ages of his ignorance before he knew what true feminine beauty was. A woman's beauty resided in her *difference* from a man; a truly beautiful woman should *not* have a little scrawny, boyish bottom—that was an aesthetic evaluation imposed by faggy fashion photographers. Melody's behind was the *true* behind of a woman—lovely, beautiful, classic in its perfect Hera-like proportions . . . those plump, rounded, generous buttocks were the ideal of feminine beauty, and very sexy besides. A sudden impulse came to Jim to put his hand on Melody's true behind.

"Yes, I guess we might drown," he said. "Of course, if we drown, nothing matters any more."

"Yes, I know," said Melody in a voice that sounded a trifle strange.

Jim looked down again at the classic, perfect, true behind in his lap. Why not? If they were going to drown and die, what did it matter? It could not hurt Charles or Linda or himself or her or anyone else if they would soon be on the bottom of the ocean. Why not? Her legs were slightly apart and the thought occurred to him he could place his palm on the cleft of her buttocks and reach with his fingers down underneath and. . . . Jim winced in shock: what an awful idea! Of course he would not do any such Goblin thing to her, after all that had happened. As he thought he would not do it, Jim lifted his hand and did it.

Dizzy and horrified by his dreadful conduct, Jim sat there with the plump, round cheeks under his palm. But in the midst of his shock, a dreamlike serenity possessed him. It seemed the most natural thing in the world for him to move his fingers down far underneath her and press his fingertips against her pubic bone, which he could feel clearly through the thin rayon material and through her own feminine flesh —yes, he could feel it, pubic bone, wider in women, the basic arch of human life. He also could feel to a certain extent the familiar but ever amazing design of that most remarkable part of any woman's body, the place where life enters and the place from which life is born—the better half, so to speak, of that dynamic, high-powered organization ready in a flash to throw an exciting Special on the air, a Special that might not be as great as a Spectacular but day in and day out reached quite an audience.

It rather shocked Jim Kittering in the midst of his shock, this final and complete proof that Melody was not an angel from heaven but a female human being on the earth. Of course, he had expected to find exactly what he found, but it still was something of a shock. And it was not quite the same thing as touching her hand or finger, either.

However, Jim felt a calm in the midst of the shock within the shock, a bit like being in the eye of a hurricane that in turn was in the eye of another hurricane. In dreamy absorption, Jim pressed his fingers against the place from which life is born, as calmly as a doctor performing an examination to determine if everything was there in its correct location. He thought he could detect with his fingertips a thin padding of pubic hair under the material of her dress and panties.

She'd had no children and was rather girlish in this area. Insofar as he could tell, everything was as it should be, but the matter needed closer investigation. The obstructive material of her dress and panties prevented necessary research. The thing to do was pull up her dress and lower the panties over her true behind, then he could conduct the examination properly.

During Jim's handicapped but unflinching exploration of the most intimate part of her body, Melody herself, after a slight quiver of shock and a brief contraction of the muscles of her buttocks, had not made an uncooperative move or said a word. She lay there motionless across his lap, with her face on her arm and her eyes shut. It was as if she had gone to sleep, but she had not. Not long after Jim put his hand on her, she had moved her legs a bit farther apart and since then had several times shifted her hips in an obvious effort to help out and make the examination easier.

Calmly, although his heart was pounding so loudly he could not hear Hurricane Beulah, Jim reached down and pulled at her dress. But the dress was twisted around her and would not come up. What could he do about this?

"Honey, raise up for a second," said Jim in a voice that was strange and hoarse in his ears.

"What, Jim?" she asked. Her voice also sounded strange and hoarse, and seemed muffled; he could hardly hear her.

"Raise your hips just a little, honey, so I can pull up your dress."

"Oh," she answered, "you mean like this?"

"Yes, that's good," said Jim as he pulled the rayon material well above her hips, thus completely exposing her panty-clad behind. And it was indeed a lovely, beautiful behind, even with those obstructive white panties on it. Jim put his hand on the small of her back and slid his fingers under the thin elastic band of the panties, then paused to take a needed breath of air and consider the situation. His hand now was on her warm, bare bottom, his palm in the plump cleft of her buttocks, and his fingertips just touching a silky wetness.

Jim and Melody, in all innocence, had been unaware that greater winds than Beulah doth blow. As a consequence, they had been blown off the bolted-down chairs, a very indecorous thing and an awful surprise to them both. However, in all fairness to them, Beulah had served another purpose than to provide a light spring breeze to cool brows fevered by the dreamy dance around a column taller than a hurricane's eye. The greater storm would never have been generated by the golden yellow sun and the deep blue sea but for the providential breeze called Beulah. God's love would have lasted to Bluefields and man's nature would not have had its May Day.

As he stared down at his hand on Melody's naked behind, Jim recognized May Day for what it was and the dreamy dance was interrupted. He snatched his hand from her, pulled frantically at her panties to get them back up, and grabbed at her dress to pull it down as he said:

"Melody, I'm sorry! Honey, now I didn't mean to do this! Here, pull your dress down—let me help you, that's right! Oh, I'm sorry, I didn't mean to do that, I really didn't!"

Melody stood up, holding to the table for support. She was quite pale and small twin streams of blood had run from her nose. She raised her hand and touched her fingers at a bump-bruise on her forehead that already had turned a dark purple. "I hit my head," she said. "On your knee, I think. And I lost my deck sandal. Where'd it go? My glasses are gone too, I can't see."

"Sit down," said Jim, "sit down and I'll find the sandal."

The sandal was ten feet away under another table. As he stooped to pick it up, the shame of what he'd done made him groan half aloud. Now she would think he didn't love her, that all he wanted was to do Goblin things to her—and what a Goblin thing it was, approaching her from the rear like that! Poor darling, she must have been terribly embarrassed, although she didn't seem to mind. Head sheepishly bowed, Jim took the sandal back to her and sat down at the table beside her as she slipped it on her foot.

"Honey," he said, "I could shoot myself. I don't know what came over me. I didn't mean to do that, I really didn't."

Melody turned and stared rather emptily and gently at him. "I can't see . . . do you know where my glasses are?"

Jim found the glasses under his chair and gave them to her. One of the lenses was so badly cracked that only a splinter of glass remained in it. "They're really busted," he said. "Lucky you weren't hurt bad."

"You stopped me or I would have been, I think." Melody picked out the splinter in the broken lens and put on the glasses. "I can see with one eye. That's better than practically nothing. I'm so nearsighted it's pathetic."

"Honey," said Jim, "I hope you believe me. I do love you, Melody, and I didn't mean to do that just now."

"It wasn't your fault," she answered. "I tempted you. I deliberately tempted you, I lay there and pretended I was hurt and couldn't get up."

"But you *are* hurt."

"No, I'm not, not really. I tempted you. I have no character at all, Jim, none. I'm simply a weak and wicked person."

"Oh, now look, you weren't to blame at all. I took complete advantage of you when you were half stunned and helpless. Look at you—your glasses broken, a bad bruise on your forehead, and your nose bleeding. I'm completely responsible."

"I knew what I was doing, I wasn't stunned. Is my nose still bleeding? I must look awful."

"I'll get a cloth from the bar," said Jim.

By the time Jim picked his way back to the table with a dampened towel, an awareness had returned to them both of the lesser wind called Beulah. Although they had forgotten Beulah, Beulah was still there, blowing and screaming in fury outside the portholes of the lounge.

As he wiped the blood from her nose and mouth, Jim said: "The storm seems worse. The waves look higher and I think the wind is blowing even harder."

"Yes, I think so too."

"Maybe that's why it happened just now. The storm. We were both thinking we were going to drown and die, remember?"

"Yes. Yes, I remember that. But it's not much of an excuse."

"No, I suppose not. Except if we drown and die we couldn't hurt anybody else."

Melody slowly nodded, a pensive expression in her eyes. Then for half a minute or so she was silent as she dabbed at the traces of blood on her face. Finally she said, "The storm is pretty bad, isn't it?"

"It's terrible," said Jim.

"Every now and then I hear a noise somewhere, or a vibration. A kind of bump or crash somewhere in the ship."

"Yeah, I think some of the cargo must have broken loose when that big wave hit."

"That's serious, isn't it?"

"If it's one of those so-called medium transformers, it's *very* serious."

Melody stared pensively out of the portholes. "The waves are higher," she said.

"And the wind is stronger," said Jim.

"Yes, but we'd hurt *ourselves*."

"How?" he asked.

"I mean if we . . . I mean . . . like yesterday. You know, the stateroom. We would hurt ourselves, Jim."

"How?"

"Well . . . we'd feel badly."

"We love each other, honey. We wouldn't feel badly as long as we weren't hurting anybody else."

"Yes, but even if we drown and Charles and Linda never could know or be hurt, God would know. God would see us, Jim."

Jim hesitated. It would be best not to get involved with her in a discussion of whether or not God would see them. "I don't think God would blame us, Melody, under these conditions. The point in . . . God's law is to have rules so you don't hurt other people."

"No . . . no, the point also is to have rules so you don't hurt yourself."

"Melody, we *love* each other. How would it hurt us?"

Again, for quite a while she stared at him in grave silence. "I . . . I . . . it . . . I think we would feel badly."

"You said that before, and I don't think you believe it. We wouldn't feel badly, honey. We love each other, we'd feel wonderful."

"Maybe you're right, maybe we wouldn't feel badly. But the ship might not sink."

At this moment, luckily, another huge wave crashed down on the passenger deck and the top of the *S.S. Lorna Loone*. It wasn't an awful monster like the other one, but it was a good one. The lights in the lounge flickered out for a moment and Jim heard again a crashing and splintering sound from somewhere in the innards of the ship.

"I think it will," said Jim. "I really do. I think we could practically go to your stateroom right now and be perfectly safe."

"Oh, I don't think so."

"We don't want to wait *too* long or the thing will sink on us before we can get there. I'm sure it's going to sink, Melody. Let's go to your stateroom."

"*No!*" she answered. "*You're* being weak now, Jim. This is not your better side. Why, this ship might not sink at all, then where would we be?"

At this point, fortunately, the *S.S. Lorna Loone* took such a terrific roll to starboard that Jim and Melody had to hold onto the bolted-down table to avoid being thrown to the floor. "See?" said Jim. "We almost capsized that time. Let's go to your stateroom right now."

"No. I absolutely won't, it might not sink!"

"Melody—"

"No! No, Jim! I can see I've got to be strong for both of us, which is only fair since you've saved *me* twice. We can't go to the stateroom. The point is we can't be absolutely sure the ship will sink."

Jim sighed. As long as the *Lorna Loone* was even half afloat, she would not go near the stateroom. "I suppose you're right," he said. "If you were worried and anxious about it, it wouldn't be any good anyhow."

"I'd be worried. Sometimes ships go through terrible storms. We absolutely can't go to the stateroom, Jim, we really and truly can't."

"Okay, honey."

Melody was silent for a while as Beulah howled and shrieked and the wind that doth blow gathered its greater power to let go another blast. "However," she said, "I think we could go sit on the sofa and you could kiss me."

Ten minutes later Jim lay half across Melody on the sofa as they kissed each other with wild, frenzied, tender passion, wholly oblivious of the pitching of the ship and the roaring of Beulah. He had kissed her before and she had kissed him, but not like this. It had taken only a few such kisses before Jim unzipped the zipper at the side of her dress. His hand, with a bit more dignity, was in the front of her panties this time. He had completed successfully the examination he had begun before and the procedure had aroused her so much he was afraid he might soon lose the patient, or at least lose her temporarily. She was breathing very heavily as she kissed him and grinding and twisting her body against his hand. He did not want her to exhaust herself in this manner but to save herself for the stateroom, which had to come soon even though she refused almost hysterically to get up off the sofa. Every time he suggested it, she said: "No, it might not sink!" He really did not like to see her wear herself out in this manner, although this patient was healthy and would make a quick recovery, but there was nothing he could do. She had a grip like iron on his wrist and would not let him take away his hand. Melody, he had discovered, was very strong, almost as strong as he was.

A giant bruiser of a wave, a really bad one that briefly penetrated his consciousness, thundered on the passenger deck and the side of the lounge just behind Jim and Melody, almost throwing them off the sofa. Melody pulled her mouth from his, gasping for breath. "I think I'm going to do it," she said in a choked voice. "Oh, darling . . . oh, Jim, how I love you . . . don't stop, in a minute I will. . . ."

At this delicate moment Florence opened the door and entered the lounge. Jim could see her over Melody's side and shoulder. Melody, whose glasses were off and whose eyes were shut tight, did not know Florence was on the same planet with her. Jim attempted to pull his hand away and said: "Florence . . . Melody, *Florence* is here!"

"What!" Melody opened her eyes and turned her head toward the lounge door and frowned nearsightedly at Florence. "Is that you, Florence?"

"Gray-et Godd, holy catfish!" said Florence. "Are you *both* out of your minds?"

Melody fumbled on the sofa for her glasses as Jim took his hand from her dress. "It's all right, Florence!" she said. "The ship is going to sink."

"It's *all right*, because the ship is going to *sink?*"

"Yes, it *is* all right, and it's my idea as much as Jim's. We're not hurting anyone or ourselves either. Besides, it's none of your business, Florence. You go away!"

"Yes, Florence," said Jim coldly, "you are intruding in a very rude and inconsiderate way. Get the hell out of here."

"That's right!" said Melody angrily. "Stop interfering!"

"You really *are* out of your minds!" said Florence in amazement. "I never saw anything to equal it! Here you are, smooching and petting like a couple of insane teen-agers, when this ship is damn near about to go to the bottom of the sea!"

"Is it?" asked Jim. "I told you, Melody. Come on, let's go to the stateroom while there's still time."

"Go to the stateroom while there's still time for *what?*" asked Florence. "Are you stark mad?"

"No, we are not!" said Jim angrily. "If we're going to drown, we might as well have a little happiness first. Now, you get out of here! I want to talk to Melody, this is serious, get out, Florence!"

"I *can't* get out, you nut! I have got to stay in the lounge and so have you. It's captain's orders. He has to know where the passengers are when the crew lowers the lifeboats, so stop telling me to get out."

"Lifeboats?" asked Jim.

"That's right, lifeboats. I assume you are not so intent on bed that you care *nothing at all* about saving your ridiculous lives?"

"Well," said Jim, "no."

"Your husband and wife might want you to live."

"I didn't think about lifeboats," said Melody. "How can they lower lifeboats in a storm like this?"

"I'll explain the captain's plan to you," said Florence wearily. "Now, if you don't mind, I'd like to sit down on that sofa by you two insane smoochers. I took an awful fall up on the bridge when that big wave hit and I've hurt my side. May I sit down?"

"Oh, of course," said Melody. She had remembered that her dress was open and that her stomach and bra and panties were visible. Blushing, she zipped up the dress with a little guilty smile at Florence. "I'm sorry. I'm sorry, Florence, I got upset."

"I guess to hell you did," said Florence as she sat down, a hand against her ribs and a pained wince on her face. "You two amaze me. Don't you realize the ship almost went down when that big wave hit? Do you know how close we came to capsizing?"

"We knew it was bad," said Jim. "But I don't see how they can possibly lower lifeboats in that sea, or how lifeboats could survive in it if they did. What's the captain's plan?"

Florence was searching in the pockets of her suit with a frustrated frown. "Providence Island," she said. "I've got to have a cigarette. Give me one, Jim."

"I ran out an hour ago."

"Oh, hell. My nerves are absolutely shot, I've got to have a cigarette. Aren't there any in here at all?"

"No. What's that about Providence Island?"

Florence settled back on the sofa, again wincing as she held a hand against her ribs. "All right, I'll tell you the captain's plan, then I'm going to my stateroom for a cigarette, orders or no orders. First, since you both obviously are in a dream, you'd better brace yourself. Are you the hysterical type, Melody?"

"No," said Melody.

"All right, the ship is on the verge of sinking, for several different reasons at the same time. Number one. *This* is one of the worst hurricanes in history—the captain, the first mate, none of them can believe it. I was up on the bridge, that's where I went and that's where I was when the big wave hit. The hurricane itself will sink the ship sooner or later and it might do so at any moment. Number two. The medium transformers have broken loose, first one, then another, then all of them. Even in your insanity, couldn't you hear them crashing around—in fact, don't you hear them *now,* when the ship takes a bad pitch or roll?"

"I thought that's what it was," said Jim. "We heard it."

"Those transformers are very heavy and in this kind of weather it's humanly impossible to secure them. They are sliding back and forth and might do one of several things, such as knock a hole in the side of the ship itself, in which case our troubles are quickly over. More likely, they'll knock out the less strong partition or bulkhead that separates them from the wheat. In which case the wheat will shift and our troubles will *also* be quickly over. Number three. Two of the pumps have stopped working because of short circuits caused by the storm, and water has gotten in the wheat, a considerable amount of it. The wheat is swelling like Serutan. It has already half cracked one bulkhead and can crack the ship itself wide open. You remember the *Castillo Montijuich,* Jim."

"Yes. What about Providence Island?"

"That's our chance, and our only chance. The ship can't possibly make it to Bluefields but it *might* make it to Providence Island. I am sorry, Melody, but you were wrong about the location of that island. It's much nearer than you thought. According to the captain, we're only a few miles from it—or the idiot *thinks* we're only a few miles from it."

"If we can get to an island, why do we need lifeboats?" asked Jim.

"There's no harbor on the island, or at least the captain *thinks* there's no harbor on it. The idiot lost all his charts of this area when he set that stupid fire in his stateroom. But the first mate also is sure there's no harbor. It's almost no better than the open sea."

"I don't see how it helps us then," said Jim.

"I said *almost.* The island *does* have hills. The captain's plan is to come in on the leeward side of it, where the hills would protect us enough from the wind so they could launch lifeboats. The reef comes in there very close to the island and there's an opening in it. Not wide enough for the ship, but wide enough for a lifeboat. We'd have a chance to go through the reef and beach the lifeboat and live."

"You see?" Melody said to Jim, "We might survive after all. Thank God I didn't go to that stateroom."

"Hmmph," said Jim. He could not at once adjust himself to the prospect of living and he felt disgruntled. It was just *like* the goddamned *Loony Goony* somehow to straggle through this thing and survive.

"In fact, I shouldn't have done what I did," said Melody. "I feel *awful.* But then . . . how was I to know they could do that with lifeboats?"

"Cheer up," said Florence. "They probably can't."

"You said they could," said Jim.

"I said there was a chance. The chance is about one in ten thousand, maybe. Even on the leeward side of an island with hills, the sea will be very rough in a storm like this. They *might* get a lifeboat down and the lifeboat *might* get through the reef to the beach. The odds probably are closer to a hundred thousand to one, maybe not even that good, because first we've got to *find* Providence Island, and the captain doesn't know where it is or where *we* are either, for that matter."

"Hell, it's going to sink, then," said Jim.

"Maybe not, there's a chance. He knows approximately where we are, and approximately where the island is. Furthermore, you were wrong about something else, Melody. There *are* other islands in this part of the Caribbean. Roncador, Serrana, Swan Island, and five or six more—most of them are just sandy cays, but some would give us protection. We might run across one of those islands looking for Providence."

"When do they expect to get to Providence Island, assuming they get there at all?" asked Jim.

"They don't know. Maybe half an hour, maybe two hours, maybe never. So." Florence stood up. "There might be a cigarette in the life-raft closet, Odd used to keep some in there."

Jim took Melody's hand as Florence walked over to the life-raft closet, holding her side. "We're not going to make it, honey," he said. "It really is one chance in a hundred thousand. Are you afraid?"

"Yes, of course," she answered. "I wasn't before, but now maybe we won't die, I'm afraid."

"So am I," said Jim. "Well, I hope I don't go to hell."

"There's no hell," she answered. "Hell is on earth."

"I'm surprised, I thought you believed in hell."

"Charles does, but I don't. I only believe in heaven."

Jim smiled and squeezed her hand. "I don't even believe in that. I believe heaven is on earth too. And I think I know where it's located right now." Jim paused, his eyes fixed intently on Melody as Florence rummaged around in the life-raft closet. "We don't have a chance, Melody. When Florence goes after her cigarettes, let's go to your stateroom, honey."

Melody hesitated a long, long time, then said, "We can't, the captain won't let us."

"To hell with the captain."

"*No*," she said. "There's a chance we might live."

"But Florence will come back and bother us."

"I know. But I can't go in the stateroom. I can't, Jim. Not unless I know for sure we're going to drown."

Impossible. Hopeless. Whatever "wicked weakness" Melody had had was gone. She would *not* go into that stateroom unless the ship had water gurgling into it. If he got her, it would be pretty hasty love-making, because the ship would actually be going down. "Oh, crap!" said Florence. Jim caught a glimpse of her as she angrily yanked the chain to turn out the light in the life-raft closet, and a great inspiration hit him. *The life-raft closet*. But of course!

"There're cigarettes in there somewhere but I can't find them. I'm going to duck down to my stateroom and get a pack."

Jim put his arm around Melody's waist and said: "We'll hold the fort."

Florence smiled. "Watch out for Indians. They are sneaky."

"We shall keep the musket loaded," said Jim.

"Huh," said Florence. "You are both crazy. But I gather you *did* straighten out your misunderstanding. It appears to me you don't hate him any more, Melody."

"No, I don't hate him. And I'm sorry I talked to you the way I did, Florence. I'm very sorry."

"Forget it. I'll be back in a minute." Florence turned in the doorway of the lounge, her face mottled with fright and a hand pressed against her side. An ironic amusement was in her eyes, despite her fear of death and the pain in her ribs. Absorbed in Melody as he was, Jim felt a surge of admiration for her. The account she had given of the predicament of the *S.S. Lorna Loone* was both lucid and courageous, and even in dire extremity she had enough stuff in her to be amused by them. As her agent Al Ingerman would say, Florence had "real class." Jim smiled across the lounge at her; he would really have to write a good show with her someday, if they didn't drown in a few minutes. "Well," said Florence, "keep an eye out for those Indians. They are extremely sneaky."

"Yes, I know," said Melody, "and don't worry, we will." She turned to Jim as Florence disappeared and put her hand sadly on his shoulder. "I kissed you a few times, anyhow. That's something. Do you want to kiss me once more while she's away?" Jim was silent; he was waiting for Florence to be gone. "We might as well, Jim . . . we won't be able to when she gets back."

"Let's go in the life-raft closet," said Jim. "Florence won't know we're in there."

"The life-raft closet? You mean . . . the *life-raft* closet?" Melody turned her head to stare in the direction of the shut door to the left of the bar, then turned back to Jim. "We can't do that."

"Why not? Why can't we?"

"Well . . ." said Melody, her eyes intently on the closet door. "But what's in there?"

"Nothing," said Jim. "Deck furniture, cases of soda, life preservers. We can blow up the life raft and sit on it. Florence won't dream we're in there, she'll think we've sneaked off to some stateroom."

"Blow up the life raft," said Melody, eyes fixed on the closet door. She shook her head. "That doesn't sound like a good idea to me. We can't do that."

"Melody, we've got *one* chance in a hundred thousand. They'll never find that island and if they do they'll never launch a lifeboat and get it through that reef. This ship is sinking for three different reasons—you heard Florence. Please, let's go in there before she comes back."

"But . . . that life raft . . . I don't know."

"Melody, we're going to drown and die! I want to hold you in my arms—not make love to you, just hold you in my arms! Please, darling, let's go in the life-raft closet!"

Melody was silent for three seconds, then said: "All right. But promise you won't make love to me."

"I promise," said Jim. "Come on, hurry!"

She was still reluctant and Jim had to pull her by the hand across the lounge to get her into the closet door. There was not much time.

Florence would be back any moment. As quickly as he could, he opened the door, pulled the hanging string to turn on the closet light, and bent down and spread out the rolled-up life raft. There was a ring on it somewhere; it inflated automatically from a cylinder of gas—where was the ring? The thing would fill the entire closet and it had to be inflated before they went in there.

"I can't find the ring!" said Jim desperately. "Where's the ring?"

It was impossible to wait another second; Florence would walk in and everything would be ruined. He'd have to inflate it while they were in the closet. Jim grabbed Melody's hand to pull her into the little musty and low-ceilinged room, but she balked.

"You promised! Remember!"

"I know, come on!"

"No, promise me again! Really promise!"

"I promise I *won't* make love to you, Melody."

"All right," she said. Her knees were trembling as Jim led her into the closet and shut the door. They continued to tremble as Jim crawled around on the spread-out raft looking for the ring.

"Help me find this thing, honey!" said Jim, but then he saw it at the corner of the raft and scrambled toward it and gave it a violent pull. At once, POOOOF!—the life raft exploded into shape beneath his hands and knees like a giant mattress, shoving deck furniture to the wall and crowding against Melody's legs. Jim looked up at her. "Are you all right?"

"Yes," she said.

Safe! Florence would never guess they were in there. "Come sit by me," said Jim.

Melody stared down at him. Her knees were still trembling. She wet her lips and swallowed, fright in her eyes. "Remember," she said, "you promised."

"I won't do anything but kiss you, honey, really I won't," said Jim. "Come sit by me."

"All right," she answered. Slowly, she pulled her legs free, stepped onto the inflated raft, and sat down beside him.

Twenty minutes later, Jim and Melody lay on the raft with their arms tightly around each other and their bodies very close together. Melody's dress and sandals and glasses were gone; she wore only her bra and underpants. Jim was similarly unclad; he had on his jockey undershorts and nothing else. Jim had intended to keep his promise, but it was impossible for him to do so. The feeling of her half-naked body in his arms drove him wild. He felt a desire for her of a kind he never before had known in this world. Her body was beautiful beyond his dreams and he had abandoned his promise and was bent on making love to her.

However, she was resisting to the best of her ability, although she too was in a waking coma of desire. She would not let him get anywhere near the panties; she'd permitted it in the lounge but evidently felt it was too dangerous, too much for her on the mattresslike raft. She was strong and would grab his wrist with a grip of iron if he tried to put his hand anywhere below her waist. Several times, in the midst of maddeningly passionate kisses, Jim had tried to take off her brassiere, but she would not allow that either, although her resistance was less in this area. He would get one hook of the bra unfastened, then she would reach around behind her and refasten it. How could he get the bra off? She wouldn't be forced. The thing to do was to ask her to take it off herself.

"Melody, take off your bra, honey."

"I can't."

"*Please*, darling. Take it off."

She took a deep breath, her nearsighted eyes staring into his. She could see him from this distance. A heavy sigh came from her. "Can't you just kiss me?" she asked.

"I want to see your breasts. Please, darling."

Another heavy sigh came from her as she stared into his eyes. "All right," she said. "But not my pants!"

"No, not the pants," said Jim.

Melody sat up and reached both hands behind her, facing Jim and staring at him with an expression of pale fright. He could see the muscles of her arms move as she worked with her hands to undo the hooks, then suddenly the brassiere loosened and she slowly pulled the straps down over her arms. Even more slowly, she held out the bra in her fingers and dropped it off the raft, then sat staring gently at him, her shoulders back with a Hera grace.

"You're beautiful, Melody," said Jim, who was moved almost to the point of tears. "You're the most beautiful woman in the world."

And in the eyes of Jim Kittering, she was. Whether or not she carried too much weight, almost any judge of womanly beauty would have conceded she did have beautiful breasts. Although her breasts were very full, they were firm and stood forth on their own. Her nipples and areolae, which were girlish rather than womanly, were tilted slightly upward and the semicircles where her breasts joined her chest were not overhung. Melody was one of the rare women who needed a brassiere only for comfort and not for aesthetic reasons.

Ten minutes later Melody said: "No, I won't take them off! I won't! I want to, you know I do, but I won't, I can't!"

"Melody, listen," said Jim, "listen to me, honey. I know I promised, but it's ridiculous. We've got one chance in a hundred thousand of living through this, probably less. We're going to drown and die, honey—they haven't found that island and they won't, and even if they do it won't make any difference. We're going to die, darling—don't deny us the only thing we have left!"

She began to cry. "But Jim . . . Jim . . . please don't ask me, don't ask me like that!"

"I want you, honey, I want you in my arms, I can't help it!"

"Oh, please don't ask me or I'll do it! Please don't ask!"

"Melody, the ship is going to *sink!*"

"But we can't be sure! It might not!"

"Melody, God would understand this and forgive us even if it *didn't* sink! But it will! You haven't got a thing to worry about! This ship is going to *sink*, Melody, I promise you it will, I guarantee it!"

"Oh, please don't ask me! I can't help myself either, don't you understand?"

"Melody!" said Jim with all the longing in his heart, and there was plenty of it. "I want to hold you in my arms!"

"All right," she said. "I will."

Jim quickly took off his jockey shorts, a thing he had not done while she herself still had on her panties. Naked, he sat and watched her as she pulled the panties down over her hips, over her knees, and off. Naked as the day she came a female child into the world, Melody lay there on the raft and stared up at him, an arm behind her head and tears still in her eyes. The moment of irresistible truth had arrived: a storm greater than Beulah had overwhelmed them and May Day was here.

As Jim lay beside her, moved half on her body and put his hands on her breasts, she said: "God forgive me. I couldn't help it, I couldn't. . . ."

Jim moved upon her, placed his hands on her shoulders, and lay his face between her breasts. "I love you so much," he said. "Oh, Melody, Melody. . . ."

Her body arched as she raised her pelvis hard against him and wound her arms around his back. "Oh, darling!" she cried. "Jim, I love you!!"

From somewhere, Jim heard another voice exclaim: "What the hell!" It was Florence and she had heard Melody. Disaster! Quickly, Jim propped on an elbow to put the Special on the air before the God's Love Marching Society could cancel it again. But—too late!

"What in the name of *Christ* do you two think you're doing?" yelled Florence. "Get up off of there! Get up this second!"

It was unbearable. For a brief instant the Special had almost flickered into a full picture, but the sound of Florence's furious voice startled Melody and caused her to give a violent wrenching twist of her hips; thus the flickering image swirled in upon itself and went out. To be so close, to be right there with the Special a tenth of a second from the air waves, to be pre-empted at the very last possible moment by another damnable Spectacular—it was intolerable.

"Get the hell out of here, Florence!" yelled Jim in a rage. "This is none of your goddamned business!"

"That's right!" said Melody. "Go away, Florence, you're embarrassing me! Go away, get out!"

"You goddamned fools!" yelled Florence. "They're lowering lifeboats! Providence Island is *three hundred yards away!* I've risked my life to come look for you again! Will you get up? Will you?"

Jim and Melody for several seconds stared in stunned surprise at Florence, then frantically scrambled to their feet and simultaneously bent down again, heads turning from side to side as they looked desperately for their clothes.

"I can't find my dress!" cried Melody. "I can't even find my pants, and where's my bra?"

"I can't find anything either!" cried Jim.

Weirdly, their clothes seemed to have vanished. It was not so weird as it appeared. As they removed their clothing bit by bit, they had placed it to the side of the life raft on the floor and the pitching of the ship had caused it to slide far back underneath the stacked deck chairs along the wall.

"There's no time for clothes!" said Florence. "They've already got one lifeboat lowered and the other one's half down!"

"But I can't go like *this!*" exclaimed Melody in horror. "I'm stark naked!"

"Will you *please* come?" asked Florence, half crying. "They won't wait for us!"

"But . . . but I can't go *naked!*" wailed Melody. "All those *men!*"

"They've seen a naked woman before. Melody, *please,* I risked my life for you, can't you risk nudity!"

"She's right—Melody, come on!" said Jim.

"Well . . . my panties anyhow—where are they?"

Florence shut her eyes tight and made fists of her hands. Then she looked at Melody and said calmly: "Melody, we can get to the beach if you'll just come. We're not only on the leeward side of the island, we're in the *eye* of the hurricane at this very minute and the sea is much calmer. The boats can make it through the reef! Will you *come,* Melody, and save your life and mine and Jim's too?"

"Yes, all right," said Melody.

"Hurry, for God's sake!" said Florence.

As they rushed across the lounge, Jim saw weird and eerie sunshine through the lounge portholes. He also noticed that the wind had died down. The sea was still extremely rough, with giant waves and even more gigantic rolling swells. However, it was not as wild as it had been; at least now it was possible to distinguish between the water and the air above it. A lifeboat could probably be lowered successfully if the ship did not take too bad a roll at the wrong moment. With tremendous luck, a lifeboat might even get through a reef.

As they hurried toward the lounge door, which Florence in her haste had not stopped to fasten with the loop of twine, the *S.S. Lorna Loone* hit a huge swell and slowly pitched high in the sea and rolled over, over, over and down, down, down as a terrible rumbling and thunderous groan came from its bowels. Jim, Melody, and Florence fell to their hands and knees as the swinging lounge door slammed shut with a crash.

"The wheat shifted!" said Jim. "That's the end of the lifeboats and the ship too—but there's still a chance, we might be able to swim ashore if it isn't too far."

As he spoke, Jim crawled on his hands and knees down the steep incline of the lounge floor and grabbed the door and pulled at it. He could not open it. The damp and swollen plywood was stuck immovably in the frame.

"Help me!" he cried. "Florence, you and Melody! I can't get this thing open."

"It doesn't matter," said Florence in a hopeless tone. "We could never swim through that reef. I saw it."

"We could try! Come on, Florence, help me, damn it!"

"It won't open, Jim," said Melody, who already was beside him and helping him pull at the knob.

Melody was right. All three of them could not budge the door even a fraction of an inch.

"Maybe we can get out of a porthole!" cried Jim, who had an awful feeling of claustrophobia. To drown was bad enough, but to be trapped in that lounge and drown was downright horrible. And the ship could not float for long, tilted over at whatever horrible angle it was. The lounge floor was so steep Jim could barely get up it to the porthole over the sofa.

"Impossible, Jim," said Florence. "You can't get through that thing, it's only about ten inches wide."

"I don't think you can either," said Melody.

"Well, I can sure as hell try!"

Florence and Melody were, of course, right. Jim got the porthole open and managed to stick his head and neck through it, but the diameter was simply not large enough for his shoulders to pass. The sight he saw, however, took his mind off his claustrophobia.

"There's the island! And one of the lifeboats upside down! I can see the reef and an old wreck on it, and this thing—"

Although the sun was shining with an eerie cheerfulness and a circle of blue sky was directly overhead, the sea was still very rough, with huge waves and even huger swells. The half-capsized *Lorna Loone* dipped down in a giant trough and Jim lost his footing on the slanted lounge floor and slipped from the porthole, almost falling all the way down on top of Melody and Florence. The observation that had been interrupted was that the ship, in some impossible crazy way, was still running and headed directly toward the reef. But on second thought he decided not to finish his sentence; there was no point in terrifying the women.

"I think this damn fool ship is still running somehow. I guess the propeller is still in the water and the engines are going, but there sure as hell isn't anybody up there on the bridge at the wheel. I saw one lifeboat turned over."

"It wouldn't have done us any good if we'd gotten out," said Florence.

Jim stuck his head again through the porthole. The reef was much nearer; some kind of powerful ground swell seemed to be carrying them swiftly toward it. It would all be over soon. He would say nothing to Melody and Florence until the last moment.

"What do you see now?" asked Melody.

"There's an old rusted wreck stuck on the reef," said Jim. "You'd swear it was a sister of the S.S. *Lorna Loone.* It looks as if it's been there for years."

Jim also could see the so-near-and-yet-so-far island behind the barrier reef, which was roiling furiously in the heavy waves and giant swells. They could not possibly have managed to swim over that coral; in an instant they would have been torn and broken into bits. The stupid stuck door had no meaning at all, really.

Jim sadly shook his head in the porthole as he stared at the relatively calm lagoon and the snowy white beach beyond it. In the calm of the eye of Beulah, the only sign of the storm that he could see on the island was a litter of coconut palm fronds on the beach and a number of coconut palms blown down. Beyond the beach he could see a parklike grove of coconut palms stretching toward a different type of vegetation that covered two fairly high hills, which looked like miniature versions of the Jungfrau and the Matterhorn.

"And I see the island," said Jim. "It looks very small, but it's pretty."

"Too bad we're not on it," said Florence.

"I'm afraid we won't ever be," said Jim quietly. "We're going to hit the reef."

It was true and Melody and Florence might as well know. For a moment he had thought the *Lorna Loone* would miss the reef and go back out to sea to an early watery grave, or maybe even steam on its side all the way to Bluefields in true *Loony Goony* fashion. A big wave had turned it briefly but a bigger wave had turned it back and it was now headed directly toward the reef about fifty yards to one side of the wreck. There was no point in watching. Jim lowered his head from the porthole and went down the slanted lounge floor to Florence and Melody.

"We're going to hit," he said. "But don't be afraid—maybe we'll stay on the reef like that old rusted wreck."

"How many of them do that?" asked Florence with a wry smile. "I think we'd better hold hands and get ready to die."

"Yes, I think so too," said Melody.

As Jim, Melody, and Florence reached out to hold hands and meet eternity, they were all thrown violently to the floor of the lounge by a tremendous, earsplitting, bonging crash. The *S.S. Lorna Loone* had veered and struck with terrific force not the reef, but the rusted wreck itself. The *Loony Goony* couldn't even hit the side of a reef! Jim, although half stunned and half blind from blood that had run into his eyes from his forehead, knew exactly what had happened.

"It hit that goddamn wreck! The stupid boat won't give us a chance at all! It's a pinhead, an idiot!" Jim could hear Melody groaning loudly. "Melody—what's the matter? Are you hurt?"

"My behind," she said, half crying. "I sat down on it very, very hard. Ohh, it hurts . . . oooohh!"

Jim crawled over to her. Florence seemed to have vanished. Melody was half lying by the lounge door. She was, of course, still stark naked and had both hands clutched to her bare rear end as she moaned and groaned. "Let me see," said Jim. "Roll over and let me look."

"No, I don't want to."

"Melody, good grief, this is no time for modesty! I want to see if you're hurt. Roll over now."

Reluctantly she turned on her side and he pulled away her hands. Each round cheek of her behind had a reddish-purple bruise the size of a baby's head. "You're just bruised," said Jim.

"Oooooh, it hurts!" said Melody.

"Hey," said Florence as she crawled from under a table. "Why isn't the ship moving?"

"What?" asked Jim.

"The ship isn't moving. It's perfectly still for the first time since we left Savannah."

Jim scrambled to his feet and climbed up toward the porthole. The angle was even steeper now; he almost could not get up it. "We might be on the reef," he said, "but I don't see how it's possible."

Jim stuck his head through the porthole. Wind blew his hair; a dark line was on the near horizon—Beulah was coming back, the eye was darkening, and soon would be gone on its way to Texas. The island was still there, the fronds of the palms now moving and the lagoon rippling. But the rusted wreck was gone, disappeared, vanished as if it never had been there.

"Do you know what this cockeyed ship did?" asked Jim. "It knocked that wreck off the reef and has taken its place. And we are well on it, too. The sea is very rough now and the ship isn't moving at all. Furthermore, when the storm comes back the wind will be reversed—this side of the island will be the windward side! Beulah will blow the *Loony Goony* even farther on the reef, maybe even into the lagoon and up on the beach! We are going to survive! We're going to live!"

A long silence greeted Jim's remarks; then he heard Florence begin to cry. Melody, however, did not cry. "That's wonderful, Jim, just wonderful!" she said. "But I am stark naked, I have got to find my clothes. Florence—don't cry, come and help me look. They must be in that closet somewhere and I've got to get dressed."

Florence replied, "Oh, to hell with your clothes, Melody. And to hell with *his* clothes too."

"I've got to find them. We can't go around naked. This is awful."

"You are out of your bloody minds, *both* of you!" said Florence. "I never saw the equal of such insanity in my life!"

"Neither did I," said Melody. "Thank God you found us when you did—that's all I can say, thank *God* you opened that door and stopped us before it was too late!"

"Yes, thank God for that," said Jim.

Although he felt a horrible ache of frustration, Jim was quite sincere. It was indeed fortunate Florence had discovered them when she did. However, the island seemed small and uninhabited. Would they perhaps be on it for a while? And if so, would not the moral situation be altered?

As Jim watched Melody walk across the canted lounge with a naked grace, Florence put her freckled hand on his arm and turned her head toward him in the eerie light of the eye of Beulah.

"Yes," said Jim solemnly, "thank God you discovered us when you did."

PART FIVE
Labor Day

THIRTEEN

Morgan's Treasure Cave

Dear Linda:

I don't know when you will get this letter—perhaps in a few days or weeks, perhaps in months, or perhaps never. I am stranded with two women, a dog, a cat, and a filthy-talking parrot on a tiny uninhabited island somewhere in the far west Caribbean. We have been here three weeks and have seen no ship, no boat, not even a jet contrail, just empty blue sea and blue sky with fair-weather clouds.

As nearly as we can reckon, the island lies about a hundred miles off the coast of either Honduras or Nicaragua. We had thought it was Providence Island, a little-known but historic dot in the sea once settled unsuccessfully by Puritans. It seems too small even for Providence, a tiny speck itself on the basis of our meager information, but we call it that and the name is fitting because it is a wonder we are alive; the entire crew and ship's officers were lost in Hurricane Beulah, of which I am sure you must have heard since it was a tremendous storm.

The two women with whom I am shipwrecked are a missionary's wife and a Lesbian writer. No doubt that strikes you as a seriocomic variation of Don Juan in hell. Well, yes and no. I will admit lately it has begun to seem a bit hellish around here from the Don's point of view, but then, he was an ignorant fellow with a one-track mind and there is more both in heaven and hell than he knew in his philosophy.

So here I am, abiding in chaste Christian love with two women on an uninhabited island. Doesn't sound much like me, does it? Frankly, I have been too tired to worry about it. Until recently, I have been working myself half to death establishing a safe habitation on this island. Under such circumstances, I assure you Don Juan would not be running around at night playing a guitar below balconies with a red rose in his mouth, he would be home asleep, snoring.

The women have worked very hard too, a bit reluctantly since they expected to be rescued in a day or two and saw no need for such effort. Women, I am afraid, in some ways are slightly like grasshoppers, if you don't mind my saying so. The missionary's wife is named Melody and the writer's name is Florence. They are both rather remarkable women and I am lucky to be with them, although I really have had to bully them to make them do this work and I'm sure in recent days they would have preferred the company of our pets to mine. As I said, we have a dog (Rufus), a cat (Joan) and a parrot (Robbie) with us here— these were pets of the crew abandoned in the storm. The dog has proved useful in many ways, the cat catches an occasional bat in our cave home and otherwise does nothing, and the parrot says "Fock you" all day long in a Spanish accent.

The writer Florence is a very sensitive, goodhearted, and homely woman with a considerable dry wit that seems to have been lost somewhat under the pressure of being stranded on this island. She once described herself to me with a wry irony as a thirty-eight-year-old virgin. I'm afraid she's not looking to lose her virginity. She is a Lesbian and that is bad news for us on this island. She is not, thank God, aggressive—I mean she does not smoke cigars and growl. Actually, Florence is hard to make out, she's quite feminine in many ways. I like her very much and to tell the truth I am worried about her. She seems to me very lonely and miserable and I am concerned about the problem her nature might cause us here. The thing worries me and I believe it worries Florence too. She goes off on solitary walks with the dog and seems frightened of me—she stammers, trembles, can't look at me, shrinks away. It was very bad a week or so ago . . . maybe she had her period or something. Recently, praise God, she has calmed down and is more like her old self.

As for Melody, my other lady companion here—she also has had trouble adjusting to life on the island. In fact, I am afraid she is even more miserable than Florence. She bursts into tears at the bat of an eye, complains of stomach-ache, headache, backache, weakness and fatigue, and every other ache and pain you can think of. She has fits of temper, formidable temper—and believe me, when she's angry she's no one to trifle with. Florence is afraid of her when she's mad, and so am I a little bit. But usually she doesn't get angry, she cries. Say the least thing to her and her lip begins to tremble and she goes off and broods in a corner with the cat, petting it while the damn thing purrs in her lap. At least Florence takes walks, but Melody is miserable and won't let herself enjoy anything. The only pleasure she has is playing an accordion I found in a crewman's cabin, but she seldom plays it. I guess she also enjoys her baths; she is constantly on her way to a secluded salt-water pool at the northern end of the island—Florence calls it "Melody's Bathtub." She's a study, this one. You'd think it was Susanna in the Bible when she takes down that towel and says: "I . . . am going . . . for my bath." I guess the ostentatious announcement is to warn me not to sneak up there like an elder and peep on her.

What else can I say about her? She is a devout medical missionary's wife and graduate registered nurse, devoted to her husband and I think well-married, although I gather they have some problems in some areas. (The husband recently had to be flown from South America to the Duke Medical Center with some "noncritical illness" and she has been very worried about this.) What else? She's surprisingly broad-minded and liberal in some ways, very naive and narrow-minded in others. There's a childlike quality about her, an innocence that usually is real and occasionally is affected. She can be startlingly intelligent at times, dense to the point of opacity at other times. She will tell a lie and look you right in the eye like a child when she does it, but she is fundamentally truthful. She's opinionated, intolerant, self-righteous, prudish, and almost pathologically modest. She's feminine, emotional, gentle, sentimental, and extremely tenderhearted. I guess she is also passionate and sensual, and very ashamed of it. She is twenty-eight years old and although she dresses in a most unbecoming manner she is a very handsome, even beautiful woman with a full figure, a lovely smile, and deep blue eyes that never show cruelty even when she's angry, and I believe that tells it all or most of it anyhow.

So these are my two women, my two grasshoppers on this island. They still insist we will be rescued soon by fishermen, but their faith is waning and I myself see no likelihood of it. The island, I am afraid, is in the midst of absolutely nowhere. It is too tiny to be inhabited by more than a handful of people, has no harbor at all, insufficient level ground for a landing strip, and I do not see what practical use it could be to anybody at any time and I don't know why anyone would come here. We might be on the place God knows how long, months or even years, until some wandering yacht or survey ship happens to come by. But neither Melody nor Florence will admit this as yet. They keep saying fishermen will come and that an alarm is out for the *S.S. Lorna Loone* and the Navy is looking for us.

I don't think so. The ship had no radio the last thirty hours and it sent no distress call. There's no way the Navy or the Coast Guard could know within five hundred miles where this ship might be and I'm sure they will merely assume it sank to the bottom of the ocean.

Which it damn near did. Only an accident saved our lives—we were trapped (or *thought* we were trapped) in the ship's lounge during the worst of it and none of us remembered the emergency exit to the passenger deck through the life-raft closet. It was lucky we didn't because the lounge was much the safest place for us. We huddled in there claustrophobically all night long while the wind screamed and almost blew the wreck off the reef. I had expected the wind would blow it up farther on the reef, but the wind did not blow straight toward the island but diagonally. The captain, a kind of drunken idiot, was supposed to be approaching the island leeward to the wind, he said so to Florence, but I think he got mixed up about the direction in which cyclonic disturbances revolve in the Northern Hemisphere! At any rate, the returning wind almost blew us off the reef; we could hear the hull scraping on the coral and feel the thing shuddering.

The irony is we weren't trapped in there at all. The next morning, when I was struggling to open the jammed lounge door, it suddenly struck me there was an emergency exit behind the deck furniture in the closet. I wonder if I knew about it subconsciously but felt we were safer in the lounge?

Well, this is certain: if we had gone on deck during the storm we would have been blown overboard, and we probably *would* have gone on deck when the ship started crunching on that reef. I think I knew about the emergency exit but suppressed the knowledge out of an instinct for survival, an amazing thing when you stop to reflect on it. I wonder how many truths of vital importance we hide from ourselves—knowledge too painful, too dangerous, or too destructive? Or knowledge we simply prefer not to face because we cannot cope with it?

In any event, forgetting the emergency exit was a "fortunate" thing. It was simple enough the next morning to move the deck furniture and open the door to the passenger deck. The ship is lying half on its side on the reef and the decks are so tilted it's difficult to get around on it, which is one reason we've had to move to the island; the ship would be unlivable even if it were safe. And it isn't. We had to abandon the ship because of the danger that it might at any moment slide off the reef and go down God knows how far to the bottom of the ocean.

There is no trace of the old wreck originally lodged on the reef. This island is of volcanic origin, a pinnacle mountaintop just breaking the surface of the sea. The reef is mostly very close offshore; the wreck is only about eighty yards from the beach, and the lagoon is not much wider at the north end of the island, maybe two hundred yards or so. The water on the ocean side is dark blue and I'm sure is very deep.

The wreck is just hanging there; it grates on the coral whenever a big wave or swell hits it. The fool ship may stay there for years, but it wouldn't surprise me to look out some morning and find it gone. Anyhow, we had to get off the wreck as soon as possible. Both the ship's regular lifeboats were destroyed in the storm and I don't think I could have launched or handled one of them in any case. We managed to squeeze the life raft through the door and get it out on the passenger deck and drag it along to the freight deck over to the lagoon side of the reef and launch it. The bow of the ship is across the coral and slanted down nearly to water level. We went in the hold and found a gigantic pile of cases of Dinty Moore beef stew, plus a smaller pile of cases of grapefruit juice. We took three cases of the stew and three cases of the grapefruit juice and lugged them up on deck and put them in the raft and paddled the thing across the lagoon to the beach, and thus we were delivered to the shores of Providence Island where we now abide in chaste Christian love and reasonable comfort.

Since we first stepped out of peril onto the island, I have made I don't know how many trips back and forth hauling food and supplies from the wreck to the beach. Hundreds, I don't know; all I know is that it's the hardest work I've ever done. Paddling ashore is nothing, it's the hauling that damn near killed me. It'd be brute labor at best and the difficulty of getting around on the canted decks makes it infinitely worse. I'm simply not used to such physical exertion and for most of the past three weeks have gone to bed every night so exhausted I could barely hold my head up.

Well, chaste Christian love kept me going, plus no alcohol, no tobacco. Yes, that's right—not only do we have no sex on this island, we have no cigarettes and no whisky! On the second morning Melody played a diabolical trick on Florence and me. While Florence and I were crawling through the crew's living quarters, the pious little bitch threw every bottle of rum, gin, and whisky overboard, then capped it off by throwing all the cigarettes overboard too! Florence and I were so infuriated we could have killed her. She sniffled and wept phonily and said she was trying to help us.

However, believe it or not, both Florence and I are glad she did it. I have come to think it was the right thing to remove alcohol from the scene here. Besides which, I feel better than in years. Imagine it—no cigarettes and nothing to drink for three weeks! Fantastic! I feel fifteen years younger and am amazed by the energy I have. I sleep better, see better, the smoking cough is all gone—it's like being out of jail. I don't need sleeping pills here or push pills either, and figure I have lost about ten pounds; am sun-tanned, healthy—you wouldn't know me.

Of course, being so healthy and everything does have its drawbacks, such as *frustrato terrifico*. Chaste Christian love is subtle; it builds you up and then tears you down. I've noticed it especially these last couple of days, which we have spent resting from our labors. The mind tilts, the mind reels. I haven't felt like this since I was sixteen. Do you know something? It has been *one month* since I've had any contact with humanity's better half and that's incredible.

However, as someone once said, "sex isn't the most important thing in life," and if you don't believe me ask our pets—they are all celibates and don't seem to mind it a bit. The women love the animals beyond belief and I am glad for their sake we have them. I found two of them on one of my early trips back to the wreck our first day here, the dog and the parrot—the cat turned up next day meowing in a cupboard in the galley.

Florence, who gives names to everything, calls the dog "Rufus" on the grounds that he looks like her editor in New York. She has an awful-looking editor if that's true. I'd thought I heard a dog whining even before we left the ship and when I went back I found Rufus in the cabin of one of the crewmen. He heard me while I was poking around the ship and began to bark. The parrot was cursing in the next cabin. He has a very filthy tongue, this bird, and says a number of things but mostly a tiresome, Spanish-accented "Fock you"—it's croupy and indistinct and Melody kept asking, "What's he saying?" I finally explained it to her. She eyed the bird with compassion and interest. "Why, the poor thing," she said. "How could anybody be so mean? I'll have to teach it some nice words." Florence calls the parrot Robert E. Lee for some reason. As I said, she's a namer. The cat was singed in the radio-shack fire and she calls it Joan of Arc.

The way the women carry on over these pets is slightly disgusting, but I suppose they are frightened to be stranded here and the animals reassure them or something. I'll admit the dog has earned his keep. He is fairly large and of a mixture of breeds; he seems part Irish setter, part standard poodle, and part God knows what. He is a kind of brindle color and has woolly jaws and a solemn expression. As Florence says, he is a serious dog, an intellectual and thinking dog. The animal means a lot to her and he certainly has been helpful. He has twice caught and killed iguanas and four days ago caught a small, wild pig. Much more important, he also discovered "Morgan's Treasure Cave" and a fresh-water spring. Not much water and even less treasure, but some water anyhow and the cave gives us our happy little home where we abide together in chaste Christian love on Providence Island.

Maybe it really is Providence Island, but if so the Puritans were out of their minds to try to found a colony here. It is a tiny place more or less circular, with a reef on one side and jagged, rough rocks on the other. The reef is on the easterly or windward side, exposed to the trade winds, which blow very pleasantly nearly all the time. The climate here for the most part is Paradise Type One—balmy, mild, dreamy tropical, with some rain in heavy quick showers. The surrounding water is very beautiful; you know, of course, the jewel-like greens and blues of the water of the Virgin Islands far to the east of here . . . well, this water seems to me even more beautiful, though I suppose it is about the same as that of St. John or Magen's Bay.

The eastern side of the island is much more lush than the Virgins, however. It rains here more and we have found (or rather, the dog found) a small fresh-water spring and pool at the foot of the southern hill. The little beach is one of the best I have seen anywhere. Imagine a perfect crescent of sand and fantastic emerald water that is crystal clear, with a beautiful coconut-palm grove in the background. But the most striking feature of the beach, aside from the incredible water of the lagoon, is a beautiful sheer rocky cliff that overlooks a little horseshoe cove at the northern end. The cliff is only a few yards from the beach and even has a huge shade tree on a small knoll at its base. It's a very beautiful island and would make a fabulous location for a modern resort hotel of the kind that has ruined so many islands in this sea, but since the only way to get here is by small boat, I guess it will be spared until Detroit perfects a practical flying saucer.

The basic topography of the island consists of two good-sized hills with a "meadow" in between. The hills, especially the northerly and more rugged one, are covered with dense bushes, cacti, and a few trees —mahogany trees, Florence says, although who knows what they are. The lower land between the beach and the hills—on the eastern or windward side of the island—has a beautiful parklike grove of coconut palms, which I do not think are native to the Caribbean and therefore must have been planted at some time by people.

This made me feel at first that maybe workers would come here to "harvest" the coconuts; on one of my shows we had a commercial showing this, the "copra" and how they get the oil and make shampoo out of it, and how the natives go out every six months singing songs and so forth. I was sure for about a minute this place was a coconut farm. But no—we'd see the piled-up debris of previous such "harvests," big ratty piles of coconut choppings, and we'd also see spur markings up the palms from being climbed. There's no indication these palms have been touched for years or even decades.

I think the trouble is there's no harbor and only a tiny opening in the barrier reef. The leeward or westerly side of the island is rocky, barren, and impossible to reach by any kind of boat. There is no reef; the entire coastline of this side of the island is made up of piled, jagged, face-of-the-moon rocks. This is where most of the iguanas hang out. Florence likes it and goes over there with Rufus. But to sum up, I do not see how any boat other than a very small one could possibly make a landing on this island.

We call the two hills the Matterhorn and the Jungfrau—my own small contribution to local place names. The cave is located about two-thirds up the one we call the Jungfrau. The other hill, the Matterhorn, has a great deal of prickly cacti and many bushes all over it and we have not explored it too much. But I don't think anything is up there, it is just a hill. It does have a magnificent view from the rock ledge on top, an odd sofa-shaped formation Florence calls "Morgan's Armchair." It's closer to the beach and the lagoon than the Jungfrau. The view is of the lagoon and it is spectacular. You can also see the northern end of the island, including the little crater-shaped pool known as Melody's Bathtub. (In fact, I once had a clear if distant view of Melody taking her bath, so I guess an elder did peep on Susanna after all. Not intentionally, however. I was up there looking for a ship or a sail and happened to glance down and see her. She has a figure that can be recognized some distance away.)

The other hill, the Jungfrau, is to the south of the island and is slightly larger but not nearly so steep and rugged and bushy. It has a plateaulike summit of rounded rock we call "Morgan's Pillow." The view from here is also magnificent, a spectacular panoramic vista of the entire island but especially the narrower part of the lagoon, the palm grove, and the southern and western rocks.

There's a freaky feature down at the south end of the island, a sort of blowhole channel eroded through solid rock. It's inland fifty feet or so but connects subterraneously to the sea. When a big wave comes ashore, air is caught and compressed and all of a sudden, *Whoooosh*—up comes a spume of air and spray, mostly air. If you hold out a palm frond, the blast will snatch it right out of your hand and blow it fifty or sixty feet in the air. It makes a kind of "thoomping" noise and the effect is a bit like the Jolly Green Giant suddenly and mightily breaking wind. Florence calls this "Morgan's Asshole," to Melody's horror.

"Oh, what a name," she says. "Oh, what a vulgar remark, Florence."

Her priggishness provokes me sometimes. She is always criticizing me and Florence for our filthy language. I am often tempted to shake her up, really shock her, suggest to her that language is not filthy—only man's inhumanity to man is filthy. "Now Melody, every person has an asshole, even Morgan, even you." I'm afraid it would just make her cry. Her modesty is even more ridiculous and exasperating than her priggishness. You should see the clothes she wears—full-length dresses in the tropics. There is one dress I especially hate, a pale gray thing she had on when I first met her.

However, *both* these women are almost pathologically modest—Melody out of prudery and Florence out of shame at her lack of voluptuousness. My favorite spot on the island is the little horseshoe cove under the cliff not far from the big tree on the knoll. I often swim there, but neither of the women will swim with me. Florence sometimes sneaks down the beach and swims by herself, but Melody, never—she has no suit and is too modest to borrow Florence's, which she says is too small for her. Madness. Such shame at the appearance and image of the human body is pathetic.

(However, Melody's modesty is weakening. She has lately begun sleeping with her pajama tops unbuttoned at night and her breasts bare. Florence gets *more* modest, though. The other day by accident —and believe me, it *was* an accident—I happened to intrude on her when she was naked and I thought she would literally collapse and die. The irony, surprisingly enough, is that Florence has a rather pretty figure, sort of like a young girl—little breasts and everything, including hips more feminine than you'd think to look at her in the mannish suits she wears. Of course, she has freckles all over and she *is* kind of thin. I'm not saying she's Sophia Loren. But physically she's a woman, there's no doubt about it. As for Melody, there's no reason on earth for *her* to be ashamed of her body. They are both nuts. To see the blushing and the gasping is enough to make a man become a philosophical nudist.)

I keep getting off on my grasshoppers. It is now night and before it gets too late I want to write you about "Morgan's Treasure Cave." We found it, or rather Rufus found it, our first day ashore. Inspired by the affection shown him by the women (Florence actually hugged him and kissed him on his woolly jaws) and happy to be free on land, the dog went racing all to hell over everywhere and after a while commenced a terrific ruckus.

Florence went to see what was going on and found him in a good-sized cave barking at some tiny bats that were swooping all over the place. I lighted a palm frond and smoked out the bats and we have been living in the cave ever since, which Melody decided at once was probably where Morgan buried his treasure—thus the name, "Morgan's Treasure Cave."

It was a very fortunate discovery, because the cave gives us ideal shelter. It is cool during the day and it is dry. I think this is the rainy season because it rains like hell on the island once or twice a day—clouds suddenly accumulate and down she pours like cats and dogs for half an hour, then it's all over and the sun comes out. I don't know what we would have done for shelter if Rufus had not found the cave, because the fact is, even in Paradise one needs protection from sun, wind, and rain.

The entrance to the cave is large but half hidden by bushes and I don't know if we would have found it without Rufus. Maybe, but the entrance is not all that easy to see even though it is big enough to drive a car through. The cave consists of one large chamber about forty feet long and varying from twenty to twenty-five feet wide, ending in a very narrow opening that leads on, I suppose, to more cave, but we cannot get in there and neither can the dog. The cat goes in there but doesn't report anything back to us about it. A few bats still try from time to time to go back in there—we have swatted and killed most of them—and the cat chases in after them and catches them and eats them.

During these past three weeks, until a couple of days ago we were constantly hauling food and supplies from the wreck and have rigged up a home here and it is not too bad. Our "bedrooms" are located to the right side of the cave as you enter, where the ceiling slopes down fairly low. I have my "room," and Florence and Melody have theirs, a bit bigger than mine, and we also have a "living room." We have strung ropes and draped blankets over them so as to form partitions, which provide at least a little privacy, if not much.

You'd be amazed at the effort required to do this and I'm afraid I've had to bully the women slightly in order to get them to help me. They kept saying we'd be rescued any day now and there was no need to wear ourselves out. Frankly, although women are wonderful and I love them, it can be aggravating to be stuck on an uninhabited island with a couple of them. It's hair-raising, the struggle I have explaining the simplest thing to them, such as: "Suppose we *aren't* rescued any day now?"

Since the wreck could have gone off the reef at any time, it was an urgent necessity to get food and supplies off it as soon as humanly possible. We are now, thank God, comfortably settled, the brute toil is over. I have hauled enough food from the wreck to last us for years—most of it, eccch, Dinty Moore beef stew (we are already sick of it). We have real mattresses, sheets, and blankets and even a few modest pieces of furniture, all of which I managed to transport on the life raft. Morgan's Treasure Cave is quite cozy, you might even call it "homey."

It is late and I am tired. I am typing these pages on Florence's portable typewriter, which she insisted on lending me even though she is writing something herself. I have for light a kerosene lantern and I am staring at a blanket partition on the other side of which is the women's "bedroom." Not much of a partition—the blankets don't really hold together too well. And not much of a bedroom either—mattresses on the stone floor, packing cases for end tables, clothes hanging on railroad spikes driven in the wall.

Well, it's not the Ritz and it's not a Y.W.C.A. dormitory. No, it's Morgan's Treasure Cave, piled and stacked high with the precious wealth of chaste Christian love. Yes, indeed, wall to wall and floor to ceiling, we have it here, the thing men seek and seldom find, a priceless trove of pure, uh-huh, love. And I'm getting slightly fed up with it, too. I suspect I am not the only one who is getting weary of chaste Christian love, if you want to know the truth.

The women also have a kerosene lantern and they are awake. Florence, I believe, is writing a poem. Melody earlier in the evening was writing something too, but the last time I peeked through the blanket she was reading the Bible, propped on a pillow with her pajama tops unbuttoned and her breasts bare. As I said, her modesty is weakening. She was aware of me, I am sure. She looked up from the Bible, stared in pale silence toward the blanket partition, and made no effort to cover herself. Tonight at dinner she reached across me for salt and leaned her breast against my arm. She did the same thing at lunch, a bit less obviously. It has been apparent for about a week she is even more sick and tired of chaste Christian love than I am. She is trying in a rather transparent way to seduce me and if she keeps on she is going to succeed gloriously.

A small thing, not of too much significance perhaps, but not altogether reassuring either. I happened to wake up early this morning and peeped through the blanket and found Florence in bed with Melody. They were both sound asleep, both naked from the waist up. It was a touching little tableau. Melody was asleep on Florence's shoulder and Florence had her arms tenderly around her. I'm sure there was nothing "Lesbian" about it, at least not on Melody's part; she behaved in the morning as if nothing at all had happened. But I don't think Florence's feelings were altogether sisterly. She, too, I have no doubt, is sick and tired of chaste Christian love.

Let's face it: chaste Christian love is the greatest, but it gets tiresome after a while. That's the truth, Linda. Of the two hundred monkeys that roam this earth, 199 of them are hairy and mate by the moon; the other is hairless and mates by the stars. I certainly agree with your favorite truism that "sex is not the most important thing in life," but let's be sensible, it is not the least important thing either. In fact, after food and shelter, I'd say it rates fairly high on a list of human needs, wouldn't you agree? Of course we have successful celibates in this world, a few of them, but I think a sex life even without love is essential to the mental and spiritual health of nearly all men and women. Combined with the deeper need for love, it's an overwhelming necessity as fundamental to life as oxygen is fundamental to blood. I know this is true as far as I am concerned and I am sure it is equally true of Melody and Florence. Therefore, from a strategic point of view, I wonder how long chaste Christian love can or should endure in Morgan's Treasure Cave?

I am very tired and very depressed. Have read through this letter and apart from my description of the island—which is harmless enough if not too inspired—I'm afraid it's impossible. The difficulty isn't just the collapse in the last few paragraphs; the entire letter is impossible. A pinhead could read my comments on Melody and know I love her and she loves me, that we are both half crazy with desire and on the very verge of the sin of sins—all of that was plain even earlier in the letter, and it is not a matter I had intended to discuss with my wife.

Well, the fact is, I am in a serious dilemma on this island and I don't know what I should do. I guess I have just wanted to "talk" to somebody about it. After all, I can't talk to Melody or Florence and the parrot only says nasty things to me.

It is *not* a simple problem. Perhaps it *sounds* like a simple problem —the magazine cartoon of man and blonde on a spit of sand beneath a palm implies a total and delightful absence of responsibility, and I guess for that reason is a common daydream of men and of many women. Whee, perfect license, and inevitable, too! Imagine any woman you like on that spit of sand beneath the palm—she's yours. Imagine any man you like—he's yours. The most beautiful or handsome movie star thus becomes the plausible lover of a pimple-faced stockroom clerk or a flat-chested secretary.

However, I am afraid there is no such thing as total and delightful absence of responsibility, not if you stop to think for a moment. The truth about the situation here, painful and tiresome as it may be, is that a love affair between Melody and me on this island could destroy her marriage and her life. Unless we assume we will be here forever—an unreasonable assumption—that is the grim reality and it must be confronted. In the first place, she'd probably get pregnant, we have no means of preventing it exactly. Suppose she goes to her husband three months from now, six months from now or a year from now, either pregnant or with a baby and he says, "Jezebel! Whore of Babylon!" and throws her out?

And he might react in just that way. From what she tells me, he is naive and has problems and fears about sex. But he is a good man and loves her and is a well-suited husband for her. And she loves him too—not romantically, the way she does me, perhaps, but she loves him in a human way that might even be deeper really. Wouldn't it be very sad and even tragic for her marriage to be destroyed? Wouldn't it be worth a little effort and sacrifice to prevent such a thing, especially since—who knows?—we may be rescued from this island tomorrow or next week?

Florence is another reason to leave Melody alone. As things stand, I believe Florence can control herself, but what would happen to her if I were living and sleeping with Melody in the enforced intimacy and lack of privacy of Morgan's Treasure Cave? We all must have shelter, there is nowhere else for us to go or Florence either, and we could not send her away alone even if there were. It's a slightly clinical but unavoidable thought: a man and woman cannot make love in utter silence—Florence would hear the kisses, the sighs, the heavy breathing, and all the sounds of love. How could she stand such a thing?

I don't think she could. It would be the torments of Tantalus for her, when she herself has nothing, nothing at all but her dog Rufus to keep her company on her lonely walks. Any fool could predict what would happen. It would be unbearable for her and sooner or later she would go to Melody . . . and who knows what the consequences of that would be?

There's no predicting, but I'm convinced the greatest danger would be to Florence herself. Whatever her fears or foibles, she is a hypersensitive, highly emotional, and very intelligent woman. No matter what happened as the result of some kind of "pass" at Melody, Florence would be in trouble. Perhaps there are more feminine women who are *less* homosexually inclined than Melody, but if so, I have never met one; I'm sure she doesn't even know what a "Lesbian" is, not really. Almost certainly she would be appalled and shrink back in horror, in which case Florence would face total isolation. On the other hand, Melody is very tenderhearted and I suppose it is possible she might briefly tolerate a certain amount of "unnatural" behavior out of pity. I don't think Melody could endure such a thing for long. And I don't think Florence could either. I believe she has severe conflict about her "Lesbianism." Maybe I am wrong, maybe she would feel no guilt at all, no remorse on my account or Melody's, but I had a dream last night Florence killed herself, I dreamed I found her broken and bleeding body on the rocks of the western shore of this island.

I am afraid the argument in favor of chaste Christian love is overwhelming. 1) An affair between Melody and me would probably wreck her marriage and thereby wreck her life as well. At the same time, 2), such an affair would subject Florence to unbearable pressure that probably would lead to some kind of an emotional breakdown and perhaps even worse.

The situation on this island *is* a variation on Don Juan in hell—the Don with a conscience, the Don looking ahead at the consequences of his acts. I think the best thing for me to do would be to castrate myself as quickly and painlessly as possible.

I have read over this letter again, and have read over the last crucial pages of it twice. I have also thought about this entire dilemma for a sweaty half hour and I see no way out. The argument is irrefutable. I have locked poor Don Juan in hell and thrown away the key. An affair between Melody and me *would* in all likelihood wreck her marriage, and such an affair *would* put unbearable pressure on Florence. I find no justification to risk wrecking that marriage and also risk driving an emotionally crippled woman to self-destruction. The Don must burn.

Well, it will be an achievement of sorts to go down in history as the man who was shipwrecked on an uninhabited island with an attractive, passionate, loving woman and couldn't get laid. Yes, that will be a record. They will shoot, so to speak, at that record for a long time.

Or am I being a bit masochistic about this thing? Am I making a real moral evaluation or am I punishing Don Juan for his previous crimes? Would chaste Christian love be beastly and unfair both to these women and me, and is the argument in its favor a rationalization to avoid rather than accept human responsibility on this island? Am I reacting to Melody and Florence not as the human beings they really are but as ghosts of a red-haired bridesmaid in a boathouse and a wife driving away in the rain?

Or was I right to begin with? Are the above questions a half-formed but cunning rationalization to get the Don out of hell? Is chaste Christian love, horrible and absurd though it is, the only moral answer on this island?

I don't know. Why did I ever sit down in that living room and start thinking about that squid and his goddamn shell?

I guess the answer is fairly obvious and I'm afraid the irony of this letter has long since become apparent. I don't want to hurt these women, I want to help and protect them both. I want to do the right thing, I really and truly do, but I don't know what it is. And so, ironically enough, I ask another woman, or her shadow, in a letter I cannot mail, to tell me what is right.

The truth is there is no one to tell me. The day has come when I have to decide it for myself.

Blonde, blue-eyed, beautiful Linda, are you there? I won't destroy this. The day may also come when you should and must read these words. Until then, I send you my love from Morgan's Treasure Cave.

FOURTEEN

Hell's Half Acre

Dear Diary:

This beautiful Sunday on the island finds me depressed and badly bewildered. "Mysterious machine of the mind," indeed. An almost Mandarin tact guides him. Yes, an Oriental subtlety. I can't keep up with him, I admit it, he has me confused. Although I am sure he does not believe in the Dragon, he insists on pretending he is worried about an "unnatural" interest on my part in Melody, whom he continues for some obscure reason to torment with loving chastity. The son of a bitch is as oblique as Fu Manchu. According to sheep's entrails I examined recently, this is what he really thinks:

"There is no Dragon, Florence, no Dragon at all. Dragons need belief in order to live and I don't believe in yours. I have looked into your heart and I know what is there. The more I mockingly pretend to believe in the Dragon, the more I talk with you of the mysterious machine of the mind, the more I stare at you with pain and sympathy and an amusement that is not cruel . . . the more the Dragon sighs and cries and dies."

Speaking of Dragons, a tawny-haired, ferret-eyed, small-minded girl named Verta Killington Rhabb told me an interesting filthy story several years ago about a couple of Dragons living in a stinky den down in Hell's Half Acre and I would like to tell you that story now, dear Diary, except it's too filthy and ghastly and awful. The story itself isn't so bad—the Vaseline and the blood and the semen do not bother me much—but the ending is pure wormheart. A nasty comedy suddenly contains a grain of truth and that's unendurable.

As Tolstoy said to Gorky: "You can't write that!" Gorky had told him about a drunken peasant woman with her skirts up and urinating all over herself in a railroad station while her children watched in horrified shame. It was filthy and ghastly and awful, and kind of funny in a gruesome way, just like Verta Killington Rhabb's tale about the Dragons. "You can't write that, it's too dreadful," said Tolstoy. But then he reconsidered and declared: "No. You *must* write that."

Oh, to hell with it, it's too filthy. What do the Russians know about it, anyhow? They're great when it comes to political theory, but they just never could get the hang of fiction. As the old lady said as she took her son-in-law's eyeballs out of the refrigerator, "Life is hard enough as it is, without reading about nasty people who eat eyeballs." Dragons? I don't see any Dragons, except maybe a few.

Since there are a few, I will describe the Dragon's abode. That is as close as I will allow myself to approach the revolting subject, unless the temptation to tell an interesting filthy story overwhelms me against my better judgment.

On the western side of the island, iguanas run and hide among purple rocks and little wild pigs hunt sure-footed on jumbled boulders for shellfish in the sea—uggch, terrible.

On the barren western coast of this lost speck in the sea, iguanas scurry on lizard business and little pigs crunch decaying clams in rocky pockets as foam spreads over trotters balanced in a delicate precision —uggch! Are you crazy or something, some kind of nut? Simple!—the way is not "Look, Daddy, the Dragon lives here!" but rather, "Father dear, can you detect a faint scent of sulphur?"

Decaying clams, indeed. Might as well say rotten seafood. Try again, please. Concentrate. Keep it simple. Pretend *he* is reading it, that ought to inspire you. After all, look what he said about the girl on Cape Cod: "A strange book for you to write, Florence. The girl was so lonely, so terribly lonely, and you don't seem lonely to me at all." Mao himself couldn't top that, it's out of Fu Manchu's league. But never mind, once again, please. Concentrate and keep it simple.

On the dead western shore, iguanas scuttle and little pigs splash in rocky pockets of the sea. The dog loves this desolate land, in particular the stone promontory at the northwestern end of the island. He barks, he runs, he plunges into small rocky pools and shakes his coat in the sunshine. It gives us much joy and relief, this area of desolation where roaring waves cascade ashore and form rock-bound ponds in which mute iguanas and little pigs wade.

The song is there but I can't recognize the melody. Ah, well, *c'est la guerre*. Dear Lord, why is it I so love such words as scurry, scuttle, cascade, and promontory? Why is this, dear Lord, who made us all and gave us our foolish nature and character, along with our hopeless and absurd wishes and wants? "The great writer is not afraid of banality," said Tolstoy. Me, I'm terrified of it. That's why I write occasionally with artful cleverness and never with Tolstoyan power. I have known the limits of my gift for three years. But then, writing has never been enough for me, I have always been miserable.

I call it "Hell's Half Acre" and a strange mansion rises there, a most peculiar dwelling place lonely and made of dead rock; the architecture is odd, windows it has none, and neither warmth nor water, just a dark and gloomy den, that's all, a suitable place for a Dragon to hide and snort occasional preternatural smoke or even once in a while blow a breath of reluctant fire at some unwary maiden who might wander by. An absurd habitation for a living and breathing woman able to bring into the world a Tolstoy or a Beethoven or just a normal human child . . . but satisfactory to a Dragon.

"Absurd"—another word I got from him, among many. I find myself talking like him, thinking like him, joking like him, stretching in the morning like him, sighing at sprinkled diamonds in the night sky like him—I do everything like him, except love Melody like him.

I got very annoyed with her this morning, partly, I suppose, because of guilt about last night but mostly because of her unbearable misplaced compassion. I have a neurotic fixation on him, certainly; I had that even as long ago as Savannah. I don't deny the fixation, I don't even deny a certain amount of perverse sexual attraction; I dreamed last night, as I have dreamed repeatedly, that I was naked in his arms and he was kissing me and about to make love to me. So much for dreams. When I am awake I can't endure him to touch me. It's idiotic to consider my neurotic fixation an equivalent to her romantic and unqualified love for him.

But that's what she did. I was laughing this morning at something he had said, something very funny—and he can be very funny—and I caught her staring pensively and rather sadly at me. She knew what I was laughing at but she asked me anyhow and I told her and she said: "You like him very much, don't you?"

I am afraid I gave her an icy stare and replied: "The son of a bitch reminds me of my brother and my father rolled into one. *You* might not mind being called a 'grasshopper,' Melody, but *I* resent it. And I resent the way he has bullied us and ordered us around and worked us half to death, you with your period last week and bad cramps and me with broken ribs not even completely healed. He's a hateful bully and he's so vain he thinks *any* woman would love him. Well, I'm not *any* woman. I'm not his grasshopper and I'm not his slave either. As for 'liking' him, I'll be glad to get off this island and see the last of him, if you want to know."

It bothered her all morning. Melody is the kind of woman who won't change her mind once she's got a notion in her head. "Dear Florence," she says to me at lunch, my hand in hers and tears in her eyes, "I do love you, please always be my friend." What a pain in the ass she is. That sweet compassion of hers is too much to endure, all the more so since it's so godawful authentic; she *does* love me and her tears of sympathy were real, if misplaced and inappropriate.

Oh, yes, they were real and her sweet compassion is godawful authentic—except when she's having one of her frustration fits, and lately that's damn near all the time. I have never seen or heard of a woman so frustrated. It has made her physically ill. I wonder if she knows enough to masturbate, and fantastically enough I'm not even sure she does. *Incroyable! Le dégouttement très pathétique! Le petit jugement dernier n'est pas la grand airelle!* Well, I never hear her snorting—if she does, she's awful furtive and sneaky about it—but then, she would be. I almost think she just lies there and cries. Maybe she doesn't know how. Maybe "Self-Abuse: Its History and Practice" is not included in the curriculum at Tom Armour University. I am sure she must have picked up the arcane skill somewhere; the truth, of course, is that it helps very little. The scene with her last night was pitiful; even this cold reptile heart was moved. Poor darling, poor thing; how can I even pretend to laugh at her, knowing as I do she would never laugh at me . . . and there's more to laugh at here than there.

Quite a bit more. So much more, it is . . . "absurd." Yes, I got that from him. He uses the word in a special way. To him it makes sense. In idiotic foolishness lies truth. A mysterious machine, the mind, he says, a strange mysterious machine, the workings of which we ourselves cannot follow. We talked an hour about it yesterday. I love to talk to him. I want to scream if he touches my hand, but I love to talk to him. Neurotic fixation is putting it mildly. The sound of his voice gives me pleasure. I never tire of talking to him, never, but if he touches my hand I want to scream and jump in the sea.

I wonder why that is. If he touches Melody's hand, *she* doesn't want to scream and jump in the sea. On the contrary, she wants to scream and jump in the sea because he *doesn't* touch her hand. And "jump in the sea" is no empty figure of speech. I know my own dark impulses on that promontory; and two days ago, when Melody walked with me there, she paled with fright as she stared at the rocks and roiling waves, locked her arm in mine, and said: "I have an urge to jump. Don't let me."

It's absurd. Yes, "absurd." *I* have an impulse to die for fear he will, *she* has an impulse to die for fear he won't. And yet she naively thinks my feelings are identical to her own, that I love him and want him just as she does. She is half right, and half right is not right enough. I only love him and want him in my dreams, and dreams are not and never can be reality. Furthermore, if my interpretation of the sheep's entrails is correct, then *he* is not *half* wrong, he is *totally* wrong. The Dragon lives and blew a breath of fire not twenty-four hours ago—furtive and hidden fire, to be sure, but fire.

Speaking of Dragons, an orange-haired, weasel-eyed, and rather stupid girl named Verta several years ago told me an instructive story about a pair of them living down in the Village. They were happy in a Dragon kind of way, but after a while the more "feminine" of the two decided their life was a bit empty and unfulfilled and they ought to have a baby. The "masculine" one was badly upset at first and snorted smoke, but after considerable discussion in the den became enthusiastic and agreed it was a hell of an idea, that a darling little baby Dragon was just what they needed around there to bring a little cheer to the place, to light up its shadows. Of course the process of obtaining a little baby Dragon would be a horrible ordeal, but with fortitude and a few tranquillizers it could be endured. So the Dragons went to a bar and found a young drunk sailor boy and picked him up and lured him to the den. They got him down and took his pants off, but he was terrified to death of those ghastly Dragons and his thing wouldn't work. Nope, his thing was intimidated, scared silly. It was a distressing situation. The "feminine" Dragon, who had a good figure and was pretty, sat on him naked and everything but it only terrified him worse. She kissed him on the mouth, not passionately but on the mouth—no result. She took his hand and put it on her breast—no result. She squatted on him, rubbed on his thing, and bounced on him like she was riding a horse—no result. His eyes just opened wider and wider. He finally began half crying and the Dragons decided he was too young and let him go. But they weren't ready to give up, hell no. The next sailor was older and less drunk, but he got nervous too when they came at him. Of course, Dragons don't know anything about feminine wiles and besides, they wanted to get right down to business. At first the sailor had been eager, but when the "masculine" one grabbed him by the belt to take off his pants and the "feminine" one started unbuttoning her blouse, he began to talk and mutter about "getting back to the base," and tried to saunter toward the door, sweating, his eyes bugging slightly . . . they had to wheedle him and pull him back and give him a lot more to drink, quite a lot more, and even then it was an awful struggle. The "masculine" one had to hold him while the "feminine" one got on him. At first his thing wouldn't work either, but she kept sitting on him and rubbing on him and finally it did. The "masculine" one ran to get some Vaseline and then commenced the agony of the "feminine" one—oooh, it killed her, it was so big, but she was determined and kept sitting on it and pushing down and she finally got the horrible thing all the way in her. The sailor became interested at this point and began making movements and this was painful to her, but she gritted her teeth and endured it even though it seemed he would keep it up forever. Then suddenly he groaned and moved harder and she felt baby Dragon stuff coming out of his thing and going into her. Eureka! A triumph! But alas, no luck. It all ran out in that position, she could feel it down her leg, and though the "masculine" one hurried and got a spoon and they tried to scoop it off her thigh and get it back in, they couldn't, it was all mixed with Vaseline and blood and most of it got lost. While they were trying to spoon the baby Dragon stuff back into her, the sailor grabbed his pants and ran out the door and staggered down the stairs. Well, the Dragons decided sailors were no good, it had to be done not once but a number of times and with the man on top. So, to make a long story short, they found a man somewhere, a door-to-door salesman, I think it was, some man who looked like he had good genes, and they paid him money to do it on top three or four times to the "feminine" one. That is, three or four times on different occasions, with the "masculine" one holding her legs up to counteract gravity. It didn't hurt the "feminine" one any more but it distressed her terribly—she was beginning to have bad dreams, suicidal impulses, psychosomatic ailments. But then—true Eureka! She missed her period, rabbit test positive—the "feminine" Dragon was pregnant! Joy! Hosanna! There, in her tummy, a little precious baby Dragon, growing and getting scales already! A miracle! But the bad dreams didn't go away, the suicidal impulses didn't stop, the psychosomatic ailments got worse. Six weeks later the "feminine" Dragon had a nervous breakdown and, a week after that, an abortion. Moral: Dragons don't want babies, they just *think* they want babies.

Although I know from my limited experience with her that Verta Killington Rhabb is a tawny-haired, ferret-eyed, small-minded liar, I believe her story. I don't think it is just an apocryphal self-hate tale, it has the ring of truth to me. I think it really happened. In fact, I think it happened to Verta herself, that she was the "masculine" Dragon and that little blonde girl she lived with some years ago was the "feminine" Dragon. No doubt the story is exaggerated here and there to make it even more filthy and appalling, but I think they really did have a misadventure or two with one or more sailors and then found some man who for a price was willing to impregnate her, and that she then had a nervous breakdown and an abortion. It's a true story, a wormheart tale. And of course the filthy thing about it is not the degradation of Verta and her friend and these men, but the ending of it, the killing of the baby, that is what is filthy. Well, maybe I am not a complete and true Dragon after all, because I would have had it if it had been me. Better to bring a little Dragon with scales into the world than nothing at all. Besides, it wouldn't have been a Dragon, it would have been a human child. A hateful story, that's what it is, and I don't think Tolstoy would have considered it worth putting on paper. I'm sorry I did, because now I am even more depressed and bewildered than before.

Verta and her friends laugh in hysteria at that tale, utter wild hysteria, but I don't laugh at it, it makes me want to cry. Is Jim *right* to disbelieve in the Dragon?

Well, it's true I seldom move in Dragon circles, I almost never see them, I am not a part of that world. They don't distress me, I understand their feelings, they don't bother or upset me—they bore me to death, that's all. I don't really *like* women for the most part. And yet in my observation most Dragons don't like them either, really. I don't know *what* to think and I don't know what *he* thinks. All I know is that to judge by the episode of last night the Dragon lives.

It is late at night and I suppose Melody wants the lantern off so she can sleep. She looks up from her pillow and smiles at me and says no, the light does not bother her, in answer to my question. Now she shuts her eyes and stretches her arms behind her head, her breasts naively bare. What an innocent she is. Another woman would be doubtful of such a person as me, but not Melody. She's an exception to the rule that I don't like women. I really love her and would never want to hurt her. Let her have him, I hope she is happy.

She really *is* an innocent, almost unbelievably so, but I guess there are other women like her in the South and in small towns. Although there will never be a repeat of the episode if I can possibly help it, I have been in her bed, have held her half-naked body in my arms, and she has slept like a child with her head on my shoulder—and I am absolutely certain she didn't know, she didn't think, she didn't even dream there was anything even remotely Dragonish about it. That might sound slightly incredible, but it's true.

She started this bare-breasts-in-the-tropical-night thing several days ago, I guess in the hope he would see her through the blanket partition and pay some attention to her. "Oh," she said, in a voice loud enough for him to hear, "It's so hot, Florence. I'm going to sleep with my tops unbuttoned. It'll be more comfortable."

Yes, more comfortable. She wanted him to think about it and I'm sure he has. Her breasts are her best feature by far; they are large and firm and perfectly shaped, a pure Meerschaum white with no trace of veins and beautiful girlish nipples set in baby-bunting pink. That's a fairly Dragonish description, I suppose, but I don't see how anyone could help but admire such beauty. And it's so unexpected, you'd never dream it from the clothes she wears. If I had breasts like hers, I'd probably have six children by now.

So how did I wind up in bed with her? It was the result of a Dragonish impulse that took me completely by surprise. I have not allowed myself on this island even to think about Melody in such terms; and luckily, although I love her and admire her beautiful breasts, I am not especially attracted to her. So how did it happen? Well, I woke up very late last night, heart pounding and out of breath and perspiration on my face and in my eyes. It was another of those goddamn dreams. As I said, I love him in my dreams. This time, he was not only kissing me and lying naked in my arms, he was actually making love to me or starting to do so—a very unrealistic dream, since it didn't hurt me at all but on the contrary was ecstatically pleasurable. I think I would have had an orgasm in another few seconds if I hadn't awakened, and I wonder if that would constitute a loss of virginity, psychologically anyhow? I'm afraid not. Besides, he wasn't actually doing it, he was just "about" to do it—the truth is I don't know what the sensation is really like and my dreams have to become fuzzy or stop at that point. But at any rate the dream made me feel horribly sexy and restless, and suddenly an insane impulse came to me. Self-abuse doesn't help much but I was considering it when the idea popped into my mind that Melody was even more frustrated than I was and since she was asleep half naked on a mattress two feet away, why not go and get in bed with her? What the hell, why not? I could kiss her, hold her in my arms, feel her pretty breasts—a splendid idea! Why, mutual masturbation was normal as apple pie, it was rampant in every girl's boarding school in the country and just what we needed in Morgan's Treasure Cave!

The insane impulse was so strong I was appalled. Terrified. Horrified, in fact. Such a thing couldn't succeed—she would gasp, cry out, push me frantically away, call to Jim, he would get up, light the kerosene lantern, stare sternly at me: "Florence, now what do you think you're doing? We can't have this kind of thing on this island. Now, goddamn it . . ."

And then I heard in the darkness: "Snnf! Snnff!" She was awake, crying, miserable. Golden opportunity! In a trice off go my own pajama tops and I am sitting beside her, my hand on her arm. I whisper: "Melody?" A doleful sigh from her, very, very doleful, chock-full of despair. I lie beside her and prop on my elbow, my left arm across the sheet on her stomach. "Why are you crying? Are you unhappy?"

"Oh, yes, yes, yes," she whispered, and I listened for several seconds to choking, suppressed sobs. Then another whisper: "Bend over, I don't want him to hear."

"Let me get under the sheet," I said.

"All right," she said, "come in bed with me." Up goes the sheet, me under it, then soft arms around me, wet tears on my shoulder. "Oh, Florence, I love him, what can I do? I love him, I love him. . . ."

"I know," I said. "It's hard for you."

"It's impossible. I've tried, but it's impossible. I want him so much, I can't resist. I can't, Florence, I know I can't."

"Well, if you can't, you can't."

"Yes, but what about Charles? What about my husband?"

"Well . . . is he a nice man, kind?"

"Oh, yes, very nice, very kind."

"Then maybe he'll understand and forgive you."

"Oh, no. No no no. He couldn't understand such a thing as this. Never. You don't know him, he'd never understand it. . . ."

We discussed it to no avail at considerable length, even though she was so exhausted she was practically going to sleep in my arms. I'm sure it didn't even vaguely occur to her I could have had any "unnatural" feelings toward her, and oddly enough, at this point I didn't. It's impossible to have a person weep in despair on your shoulder and not be affected. I felt nothing but pity for her. The Dragon was shriveled.

Finally, in a sleepy whisper she said: "You are so sweet to me. I don't know why, as weak and wicked as I am. You must have been very unhappy sometime yourself to be so understanding. I just can't *help* it, Florence, I love him and I can't think about anything else. What am I going to do? It's terrible, awful. I can't think about *anything* but him."

"Well," I said, "go on to bed with him, then."

"Oh, no," she answered. "I can't . . . my husband . . . I . . . I can't."

"Then control yourself," I said sweetly. "Take walks, think about other things."

"I know, I know," she whispered. "I've tried that, but it doesn't work. All I can think about is him."

Melody sighed in heavy gloom, and so did I. There really was no solution for her problem, none she herself could make or find.

"Maybe we'll be rescued soon," I said. "Why don't you go on to sleep? Aren't you tired?"

"I've never been so tired. I'm tired all the time. But I can't sleep. Will you stay here with me for a while? Do you mind? I think I could sleep if you'd stay a little while."

I didn't mind. She went to sleep in my arms in about two minutes, emotionally and physically exhausted. First light, steady breathing, then heavy, then soft, slow breathing and complete relaxation, her hand limp and floppy as I lifted it from around my side. I put my hand on her breast and felt the thump of her heart. There was no reaction from her at all, she was sound asleep as a child. I had no temptation to do more and pulled up the sheet and put her limp arm back around me and my own arms around her.

What difference would it make if she was asleep?—and I didn't want to wake her up and worry and upset her. Besides, the Dragon's fire had been extinguished. I felt nothing but pity and love for her . . . well, nearly, but not quite. Coiled and skulking in some hidden hole, faint wisps of smoke came from the Dragon's nostrils. I was aware of her beautiful breasts against me, of her soft breath on my neck, of her hair against my cheek and her tears drying on my shoulder . . . I myself slept so soundly I didn't awake until quite late and to judge from his manner at breakfast I think he saw us in bed together.

I have felt badly about it all day. Nothing like this must happen again. It's true the whole thing turned out to be "innocent" enough, but I think Melody, without being at all conscious of it, did respond to me and I think if I had made some kind of approach to her she would have responded more, and consciously. I don't want that. He would hate me for it, and so would she, too, really. The worries I have had on this account have made this a bad day in my unhappy life and have led directly to the writing of these wretched pages.

So much for my ill-advised and misbegotten effort to practice self-therapy by starting a "diary" on this island.

A final, dismal thought. What will I do when they become lovers? It's bound to happen soon; if I know him at all, he can't possibly continue to be so cruel to her. And believe it or not, dear Diary, I want it to happen, I truly do, I want her to have him and I want him to have her; I am not really jealous, I love them both. But here, in this cave? What is to become of *me*? No. I can't stand that, not even if they make love in the afternoons when I'm not here. I'll move out, I'll go sleep in a pool with the pigs and iguanas.

But I guess, realistically speaking, "love in the afternoon" is the only practical answer. Thank God for Rufus and the island, thank God for the purple rocks, the waves, and the sun. I can always go there with my dog. Rufus will save me, there is a soul in him, a spirit. He looks at me with his beautiful brown eyes and he loves me, he does not know I am ugly and a Dragon lives in me.

Self-pity is too much, it is time to blow out the lantern and go to bed. Nature will solve my problem in another few years.

A truly final thought: I wonder what my kindly and ultracivilized editor in New York—the original Rufus—would think if he could read these words? Poor Rufus would collapse. The bad prose would not shock him, he has known me to write badly before, but the content . . . I shudder to think of it and must make a visit to the purple rocks and commit these pages to the merciful oblivion of the sea. It would be a disaster if Melody should see and read this, and an intolerable disaster if Jim should see and read it.

To bed, sleepyhead, but still I wonder . . . I wonder . . . why did he ask that wholly unnecessary question on the plane to Atlanta? He had seen me stare at the pretty stewardess and knew of my Dragon nature—why did he look at me with pain and sympathy and an amusement that was not cruel and ask that seemingly crude question? And why did he take my hand beneath magnolias and live oaks and look in my eyes and say, "I'm sorry, please forgive me. It's a beautiful little park."?

Ho ho ho, said Santa Claus. Get a grip on yourself, kid. The reindeers are in rut this time of year and don't want to haul sleighs through the sky. To hell with him, he's a vain and hateful bully, worse than buddy boy and Father dear combined. Even if Melody did not have him hypnotized by her alabaster breasts and gentle blue eyes, I would still shudder at the touch of his hand. He has aroused senseless hope in a hopeless person and nothing is more cruel. That is the truth, and I hate him and fear him. Dreams, dreams, dreams . . .

I will throw these pages early in the morning to the pigs and iguanas as they splash in the rocky pools of Hell's Half Acre.

FIFTEEN

The Elysian Field

Dear Charles:

I am afraid the time has come for me to write you a letter that will cause us both heartache. This morning my companions here on the island went with me to a lovely meadow we call the Elysian Field for a simple Sunday service. I read the 91st Psalm, which as you know contains the beautiful passage:

"There shall no evil befall thee, neither shall any plague come nigh thy dwelling. For he shall give his angels charge over thee, to keep thee in all thy ways."

As I read those words in the midst of a beauty equaling Paradise, a beauty not only of God's nature but of man's own heart and soul, I found the courage to write you this letter, in the faith that in God's love no evil can befall us and no plague come to our home, in the belief God's promise is eternal and absolute and he shall forever and always give his angels charge over thee and me.

There are hurtful and terrible things I must write to you, but first I want to tell you where I am and what has happened to us all. I have tried without much success on several occasions to write you before. I have been too exhausted to write coherently and too full of fear and confusion to write honestly, thus have torn up my earlier unfinished efforts.

As I write you this I am still so tired I can hardly sit up and so worried about your illness and the concern you must feel for me I can hardly write at all. Let me hasten to say I am safe and hope to mail this letter to you in a few days, by which time I trust and pray we will have been rescued from the little island upon which we are stranded.

I'm thankful the radiogram said your illness was not critical or I would truly be out of my mind with anxiety. But I can't understand why it was necessary to fly you back from Bogotá to the United States. It must be something serious or they wouldn't do that. I wish they'd told me more in the radiogram. All I can do is pray that you are all right and hope by the time you receive this you will be well.

As for myself, I am by God's mercy safe. The ship was wrecked in the hurricane but the lives of three of us were spared—a man, another woman, and myself. The man's name is Jim Kittering and the woman's name is Florence Carr; she is a well-known author and he has an important job in television. They are both wonderful friends to me and it is "Providential" I am with them.

I say "Providential" because the island we are on is called Providence, or at least I myself think so. Jim believes it is too small and Florence is undecided. But it is "Providence Island" to me, whatever its name. I feel that way about it because of the people I am here with. Jim Kittering is a very kind man and he has been a true and wonderful friend to me. He has also been very kind to Florence. He is married and has two children, young girls. The work he does puts him under great pressure and he and his wife have had some troubles and recently were separated, but I have no doubt they will get back together, he loves both her and the children very much. Florence also is a fine person and a true friend. It is "Providence Island" for me to be here with them.

Florence and I are especially fortunate that Jim is with us on the island. I don't know how we would have survived without him. He has made us a nice home in a cave found by Florence's dog (she calls it Rufus, it was left on the ship along with a cat and a parrot) and Jim has done many other things for us as well. It is lucky for Florence and me he is the kind of man he is; I am sure you will realize it could be very serious for two women alone on an uninhabited island with a wicked man. Jim does not belong to any church but he is a good man and I am absolutely sure he will not harm either of us in any way, but on the contrary will look after us as if we were his sisters.

I want to write you about the island and the wreck and everything that has happened, but I am very tired. We have been working constantly to fix up this cave so we can live in it for as long as need be. Jim insisted on it, that we be able to survive in case rescue is delayed. He has exhausted himself hauling food and supplies from the wreck, and Florence and I are exhausted too. She broke her ribs when a huge wave struck the ship during the storm, and later when the ship hit the reef I myself was thrown down and badly bruised—it's nothing serious, except for two weeks I could hardly sit down. Now, after three weeks here, I am glad to say we are both better and the hard work is done.

I do hope we will be rescued soon and I believe we will be. I'm sure they have been looking for us and fishing boats must come here sometime, there are a lot of fish in the lagoon. I am not only anxious about your illness and concerned about your being worried about me, I am so eager to see you because there is much I want to tell you that I really cannot put in a letter. I mean, I cannot explain it in words, I could never explain it in words, but I believe because of this accident our life together will be very different in the future.

I hope and pray we will be rescued soon. I am so anxious to see you, Charles. Even as tired as I have been these last few days, I have thought of you again and again. I have thought of how fortunate I am to be married to such a kind and wonderful man, who is able so much more than I am to give of himself to others. I love you very much and do hope and pray to see you soon.

Charles, I have learned something very important since I saw you last. The thing I have learned is that love means an understanding of one's own weaknesses. It is not enough to understand other people's failings, we must understand our own too. By forgiving ourselves, we can forgive others, and thus true love becomes possible. I believe this is very, very important.

But do you think I mean we should "accept" our weaknesses? I wish I were a writer like Florence and could express it in words—I say it but I can't make clear what I mean, the full meaning does not come through. Of course we should never take license to be weak, this is the coward's way out. "I can't help it, I am weak." No, I don't mean this. Do you know at all what I am trying to say?

It's by seeing our own human side that we can see the human side of others and can love and understand them. Because, Charles, no matter how hard we try, no matter even with resolutions and prayer, isn't it true we are all human beings, the "children of God"—and don't children by their very nature often stumble and fall? And if a child stumbles, do we hate the child? No, of course not, we run and help it, we show sympathy and take a little child in our arms when it cries. Wouldn't anyone do this? And we are all children in so many ways, but when a grown person is hurt and cries, who will help? There is so little love and sympathy between grown people that when we find it life becomes "like unto paradise" and an ordinary meadow with wildflowers a true Elysian Field. Instead of studying man, for whose happiness and worth and fulfillment the law is designed, we have studied the empty and meaningless law itself with cold hearts and cold minds, and thereby have turned the Elysian Field into a dismal and inhuman swamp.

I know we have argued about all of this before, even as far back as schooldays. I have not forgotten the number of times you and other friends saved me from being expelled from Tom Armour for my heretical and radical views. It still is a mystery to me how I ever graduated from there. I suppose it is because I *look* innocent, but certainly I am not, I am a "radical," as you say, perhaps even more than you realize. Perhaps more than I have dared let you realize. If it were up to me, whole reams of the Bible itself would be dismissed as superstitious, useless trash.

I'm sure that must shock you, although I have told you before in less harsh terms the same thing. You have a way of not listening to me. If it's a thing you don't want to hear, you don't hear it. I wonder if I can penetrate your deafness if I try. Some of the Bible contains great moral wisdom, some of it contains inspired and beautiful poetry, but most of it is junk, Charles. I have been reading it lately and thinking about it. I would say about five percent is worthwhile, and the rest is *junk*.

Yes, I am trying to shock you. I can't believe you yourself are as naive as you pretend. How could you go through medical school and believe all the things you say you believe? You don't always act on the things you say you believe. Do you remember failing to report to the police the boy who visited us in Knoxville in a stolen car? Do you remember helping the young student nurse obtain a criminal abortion? There is a contradiction between your heart and your beliefs, and can you guess which of these I respect? Do you know why I love and admire you and married you in the first place?

Oh, Charles, I can't tell you how I feel, I am making a ruin of this letter because I cannot find the words to say what I want to say. I do wish I could get off this island! I am tired all the time, I've been so depressed here and have such terrible dreams. And I can't sleep or, if I do, a nightmare wakes me up. I finally went to sleep last night around two o'clock and woke up an hour later with an awful dream. It was horrible, dreadful. There's this place Florence likes, a cliff about fifty feet high with jagged rocks down below. Big lizards are there and Florence says wild pigs sometimes come too.

She calls it "Hell's Half Acre" and that's what it really looks like.

The dream I had about it frightened me worse than almost anything I can remember. I was there on the cliff and the light was strange and suddenly the rock began to move and I couldn't stay on my feet. I tried, but twice I fell down and when I did, the lizards (they were all over everywhere) rushed up at me and tried to bite me on the legs and push me over the cliff. I got very angry and threw rocks at them. Then I think I killed some animal, not a lizard but some worse animal, I believe a kind of half hog and half man.

There was blood all over everywhere and the animal was screaming, it was dying, screaming and dying. I felt awful, but it had tried to kill me, tried to push me over the cliff with its nose—it was pushing at me and making a horrible slobbering noise and also trying its best to bite me, and I didn't know what to do so I threw a big rock at it and killed it. The ground was still shaking and I was about to slide off the cliff and be killed myself when Jim came running and jumped down and grabbed my hand and pulled me back just in time. I was crying, hysterical. He put his arm around my shoulder and the ground stopped shaking and he led me away, but I could still hear the animal screaming as it died. That was the worst part, killing that animal and hearing it scream. I can still hear it screaming, even now.

The dream might not sound so terrible, but it frightened me worse than anything since I was a child. I woke up crying and couldn't go back to sleep even though I was so tired I was nearly crazy. I don't think I have ever been so miserable and frightened. Luckily, Florence woke up and heard me crying and came and got in bed with me or I think I would have died. I really think I would have died, at least I felt that way.

Florence acts kind of gruff, but she is so sweet and kind I can't tell you. I will always love her. She held me in her arms so tender I can never forget it. And the next day I realized how hard it must have been for her to think of me, because she has troubles and worries of her own. She didn't think of herself, she cried with sympathy for *me*, and held me in her arms in the most beautiful way and I will always love her for it.

The truth, I am afraid, is that Florence has a bad problem on the island here. You see, she is not very pretty and I don't think many men have been interested in her, but Jim has been kind and sweet to her, he has shown that he likes her and admires her and cares about her, and I'm afraid she has fallen completely in love with him. I didn't quite realize it until this morning when I saw the way she was looking at him, then watched the way she was laughing at something he had said. I tried to talk to her a little about it and I think hurt her feelings. She denied it in a pathetic way that convinced me she loves him even more than I'd realized.

Of course, he's married and it's hopeless. Florence herself has never married and I don't think she has had much experience with men at all, which makes it all the harder for her. To fall in love at last and for it to be a married man must be awful for her. She is a typical spinster, wears suits, has canaries in her apartment, leads a very lonely life. I don't think Jim loves her, but he likes her very much and although I say it's "hopeless" I almost feel . . .

Well, you wouldn't understand what I was going to say, so I won't say it. There's no point in my writing something to you that you simply would not ever understand. But I don't know, I can't go on the way things are. I have reached the limits of my endurance, Charles. We have got to get our marriage on a different basis, so I will say what I was thinking about Florence. Yes, I will say it even if you don't understand it. My thought was that if we are here on the island for a long time more, then I almost feel it would be a good thing if Jim lives with Florence here, and not as brother and sister but as man and woman. In fact, I don't almost think that, I do think that. Maybe it would be adultery because of his wife, maybe I am wrong; I know you will think so, that my idea is pagan, barbarous, sinful, wicked.

The reason I feel as I do is because of Florence. But first Jim. He has been unfaithful to his wife before, he told me so. And she has been unfaithful to him too. That is the real reason they are separated. Such things happen in the world, Charles. People are weak and don't always act perfectly. Sometimes it is a good idea not to act perfectly, because what seems perfect isn't perfect at all but horrible. It won't hurt Jim or his wife for him to live with Florence on this island. Not a bit. You can't convince me it would hurt them, because I know it wouldn't.

And it would help Florence. Like most spinsters, she is very afraid of men. For example, even though she loves Jim, she hides it from him as much as she can and from me too, for fear I might tell him or reveal it to him. She is terrified of men. Also, she has an awful complex about being ugly. The truth is she is not as ugly as she thinks she is. I wish *I* had her figure—without her clothes, she is slender and pretty as a girl. There's nothing wrong with her looks and some man would be very grateful and happy to have her love, all the more since she is a brilliant and sensitive woman and a talented writer, a person of real character who has achieved something and can achieve more.

It would be the best thing in the world for Florence to have an "affair" with Jim on this island. Because this would give her confidence, it would get her over her fears, make a complete woman of her not only physically but emotionally and spiritually. She would learn to give love to a man, to relax and not be afraid with a man. She would learn that a man can be attracted to her and want her and make love to her, that she is not a leper or something but a desirable woman. It would change her life forever. She would go back to New York and find a husband of her own and have a child and be fulfilled and happy instead of lonely and miserable in that apartment with her chirping canaries. *You* call it adultery, and *I* call it salvation! And if you don't like it, then I don't care, I don't care one bit, because I am thinking of Florence and not some rigid rule that doesn't serve the purpose of either God or man—I want to *help* Florence and *you* want to smother her and let her die. Yes, that's what you want, Charles, it's exactly what you want, you and all the people who think the way you do. You talk of Christian love, but it isn't love of any kind, it's narrow fear and mean-hearted hate that goes against everything that makes life beautiful and worth living. The prophet meant not an empty love of God, but a true love of God, a love of God's children and a love of life itself—then, and only then, "He shall give his angels charge over thee."

Otherwise, devils will rule you, as they rule you now, Charles, to my grief and woe during the last three wretched years of our marriage. You said to me I was "abnormal" just before you left for Bogotá. I cannot begin to tell you the pain that remark has cost me. I thought perhaps it was true. I also thought there was something wrong with me, that I was so unattractive no man could want me. How many times have I cried myself to sleep because of that thing you said? It's not true, it's a cowardly lie. I am no different from other women. Every woman wants to love someone and to be loved. And I am not unattractive, a man can want me and love me too.

Charles, it is unbearable to me to go back to things the way they were. Two days ago, when I went with Florence to that cliff, the thought came to me that maybe we would be rescued soon and I would see you again, and I had an urge to throw myself down on those rocks and die. I can't stand it any more! I can't, I can't endure it! How could you say such a thing about a person you love? How? I don't think you love me at all. . . .

I have read this letter through carefully and to say I am so tired I don't know what I am writing is no excuse. The design is plain, the intention obvious. The whole point is to justify my being unfaithful. Moral law is meaningless, therefore Florence should live with Jim. My husband doesn't love me, therefore I should live with Jim too. I am exhausted and I am going to sleep and I hope a better vision of paradise on earth will come to me in my dreams.

Oh, God, deliver me from this island! The truth is, I am a weak and wicked woman with sin on my mind, ready and willing to use any excuse, any argument, any justification, even the 91st Psalm. "He shall give his angels charge over thee"—yes, me, a naked angel on one side of him and Florence, a naked angel on the other. That was my inspired vision when I read those words this morning in the Elysian Field.

PART SIX

St. Valentine's Day

SIXTEEN

Bluebird Feathers

At breakfast three weeks and three days after the wreck of the *Lorna Loone,* Melody said: "I had a dream last night. I dreamed thousands of pretty bluebirds came to the island, a great cloud of them. They were all over the hill nestling in the thistles. It was beautiful. Bluebird feathers were everywhere, floating in the air like snow."

"A great dream," said Florence, "and you ought to do something about it."

"Do something about it?"

"Never mind," said Florence, "I was just talking."

Melody sat at the "dining table" in silence, eyes fixed pensively on her plate of Dinty Moore beef stew. The sunshine from the entrance of the cave lighted her hair and head with a faint saintly halo. She wore this morning her most modest dress, the pale gray garment she had had on when Jim first saw her from the cobblestones at Savannah. Her fork made a little clatter on the plate as she put it down, lifted her head, and stared in puzzlement at Florence. "How could I do anything about a dream?" she asked. "What do you mean by that?"

"Tell me what happened in the dream," replied Florence.

"Nothing happened. There was no question of anything happening. There were just bluebirds everywhere."

"I see. Lots of bluebirds."

"Yes, bluebirds. And their feathers."

"Um-hmm," said Florence. "Did you do anything with the feathers?"

"How could I do anything with the feathers? I don't know what you're talking about, Florence. I don't understand you at all. What could I possibly do with the feathers?"

"You could make a nest out of them, I suppose."

"A nest?"

"Or a bed, maybe," said Florence. "I should think bluebird feathers would make a lovely bed."

Melody picked up her fork. "All right, Florence," she said. "It happens to have been just a dream, that's all. I've dreamed about bluebirds many times before. I even dreamed about them as a child."

"You're ahead of me," said Florence. "I don't dream about bluebirds, I dream about less elegant creatures."

"I don't care what you dream about; it doesn't interest me."

"Sorry," said Florence. "I was just making light conversation. Actually, it's a lovely dream, bluebird feathers falling like snow."

Melody bit her lips together and did not speak again until after Florence had left for her morning walk. She then turned to Jim and said: "I want to talk to you about something important."

"Yes, I think we should talk," he answered.

"It's very important, Jim. Very, very important. I thought this morning would be a good time, while Florence is off on her walk with Rufus."

"I think it's an excellent time," said Jim. He could not quite control a slight tremor in his voice. The bluebirds, he was sure, would arrive on Providence Island very soon. In fact, a few feathers already had fallen.

"She can't mind her own business, you know," said Melody. "Of course, the way we're living here, I know it's hard for her. But I get tired of those little remarks. Do you suppose she was eavesdropping last night?"

"Oh, I don't think so. Florence wouldn't do that."

"No, I don't think she would either. But she might have heard us without intending to. Jim, it took me till all hours to go to sleep last night. I don't know when I finally did, it must have been almost morning."

"I had a little trouble dropping off myself," said Jim.

"I can't stand another night like that. You may not believe it, but I almost got up, a dozen times I almost did. To tell the truth, around four o'clock I did get up. I couldn't control myself, it was as if it wasn't me doing it but somebody else. I got up in the dark and stood there by the blanket partition for about five minutes with my knees shaking and I still don't know how I ever got back to my bed. Jim, I can't go on like this and that's why I want to talk to you."

"We should have talked before," he answered. "I'm afraid neither of us has been very realistic."

"I certainly haven't been," said Melody. "I'm just not used to being honest about such things. I've never been honest about it before in my life, but I've got to be now."

Jim had felt it coming. On the evening before, after a gloomy afternoon spent writing and tearing up still another letter to her husband, Melody had entertained Florence and him for a couple of hours by playing the ebonite and mother-of-pearl accordion he had found in a crewman's cabin on the wreck. She had a natural musical bent and had learned during her childhood to play both the piano and the accordion by ear. Pleased by Jim's and Florence's praise, she played first one thing and then another with a childlike enjoyment, first hymns and semisacred country music and then, to Jim's surprise, a number of songs from Broadway musicals and other popular tunes he would not have expected her to know. As she played, she smiled, made jokes, and laughed, and the look of chronic, nagging melancholy left her eyes. It was the first time Jim had seen her happy since before the hurricane.

Later in the evening, after Florence had gone to bed, Melody stood with him in the entrance of the cave and stared at the sprinkled, diamondlike stars of the tropical sky, arms locked across her breasts and a wistful expression on her face in the dim light. "It was fun," she said, "more fun than anything since we've been on the island. I'm tired of being miserable, Jim. I'm so tired of being miserable I don't think I can stand it any more." Jim put his arm around her waist and Melody leaned toward him, a hand on his shoulder and the fresh scent of soap and salt water in her hair. "Jim, will we *ever* get off this island?"

"I don't know." Jim tightened his forearm in the curve of her waist and spread his hand on her soft stomach. Madness! Not madness what he was doing, but madness he had not done it before. *This*, on the island, an overwhelmingly attractive woman who belonged by all the logic of life itself in his arms, and he had stayed away from her and she from him? Such insanity was caused by excessive reflection on morals. Only the wicked reflect on morals. Sheer madness! What more truly moral thing could he do than put his arm around her curving waist and gently but firmly spread his fingers on her soft, womanly, human stomach? "I don't know if or when we'll be rescued, honey," said Jim. "I suppose we will sometime."

"I think we will soon," replied Melody in a surprisingly calm voice that continued serenely without pause as Jim's hand moved down between her thighs, "but I don't know what good it will do. My husband either can't or doesn't love me. We've hardly lived together at all the last three years. Or at least that's the way it seems to me. He says I'm abnormal and maybe he's right. Jim, you'd better not do that."

"Hadn't I?"

"No. No, you'd better not."

"Why shouldn't I?"

"Oh, I don't know. I don't know anything, maybe Charles is right." Melody's voice was becoming less calm. She turned toward Jim and put her hands on his shoulders. "All I know is I've tried, but I can't help it. And it isn't just that I love you. I'm a woman and I want to live. That's what I really want, Jim, I want to live."

Jim put both arms around her and pulled her toward him. "Sounds reasonable."

"Yes, but it isn't," said Melody in a tiny voice. "You'd better not kiss me."

"I think I had better," said Jim, also in a half whisper.

"No, I don't think you should."

"Why not?"

"Well, you had better not."

During this exchange of semimindless words, Jim tried to find her lips but only succeeded in kissing her cheek, her neck, and her hair. Melody rested her hands on his shoulders and made no attempt to pull away from him, but she would not kiss him.

"Melody, hold your head still, you can kiss me."

"No, I can't. If I do, I'll sleep with you."

"Don't worry about that."

"I have to worry about it."

"No, you don't."

"Jim, please, let me go."

Jim took her chin in his hand and said, "Just kiss me once."

"It won't be once," she answered, "you know that."

As he found her lips after three weeks and three days and felt her arms tighten around his neck and her woman's body press against him, any small moral doubts Jim Kittering might have had were obliterated by love and desire. As he continued to kiss her with a geometrically progressive passion, he forgot all of his argument on behalf of chaste Christian love. The battle was over, finished, done with, and for her as well as for him. The violence of her response made that perfectly plain. However, although she kissed him repeatedly in the most passionate manner imaginable and did not prevent him from pulling her dress over her shoulders and taking off her brassiere, Melody would not go to his bed and she would not go to the beach either. Bosom bare, breathless, hands and knees trembling, she shook her head and would not budge. The most he could get out of her was a statement she "might" after Florence was asleep.

"Look, you're a grown woman, Melody, and I'm a grown man. We're not teen-agers in a parking lot."

"Of course we're not, that's just the point. I realize that."

"All right, then what do you mean, you *might*?"

"I mean, I might when I'm sure Florence is asleep. It's perfectly obvious what I mean, Jim."

"Will you or won't you, Melody?"

"Well . . . I have to think."

"Look, I can't lie there all night wondering. Will you come or not?"

"I don't know, I might."

"Melody, that's no answer. Are you worried about Florence?"

"Of course I'm worried about Florence. She's right there."

"All right, then let's go to the beach."

"Oh, no, I can't do that."

"Why can't you?"

"Because something will happen."

"Oh, for God's sake, you said you might come to my bed, didn't you?"

"Yes."

"Well, if you did, something would happen, wouldn't it?"

"Ah-h-h . . . yes, I think it probably would. Very likely."

"Melody, if you got in bed with me, it'd be a dead certainty we'd make love—isn't that true?"

"Yes."

"All right, if you're worried about Florence, then why can't you go to the beach?"

"Because it's impossible, Jim, that's why. I can't, like that, I just can't."

"I see. You can't, like that. But you 'might' come to my bed later tonight if you're sure Florence is asleep."

"Yes, I don't promise, but I might. Please let me go on to bed now."

Jim had been sure she wouldn't come and was glad she didn't. A mere seduction of her seemed to him wrong, inappropriate, vulgar. This was not the way he felt about her. Although he spent half the night in agonized frustration waiting for her, he went to sleep relieved that she did not come. The proper thing was not to kiss her and take off her brassiere and seduce her like a teen-ager, but rather a rational, deliberate, sensible decision to live together as man and woman on the island. Well, she had wanted to think about it and undoubtedly had done so, and then she had dreamed about bluebirds.

Thus, on the following morning, the picture seemed quite clear to Jim Kittering. A great cloud of bluebirds was on the horizon and the feathers of advance scouts already were floating in the air. "Honey," he said, "the time has come for us both to be honest. Do you want to talk here?"

"No, let's go somewhere else."

"All right, we'll go to the cove then."

When they reached the thin strip of beach by the cove, Jim put his hands on his hips and stared across the emerald water of the lagoon toward the wreck on the reef. The morning sun turned the rusting wreck a soft red. "Still there," said Jim. "I don't think it'll ever slide off that reef. The damn thing'll be there a hundred years from now."

"I'm glad it didn't slide off while you were on it," answered Melody. "Florence and I used to worry about that a lot. Especially Florence, she's the anxious type underneath. Once, when the wind was blowing and you were out there, I thought she'd have a fit. She wouldn't watch. She became almost hysterical and began to cry."

Jim dropped his hands from his hips in surprise. "Florence became almost hysterical?" he asked. "Because of me? Are you kidding?"

"No, I'm not. She said, 'He's going to drown,' then began to cry and ran in the cave and stayed there till you came back."

"Florence did that? I don't believe it. Florence wouldn't cry about me."

"She would and she did. She cried this morning, didn't you see her?"

"I sure didn't, and you're crazy."

"No, I'm not crazy. I almost wish I were, but I'm not."

"All right, why did Florence cry this morning, and when?"

"She cried because I dreamed about bluebirds and she thinks we're going to be lovers. She made those little remarks and I snapped at her, then when I looked over at her she had tears in her eyes. She's jealous of me."

"You're out of your mind," said Jim. "Florence isn't jealous of *you*—and we haven't come out here to talk about her."

"As a matter of fact, Florence is one of the things I *do* want to talk to you about."

"Huh," said Jim, who was disconcerted by this tack taken by Melody. What possible purpose could she have in bringing up Florence in such a way? "Florence or no Florence, this sun's pretty bright. Let's go sit under the Hanging Tree, we can talk there."

Melody had become more and more nervous as they approached the beach. She now stared apprehensively at the big tree at the foot of the cliff. "All right. But I wish you wouldn't call it the Hanging Tree."

"I didn't give it that name, your friend Florence did. What would you rather I call it, honey?"

"I don't care, anything you like, but not the Hanging Tree. Why do we need a Hanging Tree on this island? Why does anyone need a Hanging Tree anywhere?"

"Well, you've got to hang people someplace," said Jim. "But never mind, we won't go into it—let's sit under the Tree of Life and talk."

Melody's eyes were frightened behind the more modern-looking tortoise-shell glasses she now wore in place of the broken steel-rimmed spectacles. These were glasses she did not wear as a rule because Charles considered them "too Hollywoody."

"All right," said Melody, "we'll talk. But . . . do you want to take a swim first?"

"A swim?"

"Well, yes."

Jim had a sudden mental picture of Melody frolicking and splashing in flimsy underwear in warm emerald water. Was such swift spiritual development possible? Although she bathed at least once and often twice a day in a small salt-water pool dubbed by Florence "Melody's Bathtub," she had not been swimming for the sake of pleasure a single time since they had arrived on the island. She "had no bathing suit" and was too modest to swim in her underwear, and too modest even to borrow Florence's bathing suit, which she said was too small for her. The fact that both Jim and Florence had seen her stark naked for quite a while during the hurricane was a thing she had put out of her mind. "You mean . . . both of us, go swimming right now?"

"Oh, no, no, no, not me," said Melody, "you—I don't have a suit."

Jim had been fighting off a headache ever since he awakened and a faint stab of pain came between his eyes as the vision of Melody in her wet underwear vanished. This interview was not going quite as expected. "I don't want to go swimming all by myself," he said. "Besides, I thought you wanted to talk to me."

"I do. But I thought you might like to swim first."

"No, let's talk."

In a weak voice, Melody said: "All right."

Jim took her hand to help her up the little knoll at the foot of the cliff. The Hanging Tree or Tree of Life, whatever its proper name, grew in a scalloped and overhung recess of the cliff face and formed a shady bower.

"Let's sit here on the slope," said Melody.

Resistance, thought Jim. "No, it's not comfortable," he answered. "We'll sit under the tree where it's level."

"This is comfortable."

"It's right in the sun, Melody. Let's sit under the tree in the shade. Come on."

The Hanging Tree had leaves different from those of any other tree on the island and in Jim's belief was not native to Providence but had been planted by some visitor long, long ago. What visitor? he wondered, as he pulled Melody up the knoll and sat down with her in deep shade beneath the spreading canopy of olive-green foliage. Sir Henry Morgan himself, maybe? Was Morgan's Treasure buried, perhaps, beneath this tree? The talk with Melody thus far had been rather peculiar—first that cryptic notion about Florence, then the senseless suggestion he go swimming alone, and finally the resistance on the slope. However, Melody had been thinking all night and she was not an unintelligent woman.

And she was thinking now, head bowed over her hands in her lap as she sat on the sand beneath the hanging boughs. "Well," said Jim, "what did you want to talk to me about, honey?"

Melody adjusted her pale gray dress over her knees, lifted her eyes, and said in a calm voice: "Jim, I don't think we're going to get off this island any time soon. We've been here over three weeks now and we haven't seen anything at all like a boat. I think we might be here for a long time, maybe for months, perhaps many months. It could even be a year or two."

"I've said that from the beginning, honey. The island is in a remote area, it's very tiny, it has no harbor. The reef is too dangerous for fishing boats and too dangerous for pleasure yachts. We could be here a long time."

"Well, if we're here for a long time I'm going to need your help. That's why I've asked you to come talk with me this morning. Jim, I can't do it by myself."

"Can't do what, honey?"

"I can't resist unless you help me. Not for a long time, not for months. I could hardly do it even these few weeks, and last night I didn't have any will left at all. I haven't been honest about my feelings, but I'm being honest now. Jim, I can't control myself all alone, you've got to help me."

Jim reached in reflex to his shirt pocket and felt a little pang; it was at moments like this he wanted a cigarette. "Help you? I'm not sure I exactly understand."

She had been calm at the beginning, but an extreme nervous tension now seized Melody. She stared intently at him through the tortoise-shell glasses and twisted her fingers with a wringing motion in the lap of her pale gray dress. "I'm not as old-fashioned as you think I am," she said. "I know you're a man, and a man needs love. A woman's love . . . or most men do, anyhow. I realize that, I know it isn't fair to ask a man to . . . live alone for such a long period of time, or for what might be a long period."

"Women are no different, Melody. A woman needs love too."

"No, I don't agree with that. I think women aren't the same. If a woman knows nothing is going to happen, she can adjust to it. But for a man I think it would be very difficult and that's why I'm suggesting Florence."

Jim stared emptily at her. "You're suggesting Florence?"

"Yes. You could live with her here. I'm sure she would be willing, she loves you."

Again Jim reached to his shirt pocket for a cigarette that wasn't there, then he rubbed at his jaw in consternation. It was a development he had not anticipated. "Well, now," he said, "that would be difficult. That would pose a few problems."

"I know. Of course, it would still be adultery, you're married. But you and your wife *have* been unfaithful before and you *are* separated. I don't think it would be much more added danger to your marriage, although of course it would be to some extent. Any such thing is bound to be dangerous. You and Florence might fall in love seriously."

This madness had to stop. "Melody," said Jim gently, "I'm afraid you're barking up the wrong stump. Florence doesn't love me, she's a Lesbian."

"She's . . . what? She's a what?"

"She's a Lesbian. She isn't attracted to men, she's attracted to her own sex. It's you Florence loves, not me."

"Don't be silly," said Melody. "That's the most ridiculous idea I ever heard of. Florence is no such thing."

"Honey, I'm sorry to tell you this and I don't mean to upset you, but there *are* women like that in the world. They can't help it, they're not to be condemned or blamed for it—"

"I know there are women—"

"Just a minute, please, let me finish. I was saying, there are such women. As a result of painful early experiences they can't—"

"I *know* there are such women, but Florence isn't one of them!"

"I'm afraid she is."

"Jim, she *isn't!* Don't you think I would know? She's not like that at all. How could you believe such a stupid thing?"

"Well," said Jim with an uncomfortable smile, "her clothes, for example. Mannish suits, Melody—"

"She wears those suits because she feels unattractive and inferior. She's afraid to compete, that's all."

"That isn't all. I caught her staring at a pretty stewardess on the plane going to Atlanta."

"So what? I often stare at pretty girls."

"Not the way she did."

"Listen, you're wrong. I know you're wrong and I think you know it too. You don't believe this about Florence."

Jim started to answer angrily, then paused for a moment to think. It was true he'd always had certain doubts about Florence's Lesbianism. Perhaps Melody was partly correct. But only partly. "I'm afraid you don't know what you're talking about," he said. "Florence forms emotional relationships with women, not with men."

"What spinster doesn't, if men don't want them? What else has Florence got but girl and women friends? This is silly, I don't even want to talk about it. I know you're wrong because I know she loves you, and one of those women wouldn't."

A half-wincing squint came on Jim's face as he stared out at the emerald water of the lagoon beyond the umbrella-like limbs of the tree. Melody's absolute conviction was strangely persuasive, and if she was right, the situation on the island was not at all as he had thought. "Tell me something," he said. "How did it happen Florence got in bed with you the other night?"

"I asked her to. I'd had a nightmare, I was crying and miserable."

"What happened when she got in bed with you?"

"*Nothing* happened. She was very, very sweet to me, that's all. Jim, you couldn't be more wrong. Florence is just as feminine as I am, in some ways more so."

Jim's vexed irritation slowly disappeared as he stared out at the luminous water of the lagoon. It was true Florence in some ways was more feminine than Melody. Her irony and tough talk did not go very deep. In fact, it was ninety-five-percent bluff and so in all likelihood was the Lesbianism. Well, he'd always been dubious of Florence's Lesbianism. The mannish suit seemed like a disguise somehow. He'd doubted it on the plane too. She had *not* looked at the pretty stewardess *exactly* as a man would, but with a kind of rueful sadness.

"You're right," said Jim. "I guess I just didn't want to take it on. But you're wrong in thinking she loves me."

"I'm sure she does. And I'm sure she'd be willing to live with you here on the island. Of course, she's very afraid of men and very afraid of you too. You'd have to be . . . tactful with her—you know, gentle and understanding and yet firm. It would be difficult, she's very afraid, but I'm sure you could get her if you were persistent and showed you really wanted her. She loves you very much and—"

"Now look! Just a minute. Calm down. Maybe Florence isn't an out-and-out Lesbian, but I don't love her."

"Yes, but you like her very much."

"Melody, I don't want Florence, I want you!"

"Yes, but that *would* be immoral. With Florence, I don't think it would be. Not really. Or at least, not much."

Jim's headache was not getting any better. The very idea of giving up Melody for Florence gave him a shooting pain between the eyes. "Not much!" he exclaimed. "Melody, what a screwball you are! And what a notion for a missionary's wife to have. Will you tell me the difference between my committing 'adultery' with *Florence* and my committing 'adultery' with *you*?"

"Yes, I will," she answered. "First, Florence. I know it's adultery, technically and even literally, but as I said, I don't think it would be dangerous to your marriage. As for Florence, of course it wouldn't be permanent, but I believe it would help her, give her confidence, make her act more normal toward men. It would also help her here on the island, she'd be happy while it lasted, anyhow. Of course she might get pregnant and that's a problem. But she told me once how much she loves children and how she's often dreamed of adopting a child. I think she'd be happy to have a baby even if she weren't married. In fact, I'm sure of it. And nobody in New York would blame her, on this island and everything. It would be the best thing that could happen to Florence, much the best thing, and to me it isn't adultery, not really. And I think you should live with her."

"I think you're out of your head," said Jim. "That's the craziest speech I've heard all week. Florence wants a baby."

"She's not all that old and set in her ways, and she does love children. Even more important, she loves you."

"She *doesn't* love me and I'm getting tired of you saying that."

"I happen to know she does."

"I'm sorry, but you happen to be wrong. And you're wrong in thinking Florence is capable of a love affair with a man. She might not be an actual Lesbian, but she's extremely neurotic toward men. She shudders in revulsion if I touch her even accidentally. God knows *what* she'd do if I went to her and said, 'Florence, I want to live with you.' She'd probably scream and jump in the ocean and start swimming toward Central America."

"I don't think so. She'd be afraid, but she wouldn't jump in the ocean. Even if she argued and carried on and resisted, deep inside she'd be overjoyed. It would be the most wonderful thing that ever happened to her. Florence loves you, Jim."

Wearily, Jim put the palms of his hands over his eyes and his fingers in the roots of his hair. How had they become bogged down in this mad conversation about Florence? "Melody," he said, "arguing with you is like arguing with this goddamn tree. You get an idea in your head and you won't give it up. Now listen. Florence might—I say, she *might*—have a kind of romantic fixation on me. I'm aware of this, I've watched her, I've seen how she acts. But believe me, she'd get over it damned quick if I even looked at her seriously."

"A romantic fixation?" asked Melody. "Is that what you think it is?"

"I wouldn't even put it that strongly," said Jim as he tried to think of some way to get the conversation off Florence.

"I guess you really *don't* want to take her on," said Melody. "Well, I know she isn't very pretty. And I suppose that's all most men want, they don't care what a woman's like inside. They just want prettiness."

"Melody, will you listen? Florence is a daydreamer, all writers are."

"Well, she's just a suggestion," said Melody in a remote tone. "It's none of my business, it's completely up to you and her. If you feel it's wrong or if she does, then I certainly wouldn't disagree with you."

Jim paused, badly discouraged by the conversation thus far. The great cloud of bluebirds seemed to have turned around and headed back toward Texas. "Look, honey," said Jim gently, "I'm sure you meant well by your suggestion, and actually it's a kind of remarkable thing for you to say. But I love and want *you*."

Melody's eyes softened as a little smile came on her face. "That's a different situation, as I said."

"How is it different?"

"It wouldn't mean the same thing to me and Charles that it would to you and Linda. If I have a love affair with you on this island, it will be the end of everything for me and my husband."

"I don't think that's necessarily true at all."

"I think it is. I might be wrong, but it's a chance I can't take. You will have to admit, an adulterous affair often leads to divorce."

Jim hesitated. It always startled him when Melody started talking rationally. "Yes," he said, "an affair can lead to divorce, sure. Going down to the corner for a pack of cigarettes can lead to divorce."

"An affair is more dangerous, wouldn't you say?"

"Yes, I suppose so."

"It could lead to more than divorce. Jim, if you and I live together on this island, it's possible we would become very involved with each other."

"We're already involved, honey."

"If I live with you here, I think we would become so involved we might want to get married. Maybe not, but even so, we have to consider the chance. Jim, even if you didn't have a wife you love and I didn't have a husband I love, you and I would not be suited. I couldn't fit in your life. I don't have the same interests you have and I wouldn't know what to say to your friends or the people with whom you work. And you wouldn't fit in my life. The fact that we love each other doesn't mean we could be man and wife and fulfilled together, even if we were free, and we're not. Now, will you tell me if you agree with me?"

"Well," said Jim, "maybe I do. But I think you're being a little cold-blooded about this, honey."

"In what way?"

"You are leaving out my feelings and yours."

"No, I'm not. I said we love each other. But it's one thing on the boat or here on the island, away from everything and everybody. It would be another thing back in the world. I'm a trained nurse and have a religious calling."

Jim Kittering smiled. A grogginess had come upon him. "Well, I know you're an idealist," he said.

"No, Charles is an idealist, not me," said Melody. "I've never been an idealist, I don't believe in ideals, I believe in feelings. So does Charles, deep inside. In my opinion, all people who really do anything believe in feelings."

*Any*thing, thought Jim, to get the subject off Charles. This was worse than the discussion about Florence. "Intelligence plays its part, Melody. You didn't graduate as a nurse because of your sympathy for the patients, but because you learned things."

"Of course you've got to use judgment. That's what we've got to do now, you and me. I studied to be a nurse because this is my life and my work. You have your life and your work, Jim, and although I think in your way you want to help people too, the means by which you do it are very different from mine. We couldn't have a common life together and if we forgot our responsibilities and tried it we would fail, and the result would be heartache for all concerned. I don't want that, I don't want to risk it. We might not have the strength to give each other up when we leave the island and we are not suited to each other. That is the point I'm making and this time I want a real answer from you. Do you agree with me or not?"

Badly depressed, Jim gazed out at the white-topped waves along the curving line of the reef. The world beyond was many miles away, but Melody was right. He could not see himself organizing a Sunday-school picnic and singing hymns in church and he could not see Melody making conversation with a Gibson on the rocks in her hand at a New York cocktail party. Jim said, "I agree with you, honey. We wouldn't be suited as far as marriage is concerned, even if we were free."

A sadness came into Melody's face. For a moment she bowed her head and stared down at the lap of her pale gray dress, then she looked up at Jim and said: "I guess I hoped you wouldn't agree with me. But it's true, Jim. We really aren't suited to each other."

"In the outside world, maybe not, but we're here on the island now."

"We won't be on the island forever. We have to go back and we can't forget that. Don't you agree?"

"I don't think we'll be here forever, no."

Melody said quietly: "Charles and I *are* suited, Jim. He's a good husband for me and I'm a good wife for him. We have the same interests, the same work, the same friends. Of course we have some problems, every marriage does. But Charles and I are almost perfect for each other."

With an effort of will, Jim forced himself to nod gravely. He was determined to resist the temptation to remind her she had said the night before Charles could not or did not love her, that she and her husband had hardly lived together at all for the past three years.

"This is looking at it from a practical point of view, but there's another way to look at it more important than anything practical. I'm talking about love in its deepest sense. I love my husband, Jim. Charles is a wonderful man, whatever his faults. His feeling for others is greater than that of anyone I've ever known. He can see into people in ways I can't do and he can grow far beyond where he is now. The power he has is very rare and it's my duty to help him fulfill himself. I owe him that just as he owes me the same. If love has any meaning at all, loyalty must go with it. I can't commit adultery with you on this island. It would destroy my husband and me too. If you love me, if you care about me, then please help me."

"Melody . . . I admire your loyalty and I respect it. The point is, we're stranded on an uninhabited island and we might be here a long time. I don't see how any sensible man could object if his wife lived with someone else under these conditions."

Spots of color came into Melody's cheeks. In silence she stared at the pale gray dress over her knees, then looked up and said: "Jim, I would get pregnant. I'd get pregnant right away, I know I would. Think about that and what it would do to Charles. All our trouble comes from his not being able to be a father. Jim, he wouldn't be able to stand it."

"Oh, Christ," said Jim. "I'll do whatever you want."

Jim felt her hand on his arm. "I'll always be grateful. You don't know what this means to me or what a difference it makes. Here, I have a Bible in my pocket."

"A Bible? What for?"

"Jim, I know you'll keep your word. But I want us both to put our hands on the Bible and swear. It will help us."

"Oh, come on now, Melody!"

"Please, I want us to. It's important to me. I know we both already swore when we were married, but the island is like another world. I want us to swear in this situation here."

Jim looked at her in deepest gloom. "All right," he said, "what do you want me to swear?"

"This. 'I solemnly swear I will not commit adultery with Melody on this island, so help me God.' That's what I want you to swear, then I will swear the same thing about you."

Jim put his hand on the Bible with a helpless little shrug. He felt like a swimmer treading water in the North Atlantic. It would be impossible to get out of such an oath. The thing was fatal, the water deep and cold and dark. What was he doing in the icy North Atlantic when a warm and beautiful emerald lagoon was only a few yards away? And where had the great cloud of bluebirds gone? Head bowed, Jim stared at the Bible and at the pale gray dress behind it, then looked up into Melody's eyes and asked: "This is what you want?"

"Yes."

"All right," said Jim. "I solemnly swear I will not commit adultery with Melody on this island, so help me God."

For a moment Melody was silent. She seemed stunned with relief. "All right," she sighed, "now I'll swear." Jim held the Bible for her and she said: "I solemnly swear I will not commit adultery with Jim on this island, so help me God."

"Okay," said Jim. He stood up, put his hands on his hips and stared down at Melody, who continued to sit on the sand by the gnarled roots of the tree. "That's that."

A sad little smile came on Melody's face. "Do you hate me?" she asked.

"Of course I don't," said Jim. "I don't think you're wrong either."

"You really don't?"

"No, I think you're right. I think you ought to be faithful to your husband. And I think I ought to help you. I didn't want to face it, I guess I dreamed last night about bluebirds too. But that's all it was, a dream."

"Yes, that's all," said Melody. "A dream."

The oath, however, was the dream. The great cloud had not swerved or turned back toward Texas, it was on the way. Advance scouts already were chirping in the thistles of the Jungfrau and pale blue feathers were falling like snow.

SEVENTEEN

Sea Gull Blood

Four weeks and four days after the wreck of the *Lorna Loone,* Jim and Melody and Florence were awakened early one morning by a terrific squawking. Before any of them could get up to investigate, Rufus came padding into the cave with a sea gull in his mouth and dropped it on Florence's stomach. Florence screamed and the bird fluttered over onto Melody's bed and onto Melody herself, who for the sake of comfort in the tropical night slept with her pajama tops unbuttoned. Melody screamed even more loudly than Florence, twisted backward on her mattress and shoved away the dying bird, then jumped up and ran into Jim's arms with sea gull blood on her breasts.

At breakfast that morning, while Melody brooded and Florence sulked, Jim slowly became more and more annoyed with both of them, especially Melody. These episodes were becoming unbearable. And so was Melody's disposition.

"Well," said Jim, "now that this charming and delightful breakfast is over, sea gull blood and all, the day awaits us. It's your watch, Melody."

"What?" asked Melody.

"You heard me. I spoke perfectly plain and you heard me perfectly well. Don't look at me innocently as if you don't know what I said, because you do know what I said. I said it's your watch this morning."

"No, it isn't," she answered. "It's your watch."

"It is not my watch, it is yours. You are acting like a child. You know damned well it's your watch."

"I know damned well it isn't," said Melody in an aloof, ladylike tone. "And so does Florence. Ask her."

"Leave me out of this," said Florence. "I don't want to get in any arguments with you two. Besides, who cares? There're no ships out there anyhow."

Jim picked desultorily at his breakfast, which consisted of still another plate of Dinty Moore beef stew. He was sick unto death of it. But he was even more sick of the irresponsible way these women were acting. Jim stabbed at a gravy-covered piece of potato with his fork and said: "You are a pair of grasshoppers."

"You are a grasshopper yourself," answered Melody.

Jim ignored her childish riposte. It was one of the woman-simple methods she used in arguments: accuse her of something and she would accuse you right back of the same thing. She also depended heavily on flat contradiction. With an effort, Jim swallowed the potato and said: "I have never seen such irresponsibility in my life. You complain about wanting to get off the island, you whine and cry all the time about how you want to be rescued, but you won't lift one little pinky to do anything that might increase the odds in our favor. You're grasshoppers, both of you."

"So are you," said Melody.

"Oh, shut up, Melody!"

"Don't you dare tell me to shut up! I'll throw this beef stew right in your face and don't you think I won't!"

Jim not only thought she would, he knew she would. Her hand was on the plate and fire was in her eyes. It was quite a contrast to the scene between them half an hour before when he had wiped sea gull blood from her breasts and she had put her arms around him and kissed him repeatedly on the neck. Quite a scene, that. It was the strongest erotic contact between them since the oath and Jim had a miserable ache in the pit of his stomach. She no doubt had an equivalent reaction, a misery in her vitals of whatever kind it was women got from being powerfully aroused to no result. These episodes were truly becoming unbearable. How in Christendom did she expect him to keep the oath, the way she was behaving? The very idea, running into his arms and putting her bare breasts against his chest like that! It was outrageous, intolerable, and unfair, and now she was about to throw stew on him for good measure, the evil-tempered hateful bitch.

"All right, you needn't throw that stew at me," said Jim. "Don't you do that, Melody, don't throw that at me."

"Then don't tell me to shut up."

"My point is that you and Florence are not being logical. If you want to be rescued, you've got to go out there and look for a boat."

"There aren't any boats. And I'm warning you, don't you tell me to shut up. If you tell me that one more time, you'll be sorry."

"There aren't any boats *at the moment,* Melody. But there might *be* a boat sometime and—"

"You aren't being logical yourself. How do you know there isn't any boat at the moment? All you can see is part of the lagoon from the cave. There may be a boat on the other side of the island this very minute."

"Ha-ha-ha-ha," said Jim, as he stabbed in exasperation at another piece of gravy-covered potato. Only a fool would argue with a woman. The thing to do was drop it.

"And what's so funny, may I ask? There might be a boat."

"Yes. That is true, Melody. It was the point I was trying in my pathetic way to make, dear, when you interrupted me with that logical gem. Yes, there may be a boat and one of us should be out there to see it so that we can light the bonfire of palm fronds I so laboriously piled up while you *grasshoppers* stood and watched."

"All right, call me a grasshopper one more time, call me a grasshopper just one more time and you're going to get a plate of beef stew right in your face."

"All right, Melody, I apologize," said Jim, who did not want beef stew in his face, although he briefly considered letting her throw it on him and throwing his own on her in return. That wouldn't work, because then she would throw the plate at him and he could hardly throw his own plate at her and hurt her. "But I must say that for a missionary's sweet wife you have a pretty violent temper."

"I don't have a violent temper at all," she answered. "I just don't like to be told to shut up and be called a grasshopper."

"Frankly," said Florence, whose gaze was on her plate, "you both make me sick."

Melody turned quickly toward her. "Why do you say that, Florence? Why do you say we both make you sick?"

"You make me sick because of what you've done to yourselves."

"And what do you mean by *that*, Florence?"

Florence shrank down on the packing case upon which she was sitting, but refused to give up. "I think you know what I mean."

"I don't know at all," said Melody, "and I'd like to know."

"All right, I'll tell you, then. It's none of my business, but I have to live here with you both so in a way it *is* my business. I'm caught in the middle of this war between you two."

"War? What war? Are you crazy?"

"No, I'm not crazy. You and Jim are crazy. You should never have sworn that ridiculous oath." Florence turned to Jim. "And it's you I blame more than Melody. You ought to have known better, Jim."

"You're wrong," said Melody. "It wasn't Jim's doing. I made him swear the oath."

"I did it voluntarily for the good of us all," said Jim. "You don't know what you're talking about, Florence."

"You certainly don't!" said Melody.

Florence shrugged. "Okay, so the war goes on."

"All right, Florence! My patience is *just about* at an end."

"Are you going to throw the stew on me too, Melody?" Florence rose from the dining table, which consisted of three cases of the Dinty Moore beef stew with a blanket spread on top. "I am going for a walk with my dog and will leave you to your war. Maybe you'll strangle each other and settle everything. Do you want to throw the stew on me, Melody?"

Melody was silent, a hand over her eyes. She had begun to cry when Florence rose from the table. This was the pattern, temper and then tears; or, more exactly, desire and then temper and then tears. Glumly, Jim watched Florence walk out of the entrance of Morgan's Treasure Cave into the sunshine. He had quite an ache in the pit of his stomach. The scene that had occurred half an hour before had been unbearably sexy—so much so, the very memory of it made him dizzy.

"Melody," said Jim.

"What?"

"Honey, we can't get into situations like that. We can't, we just can't, that's all, or . . ."

"I know."

The thing had taken them all by surprise. They'd been up late the night before, singing and playing the accordion, and they were all sound asleep when the terrific ruckus began. Jim thought some wild, dangerous animal had invaded the cave even though he knew there were no such animals on the island. Half awake, he had stumbled in his undershorts to the blanket partition and the next thing he knew Melody flew into his arms, her breasts bare and smeared with sea gull blood.

"Oh, Jim! Oh!" she cried. "Oh, it frightened me to death! I didn't know what it was, I was asleep. . . ."

"It's just a sea bird the dog caught. Relax, Florence is taking it out."

The scene had been terribly sexy. Although he was half awake himself and as unnerved by the raucous squawking as the women, Jim had been instantly and horribly aware of Melody's soft, naked, pillowlike breasts against his bare chest. Over Melody's shoulder he saw Florence walk out of the entrance of the cave holding the dead sea gull by its feet; she would probably go on to the latrine, which was located behind a bush fifty feet down the hill from the cave. There was time. His hands were on Melody's shoulders in a rather brotherly way but as he saw Florence leave the cave he slid them under her pajamas onto her back. She had a beautiful back, truly beautiful, with wide handsome shoulders, a strongly arched spine, and skin like warm silk. Eyes closed, his right hand in the small of her back and his left hand between her shoulders, Jim gave a deep sigh and pulled her body more tightly against him. This was more like it. He could feel her mound of Venus with hard pubic bone behind it. To hell, he thought, with chaste Christian love, to hell with it once and for all, enough was enough. He hadn't realized how starved he was for a woman in his arms.

Melody's head was on his shoulder and her hands on his back below his shoulder blades. "Jim, I . . . I'm not completely dressed," she said in a doubtful voice. As she spoke, her body pressed against him and her arms tightened around him. Slowly, with an involuntary remorselessness, her pelvis twisted to one side and then to the other, as a heavy sigh like his own came from her. Jim felt her lips on his neck. "Oh, darling," she whispered. "Darling . . . Jim, Jim . . ." Again her lips kissed his neck, and again, and again. Her arms were around him so tightly it was difficult for him to breathe.

In a daze, Jim could hear Florence outside the cave scolding Rufus. "Bad dog, bad dog!" What an armful Melody was. God in heaven, what a woman. The breasts against his chest really and truly felt like small pillows.

"Jim," whispered Melody, "I can't stand this."

Florence did not seem to be going away. She was just outside the entrance of the cave, half scolding and half praising the dog. "Neither can I," said Jim. He moved his hands down Melody's back and slid them into the bottoms of her pajamas and spread his hands on the cheeks of her buttocks and pulled her more tightly against him.

"Did you hear me? Jim, I can't stand it. Please don't."

"In a moment," he answered.

Jim heard a sound, looked up, and saw Florence in the entrance of the cave. "Oh," said Florence, "excuse me. I'll come back later."

"No," said Melody, "that's all right. You can come in. It's nothing."

"I'll come back."

"Florence, I tell you it's nothing. Stay there. It's absolutely nothing."

"Nothing? It looks to me like he has his hands on your ass."

"Jim, will you let me go!"

"Of course, sure, I'm sorry," said Jim, as she pushed at his chest and twisted out of his arms.

"It's nothing, Florence," said Melody with a glazed smile. "I was frightened by the bird. Come right on in."

"Well, if you insist. I don't want to get in your way if you want privacy."

"Oh, no, no, no," said Melody smiling. "I wouldn't dream of it, it's time for breakfast."

Jim rolled his eyes toward the rocky ceiling of the cave and shook his head. Melody, at times, could pretend the obvious truth was not the truth at all. Her performance in this case was rendered all the more ludicrous by the fact that she seemed to have forgotten her pajama tops were unbuttoned and her breasts exposed. "Well," said Jim, "you have blood on your chest from that bird, let me get a handkerchief."

"Oh, I do have blood on me, don't I?" said Melody casually.

"You both are slightly bloody," said Florence, "and so am I. That sea gull bled all over the place."

Melody made no effort to cover herself. Hands on hips, she stared into Jim's eyes as he walked up to her with a handkerchief. Blood was smeared on her left breast and a red trickle had run down between her breasts toward her stomach, which also was exposed. The pajama bottoms were loosely tied and hung down below her hipbones so low they were practically falling off her. Jim could see not only the girlish, dentlike navel on her stomach but also a half-inch line of dark curly pubic hair above the tied bow of the pajamas. The artificial, everything-is-just-fine smile on her face was gone.

"Here, honey," said Jim as he held out the handkerchief. Melody did not answer and did not move. Hands on hips, she stared broodingly into his eyes. Slowly, Jim took the handkerchief and began to wipe the blood from her breasts. He had the task about half done when she put her hands on his shoulders, rested her head on his chest, and began to cry.

"Oh, for Christ's sake," said Florence. "I'm getting out of here."

Jim patted Melody on the shoulder as Florence walked out of the cave. "Now, look, don't cry," he said. "There's no reason to feel bad, honey."

"Oh, Jim," she answered, "it was all my fault. I'm sorry."

"Don't worry about it," said Jim.

Melody drew back from him and buttoned the tops of her pajamas, which were a blue and white silk polka dot pair he had bought at Saks Fifth Avenue. Melody's trunk, which contained most of her clothing, was soaked in water down in the hold of the wreck and she had few of her things on the island. She had admired the pajamas and asked if they were expensive, and had been horrified and unbelieving when he told her he'd paid sixty dollars for them.

"How can you tell me not to worry about it?" she asked. "When I act like that, completely shameless, awful, terrible, how can you say to me, 'Don't worry about it.'? I don't understand you. And I don't understand myself either, how I could behave like that. I guess I just don't have any willpower or character."

"Don't talk silly, honey."

"I'm not talking silly, I'm telling the truth. I don't have any willpower or character and that's all there is to it."

"I think there's quite a bit more to it."

"I don't. You can have your theory it's right to do a thing because you want to, but I don't agree."

"That isn't my theory. You know it isn't. Furthermore, you have a great deal of both willpower and character."

"I wonder what your wife would think. I wonder what Charles would think if he could have seen the way I was acting. I wonder what any decent, civilized person would think. Except I don't wonder, I know. Even an oath sworn in the sight of God doesn't make any difference to me, and you tell me, 'Don't worry about it.' I deserved that remark from Florence about you having your hands on me. Of course I did. Completely. It was my fault, the whole thing, I used the bird as an excuse."

Temper followed by tears was one pattern, passion followed by guilt was another. It was impossible to talk to her in this frame of mind. "I'm sure we both were partly to blame," said Jim.

Later, when Melody went down the hill to go to the bathroom and wash for breakfast, Jim called to Florence over the blanket partition: "Are you angry with me?"

"No," answered Florence. "Why should I be angry?"

"You seemed angry." Silence, broken by a faint sound of rustling clothes as she dressed. "Can I come in? Are you decent?"

"I suppose so, more or less."

Jim pulled aside the blanket. Florence's hands were raised behind her to fasten the hooks of her brassiere and Jim stared at her in surprise. "Hmm," he said, "more or less, yes."

"What's the difference? Will you tell me what difference it makes if you see me in a bra or not?"

"You *are* angry," said Jim.

Florence shoved her arms into the sleeves of her shirt and yanked the shirt together and began to button it. "I'm just sick of you tormenting her," she answered. "And a little weary of watching you torment yourself. Why in the world did you *ever* swear that insane oath with her?"

Jim smiled. "You women amuse me. You advise me to stop tormenting Melody and go to bed with her. On the other hand, *she* advised me eight days ago to go to bed with *you*."

"*Me?*" asked Florence.

"Yes, she says you love me."

"That's very funny," said Florence, "but you haven't answered my question. Why in heaven's name did you swear that oath with her?"

"I had no choice," answered Jim. "It was impossible for me to refuse, Florence."

"You could have refused very easily. You could have just said no. The truth is you agree with her—or at least you *did* agree with her. Do you still?"

"I couldn't possibly refuse her, Florence. But if you want to know, yes, I agree with her. I don't think I ought to have an affair with her and get her pregnant and wreck her marriage and ruin her life, no. And we're not going to break that oath. We're human and because of the accident this morning we were tempted, but nothing is going to happen, Florence. Nothing. I guarantee you."

"Do you know what? There's a fanatical glitter in your eyes and I believe you."

"Oh, to hell with you," said Jim. He walked out of the "bedroom" and angrily yanked shut the blanket partition. Florence was jealous and wanted Melody for herself. She didn't want him to break the oath, but was angry because she thought he would break it.

Thus, at breakfast on a beautiful morning four weeks and four days after the wreck of the *Lorna Loone,* while Melody brooded and Florence sulked, Jim Kittering slowly became more and more annoyed with both of them, especially Melody. An idiotic argument occurred at the very beginning of the meal on the question of whose turn it was to get water.

"It's your turn, Melody," said Florence.

"No, it's Jim's turn."

"It is *not* my turn," said Jim. "I got the water yesterday."

"All right, and I got it day before yesterday," said Melody. "It's Florence's turn."

"I cooked the stew," said Florence. "It isn't fair to me to have to cook the breakfast and get the water too."

"You opened a can and struck a match and held it for three seconds to that kerosene stove *I* lugged all the way up that hill," declared Jim, "after taking it off that wreck at the risk of my life."

"I also set the table," said Florence sulkily.

"Florence, it's *your turn* to get the water," said Jim. "I never heard such a chauvinistic, *mealy*-mouthed argument in my life."

"Oh, shit!" said Florence. "Life in this cave is disgusting!"

"It is when people talk like that," said Melody primly. She turned to Jim as Florence threw her napkin on the table and walked out with the pitcher. "And *you* are no better when it comes to that kind of language. In fact, you're worse."

Jim resisted an impulse to say something obscene to her, contenting himself with a mere: "Uh-huh."

"You needn't say 'Uh-huh' to me in that rude way as if I'm a stupid child. I'm just as intelligent as you are and I resent being patronized. Furthermore, what I said is true. Your language is worse than Florence's, by far. You talk in a very filthy way, like a little schoolboy trying to shock someone."

Jim gritted his teeth, smiled, and said, "All right, Melody."

"And I wish you'd stop it."

"I will try and stop it."

"I mean *really* try and stop it."

"I will really try."

Melody was silent for a while, then said: "Actually, I think it was your turn to get the water, Jim."

"Um-hmmm."

"Florence got it yesterday."

"Mmm."

Again she was silent for a while. Jim knew from experience she was working herself into the mood to say something really nasty. He was determined not to play. Let her say anything she wanted to and he would agree with it or at least make no comment. However, on this occasion she caught him by surprise and threw him.

"Jim?"

"Yes, Melody."

"You have no moral sense."

Briefly, spots of fury winked before Jim's eyes. Damnable bitch, to say such a thing after he'd worn himself out working for her and had sweated blood worrying about her. Through his teeth, Jim replied: "Don't I?"

"No, I'm afraid you don't. You have no more moral sense than an animal in a barnyard. Going around all the time without your shirt is the least of it. It's the way you act, the way you talk and smile and everything else, and I'm sick and tired of it! I can't endure your behavior any longer! Do you understand me?"

"No, frankly, I don't. A saint might understand you, but not me."

"Well, I understand *you.* It took me a while, you fooled me, I admit, but now I know you for what you are, Jim. I had a horrible dream about you the other night. I dreamed a big inhuman hog-man was trying to push me off a cliff, and that inhuman hog-man was *you.* Yes, you, Jim. *Charles* came along and took my hand and saved me, after I'd thrown a rock at the hog-man and killed it."

Again spots winked before Jim's eyes. The impulse to throttle her was almost overwhelming. "So you think I'm a hog-man, huh," he said. "After I've driven myself half crazy staying away from you and worked myself half to death trying to help and protect you, that's what you think of me."

Melody stared at him with an implacable anger in which there was not even the faintest shred of gratitude. "You're a hypocrite," she said. "You don't live by the things you say you believe in. What's more, you didn't work all that hard. Most of the time you made me and Florence do the work."

"You and Florence, *work?* Ha!"

"And me with awful cramps from my period for four days there, and Florence with her ribs broken and her side all hurting. That's your idea of being a gentleman. Wonderful."

"What do you expect of a hog-man like me?" asked Jim.

It was a painful meal and the misery didn't end after Florence had gone. As a rule, once she began to cry, Melody became contrite. Not this time. The days of contrition were over. It had started quietly with an effort on his part to make her realize such scenes as that inspired by the sea gull could not be allowed to happen.

"Honey, we can't get into situations like that. We can't, we just can't, that's all, or . . ."

"I know."

"I don't want to talk to you in a clinical way, I know you hate that kind of talk, but we've got to face the fact that beyond a certain point *no one* can control himself . . . or *herself* either, women are no different."

"Beyond a certain point, it happens," she answered. "I'm very aware of that."

"I hope you are."

"I am. I'm not a child."

"Then we mustn't get in such situations again."

"No, of course we mustn't." Melody was silent for several seconds, then said, "Jim, I'm sorry I threatened to throw the beef stew on you."

"That's all right, you were upset because—"

"I'm also sorry I called you a hog-man. Of course you're nothing like that, you're just immature."

Jim forced himself to wait before answering her, but it was impossible for him to remain calm. She was beyond doubt the most infuriating woman he had ever known. To be called immature was worse than being called a hog-man. "Look," he said, "you want to fight with me because of what happened this morning. Well, I am not going to play your game, Melody. It was you who came running into my arms, not me into yours. And I must say, that's the oldest cliché there is. 'Oh, the thunder—darling! Oh, a mouse—darling!' In this situation, it was a convenient sea gull."

"How can you tell such a lie? You know that bird frightened me, I wasn't putting that on."

"I'm sure it frightened you, but you admitted yourself you used it as an excuse and now you're blaming *me* for it and calling me a hog-man and immature."

"Yes, but you wouldn't let me go. I asked you to, and you wouldn't, and now you say it's all my fault. That's the coward's way, Jim. Only a moral coward puts all the blame on somebody else. And that's what you are, Jim, an immature moral coward."

"I don't want to talk to you," said Jim.

"That makes two of us," she answered. "I don't want to talk to you either. You are the most cruel and hateful man I've ever known."

"Oh, go to hell," said Jim.

Melody's eyes flashed toward the kerosene stove and for a moment Jim thought she would throw a pot at him, but she didn't. A pot was not enough. In an unnaturally calm voice she said: "That is the end. Do you hear me?"

"Sure, I hear you. A hog-man has ears."

"Then listen to this. You *are* a hog-man, Jim, and you've done your best to ruin and destroy me in every little subtle way you can."

"I'll tell you what *you* are, Melody. You're an oversexed hysterical nitwit and a phony Christian, and you can take a flying jump and kiss my ass."

Jim was sure she'd throw a pot at him this time and he didn't give a damn if she did, but again she didn't. "You are right," she said. "I *am* a phony Christian, and the other too. A good Christian and a decent woman wouldn't feel about you the way I do. I hate you, Jim. I hate you for what you are and for what you've aroused in me. But it's finished and ended. I will not speak to you again while we're on this island."

"Thank God for something," said Jim.

Melody spent the morning writing a long letter, undoubtedly to her husband. In tears, she tore it up around noon. She had eaten practically no breakfast and ate no lunch at all. In a wan tone she explained to Florence: "I have no appetite." She wouldn't speak to Jim and wouldn't even look at him. He was on watch that afternoon at Morgan's Armchair and was glad to get away from her; the sun-baked rocks and cactus thorns of the Matterhorn were a relief in comparison. Jim caught a glimpse of her at two o'clock on her way to her daily bath and deliberately turned and scanned the sea in other directions in order not to look at her. He'd regretted almost immediately his final insult, especially the part about her being "oversexed," but he didn't want to look at her or think about her. As far as he was concerned, the best thing that could happen would be for a flying saucer to pick up the damnable bitch and take her to Venus. Nevertheless, as he gazed out at featureless blue sea and empty blue sky, Jim wondered how long this impossible war could continue. If a flying saucer did not take Melody to Venus, what then?

Upon his return in late afternoon, Florence met him at the entrance of the cave and reported that Melody was lying on her bed reading the Bible and weeping and brooding.

"What do you want me to do about it?" asked Jim.

"I just thought you might like to know how things stand," answered Florence. "She says she hates you and would rather be dead than stay on the island with you."

"She told you that, huh?"

"Yeah. She wants me to help her build a raft so we can float to Central America."

"Oh, Christ," said Jim wearily. "I thought of a raft the first day, Florence. The wood of the trees on this island is heavy as iron. It won't float."

"She also mentioned the life raft from the ship."

"It's half full of water," said Jim, "and there's no way to rig a sail on it. We wouldn't have a prayer."

"Looks like we're stuck then, doesn't it? Here we are and here we will remain, until fate whimsically releases us."

"Yeah," said Jim.

"Well, I'm sorry the way I myself acted this morning. A little loss of control there."

"You were nothing compared to *her*. She's become impossible. And so have I. You should have heard the things we were saying to each other."

"I can imagine. It must have been gruesome." Florence lifted a sardonic eyebrow. "And by the way, speaking of the things people say, I hope you didn't take seriously the thing Melody said about my feelings toward you. She's very romantic and naive."

"She's crazy," said Jim. "I never realized it before, but she's crazy."

Florence smiled. "She isn't crazy. She's just emotional and very naive."

"She's crazy in the sense that she has no grasp of the reality of her own nature and no grasp of the reality of her situation here on the island. Can you imagine it? She actually in all seriousness offered you as a kind of substitute for herself. I wonder how she'd be acting now if I'd taken her up on it, if you and I were living together and she was all alone."

Florence again lifted an eyebrow. "If you'd taken *her* up on it? Wouldn't *I* have something to say about it?"

"Well, you could reject me, of course. But she suggested I try."

"I suggest you don't. I don't want to make hostile noises at a man I like as much as I do you, Jim, but I'm afraid I would scratch your eyes right out of your head."

Jim nodded thoughtfully. Florence sat in the entrance of the cave with her arms around the neck of her dog Rufus, who was panting in a "smiling" way and seemed to enjoy it. As she talked to Jim, she embraced the animal with a tender protectiveness, arms tightly around him and a hand on his shaggy head. Her small breasts were against the dog's side. There was, Jim felt, something incongruous and pathetic about her love for Rufus. He smiled and said: "You really love that dog, don't you, Florence?"

"Yes," she answered, "but that's irrelevant to what I just said."

Jim hesitated. Her arms were now even more tightly around the dog and the look of fear and dread in her eyes was unmistakable. "You know, it's funny," he said. "I've worried a lot about you since we've been on the island. One of the reasons I swore that oath with Melody was because of you."

"Because of me?"

"Yes, I was afraid of what would happen to you if Melody and I became involved here. It seemed to me this would be very bad for you, but do you know something? I think I was dead wrong."

Florence's freckles stood out like measles against the pallor of her face. "Why do you think that?"

"Well, wouldn't you rather have a human being in your arms than a dog?"

"No, I wouldn't."

"I think you would."

Florence stood up. "I hope for your sake you never act on that opinion," she said. "It'd be a pity for you to have to go around the island tapping with a cane."

How could he have been so stupid, how could it have taken him so long to understand Florence? Even now, shaking at the knees and gazing at him in stunned fear, she had her hand gently around the dog's neck and her leg against his side. Crazy and impossible as Melody's idea had been, she was fundamentally right about Florence. "You'd scratch out my eyes and blind me, huh? You'd do a cruel thing like that to me?"

"I sure as hell would," said Florence. "Come on, Rufus, let's go for our sunset walk. The man is talking filthy."

Jim watched Florence walk off down the hill with Rufus, then he turned and looked up at the rock formation called Morgan's Armchair on top of the Matterhorn, the wilder of the two hills on Providence Island. The sunset from on top of the hill was very beautiful. Sunset also was very beautiful in the lagoon, which changed color as the light reddened and dimmed.

Jim got up and walked into the cave. The blanket partition of the women's bedroom was drawn. He went over to it and asked: "Melody, are you dressed?" Silence. "Honey, we can't get off this island and we can't live here without talking to each other. Are you dressed?"

Jim heard her take a deep breath and sigh, then he heard a sniff, and another sniff, and finally: "Yes, I'm dressed. What do you want?"

"I want to ask you something. Can I come in?"

"No, not right now. I'll come out in a minute."

"Okay," said Jim. He walked over to a canvas deck chair in the living area of the cave and sat down. A few seconds later, Melody pulled open the blanket partition and came out of the bedroom, her glasses in one hand and a handkerchief in the other. Head bowed, weeping and biting at her lip, she sat down in a deck chair across from Jim. "Florence has gone for her sunset walk with Rufus," he said. "Would you like to go for a walk with me?"

A weepy expression came on Melody's face and her shoulders shook as she suppressed a sob. Again she bit at her lip, sniffed, rubbed her eyes with the handkerchief, and replied: "It's only an hour before supper."

"I know, but that's long enough for a walk. I thought maybe you'd like to see the sunset from the top of the hill. Or maybe you'd like to go for a swim."

"A swim?" Melody fumbled in her lap for her glasses and put them on. "Well," she said, in a voice so low Jim could barely hear her, "I . . . I don't have a suit."

"You could borrow Florence's."

"It . . . it's too tight, uncomfortable."

"It was just an idea. I thought you might like to go swimming, since you never have here on the island."

"No, I never have, that's true. And I . . . I've often thought of it, I love to swim. But Florence's suit is much too tight."

"I should think it would be."

"It is, I tried it on, it's very uncomfortable. Of course, I suppose I could swim in my underwear. Once I was in the water it wouldn't matter."

"It wouldn't matter anyhow," said Jim. "A brassiere and panties are about as much bathing suit as anybody wears these days, honey."

"Yes . . . I suppose so, but . . ."

"Or we could just go for a walk. Whatever you want."

Melody dried the tears from her cheeks with her handkerchief, cleared her throat, and said, "It might do me good to get out of here a little."

"Shall I put on my trunks, in case we decide to go swimming?"

"Well, yes," said Melody.

In the palm grove a few yards from the beach, Melody's voice began to tremble as she discussed the weather. "I thought it would rain this afternoon," she said. "You know, when the clouds came up. But it didn't, it never did rain."

"Sometimes it doesn't."

"No. But sometimes when you think it won't, it does."

"That's true," said Jim.

The lagoon was dark green but still luminous as a jewel in the late afternoon sunshine. The beach remained a crescent of pure white with tiny mica sparkles and bits of irridescent seashell. Melody had given up her feeble effort to converse on the weather and Jim felt a pity for her. She was fiddling nervously at the neck of her gray dress, the same hateful dress she had been wearing when he first saw her by the gangplank of the *Lorna Loone*, but although he thought of the dress as hateful Jim had a certain ambivalence toward it—he had, after all, fallen in love with her when she had it on.

Very pale, very frightened, Melody stared out at the beach and the emerald water. Slowly, she raised her hands to the neck of her dress, undid one button, another, and another, then paused. "I'm sorry, I know it's silly, but . . . would you turn your head for a moment?"

"Sure," said Jim. He faced the lagoon, folded his arms across his chest, and waited. He heard a faint lap of waves on the sand and the sound of his own heart beating in his ears, then a rustle, another rustle, and a light whisper that had to be the gray dress falling to the sand.

"You may as well turn around," said Melody. "It's foolish of me, you've seen me with nothing on at all."

"Yes, I have," said Jim. Melody stood before him in her brassiere and panties, a shy expression on her face and her shoulders uncharacteristically slumped in such a way as to exaggerate the depth of the valley between her breasts. As always, the Hera-like voluptuousness of her body hit him with a slight shock. He knew the body was there, but the revelation of it was like a trick of magic. The gray dress about which Jim had feelings of ambivalence lay on the sand at the foot of a coconut palm. He took her hand and said: "Let's go swimming before it gets dark."

"All right. But do you have a pocket?"

Jim lifted the underwater mask he'd tied to his trunks. "Sure, a big one here under the mask."

"Keep my glasses for me, then. I just hope I haven't forgotten how to swim."

Melody had not forgotten how to swim. Her nervousness and shyness disappeared after she waded into the water. Since she'd never seen tropical fish in their natural habitat, they swam out near the rusting wreck of the ship in order for her to look at the reef and the fish through the underwater mask. Jim managed to fit the mask over her glasses and she ducked down for a look. Her reaction to the spectacular reef and fish did not surprise him; he had expected some sort of religious or at least mystical comment. "It's beautiful beyond words," she said. "I don't see how anyone can look at that reef and those fish and not believe in God."

Gradually they worked their way up the beach along the line of the reef to the deeper pool by the cove. Melody was a strong swimmer, as she had claimed during the hurricane. She swam with an old-fashioned but powerful Australian crawl and it was difficult for Jim to keep up with her. He was winded when they reached the cove, but she was not. In shallow water to his waist, Jim stood watching her do underwater somersaults, first her feet, then her head and shoulders breaking the surface of the lagoon. Smiling, she called to him, "Can you do that?"

Jim put on the underwater mask, swam out to her, ducked under the water, and there she was in a soundless crystal world, arms and legs slowly moving. He could see the indented lines of her brassiere but the rayon panties were so transparent he thought for a moment they had either come off while she was swimming or that she herself had taken them off. Jim swam under her and surfaced behind her and pulled her hair. Treading water and smiling, she turned toward him.

Jim grinned back at her. "Under water it looks like you've got nothing on at all," he said.

"It *feels* like I've got nothing on," said Melody, "except for the bra. Water keeps ballooning in the cups."

"Take it off, then."

"My bra? Good grief, what would people think?"

She was smiling and joking, her lips pressed together in a manner Jim found very attractive. There was also a childlike flirtatiousness in her eyes that he found extremely charming. He pushed the mask up on his forehead, reached behind her with one hand, got a hook of the bra unfastened, and sank bubbling under the water. Again, but dimly, without benefit of the underwater mask, he saw her arms and legs moving in slow motion through the crystal-clear water. He dog-paddled to the surface and heard her laughing at him.

"Ha ha ha, serves you right—that's what you get for being so fresh."

"I was just trying to help you. You said water balloons in the cups."

"It does."

"Then take the silly thing off."

"All right. But keep it in your belt and give it back."

"Okay."

"Do you promise?"

"Yes, sure, I promise."

Thrashing powerfully with both legs and smiling at Jim, Melody reached behind herself. She managed to keep her head above water. "See? It's off." The brassiere landed in the water beside Jim. Deliberately, he ignored it. "Hey, don't let it sink! You'll lose it and I won't be able to get out!"

Jim put on the underwater mask, dived for the brassiere, and found it floating limp and empty three feet below the surface. Melody's arms and legs still were moving in slow motion and so now were her breasts, lifting and rising gently, free of the brassiere and more beautiful than any angel or parrot fish or any coral reef. Her breasts moved with the current of the water; the nipple centers moved a little bit together, a little bit apart, went slightly up, went slightly down—she looked cross-eyed, cuckoo, startled, and absorbed in her navel by turns. Fascinated by the gentle feminine eyes staring at him in the clear water and charmed by the varying expressions caused by the current, Jim forgot the necessity to breathe and came to the surface, gasping.

"Did you find it?"

Jim held up the bra. "Yeah, but I had some trouble. A couple of eyes were staring at me down there."

"You shouldn't look at such things."

"I couldn't help it. They were looking at me."

"Turn a somersault and get it out of your mind, then you'll feel better."

"I don't feel bad."

"Go on, turn a somersault, I want to see you do it."

Jim turned several somersaults to oblige her, then said, "Okay, that's enough, let's go ashore."

"Well, give me my bra."

"You don't need it."

"Yes, I do, give it to me."

Jim handed her the brassiere and she swam toward shore till her feet touched sand, then she put on the bra, took his hand, and walked with him to the beach.

"Did you like it?" asked Jim.

"I loved it."

"I should have taken you swimming before."

"Yes, you should have. Except I probably wouldn't have gone. I had to get completely miserable first."

"Yeah, maybe so." Jim glanced toward the big tree at the foot of the cliff, the tree under which he had sworn not to commit adultery with Melody on Providence Island. Out of nowhere the recollection came to him of a rather bad motion picture starring Gary Cooper and a Swiss or Austrian actress not too active these days. "The Hanging Tree" it was called, with a murky ballad that sobbed optimistically that nothing was closer to the Tree of Life than a good old fundamental Hanging Tree. And he had thought his play with the names of the tree was rather cute. Banality was sly as Asian flu and one ballad leads to another. "Oh, I committed adultery with my darlin' beneath the Hangin' Tree of Li-i-i-fe, though we swore we wouldn't do no such thang. . . ." Jim could hear it, he could see Hob approvingly narrow his eyes and make a little triumphant circle with his thumb and forefinger.

"Why are you smiling?" asked Melody.

"Just thinking of something," said Jim.

"What?"

In a sudden daze, Jim stopped to consider. There was still time, nothing had to happen, compulsion was only a word. He could lead her to the palm grove, help her into her pale gray dress, and take her back to the cave. Of course, it would be a hog-man kind of thing to do, a cruel and hateful thing . . . indeed it would. To hell with appearances and to hell with Hob.

"I was just thinking how pretty you look with that dress off," said Jim. "I don't want you to ever put that thing back on, just leave it where it is in the coconut grove."

Melody smiled. "You know, I hate that dress myself. I've always hated it."

"Leave it lie, then." Jim took her hand. "Let's go sit under the tree."

Her smile faded slightly. "That tree?"

"Yes. It's only a tree."

"All right," said Melody.

The sun was getting low behind the hill, but there was still plenty of light beneath the umbrella-like limbs of the tree. As Melody sat beside him on the sand, Jim could see the nipples of her breasts and the dark triangle of her pubic hair through her wet underthings. The shyness had come upon her again. Timidly and nearsightedly, she stared at him in silence. "I know you just put this back on," said Jim, "but let's take it off again." He reached behind her, unfastened her brassiere and pulled it off, then put his arms around her and kissed her. She returned the kiss and he kissed her again, and again, then placed his hands on her shoulders and said, "Sit back and raise up for a second." Melody leaned back on her elbows and lifted her hips clear of the sand as he pulled down her wet panties. He then took off his own swimming trunks and a moment later found himself in a position similar to the one he'd been in when Florence burst upon them in the life-raft closet during the hurricane. The only difference was that Melody had her ankles locked and her arms across her breasts. Jim put his hands on her shoulders and his knee between her legs.

"Jim . . . we swore we wouldn't."

"I know," he said. "We're going to break the oath."

Melody slowly uncrossed her ankles and put her hands on either side of Jim's face. Her legs were still together, her eyes opened wide in an effort to see into his own. Jim felt her legs move apart. For a moment he hesitated, then in dreamlike shock he felt the warmth of her body. "Oh, darling," she whispered, "I love you, I love you. . . ."

It had taken Jim a month to get the Goblin Special back on the air, but it did not seem to him a Goblin Special at all. Hands on her breasts, enveloped in the warmth of her body, Jim stared into her eyes and whispered: "I love you too . . ."

EIGHTEEN

On Top of Old Jungfrau

Jim awakened at dawn with the feeling that something catastrophic had occurred. For a groggy half-minute he could not think what thing it was, then he remembered the bluebird feathers, the sea gull blood, the Hanging Tree of Life, and all the rest. He whispered, "Oh, God." Something had to be done about this. If the memory of events made him want to jump in the ocean, what would it do to Melody? Jim got up, silently dressed, climbed to the top of the hill, and sat down on Morgan's Pillow, then for an hour struggled to find a way to modify the feathers, the blood, and the tree. It was there the idea came to him, on top of old Jungfrau in the pearly dawn.

A tense, awkward silence prevailed during the first five minutes of breakfast, which consisted as usual of inescapable Dinty Moore beef stew and tongue-furring canned grapefruit juice. Florence, whose eyes were pink from weeping and who was in an unconcealable dither of nerves, finally could endure it no longer. "Well," she asked, "is anyone going to say anything?"

"Mmm," said Jim.

"Very well, *I'll* say something. Frankly, I am glad. The situation around here had become impossible and I'm happy for you both."

Melody, who looked ill, glanced up briefly at Florence. She seemed to have lost the power of speech.

"Look," said Florence, "I know it's none of my business, Melody, but when you come in stark naked at three in the morning we *can't* just pretend nothing happened. Isn't that true?"

"Yes," said Melody, her gaze fixed on her plate of beef stew, which she had not touched. "I don't mean to pretend."

"And I don't mean to poke my nose where it doesn't belong either," said Florence. "But we have to live together in this cave, Melody, all three of us, and I think there are a few things we had better face honestly here and now. Don't you agree?"

"Yes."

"All right. First of all, living arrangements. This cave, I regret to say, provides damned little privacy. I see nothing we can do about it, we can't build you a boudoir with two-by-fours and plaster and flocked wallpaper with rosebuds. But in view of last night I assume that you and Jim will now want to share our present bedroom."

"I don't want any breakfast," said Melody.

"What did I *say?*" asked Florence.

"Nothing. I don't feel well."

"Melody, I don't want to embarrass you and I don't want to interfere with you and Jim in any way. But we've simply got to decide a few things, such as living arrangements here in the cave, who's going to sleep where, and so forth. I assume, Jim, you will want to change bedrooms with me?"

"Maybe we'd better talk about it later," Jim said.

"I want to get it settled here and now," replied Florence. "It's on my mind and it bothers me. I agree to change bedrooms, that's reasonable. But, as I said before, there's very little privacy in the cave. God knows I'm not an expert in this area or what you'd call an authority . . . but don't people in love want privacy?" Jim lowered his eyes in discomfort. Florence was indeed in a dither of nerves; Jim was afraid she would begin to cry at any moment, yet there seemed no way to shut her up except to jump on her and hurt her feelings. Head bowed, he listened to her. "I guess people in love do, I'm sure they do . . . I mean, want to be alone, but I have to stay in the cave, there's nowhere else for me to go, at night I have to stay here. But I can go out during the afternoons and walk. . . ."

Melody stood up, a hand on her stomach. "I really don't feel well," she said.

"Melody, I don't *want* to be in the way, but where can I go?"

"Florence, we'll talk about it later," said Jim.

"I can't sleep in the cactus bushes, what's to become of me? I don't want to invade your privacy, but I can't help it in this . . . this damned cave!"

"I said that's *enough,* we'll talk about it later."

Florence turned to him in shock, a thin film of tears in her eyes. "Jim . . . Jim, I'm just trying to be calm and sensible. You don't have to shout at me like that."

"I didn't shout at you."

"Please excuse me," said Melody, hand on her stomach and eyes averted from them both. "I'm going to lie down, I feel sick."

"Sit down and eat your breakfast, Melody," said Jim. "The reason you feel sick is because you haven't eaten anything since day before yesterday."

"No, I really am sick."

"You're not sick, your stomach is empty, that's all. Now, sit down and eat, then I want you to come with me to the Elysian Field. There's something I'd like to discuss with you."

"What?"

"Come on, honey, eat some of the stew."

"Oh, Jim, I can't. I'm sick to death of it."

"We're all sick of it, but eat it anyhow, then you'll feel better."

"What is it you want to discuss?"

"I'll tell you later. Eat some breakfast."

Jim managed to coax and nag her into drinking a glass of grapefruit juice and eating half a plate of stew, at which point Florence made a choking sound and abruptly got up and walked out. "Oh, Christ," said Jim. "I guess I spoke too rough to her, but what could I do? She'll just have to adjust, that's all."

"Adjust," said Melody. "How can she adjust when her heart is broken? I told you how she feels about you, now maybe you'll believe me."

"She's just in a generalized dither," said Jim, "and on your account as well as mine."

"She's in a dither on my account, all right. She looked at me this morning as if I have snakes for hair."

"That's completely your imagination, Melody. Florence is a hypersensitive person and she's upset, but I'm sure she's sincere about being glad about . . . last night."

"She wants to be glad, but she isn't." Melody stared morosely at the remains of her stew. "Jim, I can't eat any more of this."

"Eat just a little more."

Melody reluctantly picked at the stew with her fork. "I didn't know she saw me. I thought it was dark and raining."

"The moon was out a little. I guess she saw you when you came in the entrance."

"Well, I knew she was awake. When I came in she didn't make a sound, but later I heard her crying. She had her face buried in the pillow but I could hear her. Then this morning she looked at me like I was a vampire and my hair was all snakes. She's very jealous, Jim. Very, very jealous. I hope she gets over it."

"I'm sure she'll get over it. What else can she do? Frankly, at the moment I've got other things to worry about than Florence."

"It should have been her under that tree, not me," said Melody. "I told you that in the first place, but you wouldn't listen. But don't worry, I'm not going to burden you with my conscience or recriminations or anything like that. And I hope you won't either. There's no point."

"I know. But there *is* something I want to discuss with you. Let's take a walk to the meadow."

"Oh, Jim, I can't, I've got to lie down. I have a bad headache, I'm sick to my stomach and I feel terrible, awful . . ."

"I know how you feel. Come for a walk and you'll feel better."

In the Elysian Field, the meadow between the two hills of the island, Melody's spirits did seem to improve slightly. Jim led her to a little sheltered grassy pocket in the center of the meadow and they sat down and watched puffs of fair-weather clouds pass over the island.

"It's a beautiful day," said Melody.

"Yes, it is," answered Jim. "The sunrise was fantastic this morning at Morgan's Pillow. The whole island turned red, then pearly pink, and the ocean shined like gold."

"Is that where you went, up on the hill?"

"Yes. I woke very early and went up there because I wanted to think. And that's what I did. I thought about everything from beginning to end."

Melody stared into her lap. "Did you?" she said.

Jim glanced around at the Jungfrau on one side of the meadow, then turned and looked at the Matterhorn on the other side. The idea he'd had at Morgan's Pillow seemed to him both logical and inspired, but how could he bring it up without sounding ridiculous? "It's very beautiful here," he said, "on the island."

"Yes, the beauty of the island helps. At least we're not stuck in some ugly place. It's all beautiful, except those horrible rocks Florence likes."

"Even the rocks have a beauty of a kind."

"I suppose so. Jim, I'd like to go back and lie down soon. What was it you wanted to discuss with me?"

Jim felt a slight shortness of oxygen, despite the trade wind that blew with a gentle constancy through the valley between the hills. He took a deep breath and said: "Well, Melody . . . no recriminations, no *mea culpa* tears, I agree with you, what happened happened. But as I told you at breakfast, there *is* something I want to say to you. First, I want to say that I love you. After last night, I think it's important for me to say that and for you to realize it's true. I do love you and I want your happiness more than I want anything else. Do you believe me?"

Melody's eyes softened a bit. "Of course I believe you," she said. "I know you love me."

"All right," said Jim. He took another breath and said: "Melody, we might be on this island five years. Now, I think you love me the same way I do you. I think you want me to be happy just as I want you to be happy. Therefore, I suggest we get married."

Melody stared thoughtfully at him. "You suggest we get married?"

"Yes."

Melody slowly shook her head. "Jim, I'm sorry, we talked about that. I do love you, but there are other people involved and we aren't suited. We really aren't, Jim."

"We aren't suited for the outside world, but I don't mean that. I'm asking you to marry me here on the island."

"Marry you here on the island?"

"Yes."

"But I'm already married and so are you."

"True, but we are not married on this island, we are single on this island. *Very* single. And we can't go on being single on this island, Melody, it's impossible. You know that as well as I do."

"But how can we get married if we're already married?"

"You don't understand. We are not married here, we are married in the outside world. Here, on this island, we are single. Therefore, I suggest we get married and live together as lawful man and wife for such time as we are on the island."

"I see. You mean for such time as we are on the island?"

"Yes. Until we return to the outside world."

"Such a marriage wouldn't be legal."

"I have thought about it, Melody. It would be legal."

"But who could marry us here?"

"I'm sure Florence could do it."

"*Florence?*"

"Yes, she could do it."

"Jim, you're crazy. She's not a minister or anything like it."

"That's only a technicality. It wouldn't matter as long as she said the words and we answered."

"But we aren't divorced. You're talking completely crazy. Why, even if Florence did marry us in some kind of ceremony, you'd still be married to Linda and I'd still be married to Charles. It would be a form of double bigamy, Jim, if it was anything at all."

"No, it wouldn't. On the island we would only be married to each other, honey, so it wouldn't be bigamy. And it wouldn't be adultery either. It would be a strictly lawful marriage. I'm sure any reasonable court anywhere would accept it as lawful."

"*Lawful?*" Melody was staring at him in absorbed fascination, her headache and her stomach-ache now forgotten. "I don't see how it could be lawful."

"Let me explain it to you as I see it. First, laws—that is to say, society's laws—are made by people. We are the people on this island and therefore it's up to us to make the laws on it. Actually, we already have laws here. Such things as all of us helping keep the cave clean and orderly, sharing the food we have, not hurting each other, and so forth. For example, if Rufus catches a wild pig, we have a law that we share equally, because we are all sick of beef stew and it wouldn't be fair otherwise. Isn't that true?"

"We don't actually have a law about it."

"We have an unwritten law. Suppose I tried to eat all the roast pork and wouldn't let you and Florence have any? You'd quote that law at me pretty quick, wouldn't you?"

"We would say it's unfair, there ought to be a rule . . ."

"That's all any law is, honey, a rule. And if we can have a law about sharing food, we can have other laws, including marriage laws. There's nothing to prevent us from convening the legislature—you, me, and Florence—and passing a law that my marriage to Linda and your marriage to Charles are hereby declared null and void on this island, until such time as Linda and Charles show up in a row boat."

"But Jim, you know they won't."

"No, they won't. Therefore, in reality, our marriages to them *are* null and void on this island, and such a law would only be taking sensible recognition of that fact. This is a basic function of law, to take sensible recognition of the truth. All great courts do this."

"Well, it's true Linda and Charles aren't here . . ."

"No, they're not, therefore from a standpoint of law our marriages to them don't exist on this island. I am sure that would be the decision of any competent court if the question were put to a serious test."

"Well, maybe from the standpoint of law . . . I don't know, they decide all kinds of funny things these days."

"Melody, the Supreme Court wouldn't consider it bigamy. I'd bet my last dollar on it."

"The Supreme Court . . . they're against prayer in the schools, too. Maybe they wouldn't. Maybe not. But there's more to it than that, Jim."

"Yes, there is," said Jim. "There's a lot more to it than anything the Supreme Court might say about Linda and Charles or you and me, because another person is involved."

"Another person?—you mean Florence?"

"No, I mean someone much more helpless than Florence. I mean your baby, if you have one."

A worried indentation appeared on Melody's forehead. "Yes," she said, "the baby. I've tried not to think about that this morning and I'd rather not talk about it. But you're right, someone else is involved."

"Let's say, might be involved."

"Is," she answered. "I'll have a baby."

Jim smiled. "You think you have morning sickness so soon?"

"I might not have morning sickness yet, but I will. If I'm not pregnant already, I will be soon. I can't help myself." With a wan smile, Melody put her hand on his. "I want you now a hundred times more. I want you even with a headache and sick to my stomach. You'd think I'd have something else on my mind, but no. Not me. Believe it or not, I woke up this morning feeling passionate. Charles is right, and so are you. I'm oversexed."

Jim squeezed her hand in exasperation. "Now listen," he said. "I will always regret saying that to you, because it's ridiculous. Believe me, you are a perfectly normal woman, Melody."

"It's normal to be made love to three times and wake up four hours later and want to be made love to again? That's normal?"

"It certainly is. You've been bitterly frustrated for months. I assure you any normal woman would react exactly as you have, especially if she had a strong emotional attachment to the man."

"Maybe so, but I don't believe it. I don't think other women feel the way I do."

"You're wrong—and dangerously wrong. We have more important things to talk about, but let me say this. Nature, in the course of evolution, has overcompensated the human sex drive as much as the brain itself is overcompensated. These things are the basis of civilization itself. People are a thousand times sexier and smarter than other animals and that's why they're human. Now you'd better learn to live with this fact about yourself and stop mewling about it like a child. You'd be better off and so would your husband."

Open-mouthed, Melody gawked at him. Finally she said, "That's ridiculous. Sex is just an urge. It isn't the basis for civilization; love and cooperation are the basis for civilization."

"That's what I just said," answered Jim. "Power of mind and a capacity for love define a human being. I don't mean by sex a simple moronic urge such as animals have, but a complex emotional, spiritual, and physical phenomenon that defies analysis. But let's suspend this discussion—I want to talk to you about the baby you might have here. The point is, you might have a baby and that's the main reason I think we should get married here. After all, marriage isn't—"

"Oh, Jim, stop talking about our getting married, that's *crazy!*"

"As I was saying, marriage isn't just a license to go to bed together, it's hardly that at all. The main purpose of marriage is to protect the young, that's what the institution is really for. And since I love you, I want to protect you and your child."

Melody pursed her lips in a prim manner, a coolness in her eyes. She obviously didn't like being told her brave confession of wickedness was mere mewling. "That's sweet of you but I don't see how you can. I'm afraid it'll be up to me and others to take care of any baby I have."

"What others?"

"Well . . . those who care about me."

"I care about you. I told you when we first sat down here I love you and want your happiness more than anything else, and you said you believed me."

"All right, then you tell me I'm mewling like a child."

"You were."

"That's your opinion. But actually, when I said those who care about me I meant my husband. Whatever our feelings toward each other and no matter what's happened, I *am* married, Jim, and Charles is my husband."

"And nine days ago you told me at great length how you didn't think he'd be your husband long if you were unfaithful to him and got pregnant on this island."

"I also said he has more feeling for other people than anyone I've ever known. Charles will forgive me."

"I hope he will, but you didn't think he would last week, Melody. You told me flatly he couldn't endure to accept and raise another man's child as his own."

Melody's lip began to tremble. "Why are you trying to make me feel bad?" she asked. "Don't you think I feel bad enough as it is?"

"I'm not trying to make you feel bad, I'm trying to make you face this situation as it is, for your good and for the good of any baby you might have."

Melody's lip trembled more. "I might not even have one. The doctors could be wrong, I might be like Charles and unable to have children."

Jim waited patiently while she took out a handkerchief and began to cry into it. A few tears and she would calm down and perhaps be able to talk rationally. It was senseless, in any event, to point out to her the irony of tears caused by fear that she would get pregnant followed by tears caused by fear that she wouldn't. As he sat watching Melody weep in her handkerchief, the thought occurred to Jim Kittering that the emotional nature of women really was different from that of men, and that the difference could not be wholly due to culture, training, or attitudes. It was a reactionary viewpoint, perhaps, but it was true all the same. In a sense, women *were* grasshoppers. The emotional qualities needed for motherhood were different in kind from the reasoning powers needed for the hunt—and that was the division of labor from time immemorial; the raising of children by women and the providing of food for women and children by men. As Melody wept over her fear of pregnancy and her fear of non-pregnancy, Jim wondered if Linda was the same. He'd never really thought so.

Melody finally dried her eyes and said: "I'm sorry. I'm not behaving very well this morning. I'm ill. It's that stew, I'm so sick and tired of it I could scream."

"Maybe Rufus will catch us another pig," said Jim. The wild pigs were extremely elusive, but it had happened once; the dog had killed a pig and they had skewered and roasted it. "If I'd found a gun on that stupid ship I'd go hunting for one. But let's get back to the question of what's going to become of you, now that you're a fallen woman. Okay?"

"I suppose so, if you insist. But I don't know what good talking about it's going to do."

"It might do some good. Shall we try?"

"All right, but stop bullying me."

"I'm only trying to help you, honey. The truth is we've got to face two facts. One, you might have a baby. Two, your husband might divorce you, he might not be able to endure your sleeping with another man and bringing home that man's child. Is this right, what I say?"

Melody slowly nodded. "Yes, it's right. He might divorce me."

"All right, then you face the possibility or even the probability of having a baby all alone in the world and of then having to raise a child by yourself."

"I admit I've worried about it," Melody said. "Of course many children don't have fathers. Their fathers die or abandon the mother or there's a divorce. But it would be hard. I couldn't expect financial help from Charles and it would be difficult for me to support and raise a child by myself, although I'm sure it can be done. I'll just have to do it, that's all."

"No, you won't," said Jim. "A marriage between us on this island would certainly be a legal acknowledgment of my responsibility for any child you have as a result of your relationship with me here. It would stand up in any court in the world, honey, even if only as proof of paternity."

"Well . . . yes, as far as that goes, I think it would."

"It goes pretty far," said Jim. "I'm not proposing a mock marriage to you, but a marriage with a real meaning and purpose. I suggest in any event a financial agreement between us concerning any children we might have. Don't you think that would be a good idea?"

"Yes, I suppose so, if you want to do it."

Melody seemed to have forgotten completely her headache and stomach-ache. She had crossed her legs beneath her and had folded her hands in her lap and was much calmer. The tears, no doubt, had helped. Evidently it had not occurred to her she would not be abandoned and she gazed at Jim with an absorbed interest.

"All right, in the event Charles won't accept you and your child, assuming you have a child, then let's say Child Support Law Number One of Providence Island will apply. Our marriage here would not be legal in the outside world, but I would have a continuing responsibility to you and your baby if your husband won't accept you. If he doesn't, you will inform me of this and I will arrange through a lawyer to send you support for the child till it's twenty-one. I make very good money and I'm going to make more, so the support payments can and should be fairly generous—let's say eight hundred dollars a month. Also, I will name the child in my will as an equal heir with my other children and I'll take out insurance to guarantee support if I die before the child is twenty-one. And of course I'll pay any nursing or hospital expenses you might have in childbirth. Does this seem okay to you?"

Again Melody gawked at him in stunned disbelief. "Eight hundred dollars a month?" she asked. It reminded Jim of her reaction to the information that he'd spent sixty dollars for a pair of pajamas. "Jim, that's too much."

"No, it's reasonable in terms of my earning power and what I suppose would be the standard of living you'd want and expect."

"You'd be depriving your wife and your own children."

"This would be my child too. And as for depriving my wife, she's an heiress. Linda will inherit at least three million dollars when her grandmother dies, and her grandmother is eighty-something."

"Oh," said Melody, her eyes opened wide with awe at the thought of such a fortune. "It still sounds like an awful lot."

"Actually I think it should be more, perhaps a thousand. We'll check with the lawyers and see what they say."

"No-no-no, I wouldn't want a thousand. Eight hundred is enough, more than enough."

"Well, we'll make it eight hundred in the agreement, then see what the lawyers say."

Melody was awed. For a poverty-loving Christian, she had quite a thing about money and even after a month still snooped around the island looking for Morgan's Treasure. "Eight hundred dollars a month," she said. "That's very generous of you, Jim."

Jim shrugged. "Not really. A court would make me pay that much in a paternity suit."

"I don't think so. But let me ask you something. If all this happens and you support the child . . . would you see it?"

"That's a hard question and a hard choice, but I think it would be better for everyone concerned if I didn't. There would be the danger of you and me becoming involved again and that wouldn't be fair to Linda or to you either. If things don't work out with Charles, you should be in a position to marry someone else who could be your husband and a father to your child."

"I think that's right and sensible. But you'd have none of the rewards of being a father, you'd just have to pay and pay and pay. And think of this—suppose I *am* pregnant and a boat did come this afternoon, do you know what it would cost you to have made love to me one night?"

Jim looked up at the puffs of cloud that floated over the island, multiplied to himself, and said, "About two hundred thousand dollars."

"Isn't that ridiculous?"

Jim grinned. "It would have cost me cheaper if I'd behaved under that tree."

"It's ridiculous for it to cost you two hundred thousand dollars to sleep with a woman once. Why, I never heard of such a price as that."

"You can't figure it that way. You aren't a hooker, honey."

"What?"

She didn't know the term. "Prostitute," said Jim. "Besides, it isn't as much money as it sounds like added up. It's only about ten thousand a year. I make much more than that and I'll make even more."

"It's still ridiculous for it to cost you such an amount."

"What would it cost *you?*" asked Jim. "This is why we have marriage, so men will pay as much for that one night as the woman pays. Share the pleasure, share the pain, and meanwhile the human race survives in all its misery. But I doubt if a boat will show up this afternoon. I'll probably get more for my money than one night."

Melody smiled. "You probably will."

"Maybe even twenty nights."

"That's ten thousand dollars a night. I hope I don't think—good grief, this is costing him a fortune, I'd better kiss him right."

"You'd kiss me right for nothing," said Jim, "and I think you'd better marry me while I'm in a virtuous mood. I'll draw up Child Support Law Number One this morning, and you and I and Florence can all sign it. I'll make carbons so we all have a copy. I'll also draw up Nullifying Marriage Law Number Two and we can sign that one. It will declare null and void our marriages to Linda and Charles on this island, then we can get married ourselves."

"Jim, I'm very grateful for your offer to help me with the baby," said Melody with a smile, "but we can't get married, that's silly."

"Why is it silly?"

"Jim, it's impossible. You can't just declare our marriages null and void, you don't have the power."

"*I'm* not declaring them null and void, all the people on the island are declaring them null and void, and if that isn't legal, I don't know what is."

"It might be legal according to some modern court, I don't know, but even if it is, what's legal isn't everything. There's more to marriage than that."

"This is the second time you've said there's more to it than that, and for the second time you're right. Of course there's more to it. Law is only half of it—"

"Jim, you are only trying to make me feel better and I'm grateful, you've been very sweet. But you don't have to, I'm all right. I'll live with you here and it won't bother me—"

"Will you shut up and stop interrupting? I am trying to talk to you about something serious and you keep interrupting me like an idiot. It's intolerable. Will you shut your rude grasshopper mouth and listen, or do you want me to get really angry!"

It was dangerous, but she had to be sidetracked at all costs or there'd be woe on that island. Jim glared at her in a simulation of male rage. The thing to convey was that he might strike her at any moment.

"I . . . I . . ." said Melody. Once again she gaped at him with her mouth open, as if she'd never quite seen him before. "I'm sorry, I didn't mean to be rude . . ."

Great, thought Jim. Superb male rage. Of course, having made love to her was a fundamental help in taming her female temper, but he was entitled to use that edge. One thing was sure: the days of her threatening to throw beef stew on him were over.

"Then be quiet and listen to what I'm trying to say to you."

"All right, I'll listen."

"I was saying when you interrupted me that of course there's more to marriage than a simple question of law. Law is only half of it. Marriage is concerned with moral issues as well as legal issues. There's an intimate, even symbiotic relationship between all law and morality, but civil law and individual morality are recognizably distinct areas of the framework upon which human society is organized and constructed." Jim was glad for once of his philosophy major and even gladder of his prep-school debating days. He was almost impressed himself, and Melody again was gawking at him. "Understand?"

"No . . . no, not exactly."

"The thing I am getting at I would call a question of ethics. You'd call it a question of God. Okay, I don't mind the word God. I don't believe in God, but I don't mind the word, we're talking about the same thing whatever word we use. The point is, any law dealing with marriage should not be unethical or immoral—or, if you like, unacceptable to God. For this reason, marriage laws are considered in a special category by practically all civilizations. That's why we call marriage a sacrament."

Melody's shock at his male rage had diminished. She now had an odd little half-amused, Mona Lisa smile on her face that Jim could not quite interpret. "You call marriage a sacrament?"

Jim shrugged. "Everyone does, in a sense."

"Not everyone. The Roman Catholics and the eastern churches do, along with baptism, confirmation, the Eucharist, penance, extreme unction, and holy orders. The Protestants only recognize baptism and the Lord's Supper."

Jim Kittering smiled to himself. Thank God he'd had the foresight to look up "sacrament" in the dictionary when he got back to the cave from the hill that morning. "You're talking about the word in terms of organized religion," said Jim. "Sacrament also has the broader and deeper meaning of a covenant between God and man, or a covenant between a man and his fundamental feelings of right and wrong. 'I shall not kill, even if I die myself' is the covenant, for example, of a conscientious objector. 'I shall love and protect this woman and her children' is another covenant. Marriage is a sacrament and marriage laws are in a special category, just as I said."

Melody's chin was in her hand and she was staring at him in fascination, although the faintly amused smile was still in her eyes. Jim could not quite make it out. It was not a contemptuous or hostile smile, but it was amused. "Well, yes," she said, "I'll have to admit that in a broader sense you're right. And I think I understand now what you're trying to say."

"Tell me. What am I trying to say?"

"As I understand you, you are saying that a law nullifying our marriages on this island and permitting us to be married here would be not only legal, but also ethical and moral and in that sense acceptable to God."

"Yes," said Jim. "That's exactly what I'm trying to say, and that's exactly what I believe. And I think you believe it too, whether you'll admit it or not."

Melody smiled. "You seem pretty certain of your own opinion, whatever mine might be."

"I'm certain of my opinion, yes, but of course I may be wrong. I'm sure there're many people who wouldn't agree with me. I imagine your husband wouldn't and most of your friends wouldn't. This is the prime problem—what's acceptable to God and what isn't. I can only go by my own opinion, and that's all anyone can do."

"No, you're forgetting we have guidance, Jim. There's the guidance of God's law in the Bible. And for this very reason we can't just make up new laws to suit ourselves."

Jim knew very well her views on the imperfection of the Bible and felt a little triumphant tingle. "Well now, honey," he said, "I don't want to get in a theological argument with you, but I'd say that even though the Bible may be in part God-inspired, I don't think it's finished and complete any more than I think the human race is finished and complete. When God's law is written, Gabriel will blow his horn and we'll all go up to heaven because our time on earth will be done. Don't you agree?"

Melody's little smile was gone; she now had a look of dreamy absorption. She loved God-talk and he'd counted on that. Nothing suited her better than a penetrating discussion on God and morals. "Yes, I do," she answered. "I don't believe God's law is all written, not yet." The little smile returned. "But how do you know *this* is one of God's laws?"

"I believe it is," said Jim. He knew what her next question would be. Except for her enigmatic little smile, the conversation was going as he had planned and hoped.

"I'm not sure I understand completely what you mean. Are you trying to tell me belief makes a thing right?"

"Yes."

"I don't see why that's necessarily so. Suppose we believe something wicked and wrong?"

"That's our problem. We mustn't believe things that are wicked and wrong or we don't survive. We must believe things that are right."

"But if God's law isn't all written, how can we tell the difference? How do we know what's right?" It was eerie. The only distracting factor was the little smile in her eyes. "What do we base our judgment on, Jim? It can't be based on nothing."

"I'd put it one way and you'd put it another. I'd say primary postulate, you'd say faith. But however you put it, primary postulate or faith, that's the only answer there ever was or ever will be."

"I'm not sure I understand you exactly. I think I do . . ." It was very distracting. Jim could not make out her smile. Melody seemed amused by him and yet she wasn't. "Yes, I think so, but can you give me an example of what you mean?"

"I'll give you several," said Jim. "How do we know God exists?

How do we know life is worth living? How do we know love is real? How do we know it matters if a baby cries?"

In silence, Melody stared at him as the trade wind blew her hair. Finally she said: "Then faith or primary postulate, as you call it, would mean to answer yes—God does exist, life is worth living, love is real, and it matters if a baby cries. We don't know these things?"

"Nobody knows those things," said Jim, "but most people assume a few of them are true."

Once again Melody was silent, legs crossed beneath her and hands folded in her lap as the trade wind blew her hair. The little smile was back in her eyes. "Well," she said, "you're right in thinking Charles and most of our friends wouldn't agree with you. They wouldn't consider it a sacrament, Jim. They'd consider it a sacrilege, and a dreadful one at that. A mockery of the law of both man and God."

"I don't doubt it. Most of my own friends would consider it meaningless sentimentality."

"I don't see how they could think *that,*" answered Melody. "It would give me and any baby of mine more protection than anything you could do. I don't need or want such protection, you'll help me anyhow if it's necessary, but a marriage would guarantee it. No matter what people thought about it, the baby and I would have a certain position. The father loved me and tried to marry me, even though he couldn't and it was only a sacrilege."

Briefly, Jim thought of going over the argument again but rejected the idea as useless. He had done his best, but it was too much. Woe would prevail on the island, that was all, woe and adultery without end. "Yeah, I tried," he said. "I sure did. But I guess I can't ask you to do a thing you think is a sacrilege."

Melody opened her eyes in surprise. "What?" she asked. "*I* don't think it's a sacrilege. Charles might think so, but not me."

"You don't? Then what *do* you think?"

The little enigmatic smile reappeared once more in Melody's eyes. Solemnly she replied: "I think it's a sacrament. I think if we promised to love each other as man and wife on this island it would be a real marriage."

"Then you *will* marry me here?"

"Yes, I will," said Melody.

"You will?"

"Yes. When would you like the wedding to be?"

"The sooner the better. How about this afternoon?"

"All right."

"I think a simple, dignified ceremony," said Jim. "Nothing elaborate."

"No, simple."

Jim took her hand and helped her to her feet. He still could not quite believe it and was half afraid she might change her mind. "We'll have to get ready. I'll have to write those laws and also a ceremony for Florence, and you'll have to find a suitable dress."

"Yes, I will have to find some sort of dress." Melody smiled again as she put her hands on his shoulders. "Now that we're engaged, don't you think you ought to kiss me?"

Jim kissed her lightly on the lips. "Anything but that pale gray dress—you know, the one we left in the coconut grove last night. That one isn't suitable. It ought to be a white dress. A long, white dress."

"I'll see what I can do," said Melody, with still another baffling little smile.

"You look like Mona Lisa in tortoise-shell glasses," said Jim. "Why are you smiling at me like that?"

"No reason."

"Hmmph," said Jim, puzzled. "Must be some reason. What are you thinking?"

"I probably shouldn't say it, but I was just wondering if your wife understands you."

"What on earth made you wonder that?"

"I don't know. It always surprises me about you, but at heart you're very old-fashioned."

Jim smiled. Little did Melody know. "Linda understands me," he said, "only too well."

"I hope she does," answered Melody. "But you're a very deceiving man, or maybe I should say deceptive. There's quite a distance between what you think you think and what you really think. I agree with Florence about that."

A triumph, thought Jim, as he put his arms around Melody and his cheek against hers. He had handled her perfectly, she had bought this slightly ridiculous marriage with no reservations at all. A silent "*Whew!*" came from him and he lifted his eyes ironically heavenward when she could no longer see his face. A triumph of Thespian art, that was what it was. What a performance! He'd even managed subtly to persuade her he was "old-fashioned"—a stroke of sheer genius, that, the dramatic art carried to its ultimate. He had given, Jim felt, a masterly performance.

To Jim's and Melody's surprise, Florence seemed overjoyed by the news. "That is the greatest thing I ever heard of," she said. "I love weddings anyhow, but a wedding under these conditions is just too great to think of."

As discussion of arrangements continued, Florence's enthusiasm did not diminish. "Let's get this straight," she said. "Jim will be standing in place and *I* will be off to the side with the accordion. You'll have to be out of sight somewhere, Melody, behind a bush or something. Then when I start to play the 'Wedding March,' you will come forward and take your place by Jim and I will step around in front of you and marry you."

"Maybe I ought to play the 'Wedding March' myself," said Melody. "You really don't play it very well, Florence."

"Melody, you can't play the music at your own wedding," said Jim. "You're the bride, that wouldn't make any sense at all."

"Don't worry," said Florence. "I'm going to practice all morning. You can correct me and give me a lesson while you work on your wedding dress."

"All right, but you'll have to practice hard, Florence. I don't want it to sound silly, this wedding is unusual enough already."

"I'll practice hard, don't worry, I can learn it," said Florence. "But I can't learn the ceremony too—especially if it's going to be some new, different ceremony nobody heard of."

"You can read the ceremony, Florence," said Jim. "I'm going to write it this morning and I'll make a neat copy so you can read it."

"This is awful," said Melody, who was in the midst of an anxious search through the dresses of her closet, which consisted of a stretched wire in the corner of her bedroom. She had already emptied both of her suitcases on the mattress-pallet. "Just awful. I don't have anything to wear that's the least bit suitable."

"It'll have to be that white dress," said Florence.

"I know, but it doesn't look like a wedding dress at all."

"You can adapt it. Sew some frills on it or something."

"I don't know, but I'll have to try."

"Florence, where'd you put your typewriter?" asked Jim.

"On the crates of grapefruit juice under a towel," said Florence as she took down the ebonite and mother-of-pearl accordion from a railroad spike driven into a fissure in the wall.

"You're always hiding it," said Jim.

"I ought to throw it away and go to the Klondike and live with the Eskimos," said Florence. "That typewriter eats the meat right off my bones. The Eskimos would fuck me and fatten me up."

Jim winced, but Melody was in the bedroom burrowing at the bottom of one of her suitcases and had not heard the remark. Florence often made such little jokes about herself. For such a shy and hypersensitive woman, her language could be pretty rough at times. Surreptitiously, Jim glanced under and around his shoulder at Florence, but she was in a bland good humor.

And thank God for that. Apparently, while he and Melody were working out their immediate destiny with God-talk in a trade wind, Florence had found some kind of answer to her own problem. Her dither of nerves was gone and she seemed genuinely pleased by the wedding. Her first reaction had been astonished disbelief, but then she had laughed almost hysterically and put her hand on Jim's arm and said: "You're going to make an honest woman out of her—beautiful!" She had then actually put her arm for a moment around his waist and said: "You always surprise me. This is one I wouldn't have thought you were capable of." An intricate girl, Florence, thought Jim as he found the portable typewriter under the towel. Putting her arm around him like that, unafraid. She seemed to lose her morbid fear of him in moments of emotion.

Jim placed the typewriter on a blanket-covered case of Dinty Moore beef stew. "Before you start practicing, Florence, and before you get involved with that dress, Melody, let's decide where we're going to have this wedding. Does anyone have any ideas?"

"Well," said Florence, "I know the island better than either of you, and I'd say the best place is down at the southern end. It's very beautiful. There's a level area of rock, the waves are very big, and the wind makes a haunting musical sound as it blows through the . . . rock formation . . . the, er, channel there."

Jim shook his head. "Melody won't go for that, not in this century."

"I sure won't," said Melody as she held out her white dress and stared dubiously at it. "I'm not getting married in any place with a name like that."

"But it's beautiful, Melody. What difference does it make what name it's called?"

"What difference? You wouldn't even mention the name out loud yourself, that's the difference."

"Let's change the name then. Let's call it Morgan's Blowhole or Morgan's Pipe or something."

"I'll always think of it by that other name," said Melody. "Besides, it makes a funny noise. I'm not getting married anywhere with a thing making a noise like that."

"I agree with you it's a beautiful spot, Florence," said Jim, "but it's a bad idea. Think of some other place."

"Umm . . . The Elysian Field?"

"No, we got engaged there," said Melody. "We ought to get married somewhere else."

"All right, how about Hell's Half Acre out on the point there? That's even more dramatic."

"She doesn't like that name," said Jim.

"No, she doesn't," said Melody, "or the place either—all those horrible lizards and things."

"Well, let's see . . . how about Melody's Bathtub up at the north end of the island?"

"I don't want to get married someplace where I wash my back," said Melody. "That's a terrible idea, Florence."

"Okay, I've got another thought. A great thought. The horse-shoe cove under the Hanging Tree. That's beautiful, perfect."

"I don't think so," said Jim.

"I don't either," said Melody.

"What's wrong with it? It's lovely under the tree there."

"Florence, that's not a good idea," said Jim. "*Hanging* Tree, what a place to get married. You keep getting one bad idea after the other. Melody wants a *nice* place to get married and so do I."

"I suggested the Elysian Field and you didn't like it. How about the beach across from the wreck?"

"No, I don't want to look at a *wreck* while I'm getting married."

"Okay, the coconut-palm grove back behind the beach. You wouldn't be able to see the wreck from there."

"No, but it's too closed in," said Melody. "We wouldn't see anything else either, except coconut palms."

"All right, how about the cave itself, right here?"

"No, that's even more closed in."

"Then I give up. There's no place else on the island, I've covered everything."

Melody was frowning at her white dress. "Well," she said, "I do have Charles's mother's lace tablecloth. You remember, Jim, it was in the top part of the trunk and didn't get wet?"

"Yes," said Jim. "Think of some other place, Florence. We've got to decide this."

"I could cut up the tablecloth and add it as a sort of fringe to lengthen the dress," said Melody, "and wear the rest as a shawl, a kind of—what do they call it, *mantilla* or *mantillo?*"

Florence laughed and shook her head. "*Mantilla* is the word you want. *Mantillo* means manure."

"Good grief, and I'm supposed to have studied Spanish. But I *could* cut up the tablecloth. Of course Charles's mother would whirl in her grave."

"Think of a *place*, Florence," said Jim.

"The best place by far is the first one I suggested. Morgan's, excuse me, Asshole. And I really think, Melody, it's high time you got over your squeamishness. You were a nurse in a hospital, you must have seen assholes before, what are you scared of?"

"I'm not scared. Who's scared? That's silly, Florence."

"You're letting a name, a mere word dominate you. And that's nonsensical. I think you ought to conquer your squeamishness and prudery and get married there."

"Get married there yourself," said Melody.

"Me? I'm never going to get married *any*where. I'm not the marrying kind, but you are and you ought to get over your prudery. It's ridiculous."

"Get over my prudery," said Melody. "I'm tired of being accused of that. You're both more prudish than I am, by far."

"That's an original idea. Did you hear her, Jim? We're both more prudish than she is. Did you hear that?"

"Yes, I heard it. But you can stop arguing, I've thought of the place for the wedding. The ideal and perfect place, in fact the only place. Right above our heads."

Thus, at four o'clock that afternoon Jim stood on Morgan's Pillow on top of the Jungfrau in his best suit, with a clean shirt and necktie and his hair brushed and combed. Rufus, who had gone along with them, became agitated as Florence gave a preliminary squeeze at the accordion and caused it to make a wheezing groan. "Woof!" said the dog. "Woof, woof!" Jim stared emptily as the dog ran forward, stopped, hunched over, and barked again as if to say: "There are strange unnatural things going on here and I don't like it." To his surprise, Jim felt a bit trembly at the knees. That was peculiar, he felt almost as he had felt when he married Linda. Well, it *was* a marriage of a kind. As Melody herself had pointed out, it could cost him close to a quarter of a million dollars and if that wasn't a marriage it was certainly an involvement. But Jim felt a gathering nervousness that had nothing to do with any financial commitment and this surprised him. The sight of Melody in her improvised wedding dress with the lace tablecloth fringe had given the whole thing a sudden strange reality. It was ridiculous and yet there was something real about it.

"Are you ready, Melody?" called Florence.

A voice came from behind a clump of shrubbery at the edge of the hilltop: "Yes, I'm ready."

"Okay, here goes." Rufus began to bark again as Florence's fingers moved uncertainly on the keyboard of the accordion. "Shut up, Rufus. Wait a second, Melody." The dog jumped back, hunched over with his head low to the rock of Morgan's Pillow, and barked as Florence wagged a scolding finger at him. "Sit, Rufus! Sit!"

"Maybe you better send him home," said Jim.

"He won't go. But he's sitting now, he's all right. Okay, Melody, here we go again."

Florence's fingers moved and with a thin wheeze the accordion began to make a noise that sounded more or less like "Here Comes the Bride." Jim gulped nervously as Melody appeared at the edge of the bushes and came walking slowly toward him in her white dress with the lace fringe. She'd taken off her glasses and held a dozen wild flowers in her hands. Jim anxiously looked down at Rufus; the dog again was barking, head scrunched low to the rock and shoulders humped as if to make a mock charge at Florence. He'd never bite her, the dog adored Florence, but he might make a mock charge at her; the accordion bothered him, and no wonder—Florence was making numerous errors. Jim ground his teeth in exasperation. The dog and Florence were ruining everything, the wedding was a mess. Jim looked up as Melody took her place by his side and was startled to see a smile on her face. How could she smile like that when Florence and the dog had made everything ridiculous, and what was Florence sniffling about?

"I'm sorry, weddings always make me cry," said Florence, "and this one especially gets me." She put down the accordion and walked up to them. "Do you have the script?"

"It isn't a script, it's the words of the ceremony," said Jim. He took the typewritten page from his breast pocket and handed it to her.

"All right," said Florence. "Will you join hands, please?"

Jim took Melody's hand and faced Florence, who cleared her throat, then read in a grave tone:

"We are met here to join together as man and wife you, James, and you, Melody. However, the circumstances of this marriage are exceptional in that you, James, and you, Melody, are already married to someone else. Therefore, this community, consisting of the entire population of this island, has debated, voted upon, and duly enacted two laws in response to this situation: Child Support Law Number One and Nullifying Marriage Law Number Two. Do you agree that these documents together shall constitute your marriage license for this wedding?"

"Yes, I agree," said Jim.

"I agree too," said Melody.

"Dearly beloved, we are gathered here today in the sight of God to join together in holy matrimony you, James, and you, Melody. Matrimony is an honorable estate instituted of God and a shrewd if not always successful attempt by man to insure the perpetuation of the human species and to fulfill the deepest longings for love and companionship to be found in the human heart. Thus, I require and charge you both, as you will answer at the dreadful day of judgment when the secrets of all hearts shall be disclosed, that if either of you knows of any impediment why you may not lawfully and in true love be joined together, you do now confess it, for be well assured that if any persons are joined together otherwise than as God's law and man's conscience doth allow, their marriage is not lawful and will bring neither fulfillment nor joy."

"Well, I'm married in New York," said Jim, "but I'm not married here, according to the laws of this island."

"I'm married in the outside world too," said Melody, "but I'm not married here, according to this island's laws."

"There is no impediment," said Florence. "Will you, Jim, have this woman to be your wedded wife on this island? Will you love her, be kind to her, respectful to her, and keep her in sickness and in health for so long as you both shall live on this island?"

"I will," said Jim.

"Will you, Melody, have this man to be your wedded husband on this island? Will you love him, be kind to him, respectful to him, and keep him in sickness and in health for so long as you both shall live on this island?"

"I will," said Melody.

"Those whom God hath joined together let no man put asunder . . . on this island. In the authority vested in me by law, I now pronounce you man and wife on Providence Island."

Jim resisted an impulse to raise his hand and scratch his chin. The ceremony, he felt, had been perhaps a bit *too* simple. Of course he'd spent most of his time writing the two laws, which were much more complicated and in a way much more important. The ceremony did cover the fundamentals, anyhow.

"You may kiss the bride," said Florence, "if you want to."

"I hope he wants to," said Melody with a smile. "Give me my glasses, Florence, so I can see him."

Melody put on her glasses, opened her arms, smiled again, and Jim embraced and kissed her.

"A lovely wedding," said Florencc, "just lovely. A beautiful bride and a handsome groom, and as far as I'm concerned you've got nothing to worry about when the dreadful day of judgment comes."

"It comes every day if you ask me," said Jim, who felt badly let down.

"You really do look beautiful, Melody," said Florence. "If I had a camera, I'd take a picture of your smile and keep it always."

"We love you too, Jim and me both," said Melody as she put her arms around Florence and accepted a kiss on the cheek.

"Well, I am going for my usual sunset walk with Rufus and I'll be back around seven," said Florence. "Congratulations to you both."

With a feeling of dismal anticlimax, Jim watched Florence walk off down the hill with her dog. It was true Melody had smiled, but she was not smiling now and the whole thing was a ridiculous fiasco from barking dog to the lace-tablecloth wedding dress. He had thought it would help her, reassure her, encourage her, make her feel less guilty and miserable, make her feel that he really cared about her, but it had fallen flat. She was ashamed, depressed, she could not look him in the eye. Even Florence, who had gallantly tried to say what she thought they wanted to hear, had been embarrassed and anxious to get off that hill.

"I guess we better go back to the cave and get out of these . . .

clothes," said Jim. "I mean . . . out of these wedding clothes and into normal clothes."

"Yes," said Melody, head bowed. "I suppose so."

How do you win? Jim wondered. They did not speak going down the Jungfrau and reached the cave at quarter past four. Unbelievably, the wedding had taken only fifteen minutes.

"Florence moved her things to your bedroom," said Melody.

"I know."

Eyes averted from each other, Jim and Melody walked into the larger of the two bedrooms and then, at a total loss, stood there between the two mattresses on the stone floor.

"I thought of asking Florence to read that quotation from the 91st Psalm," said Melody. "You know, 'He shall give his angels charge over thee.' She can't last long and it might have made her feel better. But she was very sweet, I admired her so much."

Unsure of what to do, Jim took off his necktie. "How could that have made her feel better? And what do you mean, she can't last long?"

"She's so alone. She's very brave, Jim. I can't tell you how much I admire and love her."

"I like Florence too. But I don't understand what you mean about the 91st Psalm. That quotation has meaning for us, I know, but . . . Florence?"

"If it has meaning for us, it would have meaning for her too, wouldn't it?"

Still unsure of what to do, Jim took off his jacket and put it on a hanger and hung it on the stretched wire. "I'm not sure I know what you're talking about," he said.

"I'm not sure either." Melody pulled the blanket partition shut and slid her makeshift wedding dress over her shoulders and let it fall to the floor, then unfastened her brassiere and took it off. "It just seemed pathetic to me when she said she'd be gone till seven. That's almost three hours. Ordinarily her sunset walk takes an hour."

"I guess she thinks . . ."

"Yes, I guess she does," said Melody. "I'm afraid she doesn't know much about anything. It was pathetic."

"Well, I'm sympathetic to Florence, but . . . let's talk about something else."

Melody sat on her mattress-pallet in her panties. "Jim, I've had a very hard day. One of the hardest days I've ever had in my life. I still have a kind of headache and my stomach hurts. Would you mind if I didn't talk at all? I'm exhausted and I want to lie down and sleep. I've wanted all day to lie down and sleep. May I lie down and sleep?"

"Why, sure, honey," said Jim. What was the matter with her? In bewilderment, Jim watched her lie down on her back and put her arm across her eyes. She seemed actually to want to go to sleep, but if so, why the tone of reproach in her voice and why had she taken off her brassiere? Jim, who had seen several snapshots of Charles, suddenly had a mental picture of a solemn-eyed, tight-lipped, rather handsome and kind-looking man in rimless spectacles. Melody was mixing him up with Charles, a natural enough thing to do since what did she know about men? Hesitantly, Jim walked over and stood beside her. "I'm tired myself," he said. "It's been a nerve-wracking day for everybody. Do you mind if I lie down too?" Melody didn't reply. Jim undressed and sat beside her on the mattress and pulled her arm from her eyes. As he had expected, she was crying. Jim put his left hand between her breasts, slid his right arm under her and lay beside her, then kissed her on the cheek and asked, "Do you want me to make love to you?"

In surprise, she turned her head toward him. "I've wanted you to all day," she said, "but how can you? It was only last night."

Melody had been startled the night before when Jim had made love to her a second time, and she'd been amazed the third time. "How are you able?" she asked. Charles, she said, had made love to her twice on two or three occasions during the early months of their marriage, but afterward had complained of extreme fatigue and debilitation. It was his view as a medical doctor that such excesses were a severe strain on the heart, the lungs, the circulation, and most of all the human nervous system—particularly insofar as men were concerned; women, of course, who had a much feebler reaction, were not so seriously affected. It did not *drain* them the way it did men. Jim had shaken his head in disbelief. It was fantastic that a man could go through medical school and believe such things, but he seemed to remember having read somewhere an article deploring the extreme ignorance and naiveté of many medical doctors in this area of human life.

"Can I?" asked Jim with a smile. "I might be able to manage."

"But you mustn't tire yourself all out just because of me," said Melody. "I'm all right, really, I can just go on to sleep."

"Go to *sleep?*" asked Jim. "*Now?* We just got married, honey, don't you remember?"

Melody smiled, then took off her glasses and stared at him, a shyness in her eyes. She always looked very shy, very gentle without her glasses. She'd looked that way when she came walking toward him across Morgan's Pillow in her white dress with the lace fringe from Charles's mother's tablecloth. "Yes, I remember it," she said. "How could I ever forget it?"

Jim propped on his elbows and put his hands on her breasts, which amply filled his palms. It baffled him now to remember he had always considered full breasts a bit lacking in true elegance and feminine appeal. In recent weeks he had reversed this superficial judgment. The soft mounds beneath his hands were sublimely beautiful, and so was Melody herself and everything about her. If only he could make her happy. . . .

"Are you sorry?" asked Jim. "Do you regret it, honey?"

"Let's don't talk," she answered. "Just . . . kiss me."

Florence didn't come back until eight-thirty. It was dark and Jim was half asleep in Melody's arms when he heard her talking to Rufus outside the cave. He propped on an elbow, struck a match, and lighted a kerosene lantern. "Florence is back," he said.

Melody put her arms around him, pulled him down to her, kissed him, and whispered: "I love you! Oh, Jim, I love you so much! Sleep in my arms tonight . . . just sleep in my arms."

Jim propped again on an elbow and stared down into her eyes. It was not passion that moved her. He had won, after all. A real inspiration had come to him on top of old Jungfrau in the pearly dawn.

NINETEEN

Iguana Bile

Florence lasted about three weeks. Jim sensed at once her helpless, abject, and pathetic surrender but he was happy with Melody and reluctant to face the problem. A rather interesting accident involving Florence and Rufus and an iguana gave him the emotional impetus to come to terms with the situation, which he felt in his heart he should have done much sooner. However, there was in Florence, as she herself said, a certain amount of "bile" that needed time to be boiled out of her.

The iguana, in Jim's opinion, was a convenient but meretricious dramatization of the thing for Florence, for Melody, and for him. Florence often had spoken of "me and my iguanas" and more than once ruefully referred to herself as filled with "iguana bile." She had even once told Jim point-blank he ought to dip her in boiling water and induce her to vomit her poison, as the Indians reputedly did to iguanas in Mexico. This, she said, would purge her and make her taste like chicken. Jim, who already had a chicken on his hands and regarded Florence as a tough bird at best, smiled and looked the other way as he had done on other occasions when Florence made her little jokes about thirty-eight-year-old cobwebs, merciful chloroform, and other esoterica.

However, although he did not want to face the onerous problem, it was as if he were waiting for some little thing. He had noticed for several days peculiar behavior on Melody's part, a certain odd, nervous agitation and a tendency to wool-gather, plus a rather puzzling inconsistency in her reactions to him sexually. Her period was due soon and he had marked it up to premenstrual tension. It was a plausible answer, but he knew it was not a correct answer. He was waiting for some little thing, almost any little thing—a stammer, an averted gaze, a hesitant reply, or even an irrelevant upset of some kind that would start the adrenals working.

A few days short of four weeks after the wedding, Jim was repairing a broken deck chair one morning when Melody suddenly appeared out of breath in the entrance of the cave, her hair wet and her eyes wide with alarm. "Jim!" she cried. "Florence is in trouble!"

"Trouble? What kind of trouble?"

"She's caught in a hole in the ground somewhere on the Matterhorn! I can hear her, but I can't tell where she is! You'd better come right away!"

"What do you mean, caught in a *hole* in the ground?" asked Jim with indignation. The very idea was outrageous. Hadn't he had enough trouble with *Melody* on that island, without *Florence* foolishly getting caught in a hole in the ground? She'd get short shrift, that was for sure. "All right. Now, you calm down, Melody, and explain what you mean about Florence in English."

"I mean she's caught, Jim, she's trapped! It's somewhere underground! I can hear her calling and Rufus is down there too, barking. Jim, you'd better hurry. I think she's all right, but she's frightened and wherever she is, she can't get out."

Jim had not shaved that morning; he sometimes put it off, because although he'd found plenty of razor blades on the ship he'd run out of shaving lather and it was unpleasant to shave with soap. Half puzzled and half indignant, he rubbed at his sandpaper-like chin and narrowed his eyes in pensive cogitation. Again, quite apart from her concern about Florence caught in some mysterious subterranean trap, there was an odd nervous agitation in Melody's manner. For some strange reason, she was having difficulty looking him in the eye. "A hole in the ground, huh," said Jim. "Well, I'd better get a rope."

"I was coming back from my bath and I heard her. It was up on the hill somewhere and I couldn't find her. I . . . I thought I ought to come get you."

"Um-hmm," said Jim. It was pretty early in the morning to be taking a bath, but Melody recently had been taking quite a few baths, or so she said, and she certainly smelled of soap. On the day before, she had taken three baths, and on the day before that, two. Why this sudden fetish for cleanliness and why could she not look him in the eye? "You had another bath, huh? I thought you and Florence were going for a walk."

"Well . . . no. I decided not to."

Jim took down a coiled length of nylon rope and slung it over his arm. Melody and Florence had been going for frequent walks lately. The odd thing was that even on watch at the top of the Matterhorn he could not see them. Where did they go? Practically all of the island was visible from Morgan's Armchair. Of course, it was impossible to see the little cove under the cliff or into the coconut palm grove or on the other side of the Jungfrau. That was probably where they were, on the other side of the Jungfrau, but what were they doing there for two, three hours?

"You decided not to go with her today, huh?"

"Yes, I . . . I thought I'd take a bath."

"Where do you go on these walks with Florence, honey?"

"Jim, we can't talk now, she's caught underground someplace."

"Yes, but where do you go?"

"Nowhere in particular. Please, you'd better hurry—she's frightened and says she hurt her knee."

"You talked to her?"

"Yes, I could hear her but I couldn't tell where she was."

If it was premenstrual tension that bothered Melody, she had a bad case of it. Her nervous agitation and abstracted manner were quite strange. Even now, in the midst of genuine alarm and concern about Florence, she had a wool-gathering look about her, as if some murky and absorbing thing was on her mind. As he walked with her down the Jungfrau and across the meadow toward the Matterhorn, Jim wondered about it and the more he wondered about it, the more worried he became.

It was strange. Three days before, Melody had rejected advances on his part after making advances herself. She had been very abstracted during dinner and even more so after dinner; then, when Florence left with a kerosene lantern to go to the latrine around ten-thirty, she had become quite nervous and agitated and suddenly got up and came and sat in his lap and kissed him passionately three or four times. Later that night, when they'd gone to bed, she again kissed him passionately but then pushed him in the chest and said she was too tired and besides, Florencc wasn't asleep yet.

Jim didn't like it and he didn't understand it either. Melody was always receptive, she was never "too tired," and her self-consciousness was equally unconvincing. It was true, in the beginning they'd both been inhibited by Florence's presence in the cave. They had made love in the afternoons or waited until late at night when they could convince themselves Florence was asleep. They also tried at first to be silent as a mouse about it, but in the normal course of events this inhibition had gradually broken down. Why pretend?—and why be ashamed, what difference did it make anyhow?

None, really. A week or so after the wedding they got carried away one night and forgot to be quiet and the next day Florence laughed about it, made a joke, said she was surprised they both could walk. After that, although they still tried to be reasonably quiet and not make a gross exhibition of themselves, Jim and Melody had made love any time they wanted to, whether Florence was there and could hear them or not. Why pretend, indeed? She knew what they were doing and it didn't matter if she heard an occasional kiss or heavy sigh or even more disturbing sounds, because it didn't really bother Florence, she was amused.

Yeah, thought Jim as he climbed the cactus-covered Matterhorn with a nervous, agitated, wool-gathering Melody. What a notion!

How on earth could Florence be amused? How could she or any other person find it funny to lie alone in bed and listen to other people in the throes of love six feet away on the other side of a flimsy blanket? Wouldn't she be tantalized beyond measure, aroused to unbearable desire, and, in short, driven half crazy if she were any kind of normal person at all? Of course she would, and it was a thing he had feared from the very beginning. The explanation of Melody's nervousness and wool-gathering could not be more obvious. Halfway up the Matterhorn, Jim stopped and turned to her, his lips bitten together in a thin line. "Okay," he said, "how long have you and Florence been doing funny things to each other? The last three days or is it longer than that?"

"What?" asked Melody. "What did you say?"

"Or is she merely doing funny things to you? Is that the trouble, Melody? Is that why you're acting so strange?"

"I'm not acting strange and I don't know what you're talking about."

"You *are* acting strange and so is Florence."

And that was certainly true. Florence had been acting just as strangely as Melody but in a different way. Whereas Melody was gripped by a nervous agitation, Florence exuded a spooky calm. She lay around the cave in a languorous manner, sprawled on the deck chairs as if under tranquillizers. At the same time, like a child who steals cookies and is terrified of getting caught, there was a mixture of sly defiance and fear in her eyes, as if to say: "I'm not afraid of you, I can handle you any time—but for God's sake don't spank me because I can't bear pain!"

The two women had indulged in some kind of "unnatural behavior," and Melody, to judge from her reaction, had responded to it to some degree. So Jim believed, but she seemed genuinely staggered by his accusation and he was not quite sure.

"Well, Melody? Isn't it true? You're both acting very strange, what else could it be?"

Melody slowly shook her head in disbelief. "Jim, this is the craziest idea you've had since we've been on the island. What on earth could possess me to do 'funny things' with Florence? What kind of a woman do you think I am? Even if you could think it of Florence, how could you think it of *me*, when you sleep with me and know how I feel about you? What in the world put such an idea in your head?"

"Nothing specific," said Jim, his confidence shaken. Could he have had a minor attack of paranoia? There was not a whit or a trace of guilt in Melody's gaze, not even a microscopic particle. If anything actually had happened between her and Florence, surely she'd never be able to look him calmly in the eye and deny it. He must be mistaken. Something was going on between them, all right, but it was on a psychological rather than a physical level. And yet, at times Melody could be an awful liar. He had often been amused by her ability to look him in the eye with the innocence of a child and tell an absolute flat lie. The situation, Jim decided, would bear further investigation.

"Now, let me repeat," said Melody. "While you're imagining ridiculous things, Florence is caught down in some hole in the ground. She's hurt her knee and she's frightened. Don't you think you ought to go and help her?"

"Yes, I think so. And I'm sorry if I offended you, because I don't really feel that—"

"You can apologize later. Let's help Florence now."

Two-thirds up the Matterhorn, Jim heard Rufus barking. The sound was distant and remote and seemed weirdly to come not only from underground but from several directions at once, both from out over the cliff and from somewhere under the earth. The hill was more rugged than the Jungfrau and steep on all sides except the western slope to the meadow. The eastern face was an actual cliff so steep as to be unscalable except by an expert with equipment; this was the rocky cliff that loomed over the little horseshoe cove and the "Hanging Tree of Life," which grew near its base on a raised elevation back from the thin strip of beach.

"She and the dog are down in the ground somewhere," said Jim. "But I don't understand it, the noise is also coming from over the cliff."

"Yes, it's coming from different places," said Melody. "That's what puzzled me too."

"*Florence?* Can you *hear* me? Where are you?"

A remote voice called back: "Jim? Is that you?"

"Yes, it's me, where are you?"

"I'm down here, get me out!"

"Where the hell is down here?"

"I'm in a sort of little cave! I fell in and hurt my knee—not bad, but get me out!"

"How can I get you out when I don't know where you are?"

"Maybe it's under one of the bushes," said Melody.

"The whole thing is bushes. Which bush?"

"Look for a crack in the rock!" called Florence. "Not very wide. It's hidden by a bush."

"We know that, but which bush?"

"A low one that's spread all over."

Jim folded his arms and looked around. This entire part of the hill was covered with various kinds of cactus plants and low-spreading, dense-foliaged shrubbery. "They're all low and spread all over," he called. "Sing something and I'll try and follow the sound."

"What'll I sing?"

"Oh, Christ, I don't care what you sing. Sing anything."

Florence began to yodel. "Yo-dee-lay-dee-hoo, yo-dee-lay-dee-hoo, hoo hoo hoo . . ."

"It's this way, I think," said Jim. With difficulty he picked his way through cacti and leg-grabbing dense bushes that formed a near-continuous mat rising in green waves one to three feet above the ground. The sound of Florence's voice and Rufus' barking became louder. "Keep singing, Florence."

"Ouch!" cried Melody as a cactus thorn caught her on the leg. "I can't walk through this."

"Wait there," said Jim. "Keep yodeling, Florence, I think I'm getting hot."

"YO-DEE-LAY-DEE-HOO!"

She was directly beneath him or very nearly so, but Jim still could not see any crack or opening in the rock. "This beats me," he said. "I wonder if that stupid bush over there . . ." A low-growing, thick-leaved bush grew in a slight bowl-shaped recess eight feet away, protected in every direction except to the cliffside by prickly cactus. The edge of the precipice could not be too many feet away; he could see over the rising wave of jungle-like foliage a part of the lagoon glimmering green down below. "How in hell did she *ever* get in here? Ouch! Damned cactus!"

"YO-DEE-LAY-DEE-HOO . . . HOO HOO HOO!" sang Florence.

Her voice was directly below him and unmistakably coming through the low-spreading dense bush, although Jim also could hear it coming from over the edge of the cliff. Taking care not to get stuck with cactus thorns, he bent down and pushed aside the leaves of the bush but could see nothing. "Good God," said Jim, "I never heard of cactuses growing among jungle bushes like this. The island is out of its mind."

"You are right above me," said Florence. "I think I can see your shadow through the leaves."

Jim got down on his hands and knees and crawled out over the matlike bush itself, which reminded him of the altitude-starved and wind-runted foot-high birches on top of Mt. Mansfield in Vermont. The birches were more solid, however. In desperation, Jim grabbed at a gnarled root as he felt himself begin to fall.

"Holy cow! This is the most *concealed* damn thing I ever heard of. I almost fell in it before I could see it."

"I can see your foot now," said Florence.

Jim also could see Florence. The mystery was explained. The spreading bush, which in turn was guarded by dense cactus plants, had grown over a fissure in the rock of the hill, an opening that apparently went all the way through from the western slope to the eastern face of the cliff. By pushing aside the leaves Jim could see down into a well-lighted little chamber about ten feet below. Florence sat on a benchlike ledge with her legs crossed and a sheepish expression on her face. Rufus stood beside her, head lifted to look up at Jim and his tail wagging.

"Hi," said Florence. "Sorry to be so much bother."

"No trouble at all," said Jim.

"I tried, but I couldn't climb out of here."

"Did you find her?" called Melody.

"Yeah, I found her," said Jim. "I just have to tie the rope to the roots of this bush, then I'll go down and get her."

"Can I help?"

"No, stay back, there's too much cactus. I'll get her out in a few minutes, she's all right."

"A little shook," said Florence, "that's all. I'm really sorry, it's idiotic. The dog chased an iguana and both of 'em fell down here. I heard him barking but couldn't find him, then before I knew it I fell in the place myself. It's lucky I didn't break my neck."

"I'll get you out," said Jim, "no harm done." He tied another knot in the rope, pulled at it hard to test it, then dropped the coil through the thirty-inch fissure.

"It's a great little cave," said Florence, "if you could call it a cave.

It's really just a rock formation in the cliff face. But wait'll you see it. It has a fantastic picture window right on the lagoon."

"I'm coming down," said Jim. He put his feet into the fissure, then lowered himself hand over hand on the rope down into the small chamber.

"Welcome to Morgan's *Second* Treasure Cave," said Florence with a grin. "I haven't found much gold yet but it has its points."

Jim looked around. The first thing he saw was a large and obviously dead iguana on the floor. There was not much blood, but a pool of greenish-yellow stain was on the floor by the creature's mouth and the things only vomited bile in their death throes.

"Is that thing dead, Florence?"

"Oh, yes, very dead. When Rufus kills something, he kills it. He bit half its stomach out."

"It's a nasty-looking thing," said Jim. "I wonder how sick we've got to get of beef stew before we break down and eat one."

"Ugggch," said Florence.

"They say they're good. You boil thcm. Maybc wc'll cat this onc."

"Well . . . I'm game, if you are," said Florence.

"Yeah, maybe we'll eat it." Jim lifted his gaze from the dead lizard and looked around the little chamber. At once he understood why Florence had call it "a great little cave." The room had a level floor littered with broken rock, bat guano, and bird droppings, and the ceiling was a vaulted, irregular mass of water-stained and mossy stone that lifted up to the fissure; but the floor was dry and so was the shelflike ledge at the back. The place, Jim thought, was coziness personified. It was a perfect natural shelter and the hiddenness of it gave it a primeval charm. But the most striking feature of Morgan's Second Treasure Cave was an opening the size of a ranch-house picture window that looked directly over the lagoon. The "window" was raised eighteen inches or so from the floor, which would prevent a restless sleeper—the floor was about the size of a king-size bed—from rolling over and falling down into the top of the big tree in the cove. "This is a fantastic place," said Jim. "It's an agoraphobe's dream—with a view."

"I told you it's great. Rufus has done it again. He's a thinking dog—although both of us felt a little silly, hollering and barking to get out of here."

"Melody came by and heard you?"

"Yes. She had gone to take a bath."

"She's taking a lot of baths these days."

"She likes it up there."

"I'm surprised she could hear you. The path from Melody's Bathtub doesn't go by here. This is pretty near the top of the hill, Florence."

"Well . . . the path isn't that far."

"*I* couldn't hear you till we were way up the hill."

"I suppose she was looking for me. We'd intended to go for a walk, she knew I was here on the hill somewhere."

"Um-hmm," said Jim. He looked around again at the little chamber in the face of the cliff. "One thing puzzles me. Why can't we see that window opening from the beach? I've never noticed it. Have you?"

"I think the tree blocks it. The beach is very narrow there and the reef curves in. You'd have to go out in the ocean beyond the reef to see it. From the lagoon it isn't visible."

"We can see *out* of it, though," said Jim. "Maybe it's the angle of the cliff. Oh course, it's an overhang and it's in shadow most of the day."

"I think that's it. We'd never have known it was here if Rufus and I hadn't fallen in it."

"That is for sure," said Jim. "It's lucky Melody came looking for you."

"Yes. It's a great little place, though, a real hideout. I think I'll take a sleeping bag or pallet and some books and come here and read. You know, relax and everything, away from it all."

"The madding crowd," said Jim.

Florence smiled uneasily. She did not seem to like the meditative way Jim was staring at her. "Shall we get out of here?"

"Not quite yet," said Jim. He walked to Florence and stood over her, hands on hips. "Okay, Florence, what's going on between you and Melody?"

"What? What did you say?"

Her response was identical to Melody's, but she was not as good a liar. "You heard what I said, Florence. What's going on between you and Melody?"

"Going on? Jim, I don't know what you mean. Does Melody say anything is going on?"

"No, I asked her about it and she denied it. But she was lying and so are you right now, and that's foolish. It's not a thing you can keep secret from me. What's going on?"

"Jim, there's nothing going on. We've taken some walks, that's all."

Jim stared in cold annoyance at her. He felt like putting her across his knee and spanking her. "You've got a *hell* of a nerve, Florence. Didn't you know I would find out about it? You must have, you're not an absolute idiot."

"Jim . . . we've just taken walks."

Despite his exasperation, Jim could not help but feel a pity for her. As silly and pathetic as the whole thing was, Florence took it seriously as death. Her lips were apart in paralyzed fear and a pleading, don't-hurt-me expression was in her eyes. The blood had drained completely from her face and her hands were trembling. Of course she had known he would find out, she had known it quite well and now she was terrified. With a half-conscious thought of preventing her from hysterically throwing herself down over the cliff, Jim stepped between her and the window opening of the cave and said:

"You've done more than take walks, Florence. You've been a bad girl. You've been fiddling with Melody."

"No, Jim . . . Jim, I haven't. Really I haven't."

"All right. I'll get the truth out of *her*."

Jim turned toward the rope but Florence jumped up and grabbed his arm. "Jim, wait! Please . . . don't be angry with me. I didn't mean to. Really I didn't, I swear I didn't! I was more surprised than she was, and it . . . it . . . I didn't mean to."

Jim was silent for a moment, then said, "Okay. Let's get out of here."

"But what are you going to do?" asked Florence, her eyes popped with worry. "Are you . . . I mean, you must hate me and despise me, what are you going to do?"

"I'm going to get out of this cave," said Jim. "Do you have the strength to climb up the rope?"

"Oh, God!" exclaimed Florence. Despite himself, Jim almost smiled as she raised her hands, clutched them together, and wrung them in a manner worthy of Sarah Bernhardt. He had not known Florence was capable of such a theatrical gesture. Talk about *romantic*—she was worse than Melody. "Oh, God in heaven! Can't you forgive me? I'm only human! Do you have to hate me and despise me and look at me like that?"

Jim paused to get himself under control. Her distress was genuine and it was no time to smile. Later, perhaps, he could joke with her about it. Florence, in time, would laugh at this scene, but it wasn't funny to her now. Jim stared at her in cold, stern disapproval and said: "I asked you a question. Do you have the strength in your hands to climb up this rope?"

Florence wilted as tears brimmed in her eyes.

"No, I . . . I don't think so."

"Can you hold on to it if I pull you up?"

"Yes, I can do that."

"All right, I'll climb it, then you take a firm grip and I'll pull you up. But first tie it around Rufus and I'll pull him out. Can you do that?"

Florence's hands and knees were trembling and tears were running down her cheeks. "I . . . no. I'm not clever, I don't know how to do the knots. Oh, Jim . . . Jim, can't you forgive me?"

"I'll make a sling for the dog and pull him up first."

By the time Jim got Rufus and Florence up into the cactus patch, Florence was sobbing uncontrollably, a hand over her eyes. Melody took one look at her and put a hand over *her* eyes and began to cry. It was a pathetic tableau.

"All right, now stop crying, both of you," said Jim. "That's not going to do any good. And you'd better take your hands down from your eyes or you'll get stuck with cactus thorns."

Jim led Florence around through the cactus plants to the clearer area where Melody stood. Tearfully, the two women looked at each other.

"Is your knee all right?" asked Melody.

"Yes, it's just bumped a little."

"She's lucky she wasn't killed," said Jim. "And I'll tell you this about that place. No one would ever find it, you could live on this island twenty years and never know it was there. I don't think you could find it even if you knew it was on the hill, unless you knew exactly and precisely where it was."

"Well, I couldn't find it," said Melody.

"You really are lucky you weren't hurt, Florence," said Jim. "That's at least a ten-foot drop down there."

Melody sniffed, brushed tears from her eyes, and said, "Rufus doesn't look hurt either."

"No, the only injured party was the iguana Rufus was chasing," said Jim. "And do you know what? I think we ought to get our nerve up and eat the damned thing. We're all sick of beef stew, why not?"

"Oh, I couldn't," said Melody.

"The Indians eat them in Mexico all the time. They really are supposed to be very good, like chicken. Why don't we eat it?"

"Oh, God!" said Florence.

"At least we could *try* to eat the damned thing. You said before you were game if I was, Florence. Why not let's try?"

"Jim," said Melody. "I . . . I want to talk to you. I want to explain something."

"I say let's try to eat that iguana. Florence, you go back to Morgan's *First* Treasure Cave—I guess that's what it is now—and take that big ship's galley pot and fill it with water and put it on to boil. Will you do that?"

"Jim," said Melody, "I want to *talk* to you."

"Will you do that, Florence?"

"Yes, I'll . . . I'll do it. But I want to talk to you too, Jim. I can explain a lot better than Melody. Will you talk to me?"

"I'll talk to you, Florence, sure, but later. Melody will be interested to see this new cave and I want to get that iguana, so you go on back and start boiling the water, okay?"

In a meek little voice Florence answered, "All right."

"Don't fill the pot but about half full, the iguana will displace a lot of water. I'll stop by the beach on the way back and clean it and skin it."

Florence nodded and turned with slumped shoulders and walked off, followed by Rufus, who was frisking in regained freedom despite cactus bushes everywhere.

"Jim," said Melody. "Jim, I . . . I . . ."

"Let's take a look at the cave. I'll lower you, honey. Come on, watch the cactuses now."

"But there's something I want to say."

"We'll talk down below. This way, honey."

"It isn't what you think," said Melody.

"Watch out for the thorns," said Jim. "Watch out, you'll get stuck. Now this way—no, turn like that, there, that's right. Now walk *on* the bush—no, over here where the branches are heavier."

"But it isn't what you think," said Melody.

Jim finally maneuvered her through the cactus plants to the low-spreading bush that covered the fissure that led to Morgan's Second Treasure Cave. He put the rope in her hands and said, "Now hold on tight and I'll lower you. Just don't let go."

"I won't let go, don't worry. But Jim, you're going to be surprised. It really and truly isn't what you think."

Melody shrank back from the dead iguana in its pool of bile. "Oooh," she said. "I always hated those things."

"They're completely harmless. Once in a while they bite a little bit, but that's all. And they're good to eat. I really think we ought to get over our prejudice and cook it and eat it."

"Oh, Jim, I know what you think! But will you stop talking like that? Didn't you see the look on her face and the way she was crying? Making her go boil the water—Jim, how can you be so cruel? She can't help the way she is. Jim, please. Let's go back and tell her she doesn't have to boil the water."

Jim pointed to the benchlike ledge and said, "Sit down, honey. I'm not being cruel to Florence."

"Yes, you are, you're being very cruel to her. Don't you know how upset she is and how bad she feels? I've been afraid, worried she might do something to hurt herself. Jim, please don't be mean to her."

"Will you sit down?"

"All right, but you don't understand."

Jim sat beside her and folded his arms, then waited as Melody glanced unseeingly around the cave. She finally turned toward him and he said: "Are you calm now? Or reasonably calm?"

"Jim, you're being brutal. How can you act this way? It isn't like you a bit, I don't understand it."

"I suppose you're as calm as you're going to be. Now, the question is this, Melody. I don't care what you did or what Florence did and I don't even want to know. I really don't, because it doesn't matter. The question is, what are we going to do about it."

"What I did and what Florence did? I didn't do *any*thing and neither did she! I told you you'd be surprised. It really and truly isn't what you think, Jim."

Jim sighed wearily. "Melody, for an honest person you're the biggest liar I ever met."

"But I'm not lying, it's the truth!"

"All right," said Jim. "I didn't want to go through this, but I guess we've got to get it out in the open or you'll brood about it for the rest of your life. Would a few questions help you?"

"A few questions?"

"Yes, I think a few questions. Not because I want to know, I know already, but just to help you get it out of your system. Did she kiss you?"

"What?"

"Did Florence kiss you?"

"Jim, you don't understand. She *loves* me."

"I didn't ask you if she loves you, I asked you if she kissed you. Did she?"

"Well, yes, but . . ."

"Did she touch your breasts?"

"Jim, how can you ask that?"

"Stop pussyfooting around, Melody. Answer me. Did she touch your breasts?"

"Well . . . yes, but it wasn't like you think."

"It's exactly like I think. Did she put her finger in you?"

"Oh, Jim, *really!* How can you ask such a thing as *that?*"

"Did she?"

Melody's eyelids fluttered, then fluttered again and closed as a dark blush spread in her cheeks. "Well . . . yes, she did."

"Did you do the same thing to her?"

Melody's eyes snapped open in surprise. "Oh, no. Of course not."

Jim nodded. Melody's surprise was genuine. It had not occurred to her as a possibility she might do the same thing to Florence. "And when she did this," asked Jim, "you responded?"

Again Melody's eyelids fluttered shut. "Well, a little," she said. "I couldn't help it."

"All right, did you do anything else with Florence?"

"Anything else?"

"Yes, did you and Florence do any other things together?"

"No," said Melody puzzled. "What do you mean?"

"Never mind," said Jim. "Let's sum up, then we can talk about our real problem. She kissed you, she touched your breasts, she put her finger in you, and you responded to it to a certain extent. That's what happened, right?"

"Yes."

"And the first time was three days ago?"

"Yes, but she didn't touch me with her finger then. She just kissed me and put her hand on my breasts."

"That was three days ago. The next day, day before yesterday, she touched you with her finger?"

Again Melody blushed. "Yes. Day before yesterday."

"And yesterday?"

"No, I wouldn't. She wanted to, but I wouldn't."

"And this morning?"

"Well, she wanted me to go for a walk with her and I was sorry for her and at first I said I would, then I said I wouldn't. And I didn't, I went and had a bath."

"After your bath, you came to the hill and looked for her?"

Melody nodded. "Yes. She'd cried when I said I couldn't let her do that any more. I wanted to talk to her. Then I heard her and Rufus down here, except I didn't know where she was so I came and got you."

"All right," said Jim. "Now I want to ask you one more question, Melody, and I don't want you to lie to me. I really and truly don't, because this is an important question. Don't lie, honey, please don't, okay?"

"I won't lie," said Melody, her head bowed.

"Okay, this is my question. When you went back looking for Florence on the hill, did you intend to have pity on her and let her do what she wanted?"

Melody opened her mouth to speak, then paused. "Well . . . I honestly don't know. I think I might have."

"Uh-huh," said Jim. "I think you might have too. In fact, I think you would have. And unless we do something about it, I think you will in the future."

"Jim, it isn't that I want to. I know you think there's an unnatural streak in me and maybe there is or I couldn't do such a thing at all, but I don't like it."

"Okay, then it's got to stop. I don't like it and you don't like it, so it's got to stop."

"Yes, but I don't think Florence can control herself. Jim, she really loves me. I was wrong about her and you were right. She doesn't like men in that way, she's not attracted to them. I was naive about it, I've never known such a person. But you were right, she's a Lesbian."

"Is she?" asked Jim with a faint smile. "I don't think so. I've never really thought so."

"But she *is*, Jim. I admit I didn't believe it myself and it took me completely by surprise. I was so amazed I couldn't move! All of a sudden she put her hand on me, then put her head on my shoulder and began to cry. She was sobbing, her arms around me like a child. It was awful! What could I do? I felt so sorry for her, and she felt terrible herself, she kept asking me to forgive her. And I do love her, Jim, what could I do? It isn't what you think."

Jim smiled wryly. "It's what I think down to the last dot on the i," he said. "And there's an unnatural streak in you, all right. You're too kindhearted for this world."

"I did feel sorry for her, and so should you, Jim. Instead of shaming her and making her boil that water, you should pity her. Jim, don't be cruel to her. She's so afraid of you. She kept begging me not to tell you."

"She did, huh?"

"Oh, yes, constantly. 'Don't tell Jim. Don't tell Jim. For God's sake, don't tell Jim.' She kept saying it over and over."

"Methinks the lady doth protest too much. Believe me, Florence is no Lesbian. She might be impossibly neurotic and too much for any man to handle, but she's no Lesbian."

"Jim, she *is*, I tell you. I know she is. Touching me made her passionate just like it would you."

"Look, after listening to us make love for three weeks I should think it would make Florence passionate if a bug sat on her—no invidious comparisons intended, honey; I'm sure you're more attractive than any bug. And more attractive than Rufus, too."

"Rufus?"

Jim smiled. "I was just remembering how I once saw her hugging the dog and I asked her if she wouldn't rather have a human being in her arms. I guess I knew then we'd come to this. It was sort of inevitable."

"If you understand that, then don't be cruel to her. It's pitiful, Jim, she's so lonely. She wants someone to love and she's never had *anybody*. She doesn't get along at all with those women who are like that and the only man she ever loved was a fisherman who didn't even know she existed."

"I thought you said she was a Lesbian," answered Jim dryly, "and now you tell me she loved a fisherman. What kind of Lesbian is that?"

"It was a romantic love, not a real love. It was a fixation."

"A fixation? You mean, like she has on me?"

"Well . . . yes. And that's all the more reason you shouldn't be cruel to her. She's so afraid of you, Jim, so afraid of what you'll think and that you'll hate her. *Please* don't be cruel to her, Jim. Be nice to her and go to her and tell her it's all right, that you understand."

"There's nothing I could do that would disappoint her more," said Jim. "I'm afraid you're not reading this thing clear, honey."

"What do you mean?"

Jim paused. It was a ticklish thing to bring up. Melody had offered Florence as a substitute for herself in the first place and had just allowed herself to be subjected to a distressing experience on Florence's account, but what man can predict the primordial jealousies that lurk in the female heart? It couldn't be helped, in any event. Whatever Melody's reaction, there was no alternative.

"I guess we have come to the nub of it," said Jim. "And that's the problem of what to do about Florence. This is why I had to talk to you before I talk to her. I would want your approval of what I have in mind."

Melody suddenly blinked. "You mean—you and her? But Jim, I don't think that would work."

"Because of you or because of her?"

"Because of her—not me, I wouldn't mind. Or at least, I don't think I would. It's because of her it wouldn't work."

"Well, I guess we can't assume flatly Florence is *not* a Lesbian, since, after all, she has done Lesbian-type things both on the island here and elsewhere, I'm sure. But I think we *can* assume at the very least she's mixed in her attitude. She told you she doesn't get along with Lesbians in New York and she had a fixation on a fisherman and also a fixation on me. Therefore, if it's acceptable to you and to her, I think I should live with you both on the island. Otherwise she's going to continue to torment herself and you and me too. It's the only answer I can see, Melody. What do you think?"

Melody was slightly pale. "Well . . . it would take a little getting used to. But if it would work, I think it would be fine. After all, what right do I have to keep you all for myself? Florence is a human being. I think it would be fine."

"There are precedents in the Bible, of course," said Jim.

"Yes, I know. And I definitely think it would be fine. I'm not jealous and possessive, Jim. I'll share you with Florence if she wants to. But I'm afraid you may have an *awful* time with her."

Jim gave a slight shudder. "Yes," he said, "I may."

Shortly before noon, Jim walked into the entrance of Morgan's First Treasure Cave, hitherto known simply as Morgan's Treasure Cave. He had accepted Melody's impassioned plea that the dead iguana was too much of a muchness—"Jim, you mustn't bring that horrible lizard there. She's been shocked enough, you've got to be sweet and kind to her now. Be very *gentle* with her, and maybe she will. Be very *deli*cate with her. And Jim, don't rush her. Be patient and gentle. And don't you dare bring that horrible lizard there."

Jim, who felt or at least hoped the "horrible lizard" had served its purpose, concurred. He'd picked up the thing by the tail and thrown it out of the window opening of Morgan's Second Treasure Cave. Florence, however, had taken him at his word and filled the big ship's galley pot with water and put it on the kerosene stove to boil.

"I see you put the water on," said Jim.

Florence, whose eyes were red from weeping, sat on a crate by the stove. Rufus lay at her feet, head on his paws and eyes doubtfully on Jim. "Yes, I put it on," she said. "Where's the iguana?"

"I threw the damned thing over the cliff. I'm not even sure how you cook one of them."

Florence smiled feebly. "Neither am I. But you said put on water, so I did."

"One of these days we'll have to get up the nerve to eat one. But I don't think today is the day. We have more important things to worry about than a dead lizard."

Again Florence smiled feebly. "Yes, I guess we do. Where's Melody?"

"She's gone for a walk."

"A walk? It's almost time for lunch, when will she be back?"

"Later," said Jim.

Florence stood up, turned off the kerosene burner under the ship's galley pot, and walked toward the cave entrance. As she reached Jim in the living area, she stopped and said: "I have to go to the bathroom."

"Do you?"

"Look, it's *my* bladder, I guess I know whether I have to go or not. And I do. I have to go."

"I'm not stopping you," said Jim.

Rufus, who had padded along after Florence, suddenly lowered his head and growled at Jim. "Shut up, Rufus," said Florence. "Be quiet, he's not going to hurt me."

"No, I'm not," said Jim.

Florence moistened her lips and made a gulping sound as she swallowed. "Jim, I swear I won't do it again."

"Hmm."

"What do you mean, *hmm?*"

"Nothing. I thought you had to go to the bathroom?"

"I just went. Jim, won't you believe me? I *swear* I won't do it again. I'll swear an oath to God I will never do such a thing again."

"I'm sure you'd mean it too, Florence. But those oaths seem to be a kind of waste of breath."

"Oh, God! Jim, I know it was awful of me and I feel terrible about it."

"It was just schoolgirl stuff," said Jim. "Under the blankets at boarding school. I wonder how many times that happens every night? Maybe six thousand seven hundred and fourteen? It wasn't all that awful, Florence, let's don't exaggerate."

Florence seemed indignant. "It upset and disturbed *Melody* more than you realize. Much more. The truth is, she . . . she responded to me."

Jim shrugged. "I guess she's a Lesbian, then." Again Rufus growled at him. Jim considered and then rejected the idea of patting the dog on the head. Not a good idea, the animal would probably bite him.

"Oh, Rufus, *please* be quiet! Stop growling! Jim's not going to hurt me, you stupid dog." Florence again moistened her lips and swallowed painfully. "I guess that was meant to be ironic, about Melody being a Lesbian. It's ironic, all right. You know very well the only reason she did it was out of pity for me. She's about as much of a Lesbian as Rufus."

"So are you," said Jim.

"Oh, Jim, please don't joke! This might be funny to you, but it isn't to me! Don't you know how ashamed I am to have acted that way? Jim, I couldn't help it, I couldn't—all of a sudden the impulse came over me and I couldn't help it!"

"I wasn't joking," said Jim. "You're about as much of a Lesbian as Rufus."

"Oh, God!" In a melodramatic manner reminiscent of nineteenth-century theater, Florence clapped her hands over her forehead and eyes, then rocked slowly back and forth, crooning, "Oooooooh, oooooooh, God!"

"You're not a Lesbian, Florence."

Florence snatched her hands from her eyes. "Is that so?" she asked, "I'm *not*, huh?"

"No, I don't think so. I never have."

"Um-hmm. And what does Melody think, may I ask?"

"Well, at first she was confused, but I believe she agrees with me."

"All right, this madness will never cease until I put a stop to it. What did you decide, you and Melody, in that place? You were talking to her and talking to her and talking to her! What did you decide?"

Calmly, Jim replied: "Well, we decided it would be a good idea for me to live with you as well as with her on the island, Florence, if you're willing."

"You decided *that?*" exclaimed Florence, as if the thing she had heard were not only beyond belief but beyond all imagining. "You and Melody decided such a thing as *that?* Are you *serious?*"

"Perfectly serious," said Jim. "She's willing to share me with you on the island, Florence. I don't know how much of a bargain I would be, but it might make you feel a little less lonely."

Again Florence clapped her hands to her head in a manner truly worthy of Sarah Bernhardt. "What a proposition! It might make me feel a little less lonely!"

"It wouldn't be an entirely soulless thing, Florence. I can't say I'm in love with you, but I do like you very much and I always have. And I think you're an attractive woman, too."

"Oh, shut up! You don't think any such thing! That's ridiculous! You don't want this and neither does she—it's just that I've caused trouble. Can't you believe me if I swear I won't do it again?"

"We're not trying to force you into anything, Florence. Melody and I are agreed on that one hundred percent. I've never raped a woman in my life and I never will. All we're saying is, we feel it would be best for all of us if I live with both of you on the island."

"That's nothing but a cold-blooded decision and I *hate* cold-blooded decisions! You know perfectly well you're not attracted to me in the least, and for that reason alone I say such a thing is absurd, insane, ridiculous, and out of the question!"

"I *am* attracted to you," said Jim firmly, "and may God hit me with a lightning bolt right now if it isn't true."

"You'd better not go out in a thunderstorm or your ass will look like a ragged piece of roast beef! You know goddamn well you're not attracted to me and the only reason you're suggesting this is because you think it would keep me away from your precious Melody. Well, I don't want her! You can have her!"

"I think it would keep you away from Melody, yes, but that's not my only reason for suggesting it. I'm suggesting it on your account too, and on mine as well."

"On *yours* as well? Now, what could you possibly mean by that?"

"Look, Florence, it's true I love Melody, but I'm a normal man. And human nature is not strictly monogamous, especially as far as men are concerned. It wouldn't be unpleasant to me to have two women on this island. And I think most men would be able to bear the pain of such a thing."

"Fu Manchu," said Florence, "that's what you are! Trying to make me think you want a harem here. Jim, you're the biggest liar that ever lived. I don't believe a word of it and even if I did it wouldn't make a particle of difference, because you and Melody don't have the right to decide my fate and that's all there is to it!"

"We're not trying to. All we're saying is, we think it would be the best thing for everyone concerned. Don't you think so yourself, Florence?"

Again Florence clapped her hands to her head. "Oh, God! And you say you've never raped a woman! What else is *this* but pure rape? Oh, God!" Florence took one hand from her head and reached out in a trembling manner for the back of a deck chair. It was a gesture right out of the Booth era of the Thespian art and Jim had difficulty hiding a smile. Of course the real battle would come later, but he was very encouraged. She was obviously on the verge of agreeing in principle. "This is too much. I . . . I've got to sit down. It's pure rape."

Jim sat opposite her in a deck chair and said, "I don't see how you can call it *rape*, Florence, I really don't."

"Oh, you don't, huh? Well, look at the pressure you're putting on me, both of you! Why, in effect you are passing a law on me, you are saying in so many words I have got to do it."

"We're not saying you have to do anything."

"Yes, but you're telling me your opinion and isn't that the same thing?"

"No, I wouldn't say it's the same thing."

"It certainly is. You're putting pressure on me, *moral* pressure. I've been bad, I'm a dirty girl, so I've got to be punished."

"You're not a dirty girl," said Jim, "you're a frustrated woman."

"Oh, don't give me that shit, I'm a dirty girl and I know it. Why in hell didn't I keep my hands off her? Oh, God, I knew it would come to this, why didn't I leave her alone?"

Jim resisted an impulse to ask: "Why didn't you?" Instead, he reiterated a point he had made several times before. "We're not trying to force you to do anything, Florence."

Florence put her elbow on her knee and her head in her hand. "Another wedding," she said glumly. "I couldn't stand that."

"I don't think a wedding would be necessary in this case, since you and I are a little more worldly than Melody."

"You mean . . . we should just go to bed, like that?"

"You make it sound pretty cut-and-dried, but I'd say yes, more or less. There's nothing like being decisive about these things, Florence."

"Oh, God," said Florence feebly. "And when, may I ask, do you and Melody expect this blessed event to occur?"

"It isn't up to Melody or me either—it's up to you, Florence. But I should think the sooner, the better."

"You said she'd be back . . . 'later.' When is later?"

"She didn't want lunch—you know she's always worrying about her weight. She'll be away all afternoon."

"All afternoon? Ooooh . . . oh, God," said Florence, a stricken fear in her eyes and a hand on her heart.

"I'd say the sooner, the better, definitely. It's kind of like an operation, Florence. The longer you wait, the more nervous you become. The best thing is to go ahead and get it over with."

"This is the most *romantic* seduction I ever heard of! An operation, he says, like I'm having my gall bladder out! Get it over with, the sooner, the better—oh, God!"

"That wasn't very romantic, was it? I didn't mean it to sound quite like that, Florence. This is an unusual situation for me as well as for you. I think in time, though, things will improve."

Florence took a deep breath and pulled herself erect in her chair. As if storing up mental force, she stared unwaveringly at Jim, her lips bitten together and her eyes more popped than he had ever seen them and the freckles on her face like chicken pox and measles combined. She was not as homely as she thought she was, but Florence was no beauty. Her worst feature really was the buck teeth. Jim didn't mind the freckles, he'd gotten used to them. But those buck teeth were romance-shriveling. Was it possible, Jim wondered, to kiss the poor thing and feel desire for her? Would he be able, as the boys say, to get it up? A trickle of icy sweat ran from Jim's armpit as he sent forth a silent prayer to Priapus.

"Now listen," said Florence as if reading his mind. "It's plain as day you are not attracted to me at all and you don't want me and you wish to hell you were somewhere else. I will give you and Melody both a gold star for Christian kindliness. But you are wasting your fucking compassion on me because, goddamn it, I don't *want* to live with you here! Do you *hear* me, do you *hear what I'm saying?*"

Jim swallowed as another trickle of cold sweat ran down his side. The prayer to Priapus was slightly premature. "Yes, I hear you, Florence."

"All right, then get this in your goddamned head and get it there good. I don't want to sleep with a man! I don't want a man touching me and monkeying with me and doing repulsive things to me! I never have and I never will and this is absolutely and totally barbarous! Furthermore, it is *not* Christian compassion, it is brutal coercion based on an outmoded, ignorant, and intolerant Puritanism. If you and Melody really wanted to be kind to me, you would let me be *myself*. I didn't hurt that pious little hypocrite or do her any harm at all—on the contrary, she *liked* it! And that's why you're doing this. Hypocritical Puritan guilt on her part and Puritan jealousy and insecurity on yours. I touched her sacred little heterosexual pussy and revealed to you both that a woman can excite her just as a man can, and this is the unforgivable crime in the benighted world in which you both live. So now I'm to have an operation, I'm to be punished, chastised, scourged! In Christian charity you offer me your fair white body! Well, I don't want your fair white body! I am me, myself, I, and I'm going to remain *me, myself, I!* You and Melody don't have the right to decide my welfare and my fate and goddamn it will you let me alone? I don't *want* you! You *revolt* me! I want to vomit if you *touch* me! Now go away and leave me alone!"

It was bluster, Jim was sure, a sort of desperate Battle of the Bulge, but despite himself he shrank down in his chair just a little. Somehow he managed to smile and say: "I know I'm pretty disgusting, Florence. But I always thought you kind of liked me, despite my faults."

"You . . . are the filthiest man that ever lived. My father and my brother were both hateful bullies, but in comparison to you they look like choirboys. Oh, what a filthy bully you are! Making me put water in that pot . . . and then having the Fu Manchu nerve to say you didn't bring any iguana in here. Who are you putting on? Don't you think I know your methods by now? You brought an iguana all right and you are boiling it to beat all hell. It's the most barbarian and unfair thing I ever heard of in my life, to put me in this position where I don't have any choice—except it's not going to work, I'll drown myself in that ocean before I'll let you touch me."

Jim smiled painfully. This was more like the Battle of Stalingrad than the Battle of the Bulge. She had worked herself into a truly monumental dither. And no wonder. The whole thing *was* a trifle cold-blooded and inhuman, especially for a thirty-eight-year-old virgin terrified of men. An inspiration was needed, a bit of gold thread had to be found somewhere. Jim opened his mind and waited to hear what he would say. He felt a slight constriction in his chest as the words came out.

"Well, Florence, Melody says I'm old-fashioned and I guess a man who would make a woman sit alone for two months on an uninhabited island has got a square streak in him somewhere." Jim was afraid Rufus would bite him. However, courageously he stood up, walked over to Florence, and put his hand on her shoulder. "I'm sorry," he said. "It isn't that I don't care about you, Florence. I've thought about you from the beginning. But I've been very busy with Melody, she was a problem."

As he finished his speech and realized what he had said, Jim Kittering almost groaned aloud. What presumption! What gall! And what utter incoherence! To his astonishment, however, Florence sighed as if in relief and then answered in a tiny voice: "I knew you liked me a little. I knew that all along."

Jim was afraid to open his mouth for fear of what might come out, but she obviously expected him to say something and he couldn't just stand there with his hand on her shoulder. The only thing was another step into the wild blue yonder. The slight constriction in his chest became painful as he said: "Yes, ever since we were in the little square in Savannah, I've loved you, Florence, because I understood you then."

Another mad remark! Jim winced and shut his eyes. She had been very angry with him because he'd criticized that little park and scoffed at it and said it was silly. Jim felt a hand on his hand and opened his eyes in time to see Florence bow her head and begin to cry. "I know, I know," she sighed, "and I'll never forget it. It changed my life, Jim, the thing you said to me in that little park."

Incredible. What thing had he said to her? It must have been something significant but for the life of him he could not recall what it was. The only thing he could remember was that Florence had been upset when he scoffed at the park and that he had then apologized and said he thought it was beautiful. How could this change her life?

"Well," said Florence with another sigh, her hand still on his, "I suppose you realize I'll hate you for this forever?"

"Yes, I realize that," said Jim.

"Melody really doesn't mind? She really doesn't?"

"No. She loves you."

Florence's shoulder trembled under his hand as she wept. "But you won't like it. You won't Jim. You can boil me forever and I won't taste like chicken."

"You don't have to," said Jim. "Forget that."

Again Florence's shoulder trembled. "I am a terrible coward. Will you hurt me?"

"Maybe a little," said Jim.

Florence brushed tears from her eyes with her free hand. "All right," she said, "but not here."

"No, we'll go somewhere else."

"You are going to have a hell of a time," said Florence philosophically, "a hell of a hell of a time. Your manhood will be tested and retested before you are through with this dirty girl."

That undoubtedly was true, thought Jim, but one thing at least had been accomplished. He was confronted now by brave fear, not by iguana bile.

TWENTY
The Mighty Matterhorn

Florence was encumbered by two lunch boxes, several Perry Mason mysteries, and a cotton blanket for the bunk mattress Jim was carrying, but she attempted to make light conversation as they went up the hill. Twice, as she stumbled up it, she referred to it as "the mighty Matterhorn." Consciously or unconsciously, she did not seem to have a mere protrusion of the earth's crust in mind but a grander phenomenon of nature.

At first Jim smiled with a tepid amusement, as a sandlot slugger might do when told: "You're another Mickey Mantle! That hundred-and-eighty-foot blast would have gone out of Yankee Stadium!" But when Florence referred again in tones of awe to the "mighty" Matterhorn, he began to take her seriously. Perhaps it was understandable coming from a thirty-eight-year-old virgin spinster, but nevertheless it seemed incredible to him. She was terrified to the depths of her soul by an appendage he had always considered one of the most harmless, helpless, vulnerable things in the world.

Certainly that was true. What could be more innocuous than this thing, which dangled defenseless and timid, which waited only to be hauled out and made to pee or to be tugged forth to meet a far greater, more harrowing duty? The thing had no will of its own and was no match for the sulphurous volcanic fissure into which it was doomed to sink.

Yes, doomed, and for what?—to placate feminine fury and bring little squalling creatures into an overpopulated world at a two-hundred-thousand-dollar clip each. Child Support Law Number One had been passed and it could not be rescinded. Florence might get pregnant if Melody didn't. They both might get pregnant. They might have twins—one of his grandfathers had thrown twins three times! "Doomed" was the word. The goddamned island was not only going to ruin him financially, it was going to wear the mighty Matterhorn down to the peneplain.

And that was only a slight exaggeration, if at all. Melody, in the past three weeks, already had subjected the central massif to considerable erosion; in fact she had reduced it to a very modest peak only the night before, driven no doubt by emotional tumult brought on by the problem with Florence—she wouldn't cease and desist but with whispers of merciless love kept right on immersing and re-immersing the battered Matterhorn in a lake of real fire. She was a menace—wonderful, but a menace. After months of frustration and gripped with a mad love for him, she wanted to torment the Matterhorn two or three times every day. How could it take this kind of punishment and still call itself a hill, much less a mountain? Jim flinched with embarrassment at the memory of his complacency at the beginning. "Oh, I might be able to," he'd said. Now he was saying: "*Again,* Melody? Really? But don't you think you need a little sleep?"

The mighty Matterhorn, indeed. Florence was living in a world of fantasy as far from reality as could be. That shrunken, worn-out, discouraged thing—a threat? How could he explain to her what an innocent victim it really was and thus diminish her fright, which in all truth had no basis to equal his own? There was only *one* of *him,* but there were *two* of *them*—and how many men, Jim wondered, who dream of harems and breasts and behinds galore, would find themselves wanting in Arabia? It made perspiration run down his brow as he toted the deflowering mattress up the hill like a kind of antipodal Christ fated to expire ingloriously in the cross of a woman's legs.

But he probably would not even have the Chinook grace to drop his milt, roll belly upward, and expire. There was first the problem—and it had to reckoned with—of Florence's sad lack of feminine appeal, to say nothing of the shriveling objections and obstacles she would doubtless throw in his path. Her prediction that he would have a hell of a hell of a time was no idle threat. Secondly, Charles, the poor scoundrel, had a point. Jim felt he owed a humble apology to Charles. Melody *was* oversexed! Perhaps it was the situation and she would simmer down after a while, but as of now she was tireless and insatiable. She was wonderful, a beautiful and tender lover (he had always suspected the truly great ones were there singing hymns in church), but after three weeks of near-futile effort to satisfy her, he was ready to go to the jungles of Colombia and teach the Indians about Jesus. And Florence was terrified of the Matterhorn. Ridiculous. The mighty Matterhorn was a fraud and a myth.

"Were you ever in Switzerland?" asked Florence brightly.

"Umm, yes."

"How exciting. Did you ever climb the *real* Matterhorn?"

"Not recently," said Jim.

"It isn't a silly question, a lot of people have. It used to be something, but nowadays they just scoot up it. Old women, schoolgirls, all kinds of unlikely types, they scoot right up it. American tourists with no experience! Today it's nothing! You see, they have ropes all over it. Tacked in permanent. You know, lead lines, pitons. But it was something to climb it back in the days of . . . oh, God, what was his name, anyhow, *Whine* or something? You know, that idiot who said he climbed the damned thing because it was *there?*"

"Whymper, I believe," said Jim.

"Yes, Whymper. I guess it made him whimper—ha ha ha. Forget it. Not a good joke. Rotten joke."

Jim paused for a moment on the path. "Florence, this isn't the end of the world."

"Who said it's the end of the world? I don't think it's the end of the world, I think it's springtime for Flossie."

"Okay, Flossie, but can't you relax a little?"

"Flossie is relaxed. Perfectly. What makes you think I'm not relaxed?"

"You seem slightly tense," answered Jim as he resumed the walk up the bush-covered and cactus-grown hill. Florence stumbled after him.

"You mean slightly hysterical. If you think I'm hysterical *now,* just *wait.* I'm not going to take my clothes off, I'll tell you that right now, and I don't want you to take yours off either. I've never really seen a man naked and I don't want to. I didn't look at you during the hurricane. I don't want to look at you. It would turn me into a pillar of salt. I'll do it but I don't want to look at it."

"I wish you'd calm down and stop making these hysterical jokes," said Jim as he shifted the mattress and trudged on up the hill.

"You had better let me joke. If I couldn't laugh about it, I'd scream and cut my throat. But that wasn't a joke. I really don't want to see you, it would horrify and appall me—and I don't want *you* to see *me!*" Florence stopped abruptly on the path. "Jim, I'm thin and ugly! You won't like me! You won't be able to do it! And for that reason, I'll only do it if we keep our clothes on!"

Jim adjusted the mattress on his back and rubbed his head on the shoulder of his crocodile sport shirt to wipe off sweat. "Florence," he said, "you are talking like you've had an overdose of methedrine. How in hell can we do *any*thing if we keep our clothes on?"

"I don't see why we can't do it with our clothes mostly on, if we've got to do the damnable thing at all. Let's don't do it, let's go back. I won't bother Melody, I swear."

"Oh, Christ," said Jim.

"Forget it, can't you take a joke? That was a joke."

"Yeah, okay," said Jim. He continued up the hill and Florence staggered after him, followed by a solemn and silent Rufus who seemed very doubtful about it all. They were, thank God, drawing near the cactus patch that guarded the bush that hid the entrance to Morgan's Second Treasure Cave.

"But getting back to the Matterhorn," said Florence, "the real subject at hand, frankly I don't see anything hysterical just because I say Whymper whimpered. The point is, he *did* climb the damned thing and he left nice ropes tacked all over it so tourists could climb it too. And that's what I call a real pioneer. The first mortal soul to climb the mighty Matterhorn and stand on top of its rugged peak thrust into the sky among the clouds and the birdies! Long live Whymper! He climbed it because it was there!"

They were at the cactus patch and Jim stopped. "Would you rather go somewhere else?"

Florence patted Rufus and smiled glassily. "Maybe. I do have claustrophobia."

"You said before you had agoraphobia."

"I know, but now I suddenly have claustrophobia."

Jim adjusted the rolled-up bunk mattress across his shoulders. It was smaller than the regular mattresses. At Florence's constant urging, he had taken it from the ship to provide a bed for Rufus and it smelled doggy. Jim felt silly carrying it, but what else? He could hardly relieve Florence of her virginity on that rocky floor and he was beginning to wonder if he could relieve her of it on eider down.

"Okay, I'll go anywhere you want to," said Jim. "This is your show, honey."

"I don't want to go on stage, the audience will throw fruit," said Florence feebly. Again she patted Rufus. "I've got sudden claustrophobia, all right. But we've got to go here, it has to be a place where Rufus can't follow. Otherwise when I scream, he'll bite you on the ass."

"Look, you're not going to scream, Florence."

"The hell I won't. And I honestly don't think you can manage this thing with a dog biting you on the ass. It would discourage you."

"Yeah, I guess it would," said Jim, who already felt discouraged no small amount. There did not appear to be even a stirring vestige of life in the mighty Matterhorn. Suppose he actually could not deflower her? It was too ghastly to think about. She'd never get over such a total humiliation as that and would go to her grave convinced she was an utterly undesirable and unattractive woman, which really was not true. She was thin, yes, and her face and arms were covered with freckles, but underneath the severe skirts and blouses she had an almost girlish body. He knew that from the time he'd walked in on her by accident when she was naked. She had pretty little breasts and noticeably feminine hips as well. She could not be called voluptuous, but the only truly bad feature she had was the buck teeth. Jim swallowed nervously. Soon he would have to kiss her and cope with those teeth. Maybe she would refuse to kiss him and there'd be no problem, yet how could he in all humanity fail to kiss the poor thing? Teeth or no teeth, he would have to kiss her, whether she wanted him to or not.

"Shall we thread our way through the cacti?" asked Florence.

"Sure, why not?"

"That's right, why not. I might as well die now as later."

"You won't die."

"You say I won't, but people sometimes die of terror. I could have a heart attack or a stroke."

"Well, I hope you survive."

"Don't rush me, that's all I ask. We'll have lunch, then read for a couple of hours. There's no hurry about this thing."

Florence had insisted on bringing along several paperbound mystery stories. Jim had found a few of these on the ship, mostly Perry Mason. Melody had read them, but Florence had not read any of them since they'd been on the island and neither had he. Mystery stories were not up his alley and not up hers either. Now, perhaps, they would read the Perry Mason tales.

As he guided Florence through the cactus patch and lowered her on the rope into Morgan's Second Treasure Cave, Jim thought it over. It seemed both reasonable and humane not to rush her, but was it? Wouldn't she become more and more terrified as time went by?

Would she be able to concentrate on either idle conversation or the adventures of Perry Mason? Certainly not. It would be stupid and sadistic to make her wait. Of course he shouldn't grab her and frighten her out of her wits the minute they got in there, but *Blitzliebe*, lightning love, was indicated. The ideal would be to have her down and her hymen penetrated in, say, ten minutes.

By the same logic, Jim was skeptical of gentleness and sweetness. To hell with that. It seemed reasonable to be gentle and kind to her as Melody had advised, but this might prove as sadistic as procrastination. *Blitzliebe* and merciful force were the best approach, assuming his manhood didn't desert him and render the whole question academic. If that happened—and it was a real possibility—then Heaven forfend.

Thus Jim Kittering attempted to plan the strategy of his effort to make love to a woman for whom he had felt a strange liking and sympathy the moment she walked into his office, a woman in whose presence he had precipitated a blow-up with his wife and his boss, a woman he had known would be aboard the *S.S. Lorna Loone* when he sat in his living room by emerald oblivion and dreamed of Maria Concepción. *Blitzliebe* and merciful force, he thought. Ten minutes and a slap in the face.

Maybe not quite like that, thought Jim with a flinch as he squeezed the mattress into the opening behind the bush and shoved it down into Morgan's Second Treasure Cave. No, not ten minutes and not a slap in the face. Florence was a special person, she could not be treated that way. But if not lightning love and a firm hand, then what? Reasonable speed, yes, and force too maybe, but of a special kind. Jim shut his eyes in confusion. What did that mean? God only knows. It was impossible to understand these things, he would have to trust to inspiration. Jim braced himself to meet his fate as best as possible and followed Florence down the rope into Morgan's Second Treasure Cave.

"Here we are," said Jim. "How about lunch?"

"Rufus doesn't like this," said Florence.

Rufus didn't. The dog was barking angrily in the cactus patch, so angrily Jim was afraid he would jump down into the cave.

"He'll calm down in a while, Florence. Why don't you open the picnic lunch on the ledge and I'll clear out these rocks to make a place to put this stupid mattress, okay?"

"I'm not hungry," said Florence in a half whisper.

"Sit down and relax and I'll get these rocks out," said Jim casually. "Now remember, like you said, there's no rush about this, we've got hours."

Florence sighed and answered, "All right."

By the time Jim got the broken rock on the floor tossed out over the cliff and the mattress down, Rufus had given a final indignant woof and sat on his haunches to wait for Florence to come out. Melody had only a mild interest in the cat, and Jim's pet, the parrot, had said "Fock you" one Sunday and collapsed and died, but Florence had a passionate love for Rufus and the dog followed her everywhere. Jim got down on his hands and knees and felt the mattress.

"I think most of the rocks are out," he said. "A little lumpy here and there, but it's all right." He felt the mattress again, then picked up one end and pulled out a jagged shard of rock and threw it out the window opening down over the cliff.

"Let's sit over here," said Florence. She was hunched on the ledge, her arms hugged around her and her knees together.

"Don't you want any picnic?"

"No, I can't eat, I'm not hungry. But let's sit here."

"Okay," said Jim. He stood up, walked over to the shelflike ledge, and sat beside Florence. As he did so, Florence pressed her knees together harder and hugged herself more tightly. Her shoulders and her knees were trembling. Jim put his hand on her arm and she winced. "Now, look, Florence. I am *not* going to hurt you. I just told you we've got all afternoon. Calm down, will you?"

"I'm c-c-calm," said Florence.

"I won't hurt you, I give you my word I won't. I hurt virgins less than any man you'd care to meet. Just relax, will you?"

"All right, I'll tr-tr-try."

Jim kept his hand on her arm in an idle manner. "Okay, let's talk about some harmless subject."

"What?"

Jim raised his hand and put it on her shoulder, as if to reassure her. Gently, he said, "Now, Florence, *relax,* will you? You're trembling all over. I'm *not* going to bother you, really I'm not."

"The hell you're not," said Florence with an audible gulp. "What'd we come in here for—to play parchesi?"

"That's it," said Jim.

"Uh-huh. Then what you got your hand on me for?"

"My hand isn't hurting you. Relax, we've got all afternoon. It doesn't even have to be today, for that matter. If you're too nervous we can wait till tomorrow or even the next day. Now let's talk about some harmless thing."

"All right, what?"

Jim kept his hand on her shoulder. He'd decided on *Blitzliebe*, after all. Florence didn't know it, but the tanks had already crossed the border and supporting infantry would follow soon. A brotherly kiss on the lips in a minute or so and then . . . well, a kiss that would have to be other than brotherly. Would her buck teeth, Jim wondered, interfere with her ability to kiss properly?

"Let's talk about when you were a little girl."

"No, that's a dismal subject."

"Why?"

"I was a dismal child."

"Were you really?"

"You wouldn't believe how dismal I was."

"Did you have freckles?"

"Oh, God yes. I invented freckles."

"I don't see anything so dismal about that. Freckles can be attractive in a child."

"Not in a girl, Jim. Not in a girl. Besides, I was skinny and ugly and knock-kneed and pigeon-toed and had horrible buck teeth just like now and nobody liked me."

"I'm sure somebody must have liked you."

"Nobody did, Jim. My father didn't and neither did my brother. And I don't blame them, I was horrible."

It didn't seem to be a harmless subject, but Jim hadn't wanted a harmless subject in the first place. A little force was part of *Blitzliebe*. She was blowing up her own ammunition dumps and didn't know it. The more miserable she was as a child, the luckier she was now to have the fortress of her heart under assault. A kiss now, to change the image, would be water in Death Valley—or, after a long hard winter, a true springtime for Flossie. Somebody loved her, after all. Despite himself, and against the grain of his reflective calculation, Jim felt a certain bittersweet sympathy not unakin to the feeling he had always had about Florence—of course she was exaggerating now, but, hypersensitive soul that she was, she must have suffered terribly as a child with those freckles, buck teeth, and all the rest. The *Blitzliebe* was not working too well; the tanks were getting foreign matter in their carburetors. And as for force?—well, no. He could not slap the woman who had been that little girl. There would have to be some other way. But there wasn't, her fear was too great. Jim lifted his hand to his forehead. Cold sweat was there. This was no job for Priapus, it was beyond the Matterhorn.

"Someone *must* have loved you, Florence, or you wouldn't be the person you are. What about your mother?"

"She took one look at me and died."

"Died? You mean in childbirth?"

"Well . . . no, I was about four, I guess. I was very small, I don't even remember her except as a vague shadow that was very sweet to me and loved me."

Jim sighed with relief. Someone, thank God, had loved her. The father must have had some feeling for her too. "I'm glad to hear that, Florence. Why do you say your father disliked you?"

"Because he did."

"Why did he?"

"Because I was ugly and revolting. And because he'd wanted another son. He never liked women. It was his opinion they had no brains and no talent and no judgment and no moral character and they all ought to be drowned at birth like in China. He often said so."

"Sounds like a regular Schopenhauer. I guess there are men like that, but . . . did he ever remarry?"

"Yes, because he got tired of prostitutes. Too inconvenient and expensive. But that wasn't till I was in boarding school. I never knew Eva, that was his wife. She had been, I think, a high-priced call girl."

Jim nodded, then blinked. Florence came on so straight it was hard at times to know if she was serious or not. "Oh, come on, Florence, she wasn't really a call girl."

Florence sighed. "Maybe not. But she screwed my brother."

"Did she really?" asked Jim, half convinced.

"Well, she wanted to. Maybe she didn't have the nerve."

Jim paused to reflect. "What did your father do?"

"He was an engineer for an oil company. I lived in Venezuela, Oklahoma, Texas as a child, mostly Oklahoma. He was very competent. We were also one year at Boston when he was doing research at

M.I.T. That's when I first got to know Cape Cod. Daddy died three years ago of a heart attack. I cried for four days."

Jim paused again to reflect. She had loved Daddy even if Daddy hadn't loved her. As he gazed pensively at the mossy ceiling, he moved his arm around Florence's hunched shoulders as if in sympathy. "I know," he said. "I reacted kind of like that when my mother died."

"I was also delighted," said Florence. "I felt as if I was out of jail when the hateful bastard finally kicked off."

"Let's change the subject. What was your favorite hobby as a young girl?"

"Masturbation," said Florence.

"Oh, come on, Florence—seriously, what was your main interest as a teen-ager?"

"I told you—masturbation, that was my main interest."

"All right, what were your other interests?"

"Well . . . gossip, sucking on cigarettes, cheating on exams, stealing; you know, things like that."

"You had other interests better than that—what were they?"

"Oh, Christ. I guess I liked to read. And maybe I liked to write. Mostly poetry, if you can call that slush I wrote poetry and you can't. I don't have any real talent as a writer."

"I know that isn't true and I don't believe it's true your father and brother didn't like you. They must have liked you. Didn't they like you at all?"

"Not a bit," said Florence. "My father used to call me Bugs Bunny because of my teeth. He'd say, 'Where's Bugs?' Or he'd say, 'Has Bugs stumbled home yet or did she fall in the river and drown, I hope?' My brother used to call me that too. He also used to call me Ragmop because of my awful hair. He beat me up a lot. He was very strong and I was very weak and he hated that. He'd say, 'Hi, Ragmop,' then hit me in the stomach and knock out my breath. He was very handsome and believe it or not there wasn't a freckle on him. The girls were all crazy about him. I had his picture at boarding school and they were all dying to meet him."

"Where is he now?" asked Jim.

"He was killed in Korea. I cried for five days."

"You loved him too, huh?"

"I loved them all but they hated me. And I honestly can't blame them. I was really and truly a dismal child. The worst thing is that I was weepy. God, was I weepy. I cried myself to sleep every night for four years from the time I was twelve to sixteen. I'd lie there and think, 'I love them all but they hate me,' and I would cry-cry-cry. It was revolting."

Jim shifted his position on the benchlike ledge as if to get more comfortable and as he did so moved closer to Florence and pulled his arm more tightly around her shoulders. The move was synchronized with a sad comment: "I don't think that's revolting, I think it's pathetic for you to have been so unhappy. Especially since I'm sure both your father and brother really loved you."

"They didn't. I accepted that when I was sixteen and stopped crying. Jim, your arm is making me nervous."

"I think you're exaggerating ridiculously," said Jim after a thoughtful pause, his eyes again fixed on the mossy ceiling. He did not remove his arm from around Florence's shoulders and gave no indication he had heard her. The *Blitzliebe* was not blitzing too well and he could hardly allow his tanks to be driven back over the border before his infantry could even move to the front. "Yes, I think you are exaggerating just ridiculously, Florence. I'm sure your father and brother loved you and they must have admired you for being clever, even if you weren't as beautiful a child as Goldilocks or Snow White."

"Clever? Who was clever? I wasn't clever, I was dumb."

Jim moved a bit closer to her and as his chest touched her shoulder she flinched. "Why are you flinching? That doesn't hurt, does it?"

"No . . . no, but it makes me terribly uncomfortable and I wish you wouldn't. Your arm is too heavy."

"All right, I'll put it around your waist then. It won't be so heavy that way." Jim lowered his arm and put it around Florence's waist and continued the conversation as if nothing had happened. Nothing much *had* happened, and it had to soon. He had to kiss her and he had to do it right away or the *Blitzliebe* was lost. "Florence, I can't believe you were dumb. I can accept that you had freckles, but not that you were dumb."

"Oh, Jim, I was dumb and this is hopeless! Please take your arm from around me."

"No, I won't," he answered. "I'm not hurting you and you've got to get used to me touching you."

"I can't get used to it, I don't like it and it makes me nervous. Jim, this is hopeless. Let's go back to the cave. I can't do this, it's impossible."

"It isn't impossible. Now, you just relax and answer my comment."

Florence sighed in despair. "I don't even know what you said."

"Look at me for a second. Stop turning your head away and look here."

Cautiously, Florence turned her head half toward him. "Now . . . don't kiss me. Really don't, Jim, I don't want you to."

"We've got to break the ice, Florence. It won't hurt you to kiss me, turn your head this way."

"No, I can't! Please, Jim, I really can't!"

"You mean you can't even kiss me? That's ridiculous."

"I could but there's no use. It's completely hopeless, don't you see that?"

"All right, it's hopeless, but kiss me anyhow."

"No, I can't!"

"Yes, you can. You just said you could."

"Oh, I can't, you've got whiskers all over and they revolt me! You didn't shave this morning and I can't kiss you, if I do I'll throw up!"

To judge from her sweaty pallor, it was possible she might do just that. The prospect was not very enticing to Jim Kittering and it was new to his experience. There were, of course, plenty of girls and women in his life who had not wanted to kiss him for one reason or another, but there were none he could recall who had said the experience might make them vomit. Perhaps a few had felt that way, but none had said it. The mighty Matterhorn was shrinking to near-invisibility and the *Blitzliebe* was pooping. He had better get both those metaphors out of his mind and come up with a real inspiration or he'd be carrying Rufus' mattress back down the hill in another minute or two. But she was an even more maddening woman than Melody and Jim was too irritated to abandon as yet a rational approach. No wonder the brother had hit her. She ought to have enough sense to realize the consequences of her remarks. Who could possibly love her if she behaved like that?

"The way you're acting, Florence, I'm liable to throw up myself. Don't you realize that?"

"I realize it very well. We'd *both* vomit. So don't try it, Jim."

Jim gritted his teeth. The woman was impossible. "Look, I'm going to kiss you, Florence."

"No, you're not. We are going back to the cave, this is hopeless. It's totally hopeless. I'm not physically attracted to you, Jim, I'm just not. I like you very much as a person, but so help me I swear to God it revolts me for you to touch me. I can't even stand the smell of your perspiration when you're five feet away, it nauseates me. Now please, for the last time, take your arm from around me. I don't want to make an ugly scene, but take your damned arm away and do it *now*."

Jim stopped grinding his teeth and wearily shut his eyes as the totality of his defeat sank home. How could any man cope with a woman who said such things to him? Jim opened his eyes and stared emptily at her. She was hunched on the ledge, her head turned away from him. It was all over. Florence was impossibly neurotic and that was all there was to it. What could he do? Jim stopped thinking and said:

"Now listen here, you goddamned fool! You love me and you know it. What are you going to do, throw your life away when this is the last chance you've got? Are you that big a goddamned coward and idiot? I think you are—but I'm not going to let you be! You're going to kiss me even if you puke in my mouth! Now turn your head this way!"

A little half-hysterical whimpering sound came from Florence and her body tensed under Jim's arm. He thought she'd jump up and start climbing the rope to get out of there, but instead she startled him by moistening her lips and making a joke. "Give me a week to think it over," she said.

"No! Turn your head this way."

"Give me a minute," said Florence.

"Come on, Florence, turn this way."

"Oh, Jim, I really will throw up . . . and so will you."

"Turn this way."

Slowly Florence turned her head. Jim put his hand behind her neck, pulled her toward him, and kissed her on the lips. A little tingle of shock ran through him. It was not unpleasant to kiss her and he had not noticed her buck teeth. Of course, it was an almost brotherly kiss.

"Did that hurt?"

Florence sighed heavily. "No."

Jim kissed her once more on the lips and again a little tingle of shock ran through him. It was not only "not *un*pleasant" to kiss Florence, it was pleasant to kiss her. The touch of her lips against his own did something strange to him. To kiss her gave him a bittersweet emotion he could not define.

"All right, that's enough," said Florence. "Quit while you're winning."

"Lift your arms and put your hands on my shoulders," said Jim. "Now . . . turn more to the side. No . . . even more. That's right. Now put your arms around my neck."

Jim tightened his right arm around Florence's waist, pulled her body against him, and another tingle of shock ran through him as he felt her small breasts against his chest, but despite these tingles he was unprepared for the shock that lay ahead of him. Could Florence kiss properly despite her buck teeth? Would he be able to make love to this homely woman at all? Those freckles, those teeth . . .

But there was no avoiding it. The thing had to be done, somehow or other. He liked Florence, and that would help. Jim tightened his hand behind her neck, pulled her head toward him, and kissed her, this time not like a brother, and the shock that hit him was no tingle but a jolt. The jolt was followed by a rush of overwhelming emotion. What was happening? What did this mean? Jim was so astonished he could not think. The only thing he understood was that he was kissing Florence and he was very strongly attracted to her.

Florence returned his kiss for about fifteen seconds, then made a half-strangled sound—"MmmMMph!"—and pushed with surprising strength at Jim's shoulders and twisted her head away. "Please," she said, "don't kiss me like that."

"Why not?" asked Jim, who was slightly breathless.

Florence also was slightly breathless. "Because . . . it upsets me."

"It upsets me too," said Jim, "but we have to be brave." He pulled her toward him but Florence pushed at his shoulders.

"No, don't," she said. "You don't really want to."

"The hell I don't. Of course I do."

"You don't, you couldn't like it."

"Be quiet," said Jim, "and kiss me again."

"Oh, I wish you wouldn't," said Florence in a meek voice.

Groggy with shock, Jim paused to stare in her eyes. It was totally incredible and he could not believe it although it had just happened to him. How could he possibly feel such an overwhelming attraction to this woman with buck teeth and freckles like chicken pox? It was impossible. It hadn't happened. But *some*thing had happened, there was no doubt about that.

The thing was incomprehensible and perhaps it was best not to go into it too much. Jim pulled Florence toward him and kissed her again, and this time she made no strangling noise of protest and did not struggle to get away, but returned his kiss with passion, her arms around his neck and her small breasts against his chest. As the kiss continued, she lifted her hand to the back of his head and began to breathe faster and make a tiny moaning sound. It was a fairly strong heterosexual response for a Lesbian to have, but he had always known she was no such thing. Her hand moved from behind his head to his unshaved cheek. She did not seem to mind now that he had "whiskers all over." The kiss went on and on, until Florence finally put her hands on his shoulders and pulled away.

"Oh, please!" she said. "Jim, I can't, it's upsetting me too much. I . . . let's talk now, don't kiss me any more."

Jim smiled and put his hands on her shoulders. "You kissed me beautifully, Florence," he said. "You're amazing. Why didn't you tell me you can kiss like that?"

"I didn't want to brag," said Florence, who was badly out of breath and flushed behind her freckles. "Besides, you never asked me."

"You're an amazing mystery woman," said Jim. "Do you know something? You've gotten me passionate."

"That *is* amazing, if true."

"It's true, all right. This ledge is uncomfortable, let's go sit on the mattress."

"Oh, God no, Jim, I can't. Don't ask me, it's out of the question, I just can't."

"Sure you can."

"No. I absolutely can't. I'll kiss you, but I can't go over there."

Half an hour later, after much passionate kissing and much near-hysterical struggle and resistance from Florence, Jim managed briefly to get his hand into her blouse and into the right cup of her brassiere and on her breast. He felt for a moment her nipple under his palm, then she gave a violent twist and lurch of her body and pulled with frantic strength at his hand. "NO!" she cried. Frightened, Jim took his hand from her blouse.

Ten minutes later, after more passionate kissing and even greater struggle and resistance, Jim again managed briefly to get his hand in her blouse and on her breast. Her reaction this time was even more hysterical. "Stop it! Stop it! STOP IT!" she cried, then pulled at his hand with such desperation that her fingernails left three bleeding furrows on his wrist and the back of his hand. Jim apologized, assured her he would not do such a diabolical thing again, then calmed her down with several kisses. It was an impasse. An inspiration was needed.

"Let's talk for a minute," he said. "It's strange, but do you know something, Florence? I knew we'd go to bed together someday when we were on the airplane."

"Wh-wh-what airplane?" asked Florence.

"The airplane going to Atlanta. You know, when I was so drunk and everything?"

"Y-y-yes, you were drunk. You must have been drunk if you knew that."

"I did. It had slipped my mind, sort of, until just now, but I remember thinking, 'I'll go to bed with her sometime.' It was when you were staring at that pretty stewardess." Jim hesitated, bothered by a twinge of conscience. He was making the whole thing up, he had thought no such thing on that airplane. Inspirations, however, were often lies in a sense. Jim suppressed the twinge of conscience and continued his wild tale: "At first, I thought you were a Lesbian because of the way you looked at the girl. But then I decided you weren't, you just thought you were, and that I'd go to bed with you someday to prove it to you."

"I know," said Florence, suddenly calm. "That's why you wouldn't leave the thing alone."

Puzzled, Jim asked, "What do you mean?"

"I'd told you in so many words I was, but you wouldn't leave it alone. You asked me point-blank if I was a Lesbian, and it was obvious from the ironic look in your eyes you didn't believe I was."

"Didn't I? Well . . . maybe I didn't."

"You just said you didn't."

"Yes, I did say that, didn't I? Well, this ledge is uncomfortable. Come on, Florence." Jim put one hand under her knees and his other hand around her waist and picked her up.

A numbness came into Florence's eyes, but her arm instinctively went around Jim's neck as he lifted her in his arms. "No!" she cried. "Jim, put me down!"

"We're not going to do anything today, I swear I won't touch you."

"Jim!" she cried. "Put me DOWN!"

Jim put her down on the mattress and kept his arm around her waist so she could not jump up and go back to the ledge. "I *swear* I won't touch you," he said. "It's *very* uncomfortable there, Florence, let's stay here."

"Then take your arm from around me!"

"Will you stay here?" A wild panic was in her eyes. "I *promise* I won't touch you, I give you my word. Please stay here, Florence, it's much more comfortable. Will you?"

"All right . . . if you promise. I just can't, Jim. Really, I can't."

"I know, I understand that," said Jim. He released her and leaned back on his elbows, half convinced she would jump up and go back to the rocky shelf. However, although she obviously wanted to, she didn't. A major hurdle had been passed, thanks to his spurious recollection of the flight to Atlanta, but far greater hurdles lay ahead. Jim had no idea how to proceed. Maybe there was more pay dirt in the Atlanta flight somehow or other. "It's amazing I could have thought such a thing on that airplane," he said, "drunk as I was. That's just plain amazing."

Florence moved a bit farther away from him, her eyes watching him warily. "Now remember, I can't," she said. "I know it's foolish of me but I just can't control my emotions when you grab me like that."

Jim resisted the temptation to tell her his approach to her could hardly be called "grabbing." Instead, he said: "It's amazing I'd think such a thing when I was drunk, but then, on second thought, maybe it's not so amazing after all. I know I've never really believed you were a Lesbian, not even when you first came in my office."

Florence sighed heavily. "You didn't, huh." She seemed to be calming down a little and to have accepted sitting on the mattress, but she would doubtless jump up and run back to the ledge if he tried to kiss her or even touch her. Well, she had said he would have a hell of a hell of a time and that was an understatement. How could any man seduce such a woman as this? An inspiration was badly needed.

"No, I didn't think you were a real Lesbian, I never have."

"Well," answered Florence, "most people, or at least sophisticated people in New York, think I am or suspect it."

"Yeah, the disguise is good."

"Disguise?"

"Your clothes, the way you do your hair or don't do it, no make-up, using four-letter words, that sort of thing. It fools people."

"But it didn't fool you?"

"Of course I'd read your book and that was a great advantage. A good writer reveals himself or herself in a book, don't you think so?"

"Clever ones can conceal quite a lot," said Florence in an almost normal tone. The reference to her book interested her. It interested her quite a bit and Jim suddenly had a flash. For the moment she had forgotten the dangerous situation she was in there on that doggy pallet with the mighty Matterhorn threatening and near. This was it. Exactly and precisely. There was only one possible way and the immediate thing to do was lull her and take her mind off it all and in the meanwhile give his own passion a chance to subside.

Jim saw it in a flash. The routine man-with-a-maid approach of kissing, caressing, taking off this garment and then that would *not* work with Florence. She was too frightened of his body and too ashamed of her own, and too sensitive by far to male aggression—no matter how passionate his kisses made her, an aggressive move on his part invariably triggered a cutoff. The pattern of arousal and hysteria, then more arousal and more hysteria, would sooner or later exhaust her and the hysteria would take over. This had almost happened already. It was a literal impossibility to "seduce" her and the only result of an effort to do so would be to bring her to such a state of panic and fright it would be senseless even to touch her. And that would be that. The trauma of such a failure would make a second approach to her even more difficult than this one and a third approach even more difficult yet. The grim truth was *he could not get her*. He had kissed her and she had responded; the door had opened a crack and her frightened eye was peering out, but thirty-eight iron padlocks held it shut.

However, Jim felt there was a way. The thing to do first was to lull her with a little literary analysis, which interested her but surely was one of the most lulling things in the world. This would calm her and also achieve another essential end: literary analysis, Jim was sure, could be depended upon without fail to shrivel the Matterhorn and render it harmless and pathetic. This would enable him in due course to throw the inspiration at her. Such were the thoughts, if they could be called thoughts, that flitted with the speed of true *Blitzliebe* through Jim Kittering's brain.

"Clever writers might try to conceal themselves," said Jim, "but they can't. A person reveals himself by everything he does, even by the way he says hello or the way he eats peach pie. And writing is much more complicated than either of those things. The clever writer might try to hide his true character or his real feelings, but he reveals himself without intending to. Haven't you ever read a book and thought to yourself: 'This liar is pretending he cares about humanity and the underprivileged, but he is really a vain and egotistical jackass who doesn't give a damn about anyone in the world but himself'?"

"I've thought worse," said Florence. "Of course all writers hate other writers and want to kill them and cut them up, but I've often felt that. It's ghastly sometimes, the things you can read between the lines."

"Yes, it can be ghastly, and it usually is. Let's face it, we all lie about our emotions most of the time. The talented person is a freak who sometimes doesn't do it, and if he has a developed gift for writing or painting or singing or whatever, we call him an artist. If he does his trick with great power in ways hitherto unknown and if his experience has a broad meaning for other people over a substantial period of time, we call him an artist of genius. It's an extraordinary thing and very difficult to recognize in the era that produces it. It tends to be by its very nature because no man can predict the future. Besides, it's bewildering to the ordinary mind and arouses a rage reaction, plus a sense of helpless consternation."

"You always surprise me," she said. "How could you think this up, living in New Jersey and working for the Goblin?"

"We all work for the Goblin," said Jim, "and most of us live in New Jersey. But I've always had my doubts about Hob and I've never really believed in Cherry Dale."

Florence's guard was down and so was the Matterhorn. One more fair-to-middling streak of literary analysis and she would be defenseless and the Matterhorn would be reduced to an absolutely harmless condition.

"Well," sighed Florence, "it's very interesting what you say, and I admit you always surprise me, I never can keep up with you. But I just hope you don't think *I* am some kind of genius because I'm not."

"Who knows about that?" asked Jim. "As I said, artists of genius by their very nature are unidentifiable in their own time, unrecognizable either by themselves or by others. The most we can have is suspicion. And that proves nothing, so why waste time on idle speculation? Besides, what difference does it make whether you're an artist of genius or merely an artist?"

"None, I suppose," said Florence with a smile, "assuming I'm either."

"Well, we *do* know you have at least a touch of divine fire, Florence. This much we can know—if we have a touch of it ourselves. That, of course, is essential; an ugly person can't possibly recognize beauty."

"That's true," said Florence with another smile. "And the critics who dare not to like my books are very ugly. They are real toad-frogs."

"Well, actually I think they are, because there're ways of recognizing a good writer," said Jim. She was lulled. One more streak, and then the inspiration. "You see, there's a basic difference between a good writer and a bad writer, and it has nothing to do with words or even storytelling. The bad writer hides himself, but the good writer reveals himself without fear and this is the source of his gift. He doesn't fear for himself, but speaks his own thought and reveals without hesitation the feeling in his heart, even if this isn't very flattering to him and often it isn't. You revealed yourself without fear in that book, you and the lonely girl on Cape Cod. I knew you when I'd finished reading it." The literary analysis was over—now for the inspiration, it should follow immediately. But on the spur of the moment Jim decided to wait to hear what she would say.

"I never thought much of that book, if you want to know the truth, but maybe it served a purpose after all. Maybe it got me a boyfriend."

"Sure it did," said Jim without thinking. "It was a beautiful little book, Florence, and I've loved you ever since I read it. Maybe I was primed, ready to explode. I guess I was, but it changed my life to know that someone was lonelier and more frightened than me. It *did* change my life, your book. I'll never forget the morning I was waiting for you to come to my office. I was imagining all kinds of sadistic tricks to play on my secretary and I thought you'd never get there. Florence, I think I love you and need you more than you do me."

Florence stared at him in open-mouthed amazement, then lifted her hands, put her arms around him, leaned her head on his chest, and began to cry. "Oh, Jim," she said. "You do love me. I knew you did, I knew it all the time."

Stupefied, Jim held her in his arms as she wept. It was the most insane experience of his life bar none. He *liked* Florence, he liked her very much, he always had—but love her?

Florence was sobbing, her arms tightly around him. However, it couldn't go on forever, Jim knew. He clenched his jaw as he felt her body tense in his arms, then braced himself as she drew back and stared at him through her tears. "But what about Melody?" she asked. "You love her, Jim, I know you do. And what about your wife? You love Linda too."

Jim Kittering moistened his lips. A rational reply was an impossibility. What could he say? "These things don't work by mathematics," he answered. "I know it's crazy, but let's just be patient and not worry about it, because even if I love Melody and Linda, I love you too."

Florence took her arms from around him and sat back, crossed her legs beneath her, brushed tears from her eyes, and stared out of the window opening at the luminous green and blue water down below. A little rueful smile came on her face and Jim thought he could detect a shrug of her shoulders. "Back to reality," she said. "It was lovely while it lasted."

"I meant every word I said," answered Jim. "Why is it impossible for a man to love more than one woman? It *isn't* impossible, and I *do* love you, Florence. That was the truth."

Florence smiled again. "You are a complicated man," she said. "I'll admit I have never been able to figure you out; I'm always wrong and you always surprise me. But I've got you now, Jim."

"Got me?" asked Jim. An uneasiness began to steal upon him. Florence's calm resignation was more deadly than hysteria.

"I think I finally understand you and it's about time. Jim, the woman you really love is Linda. What you want is to win her back and you can't do that unless you change yourself. It's the most painful thing in the world for a person to change himself. Melody is one of the ways you've found to do it, and maybe I'm another. I'm not saying there's anything 'wrong' with what you're doing. On the contrary, you've been very sweet to both me and Melody here. But that's what you're doing."

"I . . . I'm not sure that's exactly true," said Jim.

"Do you remember telling me on the flight to Atlanta about how your wife burned her mink coat, and how beautiful and brave and wonderful she was? And do you remember telling me about 'The Chambered Nautilus,' the poem that haunted you that night? Jim, you're building a new temple for your soul and you are using me and Melody to find mother-of-pearl."

Disaster. Jim moistened his lips and struggled to come up with an answer. "There might be some truth in what you say, Florence. But that's not the whole story."

"It's the whole story in a nutshell," said Florence quietly. "I'm almost sorry and maybe I shouldn't have said it to you. But this time, Jim, I've got you."

"No, you're wrong," said Jim. "I love you for yourself, not just to save my own miserable soul. And that's the truth, Florence."

"I think you love me in a way," said Florence with still another smile. "I also think you're an even bigger softie than Melody. There's nothing 'bad' about what you're doing, you shouldn't look so sheepish. I'm grateful to you. It's very kind of you, Jim, kinder than anyone has ever been to me and I'll be brave and sleep with you. I will, don't worry. But not today, I'm too upset."

Total ruination, thought Jim. It had been a disastrous error to tell her he loved her before sleeping with her. He should have known this would dredge up not only Melody but Linda as well. What had become of the original inspiration? He had lulled her with boring literary analysis and prepared her perfectly, then like an idiot he had waited to hear what she would say. He had then gotten carried away by his feeling for her and had made an almost certainly fatal error.

How could he get back to the original inspiration? How? It had to be done or all was lost. If Florence's virginity was intact when he pulled her up that rope out of Morgan's Second Treasure Cave, it would remain intact forever. She would live and die an unloved old maid haunted by the memory of how close she had been to her heart's desire. A few kisses, that was all she would ever have. It could *not* be allowed to happen. In a panic, Jim struggled by sheer will and longing to find an answer.

"You're right, I don't really love you, Florence. You have got me, and this time I won't surprise you because I can't, I'm all out of surprises. Of course you're right. Obviously you're right. Linda is at the root of everything I've done." Jim paused for a moment, then in a very casual manner leaned back on his elbows. He smiled and asked, "This puts us right back where we were to begin with, doesn't it?"

"Yes, it puts us back where we were," answered Florence, "except my nerves are slightly shot and I think we'd better get on home."

Jim nodded. "I think we ought to get back soon too," he said, "and I certainly agree with you we can't and shouldn't sleep together today after all of this. But it's still early and I think we ought to make *some* progress, therefore I suggest we take our clothes off."

"What?" asked Florence.

"I suggest we take our clothes off."

"Jim, are you crazy? Take our *clothes* off, are you serious?"

Jim laughed. "Actually, it's not as far-out an idea as it sounds. I think one of the big reasons you have trouble is you're afraid of my body and embarrassed about your own. You know, there's a lot of philosophical and emotional truth behind the nudist movement. Have you ever read any of their magazines?"

"God, no," said Florence. A startled expression was on her face and she was staring intently at him.

Jim, however, was not staring intently at Florence. He was staring idly at her. "One of the office boys had a bunch of them around and I was looking at them. They were very interesting. Of course they go too far, they're kind of mildly fanatical and nutty—nudism will solve all the problems of the world and everything, but they really have a point. People *are* ashamed of their bodies and it's the most senseless thing imaginable. I'll tell you what. I'll take off my clothes if you'll take off yours."

Florence wet her lips and attempted to smile. "That's exactly what I don't want to do," she answered.

"And that's exactly the reason you ought to do it," said Jim. "I'm serious, Florence. Let's take off our clothes and talk for a half hour, then we'll go back home."

"Jim, I couldn't do that."

"Why not? You'd get over your embarrassment in about two minutes. Really you would, Florence. And I give you my absolute word I won't even touch you with my little finger. And I really mean that, I'm not just saying it. Do you believe I mean it?"

"Yes, I suppose you do. But Jim, I . . . this is silly, I couldn't do such a thing."

"It isn't silly at all. Do you honestly think it's silly?"

"Maybe not completely. But I—"

"Don't you remember how you were saying on the way up the hill that you don't want to see *me* and you don't want me to see *you*, and all of that?"

"Sure I remember, and that's how I feel."

"Well, it's a ridiculous fear and don't you think you ought to get over it? In fact, don't you think you *have* to get over it?"

"Yes, eventually, of course . . . but not today, Jim."

"Look, I agree we shouldn't sleep together today. Absolutely not. But if you're sincere and really care about how Melody and I feel, we've got to make *some* progress on this thing at least. Now, we can't have you putting your finger in her, Florence, we just can't have that monkey business going on around here. It upsets the hell out of Melody and I don't like it myself. We've got to make some progress on this thing. You take off your clothes and I'll take off mine."

"Jim, I . . . no, I . . . I don't want to."

Jim shrugged. "All right, then let's kiss some more."

"No, I . . . I can't do that either. I can't kiss you any more today, it excites me too much."

"We've got to make progress in *some* direction, Florence. It isn't fair to me and Melody if we don't. Come on, let's kiss."

"Jim, really I can't."

"Now look, I'm *not* being brutal with you, I agree we shouldn't sleep together today, but you've got to *try*, Florence. What the hell—either take your clothes off or let's kiss."

The consternation in Florence's eyes would have struck Jim as funny, if he had dared to smile. She was on the horns of a dilemma she did not like at all. But she wouldn't kiss him on that mattress, it was too dangerous. She would offer him the blouse.

"I . . . I guess I *do* carry my modesty too far and I suppose I ought to get over it." Florence moistened her lips again and swallowed with a tiny gulp. "Would it be enough if I took off my blouse but left the bra on?"

"It would be a start," said Jim. "I'll take off my shirt and you take off your blouse."

Florence sighed in anxiety, worry in her eyes. "All right," she said. "But this is really slightly cuckoo."

"It isn't cuckoo at all, it's good sound psychology."

Florence sighed again. "All right, I'll take it off. But you've got to promise you won't touch me."

"I give you my absolute word," said Jim. Without further ado, he pulled his crocodile shirt over his head, pulled off his undershirt, then looked up with an innocent, bare-chested smile at Florence, who had not moved. "See? My chest. The normal chest of a human male in reasonable health, and I hope not too revolting to look at."

"Oh, I've seen your chest before," said Florence. "That's nothing."

Jim folded his arms and waited, a bland expression of mild boredom on his face.

"Now look," said Florence, "you really promise you won't touch me?"

"Of course I won't," said Jim.

"All right. But this is ridiculous. Completely ridiculous. There's nothing for you to look at." An angry blush appeared in Florence's cheeks as she undid the buttons of her blouse and took it off. "See? I don't have any figure at all."

"Okay, take off your bra now," said Jim.

"No."

"Take it off, Florence. I saw you in your bra the other day, that's no progress."

"But I don't have anything to show you, what's the point?"

"Come on, stop stalling. Take off the bra if you don't want me to kiss you."

"But you said you wouldn't touch me."

"I won't touch you if you play fair, but you're cheating, Florence."

"Oh, hell! Go ahead and look, then! Here! Just see how pathetic I am, if that's what you want—I don't give a damn!"

Angrily, Florence unfastened the hooks of her bra, yanked the straps down her arms, and flung it on the mattress. She then folded her arms across her stomach and glared at him. Her breasts were not hidden by her arms, but she was not making the most of them.

"You have pretty breasts," said Jim.

"I don't have any at all. And that's why this is silly, there's nothing for you to see. Are you satisfied now?"

"No, take off your skirt."

"I certainly will not!"

"Okay, then I'll take off my pants," said Jim, and he calmly proceeded to do so as Florence stared at him in open-mouthed shock. He did not, however, take off his undershorts.

"All right now," said Florence nervously. "Don't take off anything else."

"You take off your skirt now," said Jim.

"No, I won't."

"You've got panties on, don't you?"

"Yes, but I'm not going to take off my skirt."

With calm persistence, Jim nagged at her for five minutes and got nowhere. "All right, I'm taking off my underpants," he said. "You might be a coward but I'm not."

"Wait a second, wait a second," said Florence. "If I take off this *goddamned skirt*, will that be enough for you?"

"It would be substantial progress," said Jim, "and I think beneficial to you psychologically."

"Beneficial, shit!" said Florence. Angrily she unzipped her skirt at the side. "You keep your goddamn underpants on and believe me, this is the last thing I'm taking off!"

Idly, Jim lay propped on an elbow and watched her wriggle out of the skirt. The inspiration was working beautifully, even better than he had dreamed. Florence, poor thing, wanted to take off her clothes and wanted to lose her virginity too. But he could not do it for her; she was her own jailer, he could not "seduce" her and he could not "get her"—she would have to unlock the padlocks herself.

"All right, now you see how thin and ugly I am and I hope you're satisfied. I have no figure at all, none whatever."

It was not true. Florence's breasts were girlish and attractive and her hips were unmistakably feminine, not boyish. She had, Jim felt, especially attractive legs, long and graceful like a girl athlete or swimmer. And she had a cute navel of the rather unusual button type. Jim smiled as he remembreed his *déjà vu* illusion of Maria with the button navel.

"You have a lovely body, Florence," he said. "What's the matter with you, are you out of your mind, some kind of nut? You have a beautiful body. Good grief, there's nothing wrong with you at all. Now take off your panties."

"I'm not taking off one more goddamned thing," said Florence. "Furthermore, your name isn't Jim Kittering, it's Baron von Münchhausen. What a liar you are. I don't have a lovely body, I'm scrawny as a crow."

"You have a graceful, attractive, and feminine body," said Jim. "And a lot of women would be delirious with joy to have one like it. Haven't you ever heard Melody say she admires your figure?"

"Melody's nuts," said Florence. She had stopped blushing and was not hunched over as before. Her breasts had been bare now for quite a few minutes and she seemed to have forgotten they were there. And why not? Once he had seen them, the pain was over.

"She's not nuts and you have a nice body," said Jim. "Take off your underpants, then we'll talk a while and go home."

"Jim, I'm *not* going to take them off and that's final."

Jim paused, his gaze calmly fixed on her. A dangerous moment had been reached but there really was nothing she could do. "All right, I want to tell you something. Florence, I am a normal man. I look like every other man in the world who happens to be white, circumsized, and around forty years of age, though I like to flatter myself I look around thirty."

"Don't you take your pants off!" said Florence.

"You won't turn into a pillar of salt," said Jim. "In fact, this is going to be a terrible anticlimax, Florence."

Florence turned her head away as Jim took off his undershorts. "I don't want to see you," she said.

"You're acting like a little baby," said Jim. "But then, you *are* a little baby in certain ways."

Florence sighed and turned her head back toward him. She was silent for half a minute, then smiled and said, "I guess I *am* pretty childish. I'm sorry to be such a fool, Jim, I don't know how you can stand me."

"I'm just glad you haven't turned into salt."

Florence glanced down at his lap, shrugged at the insignificant Matterhorn, lifted her eyes, and said, "I've seen men before. My father and my brother both. You know, in the bathroom, here or there."

"What were you so horrified of, then?" asked Jim, who knew perfectly well what she was horrified of—it was not some unaroused brother or father shaving in the bathroom, but rather the Matterhorn in a mood for rape.

"I don't know. I guess I'm just crazy."

"You're not crazy, you're hypersensitive. But I hope you see how harmless I am and that it doesn't make one damn bit of difference if I have my clothes on or not. I'm still the same person and we're still talking the same way as before. Isn't that true?"

"Yes, of course it's true."

"Okay, then what follows logically?"

Florence swallowed. "You want me to take off my panties, I guess." Jim said nothing and after a few seconds Florence swallowed again. "I feel like an idiot, an idiot that anything so silly is necessary for me. But I guess it is . . . Jim . . ."

"You don't have to worry," said Jim. "I already promised not to touch you and I mean it."

Florence hesitated. "You really won't?"

"I really won't," said Jim.

"All right, so I'll be naked. I practically am already."

Jim lay back on the mattress and stared up at the ceiling as Florence pulled her underpants down and off. The question was—how soon? He had a feeling it was possible very soon. In fact, at once, as soon as she had no clothes on at all.

"September Morn," said Florence. "I haven't got on a stitch, so you can't say I'm a complete coward."

"No, you're not." Jim turned toward her and smiled. "Of course I had seen you already when I walked in on you that time."

"Yes, you did," answered Florence. Her voice was shaky.

Jim looked back up at the mossy ceiling, an arm behind his head. Her voice was definitely shaky. Well, Florence was no fool. She knew on some level of consciousness that he had *not* gone to all the bother of coaxing and nagging her into a mutual strip tease in order that they might sit there and have a discussion of the philosophy of nudism. Jim kept his eyes on the ceiling as he said:

"I promised I wouldn't touch you, Florence, and I won't. I really and truly won't. But you can touch *me*, you can even kiss me if you want to. I won't move, I won't grab you, I won't do a thing, so help me God. I really won't, Florence."

Silence. Then in a very shaky voice: "Well, I don't want to touch you . . . and I don't want to kiss you either."

"I know you don't want to, honey." Jim glanced at her casually. "But it might help break down your inhibitions if you kissed me when we had no clothes on."

Again, silence. Then: "Maybe it would. But even if I did, Jim, you know you wouldn't just lie there and not move, you know that. You wouldn't just lie there."

"I certainly would." Jim looked back up at the ceiling, a mild boredom on his face. "I'd return your kiss and that's all."

"But I don't want to kiss you. It would just upset me. And you'd move. You couldn't just lie there. How could you just lie there?"

"I could just lie there by just lying there."

"Yes, but *would* you?"

"Of course I would. If I tell you I would, I would."

Another silence. Finally, in a very weak voice, she said: "I . . . I really don't think I want to get all upset."

"One kiss wouldn't upset you. Really it wouldn't. And I think it would be progress for you to learn that kissing me *without* clothes on is exactly the same thing as kissing me *with* clothes on."

"Well . . . I know it's the same."

"You don't know it's the same until you do it. You should put your hands on my shoulders and kiss me and then you'll know it's the same."

Jim heard her swallow. He was still looking with an expression of mild boredom at the ceiling. Twice he had felt a slight twinge of involuntary life in the Matterhorn, but he had sent urgent messages to it to behave itself or he'd throw another literary analysis at it. "Oh, I don't know," sighed Florence, in a very, very shaky voice indeed. "Maybe at that it might . . . get me over . . . some of my inhibitions."

"I think it would benefit you psychologically," said Jim. "Why don't you kiss me once, anyhow?"

Another long silence. Jim resolutely kept his gaze on the ceiling.

"You do promise you won't grab me?" asked Florence.

"I promise absolutely."

Again Jim heard her swallow, then he felt a shift of her weight on the mattress and a moment later her hand on his shoulder. Her face came into his line of vision as her other hand touched his other shoulder. "Now . . . don't break your word. If you do, I'll never believe you again."

"I won't break my word," said Jim.

Slowly, Florence leaned down toward him and kissed him in a sisterly fashion on the lips. She lifted her head and stared intently at his face. Jim said nothing and didn't move. "Well, I kissed you." Florence waited as if for him to challenge her assertion, but he didn't. With an innocent calm he returned her gaze. "I did . . . but I guess it wasn't much of a kiss." She moved a little closer, shifting her position on the mattress, leaned down and kissed him again, this time in a somewhat less sisterly fashion. Jim returned the kiss but otherwise did not move. "That wasn't much of one either," said Florence in a half whisper. "I guess if this is going to be any kind of test, I may as well really kiss you."

"You may as well," said Jim.

Florence sighed. "Don't grab me," she whispered, then lowered her lips to his and kissed him with passion.

Thus, after a sputtering start, the *Blitzliebe* won the war after all, thanks to a few inspirations here and there. Florence put her breasts down against his chest and her arms around his neck on the third kiss. She agreed with Jim after the fourth kiss he would not be "grabbing" her if he put his arms gently around her. After the tenth kiss or so she agreed he would likewise not be "grabbing" her if he gently put his hand on her breast. Half an hour later, Jim was on top of her and her legs were apart.

"Don't hurt me," she whispered. "Please don't."

"I won't," said Jim.

"If it hurts, will you stop?"

"Yes."

Jim had heard somewhere that older women who remain virgins often develop a thickened and tough hymeneal membrane and unfortunately this proved to be true of Florence.

"Ooooh!" she cried. "Stop, that hurts!"

"Bad?"

"Yes, it's bad, very bad."

"Can you stand it?"

"No, I can't! It really hurts! Stop, you promised you wouldn't! Oh, Jim, stop it, please! It hurts me! Stop!"

"Hold still and quit wriggling," said Jim.

"But you're hurting me and you said you wouldn't!"

It was not hysteria; he was really hurting her and that was a pity. Jim, despite all the girls and women he had known, had never slept with a bonafide virgin before and he found it a curious experience. She had a very tough membrane. He could penetrate her without difficulty for what seemed to be a couple of inches, then he would feel it, a soft weblike thing. It was flexible, but when he pushed against it she would cry out with pain. However, he was making progress. A trace of blood already was on her thigh.

"Raise your knees a little," said Jim.

Florence was sweating and half crying, but she was not hysterical. As Jim had expected, to lie naked in his arms and kiss him and have him touch her breasts and other parts of her body had aroused her so enormously the hysteria didn't have a chance. One iron padlock after the other had fallen and none was left. The present problem was merely a matter of pushing open a half-stuck, creaky door, that was all.

"Like this?" asked Florence.

"No, a little more, it won't hurt you so much. That's right. Now, grit your teeth, honey."

Jim took a deep breath, guided the Matterhorn to the proper spot, felt the blocking web, pulled back a little and thrust forward hard. He felt the web give and thrust forward hard again, and again.

"OH-HHH!" cried Florence. "Jim, that *hurts!* OHH-HHH, Jim, it hurts me!"

Jim had been so concerned with putting an end to her misery, he was startled to find himself an involved witness—very precipitately, although that had been his intention and in this case it was certainly desirable—to the cleverer of the two tricks the mindless Matterhorn knew. With an effort of will, he kept himself motionless in order not to hurt her any more than necessary; he endured the overwhelming seismic shocks as an even more overwhelming bittersweet emotion flooded his heart and soul and confirmed an inner knowledge. But like Columbus, who did not realize he had found America, he remained mostly in the dark. The endless kissing and petting of her pretty little body, he thought, had aroused him terribly. She was a woman, after all.

"Jim, it *hurts* me!" cried Florence. "Oh, please, it hurts me terribly! I can't do it, Jim! I've tried but I just can't, ohhh-hh, it hurts! I can't do it!"

Florence gasped with pain as Jim withdrew from her and rolled off her to his side. He propped on an elbow and said, "You've already done it."

"What?"

"It's all over. You're not a virgin any more."

Florence stared at him in sweaty disbelief. "All over? But how could it be so quick?"

"I didn't want to hurt you so I made it quick."

Florence still couldn't seem to believe him. "You really did it?"

"Sure I did. Couldn't you feel it?"

"Couldn't I *feel* it? Christ, the damned thing was in me nine feet, I guess I felt it. But I didn't know a man could do it so quick."

"It usually takes longer," said Jim.

"I should hope so. Will it hurt me next time?"

"You are my first virgin, Florence. But from what I've heard, it'll hurt you the next time but not nearly as much. And the time after that, it won't hurt you at all."

Florence sat up and peered down between her legs. "Good God, I'm bleeding all to hell," she said. With keen interest, she bent over and pushed aside pubic hair to examine her injury. "Fantastic. Incredible. I did it. Look at the blood."

"You had a tough hymen, I guess. Did it hurt an awful lot?"

"Jim, it killed me. I thought I'd die."

"I'm sorry."

"Good *God*, look at the blood. It's pouring, we're going to ruin the mattress."

"It'll stop," said Jim.

Head bowed, Florence again was examining herself with keen interest. "What's this stuff all over me?" she asked.

"That's me."

"*Fantastic*," said Florence. "This is too fantastic for words. I've been fucked. It's a miracle. I never thought I'd see this day, Jim, I never thought I'd see it. A man has actually fucked me."

"It wasn't easy," said Jim.

"Oh, I know, I was impossible. Utterly and totally impossible, I couldn't help it I was so scared, and there's really nothing to it at all, that's the irony."

"Yeah," said Jim, "that's the irony."

Florence turned toward him, lifted her hands to his shoulders, and kissed him on the cheek. "You're a pretty good seducer," she said. "I honestly didn't think you had a prayer, I really didn't. I didn't think there was the slightest hope, until . . ."

"Until when?" asked Jim.

"Well . . . when I took off my panties, I guess it was then. As they came down over my ankles it occurred to me I was probably going to get laid. But I didn't see how you could manage it."

"I didn't," said Jim, "I left it up to you. And by the way, it isn't true I don't love you. You remember I said I didn't, that everything I've done is because of Linda? I was lulling you, Florence. I do love you."

Florence smiled and kissed him on the cheek again. "You're a liar," she said. "And I hope you realize I'll always hate you for this. You've made a woman out of me."

It was true, and Jim returned her smile with a certain pride. He had not abandoned her to a life of lonely unfulfillment; the mighty Matterhorn had come through.

PART SEVEN
Midsummer Night

TWENTY-ONE

Una Máquina Misteriosa

Since Jim Kittering had always known American intelligence covered the entire Caribbean with spy-plane overflights by ultrahigh-altitude aircraft, the means of effecting prompt rescue from Providence Island had existed from the beginning, but Jim did not think of it until Morgan's Treasure was found and that did not happen until they had been on the island almost four months.

Jim subsequently wondered why he had not thought of this simple thing. Of course, the information he possessed was an obscure piece of trash that hardly could claim a throne upon which to sit in his brain. Something about the C.I.A. just didn't sound to him like home and Mother, even though he realized his dubious attitude was probably an injustice to this invisible organization dedicated to protecting the interests, if not always the ideals, of fair America.

Jim also was aware that if he could dream of being caught with Melody in a Nicaraguan revolution and confined with her in a room with a large bed, then it was very possible he did not *want* to be rescued—or at least not immediately; four months was about right. It was a long time to subsist on canned food, but then, man does not live by Dinty Moore beef stew alone.

However, although the information had been in his head, it was unavailable to him and Jim could only shrug in the face of this remarkable failure of mind, if failure it was. He did not even remotely think of those planes with their cameras; the trashy fact of their whispered flight through the lower reaches of the stratosphere did not enter his consciousness at all until the day he and Melody and Florence hung up the wild pig and found Morgan's Treasure.

More remarkable, perhaps, than Jim's lapse was the fact he seemed in some strange subliminal way to have conveyed to both women the knowledge that he himself knew of a way to get off the island. How he could have done this was beyond his comprehension, but so it seemed. They both came to him and said in effect: "Look, we've achieved what we wanted, let's get off the island now. Call a taxi."

Jim himself had had a rather restless and irrational feeling for a week or so that the purpose of the island had been served and they should now think seriously about ways to get off it. Melody and Florence, although they were as happy living with him as he was living with them, also felt this restlessness. They both became more conscientious about keeping their "watches" for an approaching ship or sail and each came up with a couple of completely impractical ideas for ways to get off the island.

It was a nonrational feeling, but the island did seem to have served its purpose and now the outer world, the bigger world, the real world beckoned them all with its multitude of overwhelming problems, such as Goblin bosses, bewildered unfaithful wives, impotent husbands, the loneliness of the dunes of Cape Cod, plus hydrogen bombs, black and white power and saffron smog, and all the rest. Back to the fray, thought Jim, let's try it again.

Certain things had indeed been accomplished on the island and these things seemed to Jim significant and rather interesting. Melody, for example, was pregnant beyond doubt. She had missed one period, then another; she also complained of tenderness in her breasts and had been sick to her stomach every morning the past few weeks. It was possible to see a slight swelling in her abdomen and Jim could feel her enlarged uterus with his hands. Melody would have a baby; she had gotten pregnant just as quickly as she'd thought she would—very possibly, it had happened the first night he was with her.

Melody was no longer "oversexed." She was still responsive at almost any time and remained a very passionate lover, but the insatiable tirelessness had disappeared. She would make love to him now and two minutes later he would hear her snoring in his ear, arms and hands limp as rags and her heartbeat and breathing steady as the sea. She was a different woman. Previously, her tendency had been to keep after him and pester him half to death till all hours, but this had stopped. On several occasions, when Jim had wanted to make love to her a second time, she had actually gone to sleep and begun to snore softly in the middle of it all, her body dreamily half responding to him and her arms limp on his back. Melody's fearful insatiability was gone, so gone it would have been difficult for Jim to have imagined a more totally normal woman. Perhaps she had gotten some of her frustration out of her system, or perhaps it was the knowledge of her pregnancy that made the difference. Whatever the explanation, she was not the same woman who had gotten aboard the *S.S. Lorna Loone* in Savannah, and she said to Jim one day:

"Now that I'm pregnant, we ought to get off the island, because it's dangerous to the baby for me to have it here without any doctor. I know as a nurse the things that can go wrong. I could have a brow presentation or other trouble where you really need a doctor. We'd better get off the island now, Jim."

An even greater change, perhaps, had occurred in Florence, although she was not pregnant and it was less obvious. The change in her physical appearance was the most dramatic thing. During the seven weeks since the loss of her virginity she'd gained almost twelve pounds. Her bra now was too small for her and her figure was unmistakably feminine. Florence was still slender, but the starved look was gone. Her eyes were no longer nervously popped and the lines of her face had softened and changed. The way she handled her body, her gestures and movements, also had changed.

However, the greatest change in Florence was an emotional or psychological change. Previously, she had been—for all her jokes and underlying warmth—withdrawn and guarded, for the most part incapable of showing or expressing affection. She rarely had been able to allow Jim to touch her even casually and she could not use words that could be construed as terms of endearment. Florence had not lost her astringency and, sadly enough, she had not been able to respond without inhibition to his love-making ("I just can't do it," she said), but the affection she daily showed both to Jim and to Melody was phenomenal. She actually called him "darling" and Melody "my sweet sister." It was an amazing way for Florence to behave. She was forever touching Jim, kissing him, putting her hand on his arm or shoulder, leaning against him, and she loved to sleep in his arms, which created a slight problem because Jim himself had never much liked literally sleeping with a woman.

Florence, furthermore, although she could not "do it with a man" did seem to derive considerable pleasure from the act of love. Jim told himself her frustrating failure (to make love to him, she said, aroused her unbearably but nothing ever came of it) was a trivial thing and did not matter; and he told her this, too, he explained that truly successful physical love takes patience and time and many girls and women have difficulty. "It's a trivial thing and it doesn't matter," he said. Florence did not believe him and Jim did not believe himself.

Nevertheless, the change in Florence was remarkable. She had become a feminine and loving person and now beyond doubt would make some suitable man a very good wife. Jim was not surprised when one day the truth came out about Rufus—not the four-legged Rufus of Providence Island, but the original Rufus, her editor in New York, a well-to-do, cultivated, and rather shy widower with two grown children. Florence was not the same human being who had walked into his office that September morning and Jim was not shocked to hear her say:

"Now that you have made a reasonable facsimile of a woman out of me, we really ought to get off the island—because if we don't Rufus is liable to go ahead and marry somebody else. He loves me, poor man, and we've been kind of semi-engaged for the past three years, but of course it was impossible. I think I'd better take him up on it while I've still got the chance."

From certain things Florence had said, Jim had suspected there was an impossible "semi-engagement" to Rufus, of whom she often spoke with a wry affection. It was an impossible semi-engagement no longer. Florence, with some stubborn help on his own part, had liberated herself and she would marry Rufus now. There was still time for her to have a baby and Rufus, she said, wanted her to have one. "Yes," she said, "I really *do* think we ought to get off the island now, Jim. We've been here long enough."

Such were the more noticeable changes that had occurred in Melody and Florence. Jim Kittering was less aware of the changes that had occurred in himself. The thing that had attracted his attention was the fantastic virility that had come to his aid in the situation. He had been seriously concerned he might not be able to handle two healthy, passionate women, each of whom would expect him to make love to her on "her night"—he had feared he couldn't do it and there would be squabbles between the women, that one or the other of them would feel unloved and neglected and would get jealous and start to pick fights and they would pull each other's hair and throw crockery.

It had not turned out like that. There had not been one moment of real conflict between Melody and Florence during the seven weeks he'd lived with them both. They called each other "sisters" and each seemed to feel a tender love for the other. "Where's my sister?" Florence would ask. Melody often would put her arms around Florence and say some such thing as: "She's my sweet sister." There was, to Jim's relief if not surprise, no repetition of the schoolgirl "Lesbianism." The love between the women had no unnatural overtones he could detect and he was sure none was there.

Jim was less aware of the changes in himself and even less aware of the meaning of those changes; he ascribed much of the success of his "multiple marriage" to his phenomenal virility. He also marked up a good part of the success to what he called the System. They had worked out what proved to be a sensible *modus operandi* for the division of the sexual responsibilities that were, naturally, a considerable factor in his human duties as a "common law" husband to Melody and Florence.

The *modus operandi* was that Jim always slept on the big mattress in the larger of the two bedrooms in Morgan's First Treasure Cave, whereas the women moved from one bedroom to the other each day; Melody would sleep with him one night, Florence the next night, Melody the next, and so on. The suggestion had been made by Melody (this was before she'd gotten pregnant and simmered down) that in the event one or the other of them had her period, she would stay in the smaller bedroom and the other would sleep with him during that night or nights in order not to "waste" those nights, but Jim had said: "For crying out loud, no! I've got to *rest* once in a while—those nights will be my nights off!"

Thus far, Jim had not had much rest and he hadn't wanted any. To his amazement, he had proved sexier than both women combined. As he had "deceptively" told Florence in the course of his effort to win her, it was not painful to him at all to live with two women on that island. He went with renewed vigor from one to the other with an enthusiasm that was incredible. He would think: "Ah, Florence tonight, wonderful!—the sweet way she kisses me, great!" Or: "Ah, Melody tonight, wonderful!—the sweet way she kisses me, great!"

It awed him; such virility was unknown to his experience. Florence had gotten her period twice during the seven weeks and this gave him in theory a number of nights off. To his amazement, he found himself feeling frustrated and he wound up sneaking love from Melody during the afternoons while Florence was off on her watch—he practically had to seduce her; Melody was reluctant and had a tut-tut attitude about making love to him on Florence's "day," even if Florence was *hors de combat.*

Combat, however, was not quite the word, in fact it was not the word at all. There had always been in his love-making to women—just as there had nearly always been in their response to him—a certain amount of exploitative, aggressive emotion, a kind of "Ha, ha, got you!" attitude. The feeling he had toward Melody and Florence did not include the faintest trace of any such emotion or attitude; on the contrary, he felt a tender love for them both that seemed to him nonsexual. It was a paradox he did not examine too closely—that nonsexual feelings could inspire a prodigious sexual performance.

But perhaps it was not quite as prodigious as all that. It seemed to Jim to be more a matter of habit than anything. What could be more natural than to make love upon waking up in the morning, especially if the woman was right there in your arms (Melody, too, wanted him to sleep "literally" with her) and receptive? Surely at night there was nothing better to do. And what could be a pleasanter way to pass an hour or two than love in the afternoon?

It was a habit, that was all. He had gotten into the habit of making love at least twice and often three or more times a day; he was physically accustomed to this, attuned to it, and needed it. The women, on the other hand, had become accustomed to love every other day and it did not seem to bother either of them too much to sleep alone on her day off. Jim was sure one woman and two men could have made a similar peaceful adjustment, if they loved one another.

Another perhaps not insignificant change Jim noticed in himself was that his lifelong post-coital depressions were gone. Maybe he was too busy to have time to get depressed—such was his amused reflection when it occurred to him, shortly before the discovery of Morgan's Treasure, that "After love animals are sad" was no longer his motto.

What a scene, thought Jim with an ironic inner smile on the day Rufus caught and killed the wild pig. What a sweet and downright square scene it really was, he and his two "wives"—well, it would surprise his real wife very much. And speaking of Linda, what had become of her during the past four months? Had changes occurred in her as they had occurred in him? Undoubtedly. Leaving him and living apart from him of itself would cause tremendous changes in

Linda, and there were other factors that would cause change as well. She'd probably gotten a job as a librarian or teacher and this would be a significant experience for her. But the enforced chastity of life at Gram's would be the biggest thing working for change in Linda. Her problem was different from his own and what she had wanted and needed was to *get away* from sex and men and the whole enslaving schedule of pleasure for its own sake. Yes, there would be changes in Linda and the time had come to leave Providence Island. Such were Jim Kittering's thoughts on the day Rufus killed the wild pig.

The dog had done it twice before. There were not too many of the little wild pigs on the island and they were elusive. The captain and crew of the *Lorna Loone* seemed to have taken all firearms with them when they abandoned the ship; Jim had not been able to find any gun with which to hunt the pigs or he certainly would have done so. They were all very weary of Dinty Moore beef stew (an admirable and life-sustaining product, but monotonous three times a day for four months) and the few canned chickens and caviar had all long since gone. Twice they had had wild roast pig and it was so delicious they almost got drunk on it.

Thus, when the dog chased down and killed a pig on the beach on a January day warm as summertime but with a pleasant trade wind, Jim and Melody and Florence were elated. A barbecue was just what they needed to take their minds off the restlessness of recent days. Jim cleaned the pig down by the beach and washed it and carried the carcass to Morgan's First Treasure Cave, then tied a rope to it and looked for a vacant railroad spike to hang it on while they built a fire on a level area near the cave entrance.

"Don't hang it there," said Melody. "It'll drip on my clothes."

"Don't hang it there either," said Florence. "The blood will drip and get on the mattress."

"I don't want to put it on the floor, it'll get dirty," said Jim. "I'll put it here."

"No, it'll ruin the dining table," said Melody.

"It sure will," said Florence. "Drive another spike in the wall and hang it down there, away from everything."

"All right," answered Jim. "You and Melody hold it by the legs and I'll get the hammer."

Jim picked up the hammer and took another big railroad spike from the box he had found beneath the bunk of the captain's cabin on the ship. It was a mystery what the mad fool had wanted with those railroad spikes, but they had come in handy in the cave; he had driven them into cracks in the walls to hang things on and to tie the ropes upon which the blanket partitions were strung.

"Here's a crack," said Jim. He put the spike in the crack, banged at it with the hammer, lifted the hammer to bang at it again, then paused. "Hmmph," he said. "This is a funny crack." The spike had gone in quite a distance and a peculiar whitish powder had sprayed out upon his hand from the blow. "This is a very funny crack." Jim hit the spike another blow with the hammer. "This is such an extremely funny crack . . . it isn't a crack at all. It's a mortar joint."

"A *what*?" asked Melody. "What did you *say*?"

"How could there be a mortar joint in the wall of the cave?" asked Florence.

"Morgan's Treasure!" cried Melody. "We have found Morgan's Treasure!"

Jim banged at the spike with the hammer. "I don't know about Morgan's Treasure," he said, "but this is a mortar joint. And this is a rock, an individual rock about the size of a basketball. Look, here's the outline of it, with mortar all around it."

"I *told* you Morgan's Treasure was somewhere on this island!" cried Melody. "And you laughed at me! But we've found it! What else could this be?"

The railroad spike met no further resistance; it had gone right on through an apparently solid wall into air. Jim could feel a tiny draft through the hole. "There's some kind of room behind here," he said. "Maybe it connects to that opening where the cat goes and the bats used to live. I can feel air coming from it."

"Who would make a mortar joint in this cave and then plaster it over to make it look just like the ordinary wall of the cave?" asked Melody in great excitement. "Who would do that, if they didn't want to hide something?"

Jim was banging away with the railroad spike and hammer. "The rock is loosening. I think I can get it out."

"I wonder what's behind there?" asked Florence.

"Morgan's Treasure!" exclaimed Melody. "What else could it be? And do you know what it's worth? Millions and millions of dollars! We'll all be rich! Rich as sin! Hurry, Jim, get the rock out!"

"I'm hurrying as fast as I can," said Jim, who was infected by Melody's excitement. There *was* something behind that phony extension of the cave wall; whoever had built it had gone to a great deal of pains to make it look natural. And the mortar seemed crumbly, rotten with age.

"I think it does connect with the cat hole," said Florence. "See, the cat hole is only a few feet away."

"Morgan was known to be in this area," said Melody, "and he reached England with a lot less treasure than he had when he left Panama. They've never found it! Hurry, Jim! It's the greatest buried treasure of them all! Fifty million dollars, a hundred million, there's no telling, it's the greatest . . . treasure . . . known . . ."

"The rock is coming out," said Jim, who had visions of piled ingots and bags of pearls and baskets of priceless Indian gold jewelry and all the rest—a treasure, as Melody said, beyond anything known. "It's out! Watch out, let me put the rock down, Melody, stand back a second!"

"Oh, God, oh, God," said Melody.

"If it's really so much money, what'll we *do* with it?" asked Florence.

"Oh, don't worry about *that!*" cried Melody. "We'll find things to do with it, the world is starving! Why, the Indians alone, the ones they stole it all from, we'll give it back to the Indians, schools, medicine! Jim, what do you see?"

Jim had stuck his head through the hole into a small chamber that had once been a part of the cave itself. A dim light came from somewhere.

"What do you *see?*" cried Melody in a pleading tone.

"Crates," said Jim, "and a submachine gun, and a large tin box that looks watertight."

"Crates?" asked Melody in a feeble tone. "Crates and a submachine gun and a tin box?"

"Doesn't sound much like Morgan's Treasure," said Florence.

Jim withdrew his head from the hole, a pale fright on his face. "It's a cache of munitions," he said. "Help me pry out the rest of these rocks. All of this wall is phony here."

"Munitions?" asked Melody sadly. "That's . . . terrible. Who needs munitions?"

"Maybe nobody," said Jim. "But some unpleasant people think they do. I just hope it's *our* unpleasant people instead of *their* unpleasant people, although I'm not too sure it would be a big improvement. Come on, help me get these rocks out."

Ten minutes later, Jim had managed to make a hole in the wall large enough to crawl through and he was in the little chamber. Florence climbed in after him, but Melody was too disappointed and disgusted to bother. Jim could hear her outside muttering about war and guns and the foolishness of human beings. As he had suspected, the crates were full of automatic pistols, rifles, submachine guns and ammunition, plus a few hand grenades and other toys Sir Henry Morgan never heard of. In all, there were thirty-nine cases, enough to equip a sizable guerrilla force. Although the guns seemed to have been there a long time, they were all brand new and covered with sticky grease and wax paper. The crates were stenciled "BRNO," which Jim knew was a munitions center in Czechoslovakia, and a clammy fear seized his heart. His eyes fell on the tin box, which was padlocked.

"Madness," muttered Melody. "Most foolish thing I ever heard of, hiding stupid *guns* on an island like this, a beautiful island, yes, and they've got to put murdering *guns* on it—"

"Melody, be quiet for a second," said Jim, "and hand me the spike and hammer."

"But it's ridiculous, *guns*—"

"Give me the spike and hammer!" exclaimed Jim. "Don't you realize this could cost us our lives? I've got to find out what's in this box."

"Cost us our lives?" asked Florence.

"Our lives is damned right," said Jim. "These guns were made in Czechoslovakia. I've got to open this box."

Jim banged at the padlock with the hammer and railroad spike and managed after five minutes of effort to open it. Sweating and trembling with fear, he lifted the lid. A compressed pile of stacks of green dollars poured out. "Dollars!" he cried. "Dollars, and a lot of them! Thank God. It's the C.I.A. and they might not kill us if we're lucky."

"Dollars?" asked Melody.

"What are you talking about?" asked Florence.

"There must be two hundred thousand dollars here, maybe even more," said Jim. "And it's been here for at least four months, we know that. To judge from the condition of these crates, probably longer. Revolutionaries wouldn't leave this much money lying around unused; only a bureaucratic organization would be capable of such a wasteful thing. It's the C.I.A., it's our side."

Jim went back into the regular part of the cave and with the help of Melody and Florence counted the money, all of which was in five-, ten- and twenty-dollar denominations. The total was $287,335.00.

"Well," said Jim, "it's definitely the C.I.A., in my opinion. But those Czechoslovakian guns scared the hell out of me and they still do. I guess we can't be sure. We'll have to move *at once* to Morgan's Second Treasure Cave and stay there totally out of sight till the C.I.A. gets here."

"Till *what*?" asked Florence.

Jim gave a little helpless shrug and smiled a bit sheepishly. "I don't know why in God's name I never thought of it before. It just never crossed my mind and so help me I racked my brain to think of some way to get off this island. There's an easy and obvious way and you'd think a pinheaded idiot would figure it out in five minutes."

"Well, I'm not a pinheaded idiot and I didn't," said Florence.

"I'm not a pinhead either," said Melody.

"You're women and you don't think about such things," answered Jim, "but any man who knows anything about the world should have come up with this one, it's so simple. Look, this island is in the midst of the most sensitive political area in the Western Hemisphere. Numerous revolutions, guerrilla actions, and insurrections have occurred in the Central American countries to the west of here. And what have we got to the east only a few hundred miles away? *Cuba.* The area beyond doubt is under constant surveillance. High-altitude spy planes photograph this island all the time, along with every other island in this sea, and you can bet those pictures are studied for the slightest sign of any suspicious activity. Well, you wanted me to call you a taxi and I will. We've had the whistle in our hands the whole time. All we have to do is make an appropriate sign on the beach out of palm fronds and the C.I.A. will show up in two days."

There was no help for it. The discovery of Morgan's Treasure inevitably had dredged the knowledge from his mind and ended it all.

TWENTY-TWO

The Threat of Liberation

In the silence of the island the tongue of the Goblin wriggled in the anus of reality, withdrew, and spoke: "*Guns and money! Hee-hee-hee-hee!*" Fearful however, as the Goblin's giggle was, the threat of liberation conveyed a deeper fright.

Jim smiled ruefully at his two startled "wives," who doubtless would share his own poignant sadness and fear. The idyll was almost over and it had been so innocent really, so mild and harmless, the whole thing could be considered a bit square. What else could one say of sweet little make-believe weddings and gentle, mighty Matterhorns? Were they armed to face a world of Goblin giggles and death in which time did not have a stop and no enchanted island could give them all a second chance? Jim was not so sure.

The only thing they could do was walk on in darkness through the funny flowers of the Elysian Field, walk on in fear, and cling to one another with desperate love during the few hours that remained. A month before, he had noticed *Cannabis sativa* growing wild in little patches all over the meadow; the doomed Puritans, it seemed, knew a trick or two of which Melody had never heard. Perhaps now the time had come to make some use of this natural product of the Elysian Field. It would be a way to shut up the Goblin.

Jim smiled to himself. Melody often spoke of the "funny little flowers," but he'd never had the heart to inform her of the real nature of those little flowers. He had mentioned it to Florence and she had agreed *Cannabis sativa* was a thing they could get along without on the island. Besides, Melody dearly loved the Elysian Field; they'd always conducted brief Sunday services on the meadow. It would be a terrible blow to her to learn the place was growing wild with marijuana, a plant that was native to the area and very common. Jim's hunch, though, was that the Puritans had planted it as a sort of spiritual supplement to the rum they made.

He also had a bottle of rum of which Melody was unaware and rum was another excellent Goblin shutter-upper. A judicious combination of rum and pot should be enough to pluck out the Goblin's tongue altogether. Jim had discovered long ago beneath the captain's bunk a bottle of hundred-and-sixty-proof Jamaican rum Melody had missed. He'd mentioned this to Florence too, and they'd talked of having a "cocktail party" sometime, but had felt this would upset Melody and they had never gotten around to it.

Well, the third wild pig was dead and bleeding on the floor and it was sad they would have no time to roast it and sad the hour had almost come to say goodbye forever to Providence Island. Surely, the need to humor Melody was over. Perhaps it would even be a good idea to broaden her horizon a bit. She was a very sweet but very naive creature with all kinds of irrational prejudices, and thereby ill-equipped to face the realities of the world. Florence, too, in her way was extremely naive and still was blocked by shame and inferiority feelings she should master.

And besides, the thought of the end was depressing as well as frightening. Maybe they would find time to barbecue the wild pig, take a drink of good Jamaican rum, smoke a funny cigarette or two, and have a goodbye party, a sort of fare-thee-well and God-go-with-you. Yes, maybe . . . if time could be found for frivolity in a situation of such danger. The guns and money were a true Goblin whisper and a warning: the island, having served its purpose, had turned ugly.

"Get off in *two days*?" asked Melody. "But what message in palm fronds—what message could do that?"

"I should think 'Love you, Fidel' will do it," said Jim. "That ought to bring them running pretty quick. It might take a little longer than two days, but I'll bet we'll be off the island in a week."

"Are you sure, Jim?" asked Florence in a feeble voice. "They really photograph the island?"

"I am sure they photograph it and rephotograph it all the time," said Jim, "and I can't tell you why I never thought of it before. I don't say I knew it for a fact or that I know it now for a fact, but it figures. It figures overwhelmingly. With a hostile Communist government to the east and weak, vulnerable, exploited countries to the west, you know damned well spy planes are constantly photographing this island and every other speck of uninhabited or hostile land in this sea."

"But why haven't we seen the planes?" asked Melody.

"Why didn't the Russians see them when they first flew over Russia? Honey, they're ninety thousand feet high, or a hundred thousand feet, God knows how high. But believe me, they're there. This island is under surveillance, it's got to be."

"They do photograph Cuba, I know that," said Florence.

"Yes, they do," said Melody in a rather sad voice, "and they must photograph this island too, and others as well. I guess that means . . . we'll get off."

"Yes, it does," said Florence in an equally sad voice. "That's what it means."

"I think so," said Jim, "but our troubles are by no means over. In fact, we're in extreme danger no matter how you look at it."

"Why do you think that?" asked Melody.

"Extreme danger from what?" asked Florence.

"In the first place, we can't be certain these guns and this money were hidden here by the C.I.A.—they are Czechoslovakian guns, remember, and Cuban guerrillas might have hidden them on the island. If so, there's a chance—remote, but a chance—they might show up before the C.I.A. can get here. That's why we must move immediately to Morgan's Second Treasure Cave, which happens, thank God, to be a perfect hideout. We can't be found there except with bloodhounds. In the second place, the C.I.A. has purposes of its own and we don't know what they are. The taxi we're calling might just possibly give us a one-way ride to nowhere. That's why I've got to dispose of this money at once. But first we'll borrow three thousand dollars for expenses, I think that's reasonable. In the third place, although this is unlikely, these guns and this money might not belong to either the C.I.A. or the Cubans, but to independent gunrunners who won't be Sunday-school teachers. However, it's an awful lot of money for independents to leave lying around for four months or longer and I think we can rule out this possibility. Let's count the money, I have work to do."

In bewilderment, Melody and Florence helped count three thousand dollars in twenty-dollar bills. They seemed half convinced Jim was crazy and did not like it when he refused to tell them what he intended to do with the money that remained in the box, a not inconsiderable sum of $284,335.00.

"Where are you going with the box?" asked Florence.

"I'm going to get rid of it," said Jim. "Is the last pile exactly a thousand, Melody?"

Melody seemed to be enjoying herself. "Nine hundred and sixty, nine hundred and eighty, one thousand. The last pile is accurate. We've got exactly three thousand dollars or one thousand dollars each. But can we keep it?"

"I said we're borrowing it," replied Jim. "And I want to be sure it's no more and no less than three thousand."

"What are you going to do with the rest of it?" asked Melody.

"Yes, where are you going with the box?" asked Florence.

"I told you, I'm going to get rid of it."

"But there's a fortune in there. What are you going to do with it, Jim?"

Jim took the tin box from his shoulder and put it on the floor. "Now listen," he said, "I don't want either of you following me. I am going to dispose of this and I want you both to stay here in the cave till I get back. Don't tiptoe outside and peep to see where I go, because I don't want you to know the fate of this box. Is that clear?"

"Yes," said Melody, "but why don't you want us to know?"

"I have my reasons and I'd just as soon not tell you, if you don't mind. Let's just say that ignorance under certain circumstances might save you from a very unpleasant experience." Jim picked up the box again and placed it on his shoulder. "I'll be back in a few minutes. Now, *don't* follow me and *don't* look to see where I go. Just stay right here and get your things ready to move to Morgan's Second Treasure Cave."

In order to throw them off in case curiosity got the better of them, Jim started off in a northerly direction toward the Matterhorn and the path that led to Melody's Bathtub. He looked back several times to see if the women were peeping after him. Curiosity, in his opinion, was the greatest vice and greatest virtue of women and a real puzzler, since their minds worked on a parataxic emotional level that seemed hardly "practical" at all. They were not curious about the habits of game or the origin and composition of stars, but to be kept uninformed about a practical matter drove them frantic with desire to know the facts. Stars made no difference, but they had to know such things as: "Does he love me or will he abandon me and let me die? What can I do to make him want me so much he'll come back? Where is he going with that box full of money that could buy loads of pork chops?"

Strange creatures. If they didn't know the answer to a practical matter, it tormented them and brought on parataxic behavior that made no apparent sense at all. Or to put it less invidiously, their genius resided in emotional pragmatism; they were engineers, not inventors. Of course there was overlapping of endowment in the sexes and such categories were merely convenient formulae by means of which to observe tendency and measure probability.

But there was no doubt the tendency and probability were there. A gifted woman could construct an emotional Rube Goldberg machine so complex as to be beyond belief—and the thing would *work*, the goldfish would be electrocuted and the monkey would get the banana and the baby his bottle. Some men, rare and inexplicable screwballs, had this faculty too, thus combining in themselves the genius of both sexes; and other men had the faculty to a degree—he himself had built an emotional Rube Goldberg machine or two in his day. But there were not many men who could function as brilliant engineers and inspired inventors also. Emotional engineering was mainly a feminine achievement.

Whatever the meaning of female curiosity, his ominous tone seemed to have impressed Melody and Florence. Jim saw no heads peeping from the cave entrance. He circled the northeastern flank of the Jungfrau, cut southwest through the Elysian Field and its meadow of funny flowers, and headed due south across the purple rocks of the western shore.

Melody and Florence had their most essential clothing packed by the time Jim got back to the cave. They also had filled a crate with silverware and dishes and other things needed to set up rudimentary housekeeping in Morgan's Second Treasure Cave.

"Now for the guns," said Jim. "I'm afraid they'll be a little harder."

"Where did you put the money?" asked Melody. "I mean, Florence and I think we ought to know, we're not children."

"No, we're not," said Florence. "Where did you put it?"

"The problem now," said Jim, "is what to do with these guns. Logically, there's only one answer. I hate the thought of the effort involved but I'm afraid I've got to lug those crates all the way across the island and throw them in the ocean off the cliff at Hell's Half Acre."

"Why have we got to do that?" asked Florence.

"Because the ocean is a mile deep there," answered Jim. "If we throw the junk off that cliff it'll be gone, gone, gone."

"Why should it be gone?" asked Melody.

"Yes, why not leave the stupid guns where they are?"

Jim shook his head and sat down on a deck chair. "It's amazing," he said. "Both of you are perfectly intelligent; don't you see we have to get rid of the guns at once? Don't you remember my pointing out we can't be sure they don't belong to Cuban revolutionaries? And don't you remember my pointing out they might come to the island before the C.I.A. can get here?"

"I don't follow you," said Florence. "What are you, a peacenik? Why should we break our backs lugging those crates all the way across this island?"

"It's got nothing to do with my being a peacenik," said Jim. "We've got to throw those guns to the bottom of the sea to save our lives."

"I don't understand how it could save our lives," answered Melody. "It's not that I care a thing about the guns, but won't it make them mad, whoever the guns belong to, if we throw them away?"

"They are mad already," said Jim. "Our very existence on this island makes them mad."

"But they don't know we're here," said Melody.

"They *will* know we're here, and when they do they'll be mad, I guarantee you. If guerrillas come here we have got to make them think the C.I.A. has arrived ahead of them and taken us and the money and the guns off the island. If they find the guns, they'll know the C.I.A. hasn't been here yet and we're here *some*where on the island. They'd track us down and find us even in Morgan's Second Treasure Cave. They'd bring in bloodhounds from Cuba if necessary."

"I can see your reasoning," said Florence. "But why not just leave the guns and money alone and let them have it?"

"No good. We can't patch that 'treasure wall' in the cave, we have no mortar, and they'll know we know about the money and guns. We can't possibly eradicate the signs we've left in living here four months, so they'll know we've *been* here, and with the money untouched they'd know we're *still* here because no one would go off and leave two hundred and eighty-odd thousand dollars just lying there. Therefore, they'd hunt us down."

"But why? What harm could we do them?" asked Melody.

"Plenty," said Jim. "They'd know we're hiding somewhere and they'd have to assume we can see them even if they can't see us, which in fact we can from Morgan's Second Treasure Cave—there's a lovely view of the lagoon from that picture window. We could describe them and describe their boat and tell the C.I.A. how many guns they had here and how much money. It could and probably would cost them their lives and the success of their operation *not* to hunt us down."

"How would they know the C.I.A will come here and we could inform on them?"

"We want to get off the island, don't we? They'd know because of our sign on the beach. Cubans are aware of the overflights and they'd realize such a sign would be investigated by the C.I.A. It would make them desperate to hunt us down at once and shut our mouths, although of course they'd realize we're just innocent victims of shipwreck once they took a good look at the *Lorna Loone* on the reef. And by the way, if that stupid ship *hadn't* knocked that old wreck off the reef and taken its place, the overflight photographs would have shown a *new* wreck here shortly after Hurricane Beulah—it would have been investigated and we would have been rescued long ago. We can thank the *Loony Goony* and my defective brain for our vacation here. The only catch is, it's a vacation from which we might not return."

The logic of the situation was obvious, yet the women didn't look particularly worried. It was a matter of the habits of predators and it didn't interest them. They were hardly frightened at all and Jim wondered what he would have to do to convince them of danger.

"I suppose you might be right, but I can't carry those crates," said Melody. "They're too heavy, it might hurt the baby."

"I can't carry those crates either," said Florence. "I can't even pick them up, it's too hard for me. You're as bad as my brother, he was always expecting me to be as strong as he was."

"Of course it's too hard for you, I don't expect either of you to carry them," said Jim. "I'll have to do it myself and I dread it. Some of those crates weigh well over a hundred pounds. All I was trying to do was explain the situation to you so you'll understand it."

"Okay, throw them in the ocean then," said Florence. "It's all right with me."

"I don't care either," said Melody. "Go ahead and throw them."

"I intend to," said Jim. "But before we do *any*thing else, we've got to set up housekeeping in Morgan's Second Treasure Cave."

"Um-hmm," said Melody.

"Mm, yeah," said Florence.

Both the women had doubtful looks on their faces. They also had a prim tenseness around the mouth.

"That's another thing we wanted to talk to you about," said Melody.

"It sure is," said Florence.

Jim shrugged. "All right, talk then."

"Well," asked Melody, "how can we sleep in that cave when there isn't room in it?"

"Yes, how?" asked Florence. "We'd be crowded to death, all three of us sleeping there."

Jim Kittering ground his teeth with exasperation. "Okay," he said. "Now listen to me. I believe it's ninety percent sure these guns and that money were hidden here by agents of the C.I.A., but I'm not taking a ten-percent chance that I'm wrong. If this cache was put here by fanatical revolutionaries and they come here and find three pink-skinned Yankee imperialists on this island, they will never leave us here alive. They couldn't afford to and they wouldn't. They'd kill us. That's at best. At worst, they'd subject us to unspeakable tortures to find out where the guns and the money are, and that would probably include gang rape for you both and worse. They would then blow out our brains or cut our throats and bury our bodies in the sand."

Melody said in a frightened voice, "I still don't see what harm we could do them."

"He said they'd be afraid we'd report them to the C.I.A. and get them killed themselves," said Florence.

"But that's awful," said Melody. "A man who's not an enemy and two helpless women . . . what kind of men would they be?"

"Idealists," said Jim.

"I think maybe you're right," said Florence. "They would be dangerous. But Jim, we can't live in that cave. It's too small and there's no way to get in and out of it."

"I have a small rope ladder from the ship and you and Melody can easily climb it."

"But there's . . . there's no *bathroom* over there," said Melody.

"You can squat in the cactus patch. Think of a serious objection, if you've got to waste time arguing."

"All right," said Florence, "a serious objection is it's simply *too small* for three people to live in."

"It isn't too small. There's the ledge to put our food and clothes and other supplies and the floor is big enough for a mattress. I can't get a regular-size bed mattress through the fissure, but I can lower it on a rope over the cliff to the window opening and pull it in that way."

"*One* mattress?" asked Florence.

"There's no room for any more. But we've got a Beautyrest Queen, extra wide, it won't be so bad."

"You mean, we'll sleep on *one* mattress, all *three* of us?" asked Melody.

"Not me," said Florence, "that's too icky, I won't do it."

"I won't either," said Melody. "Why, that's . . . that's *uncivilized*."

"We will worry about this tumultuous problem later," said Jim. "At the moment I'm trying to save your lives, and mine too."

"I am *not* going to sleep with you and Melody on one single mattress in that goddamn place," said Florence, "not even on a Beautyrest Queen. I absolutely won't."

"Neither will I," declared Melody. "That's the most embarrassing thing I ever heard of, Jim, and you ought to be ashamed to suggest it."

Jim shook his head in disbelief. "You haven't heard a word I said, either one of you. I thought you'd gotten over your morbid modesty here, but you haven't. In the face of death, all you can think about is grasshopper nonsense. It's fantastic. You ought to know better, Melody, and God knows you ought to know better too, Florence."

"I agree with her," said Florence in a hurt tone, "and what you're doing is punishing me for the way I acted before. You know I regret that and you know how much it embarrasses me to be reminded of it, but that doesn't matter to you. You're willing to humiliate me like that in front of Melody just to punish me."

"Jesus H. Christ!" said Jim. "The logic of a woman defies description!"

"Is that so?" asked Melody. "Well, I agree with Florence. All civilization isn't gone on this island, no! Why, it would be like ancient Rome—or like in Hollywood at those parties on the floor and everything, or *Playboy* with all the girls running around naked and going tee-hee . . . people, people who do those *awful* things! Not me!"

"Me neither," said Florence. "I say it's spinach and I say the hell with it."

Jim stared at them in stupefaction. Could they actually refuse to go to the cave for such an idiotic reason? Yes, they could and they would. Well, they were living in caves and the time had come for the cave man's club, and woe the hunter who didn't have it in a pinch. He'd have to conk them a good one. "Jesus Horatio Christ!" said Jim. "Don't you realize we have *serious* things to worry about? You're in danger of getting your head blown off and what are you fretting over —a 'Roman' orgy, a 'Hollywood' orgy, and even, God help us, a '*Playboy*' orgy! Good God!—with *one* man you've both lived with for weeks and whom you love? We wouldn't even get in the *minor* leagues of orgydom! Let me tell you, the Vandals and the Goths sacked Rome a long time ago, Hollywood is more square than Main Street, and they make entirely too much money at *Playboy* to bother with orgies. On top of all that, an orgy by its nature is based on hostility, nastiness, and vulgarity in which there is not a trace of love or human feeling. We couldn't have an orgy if we tried. We wouldn't even qualify for the orgy Peanut League! Now, have I disposed of this idiotic grasshopper problem?"

"Maybe," said Florence sulkily, "but the cave *is* too small, Jim."

"Florence, for God's sake, I love you both and you both love me. How could we have an 'orgy'? It's impossible, honey."

"Well, I don't think Cubans are going to come here even if the guns and money are theirs. They haven't for four months and it would be too much of a coincidence for them to show up right now."

"I agree," said Melody. "The cave is *too small* and it's unlikely Cubans will come here in the next few days."

Woe the hunter. A better conk was needed.

"I said that myself originally," answered Jim. "Of course it's unlikely guerrillas will show up at this particular time, but how can we dare assume they won't when it'll cost us our lives if they do? And it *would* cost us our lives—they'd kill us even if they might not want to. We can't take a chance that they won't arrive. And I don't trust the C.I.A. all that much either. Who knows what sort of C.I.A. agent might show up here? I'd like to look him over before I come out of that cave. They hire all kinds of cutthroats and scoundrels, men who would kill you as quick as they'd light a cigar. Some of them might not be too bad, but how do we know we'll get a reasonable one? Suppose they don't want it revealed they have guns and money hidden on this island, suppose they decide the greater interests of 'world peace' require us to be discreetly eliminated? Who would ever know or care? We were lost in the hurricane, no one would ask any questions—and of course it would all be to preserve fair America. I grant you they might not think in such extreme terms. This insane clutch of Iron Curtain guns and Yankee dollars might not be terribly important to them. But we *don't know that* and we don't know what kind of agent will show up here. And when you don't know, you are cautious if you have any brains at all. So get this in your heads. We are going to Morgan's Second Treasure Cave and we are going to hide just like rabbits when wolves are out looking for them. I love you both too much to let someone harm you. I'm going to protect you and take care of you even if you haven't got enough sense to do it yourselves, because the very thought of some bastards coming here and hurting you drives me wild. Now, that's the *end* of this discussion! Do you understand me?"

"Oh, he's so intelligent," sighed Melody, "and he's right. The C.I.A., they're bad people."

"Yes," sighed Florence, "they're a bunch of no-goodniks."

"Okay, that settles it," said Jim. "We'll leave at once for Morgan's Second Treasure Cave."

Thus, Jim was at last able to convince Melody and Florence that thirty-nine cases of guns and twenty-eight ten-thousand-dollar bills on the island constituted a real threat to their safety. But they both made him promise there would be no orgy.

"It would be degrading," said Melody.

"And humiliating," said Florence.

"Don't spoil it, it's been so lovely here," said Melody.

"No, don't spoil it, it's been beautiful," said Florence.

Jim had to smile. As he had told them, an orgy was impossible—and thank God for that. It was doubtless square of him to think so in this world of bold sexual revolution, but orgies had always seemed to him rather unpleasing aesthetically; or at least Jim imagined it would be so, he himself had never participated in an orgy. Hob often had invited him with a giggle to his parties, but he had always shrunk back in embarrassed distaste. Of course, the girls at Hob's parties were mostly tough little hookers and swingers, with an occasional horrified innocent thrown in for the Goblin's delight—young things who sometimes fainted when they walked in and saw everyone with their clothes off; these were the ones up whose behinds the Goblin liked to put his tongue, a cute trick that seldom failed, as he said, to horrify them just beautifully, the poor little Puritanistic dears.

Hmmph, thought Jim, his smile gone. The most revolting thing about it, of course, was the Goblin's blood-curdling sadism. Aesthetic considerations to one side, there was not necessarily anything depraved in his act; the depravity resided in the effect on the young girl, and for that the man really ought to be put in jail. Who could measure the impact of such an experience on a naive twenty-year-old girl whose only crime was that she was beautiful and dreamed of fame, fortune, and "being a star" . . . ? Well, as he had often thought before, some fame, some fortune, some "star," with the Goblin's tongue up her behind and a room full of amused people watching her shudder with humiliation. Loathsome, horrible bastard—somebody ought to kill him, but no one would; the Goblin would go on forever.

Jim's reflections were a bit sobering. There were, after all, gradations and degrees of Goblinism. Three people on one mattress in a tiny little cave *was* a slight problem, perhaps. What would they *do,* anyhow? It was a question Jim had vaguely asked himself but had not answered, distracted as he was by more important considerations. But, well . . . probably he would make love to them in the dark, human nature being what it was. Maybe it wouldn't start deliberately like that, but one or the other would go to sleep, an arm would become lonely and go around a waist, a kiss would be exchanged, a breast would be touched, pajama bottoms would be furtively pulled down. . . .

Obviously that was what would happen and it was not so different from what they'd been doing for the past two months. The only difference was that instead of making love to one of them with the other six feet away and a blanket hanging in between, there'd be no blanket and the other would be two feet away. It was merely a matter of degree . . . or was it? The sleeping one would awaken; then what?

"Really, Jim," said Melody, "it's been beautiful and we don't want to remember each other like that."

"I agree with her completely," said Florence. "We don't want to remember each other that way."

"Okay, you're right," said Jim. "I hadn't really thought about it. Let's make this rule. There'll be *no* love-making at *night* in Morgan's Second Treasure Cave. Anything like that will have to be in the afternoons when only two people are there. Okay?"

"Yes," answered Melody, "and I feel a million times better."

"So do I," answered Florence.

The task of moving basic essentials to Morgan's Second Treasure Cave—Jim wanted to do this before starting on the crates of guns—

took over an hour. It was noon before he got the women settled there. He carried first a case of stew and a case of grapefruit juice to the cave, then carried the largest of the regular mattresses up the hill and lowered it on a rope down over the cliff, tied the rope, went down into the cave, and pulled the mattress inside. When Melody and Florence saw it, they shook their heads in dismay.

"Takes up practically the whole floor," said Florence. "We're going to be very uncomfortable sleeping on that thing, all three of us."

"We sure are," said Melody, "and we'll have to. There's no room on the ledge for Rufus' mattress."

"It was the biggest mattress on the *Lorna Loone*," said Jim. "That crazy Norwegian steward had it crammed in his stateroom, I guess for all those lady passengers he was supposed to have made out with."

"It's big," said Florence, "but it's not big enough for three people. We'll have to lie there with our arms folded like mummies. I really don't see how we can sleep on that thing."

Melody answered with a shrug. "There's nothing else we can do. Jim, I guess, will have to sleep in the middle."

"Oh, yes, he'll have to sleep in the middle."

"Umm," said Jim thoughtfully. "Well, at least it won't be hot in here. The prevailing trades blow right through the picture window and up the fissure. The cave is very well ventilated. And the hot afternoon sun is on the other side of the hill. It's cooler than Morgan's First Treasure Cave. And you'll have to admit that's a magnificent view of the lagoon."

"It's a magnificent view of the lagoon, but three people on that mattress . . . I don't know," said Florence.

"I don't know either," said Melody.

Jim, too, had his doubts. It would not be comfortable at all and after the vigorous love life he'd become accustomed to, it was apt to be slightly frustrating as well. To lie there in such propinquity to two women both of whom attracted him powerfully might be more tantalizing than he had imagined. Melody would be especially a problem. During the weeks together they had made an almost perfect adjustment and love-making with her was an extreme delight and pleasure. And Florence attracted him very strongly too. Perhaps she was thirty-nine and could not complete the act, but her body looked like that of a twenty-five-year old woman and even though she could not "do it" she did respond to him very passionately. Making love to Florence was also a great delight and pleasure. Lying there on that bed with arms folded like a mummy might be rather difficult for everyone concerned. Would it *really* be Goblinish to make love to them in the dark? Well . . . yes.

"I don't know," said Jim. "Maybe we'll have to sleep in shifts or something. That seems silly, but . . . we *won't* be very comfortable on that thing, all three of us."

"Why can't you make a tent or a shelter up in the cactus patch?" asked Florence. "Then I could sleep there one night and Melody the next."

"It would be too dangerous," said Jim. "We can't disturb the area up there or anyone looking for us would find this place. I think the best thing would be to sleep in shifts."

"I suppose we could do that," said Melody.

"Yes, I suppose we could," said Florence. "There's room for a deck chair by the window. One of us could sit up while the other two sleep."

Jim, who was sweaty and stuck with cactus thorns in a dozen places from his effort to get the cumbersome mattress into the cave, mopped his streaming and itching forehead with a handkerchief. "That's probably what we'll have to do," he said. "But at any rate we can get by here for the time being and I'm going to start moving those guns. I wish you'd make a couple of more trips to Morgan's First Treasure Cave and carry over other stuff we'll need. If you see anything like a boat, then come here at once and hide. Don't wait for me, get out of sight. I'm not quitting until those guns are all gone, so it'll probably be dark before I get back. Don't worry if I'm late, just stay here with Rufus and the cat and you'll be safe."

Jim spent the next ten hours carrying heavy crates on his shoulder down the Jungfrau, across the Elysian Field, and on over the jumbled rocks of the western shore to the even wilder promontory called Hell's Half Acre, a place Florence once had liked but now seldom visited. Although Jim did not consider himself a "peacenik," it gave him a satisfaction to lift the crates high above his head and heave them out over the cliff and down upon the rocks and into the deep blue water. The crates usually cleared the rocks and hit with a great splash and sank down at once on their way to the bottom of the sea. The ocean here, Jim was sure, was very deep. Several crates smashed upon the sharp jagged rock with a splintering crash and split open before sinking into the water and he caught glimpses of deadly automatic pistols and also of cartons of ammunition as they scattered in the blue waves.

The last three hours of his labor occurred in darkness and it was necessary for Jim to drive nails into the crates and hang a kerosene lantern on each in turn in order to see where he was going. The light was not too good and he often stumbled on the rocks. By the time he finally got down to the last four crates, which were filled with ammunition and very heavy, Jim's step was slow and he had difficulty lifting his arms. He did not see how he could pick up those boxes and carry them stumbling through the darkness to that cliff, but a stubborn determination drove him on.

Somehow he managed, but just barely. When he threw the last crate off the cliff he lost his balance and almost followed it. Staggering with exhaustion and soaked through with sweat, Jim picked his way through the rocks by the dim light of the kerosene lantern and entered the moonlit meadow of the Elysian Field. In his weariness he went a bit astray and found himself in a silvery hip-high patch of *Cannabis sativa,* the plant that Melody liked for its funny little yellow and green flowers, but avoided because of the sticky, aromatic resin.

On an impulse, Jim broke off a matted mass atop one of the taller plants, an agglutination of resinous matter, flowers, seeds, and leaflets. As he walked on across the Elysian Field in the moonlight, he toyed with the idea of showing the sticky mass to Melody and telling her what it was. She would probably jump out of the picture window down into the top of the Hanging Tree with a shriek of horror. Marijuana was one of her very pet devils, along with *Playboy* magazine, square and timid Hollywood, and long-deceased ancient Rome. She really should get over her delusions and so should Florence, in a different sense.

Very tired, Jim crossed the Elysian Field and found his way past leaning ghostly palms to the beach, took off his sweat-drenched clothes, and had a brief swim in the warm lagoon with the hope it would get some of the ache out of his bones and the semidelirium of exhaustion from his mind. Was it an illusion the scent of the little flowers in the silvery field had affected his mind? Could the aromatic odor of the resinous mass he had carried in his hand have caused this weirdly agreeable sensation of being suspended in time and space in the middle of a magic and beautiful but rather frightening dream?

The warm water of the lagoon restored him enough to realize how tired he was. He'd been foolish to carry all those crates without stopping; the water temporarily cleared his head but it did not help very much the ache in his bones. Jim put on his shoes and undershorts, threw his other clothes over his shoulder, picked up the sticky mass of resin, flowers, seeds, and leaflets, and turned for a last look at the lagoon.

The moon had risen and was full. "Beautiful," said Jim aloud. It was a pity Goblin guns and money could afflict such a place, but hadn't the white man's civilization done the same thing to nearly all the islands of the Caribbean? What a horror Columbus had brought to the Western Hemisphere in his search for China—would it all be ravaged and destroyed or would an effort be made someday to restore the beauty that once was there, to preserve it and keep it as a treasure of all men? That was what was needed, thought Jim groggily, to restore the beauty of fair America, to restore and re-evaluate and recognize the miraculous thing Columbus had found.

It was a pity and a shame. The lagoon looked like a lake of luminous platinum beneath the huge tropic moon and the trade wind carried with it a perfume of fresh air and the sea. He had thought it was the most beautiful small beach he'd seen when he first looked at it. It was even more beautiful in the summery night than in the daytime. They should all go swimming at night sometime in the warm water beneath the carpet of diamond stars, it would be a thing to remember in the harsh northern clime.

In a daze of tiredness, Jim picked up the lantern, went back through the palm grove, and up the bushy, cactus-covered Matterhorn. He found the entrance to Morgan's Second Treasure Cave by help of a kerosene lantern hanging on a bush in the cactus patch and wearily climbed down the rope ladder in his undershorts, his sweat-soaked clothes over his shoulder and the agglutinated mass of sticky resin, flowers, seeds, and leaflets in his hand.

Melody and Florence were awaiting him down below with another kerosene lantern and a cold plate of beef stew. Florence wore a nightgown, Melody had on a pair of his own pajamas, and they both had nervous, glittery expressions. Melody's pajama tops were fastened by only a single button, the cleavage of her breasts plainly exposed; and Florence wore the flimsiest nightgown she owned. After all that fuss and complaint, had they jumped off grasshopper-style in the opposite direction? Or was he imagining things? The latter, probably; they had to wear something to sleep in.

"Ladies," said Jim, "I am tired. I have just carried about three tons of guns a distance of approximately twenty miles all told. But the job is done. If our Cuban friends come tomorrow morning, they won't find their money and they won't find their guns and they won't find us either. They'll think the C.I.A. has come and gone and nobody's here."

"Here's your supper," said Florence primly. "It's cold, I'm sorry."

"I'm too tired to eat," said Jim. "Would you do me a favor? I left the kerosene lanterns up above, my hands were full. Would you get them for me from the cactus patch?"

Florence stared with curious interest at the gummy mass in Jim's hand but said nothing about it. "Sure," she answered, "I'll get the lanterns. You do look a little ragged."

"I wanted to get rid of that junk," said Jim as he looked around half blindly at the tiny cave in the dim orange light of the kerosene lantern. The ledge at the rear was filled with food, clothes, and other essentials. The dog's mattress was rolled in a corner and occupied by Rufus himself, who was curled up asleep on it. Joan the cat was asleep on a pile of towels. In exhaustion, Jim sat on the mattress in his undershorts and began to take off his shoes.

"Don't you want to eat anything?" asked Melody.

"I couldn't possibly eat," said Jim. With slumped shoulders, he sat staring at the resinous mass on the floor, then picked it up and put it out of the way on the foot-wide sill of the picture-window opening.

"What's that?" asked Melody.

"*Bhang*," said Jim. She wouldn't know that word.

"What?"

"Bang-bang, like in cops and robbers, or bang-bang like on that Hollywood floor." Three pillows and a clean sheet were neatly on the mattress. Jim lay his head on the middle pillow, put an arm over his eyes, and asked: "Whose night is it, anyhow?" Silence. Florence had gone after the lanterns and Melody wasn't talking. Jim adjusted the pillow under his head, opened his eyes, and stared unseeingly at the mossy dark ceiling of the cave. It didn't occur to him at the time but he was half delirious with exhaustion and did not quite know what he was saying. "I asked, whose night is it?"

"It's mine," answered Melody in a shaky voice. "But we agreed under these conditions it would be nobody's night."

What was she nervous about? They were always getting nervous about one thing or another. "Okay," said Jim, "we'll worry about it next week. Right now I'm going to sleep."

Jim closed his eyes and heard nothing more. He did not awaken when Melody and Florence lay down on the mattress on either side of him, but they were there the next morning, each scrunched over far to the side in an unsuccessful effort to avoid body contact with him. He could feel Melody's hipbone against his left leg and Florence's behind touching his right leg. Three people on one mattress was a crowded proposition but Jim had slept well and long. He sat up and stretched his arms as both women stirred and groaned. To his surprise, he felt good; his shoulders were sore from carrying the heavy crates, but he was not a tenth as lame as he'd thought he'd be. The hard work he'd done in establishing a habitation in Morgan's First Treasure Cave had gotten him in good condition and evidently he had stayed that way. But how tired he had been the night before!—it all was like a weird dream, stumbling through the field with the lantern, swimming in the moonlit lagoon. . . .

"Okay, ladies!" cried Jim. "Up and at 'em! We've got to make our sign for the C.I.A. today and move the rest of what we need over here and if possible roast that pig Rufus killed yesterday. Come on, let's go!"

Florence and Melody groaned. They were both night people, whereas Jim was a morning person—or at least he was on the island; back in Cherry Dale he'd often had hangovers in the morning.

"Oh, God, what a horrible night," said Florence with another groan. "I can't sleep on this goddamn thing."

"Ohh-hh," said Melody, "neither can I."

"You'll get used to it," said Jim cheerfully. "Up and at 'em, girls, we've got a long and eventful day ahead of us."

It was indeed a long day and an eventful day as well. When they got to the beach after breakfast, Melody and Florence in turn went up the hill to the regular bathroom while Jim gathered palm fronds and considered what would be the simplest and best taxi whistle to the C.I.A. He finally settled upon the slightly cryptic:

FIDEL XXX

Jim explained the taxi whistle to Melody as they waited for Florence to return. His feeling was that although "xxx" meant "love and kisses" or "kisses and hugs," it also had a rather sinister and mysterious smack to it, a connotation of not only smooches for Fidel but of skull-and-crossbones, death to the white race, we will bury capitalism, and so forth. "That'll bug the piss out of them," predicted Jim. "Wait till they see that on those photographs, it'll bug the motherloving piss out of them."

Melody, during the months with him, had gotten almost inured to Jim's filthy language, but she seemed nervous and depressed this morning and not quite herself. "Oh, Jim," she said, "I wish you wouldn't talk like that. Don't you realize how disgusting you are?"

"What's the matter with honest piss being bugged out of the C.I.A.?" asked Jim. "I don't think that's disgusting, I think it's healthy."

Melody pursed her lips in prim disapproval. "It's pathetic," she said. "You think you're funny, but you aren't. There's that 'little boy' side to you and I don't guess you'll ever get over it."

"Probaby not," said Jim. "And you'll probably never get over being a prig, either."

Melody turned abruptly and walked away as Florence came toward them through the coconut grove. Florence was not herself that morning either; she, too, seemed nervous and depressed.

"How's the pig, did you go in the cave and look at it?" asked Jim.

"Piggy's all right," answered Florence. "It's cool in the cave, but I think if we're going to have the barbecue we'd better have it today. I wouldn't wait till tomorrow."

"Never wait till tomorrow to do a thing you can do today," said Jim, "because tomorrow might not come."

"Why did you bring home that mess of marijuana seeds and flowers last night?" asked Florence.

Jim had almost forgotten it. He shrugged. "Just an impulse, I was tired. Did you tell Melody what it was?"

"No. What's the matter with her?"

Jim glanced over his shoulder. Melody had walked a hundred yards down the beach and was staring out broodingly at the lagoon, arms hugged around herself. "She's angry at me. I told her what a prig she is."

"Well, she's timid. Jim, I want to talk to you. Come and sit down for a minute."

"We haven't got time, Florence. We've got to make that palm frond sign. The message is *Fidel ex ex ex.*"

As they gathered palm fronds at the edge of the grove and as Melody slowly walked forward to join them Florence said: "I found your rum."

"Rum?"

"You said you hid it under a bush behind the latrine. It's there."

"Good," said Jim. "I'd kind of forgotten it."

"Are we going to roast the pig?"

"Yes, I think so. Melody can gather some twigs and lay them. Later I can get some heavy firewood for her, bring down the carcass, and make a spit. We'll barbecue it here on the beach."

Making the message to the C.I.A. took longer than Jim had thought it would; the difficulty was that he and Florence had to go farther and farther afield for palm fronds. It was also necessary to dig them half in the sand so the trade wind wouldn't blow them out of position. Jim stopped twice to help carry firewood for Melody and to bring down the carcass of the pig and build a spit for it. It was three o'clock in the afternoon before he could make out the ten-foot letters on the beach.

"Beautiful," said Jim. "Now, we wait. It depends on how often they check the island. I should think they check it constantly, but it might be two or three days before they come over and another day or two before they look at the photographs. But it's got to work. It can't help but work. How's piggy doing?"

"Piggy's doing great," said Florence.

The smell of roast pork was delicious, but the barbecue would not be ready for several hours yet and Jim wanted to get away from the women. He'd had a painful scene with Florence around noon and a painful scene with Melody an hour later. Both women were in a dither, especially Florence. But Melody was not exactly calm either. The most fantastic thing of all was that Melody had given her approval for Florence and him to have a "cocktail party." Jim still couldn't believe it and wanted to get out of there before she changed her mind.

"There's work to do," said Jim. "You and Melody keep the fire going. I want to move some things from the old cave to the new one."

"Are you going to get the rum?" asked Florence.

Melody looked up. "It's all right with me," she said. "Really and truly, I don't care."

"I might. I probably will, we'll see."

During the afternoon, while the women kcpt fire under the pig, Jim made a number of trips between the two caves carrying various needed items, in particular the kerosene stove and a deck chair. Both, unfortunately, were too wide to go through the fissure and Jim had to lower them on a rope over the cliff as he had done with the mattress. The stove took up the last remaining space on the ledge and the deck chair fit neatly in a triangle-shaped area by the picture window.

Jim also found the bottle of rum where he'd hidden it under a bush behind the latrine on the Jungfrau. Both he and the women badly needed cheering up. They were behaving strangely, both of them, and he was still shaking with inward shock as a result of the interviews he'd had with each in turn. First Florence hit him, then Melody, and the scenes had an eerie similarity although there were differences. A little relief from the strain and stress would be welcome.

The scene with Florence, brief as it was, had upset Jim worse than the scene with Melody. Florence had the power to upset him in a way that Melody didn't. It was undoubtedly the pity he felt for her. In bed with her in near-darkness, her body might look like that of a girl but Florence remained in all truth a homely woman and there was a vulnerability about her Jim found almost too much to bear.

He had suspected such a scene was coming and for that reason had avoided talking to her earlier. But it could not be put off forever and around noon she asked him again to come in the palm grove with her.

"We really don't have time, Florence," he said. "Can't it wait?"

"Please, Jim. Come into the grove for just a minute."

Reluctantly, Jim followed her a few feet into the coconut-palm grove and sat beside her. Florence's head was bowed over her lap and when she looked up he saw she was crying. "Oh, God," he said. "What's the matter, Florence?"

"I'm miserable," she answered.

"Why are you miserable?"

"Because I love you and I don't want to leave the island. Jim, let's don't make the sign. Let's stay here, why do we have to go? We're happy here, let's stay on the island."

"Florence, we can't stay here forever, you know that."

"Yes, but I love you and I don't want to lose you. And I don't want to go back. I know it's unreasonable but I can't help it. Jim, I'm scared. I don't want to marry Rufus, I don't. I don't love him and I'm scared. Jim, I'm scared to death."

Jim did not know what to say and was about to make an innocuous remark about Florence not having slept well when she startled him by suddenly flinging her arms around him and putting her head on his shoulder.

"Oh, Jim!" she cried. "Don't you love me a little bit? I know you love me a little, I know you do!"

"Of course I do," said Jim, who was badly disturbed. It shocked him how strong his feeling was for Florence; he could not endure to hear her cry in this way or say such things to him. He had always liked Florence, from the moment she walked into his office. And of course he pitied her. Jim heard himself say: "I love you more than just a little."

"Then how can you send me to Rufus when I don't love him? It's you I love! No woman will ever love you the way I do! Linda doesn't love you the way I do—she doesn't, she couldn't and I hate her! She doesn't really love you, Jim—if she does, then why was she unfaithful to you?"

"That was my fault," said Jim.

"I don't believe it. But even if it was partly your fault like you say, she was still unfaithful, wasn't she? Jim, she doesn't love you the way I do. I'd never want another man if I were her. I'd be so happy just with you. Why should she want other men if she loves you?"

"She doesn't," said Jim. "If she'd wanted other men, we wouldn't have had any trouble. You're wrong about her, Florence."

Florence began to sob bitterly in his arms, her head on his shoulder. Jim could feel her tears wet on his neck. "Oh, I know," she said. "I know, you've never lied to me or Melody about her. But you can't just desert me, I'll die! Won't you see me when we get back? If I could see you once in a while I wouldn't have to marry Rufus! Please, Jim! I can't stand to lose you! I can't stand it!"

Jim swallowed at an ache in his throat and patted Florence clumsily on the back as she sobbed wildly in his arms. What had he done? What impossible passion had he aroused in the heart of this unloved and unlovely woman, and having aroused it, how could he desert her? And yet he had to. It was out of the question for him to go back to Linda and remain involved with Florence. Such a thing would be unfair to Linda and even more unfair to Florence.

"Oh, Jim! I can't live without you! Please don't make me marry Rufus! Please, Jim!"

Jim swallowed at the gnawing pain in his throat. The truth was, he didn't want to give up Florence. Not at all. He wanted her to be his "girl Friday," he wanted her to work with him on developing a number of new shows—with her talent and imagination she would be very useful and it would be an excuse to keep a relationship with her. Jim's intention was to quit his job with the Goblin and develop shows of his own and submit them direct to the networks. They would be good shows, honest shows, not Goblin gluck but bonafide entertainment with some real truth in it.

"Well . . . Florence . . . you're upset this morning. Maybe we ought to talk about it later when you're calmer. I know you didn't sleep well last night."

"Oh, God!" cried Florence. "You make me love you and now you do this to me? Why didn't you leave me alone? I was better off the way I was! Did you have to make me love you and break my heart this way?"

"I . . . now Florence, I didn't mean . . ."

"All right, all right! Call it a fit. That's what it is, a fit. You're going back to your wife and I'll lose you, but I'll get over it. I will. I'll get over it and marry Rufus. Don't worry, I'll get over it."

"Sure you will," said Jim. Awkwardly, he patted Florence on the shoulder as the strange hunch came to him he would play this scene with her again with the roles reversed. The thought of her marrying Rufus did not set well with him at all. Besides, they could do great shows together. Writers with real talent were hard to find. She should be not his "girl Friday," but his partner, they could form a company and develop several new series . . . and of course he would be working with her and would have to visit her often, even in the evenings . . . but Linda wouldn't mind a "business relationship" like that.

"I really will get over it," said Florence. "This is just a fit. I know it has to be this way and it's horrible of me to talk about your wife the way I did or suggest you keep on with me. I will get over it, Jim, I really will. I'll get over it and marry Rufus. He will make me a good husband. But . . . I'll never forget you and I'll always love you."

Florence, who had calmed down for a moment, began to cry again. Jim patted her. "I'll always love you too," he said.

"It's sweet of you to say it, but you don't really mean it. You're sorry for me, that's all."

"No, it isn't all. I told you that two months ago."

Florence sat back and rubbed tears from her eyes. "I've got to get a grip on myself. This is ridiculous. How can I lose my self-control so completely? I didn't intend to, I really didn't. I'm sorry."

"It's the thought of getting off the island. We're all upset."

"I know. Melody's impossible this morning. It's almost like before you made love to her when we were first on the island. She snapped at me three times for nothing at all."

"Here she comes now," said Jim.

"Oh, fuck her!" said Florence angrily. "Doesn't she see we're talking? I'm going to get angry at her if she comes in here."

Melody stopped at the edge of the palm grove and peered at them. "I need more firewood for the barbecue," she said. "Am I intruding?"

"Yes, you are," said Florence, "and I wish to hell you'd go away."

"Florence is a little upset," said Jim.

Melody said, "I'm sorry," then turned and walked away.

"My sweet sister," sighed Florence. "I hate her too, because you love her more."

"Well . . . I love you both."

"You love her more, we all know that. You picked her first, you didn't even notice me till I made a nuisance of myself. And that's just what I did. I knew if I bothered her you'd feel sorry for me and pay attention to me. It's a funny way to get yourself laid, but then, life is ridiculous sometimes."

"Insane and absurd," said Jim with a smile.

"It sure as hell is," answered Florence. "I wonder what kookie thing I'll do next. Would you believe it? I really *thought* I was in love with Melody, I didn't realize at the time I was just doing it to make you pay attention. I thought I was a Lesbian after all or at least I *kind* of thought it. It's crazy. I wonder what thing will come next?"

"More of the same, I suppose," said Jim. "We no sooner figure out one trick we play on ourselves than we conjure up another one. But it does seem slowly but surely we get where we're going."

"I'll tell you this," said Florence. "The fit is over but I have never been so unhappy in my life. I don't know how I will ever get the courage to give you up. No more fits, but that's how I feel."

"I don't feel so good myself, if you want to know," said Jim. It was true. He felt terrible. An utterly bleak depression had come upon him. Why had he thought of those C.I.A. spy planes, anyhow? Florence was right. They had all been happy on the island and now they were miserable.

The scene with Melody—which, thank God, was briefer and not so upsetting as the scene with Florence—occurred an hour later. Melody stopped tending the barbecue and walked over to him as he put palm fronds in place. "I want to talk to you a minute," she said. "Will you come down the beach with me just for a little?"

"All right," said Jim with a half-suppressed groan. As he walked down the beach with Melody and sat on the sand beside her, he braced himself.

"Jim," she said, "I know you think I'm old-fashioned, a prig and all the rest. But I can change and I will. I . . . I've always been a misfit and even if Charles will take me back I don't want him! Jim, I can't help it, it's you I love, not Charles. I can't keep the agreement we made, I just can't, that's all, I love you too much. I can't give you up even if Charles will take me back, and he won't!"

"Well, now . . ." said Jim feebly.

"It's *you* I love, not him! And I love you more than your wife, she doesn't love you!" Melody began to cry. "Jim, it's *your* baby! You ought to be a father to it. Jim, you should. And I'll be a good wife to you, I'll fit in your world! Jim, please don't make me go back to Charles. He won't have me anyhow! Jim, please marry me! You should because you got me pregnant, it would be very dishonest of you if you didn't!"

Jim awkwardly patted her on the back as she sobbed in his arms. The scene was eerily similar to the one with Florence, but perhaps that was inevitable. "I . . . I'm sorry," he said.

"I can't live without you!" cried Melody. "You never should have broken that oath if you didn't want me to love you! Jim, I can't help it, I love you so much I can't give you up—please marry me! You know you love me and we'll be so happy together, I'll fit in your world, I'll change, I'll become modern—you'll see, a lot of the things I say and do I don't really mean. I could fit in your life, I could, Jim. And I love you more than Linda—there's that, too, nothing is more important than real love. I'll watch the television shows and help you do research. I can do it, because I'm the typical audience."

Melody calmed down more quickly than Florence. This was not too reassuring, however, because Jim had a strange impression she was biding her time. Some sort of idea had occurred to her. A funny look came in her eyes and she suddenly stopped crying and apologized for being so "unfair to Linda" and so "unfair to Charles." What was she up to? What kind of emotional Rube Goldberg machine was she working on? She had *not* given up, of that he was sure. Florence, maybe, had given up, but not Melody.

"I'm really sorry, I don't know what came over me. But you said that about me being a prig and . . . it just bothered me. It seemed to me like an awful thing for you to think of me, when we're maybe getting off the island soon. Because I'm *not* a prig, Jim. You don't know the things that go on in my mind or the thoughts I have. Why, I'm not nearly as offended by those *Playboy* girls or all the rest of it as I let on. Charles is offended, but not me, because I have such feelings myself. I do, I really do. And liquor doesn't bother me all that much either. I could go to New York cocktail parties, I could. What I say and what I really feel and think aren't the same."

"Let's don't worry about it right now, honey," said Jim. "I think you might feel a little differently about everything once you get used to the idea of leaving the island. It's been a shock to us all, the thought of leaving here."

"You don't believe me. But I *could* go to cocktail parties and I'll prove it to you. Florence says you have a bottle of rum hidden on the island and you want to have a cocktail party tonight. It's all right with me. I don't mind."

Jim lifted his eyebrows in amazement. "Florence wants to have a cocktail party and you don't mind?"

"No, I don't. It's Charles who's against all drinking, not me. I'm not against a cocktail party in moderation. I'll just drink grapefruit juice myself, but you and Florence can drink the rum if you want to. I'm more modern than you think."

As Jim had known from the beginning, the threat of liberation was the real power of the tongue of the Goblin. In the silence of the island the whisper and the giggle had been heard: *"Guns and money! Hee-hee-hee-hee! You are free!"*

TWENTY-THREE

Flower Power

Melody and Florence, with smiles, had put little orchid blossoms in their hair. A glow of well-being came to Jim as he thought of his tender love for them. "Girls," he said, "the Goblin is up against something he can't understand. We have flower power going for us on this island."

"We sure do," said Florence. "Come on, Melody, have a drink and let the flower power bloom."

As they ate roast wild pig on the beach at sunset and sipped rum and grapefruit-juice "cocktails," Jim and Florence attempted to talk Melody into trying a little of the rum.

"It won't hurt you, Melody," said Florence. "Really it won't."

"I don't think so," said Melody. "I might get drunk."

"I assure you you won't get drunk," said Jim. "I wouldn't *let* you, honey. It wouldn't be any fun for you. You'd get sick and disoriented."

"He won't let you get drunk, all right," said Florence. "I can't even taste the rum in this, there's so little in it."

"Maybe I might later," said Melody. "Right now I'm enjoying the wild roast pig."

The drink of rum was so small Jim could hardly notice the effect of it, but a sense of enormous well-being had possessed him and perhaps this was due in part to a taste of alcohol after many months of total abstinence. He would never go back to the heavy drinking he had done before, but there was something to be said for good old-fashioned alcohol. The slight numbing of the critical faculty did release emotional powers too often suppressed under the strain of existence. Alcohol might be old hat compared to the modern mind-benders, but many of these would prove transitory and old John Barleycorn would continue in his plodding way to ease mankind's pain.

However, Jim felt it would not be wise to take old John with them into Morgan's Second Treasure Cave. He also felt the drinks should be small. It simply wasn't worth it to get loopy and perhaps behave in a way of which both he and the women would be ashamed the next day.

The beach at sunset was beautiful. The sun was going down over the island's twin hills and red rays of light through the valley had turned the wreck of the *Lorna Loone* a mottled pink. The white sand itself was a pale pink and the tall slanted coconut palms of the grove were a pinkish green-red. The reflection of sunset on the lagoon was a fiery red, but where the light did not shine the water remained a blend of luminous emerald and opal and beyond the reef a rich deep blue. It was the most beautiful water in the world and as usual a gentle trade wind blew toward them from the east. Jim felt the scene could not be more beautiful, yet it had seemed even more beautiful the night before under the stars.

"You should have seen the beach and lagoon last night," said Jim. "I came down and had a dip after I threw away the guns and I never saw anything like it in my life. It was absolute magic, the stars and the moon and the shining silvery water—if fairies and elves had suddenly come out of the palm grove I wouldn't have been surprised."

"We ought to go swimming at night sometime," said Florence.

"I was thinking that last night myself," answered Jim.

"Why don't we?" asked Melody. "A little later, when our dinner settles. I think it would be fun. The moon is full, I could see the lagoon last night from the window of the cave and it was almost plain as day. Let's go swimming a little later."

"Okay," said Jim, "we'll do that."

"I hate to mention it," said Florence, "but that microscopic drink you gave me is all gone."

"You shouldn't gulp it," said Jim.

"Give me another one and I won't."

"Mmm," answered Jim. "I don't think we ought to go too fast, this is strong stuff, Florence. Better wait a while."

"Oh, come on, Jim, don't be silly. I'm not going to get drunk, I *can't* get drunk. There was practically no rum in that thing at all, give me another one."

Jim hesitated. Perhaps he *was* being a bit overcautious, and besides, what could happen? Suppose they did get a little tipsy? "Okay," said Jim as he took Florence's glass, "but let's don't have a Goblin orgy, we'll all feel terrible in the morning."

"Goblin?" asked Melody.

"Put a little rum in it this time," said Florence. "Oh, *come* on, Jim, that's *nothing*. Put some rum in it, I have an empty boot, I never get drunk. I've never been drunk in my life, so help me."

"I'll make it a little bigger, but go slow on it. Really, Florence, it's a hundred-and-sixty proof."

"Goblin?" asked Melody. "That's the man you worked for, isn't it? You call him the Goblin?"

"Yeah," said Jim as he poured himself anther drink. By error, too much rum came out but he would go slow on it.

"Why do you call him the Goblin?" asked Melody.

"Because he's a horrible son of a bitch."

"What is that? I'm serious, Jim. What does it *mean* to call a man that?"

"It means he's a psychopathic and sadistic and power-mad person filled with all kinds of fears and hatred. It means he's sick like a mad dog, sort of, and very dangerous. I know you don't believe it, but there are people like that in the world and a sensible person learns to recognize and identify them and avoid them."

"I can't believe there are many such people, if any," said Melody.

"No, fortunately they're rare. Just as saints are rare. Most of us fall in between, with a little bit of saint in us at times and a little bit of Goblin, too, at times. Or at least that's what they tell me out on the golf course."

"Do you play golf?"

"No," laughed Jim. "But I might take it up. A psychiatrist once told me to play golf and pal around with the fellows and stop worshiping women. An interesting sort of duck with a beard, but fanatical like them all and full of jargon. He had one good point, about love and reverence not going together."

"I should think love and reverence would be inseparable," said Melody. "How can you love a person if you don't have reverence for him?"

"He didn't mean respect, honey. He meant unrealistic and childish worship, a refusal to allow the loved person to have any weaknesses or failings."

"I think we should try and correct our weaknesses and failings, don't you?"

"Of course. But no one is perfect and no one can be, and if we expect a person we love to be perfect we're in for a sleigh ride to nowhere. That was his point."

"It's a good point, I think," said Florence, "except it gives license to be as weak as you want to."

"It doesn't give you license to be weak yourself," answered Jim. "He meant how we feel about other people's weaknesses."

"I think I see what you mean," said Melody, "and it *is* a good point. But I've always been able, for the most part, to accept other people's weaknesses; it's my own I can't forgive."

"Neither can I," said Florence.

"Mmmm," said Jim. "Yes. There's that."

"We're getting too philosophical," said Florence. "Let's get back to the Goblin."

"Oh, I don't want to talk about him," said Jim. "The man has been on my mind all day; the guns and money we found here reminded me of him. Let's talk about that television series we're going to write someday."

"Which one is that?" asked Florence.

"The funny, honest, and entertaining one."

"We've talked about several funny, honest, and entertaining ones."

"I might have one *small* drink of the rum," said Melody. "Just to see what it's like and keep you company a little bit."

"Good," said Jim.

"I'm *not* as hopeless as you think. I've never been totally against liquor, it's only the abuse of it that I don't like."

Jim poured a small amount of rum into Melody's glass and filled it with grapefruit juice. "You're not abusing anything with *this* drink, I guarantee you."

"I'm not abusing anything with this one either," said Florence. "There's practically no rum in this at all. I don't feel any effect from it whatever."

"That can't be true," said Jim as he handed Melody her drink. "I feel it a little now myself."

"Yes, but I have an empty boot and you don't. I tell you, I'm legendary for not getting drunk. I once drank a fifth of whisky in one night and was cold sober at the end. Really."

Melody was staring solemnly at her glass. Jim felt a twinge at the thought of what it cost her to go against her principles like this. She was bound to prove to him she was "modern," whereas one of the reasons he loved her was that she was *not* modern. It wouldn't hurt her, perhaps, to be a little enlightened and rid of some of her prejudices.

"Well," said Melody, "Charles would collapse if he could see me, but—" Jim smiled as she half closed her eyes, took a sip, paused, and swallowed. Immobile, she sat there, then took another sip, swallowed and frowned. "I don't taste anything at all."

"He hasn't exactly given you a giant drink," said Florence.

"It's a good ounce. That's enough for her."

"It isn't for *me*. Jim, this is ridiculous, give me a real drink."

"I don't taste *any*thing," said Melody. "Just the grapefruit juice."

"This is gone," said Florence. "Now give me a real one and I'll tell you about that funny series we're going to write, except we aren't. Rufus wouldn't want me working all hours with my common-law husband of Providence Island. A drink, please."

"Well . . ." said Jim doubtfully. Florence didn't seem affected, but he himself could feel the rum.

"Come on, don't be silly," said Florence. "We're getting off the island in a few days if you aren't crazy, and we might as well have a party. You said so yourself this morning."

Jim reluctantly poured Florence another drink but decided to nurse his own for a while. "Okay, now tell us about the funny show we are going to write someday, Rufus or no Rufus."

"It's a show I'm afraid will never get on the air unless my character is weaker than I think it is," said Florence. "But anyhow it goes like this. Once upon a time, there was a funny, funny family of very surprising and very human people who decided to raise dachshunds on a tiny lost island in the far west Caribbean—"

"No, no, no," said Jim. "Vermont."

"—in pastoral and beautiful Vermont. You wouldn't believe the amazing things that happened to this funny, funny family in that speck of precious farmland of pastoral and lovely Vermont. . . ."

An hour later the sun was down and Jim was tipsy and even Florence seemed to be feeling little pain. Melody had had two drinks and held a third in her hand. She said she felt nothing at all, but her conversation was not quite normal and she did admit the rum relaxed her. They had moved down the beach away from the pit where they'd barbecued the pig and sat with their backs against the half-deflated life raft from the *Lorna Loone*.

At Melody's urging, Jim had gone up to Morgan's First Treasure Cave and gotten the accordion and for a while they had amused and entertained themselves by singing various popular songs and even a hymn or two.

On an impulse, while they were singing some song or other, Jim had put one arm around Melody and one arm around Florence. This made the music seem even lovelier. On another impulse he had put his right hand on Florence's right breast and his left hand on Melody's left breast. They didn't seem to mind or even to be aware of it and the comparison was interesting: his hand could cover Florence's girlish breast almost completely, but he could not quite encompass Melody's full and womanly breast. After a while, just to show it was merely an affectionate gesture and didn't mean anything, Jim lowered his hands and put them back around their waists.

"I have an idea," said Florence. "Let's go skinny-dipping."

"You mean without our clothes on?" asked Melody.

"Sure, why not? We don't have any suits and we said we were going swimming."

"All right," said Melody. "I don't mind, let's do it. Do you want to, Jim?"

"Sure, I guess so," said Jim. "But we don't have to skinny-dip, we could keep our underwear on."

"Oh, to hell with it," said Florence. "I want to skinny-dip."

"So do I," said Melody. "It's much nicer with nothing on and it's dark, so what's the difference?"

Twenty minutes later, after a delightful swim in the warm water of the platinum-shining lagoon, Jim and Melody and Florence decided it was time to get out and sit on the beach and have one more drink of rum before returning to Morgan's Second Treasure Cave.

When the water reached Melody's knees, she stopped, put her hands on her hips, and stood naked staring at the rising full moon. "Look at the moon," she said.

Florence stopped beside her and also stood naked, staring at the moon. "Beautiful," she said.

Jim walked between them and said, "Gorgeous," then on an impulse put his right arm around Melody's waist and his left arm around Florence's waist. In this fashion, they walked on through the water to the beach, Jim with an arm around each of them, and Melody and Florence with an arm, respectively, around his shoulders and his waist. Thus they walked up the beach and sat down and stared at the lagoon, arms still casually around one another.

"I don't see why we should bother to put our clothes on," said Melody.

"Neither do I," said Florence.

"After all, we've seen each other before."

"That's for sure."

"Well, *one* more drink," said Jim, "a small one, then I think the party had better end."

"I feel like getting drunk myself," said Florence, "frankly."

"I don't feel like getting *drunk*," said Melody, "but I don't feel like going to that tiny cave with one mattress and three people on it. Let's stay here awhile."

"God, don't remind me of it," said Florence. "I didn't sleep hardly at all last night."

"Neither did I."

As he poured out three more reasonable-sized drinks, not too small and not too large, Jim said: "It won't be so bad tonight. I took one of the deck chairs up there this afternoon and I'll snooze on it and you two can have the bed."

"I don't see how you can sleep on a deck chair," said Florence.

"I don't see how you can either," said Melody.

"I didn't say sleep, I said snooze. I can sleep tomorrow." Jim handed them their drinks and sat between them on the warm powdery sand. "You know, this is as close to Paradise as you can get. Think how lucky I am. Two girl friends and both of them beautiful."

"Beautiful, huh," said Florence.

"Yes, *huh*," said Melody.

Jim took a good swallow of his drink—he'd put less grapefruit juice in this time because he was getting sick of it—and set the glass on the sand between his knees, then put his right arm around Florence and his left around Melody. "Well, you *are* beautiful," he said. Jim moved his hands up from their waists. "And it isn't every day in the week a man can have one breast in one hand and another breast in the other."

"Well," said Florence, "I'm surprised you can find mine to put your hand on it. You'd miss it if you weren't careful."

"Oh, don't talk silly, Florence," said Melody. "You have a *lovely* figure, much better than mine."

"Huh," said Florence.

Jim, who had kept his hands on their breasts during this exchange, smiled with amusement at Florence. He squeezed Florence's cupcake breast in his right hand. "Nothing wrong with this," he said, then squeezed Melody's much fuller breast in his left hand. "And nothing wrong with this, either. You're both beautiful. What was it the poet said about woman in her infinite variety?"

Melody sighed. "This is getting me a little sexy."

"Me too," said Florence. "I don't know why it has that effect but it does."

Jim laughed. They were good sports. Wonderful, in fact, especially Melody—he wouldn't have thought she'd take shenanigans like this so lightly, although heaven knows it was harmless and innocent enough, he'd touched their breasts plenty of times before. "That poet was certainly right," said Jim. "Woman in her infinite variety. Truer words were never uttered. In your varying ways, you're both beautiful."

"I guess big bosoms attract some men," said Melody, "but I don't think they're so beautiful. I like your small ones much better, Florence."

"Trade with you," said Florence.

"I would if I could. I'm afraid big busts run in my family. You should have seen my mother. And my *aunt*—good Lord, she looked like she'd fall over when she walked down the street. But she was lovely otherwise."

Jim had begun gently pinching Florence's nipple and at the same time pinching Melody's. The idea of this game was to see if he could get them both to stand up simultaneously. It was a nervy little game and cutely wicked, he thought, but no harm was in it.

"Well . . . that aunt, maybe that's too much of a good thing," said Florence. "I mean, if she falls over it's too much."

"Yes, it was . . . too much, my aunt."

Melody's and Florence's voices sounded a bit distracted. This sort of thing did distract a woman. "Hey, now," said Jim. "It works, I win the game."

"What game?" asked Melody.

"Oh, just a game," said Jim. "Doesn't matter.

"I know a game," said Melody. "Spin-the-bottle, that's a game."

"Spin-the-bottle?"

"Sure, spin-the-bottle and see who gets kissed."

Jim laughed. Melody was not tipsy, he hadn't given her enough rum to make her tipsy, but she was in a rare humor—not that there was anything so shocking if he did kiss them. He'd kissed them both more than once.

"We don't have a bottle," said Florence, "except the rum bottle, and I don't want to spin that. I want a drink from it."

"Good grief," said Jim. He took his arm from around Florence and slipped his left hand down to Melody's waist as he reached for his own drink. "Have you already finished that one, Florence? You really do have an empty boot. I've hardly begun on mine."

"*Mine's* gone," said Melody, "and I still don't know what rum tastes like."

"Pour us another one," said Florence.

Jim swallowed down his own drink. Florence showed no outward signs of intoxication whatever. He could hardly allow her to make him look like a piker, but this would be the last one. "All right, *one* more, then we go home."

"Don't put so much juice in mine," said Melody. "I want to see what the rum tastes like."

Halfway through the drink, Jim again put his arms around Melody and Florence and his hands back on their breasts. "This is the most fun we've all had together since we've been on the island," he said. "And you really *are* beautiful, both of you."

"You keep repeating that," said Melody. "If we're so beautiful, why don't you give us a kiss?"

"Impossible. How can I kiss you both at the same time?"

"That's why I suggested spin-the-bottle."

"All right then," said Jim. "Whom shall I kiss first?"

"Don't spin the bottle, it's precious," said Florence. "It was her idea, so kiss Melody, but don't hurt the bottle."

"All right, I'll kiss her," said Jim. He turned, put both arms around Melody, pulled her body against his chest, and kissed her on the lips, first lightly and then passionately. Although the kissing was her own idea, Jim had half suspected she wouldn't respond to him and it really would be like a children's game of spin-the-bottle. He was wrong. Melody's response was passionate. They were both breathless when the kiss ended.

"I didn't think you'd ever stop," said Florence. "When you kiss me, does it go on as long as that?"

"I don't know," said Jim. The impact of Melody's kiss had made him dizzy. It was very sexy, somehow, to kiss her with Florence right there.

"I think we ought to go skinny-dipping again and cool off or face facts and go to bed," said Melody casually. "Where's my drink?"

"I really thought you'd kiss her all night long," said Florence. "Do I get kissed too?"

"Of course," said Jim. He turned to Florence, put his arms around her, pulled her slender body against him, and kissed her, again first lightly, then with passion as she responded to him. A sense of delicious wickedness came upon Jim. She kissed very sweetly, Florence, almost nicer than Melody, whose style was more fiery and active. It was very, *very* sexy to kiss one after the other, and what had Melody said—face facts and go to bed?

For the first time it occurred to Jim that unless something happened very soon to deflect them from the course they were following, he would make love that night to both Melody and Florence in Morgan's Second Treasure Cave. And in that fact resided a truly delicious wickedness. But they would be deflected from this course. The women would back off, they had been very opposed.

"I think you kissed Florence longer than you did me," said Melody. "I'm jealous. Will you kiss me again?"

"Sure. In a minute, let me catch my breath."

"Whheww," said Florence, "that bothered me. I'm really all stirred up. I think we ought to have an orgy."

"I do too," said Melody.

"Now, girls," said Jim.

"I mean," said Florence, "a *nice* orgy, not an ugly one. A nice one with the lantern off."

"Oh, yes, with the lantern off," said Melody, "that wouldn't be nice at all to have it on. It would be very naughty."

A chilling thrill of pure delicious wickedness ran through Jim Kittering. The women were *not* backing off—in fact they were taking the lead! *Both* of them wanted an "orgy." They were keen for it. Or were they serious? Could it be they were joking?

"Let's do it," said Florence. "We can't lie there like mummies the way we did last night and Jim can't sit up all night in that chair. Let's do it, but with the lantern off."

"I'll do it," said Melody. "I'm willing."

They were serious. "Well . . ." said Jim. Why not? He loved them both and they loved each other, it wouldn't be "Goblinish" a bit. It was not different in principle from the way they'd lived together for the past two months—he'd been slightly square about that and so had they. "Okay, I guess we better get on back then."

"Yes, let's get on back," said Melody, "and go to bed."

"And let's take the bottle of rum with us," said Florence.

"I don't know about the rum," said Jim.

"We've drunk less than *half* of it. Look. It's true, there's more than half of it still left. Let's take it with us and have a nightcap."

"All right," said Jim. "Where are our clothes?"

"Oh, let's just leave them," said Florence.

"Yes, we can get them in the morning," said Melody. "The shoes are by the barbecue, that's all we need."

They were stumbling in the moonlight through the cactus patch—and all getting a few thorn wounds in the process—before it occurred to Jim that the clothes on the beach and the barbecue itself would be evidence of recent occupation of the island to visiting Cubans. He'd have to be more careful in the future. First thing in the morning, he'd have to collect the clothes and cover up the ashes and dispose of what was left of the wild roast pig. He was too woozy to do it now.

And that was strange. How could he be tipsy sharing a mere half-bottle of rum with two other people? It then occurred to Jim the Jamaican rum at a hundred-and-sixty proof was twice the strength of ordinary rum. They had drunk between them the equivalent of a full quart of regular rum. No wonder he felt tipsy. Florence, though she did not show it, was probably tipsy too. And Melody, even though she'd not had as much as they had, was also probably tipsy. Another drink or two of that stuff and they'd all be drunk, especially now that the wild roast pig had settled and the alcohol would get in the blood faster. They had better ease off on the rum.

"I'll go down first and light a lantern," said Jim, "so you can see to come down the ladder."

Rufus was down below and greeted Jim with a wag of the tail and several barks as he struck a match and lighted a kerosene lantern. The dog was now much friendlier toward him.

"Be careful, Melody," called Jim as he saw a pair of legs and a plump behind start to descend the rope ladder. There was no mistaking who it was. Melody's behind was recognizable some distance away. He'd spotted her easily from Morgan's Armchair on a number of occasions when she was taking a bath in her Bathtub at the north end of the island. It amused him how she would meticulously soap and rinse herself not once but twice.

"I'm all right," said Melody as she stepped down to the floor of Morgan's Second Treasure Cave. "Hi, Rufus! Have you been a good dog? Jim, you know we forgot to bring him any of the wild roast pig."

Jim glanced up as another pair of legs and a slimmer behind came into sight on the rope ladder. It was amazing, the change that had occurred in Florence in the past two months. Melody was right; she *did* have a good figure—in fact, an extraordinary figure for a woman of thirty-nine. "Be careful, Florence, don't fall and break your leg," said Jim. "Here, let me help you."

"I'm just fine," said Florence. She seemed a trifle annoyed. "And I don't see any need for you to stand there and stare up our behinds."

"Just normal healthy lust," said Jim with a grin. "But don't worry, I didn't really get a good look."

"Too bad," said Florence.

"We forgot to bring Rufus some of the wild pig," said Melody, "and that's really not fair, he killed it for us."

"Can't you let him out, Jim? He could find it, he knows where we were."

"All right," said Jim. "The dog oughtn't to be out as a rule when we aren't ourselves, but I'll be up early tomorrow morning so I guess it's okay. Come on, Rufus."

Jim picked up the dog, carried him up the ladder, and shoved him through the fissure, then went back down into the cave and sat by Florence and Melody on the mattress.

"How about a nightcap?" asked Florence.

"One, and that's absolutely all," said Jim. "Really. It's strong rum, Florence."

"Okay, one more. I'll make it."

Jim watched Florence as she stood up and reached to the ledge for glasses and grapefruit juice. It was remarkable; her body showed none of the signs of age one might expect to see in a woman of thirty-nine years. He said: "Florence, you had your birthday a couple of weeks ago, didn't you?"

"Yes, worse luck."

Hadn't the jacket of her book given her age? Jim couldn't remember. The book had been published a couple of years ago and her age had been mentioned on the jacket—or was he imagining this? He could remember a rather youthful-looking picture of Florence on the cover. None of the freckles had been touched out and the smile on her face had shown the buck teeth very frankly.

"How old were you?" asked Jim.

"Thirty-nine, you know that."

Again he stared at Florence as she stood with her back to him making the drinks. There was no trace of excess flesh on her thighs, a common thing with older women. And there were no waffle-like dimples at the base of her buttocks, another common thing with women over thirty. Even Linda, who was thirty-two and had a very beautiful figure, had begun to show faint signs of these things and had complained bitterly and done all sorts of exercises and calisthenics to correct the trouble.

Florence turned around, drinks in hand. Jim ran his eyes slowly from her ankles to her chin. It was a girlish body. The graceful legs, the thin and almost silken pubic hair, the flat stomach, the small, uptilted, and lightly pigmented breasts—it was an amazing body for a woman of her age to have.

"All I can say," said Jim, "is that for thirty-nine you sure do have a youthful figure."

"She sure does," said Melody. "I almost think sometimes she fibbed about her age."

Florence laughed in amusement. "That would be a good one," she said, "to go down in history as the first woman to claim she was older than she really was."

It was true, Florence was thirty-nine. Of course she'd had no children and that probably made the difference, but even so she looked much younger in the nude than her age. She looked more attractive in the nude, too, especially in the soft orange light of a kerosene lantern. Her cheekbones were good and now that she'd gained some weight she really was not a bad-looking woman, except for the buck teeth and he himself had almost come to like the buck teeth because he associated them with her.

"I guess it's because you've had no children," said Jim.

Florence handed Jim and Melody drinks, then sat down with them on the mattress and crossed her legs Yoga style. "I wonder why I haven't gotten pregnant here. Melody got pregnant right away, why didn't I?"

"The luck of the dice," said Jim.

"Maybe I can't have a child," said Florence.

"You look healthy, I'm sure you can," said Jim. "There aren't too many barren women."

"Maybe it's because I can't do it," said Florence, "maybe that's why I haven't gotten pregnant."

"That has nothing to do with it, that's an old wives' tale. It just takes time, that's all. A few months and you'll get pregnant."

"What does she mean, she can't do it?" asked Melody.

Florence smiled. "Melody, I forgot you were there. Isn't it funny, our sitting here stark naked and talking about such things? If somebody had told me six months ago I'd do this, I would have passed out cold."

"So would I," said Melody. "But what did you mean by saying you can't do it?"

Jim listened in fascination to their talk while he sipped at his drink, which was a huge one and beginning to make him feel a little dizzy. The casual tone as they discussed how Florence might be able to have an orgasm with a man was startling, to say the least, and quite a change from the attitude they'd expressed when he first told them of the need to move to Morgan's Second Treasure Cave. Surely the rum could not wholly account for this. No doubt it had helped, but other factors must have changed their viewpoint.

"Jim makes love to me so nice," said Florence, "and I get terribly excited but I can't do it. I get right to the point and then I just can't. Something seems to stop me."

"Hmmm-mm," said Melody thoughtfully. "That's bad."

"It's miserable. I get so frustrated sometimes, I could cry. And it isn't Jim's fault. He's very patient, I just can't do it."

"I had that trouble with Charles at first," said Melody. "And he was a good lover when we were first married. Very good. But I couldn't do it. The moment would come and I'd get . . . tense."

"Yes, that's it. That's what I do, I get tense."

Melody nodded. "It's getting tense and thinking you can't. I'd think, 'Maybe I won't be able to'—and then I couldn't."

"That's exactly what happens to me. I think I can't and then I can't. How did you learn how to do it, Melody?"

"*Relaxation*," said Melody, "that's important. I mean, *emotional* relaxation, saying to yourself, 'Oh, I love this man so much, he's so sweet. And I *trust* him, I *give* myself to him, all of myself, heart and soul.' That helps, emotional relaxation."

"Yes, I should think it would," said Florence. "Emotional relaxation."

"Of course, you have to keep your mind on what you're doing," said Melody in a tone as solemn as a deacon in her husband's church. "I mean, after all, you're not just lying there. The *way* you do it, that's part of it. I can do it now nearly any way, but until you learn how, this isn't true."

"What exactly do you mean?"

"In the beginning you have to move in a certain particular way."

"What particular way?"

"Well . . . it's a little hard to explain. But there's a way that works better. You'll find it out for yourself in time."

"I don't have any time," said Florence. "What's the way?"

"It's hard to put in words."

"I wish you'd tell me, Melody, or try, anyhow."

"I know how you feel. It used to drive me crazy when I was first married to Charles."

"It drives me crazy too. It really does. I get horribly excited and nothing happens and I'm fit to be tied."

"I used to cry, I used to cry with sheer misery. Charles couldn't figure out what was the matter with me because I pretended everything was all right. It made me so nervous I'd go in the bathroom and sit on the toilet and cry in a towel."

"I know exactly what you mean," said Florence wearily.

"And do you know what? I'll bet there's loads and loads of girls and women who have this same problem, especially when they're first married. They can't do it with a man, not even their husband. They're afraid of him, that's the trouble. No emotional relaxation."

"I'm not afraid of Jim," said Florence.

Melody hesitated, her eyes down on her drink, which was almost gone. She looked up at Florence and asked: "You're afraid he's going to leave you, aren't you?"

Florence was silent for several seconds, then answered: "Yes."

"Those girls and women I was talking about, they're afraid of something too. I know I was. They're afraid of being married, afraid the husband doesn't really love them or won't, when he gets to know them, or afraid they can't cook or they'll die having a baby, or whatever. No emotional relaxation, and also they just don't know how to do it. They don't know how to move in that certain particular way."

"Yeah," said Florence glumly, "that certain particular way you can't explain."

"Well . . . I *could* explain it."

"Then why don't you?"

"If I were a writer like you, I could explain it. But . . . it's hard to put in words."

"Look, anybody who can talk can write if they sit down and try. And you talk very well."

"No, I just talk ordinary, and it's . . . too hard to put in words."

Florence gave up with a shrug and turned to Jim. "You're very quiet. Are you asleep?"

"No, I was just listening with interest to you two girls talk. And I must say, it's the most fantastic conversation I ever heard."

"What's fantastic about it? You know I've had this trouble."

"Yes," said Jim.

"You look groggy. You're not going to sleep on us, are you?"

"No, that would spoil the nice orgy."

Florence didn't seem pleased. "I don't think we ought to call it an orgy, even joking. I don't think it *is* an orgy. I love you and I love Melody, so how could it be an orgy?"

"I couldn't agree with you more," said Melody. "That's why I changed my mind down on the beach, partly. And I love you too, Florence, I really do, you're one of the sweetest persons I've ever known and I hope we can figure out a way for you to learn how to do it because it must be terribly frustrating for you."

"Well," said Florence shyly, "I . . . I'll never forget how sweet you were to me when I . . . bothered you that time. I do love you so much, you were so nice and kind to me . . ."

The women were getting drunk, thought Jim, and so was he. It seemed to have hit them all at once. The orange light of the lantern was dancing on the walls. That last whopper of a drink of double-strength rum Florence had poured was too much.

"Yes, I love you too," said Melody. "And that's why I wasn't jealous when Jim fell in love with you."

"We all love one another," said Florence. "It's beautiful. We have flower power going for us in this cave."

The woman weren't getting drunk, they *were* drunk, thought Jim. And they had flower power in that cave, all right, plus *Cannabis sativa* as well. Little yellow flowers buried in sweet resin right there on the sill of the picture window, genuine Far Eastern *bhang*. Why not infuse it in cool waters and add a mite of the resulting broth to their next drink? A mixture of funny flowers and old John Barleycorn ought to lead to true flower power indeed.

"We do love one another," said Melody.

"Oh, yes, we do," said Florence.

"*Bhang*," said Jim.

"What?" asked Melody.

"*Bhang*, like in India."

"You said that bang stuff last night. What do you mean by that?"

"I love you but I have to pee," said Florence.

"Just a second, Florence. What is all this bang-bang stuff, Jim? And why are you and Florence acting so mysterious? I want to know. If I can sit here naked with two other people, I can know what this bang-bang is. Is it just making love or is it something worse?"

"Nothing is *better* than good old-fashioned love, Melody."

"You don't understand me. I'm not opposed to all those things, and what I say and what I think and feel aren't the same. I could do a *real* orgy. You don't believe it, but I could. Easily."

"Melody," said Jim, "no one wants you to do a *real* orgy, so just calm yourself, honey."

"I have to pee," said Florence.

"You asked me if *bhang* is just making love or is it something worse, and I said nothing can be *better* than making love. It is the ultimate escape from self when it is truly achieved, a major pathway, perhaps *the* major pathway to nirvana. It amazes me the Indian mystics are not more hip to this. Their discipline seems to emphasize ascetic denial and continence, an unnecessarily difficult and perverse path, in my opinion. What is natural and preserves life can't be wrong and love is both. It's the major path."

"I have to pee something terrible," said Florence.

"What is this *bang* thing?" asked Melody. "Is it a perversion?"

"*Bhang* is certainly subordinate to love, but it can augment it."

"Now look," said Florence. "I've got to pee and I'm afraid to go up in the cactus patch because crocodiles might get me."

"Put your tail over the sill out the picture window and go down the cliff," said Jim.

"Oh, God, I can't."

"Why not?"

"I'd fall out of it down in the top of the Hanging Tree."

"You won't fall, I'll hold your hand."

"Oh, no. I . . . I couldn't go with you holding my hand."

"Tell me what *bang* is," said Melody.

"I believe you're thinking of it as *bee ay en gee*," said Jim, "whereas the proper spelling is *bee aitch ay en gee*."

"Oh, Christ, come on," said Florence as she took Jim's hand, "I've got to go and I'll fall out if you don't hold me."

"*Bee aitch ay en gee . . . bhang*," said Melody. "What is it?"

Jim stood up as Florence pulled at his hand. "Excuse me, I've got to help Florence or she'll fall into the Hanging Tree. But I can talk while we handle this little emergency. *Bhang* is a precious herb native to Asia. It is also found in Central America and Mexico and on islands of this type and elsewhere. I refer actually to the plant that forms *bhang,* not to *bhang* itself, which is a golden exudation with magical properties."

"For God's sake don't let me fall," said Florence. "I'm cold sober, but I'm a little dizzy."

"The plant happens to grow rather abundantly in the Elysian Field, Melody," said Jim, "a thing you might expect, considering the true nature of those Puritans."

"Oh, God," said Florence as Jim helped her sit on the sill of the picture window. "Don't drop me."

"You mean," asked Melody, "those little funny flowers?"

"Yes," said Jim. "Sit out farther, Florence. You'll pee on the sill itself like that, put your behind out more."

"I can't, I'm afraid I'll fall."

Jim took hold of the rock wall of the cave with his left hand, leaned over Florence's shoulder, and put his right arm around the small of her back. "Now you can't fall, I'm holding you. Move out more." Florence raised her hips and shifted under his arm and he saw her heart-shaped behind move out into the moonlight over the Hanging Tree. "You've got it in your sights, Florence. Fire away. And relax, I won't drop you."

"Don't look. Turn the other way."

"As I was saying, Melody, *bhang* is a precious herb with fantastic medicinal properties. Or rather, the product of a precious herb. You make a curative tea out of it. The resin and the flowers and the pods and the leaves and everything. I happen to have some right here. We ought to infuse it in cool water and put the sweet precious liquor of it in our next drink. What's the matter with you, Florence, have you dozed off?"

"I can't go, I'm inhibited."

"Oh, go ahead. I'm not watching you or even thinking about you, I'm just holding you."

"Ohhh-hh," groaned Florence, "I can't . . . and you *are* watching me."

"You want me to hold you, don't you? And I'm not *watching.* I might be looking but I'm not watching. Besides, you love me, so what difference does it make?"

"That's a *non sequitur,* just about the worst *non sequitur* I ever heard of."

"I don't see why," answered Jim. "Why is it a *non sequitur?*"

"Why? Holy cats, it's obvious why. The fact that I love you makes me more inhibited, not less."

"It shouldn't," said Jim. "True love means no shame at all, or at least that's what they tell me on the golf course."

"I think Jim has a kind of point," said Melody, "but there is such a thing as being . . . ladylike. I have to pee too. Come on, Florence, I'll take you up to the cactus patch."

"Crocodiles will get me," said Florence with a sigh as Jim helped her to her feet. "I guess I'll just never get over my inhibitions."

"I'll never get over mine either," said Melody. "Come on, Florence, we will go in a ladylike manner to the cactus patch."

Jim watched Florence follow Melody up the rope ladder, then stood hands on hips and stared out at the shining silver lagoon. It was, he thought, just as well Florence had been inhibited. Melody was right. Although in theory the thing seemed reasonable, in all truth it was not very ladylike.

Jim watched a dim stream fall toward the Hanging Tree of Life down below. Such matters were, after all, a depressing reminder of mortality; that was why it was ladylike and gentlemanly to perform these functions in private. Who wanted to be reminded of human limitations, of human frailty, of the terrifying brevity of life?

The luminous stream arched out into the moonlight toward the shadows below and Jim imagined he could hear over the sound of the distant surf a sprinkle in the leaves. The act of love itself, in point of fact, could be a depressing reminder of mortality, of frailty, of the shortness of life. A grimmer reminder of transience was difficult to imagine than that of a man with a woman, loins interlocked as seed searches egg. The act foretold the death of the man and the woman. At the same time, the act was an even more powerful image of life, of birth, and of immortality.

Florence came down the rope ladder followed by Melody. "Both of us got stuck with thorns," she said. "But we accomplished our mission."

"Yep," said Melody, "and I think I'm a little drunk. Tell me about that stuff, Jim."

"What stuff?"

"You know, that *bhang* stuff."

"It's a medicine," said Jim. "As I said, it makes a curative tea. That's why they call it tea. It is also called *ganja,* which means 'little helper of Jesus.' That's a literal translation from the Mogali."

"Mogali, I see," said Melody. "What other names is it called?"

"You mean the differing forms of it?"

"Hey, you guys, let's turn out the lantern and go to bed," said Florence, "and get this orgy started."

"Wait a minute, I want to hear this," said Melody. "What are the names of the different forms of it?"

"It has many names," answered Jim, "just as all great things have many names. *Bhang, gunja* or *ganja,* and *churrus* or *charas,* and many more. *Bhang* is the dark larger leaf and capsules upon which a magic resinous exudation occurs. It can be infused with cold water, strained, and imbibed to benefit. *Gunja* is—"

"To hell with it, let's go to bed," said Florence. "It isn't every day I get a chance to participate in an orgy."

"*Gunja,*" said Jim, "is the flowering top of the female plant. It is sometimes added—"

"Come on," said Florence, "let's orgyize."

"—it is sometimes added, I daresay, to fine imported smoking tobaccos on sale all over everywhere. Or possibly delicious little cakes are made from it. Think of it as looking like golden parsley. *Churrus* is the crude resinous substance alone and from it a sweet and delicate jam is made. The Count of Monte Cristo spooned it often, when not engaged in amorous combat with his favorite houri—"

"Yeah, yeah, yeah!" said Florence.

"—an olive-skinned South American aristocrat, I believe, with a rather unusual button-type navel and thin, silken pubic hair. But to conclude—*charas,* anticlimactically enough, is just another name for *churrus,* just as Charlie is only another name for Charles."

"I guess you're teasing me, whatever it is," said Melody, "but oh Lord, don't remind me of Charles. He would *die* if he could see me now, he would just die."

Jim paused, his face cautiously bland and friendly. Had this thing gone far enough? With a little wry smile he said, "I guess Charles *would* be a mite upset."

"If he were a fly on the wall, he'd fall off it," said Melody. "But I guess there's worse to come."

"I wouldn't be surprised," said Florence.

"As for my being in an orgy, Charles couldn't even *dream* of such a thing."

"Neither could my father and brother, not an orgy. That would be beyond them."

"Charles would . . . well, he'd collapse, he'd faint."

"Guess he would," said Jim with a little smile.

The little smile, however, hid a small world. Even as he had joked about *bhang*—and the double meaning of the spoken word seemed to him very appropriate—wrath was rising in Jim Kittering like a prophet of the olden time with a long white beard. Shocking, shameful! How *dare* they? The lustful little creatures—*Melody* saying such things, and *Florence!* They ought to have their mouths scrubbed out with soap and their behinds spanked—yes, their behinds in particular.

Definitely their behinds. They had *liked* it, both of them, going down that rope ladder in the orange light of the lantern with their rear ends in his face. There was no doubt about it. It had titillated them, especially Florence, who had made such a thing about it. She'd even said, "Too bad," when he indicated he hadn't seen her actual asshole. Damned nasty little bitch, almost peeing off that cliff in such a shameless way. And Melody—dear sweet Melody—talking about Charles and an orgy as if to say: "Hey, whoopee! I'm in this too!" But it was Florence who really riled him, Florence who broke his heart—listen to the vulgar way she was talking now, the lewd jokes and all the rest! Florence, a beautiful and sensitive person, or so he'd believed! Listen to her! And look at her, naked and acting like a monkey!

Yes, the little smile hid a small world and now he would really fool them. Calmly, Jim said: "Yes, I guess poor Charles would collapse. It's sad, but most people don't judge by underlying truth, they judge by outer appearance. That's why most people don't control their lives, but have their lives controlled for them."

"I think that's true," said Melody. "They're not afraid of *being* bad, they're afraid of *looking* bad."

"Yes, it's very true," said Florence. "Public opinion makes cowards of us all."

"Not if we understand the process," said Jim mildly.

Melody nodded agreement and Florence replied, "No, not if we understand it."

So far, so good, thought Jim. The time had come for the acid test.

But first he had to straighten them out on *bhang,* they were entitled at least to that; and besides, his own jokes had stuck in his craw.

"But understanding can only come from the mind," said Jim in a casual tone. "That's why I don't think funny flowers are much help. Charming, but not really illuminating. You see, *bhang* is a withdrawal from reality into delusion, into distortion, and as such it must always be a blind alley. The distorted mind filled with illusion cancels out half of what makes a man a human being, his brain. We also foist on ourselves a limited world that way, because the greatest beauty is based not on brainless dreams but on the truth, as you, Florence, well know."

"Yes, I agree with that," said Florence with a smile.

"So do I," said Melody, "though I'm still not sure exactly what *bhang* is. I guess it's some kind of drug."

"Yes, it's a drug," said Jim. "And who needs drugs, except for peritonitis or occasional amusement? Real understanding comes from the unfettered mind driven and motivated by the other half of what makes human beings human. And you know what that is, I think, both of you."

"Love, sweet love," said Florence with a flirtatious smile.

"Yes, indeed," said Melody with another flirtatious smile.

Perfect, thought Jim. Neither had the remotest inkling of the thoughts that had passed through his mind. And that was good, because Florence was shrewd. And so, for that matter, was Melody. But their guard was down. The time had come to put their little asses to the acid test. Jim earnestly wanted to know if they were grasshoppers or human beings. Were women people? Could a man love them without it being a wasting thing like tuberculosis? Did they have any principles at all or any minds? Were they the moral and aesthetic inspiration of mankind, protectors and caretakers of man's genius, pure and perfect and beautiful creatures—or *weren't* they?

"And now we come to the nub of it," said Jim with an amiable smile. "Take this situation in Morgan's Second Treasure Cave, insofar as underlying truth and outer appearances are concerned. You girls originally were all horrified and google-eyed over what you called an 'orgy.' But that's because you were trying to live up to an artificial double standard that really is the cruelest thing to women there can possibly be. The truth is that women, long known as the better half of humanity, are essentially the same as men. They have the same lusts, the same desires, the same weaknesses. They are human—no more, no less. Perhaps they don't as a rule develop certain gifts they don't want or need, but the same can be said of men who also as a rule fail to develop certain gifts they don't want or need. I don't put the beautiful sex in any special category. Human, that's all. Women go to the bathroom and get pimples on their chins just as men do. But the double standard says no, they are better, they are different. Therefore, the problem I had on the beach was to make you both aware of a *single* standard, the human standard, true equality and love between the sexes. I'm glad I got the point across to you, because the *human* thing for us to do in this cave is to go to bed without shame. And on that note, I suggest we have one more small drink and turn out the lantern."

Great, thought Jim. The acid test had been given and they both would flunk it.

"You always surprise me the way you can rattle on when you get going," said Florence. "And I certainly agree with every word you said. A single standard, that's the ticket. I think we ought to get laid now, except I have a feeling Melody and I have lost our nerve."

"I never *had* any," said Melody feebly. "Were we serious?"

Florence put her arm around Melody's shoulders. "Not really. And I guess my gags weren't very funny. I'm afraid I lost my nerve the minute we came in here. I couldn't possibly do such a thing."

"Oh," sighed Melody, "I'm so glad you said that. Florence, I can't do it in front of you. I love you, but I can't. I'm sorry, Jim, I hope you aren't disappointed, but I can't do an orgy."

Jim sat petrified on the mattress, his empty glass in his hand and his mouth half open. He'd been *sure* they would flunk the acid test, but they had *passed* it! Of course that didn't excuse their lewd behavior before, but they'd passed the acid test! Jim closed his mouth and stared at Melody with heartfelt relief and bitter disappointment, then gave an aloof shrug. "Who cares?" he asked.

"Are you angry at me? I'm just . . . *not* modern."

"I'm only *too* modern," said Florence with a wry smile. "Except I can't screw in public and I can't get drunk."

Jim stared down into his empty glass in dismal disappointment. He had been *sincere* about the single standard, really, and Melody and Florence were a couple of little cowards. They'd fooled him before, acting so natural and unashamed, but they were little cowards. In a glum depression despite his tipsiness, Jim sat and listened to Florence work herself into an emotional mood.

"It's ridiculous, but I just can't get drunk. I can't, that's all. Not that I'm not having a good time. I am. But then, I would have a good time with you and Jim no matter what. I really do hate to leave the island, it makes me sadder than I can say, because . . ." Florence sniffled as her voice broke. ". . . because I don't know what I'm going back to, I wonder if I'm going back to my . . . *old ways*." She glanced quickly at Jim—who still was stupefied by their passing the acid test—and he had a bewildered impression she wanted to see if he was listening. "Yes, my . . . *old ways*." But no, her attention was on Melody, to whom she now turned with a tender smile. "And I do love you both so much. You've been so sweet to me, such angels to me—you will always be angels to me, both you and Jim . . . even if we part."

Hmm, thought Jim, that "even if we part" thing had a real Sarah Bernhardt flavor to it and so did Melody's ultrapious flutter of the eyes as she declared, "I'm just . . . *not* modern." Were these grasshoppers putting him on, was feminine genius being focused upon him? Were they doing a job of emotional engineering, each in her way building a parataxic Rube Goldberg machine that would clank and clatter and *work?* Could such a preposterous thing be possible? Had they somehow, in some eerie manner, read his thoughts even though he'd scrupulously kept his face bland and empty of Old Testament devotion?

It was impossible. And besides, they meant it. They really didn't want to have a "nice orgy" and had merely been fiddling with the idea and leading him on—typical grasshopper whimsy, that was what it was; they'd been teasing all the time, teasing him and titillating themselves. But at least they were not a couple of depraved monkeys. Thank God for that. He'd really been afraid for a moment that an agonizing reappraisal of the entire fair sex was on the docket, a painful thing to contemplate. Such a reappraisal would reach all the way from his mother to Linda, two of the purest and most beautiful women in the world—and saintly women, both of them, who had endured his failings in pain.

Jim gave a little weary shrug. "If you don't want to go to bed, I'll sit in the chair tonight. I don't mind. It'll be a little uncomfortable but that's all right. As for our 'nice orgy,' well, sex isn't everything, or at least that's what they tell me at the poker game when I pal around with the boys."

"No, it isn't everything," said Florence. "Other things are more important, about a thousand times more so."

Melody sat forward. "I agree. It's much more important that we love one another. And we do."

"Yes, we do," said Florence, "and it's been the most wonderful thing that's ever happened to me." Another little sniffle came from her. "I do love you both so much. You've been so sweet to me, such angels to me. No one has ever loved me except you and Jim. I've always been so alone, and I've always wanted to love someone and for them to love me even if it was just a little. I'm sure a lot of it's my own fault and I don't want to be self-pitying, but do you know what it is in this world to be a homely and unattractive woman? No one wants what you've got, and how do you tell them you have it, how do you even know that you do since no one wants you or values you? I made up my mind three years ago to try anyhow, because do you know the worst thing about not loving anyone or being loved? The very worst thing? To die all alone, that's the worst thing, and if we live all alone we die all alone."

A little chill of recognition ran through Jim, tipsy as he was and filled with outraged relief at the women for backing out of everything with a schmaltzy scene. Where had he heard that before—live alone and die alone? Live oaks with Spanish moss, Bonaventure Cemetery in Savannah? How could Florence come up with the exact words and phrases that had passed through his mind beneath the back-lighted and shining canopy of silvery moss?

The little chill was swiftly pushed aside by annoyance. This parataxic emotion was typical, he thought, of the feminine grasshopper. Look at them—stark naked, damn near peeing over cliffs, poking their behinds in his face, and now subjecting him to a display of weepy sentimentality. To hell with them! He would sleep in the deck chair all night, or sit in it, anyhow, and stare at the moon while the grasshoppers snored, emotionally replete and satisfied after their Sarah Bernhardt posturing.

"Okay," said Jim with a quiet, manly bitterness. "So the party's off. I will sleep in the deck chair, I don't mind."

Both women ignored him. Melody began to weep as she embraced Florence. "I'd put violets on your grave, darling, and I'd cry for you forever because *you've* been the real angel. Who saved me on the boat and Jim too, but you? You told him to leave me alone and you were right, it would have been wrong then. And you told him to live with me here on the island and you were right about that too. You've been the real angel, Florence—" Melody glanced briefly at Jim, then turned back at once with a little grateful smile to Florence. "—and yet you have a *modern* viewpoint, you're not old-fashioned like me." Again Jim had a bewildered impression a grasshopper wanted to know if he was listening. "And you don't know how you've *broadened* my outlook, Florence, or how you've helped free me from my . . . *old ways*. I'll always love you for that."

Hmp, thought Jim, one grasshopper said she'd *freed* herself of her "old ways" and the other said she feared she would *go back* to her "old ways." Now they both were crying. Jim glowered as Florence tenderly embraced Melody and kissed her on the forehead. Why the glance over at him a moment later as if to see whether or not he'd noticed? A bit of Lesbian throwback here? No, it was sisterly. Besides, it couldn't be Lesbian throwback because Florence had never been a Lesbian in the first place.

"Okay," said Jim bitterly, "now that we've copiously blown our emotional noses, I suppose we'd better call it a party and get some rest. I have to get up early tomorrow morning and clean up that litter on the beach."

"I'm tired too," said Melody. Promptly, she lay down on the pillow on the left side of the bed and shut her eyes, ready for repose.

"So am I," said Florence. With an equal promptness she lay down on the right side of the bed and closed her eyes, as ready for slumberland as Melody.

Jim sat at the foot of the mattress and stared at their naked bodies in outrage. First he looked at Melody, with her full breasts uplifted in this recumbent position, her womanly belly handsome with its deep dimpled navel, and the girlish pubic V now modestly half concealed by closed thighs. Then he looked at Florence, with her elegant and pretty little breasts also uplifted, her flat and youthful stomach with the cute button navel, and the even more girlish pubic V also modestly half concealed by closed thighs. Damnable creatures, to hell with them!

"All right," said Jim in a martyred tone, "I will go and sit in the deck chair. Good night."

As Jim got to his feet, Melody said sleepily, "You don't have to sit in the chair."

"No, you can sleep here," said Florence with a yawn.

"Thanks," said Jim icily. "But I don't want to listen to you complain tomorrow morning you couldn't sleep because it was so crowded."

Melody turned on her side with her back to Florence. "If you get tired of sitting in the chair, you can sleep here, it won't bother me. That rum has made me very sleepy."

"Me too," said Florence with another yawn.

Damnable grasshoppers, thought Jim. They were practically going to sleep already. "I am *not* sleepy," he said. "If the lantern won't bother you, I will sit here and read something."

"It won't bother me," said Melody in a drowsy voice.

"Me either," murmured Florence as she too turned on her side with her back to Melody.

Jim found a paperbound Perry Mason mystery on the bench ledge, picked up the lantern, and went to the deck chair and sat down in it, then cursed, got up, fetched his reading glasses from the ledge, returned to the chair, opened the book, and for five minutes tried to read it. He could not get beyond the first paragraph. It was not comfortable in the chair at all and he felt woozy from the rum.

Jim took off his glasses with a weary sigh and glanced down at the mattress. The women had their backs toward each other and there was a thirty-inch space between them. Maybe if he slept for an hour or so it would clear his head and he could concentrate on Perry Mason.

"Well," he said, "I'll take a nap for a few minutes if it won't bother you, then I'll read."

Jim did not blow out the lantern because he wanted to awaken after a while. It was the only way, really, to punish them; he had to suffer at least a good part of the night in that chair. The nerve they had to pass the acid test, damnable grasshoppers!

"*Excuse* me," Jim said as he crawled forward on the mattress into the space between Melody and Florence. Both women stirred sleepily but did not answer. Jim lay back on the middle pillow, stared for a moment at the ceiling, then shut his eyes.

Ten minutes later, as he was about to drop off, Florence shifted in her sleep and Jim felt her soft and now-much-more-feminine behind touch his hip. A sleepy sigh came from her; she was obviously unaware of it. A moment later Melody stirred on her pillow and lifted an arm over her head, gave a little half groan in her sleep, half turned on her stomach, and her breast touched his arm. A sense of delicious wickedness returned to Jim Kittering full blast. *They were not asleep.* The party wasn't over yet! Jim put his right hand on Florence's hip. She didn't stir and his heart began to pound. He put his left hand on Melody's side. She didn't stir either and his heart pounded harder. No, the party wasn't over, it was finally getting started. Who should he kiss first? Jim rolled slowly on his side, put his lips to Florence's ear, and whispered: "Florence?"

"Mm?"

Lips at her ear, Jim whispered: "Turn here."

With a sleepy sigh, Florence turned her head toward him. Jim put his left arm around her waist and his right hand on her breast and kissed her for a long, long time, half rolling upon her in the process. Arms around his neck, Florence returned the kiss and twice made a slight moaning sound of relief and pleasure. Her response to him was more passionate than on the beach. As he kissed Florence, Jim reached behind him and found Melody's hand and squeezed it. Her fingers returned the pressure. Jim lifted his head from Florence and turned on his side toward Melody. Her glasses were off and she was staring at him in the yellow-orange light of the kerosene lantern with frightened nearsighted eyes.

"Oh, God," said Melody in a tiny voice, "Charles, I hope you're not looking, this is terrible."

"Just kiss me," said Jim. "Nothing is going to happen, we're all too inhibited, me as well as you. I almost slept in the chair."

"Maybe we ought to have another drink," said Melody.

"No, just kiss me."

Jim kissed Melody, and she too returned his kiss with greater passion than on the beach. He then kissed Florence again, then Melody again, then Florence, and then he asked: "Whose night is it, anyhow?"

"It's mine," said Florence. "But Melody missed her night last night. And besides, I . . . I'm still a little nervous."

"So am I," said Melody feebly. "Even with the rum, I'm a little nervous."

"Do you want to?" asked Jim.

"Yes," whispered Melody. "Yes . . . I want to."

"I do too," said Florence. "But I'm nervous . . . do you mind being first, Melody?"

Melody moistened her lips and swallowed. "No, I suppose not."

"Do you want the lantern out?" asked Jim.

"Oh . . . I don't care."

Although he was aroused by the passionate kisses, Jim felt a bit foolish and self-conscious. Did this thing have to happen? Was it really necessary? The Old Testament prophet had dropped his staff with a whoop and hoisted up his robe with a gleeful enthusiasm, but now felt just a bit silly. And yet it was impossible for him to say: "Look, girls, I apologize for all my unkind thoughts, let's forget this and go to sleep, huh?"

"Shall we?" asked Jim.

"Oh-h-h . . . all right," sighed Melody.

With a trembly imprecision, Jim put his hands on Melody's shoulders, rolled cautiously over on her and propped on his elbows. As he did so, Melody cooperatively opened her legs but gave a little weak moan of distress. Her eyes were squinted half shut.

"Are you sure you don't want the lantern out?" asked Jim.

"Oh-h-h, I don't care, but . . . Florence?"

"I won't look," said Florence as she turned on her side.

"Just for a minute," said Melody in a half whisper. "I've never done this before."

Jim leaned his cheek against Melody's shoulder, which was warm and sweaty. He closed his eyes for a moment. Even though Melody had had her usual bath that day and had just been swimming in the lagoon, he could smell the musky perfume of her armpit, which she did not shave. Melody had a strong and to him extremely agreeable body odor, stronger than Florence's, especially in the magic area between her thighs. It had at times a near-intoxicating effect on him.

Jim moved his cheek on the warm, sweaty shoulder, his eyes still shut. He couldn't just keep lying there, but Melody's very feminine and very human body odor *was* agreeable to him and to his surprise he also found her unshaved armpits very sexy. He liked her during lovemaking to lock her hands behind her head; the sight of her full breasts and the curly patches of dark hair seemed to him very, very sexy. Fastidious as she was about her person, it was an odd quirk that she wouldn't shave her armpits. This made her itch, she said. Florence, on the other hand, shaved her armpits religiously.

Something *had* to be done, they'd think he was going to sleep. Jim opened his eyes. He could see the curve of Florence's back and the vertebrae of her spine in the orange lantern light. Buckwheat freckles were all across Florence's shoulders. So Florence was "a little nervous." And Melody was "a little nervous." Well, even numbed by John Barleycorn and aroused by repeated passionate kisses, he too was "a little nervous." But the thing had to be done. There was no doubt of that, it had to be done. They would all hate themselves in the morning, but it had to be done, it absolutely had to be done.

"Oh-h!" cried Melody with a little gasp of shock. "Oh, God . . . ."

"Umm," said Florence with a little echo of shock, her back to them and her spine curved in a near-fetal position.

Fifteen minutes later, Jim had about decided Melody would never respond to him and the entire thing was hopeless when he noticed that she seemed to be beginning to breathe a little faster. Her arms, which had been half limp on his back, were around him tighter now and the movements of her body seemed more responsive. Yes, she was breathing a bit faster and also deeper. Propped on his elbows and anchored by his hands on her shoulders, Jim continued a presumable act of love that had not seemed to be getting anywhere, although as a rule her response to him was immediate and powerful.

Jim himself at first had been numbed by rum and self-consciousness and had felt almost nothing, but as time went by the sheer physical sensation of the thing could not be denied. Nerve endings seemed to awaken whether he would have it so or not. His own breathing had changed too, and for brief moments he even forgot Florence, who still lay there in a fetal position with her back to them. No, the sheer physical sensation could not be denied. Jim adjusted his elbows on the mattress and moved his hands from Melody's shoulders to her breasts. The feeling of her full breasts in his hands was always pleasant to him and it sometimes excited her very much for him to hold her in this way while making love to her. She liked him to squeeze her breasts almost hard enough to hurt her and Jim did this now as he continued slowly to enter and re-enter her body. An inhalation of pain came from her and he squeezed her breasts a second time even harder. "Hurts," she whispered. Jim squeezed her breasts a third time harder yet and thrust more deeply into her body.

Jim had forgotten Florence completely. The body beneath him was unmistakably responding now, meeting his thrusts with purpose and strength. Melody was awakening. Maybe it wasn't hopeless. Maybe not, thought Jim, as she pulled his head down toward her lips and whispered, "Please kiss me." Jim did, and now beyond doubt she was breathing harder. She lowered her hands to the small of his back and began a slow, grinding, sidewise motion of her pelvis that in the early stages of love-making always seemed to excite her. As he continued to kiss her and as she continued the rhythmic canting of her pelvis, Jim forgot not only Florence but Morgan's Second Treasure Cave as well. He could think of nothing but the sensation of Melody's body and her tongue, until she suddenly pulled her mouth from him, took a deep breath, exhaled heavily, and turned her head to the side. "Wait a second," she said, her voice hoarse and slightly breathless.

"What's the matter?" asked Jim.

"Nothing, I'm all right now. I just never did this before. Florence, do you want to watch? I can show you how I do it, I think."

Florence, who had remained lying on her side in motionless silence with her back to them, slowly looked around. "Will it bother you?" she asked.

"No, I don't mind," said Melody. "I'm just not used to this. But I'm all right now. You can watch. I think I can do it in a little while."

Florence propped on her elbow, a keen interest on her face. "If you're sure you don't mind."

"No, I don't. But I can't talk and do it, so you just watch."

"Okay," said Florence.

"I'll just say, it's like . . . *this*," said Melody as she lowered and lifted her pelvis with a slight forward revolving motion. "It's this little particular way, like this. Do you see?"

"Well . . . yes," said Florence doubtfully.

"Another thing," said Melody, "at the start it helps to do it a little like this. Jim, do it a little so she can see." Florence watched with an absorbed interest as Melody responded to Jim with half a dozen slow, sidewise, twisting motions of her pelvis. "See? Like *this*, it helps at the beginning, or at least it does me. Of course there're lots of ways and you'll learn them. I like this, though. See? On the side, kind of, like in Hawaii."

"Mmm, yes," said Florence. "Hawaii."

It was, thought Jim, beyond all doubt the most insane and absurd conversation he had ever heard anywhere at any time on any subject. "But later—keep on, Jim, don't stop. Now . . . later, when you begin to feel really excited, like *this* . . ." Again Melody slowly lowered and lifted her pelvis in a straight manner but with a slight forward revolving motion. "See? Slow at first, then faster and harder till you do it. But never do it *too* fast, that's a mistake. It's more beautiful slow and you'll do it better. Did you see what I did?"

"Yes, I think so," said Florence.

"It's that little particular way, like I did it. Now I can't talk. Jim, please kiss me."

As Jim kissed her and began to make love to her while Florence watched in absorbed fascination, he found that his powers of concentration were a wee mite defective. He had a distracting impulse to laugh in the midst of the kiss. However, preposterous and even outrageous as Melody's "lesson" was—Jim wondered what *Charles* would make of it—it had certainly been a simple, clear, honest demonstration any young wife could understand. Perhaps he and Melody should teach a course at Tom Armour University, Elementary Fucking I; such a thing would be a great boon to young Jesus-seeking, self-conscious coeds who might not know how to move their behinds *under* properly.

Melody, in any event, had broken her own barrier of self-consciousness; indeed, she had shattered it in a million bits. And now they were making love as they always did, with passionate kisses and caresses. Jim's concentration returned. Florence's presence, far from being a detraction, seemed to add an erotic and emotional dimension. In a very few minutes he and Melody became tremendously aroused and he was not surprised when she put her lips to his ear and whispered: "Can you?" It was a convention they had established; he was not expected to reply. Melody wound her arms like iron around his back and Jim moved his hands down to her buttocks, which she also liked him to squeeze almost hard enough to hurt her, especially at this moment. He pulled her against him as he began to penetrate her with thrusts deep enough to reach her cervix and she responded with the slow but very powerful under-upward motion she had demonstrated with such absolute candor to Florence. Now she was *really* showing her. Jim touched her cervix once, and again, and again, then squeezed her buttocks with nearly all his strength in fulfillment of another convention they had established between them.

"Oh!" cried Melody. "*Oh! Ohhh-hh!* Oh, Jim . . . Jim . . ."

Limp on Melody's shoulder, totally out of breath, heart pounding, Jim opened his eyes and saw Florence peering with a keen interest at him, half smiling and her eyebrows lifted. "Yoicks," she said. "Wow!"

"Ohhhh-hh," groaned Melody, "wonderful . . . but I'm half dead."

"I'm the one who's half dead," said Jim. "What you women do to us men is pathetic."

"Most fascinating thing I ever witnessed," said Florence. "You looked kind of like horses."

"Ohh-hh," sighed Melody, who was breathing deeply in an effort to catch her breath. "Ohh-hh, God, that was sexy."

"It sure as hell was," said Jim, with another deep breath as he too tried to get some oxygen into his lungs. "We'll have to hire you as a kind of baby-sitter, Florence, to watch us do it."

"I'll take the job," said Florence. "Sexiest thing I ever saw, even if you did look like horses. Or at least you did, Jim. Melody looked kind of like a walrus."

Melody laughed, very amused. "Is *that* what I looked like, a walrus? Not very romantic."

"I guess fucking *isn't* very *romantic*, exactly," said Florence. "But it sure as hell is sexy."

"At first I thought I couldn't at all," said Melody. "But I sure did do it quick once I got started. I got very excited after I showed you how to do it. Did you learn anything?"

Florence, who was sitting Yoga style on the mattress, glanced down at herself and put her finger between her thighs. "I don't know, but I'm sopping wet from watching you, I can tell you that."

"It's very easy, if you just do it like I said." Jim tried to get up and Melody grabbed him by the behind. "No, wait a minute, it hurts if you get up so soon. Just stay there a little while, then you can do it to Florence."

"Holy cats," said Jim, "you have to give me a minute to catch my breath and recover."

"Don't try and get out of it," said Florence. "You've got to do it to me after getting me all stirred up like this. I got so excited watching you I almost did it myself just sitting here."

"Maybe you won't have any trouble this time," said Melody.

However, when the time came half an hour later after another drink of rum and grapefruit juice, Florence had trouble and plenty of it. The barrier of self-consciousness might have been broken for Jim and Melody but it had not been broken for her. At first she said she did not mind Melody's presence or the lantern being on, but when the moment of raw reality came and Jim put his hands on her freckled shoulders and got on top of her she gave a little trembly moan of fright and asked Melody to look the other way. Melody did. "I'm all right now," said Florence in a quavery voice, but when Jim tried to start to make love to her she gave a gasp of shock and another moan and asked him for God's sake to turn the lantern off.

"Turn the damned thing off," she said. "I don't want the light."

"Okay," said Jim. "Relax, I'll blow it out."

"I'll sit in the deck chair," said Melody. "Forget that I'm here."

"I . . . I'm sorry," said Florence feebly. "I can't help it, I . . . I just feel a little nervous. I never did this before either."

Jim blew out the lantern and Melody sat in the deck chair and looked out at the lagoon in the moonlight. "Now I can't see you and I'm not watching or paying any attention," said Melody. "Just forget that I'm here and don't worry."

"All right," said Florence in a pitiful little voice. It was, in a way, ironic, thought Jim. The sophisticated New York artist was a hundred times more frightened and inhibited than the missionary's naive wife had been. But of course Florence was not sophisticated in this area at all. He felt as if he were raping an innocent child, although the cruelest thing he could have done to her at that moment would have been to refuse to try to make love to her.

Jim returned to the mattress and with gingerly care got aboard Florence and with even more gingerly care entered her body as she shuddered, gasped, and moaned with sheer nervousness. And then began an ordeal that probably lasted no longer than forty minutes but that seemed to Jim to last forty hours. After the passionate lovemaking with Melody, to say nothing of the deadening rum he had drunk, Jim for a long time could not get anywhere himself at all, although he finally began to feel it might perhaps be possible for him.

That is, possible if the event could somehow be terminated and she would stop tormenting him. Florence had gradually become extremely aroused but to no avail. She simply could not do it. Jim tried everything he could think of. He kissed her hither, thither, and yon, he caressed her hither, thither, and yon, he smoothed her fevered brow, he told her he loved her, he grabbed her by the behind, he seized her under the legs, he turned her on one side and then on the other, he made love to her tenderly, he made love to her fiercely—nothing worked.

It was a horrible ordeal. Jim became covered with sweat, developed a painful stitch in his side, and began to worry that he would fail her. The difficulty was, he had inevitably become affected by the sheer power of such prolonged physical sensation and was afraid he might lose control. In a struggle to control himself, he deliberately thought of unsexy things, such as doormats, road scrapers, and other such things. But it was becoming more and more difficult to shut out the raw power of the physical sensations to which he was being subjected.

Florence's suffering, however, was greater than his own. She, too, was covered with perspiration and seemed to be having trouble breathing. After her inhibited beginning, she had become extremely and even violently aroused, so much so Jim wondered how she could *not* do it. On three successive occasions she whispered in his ear such things as: "Don't give up . . . I think I will now." Or: "I'm going to soon . . . don't stop." But every time, she would give a frantic sigh and quit. They would lie there in exhausted discouragement, then he would start all over with her and the same thing would happen again. Finally, after about forty minutes, Florence cried:

"Oh, Melody, *help* me! This is driving me crazy!"

"What do you want me to do?" asked Melody, who was half visible in the deck chair in the moonlight that came through the picture window.

"I don't know, but I can't stand this! Light the lantern and tell me how to do it or I'll go out of my mind."

Melody struck a match and lighted the lantern, then sat beside them on the mattress. Jim turned sweatily to look at her and almost smiled despite his misery and weariness—she had an expression on her face that had to be her "nurse" expression; he had an instant mental picture of her in a white nurse's uniform shaking a thermometer and solemnly reaching to take Florence's pulse.

"How do I do it?" asked Florence hoarsely. Jim was in her arms, but in her anxiety she had propped on her elbows and was strained up in a half-sitting position.

"Lie back on the pillow," said Melody.

Florence lay back on the pillow with a miserable sigh. "How do I do it?" she asked.

In a gentle "nurse" tone, Melody asked: "Are you excited now?"

"Oh, God, yes! Horribly!"

"Raise your knees a little bit. Put your feet so you can move better, you can't move like that."

"You mean like this?"

"Yes." Melody glanced toward Jim, who had propped on his hands and turned his head to look at her. "All right, Jim."

"All right?"

"Go ahead, make love to her. Slowly." Jim put his weight on his elbows and followed instructions. "Now . . . Florence . . . I think, yes. You move all right, but do it a little bit more under. No . . . a little bit more *under*." Jim could not resist glancing around as Melody reached her hand under the small of Florence's back and pushed firmly at her.

"She means tilt your pelvis," said Jim, who had often attempted without much luck to explain to Florence the role of the clitoris. She seemed to think the vagina was the proper seat of sensation and that "the little devil," as she called it, was useful only for self-abuse. "Tilt your pelvis forward and your hips under."

"You be quiet, you make her self-conscious," said Melody. "I can tell her, you just make love to her and be quiet."

"Excuse me," said Jim.

"Don't pay any attention to anything he said," said Melody. "I'll tell you how to do it. Now, don't move your *hips* under, move your *behind* under and kind of go *forward*, then it's exciting. Come on, Jim."

"What?"

"Come *on*."

"Oh."

"Now," said Melody, ". . . *und*er and forward, *und*er and forward . . ."

"Am I doing it right?" asked Florence hoarsely.

"I don't know. Raise up on your hands, Jim, so I can see if she's doing it right."

Jim had a temptation to laugh. This was some missionary work Melody was doing. He said, "Okay," then put his hands down flat on either side of Florence's waist and raised his chest and stomach above her body. It was worth trying, anyhow. God knows he'd never been able to get the idea across to Florence, maybe Melody could do it.

"All right, Jim. Now, that's . . . no, no, that's not right, Florence.

Here." To Jim's surprise and perhaps to Florence's surprise too, although she showed no signs of it, Melody calmly reached her hand between them and placed four fingers upon Florence, then moved her hand down until he could feel the edge of her fingers himself. "Excuse me for touching you but it's right *here,* it's not inside. Later it's inside too, but it's right here mostly. Now roll under. *See?* See how that makes my fingers press against him?"

"Yes," said Florence in a hoarse whisper, "yes, I do."

"All right; now, when he does it, you move in that little particular way, and you'll do it. You'll have to. It'll make you do it." Melody withdrew her hand and sat back. "But don't forget emotional relaxation."

"No," whispered Florence, "I won't."

"You do love him. Think of that, and you'll do it."

"All right, I'll think of it."

"Now you know how. You can do it, Florence, if you think positively. You go ahead, I'll just lie here."

Six or seven minutes later, Florence pulled Jim's head down against her right cheek on the other side from Melody and put her lips to his ear. He thought she was again going to say she would do it soon and for him not to stop, but instead she whispered, "I do love you." A moment later she whispered, "I love you even if you leave me." Soon after this, Florence began to breathe very heavily and her arms tightened around his neck. Still, she did not say she was "about to do it" but whispered instead, "Love . . . darling!" Jim felt at this moment a magic change in her body as he was clasped by a velvetlike softness. Her vagina had become a perfect and accepting sheath and he could now feel the tip of her womb as he had felt Melody's. As the velvet sheath clasped and unclasped with a perfect firmness that was nevertheless soft and accepting and as he heard a tiny choked cry, Jim knew Florence at last was "doing it." A moment later she gave a louder cry and whispered, "Oh, darling! Love . . . love . . . love . . . love."

On the second whispered "love," Jim felt himself begin to share with another person—whose acquaintance he had first made while reading a book about a lonely girl on Cape Cod—the ultimate ecstasy and loss of self that he had known but had never before understood. It could hardly be called a sexual experience, although it would be difficult to call it anything else. The world disappeared, sex and sexiness disappeared, shame and fear disappeared; the only reality was his love for the woman in his arms, the woman who had walked into his office on a clear September day. Shaken to the depths by an emotion he could not comprehend, Jim lay in a mindless daze on Florence's shoulder and from far away heard her weeping, felt her tears wet on his face.

"Oh, Jim," she said in a whisper he could just barely hear, "if I die now, I don't care."

Unfortunately, it was an experience for which Jim Kittering was not quite prepared. In a real fright, he lay with pounding heart in Florence's arms, head on her freckled shoulder. A panic ran through him as he thought, "How can this be and what am I to do? What will happen when we get back to New York?" It couldn't be right. The purpose and aim of everything was in jeopardy. Abruptly, Jim propped on his elbows and stared in fear at Florence's sweaty, freckled face as she smiled and returned his gaze with tears of love.

"Well," said Jim in a trembling voice, "I hope that solves your problem, Florence."

Clumsily, Jim pushed himself away from her, rolled to the side, and sat on the mattress. There had to be and there was a mistake somewhere. His emotions had carried him away because something in Florence broke his heart; it was the pity he felt for her, a kind of overcompensation, plus the fact that he'd always liked her. Jim was startled to hear a sniffle and a distressed sigh from Melody. What was the matter with *her?* In annoyance, Jim glanced up at her and saw that she was staring at him with tearful reproach.

"You shouldn't push her away," said Melody softly. "You shouldn't when it wasn't like that at all."

In exasperation Jim replied: "Don't tell me what to do or what happened, Melody, because you don't know."

"Yes, I do know," said Melody with another sniffle. "I knew all along what would happen if she really gave herself to you. Maybe you loved me more on the boat and when we were first on the island, but I think you loved her more even then."

"He . . . he loves you too, Melody!" cried Florence, who was still weeping. "Don't say that, he does!"

"I'm not jealous," said Melody with a sad little smile, "or at least not much. Except . . . well, it's going to be even harder for you and Jim than for me. I don't know how I can do it myself, I really don't, but I hope when the time comes we all have the courage."

"The courage for what?" asked Jim hoarsely.

Melody lowered her eyes and answered: "The courage to say good-bye."

Florence rubbed tears from her eyes with the back of her hand and smiled. "I think maybe we will," she said. "Somehow facing it makes it bearable."

"I haven't really faced it," said Melody with a shrug.

"I probably haven't either, completely," said Florence.

Jim looked down at the trembling hands in his lap and shook his head as if to clear it. The situation in the cave had become intolerable. "Let's have another drink," he said.

"A drink?" asked Florence.

Jim looked up at her. "Yes, a goddamned drink," he said. "We don't seem to be able to have anything but square experiences on this island. Sweet little weddings, sugar-cake seductions, and nice orgies. Let's have another drink and spike it with funny flowers. There's something lacking here. What we need in Morgan's Second Treasure Cave is bonafide flower power."

The remainder of the night was a dim dream broken by snatches of ghastly recollection on the following day. Whatever the meaning of it all, the party that followed the "nice orgy" seemed to have more in common with a Goblin giggle than with flower power.

TWENTY-FOUR

The Kitty Hawk Flats

The C.I.A. taxi arrived nine days later and with stunning abruptness returned Jim, Melody, and Florence to the outer world after four months plus love and games. Fortunately, by the time the taxi came across the lagoon and up on the beach with its white-haired agent at the wheel, they had recovered from both the nice orgy and the not-so-nice orgy that followed.

But it had been truly grim on the morning after. Jim had felt like throwing himself out of the picture window down into the lagoon. Melody and Florence, to hear them tell it, had felt worse. Each said she wanted to die, she didn't want to live any more with such memories, that neither life nor love could ever be the same again.

With the help of rum and funny flowers and with an extra assist from sadness and fear, Jim, Melody, and Florence finally had managed to have an experience on the island that was not square, although their reaction to it was square indeed. And yet, horrible as it was, they all came to feel in time that the not-so-nice orgy had served a peaceful purpose.

When Jim awakened on the following morning, he thought for a brief instant he was at the far end of a local station of the I.R.T. on Manhattan Island. A strange scent was in the cave and both Melody and Florence were gone. He awakened by degrees and at first it was not too horrible, although he felt an overwhelming pain somewhere. But he'd done a very clever thing—what was it? Some masterly touch . . . oh, yes, the disposition of the money, his inspiration to lower Morgan's Treasure on a string down into Morgan's Asshole and swing it into the cecum twist.

It really was a great little touch, although Melody, poor darling, would consider him gross to have thought of it and so would Florence, who was by no means as nervy as her language sometimes seemed to indicate. Florence really was the worse of the two, she was even more shy and timid about an honest thing like an asshole than Melody, who despite her veneer of priggishness could give a squeaky little poot and giggle in amusement, whereas if Florence committed the same indiscretion she died quietly and couldn't say a word. Such little boo-boos inevitably had occurred several times with both of them; even, alas, during tender moments of love-making. "Saddle Music," Jim called it; he had always thought that would make a great title for a bawdy, realistic western. Melody, God knows, was modest enough, but at least she could giggle and admit she'd done it, whereas Florence froze with shame and could not speak. Would it help her to realize that the most beautiful women who ever lived had done the exact same thing—Helen of Troy, Cleopatra, and all the rest—that the greatest conquerors, statesmen, or divines all had committed this crime, including Sir Henry Morgan himself?

"WHAA-POOMPHPHH!"—thus spoke Sir Henry. Jim remembered it well and with a keen gratification. "WHAA-POOMPHPHH!" the Asshole had said, blowing a mighty puff of vapor and twigs and bits of palm frond fifty feet in the air. The waves were big that afternoon and the thing was farting powerfully.

Melody and Florence would both be mildly distressed by this expression of "the little boy" in him. But where *were* they, Jim groggily wondered, as he briefly opened his eyes and found himself alone on the mattress in Morgan's Second Treasure Cave. And what was that peculiar subway smell of sweat, urine, vomit, and musk that hung so heavy in the air?

"WHUU-BLOOMPHPHH!" said the Asshole, with a majestic natural candor. "WHUU-BOOMOOMPHPHH!"

Well, it had been a shrewd and practical idea with a certain logic to it. Two days before, when he saw no curious heads peeping from the entrance of Morgan's First Treasure Cave, Jim had circled the northeastern flank of the Jungfrau, cut southwest through the Elysian Field, and headed due south along the western shore toward the rock formation known as Morgan's Asshole. He'd reached the Asshole without event and pulled a twenty-foot length of strong cord from his pocket, tied the cord to the tin box full of money, and lowered the box into the Asshole. A long time before, he'd noticed about fifteen feet down a recession, a sort of cecum twist in the colon, so to speak.

"WHAA-POOMPHPHH!" Morgan's bowels were in an uproar. However, the box was too heavy to be blown out; it had landed with a clank out of sight in the pocket of rock and the next blast had obligingly blown the cord in after it. The C.I.A. would never find that box without his aid and it was delightful to think of the agent who would have to climb down in the Asshole and get farted on repeatedly while salvaging that money. And it would work, unless the C.I.A. agent was a psychopathic idiot, in which case nothing would work. Jim had carefully rehearsed the speech he would make:

"Now listen. What*ever* you are up to here, I want myself and these women taken off this island *now*. The guns are on the bottom of the sea and I've hidden the money where you'll never find it. The women do *not* know where it is. Only *I* know. Be sensible. Take us at once to the American Consulate in Nicaragua or Honduras and I'll tell you precisely where to find the money."

Yes, there had been a certain logic in it. The perfect thing to do with Morgan's Treasure was to stick it up Morgan's Ass.

Jim again opened his eyes and became aware of a shattering headache superimposed upon or perhaps caused by the strange, horrible smell. It seemed to be everywhere—in the air, on the sheets and pillows, all over the cave, a heavy and musky odor with the stink of vomit thrown in for good measure. He could not recall what had happened or why, he could not even remember what he was doing in this tiny cave. He had a terrific throbbing headache, was gripped by severe nausea, and had a floating anxiety to end floating anxiety. What dreadful thing had happened?

Jim's eyes quivered shut as he remembered first the "nice orgy." He groaned softly with a kind of whimper as the memory came to him of how he'd gotten on top of Melody and made love to her while Florence watched. He groaned again a bit more loudly as the memory came of getting on top of Florence and making love to her while Melody watched and even helped Florence "do it"—that was bad enough, the "nice orgy" was sufficiently ghastly in its own right to make him want to collapse, but he had an awful suspicion that worse, much worse, had followed.

Weakly he sat up on the mattress and put down shaking hands to brace himself, then flinched as his left palm encountered something clammy. He slowly turned his head and looked down to see what it was. It was a wide splash of half-digested wild roast pig. Dimly he recalled that Melody had gotten sick toward the end of the evening soon after the Lesbian episode—*Lesbian* episode? Yes, there had been such an episode, if he wasn't dreaming. Jim leaned to the side and vomited himself, but it was more retching than vomiting since there was nothing in his stomach.

"Ohhh-hh, God," groaned Jim. The floating anxiety had sunk like lead to the bottom of his soul. His memory of the not-so-nice orgy was mostly blotted out by amnesia, but snatches came back to him and they were horrendous.

One thing was clear: they had all gotten absolutely stinko drunk. They'd been on the verge of drunkenness when the "nice orgy" ended and those last huge drinks had smashed them totally. And no wonder. Considering that the rum was double strength, they'd each had the equivalent of two-thirds of a quart. And hadn't he also infused the *bhang* in water and added the "sweet liquor" to their drinks? Probably. In fact, definitely. It hadn't seemed to have much effect; he could remember thinking maybe the *bhang* wasn't *bhang* after all. But the plant was *Cannabis sativa* and it had to be *bhang*, and to judge from events, it had had an effect, all right.

The party had turned into an unmitigated disaster. Hadn't there been "an incredible flying machine" at one point? He seemed to remember laughing with great amusement as he instructed Melody and

Florence on "the principles of flight" and on what was necessary to cause "an incredible flying machine" to lumber down "the Kitty Hawk flats" and take off. Had that happened or had he merely dreamed it at some point during the night?

"Let it be a dream," whispered Jim aloud. "Let it be a nightmare or I'll jump out of the picture window!"

It hadn't happened. No, no. It was best not to think of it, much the best not to think of it. But *had* it happened? Was it a real memory of Florence's behind—or was it Melody's? or was it *both* their behinds on different occasions?—looming in the air above his face or was this just a Goblin dream?

"OHHHHH-HHH-HH!" groaned Jim. The thing was too horrible to endure and he simply could not think about it in his present condition. But *how* could it have happened, how could such horrors have occurred? Even stinko drunk, how could he behave like that, and how could Melody and Florence behave like that? Why, unless he was dreaming there *had* been Lesbian stuff between them late in the evening, and not schoolgirl fiddling around, either. It had happened late and they were both very, very drunk, especially Melody. He could remember her laughing and saying why not, she'd done everything else so why not that too. Then afterward she'd been sick and had passed out. Florence also had been sick and had passed out. He must have become unconscious soon after that himself and perhaps he'd been sick too—there was nothing on his stomach this morning and he seemed to remember thinking the *bhang* was impure and had made them all throw up.

It was an unqualified catastrophe. They'd gotten absolutely stinking drunk and lost every inhibition there was to lose, and then some. But even so, it was difficult to understand how such a thing could have happened. The "nice orgy" now seemed in comparison as mild and innocent as a Sunday-school picnic.

And in all truth, their behavior earlier in the evening had not really been so bad. Of course it was pretty disgraceful, but there was nothing *Goblinish* in the women's attitude or his own either. He had merely made love to them in a normal manner. Why had they kept on drinking? If they'd just gone on to sleep then, they might feel a little horrible but it wouldn't be like this. Why had they kept on? Jim groaned again, hands over his eyes. It was his *own* damned fault. The women at first hadn't wanted to drink any more and he'd had to coax them into it.

Where were they, anyhow? Jim clambered painfully to his feet and looked around for clothes. He'd better go find Melody and Florence at once. They were probably down by the ocean contemplating suicide or perhaps they had done away with themselves already.

As he dressed and then climbed slowly up the rope ladder into the bright sunshine, Jim again asked himself how such a thing could have happened. Of course, almost any human being if utterly drunk and full of drugs might be capable of such behavior.

But for that very reason the rum and the *Cannabis sativa* were neither an excuse nor an explanation. Hadn't he *known* high-powered rum would be emotional gasoline sprinkled in that cave? Hadn't he known it would lead to just such a scene and hadn't the women known this too? And if so, what earthly purpose could they all have had in bringing upon themselves such an experience? Jim shook his head as he slowly picked his way through the cactus patch and down the Matterhorn. It made no sense whatever, but he must have known and Melody and Florence must have known what strong rum would do to them in Morgan's Second Treasure Cave. It had not been all that difficult to coax the women into having more drinks and they had soon gotten into the party spirit. In fact, they'd been in a weaving mood all along. Not when the cave was first mentioned, they'd been negative then, but something had changed their minds; by the time they sat down to eat that wild roast pig the orgy was on. What had possessed them?

Jim found Florence sitting with Rufus on the promontory of Hell's Half Acre, an arm around the dog's neck as she stared moodily out at sea. He had expected to find her there. She didn't look around when he walked up but continued to gaze out at the blue sea.

"Hi, Florence."

"Hi, Jim."

"Well . . . oh, Florence, my sweet darling, my sweet angel, my . . . the . . . the . . ." Groping for words, Jim reached out and put a hand on Florence's shoulder. ". . . the woman I really love even . . . my . . . my . . . oh, God . . . how do you *feel* this morning?"

"My ass is sore as hell," said Florence.

"Mmm," said Jim, "guess it wasn't a dream."

"Guess not," said Florence.

"Ohhh-hh," groaned Jim. "I . . . I'm sorry, honey. I . . . I hope I didn't hurt you."

"I don't expect there's any permanent damage. How do you feel yourself this morning?"

"Like green and blue death. I never had such a hangover in my life. What can I say, honey? I feel awful. It was my fault for going on with the drinking, to say nothing of that goddamn *bhang*."

"We all did it. Melody too." Florence shifted uncomfortably on the rocks. "I wish she hadn't been so inventive."

"Melody was inventive?"

"Sure, that port-in-a-storm thing was *her* bright idea."

"Port-in-a-storm?"

"Don't you remember the any-port-in-a-storm thing? She also called it devil-take-the-hindmost. Said she'd always wanted to do that, but Charles wouldn't. *Christ*, am I sore. I hate to think what kind of condition *she's* in this morning."

"Umm-mm," groaned Jim. "I . . . I'm sorry."

Florence stared moodily out at sea. "I'm sorry too. It's too bad it had to end like this, but I guess it had to. I think what we did is kind of destroy ourselves. I mean, destroy our feelings for one another because we know it's going to end soon."

"Maybe in a way," said Jim doubtfully. "I guess after all of that you don't feel the same toward me."

Florence glanced up at him. "I don't feel any differently toward *you*, but I'm sure you can't feel the same toward *me* ever again."

"That's not true."

"Jim, don't you remember? Don't you remember the incredible flying machine?"

"Yeah," said Jim uncomfortably, "I remember it, more or less."

"I don't think you do remember. Let me refresh you. Without even going into all of the things Melody and I were doing in terms of the oil pump and the gas tank, *you* played the key part. We were just ordinary mechanics. *You* were Orville Wright."

"Was I?" asked Jim as a queasy sensation came upon him. "What did I do?"

"Jim, I hate to tell you, but you ignited the carburetor so the incredible flying machine would fulfill its historic destiny and take off at Kitty Hawk."

"Mmm," said Jim.

"The idea was to win World War III."

"Constructive thought there," said Jim. Now he remembered. First

Florence and then Melody. One incredible flying machine to win World War III, and another incredible flying machine to win the peace. "Very interesting. But who thought of the human pretzel to save the dollar?"

"*Me*," said Florence. "I was in there whooping it up too."

"Mmm-m-mm," groaned Jim with a slight whimper. Feebly, he patted Rufus on his woolly head and received two slow, dignified tail wags in response. Jim gave Rufus a final pat and sat down beside Florence and stared at the wave-roiling rocks at the foot of the cliff. The rocks were tempting, but there was no point. The truth was out. On some murky level of the brain, he was no better than Hob, and neither were Florence and Melody. They had all behaved like animals, and it was a fitting punishment for his pride that he himself should prove guilty of the Goblin trick he most despised.

"Well," said Jim, "as far as I'm concerned we were drunk. But I'm sorry, Florence. I really am."

"Oh, I didn't mind, I thought it was grand fun," said Florence. "And so did Melody, she had a ball. It was a real whoopee evening till we got sick. Considering there were only three of us, it was a great little orgy. More fun than a barrel of monkeys."

"Why did we do it?" asked Jim in bewilderment.

"Emotional suicide," answered Florence. "We wanted to destroy our feeling for one another so we can stand it when we leave the island."

Jim stared thoughtfully at Florence as she gazed out to sea. Did he love her any the less because she got drunk and behaved foolishly? No, of course he didn't. However drunkenly idiotic or aesthetically dubious the "not-so-nice" orgy might have been, he felt an even stronger affection for her. And yet—"emotional suicide" was what she'd called it.

"You think," said Jim, "because of your behavior my feelings toward you are different, I no longer love you?"

"Well, it can't be pleasant for you to remember. I'm not the most beautiful woman in the world, Jim, and my rear end is hardly my best feature." Florence put a hand over her eyes and began weeping. "Oh, Jim, I feel so awful," she said. "I've been so sick, I thought I'd never stop throwing up. And the worst thing . . . was me and Melody."

"You were dead drunk," said Jim.

"Florence drunk is Florence sober. I'm not going to marry Rufus. It wouldn't be fair to him. Besides, now that I know what love is like, I can't marry him. Except I can't find a man I can love, so I'll probably wind up back in the Village with the Dragons."

"Don't talk silly," said Jim. "You're not a Lesbian."

"Were you blind? Didn't you see me last night?"

"You were stinko drunk."

"I was stinko drunk, all right, but obviously I have that *tendency*. And the only thing that can save me from it is a man I truly love both heart and soul."

Even in the midst of his staggering hangover a faint suspicion came to Jim that Florence was putting on an act of some kind. That "both-heart-and-soul" thing didn't sound like her, it had a Sarah Bernhardt flavor. Was she operating the insane and absurd levers of an emotional Rube Goldberg machine? Was the not-so-nice orgy itself an integral part of such a machine? It didn't seem possible.

Jim shook his head and replied: "You aren't any kind of Lesbian, Florence. Don't you remember making love to me earlier in the evening? How could a Lesbian react like that?"

"I didn't say I *am* a Lesbian, I said I have a *tendency*," said Florence. "And besides, I love you, that makes the difference. I don't love Rufus, so if I marry him I might wind up back in the Village with the Dragons."

"I doubt it seriously. You have a loving nature, Florence. You'd love Rufus in time, I'm sure."

"Melody has the loving nature, not me. She'd love a chipmunk if it got near her. I won't marry Rufus, Jim. You've given me the courage to wait for a man I can really love."

"You have a loving nature as much as Melody, you're just shyer. I'm sure you'd love Rufus."

"No, I wouldn't. He's a kind and intelligent man and I like him, but I wouldn't love him. Besides, I can't afford to marry him because of my tendency toward Lesbianism. You saw me last night, Jim. Florence drunk is Florence sober. I have a tendency and that's why I need a man I truly love both heart and soul."

Sarah Bernhardt again, thought Jim, but it was no subtle Rube Goldberg machine. Florence *did* have a tendency, didn't she? How could he abandon her to the Dragons of the Village?

"Well, maybe you do have a tendency in that direction," said Jim.

"What I dread is going back *alone* to New York," said Florence. "I'm afraid first thing I'll do is go down to the Lesbian bars and drink too much and wind up letting one of them take me home. I haven't done that in three years, I never did it very often really . . . but the shock, Jim, of going back to that apartment all alone. I need a period of adjustment in New York and I have a very nice apartment."

"Do you?" asked Jim.

"Yes, it's very nice. Not fancy, but nice. Off Lexington Avenue in the Sixties, one of those little garden apartments. I was lucky to get it."

"Do you still have it, you suppose?"

"Oh, I think so. My niece is staying there while I'm gone. It's a very nice apartment, Jim. It has two bedrooms."

"Does it?"

"Yes. You can't go back to your wife for eight more months, Jim—why don't you come and live with me in my apartment for a while?"

"Well . . . I don't know," said Jim.

"You don't have anywhere else to live, do you?"

"No. I'm sure Linda's lawyer must have disposed of the house in Cherry Dale."

"Then move in with me for a while. It would be convenient, Jim; we would work on those shows we've talked about. And it would give me a period of adjustment."

"It's true Linda said she wouldn't see me or talk to me for a year," said Jim. "And I don't have any place to stay. Maybe for a few days . . ."

"You're certainly welcome if you want, I have an extra bedroom. And it would help me, Jim."

"All right," said Jim. "For a few days."

"Good," said Florence casually.

No, there'd been no Rube Goldberg machine, thought Jim, and this was an excellent idea. He needed a period of adjustment himself. And Melody probably needed a period of adjustment too, especially if her husband refused to take her back, and that was very likely.

"Good God," said Jim, "where's Melody? I think we'd better try and find her. Do you have any idea where she is?"

"No, when I got up she was gone."

"We'd better go look for her. I hope she hasn't jumped in the ocean."

"She's probably at Melody's Bathtub washing the hell out of herself," said Florence. "Poor thing, I wonder what's going to become of her."

"I don't know," said Jim. "I'm worried about that too."

Jim and Florence did find Melody at her bathtub, but she was not washing herself. She sat cross-legged on the sand by the little pond, idly throwing pebbles into it. She'd put on a pair of Jim's tropical slacks and one of his crocodile shirts minus a bra—he could see the dent of her nipples through the shirt. A mild surprise; he'd thought she'd have on a Mother Hubbard in reaction to the not-so-nice orgy. As they walked toward her, she looked around at them with a calm even more surprising than her outfit.

"Good morning," said Melody.

"Good morning, Melody," said Florence.

"Feeling a little hung over?" asked Jim.

Melody nodded and smiled. "I guess I do. I have an awful headache and I'm sick to my stomach. Morning sickness too, I suppose. I've been throwing up all morning, it's just stopped. I'm sorry about making such a mess in the cave. I was too sick to try to clean it up, but I will later."

"We'll all clean it up," said Jim.

"That's right," said Florence as she sat on the sand by Melody. "We all made the mess."

"Yes, I guess we did," answered Melody. She looked up at Jim with a small, wry smile. "So, I did an orgy, Jim. Now I can't talk about them in Hollywood or at *Playboy*. I'm worse than they are."

"It was my fault for letting you get drunk," said Jim.

Melody gave a little shrug. "Well, you can't say I'm a prig after that," she said. "I might be a degenerate, but I'm not a prig."

Jim sat down on the sand between Melody and Florence and reflected on her remark as he tossed a pebble into the small salt-water pool. Had he caught a glimpse of another emotional Rube Goldberg machine? Had Melody gotten dead drunk and behaved as she had to prove to him she could fit into his life and hold her own at a New York cocktail party? Would she go *that* far?

"People will do nearly anything if they're drunk," said Florence. "I feel terrible myself, Melody, just sick over it, but we ought to bear that in mind. We were drunk, very, very drunk."

"I'm glad it happened," said Melody. "Even though I feel so awful

I want to die, I'm glad it happened because I learned something last night. My eyes are opened. I understand life and people and myself now, and I never did before."

"What do you understand that you didn't before?" asked Jim.

"I understand that I'm an animal," replied Melody. "There is no God and I have no more soul than a rattlesnake."

"Now listen," said Jim, "we were drunk as hell, Melody, and under the influence of a drug as well."

"The drug didn't have any effect on me. Was it really marijuana like you said?"

"It's from the plant that produces marijuana. I didn't remember telling you."

"You told me, and I said fine! But it didn't have any effect on me, I didn't have any hallucinations. I knew what I was doing."

"The hell you did, you were dead drunk, honey."

"Toward the end, but I wasn't drunk when we started it."

"Okay, and when we started it it wasn't bad."

"My making love to you with Florence watching, that wasn't bad?"

"Not so bad. And you weren't sober then, Melody. You'd had a number of very strong drinks."

"Liquor is no excuse. What happened proves I'm an animal and an animal has no soul. There is no God, it's all ridiculous, life itself is ridiculous, and all morals are ridiculous. Of course other people could do what we did, and that just proves my point. All the laws and religions don't mean a thing. We make rules for ourselves and sometimes we can follow them a little, but underneath we're animals."

"Yes," said Jim uncomfortably, "but . . ."

"There's this question," said Melody. "How can I *ever* go back to Charles after this, even if he will have me, which he won't? I have lost my faith, Jim. And do you want to know the truth? I never really believed in God and I knew I didn't. I never had the nerve to tell Charles, and I thought I wanted him to be a missionary and that I wanted to be a missionary's wife, but I didn't really. I've learned something very important about myself. Charles's mother wanted him to be a missionary and I was playing her part because I thought it was expected of me and I had to do it. But I always hated it! Nursing people, yes—helping people in a hospital, yes—but religion, no! I've never really believed in it! Charles believes in it, but not me!"

It was, Jim felt, the truth. Melody had learned something.

"I think you're right," said Jim. "I've never really believed in you as a missionary's wife, Melody. You have some of those qualities, but you don't belong in formal organized religion."

"Of course I don't belong in it," said Melody. "And it's impossible for me now to go back to my husband and be a dutiful minister's wife. I can't do it, even if he could forgive me and accept your child. A woman who would participate in an orgy and do the horrible things I did has no business being married to a man of God. I'm not a pious and proper minister's wife, I'm an animal and last night proves it."

"Look, I feel as bad about it as you do," said Jim, "but I can't go along with you on this animal thing. People aren't animals, they're human beings and there's a difference."

"What is the difference?" asked Melody.

"People have intelligence and can love each other, that's the difference."

Melody smiled. "You love *me* after the way I acted last night?"

"Of course I do."

"Were you so drunk you don't remember what happened? Have you forgotten how I behaved, how loathsome and disgusting I was?"

"Let's keep a little perspective," said Jim. "I guarantee you you're not the only woman who ever got drunk and wanted to experiment a little."

"Well, I have been cured, I *guarantee* you *that*," said Melody with a wince as she shifted her position on the sand. "I have no further curiosity along those lines, believe me."

"That's what I don't like, the sadism part," said Jim. "I hope *you* can forgive *me* for being such a beast."

"I wanted you to hurt me, that's the worst thing. It wasn't your fault at all and besides, you were drunk."

"So were you," said Jim. "We got drunk and had an orgy."

"We sure did, and I've got no business being married to a minister. If we get off the island, I am *not* going back to Charles. I don't know where I'm going or what will become of me and the baby I'm carrying, but I'm not going back to my husband because now I can't."

The outlines of a Rube Goldberg machine shimmered in the air, then disappeared. Melody had no bonafide religious calling and she could not and should not go back to her husband, who was not only a sanctimonious jackass but an impotent hypocrite besides. Before he could think it through, Jim said:

"I agree, Charles is out. Why don't you come to New York and stay for a while with me and Florence? That is—if Florence doesn't mind."

"Sure," said Florence. "Sure, why not? We've gotten along beautifully on the island, why not?"

"New York?" said Melody. "Stay with you and Florence?"

"Yes, in Florence's apartment," said Jim. "She has two bedrooms. You need a period of adjustment, Melody. I think we all do. I can't see or talk to Linda for eight months, so we can stay on for . . . a few days at Florence's apartment."

"Well," said Melody in a casual tone, "I have to go somewhere and I suppose I could be helpful. I could do the shopping and cooking while you and Florence work on those television shows; maybe I could even find a job as a nurse in one of the hospitals."

"I'm sure you could," said Florence. "There's a shortage of nurses in New York. You can do that and we'll share the cooking the way we have here."

"Yes, and we'll share Jim too," said Melody. She smiled as Jim and Florence eyed her in mild surprise. "Oh, I'm not afraid of adultery any more. I've gotten over my old ways. Do you think we won't sleep together?"

Jim and Florence laughed. "I guess we will," said Florence. "Don't worry, Melody, we'll solve that problem."

"Yes, I think we'll solve that problem," said Jim. "And actually I'm glad the orgy happened, awful as it was. It forced us to face realities and I think this is a good solution."

"So do I," said Florence. "It's an excellent solution."

"Yes, it's good," said Melody.

"As a matter of fact," said Jim, "maybe we'll get a larger apartment after a while and settle down. You see, Linda might divorce me eight months from now. She probably will; she only agreed to wait a year because of the children. If she divorces me, I can marry one of you, maybe Melody since she's pregnant and the baby should have a legal father. But we'll stay together, all three of us, just like here on the island."

"I think that would be *wonderful,*" said Florence. "We would have Melody's baby, we could play with it and take care of it and everything, it would be like a family. And no one would have to know. I'd just be living there as Melody's dear friend and to work with you on television shows. But what if *I* get pregnant?"

"Melody and I will adopt the baby or something," said Jim. "We'd work it out."

"It sounds kind of crazy," said Melody, "but *I* think it would be wonderful too. We'll all be together, we'll love one another—it will work because we love one another. Maybe we'll all sleep in one big huge bed. After last night, I don't see why not, but I don't want any more orgies like that one."

"I'm not against one big huge bed," said Florence, "but I don't want any more orgies like that one either."

"I'll be damned," said Jim. "Do you know, this thing will *work?* Why shouldn't we stay together? We've been very happy here, the three of us. And hell, it's not unknown. In France, *ménage à trois* is very common and I'm sure it happens more in the U.S.A. than people realize. I love you both and you love me and you love each other, so why shouldn't we all live together?"

"I don't see any reason why not," said Florence.

"Neither do I," said Melody.

"Girls," said Jim, "we have just taken off at Kitty Hawk."

TWENTY-FIVE

Isla Encantada

Seven days after the night of rum and funny flowers, Jim and Melody and Florence were peacefully sun-bathing on the beach when they heard a distant roar that became louder and louder until a giant shadow sped across the sand and they looked up at the underbelly of a Navy jet pouring out black smoke as it whizzed over their heads and on over the coconut grove toward the southern end of the island.

"Here's our taxi," said Jim. "And it's the United States Navy, thank God, and not some C.I.A. agent from Central America."

Melody and Florence were naked for their sun bath and they hastily covered themselves as the jet plane, which looked to Jim like a reconnaissance fighter, turned in the sky and came back between the two hills for another low roaring pass over the beach. He stood up and waved his shirt. The jet zoomed out over the lagoon and the wreck of the ship and on out over the blue water, then turned in a huge circle to come back for a third look. Jim again waved his shirt and this time he saw a little answering dip of the plane's wings.

"He saw us," said Jim. "Did you see him move his wings?"

"Yes, but he can't land it," said Melody.

"Of course he can't," said Florence. "Melody, sometimes you're dumb, honey. He's just looking and checking."

The jet now turned over the north end of the island and began to gain altitude as it headed back out to sea. "Probably stationed at Guantanamo," said Jim. "Now they'll send a helicopter or a ship if it's too far."

Rescue, they all now knew, was near; Jim thought it would be that afternoon and so did Melody and Florence. The actual taxi, however, did not arrive until two days later.

Jim was glad they had the final two days, glad for himself and glad also for Melody and Florence. After their decision to establish a *ménage à trois* in New York, they had all made a pretty fair recovery from both the "nice" orgy and the "not-so-nice" orgy. It had been grim the morning after and grim that afternoon cleaning the mess out of Morgan's Second Treasure Cave, but thereafter things improved.

They did not further investigate the gummy exudation or the flowers and leaflets of *Cannabis sativa* and there were no more orgies —or at least there were no more "not-so-nice" orgies. When they went to bed, very tired after cleaning up the cave, Jim was sure the last thing in the world that could happen would be another orgy of any sort, type, variety, or description, but thirty minutes after they'd blown out the lantern he woke up to find soft lips kissing him and a feminine body in his arms. It was Florence. She whispered, "I feel lonely." An hour later other soft lips were kissing him and another feminine body was in his arms. "I'm lonesome," whispered Melody.

During the final days, "nice" orgies occurred every night and frequently in the morning and afternoon as well in Morgan's Second Treasure Cave. There was no trace of self-consciousness left in them and their love-making was completely frank. It was also slightly incredible. Jim had thought the activity in Morgan's First Treasure Cave had been phenomenal, but it faded in comparison to Morgan's Second Treasure Cave. Florence now could "do it" at will and she never tired. "Let's don't waste time," she'd say. "Let's do it again." A kind of erotic desperation, if that was what it was, had seized both Melody and himself as well. Melody, too, was tireless, just as she had been before she became pregnant; she would exasperate Florence by holding Jim down on her and continuing passionate body movements even after love-making ended. "Let him up," Florence would say. "He did it to you, Melody. It's my turn and I'm terribly sexy. Come on, Melody, let him up and stop being a pig." And Jim himself was tireless to a degree he never would have thought possible. He found himself making love to them both at least twice a day and often three times a day. For all practical purposes, it was a matter of continuous sex interrupted only by time out to rest or to eat or to have pleasant, dreamy, three-way conversation.

However, the feeling between them during those last few days did not seem to Jim to be primarily sexual, despite the fact that the sexual activity in the place was truly phenomenal. The main feeling was tender love and an underlying sadness. There was nothing of sex in the tender love and certainly nothing of sex in the sadness. It was a paradox he had noticed before, that the most tremendous arousal of desire came from emotions that had nothing at all to do with sex itself. The moral seemed to be that physical fulfillment was obtained not by looking for it where it seemed to be but by looking in another field.

This feeling of tender love and underlying sadness reached its peak early on the ninth morning. Jim, who had expected this would surely be the day of rescue, awakened at dawn. The women liked to sleep with their arms around him and sometimes their legs as well. He'd gotten more or less accustomed to being enveloped in feminine limbs and when he woke he found Melody asleep on one of his shoulders with her arms around his waist and Florence asleep on his other shoulder with one arm around his neck and the other across his chest. Melody awakened first, smiled sleepily, and said:

"They'll come today."

"Probably," said Jim.

Florence stirred and opened her eyes and asked, "Are they here yet?"

"Not yet."

Jim put his left hand on Melody's breast and his right hand on her forehead. He'd been "involved" with her before Florence awakened, and it was a rule such involvements were never interrupted. "This might be the last time."

"I know," said Melody.

After making love to Melody and then to Florence, Jim lay with an arm around each of them and stared at the mossy ceiling of Morgan's Second Treasure Cave. The love and games of Providence Island were over.

"It's funny," said Melody, "but something I wrote a long time ago in a letter to Charles has come true. You've got one angel on one side and another angel on the other."

"Some angels," said Florence.

"Oh, I don't think our orgy was so bad," said Melody. "We didn't hurt each other or do anything mean. We just got drunk and played like naughty children."

"Yeah, it wasn't all that bad," said Jim. "Frankly, I think that incredible flying machine might even have won World War III."

"It sure did take off at Kitty Hawk, I'll guarantee you that," said Florence.

"But seriously, isn't it funny?" asked Melody. "I really did write that in a letter to Charles. One angel on one side and another angel on the other. I was horrified at myself for getting that out of the quote from the Bible. But I knew it would end like this. I always thought, Jim, you'd have to live with us both on the island."

"I wish you'd told me earlier," said Jim. "It would have saved a hellish amount of effort and bother."

"Oh, you had to work it out," said Melody. "Angels don't come easy."

"Christ, no," said Florence, "they're hard to get."

Jim smiled and tightened his arms around them. Melody and Florence were too human to be angelic, but who could love a real angel anyhow? "I guess so," he said.

After breakfast, they went down to the beach as usual for a swim in the lagoon. Since they much preferred to swim in the nude, Jim wore only an athletic supporter and Melody and Florence were naked. Rufus went along with them and also went swimming, then shook his coat and lay beside them on the sand while they sun-bathed.

"Too bad about Joan," said Melody in a sad voice as she petted Rufus. The cat had suddenly given a meow two days before and died. "I never got to know that cat much."

"I never got to know the parrot much either," said Jim.

"It was a nice cat and a nice parrot," said Florence. "But Rufus is great. He's in a class by himself."

"Oh, yes, no doubt about it," said Jim. At this moment he glanced up and saw a small white automobile driving along on top of the water from around behind the crescent edge of the beach and the coconut grove. "What do you know about that?" he asked. "Here comes an automobile."

"There . . . there!" cried Melody. "It *is* an automobile! It's floating and running on the water!"

"Holy snails," said Florence. "How can an automobile do that?"

It was not a dream. A small white automobile was out there running along on the surface of the lagoon and leaving a little wake behind it. The thing was turning now and heading toward them, water splashing up against its fenders and along the bottom of its doors.

"When I said taxi, I didn't mean *literally*," said Jim.

The little car evidently had crossed the barrier reef in the southern neck of the lagoon where they couldn't see it because of the curving beach and the intervening coconut grove. The ship that had brought it to the island must be down at the southern end, standing offshore near Morgan's Asshole. There had to be a ship—the little aquatic car was certainly not seaworthy; a calm lagoon, yes, but not the open sea. The thing had a logic to it. The car could easily be carried on the deck of a ship and lowered to the water with block and tackle. It would be ideal for getting through a narrow opening in a dangerous reef.

"There it is," said Jim. "The C.I.A. has sent us our taxi as ordered."

"Look, there's a white-haired man in it," said Florence.

"Oh, Lord, I'm stark naked!" cried Melody.

"So am I," cried Florence, "and we didn't bring any clothes!"

As the small white car rolled up on the beach and drove toward them on the sand, Melody and Florence jumped up and began grabbing palm fronds from the FIDEL XXX sign in order to conceal their nudity. Jim stood, hands on hips, and stared intently at the harmless-looking white-haired man in the car. The car stopped twenty feet away, the door opened, and a small, white-haired, ruddy-faced man in tan Bermuda shorts and a short-sleeved white shirt stepped down to the sand, waved in a friendly manner at Jim, and came walking forward with a pleased and rather startled smile. The man had a paunch, thin spindly pale legs, and fishing hooks stuck in his shirt. For a C.I.A. agent, he certainly didn't look very dangerous.

"Oh!" cried Florence, as she dropped a palm frond and bent over to pick it up.

"Oh, Lord!" cried Melody as she held palm fronds across her body with one hand and tried to pick up more with the other.

The C.I.A. agent seemed amused. Arms folded below the various fishhooks stuck in his short-sleeved shirt, he smiled at Jim and said in a barely perceptible Spanish accent: "What have we here, the Garden of Eden?"

"You're with the C.I.A.?" asked Jim.

For a moment the man, who was the proprietor of a luxurious San Andres shop and a member of a once-wealthy and still aristocratic Bogotá family, gazed with a blank incomprehension at Jim. Then, politely, he asked: "The what? You mean . . . the American C.I.A.? You're American yourself? And you think . . . good heavens. Why do you think that?"

If the man was a C.I.A. agent, he was a master actor. He was alone, amiable and unarmed. Jim decided not to mention the guns and the money unless it was necessary. He could send the C.I.A. an explanatory letter from New York, along with a check for the borrowed three thousand dollars.

"Never mind," said Jim. "Where's the nearest land?"

"San Andres Island, a possession of my own country Colombia, is nearest. But what are you speaking about? *I* have nothing to do with your C.I.A.—I am not an American, I am Colombian. Guillermo Katto, at your service. Call me Willy. I have often visited Miami and New York."

"How did you happen to have visited *here?*" asked Jim. The man *had* to be a C.I.A. agent, but he sure didn't look it.

"My friend, it is simple. The U. S. Weather Station at San Andres had a cable from the U. S. Navy that there appeared to be a man and two women stranded here. And since I often come here fishing, I have volunteered for a look. My friend Captain Raunch of Old Providence kindly volunteered his boat, the *Lily Belle.* He is at the south end of the island now."

"Old Providence?"

"Yes, he is a native of there. It is an island about fifty miles from San Andres."

"This isn't Providence Island?"

"Oh, no, not so, Providence is much larger and inhabited. This is *Isla Encantada*—also called in English, I think, Blowhole Island. You see, there is a blowhole at the southern end."

"I know," said Jim.

"A complete misapprehension; this is not Providence. Isla Encantada, that is her proper name truly, she is a possession of Colombia. She is also claimed by Nicaragua and Honduras, and I believe Panama and Cuba too. But not much . . . practical value. A charming little place, but inaccessible. The reef is very dangerous. Thus, you see, my little go-water car."

"This is all quite interesting," said Jim, "but the ladies and I have been stranded here for some time and we are naturally anxious to get back to civilization. Would it be asking too much for your Captain whatever-his-name-is to take us to San Andres?"

"But we have come here for that purpose, my friend. And we can do it immediately with pleasure! You will be there in seven hours. With luck you will even make a six-o'clock cargo flight to Miami—I will radio for reservations if you wish. *Cert*ainly we can take you, your ordeal is over, my friend . . . if it *was* an ordeal with such charming ladies for company, and I am sure it was not."

Melody and Florence were too interested to go away, but they had been too embarrassed to speak. They stood at the edge of the palm grove with fronds clutched against them.

"Miami?" asked Melody.

"Miami *today?*" asked Florence.

"We'll dress and be ready to go in ten minutes," said Jim. "And I wish you would radio and see if you can get us reservations on that flight to Miami."

Half an hour later, Jim and Melody and Florence stood on the stern deck of a small inter-island schooner after being transported to it in the aquatic car of Señor Katto, who said he did not work for the C.I.A. They had been introduced to "Captain Raunch," a soft-spoken and powerful giant of a Negro who told them they should stay a few days and visit Old Providence. The crew were natives of Providence, too, he said. "You must visit Providence," he said. "A most beautiful island."

As the ship started, Jim, Melody, and Florence stood at the stern railing and gazed back at the twin hills of the Providence Island they had known. They had put on the best clothes they had but they looked pretty scruffy. Rufus sat on his haunches on the deck beside them, unruffled, tongue out, and panting happily as if to say: "Okay, we're on a boat now. I know about boats and it doesn't bother me. I will go where she goes, the one I love. I'm satisfied."

Both Melody and Florence were sniffling at tears. "I can't believe it," said Melody. "One minute we're on the island, the next we're gone."

"One minute you're alive, the next you're dead," said Florence. "And I'm afraid it doesn't work the other way around."

"Well . . . no," said Jim. Sadly he stared at Florence, who in her severe if not exactly mannish tropical suit already had begun to look not like herself, but like the homely "Lesbian" who had walked into his office many long weeks ago to discuss a television series to be called "Tramp Steamer." Jim had become aware during the final days that, whatever the quality of his love for Melody, his feeling for Florence was stronger. And now the time had remorselessly come when he had to say goodbye to her forever. It was a loss Jim felt he could not endure; the finality was intolerable. Surely she would see him *once* in New York, if only for lunch? Wasn't that possible—a pleasant lunch at Le Mistral or La Caravelle with great food and a couple of drinks and a little nostalgic reminiscence of Morgan's Second Treasure Cave? Jim shook his head sadly. "No, I guess it doesn't work the other way around."

Whaa-poomphphh!—as the island schooner cut through the blue waves toward San Andres and freedom, Morgan's Asshole was up to its old tricks.

"It was so sudden," said Melody, weeping.

"Yeah," said Jim. "It was sudden. I guess our white-haired friend is in there radioing to see if he can get us reservations to Miami and New York."

"New York," said Melody softly. A tearful sniff came from her. "Jim, I . . . I hate to say this . . ."

"I hate to say it too," said Florence.

Jim, who knew what they were going to say, nodded. "Yeah, I know."

"We can't go and live all together in New York," said Melody. "I have a husband who loves me and I've got to go back to him. I love you both and I'll never forget you, but I love Charles too, and I married him. I'm sorry, Jim. It would be lovely for us to live together like that if there were no one else in the world, but it was just a dream."

"Yes, just a dream," said Florence.

"I believed in it," said Melody. "I really did, until I realized the truth. You see, Charles will forgive me and accept Jim's child as his own. I'm sure he will. I know the words he'll use."

"If he doesn't," said Jim, "let me know and I'll arrange to send support as we agreed. Write me at the Plaza, that's where I'll be staying for a while."

"If *I* turn out to be pregnant," said Florence, "and if Rufus won't marry me or if in the meanwhile he's up and married somebody else, then I'll let you know too."

"Of course," answered Jim. "Child Support Law Number One. That's the foundation of the legal system of Providence Island."

"Mmm," said Melody, hands on her stomach. "I guess it's being pregnant. I used to be a good sailor, but it's rough even though we're hardly at sea yet. I think . . . I'm going in the cabin and sit down. I'll see you a little later."

Jim watched Melody walk across the deck, her shoulders back with a perfect posture even though her hands were on her stomach. Perhaps there was a childlike side to Melody, but she was no child. Jim wondered how he ever could have imagined she might abandon Charles. But painful as it was to think of her walking out of his life a few hours hence in Miami, the thought of Florence doing the same thing in New York was well-nigh unbearable.

"I doubt if I'm pregnant, though," said Florence. "In fact I think I'm getting my period right now and I wonder what it would take to knock me up. Holy snails, it's as crazy as that white automobile. I ought to be pregnant seven times over. But I think you're probably rid of me, Jim."

"Rid of you, huh," said Jim. "Won't I see you in New York ever?"

"I think we'd better not. You have your wife and she needs you. There're your two little girls, I'm sure they love you and need you too. As for me . . . I don't want to write for television, I'm a book writer, maybe not a very good one but that's what I do. I went down to talk to you and the Goblin because your voice was so nice on the phone and you kept asking me. Then I got kind of swept along, but I don't want to do it, Jim. Besides, you'd distract me, I'd never learn to love Rufus with you around."

Jim ground his teeth, an old habit he'd almost forgotten, then pointed down at the ridiculous-looking, shaggy, panting animal at Florence's feet. "*That's* the only Rufus!" he said.

"No, there's another one," said Florence with a smile. "A kind, understanding, and sensitive man who for some strange reason has wanted to marry me for three years and has cared about me for longer than that. He's always been my editor, you know. I think I amuse him with my four-letter words. A 'splendid incongruity,' he says."

"Splendid, *my ass*," said Jim. A murdering jealousy arose within him at the thought of the kind, understanding, and sensitive Rufus who hadn't won Florence. *He* had won Florence. And beyond a doubt, it was his greatest achievement on Providence Island. The injustice and the sadness of it was unbearable. As a jealous rage seethed within him, another emotion slowly took charge of Jim Kittering and helpless tears rose to his eyes. "Florence, he *couldn't* love you the way I do. Don't you know what you mean to me? You can't be heartless about this thing. Won't you have lunch with me sometime?"

A small smile appeared on Florence's face as she turned and stared at the leaning palms and rounded hills that still were not too far away. She had bummed half a package of Lucky Strikes from one of the islander crewmen when she boarded the ship and had been smoking ever since. Now she took out a cigarette and lighted it, cupping her freckled hands in the trade wind and biting her lips together. Finally she turned back to Jim and he saw she was not unmoved.

"You have a wife, Jim, and you love her. You don't need to feel guilty toward me, you've helped me, you've made a woman out of me and changed my life. So to answer your question about lunch—I'm sorry, no."

As they moved toward freedom, a final and distant puff came from the southerly end of Isla Encantada as if to bid them a fond farewell.

PART EIGHT
Independence Day

TWENTY-SIX

The Dragon Sighs

On a cold and blowing January day, after a jet flight from Bogotá marked by much reflection and a silly conversation with a pretty girl in the seat beside him, Jim Kittering stepped upon an Avianca ramp at Kennedy International Airport and returned to civilization.

In a taxi on his way to the Plaza, Jim stared out the window at the heavy traffic, the wintry Long Island parkway, and the fog-shrouded towers of Manhattan that loomed ahead. Everything that had happened was a dream. The smoggy towers ahead were reality and they were changeless. He would go back to work for the Goblin, back to the lunches with two Martinis, back to the cigarettes and the coffee, back to the amphetamines and the phenobarbital. . . .

Three days after the farewell to Melody and Florence at the San Andres airport, Jim was still subject to fits of despair. The memory of Melody walking up the steps of the plane and looking back and waving her hand at him brought tears to his eyes, and the memory of Florence at the window of the plane with Rufus' shaggy head beside her filled him with an intolerable sense of loss.

There was no regular air service between San Andres and Miami but there was a cargo flight, not a regular jet but an old DC-6 prop plane filled to the last inch with boxes and crates. Room somehow had been made to squeeze in Melody and Florence and the dog.

Jim had then been miserably stuck for three days on San Andres, unable to get off it. Hundreds of Colombians were there for vacation and to take advantage of the free-port status of San Andres. With a restless impatience, Jim watched them buy Japanese television sets and American bottle-warmers. He'd finally gotten back by going in the other direction to Bogotá, where he'd caught an Avianca jet for New York.

In his bedroom at the Plaza, the familiarity of which gave him the feeling he'd never been away, Jim tried without success to reach both Linda and Florence on the telephone. He looked up "Carr, Florence" in the Manhattan book and found the number all right, but there was no answer. He then called, one after the other, the various homes of Linda's grandmother, but could not get an answer at any of them. Could it be Gram had closed all the houses? If so, why?

At a loss what to do with himself, Jim walked across the gold rug of the bedroom and stood at the window looking out at darkening and wintry Central Park. A gloomy sight. He turned and walked into the sitting room, stood gazing without purpose at the chandelier, then went to the window and again looked out at the park. An impulse to throw himself out down on Central Park South made him smile wryly. The throw-yourself-out-of-a-window thing hadn't bothered him for months; now it was back.

Central Park looked the same from the living room as it had looked from the bedroom. Late-afternoon fog swirled through the bare tops of the trees and the macadam drives curved wetly off into the gloom, which was broken by the racing headlights of the taxis and cars. Florence probably wouldn't have lunch with him. Linda probably wouldn't either. And Melody was gone.

The leafless trees and darkening fog of Central Park were depressing and so was the Plaza, even though he'd managed to wheedle one of the nicer suites. The Plaza was Jim's favorite hotel in New York, although the Regency was more comfortable and the service better. But he was sentimental about the Plaza, he'd stayed there even back in the years when he couldn't afford it. Jim's surroundings were important to him; griminess had a physical effect upon him. The Plaza, unlike most American hotels, had a little style.

Jim turned away from the taxi headlights and darkening fog of Central Park, ordered ice and a bottle of Scotch, poured himself a drink, and decided to take a bath. In the tub, drink in hand, he remembered the young pretty girl on the Avianca jet. An exasperating thing, that. Hardly serious enough to have any meaning or significance, but exasperating. The girl had seemed so horribly young and childish and insensitive, and yet she was a senior at Smith and twenty-two years of age.

She was extremely pretty, a little blue-eyed blonde whose father was in the diplomatic service in either Paraguay or Uraguay; she reminded him quite a bit of Linda, being obviously a favored child of wealthy parents with every advantage. Her clothes were chic and expensive; everything about her—the look of serene poise in her eyes, the tone of her voice, the pleasant smile—bespoke money and position and security. She was returning, she said, from an extended Christmas vacation with her parents.

"*La Jolie*," that was what she was, and the restaurant of the same name would be a good place to take Florence to lunch. It was quiet, the food was superlative, and it had not become known to the hoi polloi the way La Caravelle had become known. Yes, La Jolie. "Frankie"—wasn't that the deliberately "wrong" name of the heavily accented and superbly trained *mâitre d'?* Wasn't he the one who so much admired the beautiful young actresses Jim often had brought there? Yes, the girl was another "*La Jolie*"—very pretty, very lovely, very beautiful, a nice thing to have, an object of art, and no doubt her father's pride.

She also was stupid and insensitive and thought he was trying to pick her up. They were practically the only passengers in the first-class section and Jim had merely been trying to be human and friendly on a long jet flight. Perhaps the cut of the suit of clothes he'd bought hastily in Bogotá didn't set too well with her; there had seemed to be a skeptical arch to her pretty eyebrow as she looked him over. But it was her response to his mild flirtation that was so annoying. She'd made a number of cool little flip remarks that in remembrance made Jim wish he'd said a few nasty things to her and put her in her place. It would have been so easy to do, she was a child, really. A little oblique withering irony would have served her right.

The girl just naturally *assumed* he was trying to pick her up. She was beautiful, so of course all men wanted her; it wasn't possible they were merely being friendly. Jim took a sip of his Scotch and ran more hot water in the tub. Worse, she had meant that "men of your generation" thing. She thought he was an old man, the little fool. She probably even imagined his sexual powers were declining. Jim had to smile at the thought of the clumsy, snorting boys with whom she made love. The girl was not without experience, she'd made a point of coolly exhibiting her sophistication, as if to say:

"Oh, of course I go to bed. Doesn't every intelligent, cultivated person? But this doesn't mean I want an old, taken, off-the-market, undoubtedly married, and not too interesting man like yourself."

The stupid little snip. Who needed her? She would be as clumsy and tiresome as her boy friends. The irony was that young girls were almost invariably horrible in bed—coarse, phony, insensitive, and downright awkward. They thought they had a thing of great value, but they didn't. They weren't even worth the five cents it cost them for their daily pill, much less the time or attention of a man who knew something of the world.

The truth, as Jim realized toward the end of his bath, was that the young girl had hurt him badly. He had not been trying to pick her up, God knows he had problems enough with women already, but he had flirted with her a little and she wasn't interested one bit. He was, alas, really and truly an "old man" to her.

Jim got out of the tub and as he dried with a towel looked at his sun-tanned, youthful-seeming body. But he was not a twenty-two-year-old boy or even a thirty-year-old man. No, he was forty-two and the mirror of the medicine chest confirmed the fact. Sun-tanned and healthy as he was, the lines of his face were those of a man entering middle age. More gray had appeared at his temples during the past four months. As his barber had said, if this thing kept on they would have to touch it up, "irregardlessly."

Yes, irregardlessly. The girl on the plane was right. The last chance had come for him and it was this fact, beyond a doubt, that had precipitated the entire adventure of Providence Island. Jim had become aware of what actually had happened on that clear September morning. He had not been acted upon by other people, as it had seemed at the time. The exact opposite had occurred—he himself had acted and had forced both Linda and Hob to behave as they had.

There was no question of it. First, Linda—it was true Linda herself wanted desperately to escape; she had become sick unto death of the empty infidelities, the senseless parties, the drinking, and all the rest of it. But she had not had the heart to save herself—not until he had hurled that impossible tirade at her over the telephone. Incoherent and childish as his accusations had been, they had given Linda both the provocation and the courage to leave him. After that phone call, she had burned up her mink coat and packed her suitcases. He had forced Linda to face the fact the marriage was sick and that a separation was the only chance of saving it, a separation that would give them both perspective and a chance to change.

As for Hob—the game of "Tailing the Goblin" had been played and won. He had known an electrician would not interrupt an important conference except for an important reason and that the man was lying when he said McAllister had told him to do it, and he had known Hob was listening on the intercom because he'd heard him breathe. He had not really thought it was the air conditioning, he had known Hob was there, and when he finished his speech on gluck he had turned to him and said in effect: "Okay, Hob, you son of a bitch. What do you think of *that?*"

Yes, he had tailed the Goblin. After such a destructive speech to the new writer Florence Carr, what choice did Hob have but to fire him—or do *some*thing to him, anyhow, something that could break the enslaving chains. And Jim had had a good idea what the "something" might be. It was an amazing thing, the lightning speed and unfaltering precision of the mind—he had picked up at once on Florence's complaint she knew nothing of boats. What more reasonable outcome than a punitive research trip? Hadn't Hob sent off another rebellious executive to Odessa, Texas, with a faggot writer for three weeks only a couple of months before? Hadn't he sent still another erring executive to the Aleutian Islands with an alcoholic, half-crazy cameraman a year ago? It was almost as if he, Jim Kittering, had set out deliberately to provoke Hob into sending him off on some broken-down "tramp steamer" with Miss Florence Carr, a homely and presumably Lesbian writer whose company Hob would think he'd loathe. In fact, it wasn't "almost as if"—that was exactly what he'd done. He had tailed the Goblin better than he'd dreamed.

There was no doubt of it. The mysterious machine of the mind had exerted its power with an irresistible force on that clear September morning. The thing that really happened was he'd blown up both his marriage and his job in a desperate bid for a freedom he did not know how to find. The only thing he knew was that the wreckage of his life had become intolerable.

Well, it had been done. Now what? Jim left the bathroom, put on underwear, poured himself another Scotch, and tried again without success to reach Florence and Linda on the telephone. It would probably be better to write Linda anyhow, the thing was too complex to express over the phone. And it probably would be better to write Florence too. Jim took off his underwear and put on pajamas. After the long flight from Bogotá, with stops in Jamaica and Miami, he didn't feel like going out or doing anything that evening; he'd order dinner sent up and he would write persuasive, intelligent letters to Linda and Florence.

As he began a long, persuasive, intelligent letter to Linda, Jim asked himself again—now what? Would Linda talk with him? Would she see any changes in him? Jim wrote on, bowed intently in his pajamas over the white and gold Plaza desk. The question echoed in his mind as his pen moved: "Now what?" What did the future hold? What if anything had he accomplished on his trip to the blue sea?

In consideration of the past four months and in view of the character of his wife, his own character, and the character of all those involved, there could be only one outcome and the answer was as plain in Jim's mind as a newspaper headline.

There was no question of the outcome, none whatever; his dilemma was no real dilemma and it contained no suspense at all. Certainly not.

Jim, however, could not read the glaring headline. Therefore, needlessly, he agonized, gritted his teeth in despair, shrank back for fear he might jump out of a Plaza window down on Central Park South, and gulped whisky in a hot tub because a young girl had hurt his feelings.

What had he accomplished on the shores of the blue unresisting sea?

The answer to his question was at hand, but Jim did not arrive at it for another nine days. The time passed swiftly, however, and in the course of those days a number of interesting events occurred. Jim learned he was in "limbo" with American International Television and Radio, Inc.—they just could not make up their minds what to do with the Goblin's right-hand man. He interviewed with some success Walter McCade, the silver-haired and silver-hearted lawyer of Linda's grandmother. He had "brunch" with his old pal John Terrence Hobson. He received a letter from Melody. He went to Florence's apartment and had lunch with her at La Jolie. Finally, on the evening of the eighth day he received a phone call from Linda in which she agreed to meet him for lunch on the following day at one-fifteen in the Edwardian Room of the Plaza.

The interview with silver-hearted Walter McCade, which was also a kind of "Welcome back to civilization," occurred five days after Jim's return to New York. To his surprise, the persuasive and intelligent letter to Linda had elicited no response and he couldn't understand it. It didn't seem possible Linda would deliberately ignore his cable from San Andres announcing his return from the dead and then ignore his long letter too.

Furthermore, there was something fishy about the lack of occupancy at the various homes of Linda's grandmother. Where was Gram? Where were Linda and the children? On the fifth day, Jim tried to telephone again and learned the phone in her grandmother's place in Connecticut had been disconnected. He tried Gram's town house in New York several times but got no answer. He then tried the home in West Palm Beach but got no answer there either, which was bewildering because servants should be at the Palm Beach house in January. There was no point in trying the summer home in Maine because the place wasn't really livable in the winter, but he tried it anyhow on the off chance that perhaps it had been opened and this was where they were. No one was there. The phone of the house in Maine was also disconnected.

It was crazy. After nearly a week back in New York, he didn't even know where his children were. Therefore, reluctantly on the afternoon of the fifth day, Jim telephoned the lawyer of Linda's grandmother. The silvery voice came over the phone receiver with a prim, sadistic satisfaction that was shocking.

"I regret, Jim, that I am unable to give you any information whatever concerning Linda." McCade, Jim knew, despised him, but at least in the past the man had always been coolly polite. The separation and prospects of a divorce made the difference. "These were her explicit instructions, that you be told absolutely nothing about her and that no messages from you be forwarded to her. You are wasting your breath speaking to me. I am sorry but I will have to hang up."

"Now, just a minute, Walter—"

"This is childish. Don't you understand, Linda is my client? I work for her, now goodbye."

"I'm coming down," said Jim, "and you will have to talk to me."

The man's extreme rudeness was a surprise. Had Linda told him she wanted a divorce? Jim took a cab down to Pine Street and after an hour of fuming was finally shown into silver-haired Walter's office by a feeble-looking old lady secretary.

"*Well*, Jim?"

"Now look, Walter. As far as I know, Linda thinks I'm dead and my children think I'm dead too. I have a right to know where my children are and I demand that you tell me."

"I didn't refuse you information concerning the girls," said Walter.

"They are in boarding school in Connecticut and arrangements can be made for you to visit them. I didn't take it upon myself to initiate a visit because I expected a father to do so on his own account."

"I thought they were with Linda and I didn't want to push myself on her, Walter. Where is she?"

"This I cannot tell you."

"Can you forward a letter to her from me?"

Walter smiled thinly. "She anticipated you would make this request and the answer is no. I cannot."

"Walter, are you a human being at all? Linda has thought for four months I'm dead and she might still think so."

"Not true. Of course I cabled her. And I'm sure the news of your adventure on the island with the two ladies must have reached her. I mean, there was considerable publicity and I'm sure newspaper accounts appeared everywhere. That Robinson Crusoe picture of you and the two ladies even made the newsweeklies."

To Jim's regret, a photograph of him and Melody and Florence in bedraggled clothes had been taken at the San Andres airport and the Associated Press had gotten hold of it. "STRANDED ON LOVE ISLAND," the headlines ran. There'd been many cute little feature stories filled with innuendoes and carrying such leads as:

"James Kittering, right-hand man and Program Director for the celebrated John 'The Goblin' Hobson, former Executive Vice-President of American International Television and Radio, here appears in surprisingly good health after being stranded for four months on an uninhabited island with Mrs. Melody Carolucy Dubbs (above right), a missionary's wife, and Miss Florence Carr (above left), a spinster novelist."

"Never mind about Robinson Crusoe, Walter," said Jim. "There weren't any dry-cleaning plants on the island and I'm afraid clothes don't stand up too well in the tropics."

"I thought you and the ladies looked as if you needed a bath more than you did a tailor or a dressmaker," said Walter. "But at any rate, of course I cabled Linda when I heard the news of your miraculous survival."

"I hope you also called the girls."

"Certainly. Children love a father no matter what kind he is. They were overjoyed and I'm sure they wonder why you haven't bothered to visit them."

With an effort, Jim controlled a rising anger. Why did the man hate him so? "I explained that, Walter. I assure you I'll go to the school this afternoon if you'll tell me where it is."

"I'll be glad to tell you. But at the moment they're not there. They are visiting their mother for the week end."

"Um-hmm," answered Jim. "You said you 'cabled' Linda, which made me think she's abroad. But evidently she's not exactly abroad if the children are able to visit her on week ends. Where is she, Walter? I want to get in touch with her."

"It's no use, Jim. You are wasting your breath and my time. I don't know how valuable your breath is, but my time is worth something."

"Now listen, Walter," said Jim quietly. It would be simple to squelch the man and make him whistle a different tune, but Jim hated to do it just as he hated to step on a bug and squash it. Surely there was some feeling in the man. "I know you have your instructions, Walter, but the situation is changed. I love Linda and she loves me and we have two small children. I'm appealing to your common sense and humanity—"

"I said it's no use. I shall *not* tell you where Linda is and she does *not* want to receive communications from you. Her feeling is this would be an insupportable emotional strain on her. She doesn't want arguments and exhortations and piteous pleas from you and frankly, I don't blame her. I might add with an equal candor, Jim, that your gross invasion of my office is not only irritating and distasteful to me it is also humanly embarrassing to me. The indignity of your behavior distresses and pains me. There's nothing else I can say to you, Jim, except to extend my sympathy and bid you good afternoon. I'm sorry, I'm busy, I'll have to ask you to leave."

Jim still hesitated for a brief moment. The extent of the man's hostility was puzzling. Of course Walter was a very stupid man. He expected now bluster and physical threats, he even seemed to be trying to provoke a physical attack. No doubt he was prepared for that—the building police or something of that order. But puzzling as the man's violent hatred might be, the bug had to be squashed. Jim smiled and said:

"Walter, think a little. You might be making a mistake that could cost you a great deal of money. Linda will have complete control over her grandmother's millions and I might have a certain sway over Linda herself. You *think* she's going to divorce me, Walter, perhaps she's even intimated as much to you. But reconciliations do occur and you could be wrong. And if you are, it might cost you a lot of money someday, unless you change your tone with me very soon. A reconciled husband can be highly persuasive in convincing a woman of the necessity to change lawyers. If Linda went back to me, I could get you fired, Walter."

"Jim, my hands are tied. Don't you understand that?"

"I think you're a perfectly competent lawyer and I wouldn't urge such a thing to Linda even though you've been rude to me. . . ."

"I have not intended to be, I have intended only to be candid."

The wretch was backing down already. "Of course there may be no reconciliation," said Jim. "But no matter what difficulties Linda and I have had, there's real love on both sides and there are two small children. You should want a reconciliation and act to make it more likely, not less so."

"Well, I . . . but nothing I said . . . of course I want a reconciliation if it's possible. Certainly. It'd be best for all concerned."

For some reason the man did *not* want a reconciliation. Was he stealing money from Gram or something? Impossible. But at any rate he was now backing down fast. Silver money was of course the key to unlock Walter's silver heart. Such men, Jim had learned, were one of the unfortunate concomitants of both success and money—*power, power, power!* It was sickening. The man had been filled with an inner glee at the knowledge of Jim's heartbreak, humiliation, and suffering. How far away from the love he and Melody and Florence had felt for one another on Providence Island, and what a revolting world to come back to. The final irony was that the disgusting wretch with his silver heart and silver soul would doubtless condemn them all to hell and gone for the way they'd lived together on the island, and he'd be totally convinced he was right. They all "needed a bath," he said. Walter's own miserable soul needed a bath much worse.

"Of course," said Jim calmly, "you have your job to do, I understand that, Walter. And you do it expertly and ethically, I've always admired that about you." The bullshit came hard; Jim had gotten out of practice. And yet how could onc fight bullshit without bullshit? If Walter did not think some good will on his part was possible, if he thought Jim would knife him anyhow upon reconciliation with Linda, then the power, power, power wouldn't work. Jim had learned that power was almost always executed with a smile. "No, if I needed a lawyer I'd come to you, Walter. Honest and able men are hard to find. I'm not asking you to do anything unethical, all I'm asking is that you listen to me just for a moment. I have a constructive proposal to make."

"Well," said Walter in a cautious but quite different tone, like a scorpion lowering its stinger a bit and looking around as if to see whether the smell was a piece of tail rather than a meal, "I appreciate that, Jim. And I'm perfectly willing to listen, if you have anything constructive to say. Naturally my feelings are with Linda, I've known and loved her since she was a child . . . and I do feel you've been a little rough on the girl. But I'm sure you love her and I'm sympathetic to you both in this situation. I know full well how agonizing these things can be, how searing and unbearable."

The yellow stuff in the squashed bug was awful. Not a word the man said was true, yet he believed it all. He did not "appreciate" Jim's praise, he was afraid of it; he was not "perfectly willing to listen," he had been compelled by his own greed to listen; his feelings were not with Linda and he had not loved her since she was a child, he had always feared her independence and eyed her with well-bred lecherous hostility; he was not sympathetic to them both in the situation, but for some reason wanted divorce and heartbreak; he did not know how agonizing such things could be, how searing and unbearable, because he did not care about human pain, a silver blob was where his heart should be.

Power, power, power!—now the wretch was "sympathetic." Such sympathy could and probably would scorch the earth and destroy human life. Lies, lies, lies, rudeness and more lies—that was the ultimate meaning of power gone mad. And how revolting, how disgusting. Even the long-shot possibility he might lose a lucrative client had touched his tender heart. What a rotten and dismal world indeed. Love and human kindness didn't mean a thing to such a man as this and there were plenty more like him.

"I have this constructive thing to say," answered Jim. "I want to make a proposal to Linda, not a plea and not an exhortation. I suggest she and I have lunch together and decide then and there if our marriage is worth preserving or not. That's my proposal and if she won't accept it I am going to start divorce proceedings myself at once on grounds of desertion."

The silver-haired Walter's mouth dropped open; the man had always believed Jim married Linda for her money—how could he threaten to walk away from several millions of dollars? "Divorce proceedings? You, Jim?"

"Yes, me. I am not going to wait a year for Linda to make up her mind. I don't have eight months more to waste. She's had four months and that's long enough. She can make up her mind now and I want you to tell her that."

"I must say I don't believe she anticipated *you* might want a divorce."

"I didn't say I wanted a divorce. I love Linda and I want her back and if you suggest otherwise to her I swear before God I'll kill you. The proposal I'm making is that Linda have lunch with me at the Plaza, a harmless lunch in the Edwardian Room. There will be no tearful exhortations or piteous pleas. We will talk to each other and consider whether or not a reconciliation is possible. You might tell Linda I feel I have changed in certain ways and I believe a reconciliation now could lead to a new and different marriage. I hope to convince her of this. If I succeed, we will have an immediate reconciliation and thus avoid waiting pointlessly another eight months. If I fail, I will agree to an immediate divorce then and there."

"In other words, you want to gamble on this one lunch?"

"That's right. But I don't think it's a gamble, Walter. I think Linda and I will be reconciled at that lunch. And I believe it's in your best interests to take a prudent view and consider it possible and be helpful in this matter."

"This proposal . . . does change the picture," said Walter in a frightened voice. "Linda's in the Bahamas, I think I can tell you that. And she certainly must be advised of a possible intention on your part to file for divorce."

"An intention only if she refuses a simple lunch with me at the Plaza. And you had better make that clear to her. I explained all this to her in a letter I sent to her grandmother's place in Connecticut, but I suppose she never got it."

"No. All mail has been forwarded here according to her instructions, so we have the letter, it's in my files. Unopened of course. She didn't want any mail from you forwarded on, you understand."

"I think you'd better call her and report this conversation to her, Walter."

"Of course I must, I have no choice. I'll do it this afternoon. Where are you staying, Jim?"

Thus ended the interview with Walter, who did not accompany Jim out into the corridor and shake hands with him before putting him on the elevator but who did say sadly: "I hope I wasn't rude before. These separations are a dreadful strain on everyone, Jim. I do want to be helpful, and I will be."

It wasn't, Jim felt, that the man had no shame; he was unaware himself what a swine he was. The sadistic delight with which he had taunted Jim for the loss of his wife and children had seemed to him a well-founded and candid reprimand, just as his semi-apology at the end had struck him as a sincere and generous gesture. The wretchedness of human nature was beyond belief; to look behind the pink skin of the skull and see the little squirming dirty worms was enough to confound a man and make him wonder if life itself was worthwhile. Most people, mercifully, had no power to look behind the skull and see the worms, and the man who had such a power was cursed indeed. What did one *do* with such terrible information? Jim had to sigh.

Silver-hearted Walter, however, was merely a minor demon of the outer world. Jim learned on the day after his arrival back in New York that his old nemesis John Terrence Hobson, otherwise known to one and all as the Goblin, had been ingloriously sacked in December. Of course Hob emerged from it with a six-hundred-thousand-dollar settlement of his contract, to say nothing of a blue-chip personal fortune of well over a million dollars, so he wasn't selling apples on the street. But at least he'd been fired, thrown out, given the old heave-ho. The Chairman of the Board and the Directors of American International Television and Radio had had enough of those falling ratings—and perhaps, although Jim doubted it, the disgraceful parties getting in the columns had influenced them too.

Jim liked to think there was a trace of moral sense in McAllister and the rest of them on the board, that Hob's sadistic megalomania had contributed to his fall. The Big-Brother-is-watching intercom had backfired dramatically shortly after Jim left on his trip to the blue sea. The leading executives of A.I.T.&R. had simultaneously offered their resignations en masse and the Goblin had giggled hysterically, made a solemn little speech about the inviolability of privacy that brought tears to his eyes, lifted his hands palm upward like Christ on the cross—and then sternly ordered on-and-off switches installed on the monitors in all the offices.

But the Goblin had shed one tear too many and it was the beginning of the end. The defeat was so total rebellion stirred among the peasants. Important executives and then even lowly secretaries began to refer to Hob as "Gob" and to smile in open derision at him as he went with his little athletic shuffle down the corridor. There was then a shocking and notorious incident that caused him to be treated with even more open contempt by the secretaries—another and a truly famed "fire-escape retreat" from one of his parties.

Jim had heard of several such fire-escape retreats in the past. This retreat, however, involved a "well-known young actress" who had fled naked down the fire escape from Al Ingerman's apartment in the old West-side mansion where the orgies were held. A police car happened by at that very moment and she ran screaming to it, and later in hysterical fury lodged a complaint that an artificial, battery-operated, plastic phallus with a buzz mechanism had been stuck up her behind and the buzzer turned on, which caused her to faint. John Hobson had done this terrible thing to her, she said. He had also, the filthy rascal, stuck the horrid gizmo up her vagina too, which hadn't caused her to faint but had been most distressing. The "well-known young actress" had been shut up or bought off, but the story spread all over everywhere to give the Goblin and his buzzing plastic pecker a true *sub rosa* fame.

There was no doubt about it, the Goblin had become reckless with his power. To play such a trick on a young girl no one had ever heard of was one thing, but to select as victim a beautiful girl who had appeared in a semisuccessful Broadway show and a number of motion pictures was something else again, it was *news*. The Goblin had gone too far. Secretaries began to make furtive buzzing sounds at him in the corridor and since he could not fire every secretary in the organization there was nothing he could do about it except rush into his dark den and put his hands on his head and giggle hysterically.

Jim liked to think there was moral sense somewhere in McAllister and the others, but it was more likely they had merely exercised good business judgment. At any rate, Hob had been ingloriously fired and others associated with him had been dragged down as well, especially those who had no talent or ability and made no real contribution to the organization.

Jim's own position at A.I.T.&R. seemed to be ambivalent, although he had one very interesting brief talk with McAllister about feature motion-picture production that led him to think he was being seriously considered for an even more important position than he'd held before. Both C.B.S. and A.B.C., of course, had gone into feature pictures some time ago and N.B.C. was known to have plans for it. McAllister felt that sooner or later American Television and Radio would have to get into the field too.

"It needs, we think, a creative man rather than just a production man," he said, with dubious and yet hopeful eyes on Jim. "A few years ago I'd have marked you as perfect for it, your best work has always been on quality specials and dramatic shows rather than on output. But the last three years, I don't know. You've had personal troubles, maybe, trouble at home?"

"Yes, I have, frankly," said Jim. "I hope to get that straightened out soon. Linda and I have been separated but I'm working on a reconciliation."

"That might make a difference. Of course Hob these last few years became very domineering with his people. Smothering. I told him so. And frankly, there's another factor. We're a little leery of the publicity you've received as a result of your island adventure. Let's wait a while, let things settle. I'll have a check drawn for your back salary, but don't bother to come in, take a rest. I can't promise a thing, Jim, you were close to Hob and there's a lot of feeling against him. We'll see."

Jim was in "limbo"—they could not make up their minds what to do with him. As Hob's "right-hand man" he was both guilty and desirable; Hob, after all, had brought in a great many dollars in his day. The right-hand-man stuff afforded Jim a wry amusement. In earlier days, maybe so, but for the past two or three years the Goblin had not listened to him or to anyone else.

"Jim," came the whisper on the phone, "Jim . . . I wept. I wept *twice*."

"Twice, Hob?"

"Yes. When I first heard you were lost. And then when you were raised from the dead. I wept twice."

Somehow Hob had found out he was at the Plaza. He called on the third day after Jim's return to say he had wept twice and to invite Jim to lunch. Jim put him off, but Hob was a hard man to put off and he called back again the next day with a dinner invitation. Jim declined rudely. "Look," he said. "I don't want to see you or talk to you. Go away." On the fifth day when Jim got back to the hotel after a "detective" visit to the superintendent of Florence's apartment building—

he had not heard from her and she did not answer her telephone—there were five phone slips with the repeated message: *Call Mr. Hobson urgent.*" Jim ignored them. At nine o'clock on the morning of the sixth day he was awakened by another phone call.

"Jim," came the whisper, "let's have brunch."

"Oh, fuck off!" said Jim. "Go away. If you don't stop bothering me, you're going to weep three times, not twice."

"I'm downstairs in the lobby," whispered Hob. "Let's have brunch. I have a proposition to make to you."

"I'm not interested in any propositions from you. Now fuck off!"

"Would you be interested in a guaranteed salary of two hundred thousand a year, unlimited expense account, plus complete creative freedom to develop half-a-dozen brand-new series with a substantial participating ownership of all the shows you do?"

Jim took a deep breath and exhaled with a shudder. Would he never be rid of this man? "Jesus Christ, Hob," he said. "Are you serious?"

"Never more so," whispered Hob. "I'm in the lobby. Let's have brunch, Jim, and discuss it. I'll wait by the jade display."

The proposition, if it was on the level, would mean not merely a doubling of his present salary but inevitably a fortune as well. The real point was "substantial participating ownership." If only *one* of six new series turned out to be a hit he would make in excess of a million dollars and there would be ways to take this money as capital gains. Jim got up and dressed and went to Le Brasserie with Hob for a nine-thirty "brunch." The Goblin liked the omelets there. He ate omelettes aux fines herbes morning, noon, and night and for some reason this had always infuriated Jim. It wouldn't be so bad except that Hob liked them soft and runny and gooey and slowly licked his lips as he ate.

"All right, Hob," said Jim, "spell it out. *Who* is going to guarantee me two hundred thousand a year?"

"I will personally guarantee it, Jim."

"Not on your life," said Jim, "not for a second. You're not talking to a stranger, Hob. I know you a little bit. Your personal guarantee isn't worth shit. What bank or company will guarantee me such a salary?"

"How about Chase Manhattan?" asked Hob with a calm whisper "Is that a big enough organization for you, Jim?"

"Yes, it's big enough."

"I'd hoped but I didn't expect you'd trust me. I'll have to sell some securities at an inopportune time, but that's all right. I will put your first year's salary in the hands of the bank and you will be issued monthly checks for sixteen thousand six hundred and sixty-six dollars and sixty-seven cents. The money will be in trust for you and that is as iron-clad as anything can be, Jim."

Jim paused as a brunette waitress put Bloody Marys before them. It was as iron-clad as anything could be, yes, but how iron-clad could a thing be when dealing with such a man as Hob?

"It sounds all right," said Jim as the waitress, who was rather pretty and had a very tight skirt, turned and walked away. "But if I didn't do what you wanted, Hob, I'm sure somehow those monthly checks would stop arriving."

Hob, head hunched, was staring after the waitress. "What Jim?"

"You heard me. You aren't interested in that waitress' ass, not right now. There'd be some way for you to stop those checks if we didn't agree."

"She swings," said Hob. "I know that girl, Al was telling me about her. But let's get back to business, Jim. You aren't being sensible. The salary part is peanuts anyhow."

"I wouldn't call two hundred thousand a year peanuts."

"Of course it's peanuts. This is a proposition that could be worth a fortune to you. Don't you realize what I'm doing? I'm coming to you hat in hand, I'm admitting how valuable you've been to me. Why, everything went to pieces after your . . . tragic loss, which thank God proved to be illusory. You see, my gift is executive, promotional, directorial. I'm a natural leader and for some reason, I've never understood it, I frighten people. I can look at them and frighten them. The thing I have in point of fact is organizing powers in terms of human effort. On the other hand, you have organizing powers in terms of human feeling and this is not an area of strength for me. It's your forte, Jim, and that's what makes you so stubborn about the work you do. Oh, you're a stubborn fellow. How many times have I tried to alter one of your shows to no avail?"

"I think you altered plenty of my shows to plenty of avail, Hob."

"You are right. Success is dangerous. I lost contact with the true sources of my strength, Jim, and that is the human material with which I work. And thereby unwittingly and with the best of motives—

I was only trying to be helpful—I abused the delicate mechanism that makes you a creative person, a man in the 'talent' category. It was stupid of me, but then, to err is human. I assure you I shan't make this mistake again. I have learned a lesson I will not forget."

It was probably true, thought Jim. The Goblin would not strangle the imagination of his subordinates to quite such a degree again. In earlier years, before he became so powerful, he had given his people more leeway and some of the shows in those days had been good.

"If you realize a man has got to breathe," said Jim as a sick sensation came in his soul. "But wait a minute, wait a minute—you said 'substantial participating ownership,' but you didn't mention any contract."

"Jim . . . Jim, *of course* I'll sign a contract with you. And it will protect your interests in any series you develop."

The sick sensation was awful. The two hundred thousand would be paid as long as he got on reasonably with Hob, a thing he could do, and a contract would protect his percentage of any new shows he developed. His tailing of the Goblin had led him straight to a fortune and an undreamed-of opportunity to do good work in a medium starved for it. What difference did it make if Hob shared in the profits? He was a promoter, that was all, and if it wasn't Hob it would be someone else more or less like him. It wasn't necessary for him to *like* John Hobson, his personal opinion of the man was irrelevant. The thing to do was to use the Goblin for his own purposes. But was this possible? Had anyone ever done it? Not exactly, no, but he would be rich, very rich and very powerful. The Goblin was making him a true first lieutenant. Jim sighed as the sick sensation spread through his soul.

"Well . . . if you *do* realize a man has got to breathe," said Jim.

"*Cer*tainly a man has to breathe," answered Hob with a pained sincerity, "especially a talented man. Coercion is the death of talent. Talent must be, it has got to be a free gift of the soul. And a brave gift as well. Let us not forget the intransigeance of the true artist. But oh Jim, this intransigeance is so easy to crush. Artists by their very nature, by virtue of the hypersensitivity and excessive emotion that makes them artists in the first place, are weak creatures. You know that Jim you know that. You see it's their little egos, Jim, their craving for praise and slavering at the mouth for recognition. How easy it is to crush the little flicker of intransigeance with a kind word. Artists are destroyed not by blame and condemnation, Jim, they thrive on that. The thing that wrecks and ruins them and makes trembling cowards of them all is *subtle praise*."

Jim could not quite understand what Hob was getting at. "What's the answer then? If praise destroys talent, what helps it?"

"*Constructive criticism*," said Hob with solemn earnestness, "and *constructive guidance* for future endeavor. Talented people are childish people, Jim, and they need and require this criticism and guidance from those who are emotionally mature and do not have weak egos."

The catch, thought Jim. Hob had not learned a thing; he had learned a few new words, that was all. The Goblin hadn't changed and the Goblin never would change. Jim smiled and replied: "You said I'd have complete creative freedom, Hob."

"You would. You'd have absolute creative freedom, but with constructive guidance. You see, Jim, human creativity is universal. I, too, have such creativity and it emerges under pressure. That is the discovery I have made in recent weeks. Jim, you don't know what my enemies have done to me. The stories they have spread, the calumnies, the slanders. But the thrilling thing is, my creativity has emerged. Try this. I see an island. Tropic palms. Blue water. I see it, a lagoon. A man—heroic, noble, pure. A woman—pure, godly, kind. Another woman—sensitive, witty, wise. I see a hurricane, a great storm."

"Hob, is there no length to which you will not go?"

"Wait, wait, I know you recognize it. But wait. I have an original contribution. Try this. I see it. A circus, a German circus, on its way to Venezuela, wrecked two weeks after man and two women are stranded on love island—"

"Love island, good God! I don't like it, I don't want to even hear it."

"I'm not through with this," said Hob with a cold anger. "You are not listening, Jim. If you were listening, then you would know I have not reached the emotional peak of what I am saying. Now, if you want me to make you rich, you must listen. This is precisely the type of childish behavior I cannot permit, this refusal to listen. So will you please pay attention?"

Fuck him, thought Jim with a sudden burst of inner rage. The horrible bastard thought he had him and already was contemptuously showing his Goblin fangs. The thing to do was get up at once and walk out, but somehow Jim Kittering didn't. "Sorry, Hob," he said.

"All right. German circus wrecked, all hands lost. But try this. Many, many *animals* swim to island and in particular a parrot. Now, the parrot teaches the man to . . . *talk to the animals.* He learns all their languages. Hub-hub the pig, a sea lion, a horse. Pirates come. Captain Hook. Sharks are a problem, invade lagoon. Many, many adventures are possible. What do you think, Jim? How does it sound?"

Jim stared in groggy disbelief at his former boss. "It sounds like Dr. Dolittle with sex, Hob."

"Sex? You mean the man and the two women? Certainly not. I'm all in favor of freedom but this is a family medium. You know that Jim you know that. We have a pure spiritual relationship between the man and the two women. After all, one is a missionary's wife and wouldn't think of sex and the other is . . . well, slightly mannish and wouldn't think of it either."

"Maybe it wasn't like that," said Jim, and at once regretted it. The island was none of Hob's business.

"I don't care how it was, we're talking about art now, not life. This is where constructive criticism comes in, Jim. We will have sex problems only with the animals. In good taste, of course. The horse is lonely, there is no other horse, and . . . well, you can work it out. He sublimates in a cute way . . . I see a windmill. He builds a windmill, I mean he operates it."

"Operates windmill," said Jim. "Lonely horse with hard on."

"Don't mock, I know this sounds like Dr. Dolittle, but all art is derivative. And that's what you're for, to make it *be* like Dr. Dolittle but not *look* like Dr. Dolittle. I'm telling you, it's a good idea, Jim. The thing could run forever. And it'd be cheap to do. The animals would be the stars and you don't need to pay animals hardly anything."

"I know, you don't even have to get the horse laid," said Jim. It was fantastic. But the most fantastic thing of all was he could well imagine Hob selling a shrewd variation of the "talking animal" idea to a network. Of course, in the form Hob presented it the idea was laughably ridiculous, but Hob knew this himself—otherwise he wouldn't be willing to pay all kinds of money to a man who could make it *be* like Dr. Dolittle but not *look* like Dr. Dolittle. The basic piracy was sound. If Hugh Lofting did it first, so what? How could you *patent* a "talking animal" or any of the other successful ideas that crop up from time to time in the world of culture and entertainment? The thing, as Hob said, could run forever. A little variation was necessary, that was all, a little disguise and the buzzing plastic pecker would be right in there. Telepathic animals, maybe—you hear their sweet trilling voices but their horrible goat mouths and donkey lips don't move. Sure, telepathic animals, solid as plastic and with a clever writer it would buzz, too, in millions of rectums throughout the land. God in heaven knows worse shows had been done and more cynical ideas earnestly proposed at television and motion-picture script conferences.

"Think you've got something there, Hob," said Jim. "But it needs garnish. Try this. Horse loses erection and dies. Dr. Dobig has to bury him. They uncover a strange rectangular slab that makes the animals telepathic. Get it, Hob? Science fiction and Dr. Squatlarge."

Hob moistened his lips. "You think you're joking but you've found it. Science fiction and Dr. Dolittle. All right, this will be our first series. We'll work together closely on this, it's my pet."

Jim stirred the swizzle stick in the Bloody Mary he had not touched but that Hob somehow had inveigled him into ordering. How could he ever have been under the control of this man? What kind of existence was it to spend insane, laborious hours attempting to pump life into utter idiocy? Was it worth a hundred thousand dollars a year? Was it worth two hundred thousand? Was it worth a million or two or three?

"I'll tell you, Hob," said Jim. "I don't want to spend what years of my life I have left working for you. Get somebody else to help you with the talking animals."

Hob smiled, unperturbed. "You think you don't need me, Jim? You can go direct to the networks yourself, is that it?"

Jim shrugged. "Since you mention it, why not?"

"They won't give you financing, Jim."

"Won't they?"

Hob still did not seem perturbed, but his eyes blinked owlishly and his whisper became more faint. "You might promote a little writer money. But for real money to do actual pilots you'll need me."

"Why? If the networks like a script they'll let me make a pilot as quick as they would you. Maybe quicker. Let's face it, Hob. That story of your buzzing artificial pecker hasn't helped your image around town."

"Hee hee hee," said Hob with a weak little grin.

A *very* weak little grin. For the first time it dawned on Jim that John Terrence Hobson was in serious trouble. The man had lost his power base and it was power by which he lived. Another thing dawned on Jim, a thing he'd realized only in part before. The truth was Hob *could not* develop a show on his own, he was utterly incapable of doing so. The Dr. Dolittle idea seemed especially ludicrous, but it was no more ludicrous than Hob's other ideas. The man could invent nothing. All he could do was force or hypnotize someone else into developing a show for him, at which point he would step in and touch it and turn it into garbage. And yet as ludicrous as the man seemed at this moment, granted a power base he was very dangerous. He had fooled many people and would fool many more. Those who did not understand him were helpless in his hands.

But Jim could not work up much anger even though he'd been John Hobson's slave. After all, it was weakness in himself that had made it possible.

"No, thanks, Hob," said Jim. "Count me out. I don't want to work for you."

"You are making the most serious error of your life, Jim," said Hob quietly. "You are not only turning down a fortune, you are incurring my ill will. I'll come back, Jim."

"Oh, I'm sure you'll come back, Hob. But not for a while. I really think that buzzing artificial pecker has put you out of business for a couple of years."

"I'll admit that smear probably hasn't done me any good," answered Hob with a smile. "But on the other hand, your being stuck on that island with those two dogs hasn't helped *your* image much either."

Jim stared uncomprehendingly at the rosy-cheeked, athletic-looking little man across the table from him. What was the fool talking about? He pronounced it "doggs"—that was "dog," but there was only one dog on the island, Rufus. An impulse to murder came to Jim as he realized Hob had meant by "two dogs" Melody and Florence.

"That's going to cost you a Bloody Mary in the face, Hob. At the very least it'll cost you that."

"Well," said Hob doubtfully, a trace of bewilderment in his eyes, "no offense intended, Jim, and I don't know why you're angry. I'm sympathetic to you for being stuck on an island with two such unattractive women. And you certainly can't say they were beauty queens.

I saw the picture of you with them and they were dogs, both of them."

Was a Bloody Mary in the face enough? At this moment the brunette waitress who had brought the drinks returned with Hob's omelette aux fines herbes, soft and runny the way he liked it. Jim waited until the waitress was gone, then he stood up and said quietly:

"I shouldn't do this, Hob. In a way, to pay any attention to you kind of degrades my feeling for the two women who were with me on that island. So let's say this has nothing to do with them. It's just to convince you I don't want to receive any more phone calls from you or any further invitations to lunch, brunch, or dinner—okay?"

Adrenalin in massive quantities surged into Jim's blood as he grabbed Hob by the back of the head and smashed his face down into the runny omelette aux fines herbes. When he got the face down he scrounged it and rubbed it back and forth on the plate with all his strength, shoulders hunched like a bear. He heard the plate crack and heard a snuffling sound from Hob. Left hand like iron on the plump neck, Jim picked up his own Bloody Mary and poured it on the thin-haired crown, poured Hob's Bloody Mary on top of that, and finally dumped an overfull ashtray on the whole mess. He then stood back and waited till the omelette-smeared face slowly lifted. Egg hung from the Goblin's eyebrows and his nose was bleeding from the force with which Jim had shoved his head down on the plate.

"Service is terrible these days," said Jim. "They just don't empty ashtrays any more."

Hob licked his lips and for a moment Jim had an impression he was eating the omelet. A whisper came: "You will never work again in this town."

"There're other towns," said Jim. "You know that old saying, Hob. Other towns, other ashtrays."

Jim turned and walked up the steps and out to the sidewalk. It was an incontestable satisfaction to be rid once and for all of John Terrence Hobson, but the problem had always been larger than Hob, and Jim had no feeling of great achievement. As he emerged into the fresh air, he took a deep breath and sighed.

TWENTY-SEVEN

The Dragon Cries

Jim finally managed to have lunch with Florence seven days after his return to New York. Long before the meeting ended on a sad-acrimonious note of goodbye, he was ready to accept Florence's own name for it: the Dismal Little Lunch.

The lunch with Florence, the brief meeting with her at her apartment, and the telephone conversation with her the afternoon before were depressing and painful indeed. The shocks came in a gray succession. The first thing that shocked him was his discovery that Florence was a liar. He had not realized this about her before. Melody, he knew, would tell a fib, but he'd always thought Florence was a truthful person. It was quite a shock to listen to her.

First she said she'd gone alone up to Cape Cod to "think about things." She had stayed by herself in a Barnstable motel called the Wild Turkey Inn. All alone, to think. Then she admitted the last couple of days her editor had come up and "half-joined" her; he had not taken a room at the motel but had stayed at his sister's home in Hyannis. The truth, as it finally emerged, was that Rufus had been with her all along in the Wild Turkey Inn.

Jim's shock that she would lie and hedge and be mealy-mouthed about it was even greater than his shock she would cold-bloodedly go to bed with Rufus in order to decide whether or not to marry him When Jim first heard about it on the telephone, he pictured a graying, fifty-year-old, cultivated, meek, gentlemanly, and rather effeminate man who spent all his time making little silly marks on manuscripts and and writing wise, encouraging letters to temperamenta authors, while living cautiously on a modest editorial salary in a nea West-side bachelor apartment. How could such a man be a threat?

It turned out Rufus was forty-three, only a year older than he wa himself. He did not have a gray hair in his head and was an excellen tennis player who had been singles champion of Hyannis a number o times. His editorial salary was modest but he didn't need it; he and hi older sister in Hyannis were the heirs of a Boston fortune that wen back five generations. They were richer than Linda and of older lineage; it was Linda's great-grandfather who'd made her money. The man worked as an editor because he liked books. The only thing correct in Jim's picture of Rufus was that he was gentlemanly and rather shy. He had a slight stammer, Florence said, and found it difficult to make conversation with strangers, except on the tennis court or in his editorial offices. The real Rufus, far from being a meek little nonthreat, was a menace.

Most of this Jim learned at the painful lunch. But even when he'd pictured Rufus as a gray nonentity, the thought of him in Florence's arms made him so sick he'd almost collapsed right there in his bedroom at the Plaza. It was, he thought, the lies and the mealy-mouthed hedging that upset him the most, but the thought of her infidelity had a horror to it that was nameless. It was a completely irrational reaction; of course she had her life to live and every right in the world to behave as she had done—but still, how could she *do* this to him? How could she weep at the window of that plane in San Andres and a few days later calmly go to a motel and get in bed with another man? And the casual way she talked about it was downright amazing. It was as if she were saying: "I went to the post office and bought a stamp and mailed a letter." But the vulgarity of her remarks was worse than the casualness. Her coarseness made Jim wince. It was as if she took an enjoyment in rubbing his nose in it, saying such things as: "Well, I had to see if I could do it with him, didn't I?" And then in a crude tone: "Oh, yes, I came beautifully." She had gotten over her heartbreak on the island pretty fast.

If he had only looked to see it, he would have realized there had always been a streak of coarseness and vulgarity in Florence. This was amply demonstrated not only by the phone conversation with her, but by her grimy apartment and by both her appearance and behavior when Jim finally managed to see her and have lunch with her. He'd gone to her apartment building and learned from the superintendent's wife that Florence was out of town. "I been feeding her birdies," the woman said. "But she's coming back tomorrow."

Jim called Florence the next day and finally reached her and after much difficulty managed to persuade her to have lunch with him.

"But what on earth's the point?" she asked. "Why should we have lunch?"

"Look, I didn't even get a chance to say goodbye to you."

"Oh, Christ, Jim, that's not true. You said goodbye to me in San Andres. It's all over, don't you realize that? It was nice on the island, but we're not on the island any more and it's finished. Lunch would be a mistake, we'd both be depressed by it."

"I really want to see you, Florence. Let's have lunch tomorrow. There's a very good restaurant I know—"

"I'm only here for a couple of days. I've got to pack my clothes, arrange to ship my books and things to Westport, have the lease of the apartment put in my niece's name, and do a million other things. I don't have *time* for lunch."

"Florence, please. I really want to see you."

"But what *for?*"

"I want to discuss your career with you."

"What the fuck do you care about my career?"

Jim had ground his teeth as he sat on the bed in his gold and white Plaza bedroom. There was a coarse streak in Florence, all right. He was very nearly tempted to tell her to forget it, but he *did* want to talk to her about her career. And he was curious to find out more about her plans and more about Rufus. Evidently she was marrying soon if she was leaving in a couple of days. And why not? After all, she had learned she could "do it" with him. A kind of masochism drove Jim on.

"All right, all right!" said Florence finally. "It's ridiculous, but Rufus predicted I would have to see you again before this is over. I showed him your letter and that's what he said and he was right."

"You got my letter?"

"Yes, it came the day before we left for the Cape."

"You could have answered. But never mind, we'll have lunch."

"Yes, we'll have lunch," said Florence grimly. "It's a mistake and you'll be sorry, but all right. Where'll it be?"

"I'll pick you up at your apartment at twelve-thirty," said Jim.

"No, I'll meet you at the restaurant."

"Florence, I want to see your apartment, the place you live."

"Oh, for Christ's sake, I'm *leaving* it tomorrow night, Jim."

"I want to see it anyhow."

"But it's a mess, clothes half packed, books in crates—"

"Florence, why are you being so unpleasant? I'll pick you up at your apartment."

"All right, what's the difference? But you won't like the apartment. You'll be sorry."

Florence was right. Jim was sorry he went to her apartment. However, he was so stunned and dismayed by Florence's appearance when she opened the door he did not even notice her apartment for the first two minutes he was in it. The shock staggered him. Despite the unpleasantness of the phone conversation with her, Jim had walked into her rather dingy apartment building confident he would be overjoyed to see her and confident she would look like herself—not beautiful, not even pretty maybe, but like Florence, like herself.

"Well, Jim. Nice to see you." Jim could not speak. Who was this buck-toothed, freckle-faced, homely woman in the gruesome and ill-fitting suit? Could it be *Florence?* "I suppose you want to come in for a minute?"

"Well . . . yes," said Jim.

"Rufus is in the bedroom, I'll get him. The Rufus you know. I'm sure he'll be happy to see you."

In a daze, Jim picked his way past crates of books and a half-packed trunk of clothing into what seemed to be a small living room that also served as a dining room and office. Unseeingly, he stared around at inexpensive prints on the walls and worn-out overstuffed furniture, then braced himself as a shaggy creature came bounding in the room, jumped up on him, and put paws on his chest.

"Hi, Rufus," said Jim.

"Told you he'd be happy to see you. I think he wonders in the back of his head what on earth became of you and Melody."

"Any . . . any trouble getting off the plane in Miami?"

"No. Why should there be trouble?"

Jim didn't know what he was saying and he didn't know what to say. "Well, I . . . I . . . shall we go to lunch?"

"I thought you wanted to see my apartment."

"Yes, of course." Jim looked from side to side and up and down, seeing nothing. "It's nice."

"I like it. I'm lucky to have had it. My niece cried with joy when I told her she was getting it back. She kept it for me while I was away, you know."

"Um-hmm, I know, you told me about her."

"It's been great for me. You see, I have a little garden out back."

Jim attempted to focus his attention in the direction indicated, but it was difficult. How in creation could Florence fix her hair in such a manner? The straw-colored hair was parted in the middle at a weird angle and stuck up from her head in two uneven lopsided masses.

And how could any woman have so many freckles on her face? And the teeth—couldn't she close her mouth and hide them or something?

"Of course, in the winter it doesn't look like much," said Florence in a sad little voice.

Jim forced himself to pay attention to the garden. Beyond paint-flaking French doors he could see a tiny, ugly, walled-in area with rotten limp stalks in the ground. It was the most dismal little garden he had ever seen. How could she point to it with pride? "It's nice," said Jim.

"In the summer it is," said Florence. "Do you want to sit down for a minute?"

"Oh . . . sure," said Jim.

Five extremely awkward minutes followed. Jim could think of nothing to say and Florence seemed to be having the same difficulty. The apartment, he felt, was as horrible as the tiny garden. Of course, Florence had never made any money from the arty little books she wrote and her standards were not the same as his own, but could there be *worse* apartments than this?

Jim found it difficult to believe a human habitation could be more grim or lacking in aesthetic appeal of any kind. The overstuffed furniture was fairly comfortable, but it was cheap and ugly and dirty and the upholstery was torn. A hideous oak roll-top desk stood in one corner, piled and stacked with manuscripts, boxes of typing paper, pencils, and other litter. Books were everywhere. Four or five cardboard boxes had been filled with them and there were plenty more to be packed; books were on the floor, on the tables, in the corners, even on top of the stove in the tiny Pullman kitchenette, the sink of which was filled to overflowing with dirty dishes. There were also many magazines and periodicals scattered everywhere.

The place had a certain lived-in, worked-in comfort, but grim was the word. The most depressing thing about it was the lack of light; the only illumination came from the French doors that opened onto the horrible little garden. In broad day it was necessary for the floor lamps to be on. And the "birdies" didn't help. This was the only so-called feminine touch Jim could see, the two cages of canaries and the single cage containing a couple of parakeets. It was the apartment of a working writer, but except for the spinsterish "birdies" it could be the apartment of a man writer.

"I guess we'd better go," said Florence. "Do you want to see the bedrooms?"

Jim resisted an impulse to say, "Oh, I don't think so." He smiled as best as possible and said, "Sure, I'd love to."

The muscles of Jim's cheeks ached from the stiffness of his smile as he stared at one miserable little bedroom after the other. Neither bedroom had the slightest feeling of femininity. The monotone curtains were drab, the floors were bare. Linda would go out of her mind in such an apartment. There was nothing really "wrong" with it, it wasn't actually grimy or dirty, it simply had no appeal, no beauty, no charm.

"Yes, very nice," said Jim in pained embarrassment as they returned to the living room.

"I guess it's pretty dinky and gloomy, but it does have the garden and that makes up for a lot. You see, it's pretty in the summer. Very pretty. I put little flowers out there and they look so beautiful in the middle of all the ugliness . . . you know, it's funny how writers quote themselves from their works. That's practically a line from one of my shitty little books. I do it all the time. I'll get my coat, let's go to lunch."

Jim slowly shook his head. One of her "shitty little books." What kind of way was that for a woman to talk? Her rough language had often seemed funny on the island but it didn't seem funny now. It was impossible to imagine Linda referring to one of her "shitty little books."

"I guess it's pretty dinky," said Florence as she got her coat. "Rufus hates it . . . and he hates this coat too. He says he's going to buy me another coat and I guess I'll let him."

Jim had nearly groaned aloud at the sight of the coat. It seemed to be made of some kind of camel fur upon which an odd glaze had been unevenly applied. It shone with gaudy spuriousness in some places and was frankly dull and ratty elsewhere. How could she wear such a coat and where in the name of God had she found it? From whence could such a coat as this be obtained? Jim could not imagine her buying such a coat in a store; she must have come across it in a garbage can somewhere.

"Oh, no," said Jim, "dinky, the apartment? It's nice."

"Rufus loathes it and I can see you do too. If you want to know the truth, I don't pay much attention to my surroundings. But we're leaving here tomorrow anyhow, me and my dog and birds are going to live in Westport."

"Is that where your editor lives, in Westport?"

"Yes, he has a house there. Rufus has two children, you know, a girl seventeen and a boy nineteen. Shall we go?"

Jim picked up his overcoat from the top of a chair; Florence had not offered to hang it up for him. "How old is Rufus?" he asked.

"He was forty-three last month."

"*Forty-three?*"

"Yes, how old did you think he was?"

"I thought he . . . was a little older. A widower and everything."

"His wife died young. Cancer three years ago—no, nearer four. She was only thirty-six."

"I didn't realize he was that young a man. When are you getting married, soon?"

"Yes, day after tomorrow in Hyannis at his sister's place."

"Day after tomorrow? As soon as all that, Florence?"

"He's waited three years, there's no point in making him wait any longer. Jim, I really think we'd better go on to lunch. I've got all those books to pack and my clothes too."

Jim slowly put on his coat, a sickness in his vitals. "All right," he said, "I hope you know what you're doing, Florence."

"Oh, yes, there's something I wanted to tell you," said Florence. "I am *not* pregnant, by the way. Or at least I wasn't two days after I got back."

"Good," said Jim in a wan voice. Somehow it seemed ironic he hadn't even been able to get her pregnant.

"I checked on it right away, in fact I had a complete gynocological go-over. I'm healthy as can be and there's no reason I can't have a child, but I'm not pregnant and I thought you'd like to know that."

"Yes, thanks for the information."

"Speaking of pregnancy, I had a card from Melody. Did you hear from her?"

"I had a letter."

"Oh? What'd she say?"

"Everything's fine. She's fine, Charles is fine, they're all fine. I'll tell you about it at lunch."

"Okay, let's go."

Purse in hand and a weird hat now on her head, Florence was

ready. Jim took one last glance at the apartment. "Dinky," alas, was not the word for it; "horrible" was the word for it. A madness had seized him on Providence Island. How could he have dreamed even for a moment of living in this apartment with Florence and Melody? He'd been totally out of his mind. Melody, seen in reality, would probably shock him almost as much as Florence.

It was, Jim felt, impossible to recapture a dream, utterly impossible. This was what he'd tried to do by going to Florence's apartment and taking her out to lunch. It was a painful mistake. The isolation of the island had detached them from the real world and had made the experience itself a kind of dream, a dream to which none of them could return.

And in that fact there was something depressing. If the truth be known, one of the reasons he had gotten so infuriated with Hob at the "brunch" was because there was a certain accuracy in Hob's description of Melody and Florence as "dogs." Of course, they were human beings and it was revolting to describe any human person as a "dog," but Melody and Florence were not very attractive women, either one of them. Melody had some good features, a very sweet smile and deep blue eyes and full, beautiful breasts, but she was a large woman and overweight. Florence also had some good features, a rather pretty little body and nice cheekbones and character in her face, but she was a homely woman and that was all there was to it. Judged by the standards of the civilization in which they all lived, Melody and Florence were "dogs." A spell had indeed been put upon him on that island and, even before that, on the *Lorna Loone*, which was a kind of extension of the island in the sense that it isolated them from the real world. It was incredible to think of it now, but during those final days in Morgan's Second Treasure Cave he had thought Melody and Florence both were beautiful.

The actual lunch at La Jolie was even more depressing and painful than the visit to Florence's apartment, because for a few fleeting moments Jim experienced something like a return to the feeling he had had for her under the spell of the island. Until then he'd merely felt awkward and embarrassed, but to feel a brief return of his old love for her was a pain of a different category altogether.

At first he'd felt nothing more than awkward embarrassment in La Jolie. It was no doubt absurd of him, since Florence's coat and suit and hat and hair-do were not really all *that* bad, but Jim could not help but flinch with embarrassment when he walked in there with her and saw the look of startled surprise on "Frankie's" face. Florence was not exactly on a par with the beautiful young actresses. She would never cause "Frankie" to lift his eyebrows and say: "Meester *Keet*ering! How-do-you-do-eet?"

The conversation about Melody was a relief from strained self-consciousness, but the thought of Melody was of itself rather depressing to Jim. Over drinks Florence said: "Tell me about Melody. What did she say in her letter? Her card to me only said everything was okay."

"It's kind of interesting," said Jim. "She wrote to tell me everything had turned out all right with Charles and I didn't need to worry about her any more. I gather they had a very touching scene when she told him about living with me and being pregnant. She's definitely pregnant, by the way. Charles says it's 'God's child' and he'll raise it as his own."

"That's sweet," said Florence. "I always thought he loved her and she loved him."

"Well, they had problems."

"Yes, but I always thought it was a real marriage. Have you seen your wife yet, by the way?"

"No, but her lawyer tells me she's flying in tomorrow evening and will call me. I hope to have lunch with her day after tomorrow."

"That's the time I'll be getting married in Hyannis. The wedding's at noon, we want to take a plane that afternoon to Nassau."

"Huh, Linda's in the Bahamas herself," said Jim. "Maybe if I don't persuade her to come back to me you'll run into her down there."

Florence smiled. "I'm sure she'll come back to you. There's no more doubt in my mind about that than there is about Melody and Charles. Of course, Charles would have to be an absolute fool to blame her for such a thing. What else could she *do* but live with you on the island? I thought she did damned well to hold out for a month, myself, with such a crush on you and wanting a baby of her own so much. And besides, Melody's a sexy woman. She did damn well to hold out for a month."

"*Crush*, huh, is that what you think?"

"No. Not crush. On the island Melody loved you."

"Yes, on the island," said Jim, "and on the boat. In the real world she loves her husband. But they've had troubles. The interesting thing is, Charles had *a nervous breakdown* in Colombia. That's why they had to fly him back to the States. You won't believe this but it turns out he has never really wanted to be a minister—his mother and Melody forced him into it, especially the mother, who seems to have been a holy battle-axe in a sweet quiet way."

"Sort of like Melody when we first knew her?"

"Yes, sort of like Melody when she got on the *Lorna Loone* in Savannah, before she started teaching lady novelists how to make love and indulging herself in orgies."

"Hoho," said Florence, "great little teacher."

Jim smiled. For a moment Florence almost sounded like herself, but it was ancient history and she was not really interested; her eyes were down on her whisky sour and she was trying to get the cherry out with an oyster fork. "Anyhow," said Jim, "it's interesting about Charles. This hang-up about being a minister was the cause of his near-impotence and all the trouble he and Melody had in bed. The man was trying to do something he couldn't do and didn't want to do, and Melody in a misguided effort was trying to help him by forcing him to do it. The more he showed signs of *not* wanting to be a missionary, the more she bucked him up, and the irony was Melody didn't want to do it herself. She sort of took over for the mother when the mother died three years ago. At the same time, Charles discovered he was sterile. The death of the mother, the wife pushing him into being a missionary, and then the jolt of finding himself unable to give her children undid the man."

"You know, I suspected something like that all along," said Florence. "The mysterious radiogram we got on the ship—why didn't it say what his illness was? I figured it was mental."

"I never suspected that," said Jim. "But I can well believe the Melody we met on that boat could be a rough customer as a mother replacement. She has a will of iron and a sense of duty six miles wide. I shudder to think of the pressure she must have put on Charles in an effort to be a 'dutiful' wife to him, and since Charles himself thought that's what he wanted, the thing got worse and worse until they were both half crazy."

"People are funny, aren't they," said Florence.

"Hilarious," said Jim. "Anyhow, when he went down to Colombia ahead of Melody, poor Charles began to collapse. When he knew she was about to arrive and would see what a mess everything was, he went to pieces completely and they had to fly him out. He was under psychiatric care for three months at Duke and made a good recovery. The shock of thinking Melody dead and his own breakdown forced him to come to terms with his life, and I guess the psychotherapy helped him too. Anyhow, he's quit the ministry and he and Melody are probably going to Alaska."

"*Alaska?*"

"They're thinking about it. They've written to Fairbanks. He's a medical doctor, you know, and Melody's a trained nurse. They want to start a clinic up there."

"My God, and I always wanted to go live with the Eskimos myself."

"Not the Eskimos necessarily, but somewhere in Alaska if they really want doctors up there, and I'm sure they do. It seems Charles was *physically* sick in Colombia too. The tropics don't agree with him."

"I'm happy for her," said Florence. "She was very sweet to me on the island, sweeter than almost anyone I've ever known. I do love Melody. I'll always love her. . . ."

Jim turned slowly and stared at Florence with a pensive frown. At this moment a waiter arrived with her oysters and his own pâté, but Jim continued to stare at Florence. She was not looking at him but down at a basket of bread, a film of tears in her eyes. Briefly, with a fleeting poignance, the spell of the island returned and Jim felt once again the love he had known for Florence in Morgan's Second Treasure Cave; in an instant, her unattractive suit and unbecoming hair-do vanished and she was herself again.

"I'll always love Melody too," said Jim. "And if you'll always love her, then why don't you love *me* any more, Florence?"

Florence did not look up for several seconds, but kept her gaze down on the basket of bread as she bit her lip and the film of tears brimmed in her eyes. Finally, with a little shrug, she looked up at him. "Who says I don't?"

"Then why are you rushing off to marry this man?"

Florence took a handkerchief from her purse and touched it to her eyes, then turned to Jim and said calmly: "Because I don't want to be a sort of half-assed mistress of yours. I have better things to do with my life."

"Is that what you think would happen?"

"Isn't it what you had in mind when you wrote me that letter?"

The moment of return to Providence Island was gone. Back in New York, thought Jim, and this time to stay. Of course his attitude was irrational; Florence had every right to protect herself, but there was something cold-blooded about her receiving his letter and immediately running off to the Cape with Rufus.

"I merely wanted to discuss your career with you," said Jim. "It was never my intention to make you my mistress, either half-assed or whole-assed, as you so elegantly express it."

"I told you this lunch was a mistake. I said goodbye to you at San Andres and we should have left it at that, instead of burdening ourselves with the memory of this dismal little lunch in this *shitty* little restaurant."

Jim gritted his teeth. She was talking in a loud, clear voice and the distinguished-looking man and his daughter at the next table might hear her; twice they had already glanced around at some raucous remark or other she had made. Jim was also indignant at her failure to appreciate the exquisite service and marvelous food. She had frowned at the waiters as if they were bothering her and hardly had touched her lunch. "Frankie" in particular seemed to annoy her, although he'd called her "ma-*dahm*" in a soft voice and been very polite. It was stupid to put it in mercenary terms, but didn't she realize this luncheon would cost somewhere between thirty and forty dollars?

"I don't want to question your culinary judgment. Would you rather have eaten at the Automat?" asked Jim. "La Jolie happens to be one of the best restaurants in the world, including Paris."

"Fuck it!" said Florence. Jim winced as he caught a glimpse of the silver-haired man and his young well-dressed daughter at the next table. They had turned around as if stuck by a pin.

"Florence," said Jim, "would you, as the saying goes, moderate your vocal delivery? The people at the next table can hear you."

"I don't care," said Florence. "I'm not afraid of them. And I say—*fuck* it! It's a dismal little lunch and a *shitty* little restaurant."

"It's dismal, all right. Dismal because you've so completely misunderstood my motives in inviting you to it."

"Okay, you asked for this," said Florence calmly. "What possible motive could you have for inviting me to lunch except to make me your mistress? And if that *wasn't* your motive, why did you just play on my feelings and try to make me back out of marrying the only man who's ever really wanted me? What else did you mean by telling me I'm *rushing* into marrying Rufus?"

Jim felt ill. The nerve she had was beyond belief. And her stupidity was incredible. He'd always thought Florence had some brains, but she didn't. A spell had indeed been cast upon him on that island. "I hate to say this. I really do, Florence, I thought you had better sense. But you remind me of a stupid little girl sitting by me on the plane coming back from Bogotá."

"I don't care what dame of yours I remind you of," said Florence. "But you're right about one thing, I *am* 'rushing' into marrying Rufus. His sister begged me to wait at least a couple of weeks so she can plan a proper wedding. His own son can't get out of school to come day after tomorrow, the boy has exams now. I'm 'rushing' to get away from *you* because the truth is, your letter tempted me more than I can tell you. It put me through hell. Of course I love you. I've loved you ever since we were in that little park in Savannah. And the thing that breaks my heart and has been the worst torment of all is I think you love me too. But you don't *want* me, Jim. This is what I faced on the Cape, you love me but you don't want me. I wouldn't even be a real mistress to you. Just like I said, I'd be a *half-assed* mistress and I don't care if they hear it at the next table or not. You'd sneak and come to see me once in a while, but you'd always be ashamed of my freckles, my buck teeth, my bad language, and my dinky little apartment. Well, I don't want a man who's ashamed of me, I want a man who loves me for myself, the way I am. And that is why day after tomorrow I am marrying Rufus Turnbull."

There was nothing Jim could say. There was no argument, no answer. Florence was mistaken to think he had intended to try to make her his "half-assed mistress," but the other things she had said were true. Outside the spell of Providence Island, they were true.

It had been foolish and pointless for him to call Florence at all, he had caused her irritation and upset for no good reason, although he did feel it was a mistake for her to continue wasting her talent writing novels no one read.

"I feel kind of like a fool," said Jim after a futile struggle to think of something else to say. "I don't know why, it's irrational. I really didn't invite you to lunch for any ulterior motive, Florence."

"I'm sure you weren't conscious of any such thing and I understand the way you feel," said Florence in a different voice. A resigned little smile was on her face. "You think you owe me something, Jim, but you don't. You are free to go back to Linda, which is the thing you really want to do. I guess I was trying to hurt you and put you on with all my talk about Rufus and me in the Wild Turkey Inn. Frankly, it wasn't all that great. But he's a good man and I like him and for some strange reason he wants me with all my freckles and other faults."

"I'm happy for you, Florence," said Jim. "And of course I want to go back to Linda. I love her, Florence. And also my two girls. I never told you or Melody, but I dreamed about them constantly, my wife and the children. It was beautiful on the island, I loved you, but here . . . what else can I do?"

It was too depressing to bear; Jim in his own turn had to look down to hide his tears. He saw a freckled hand reach toward his own hand and stop.

"Nothing else," said Florence calmly. "I knew that on the island, you never lied to me. You've got nothing to feel guilty about. Go on back to Linda, she's the kind of woman you can be proud of and happy with, she'd fit in a restaurant like this just perfectly, and I don't."

Finis. Melody was gone and so was Florence. The adventure of Providence Island was over. But Jim still felt Florence should stop writing arty little novels and enter the main arena. It seemed to him if he could persuade Florence to buckle down and be mature about her work he would save something in the situation. Her career was in a mess and what she needed was constructive criticism. While "Frankie" wheeled forward the elaborate dessert cart and two waiters poured coffee with a silent grace, Jim tugged at his collar and argued with Florence in an effort to coax her into the main arena.

"Get into the main arena, goddamn it, Florence," he said. "Not to work with *me,* hell no. There're a lot of people you can work with. I can get you a top agent. You could really fulfill yourself and incidentally make a lot of money."

"Well, I didn't want to show you this because it's so ostentatious," said Florence as she opened her purse and burrowed into it. "I'm afraid cabdrivers will pull it off my finger if I wear it."

Jim bent forward in surprise as Florence held up before him a diamond engagement ring with the biggest stone he had ever seen outside a jewelry store or a museum display case. "Good God," he said, "where'd you get *that?*"

Florence idly turned the white-gold ring with the huge diamond around and around on her finger. "Sparkles, doesn't it? It's no more real to me than Morgan's Treasure, but Rufus wants me to have it. It belonged to his wife and his mother before her."

A diamond was merely a diamond even if it was a *big* diamond, but despite himself Jim felt an awed reverence. How many hours of human labor were imprisoned in that bit of carbon crystal? What kind of superbeings could own and wear such a magnificent ring? Rufus was a menace. He had *this* kind of money behind him . . . and still got up and went to work as an editor and spent his time editing little books no one would read? It was fantastic. What made such a man tick?

"That thing must be worth fifty thousand dollars or more," said Jim in a hushed tone.

"Silly bauble," said Florence. With an expression of distaste, she dropped the ring in her purse and snapped it shut. "My point is, I *don't* need money, Jim. I can always hock Rufus's mother's ring. But I don't need money anyhow. All I've ever wanted is a little cottage on the Cape."

Jim couldn't get over the ring. He felt a bit dazed, like the devil after having holy water thrown on him. The sparkling and fiery facets of that stone had a reality beyond the piles of currency he had found in Morgan's First Treasure Cave. The audacity, the gall, the cosmic impudence of owning such frozen wealth expressed what it was to be truly rich and beyond it all. And Florence, who didn't want it or care about it, had walked right into it.

"Speaking of Morgan's Treasure," Jim said with a wistful smile, "I sent a letter and a check for that three thousand dollars to the C.I.A. On second thought I'm *sure* that little duck was an agent. I told them if it was Cuban money to send us our share."

"To hell with it," said Florence.

"But it isn't just money I was talking about, Florence. You should fulfill yourself as an artist."

"I don't . . . want . . . to write . . . for television."

"But you did before. You came to the office."

"I was curious to see what you were like."

"Florence, that's ridiculous. You didn't come there just to see me."

"I certainly did. Jim, you called me five times. Don't you remember? We talked once for almost an hour. You told me the story of your life, practically."

"But you took the job, you accepted a check from the Goblin."

Florence shrugged. "I wanted to go on that boat with you."

"Let's get back to the main arena. I repeat—why write little books no one reads? You can fulfill yourself as an artist, Florence. You can use your gifts completely."

"I'm using them already as best I can."

"How many people read your last book? A thousand? Ten thousand?"

"In hard cover not too many, but that one was in paperbound. A hundred thousand read it at least."

"A hundred thousand," said Jim. "That's pathetic. Don't you realize tens of *millions* would see your work on television?"

"Oh, fuck!" said Florence. "I don't write my books for the people who *don't* read them, I write them for the people who *do* read them."

"That's a childish attitude, Florence, very childish. Won't you at least talk to one of the top agents?"

"No, I won't. I'm a book writer, goddamn it, and I wish you'd get your tongue out of my ass. You had it there once, wasn't that enough? You sound like that fucking Goblin."

Jim hunched his head down in embarrassment. She was incorrigible. The silver-haired man and his pretty young daughter were gone, thank God, but the people at the table on the other side must have heard her. What a thing to say, and what a thing to remind him of! It was an event from which Jim Kittering had never fully recovered. Of course he'd been so drunk he didn't know what he was doing, but why had he done such a thing even drunk? Was it mere play like naughty children, as Melody believed, or was there some other meaning that escaped him? Jim could not tell. It seemed to him the episode contained a mixture of motives and a mixture of consequences as well, but what they were he could not say.

"Okay, you're hopeless," said Jim. "I give up, Florence. Go ahead and marry the man and write your books, and God go with you, honey."

"Good luck with your wife," said Florence with a smile, "and God go with you, too, Jim."

Depressing and painful as it was, the Dismal Little Lunch had cleared the decks, Jim felt, and in that sense was worthwhile. He had seen Florence as she was, not in a haze of distorting isolation but in the glaring light of the real world. Although he still liked her and admired her stubbornness, there was an incontestable streak of coarseness and vulgarity in her.

However, when he assisted Florence into a taxi fifteen minutes later and watched her ride away into a life of her own, Jim stood stricken on the sidewalk. As the taxi vanished, tears once again came in his eyes. The Dismal Little Lunch was so painful he had to cry.

PART NINE
Easter

TWENTY-EIGHT

The Dragon Dies

Jim became aware that lunch with Linda would prove to be an absolute disaster when he saw the mutation mink coat she was wearing as she walked toward his table in the southeast corner of the Edwardian Room. The coat was wrong. There would be no reconciliation with Linda and his marriage was over, finished and done with.

Jim stood up, a napkin in his left hand and the hand lightly on the table to brace himself. He could feel a trembling in his knees as the dreaded truth spread through him. Ironically, sadly, she was beautiful as ever, even more beautiful than he had remembered her; the golden hair, the serene blue eyes, the perfect smile all were there. Hers was a beauty that had about it something heartbreaking.

Linda extended a gloved hand. "Hello, Jim."

"Hello, Linda." Jim shook her hand, then pulled back a chair and pushed it under her as she sat down. He sat down himself and carefully spread his napkin on his knees.

"Here I am," said Linda. "As I said on the phone, I'm perfectly willing to discuss a reconciliation with you, Jim. I want to hear anything you can say that you feel would put our marriage on a new and different basis. We owe it to our children and to ourselves as well. But I must tell you honestly, I am not hopeful at all."

"Maybe you'll change your mind, Linda, after we've talked a while," said Jim with a calm that surprised him. Perhaps the coat meant nothing. It was pretty far-fetched to come to a conclusion on the basis of a stupid thing like a new expensive coat.

"I don't think so. But I'm ready to listen. What exactly did you want to say to me, Jim?"

"There isn't anything specific or concrete I can say, Linda," answered Jim, again with a calm that surprised him. "My thought simply was that we would have lunch and talk about this or that, anything that seems interesting."

Linda smiled and frowned at the same time, as if in a pained sympathy. "You've asked me to fly up from Nassau to talk about this and that?"

"Sure," said Jim. "We'll just talk."

"Walter says if . . . if we're not reconciled at this lunch, you want a divorce. Is that true?"

"I wouldn't put it like that. I'd say if we aren't reconciled now, I think you should go ahead and get a divorce yourself. I don't feel it's necessary for us to wait another eight months before making a decision, Linda. That was my point to Walter."

Linda nodded. "I agree there's no need to wait eight months."

"No, there isn't. A lot has happened to me in the last four months and I'm sure a lot has happened to you too."

"Yes, a lot," said Linda quietly. "I am not the same person who left you in September, Jim."

The new mink coat meant nothing. His pessimism when he first saw her was just idiotic fear. Jim glanced up at a waiter. "Do you want a drink?"

"A glass of sherry, I suppose."

"Two sherries," said Jim to the waiter. He paused as Linda adjusted her coat on the back of her chair. She wore a beautiful green wool dress that revealed in a modest way her perfect figure. "Tell me what happened when you went back to Gram's."

"She slapped me," said Linda. "Then locked me in a bedroom for three days. I finally told her I'd go on a hunger strike if she didn't let me out. It was ghastly. The girls were crying in the halls, the servants were terrified."

"What happened then?" asked Jim. "Did you get a job?"

"A job?"

"Yes, you said you were going to get a job to pay your room and board."

Linda smiled. "Wouldn't that be kind of silly, or shall we say, a trifle kookie?"

"It was your idea."

"You are mistaken. It was *your* idea, Jim. All such notions I had in those days were your idea."

Jim didn't understand her but decided he had better drop the thing. After all, it *was* slightly foolish for an heiress to work for sixty dollars a week in the library. "That's a beautiful new coat, Linda."

"Yes, I came out well on that deal. Gram was very inconsistent. She'd scream at me one minute and weep on my shoulder the next. When I told her about burning the old coat she ran into town and bought me this one. I think she paid nine thousand for it, or maybe it was more. So you see, virtue pays."

Virtue pays, thought Jim. "How is Gram?" he asked.

Linda stared at him in surprise. "How *is* she? Why, she's *dead*, Jim, didn't Walter tell you?"

"No, he didn't mention it."

"Gram died in November. A stroke, like that. I thought you knew."

"No, I didn't and I'm sorry to hear it. . . ."

"It was a blessing, really. I didn't realize it till I moved up there, but she was senile. Couldn't remember anything, rages, weeping for no reason. She'd been failing for the past three years really, but it sure didn't affect her financial judgment or maybe her luck."

"I'm sorry to hear she's gone, I always liked her."

"You wouldn't *believe* the money she made, Jim. It's simply fantastic. Everything she touched turned into pure gold. Everything. She began to get a little cuckoo about three years ago, so what did she do? All her money, most of it, was in bonds, municipals and government and a few giant corporations, very safe stuff, very conservative. She sold all the bonds and put everything in stocks. The market was down. Jim, she made a filthy fortune."

"Good," said Jim. "It's better to be rich than poor."

"I thought she was worth around three million. It turned out she really had around five. That's what she put in the market. Jim, do you know that after taxes and everything I have almost *fourteen million* dollars? It's ridiculous, really. What does one *do* with fourteen million dollars?"

"Yeah," said Jim with a grin. But he felt sick. The pessimism had returned. For Linda to talk about money in this way was wrong, wrong, wrong. "I guess you could practically live on the interest from the income. It's a lot of money."

"Her touch was fantastic. She never missed. To give you an example. She'd intended to give us twenty-five thousand dollars as a present for our tenth anniversary and had actually written you a check, but then got mad about something you did—the swimming pool or something, I don't know what it was, some extravagance. So she tore up the check and almost at random bought twenty-five thousand dollars' worth of an over-the-counter stock called *Numerex*. Now, of course *Numerex*—you've heard of it, haven't you?"

"I don't believe I have," said Jim.

"They make magnetic tape for computers and they design computer systems. Now, why did that old lady buy that stock? Why? Jim, when she bought it, no one had ever heard of it. And you know what's happened to it since."

"Actually, I don't," said Jim in a feeble voice. What did Linda care about all of this? She'd never been interested in the stock market before. How could she discuss such empty and meaningless nonsense when their own future and the future of two small children were at stake?

"She bought it at around fourteen. Their semi-annual report came out a month later and the stock zoomed to sixty, to eighty, to a hundred and forty, to two hundred. It split ten for one, went up again, split again, and on and on like that into a gold sunset. Jim, it is a great stock and it is *still* going up. That measly little twenty-five thousand is worth almost a million now."

"I . . . that's fine," said Jim. "I didn't know you were very interested in stocks, Linda."

"I wasn't, but I got the bug from Billy and I have got it bad. He's a broker, you know, and absolutely brilliant, another Gram. It's exciting. I don't need the money, but it's exciting, like a game."

"Billy?" asked Jim. "Who are you talking about?"

"Why, Billy McCade. Walter's nephew, you know him. Didn't Walter tell you *any*thing?"

The sick sensation in Jim Kittering became edged with fear—not fear for himself but for Linda. He knew Billy McCade, all right. Yes, he knew Billy. "No," said Jim. "Walter told me almost nothing."

Linda hesitated. "I suppose that was right. But at any rate I've seen a lot of Billy since I went down to Nassau in November."

"You went to Nassau in November?"

"Yes, right after Gram died. I had to get out of that house. I almost went crazy there those weeks. She wouldn't let me go out at all, then I'd sneak out and she'd cross-examine me for hours. Whom had I seen? Where was I? Did I have no morals? It was worse than . . .

well, I might as well say it—it was worse than being married to *you,* Jim."

"So . . . anyhow, you went to Nassau. Funny, I was on an island too."

Linda smiled. "Yes, I know. I saw the picture of you in the paper with the two women. And even as upset as I was, with you suddenly coming back from the dead, Jim, I had to laugh. *You,* of all people, stuck with two women like that on an uninhabited island. I almost collapsed. I became hysterical. Billy thought I would faint, he thought it was grief or something, emotional shock, but it wasn't. It was you and those *women.* I nearly died."

It was a nightmare, thought Jim. This could not be happening. He had lived twelve years with Linda and this wasn't Linda. "Why did it strike you as so funny?" he asked. "Because they weren't beautiful or something?"

"Weren't *beautiful?* Jim, the little one looked like a chipmunk, or maybe a rabbit. The teeth, I mean."

"Bugs Bunny," said Jim. "Her brother used to call her that. She loved him, though, and cried five days when he was killed in Korea."

Linda's smile faded as she stared thoughtfully at Jim. "I suppose you became . . . more or less involved with them," she said. "Such a long time and everything."

"Yes, I became involved more or less," said Jim.

"I didn't mean to hurt your feelings by making fun of them. And they weren't all that bad really. Actually, I thought the fat one had a kind of sweet smile."

It was the money, thought Jim. The money and Gram's tyranny. Linda had never had either the incentive or the chance to develop into a complete human being. Power had prevented her growth and power in the form of Billy McCade soon would destroy her with a brutal thoroughness harrowing to contemplate. What would become of the children? At all costs he would have to get the girls away from her and Billy or they would be destroyed too. Deborah and Sandra—he'd always loathed those names she had given them—would have to be saved somehow.

"How are the girls?" asked Jim. "Walter tells me you put them in a boarding school."

"Yes, I did, and they're just fine. They're in Nassau now for a few days."

It was strange, thought Jim. The minute the news of his rescue appeared in the paper the girls were whisked off to Nassau. Walter and Billy McCade, no doubt. A team. The extreme hostility of the silver-haired Walter was certainly plain now. How much, Jim wondered, would they offer him for the lives of his children? A hundred thousand apiece, maybe? No, it would have to be a little more. Three hundred thousand for the pair would be about right.

"I'd like to see them," said Jim.

"Oh, they want to see you too. They love you very, very much, Jim. Frankly, I was surprised. I mean . . . of course children love a father, especially little girls. But I never thought you were all that close to Debbie and Sandy."

"Neither did I," said Jim.

"They adore you. I have Polaroids they wrote on in my purse, I'll get them in a second. But you wouldn't believe the way they carried on when we heard you'd drowned. Debbie actually threatened to commit suicide. Would you believe that, a *child?* It frightened me, it truly frightened me. And they're nearly hysterical now. They're angry at me for having them for a visit at this point, but of course you'll see them soon."

"Of course," said Jim. "You said you have Polaroids?"

"Yes, right here. I must tell you, they don't like boarding school. But it's the only thing. I'm not in a situation in Nassau where I can have them there and the Bahama schools really won't do."

Jim looked at the two Polaroid color snapshots, one of Debbie and the other of Sandy. "Love to my dear beloved Father, Deborah" was written on the back of one snapshot and "Love to my dear Daddy, Sandy" was written on the back of the other. Both girls had visibly grown since September, especially the older Deborah. Jim felt a pain like a blade in his heart. The children knew where their protection lay. He would not abandon them. Jim put the Polaroid snapshots in his pocket and looked up at Linda.

"I'm not hungry, but let's order lunch," he said.

"Actually, I've had lunch, Arlette Sanders took me to Twenty-one. The sherry's all I want."

"Then we'll just talk," said Jim. Arlette Sanders. A name from the past and a feared name at that. Tall, high cheekbones, green amber eyes, a large red mouth, slender boyish hips, cone-shaped breasts with disproportionately big nipples, a great bush of black pubic hair, enormous labia minora that stuck out pinkly beyond her labia majora—yes, Arlette, of whom Billy McCade had said at a party, "She sucks a mean cock." And Arlette did. The fashionable, rich, beautiful, empty-witted Arlette did all kinds of things with all kinds of men, including the husband of her best friend. Five years ago Linda and Arlette had gone off alone for a week's vacation in Bermuda. This was the first of Linda's "bachelor vacations," but not the last. How many "mean cocks" had she and Arlette bestowed tender attentions upon during that week in Bermuda? And he had convinced himself Linda's first infidelity occurred three years before at his own instigation. He had even managed the incredible feat of persuading himself that some perverse and unnatural streak in his own character had forced him to push Linda into the arms of other men.

"I think maybe we'd better not talk just about this and that," said Jim. "I gather you and Billy McCade are involved romantically."

"Yes, I'm going to marry him, Jim, unless you can persuade me our own marriage is worth saving and I don't think you can."

"Billy's getting a divorce from Betty Ann?"

"Betty Ann's *dead,* didn't you hear? But of course, you've been away."

"Dead? Betty Ann is dead? How did she die?"

"It was a complete accident. She'd had way too much to drink one night and took too many pills. It wasn't suicide, it was a mistake, Jim. The coroner ruled it accidental death. She took the pills twice, that's all, then vomited in her sleep and it got in her lungs. When Billy came home from the party she was lying there dead."

Jim had once had a fist fight with Billy McCade because of Billy's wife, Betty Ann. It was not a fight Jim won. Billy had knocked him down and given him a black eye and had kicked him viciously twice in the stomach. The fight had come up because Jim had walked out on the veranda during a party at the McCades' and had seen Billy slapping Betty Ann and twisting her arm behind her back. He had always liked poor little Betty Ann, a timid girl who wore glasses, and he had once been to bed with her. She'd wept and told him Billy often beat her and on three occasions had forced her to indulge in wife-swapping. This was when she'd been married to Billy only a couple of years.

"Linda," said Jim, "I told Walter there'd be no tearful exhortations or piteous pleas, but I do want to say one thing and it's not on my account but yours. Linda, I am astounded and horrified you could take up with a man like Billy McCade. The man is a sadistic bully with the instincts of a tiger. He will destroy you, Linda, exactly the way he's destroyed Betty Ann. Of course her death wasn't suicide, it was murder."

Linda calmly took out a cigarette and tapped it on her gold cigarette case with short emphatic taps, then held it to her lips as Jim struck a match for her. Her face was composed but a little pale. "Billy McCade," she said, "is the gentlest man I have ever known."

"If you believe that, then you're the biggest fool *I've* ever known," answered Jim. "Are you out of your mind, Linda? The man beat Betty Ann with his fists, he broke her nose and knocked out her teeth."

"That is a lie," said Linda calmly. "Betty Ann was hurt in an auto crash."

"She was hurt by her husband and not once but many times. He also forced her into wife-swapping, Linda."

"That is another lie. It never happened, Jim. Never. Betty Ann was a neurotic girl, a very sick woman, and that's why she killed herself."

"I thought you said it was an accident."

"I meant accidentally killed herself. Don't try and trip me up, Jim. It's what you've always done to me, used your brains on me like a club. I am perfectly aware there probably was an unconscious wish to die on Betty Ann's part. Do you want to know the truth about her? She was a Lesbian."

Jim's hair stood on end. "Linda . . . Linda . . ."

"And she was also a Puritan. I mean a *real* Puritan. It wasn't Billy who slept all around, it was Betty Ann. She did it to hide her fear of her Lesbianism from herself, but it didn't work because then she felt guilty about sleeping around. And her Lesbian desires didn't go away. So she had an unconscious wish to die and therefore took the extra pills."

Billy McCade, psychologist, thought Jim. How long would it take him to put Linda in a coffin? The money would protect her, if Billy didn't get his hands on it.

"Let me give this advice anyhow," said Jim. "Sell your stocks and put your money in trust for Debbie and Sandy, or in trust for a foundation or whatever you want to do with it. You can't even spend the income on fourteen million, Linda. Put the money in trust where Billy can't get at it."

"But I want Billy to get at it, he's making me a fortune."

"You've *got* a fortune, you idiot. What do you need a fortune for?"

"Now listen. I haven't come here to be called names by you. The day when you can call me names is over, Jim. If you think this is the way you're going to talk me into a reconciliation, you couldn't be more mistaken. I've played Trilby to your Svengali for the last time."

"I'm sorry, I apologize," said Jim. "I got carried away."

"You certainly did. And since you mention the absurd stories about Billy being a so-called wife-swapper, I want to tell you Betty Ann wasn't the only Puritan in the world or unconscious homosexual either, and you'd better watch out for sleeping pills yourself."

"What?" asked Jim.

"Don't you realize what a complete and total Puritan you are, Jim? You, beyond a doubt, are the biggest square in the whole wide world. The extent of your Puritanism is literally unbelievable. And the cause is obvious. You have homosexual desires of which you are unaware."

It was such a nightmare Jim felt strangely unaffected, strangely calm. The world was coming to an end, the Empire State Building was falling, waves were sweeping over Manhattan Island, and thunder and lightning were crashing down everywhere, but he sat there with a placid composure smoking one of Linda's cigarettes and gazing at her as if they were discussing what play to see that night or what party to go to. And in the midst of it all, as the world and his own life came to an end, his mind worked quite clearly.

Linda, of course, was not such a total fool as she seemed. Her intelligence was very high, the trouble with her was emotional or perhaps spiritual. Melody would say "spiritual" and Florence would say "emotional," although in this case Florence might say "spiritual" too. It was obvious Linda had no actual personality or point of view of her own; she had never developed into a complete human being, thus a real personality or point of view was impossible for her.

Such people were, of course, common. They were *echo people.* In a sense they did not have souls. The essence of a human being—that dynamic combination of an independent intelligence and a capacity for love—was not inside them. Thus, they could only be echo people. When Linda had been with him, she had echoed him; and since she was a superior echo person with high native intelligence she had echoed him in a brilliant and superior manner. Now she was no longer with him, she was with Billy McCade and therefore she echoed Billy McCade.

"You are an echo person," said Jim.

"What's that?"

"Never mind. You think I have unconscious homosexual desires, huh?"

"Yes, I do, Jim. And as a matter of fact, didn't a psychiatrist once tell you so?"

"He said I had fears I was not a complete man," answered Jim. "And he was right. It's hard to feel like a complete man when your wife is in bed with all your friends. But I don't think I have any interest in sucking any 'mean cocks' the way you and Arlette did in Bermuda five years ago, before I forced you to become an unfaithful wife."

Linda stared coldly at him. A disgusted expression was on her face, but she still looked beautiful even though she was disgusted. She *always* looked beautiful. "Do you know you're revolting? There's a vulgar and common streak in you that makes me want to throw up."

A vulgar and common streak, thought Jim. It was uncomfortably close to his own perception of a "vulgar and coarse" streak in Florence, but the thing he had said to Linda was true, just as the things Florence had said to him were true. Perhaps the truth itself often was vulgar and common, vulgar and coarse. Perhaps a fear of vulgarity was a fear of life itself. Perhaps a fear of vulgarity was the most profound vulgarity that could be known, the most sickening and loathsome vulgarity of all. What really could be more disgusting than a pretentious denial of one's own humanity and the truth?

"You mean you and Arlette didn't have any fun in Bermuda?" asked Jim. "You just lay on the pink beach and let the ocean lap on your virtuous pussies?"

"You are the most revolting man I have ever known," said Linda with a tired but calm poise, "and you are making a nauseating spectacle of yourself in my eyes. I can't locate words to tell you how disgusting you are."

"I'm having trouble that way myself," said Jim. "Don't you remember the maid coming to me with the snapshots after she unpacked your suitcase? I didn't snoop; I trusted you, I believed in you, I had to believe in you. You remember, Linda. The maid who hated you and wanted me to know about your beach boy, the maid you fired a week later? Twenty-three snapshots of a muscular moron in trunks, a smug little smile on his face and biceps bulging? How much money did you give him, how many presents? But of course he was *Arlette's* beach boy, wasn't he? And you were depressed and lonely and sat by yourself and stared out at sea and wondered why you had come to Bermuda with that terrible, silly Arlette. And I bought it—like a goddamned fool I bought it and believed you. But the snapshots were in *your* suitcase, Linda, not Arlette's."

"You're not upsetting me, Jim. You are merely amazing me. I'm astonished at the incredible filth in your mind. Common, Jim. Common, common. It's snobbish of me to say it, I suppose, but I think it's your middle-class background. Success, which could include marrying money, *does* something to people from a middle-class background. Billy is right. The transition is too much for them. It's awful, in a way it's inhuman, but people should marry in their own class. How many times have I shuddered inside at the grossness and crudity of your behavior? You will never know, Jim, you will never know. Billy is right and so was Gram. I should never have married you."

"Deep thinker, Billy," said Jim, "and a real philosopher, Gram. I'm a donkey and you're Citation."

"I will leave it to you to speak ill of the dead," said Linda, who now was quite pale with anger, "but as for Billy, he is at *least* as intelligent as you are, Jim, and a *lot* more fun to be with."

Of course, thought Jim, an "echo person" had likes and dislikes; it was more "fun" to echo one master than another. He himself had been a bad, harsh, square, puritanistic master—making her cry and caterwaul in the bathroom at five A.M. merely because she'd gone to a party without her panties and fucked Herb among the hats and coats . . . yes, that kind of denying thing; it was a strain on an echo person who knew nothing at all of life beyond the pleasure principle. The world turned in order that beautiful Linda might consecrate herself to pleasure—nothing demanding, like a child, just pleasure, pure pleasure. He'd begged her literally on bended knee for a son, but she'd had her tubes tied three years before. The pill bloated her, made her tummy stick out two inches. And as for a son, there were too many people in the world anyhow, and she'd had a dream she would die if she had another baby. No tubes, no muss, no fuss, no panties to parties. And then having to go boo-hoo-hoo in the bathroom at five A.M. because the master thought it was horrible? What a drag. An echo person had likes and dislikes just like a real person. Florence didn't like the way "Frankie" called her ma-*dahm* and scooped the chicken with delicate spoons on her plate, eyebrows lifted in dismissal of her as a human being, and Linda didn't like to have to go sob in a towel for a harmless thing like fucking Herb.

". . . yes, he's a *lot* more fun and I'll tell you why. Billy loves me for myself and he let's me *be* myself."

Probably true, thought Jim. But who *was* "herself"? Well, she was an incomplete human being, and an incomplete human being was a child—and what did a child want, need, like, and require? The fulfillment of its hunger for protection, pleasure, attention, among other things, and what was more protective, pleasurable, or attentive than an erect penis, not only as a tribute to a woman's beauty but as a workhorse for her delight? Who was Linda "herself"? She was an echo person looking for protection, pleasure, and attention, and Billy helped her find it. He pointed and said, "There. There's some, go after it. And darling, don't you worry, I'm no Puritan—but before you and Bobby or Johnny or whoever go down to Bay Street to get the Sunday *Times*, sign this little paper, dear." Far be it from Billy to put a moralistic damper on her fun. He would not indicate by a vulgar and common lift of the eyebrow that he knew she and Bobby or Johnny would get the *Times*, park the Continental in the shadow of the wall behind the house, pull down panties with excited haste, and unzip fly. No, Billy was a gentleman.

"I see," said Jim. "Billy lets you be yourself. How long have you been involved with him, Linda?"

"All right, I'll answer that. I'm not afraid of your opinion any more, Jim. Billy and I became lovers about a month before Gram died, but it was difficult, I couldn't see him. She liked Walter, but Billy had too much life for her. *Has* too much life; Gram's dead, not Billy."

Linda was becoming a trifle incoherent in her anger, which was building like a storm in the quiet Edwardian Room of the Plaza as red-coated waiters moved hither and yon and the lunch crowd thinned out. "Go ahead," said Jim. "Gram liked Walter but not Billy."

"She liked Billy but she didn't understand him. She was ill. You'll not turn me against Gram, she was a great woman and a great lady and I'll always love and revere her."

"You and Billy, huh?" smiled Jim. "You were saying?"

"I am *not* afraid of your opinion, Trilby is free. We became lovers a month before Gram died. He was involved already in the Bahamas—he has plans for a giant project there, a tremendous development on an untouched island, with maybe a casino. When Gram died, I went to him. He's an electric man, you don't know the things he's done and the plans he has. Billy is a genius, he's just never had real financing, the banks are run by conservative idiots who don't know what's happening in the world."

"You were telling me about you and Billy personally."

"You think I'm afraid but I'm not. I couldn't take the girls with me for the reasons I told you, but I went to him. We have lived together openly and frankly since November."

"When did Betty Ann kill herself?"

"It was around Christmas. But they had separated in October. I didn't break that marriage up."

"Wasn't he living with her when she died? You said Billy came home from a party and found her dead on the bed suffocated by her own vomit—isn't that what you said?"

Jim was still icy calm as the furious destroying waters rushed over Manhattan Island, but Linda was white now and her rage was mounting. He wondered with an almost casual curiosity what her final outburst would be like. She'd already called him a homosexual, what next?

"She was visiting, Jim. Billy wanted to help her. She had been in great distress and had threatened suicide several times. Betty was involved with a Lesbian night-club singer, emotionally involved with her if not physically, and Billy had them both down to talk about it with them and try to make them understand themselves."

Billy McCade, psychologist. The thought of Billy telling pitiful little Betty Ann she was a Lesbian had a horror beyond measure. It was murder, all right. How could Linda be so blind to the man's monstrous cruelty? The answer was plain. She was an echo person and could not really think for herself or feel for others; she could not understand Billy was a murderer and would destroy her, because Betty Ann's agony meant nothing to her at all. Five minutes of independent intelligence and a trace of compassion would have exposed Billy McCade before her eyes in all his monstrosity; but she was an echo person with no real mind and no real heart, and therefore in one way or another Billy would destroy her. One tear, one single tear for Betty Ann could save her, but Linda was an incomplete human being and the tear would never fall. "Those who can't cry must die." Truer words were never spoke.

"Where were *you*, Linda, when Billy was explaining to Betty Ann she was a Lesbian?"

"I . . . I was in the house. But in the other wing. I didn't live with Billy while she was there and that's the truth."

"Okay, you've been with Billy for about two months. You said you're not afraid of my opinion. Let's test that, let's see if Trilby is free. First, and this is a serious question—you *do* love Billy?"

"I adore him. I glow when he touches me. There has never been in my life a man like him. Yes, I love him! It's because of him I know what love is like. And he is *not* a sadistic bully. He is the most gentle, tender, and *giving* man I have ever known."

"I'm sure he's very giving," said Jim. "Second question, Trilby. You adore Billy, he makes you glow, it's because of him you know what love is like—how many times have you been unfaithful to him in the past two months, or do you know?"

"What?"

"You mean he hasn't pushed you into the arms of other men? It isn't the way it was with me? You've been to bed with no one else since you've been involved with him? He makes you glow and that's enough? His tender, gentle, and *giving* love is all you want? Hmm, Trilby?"

Linda moistened her lips and swallowed, a fright in her eyes that undercut Jim's anger but left undisturbed his deathlike calm. What was the point? Why beat her down? He should pity her, God knows the fate before her demanded it. And besides, who did he have to blame but himself? Her wealth and her beauty had lured him into a marriage that had wrecked his life, but it was his own doing.

He could not even claim ignorance as an excuse. He had known what she was like even before he married her. Why else had he felt such a terrible fear the day before the wedding at Gram's summer place in Maine? Would he have been frightened out of his wits if he'd been marrying Florence or Melody? No, he wouldn't have been frightened to marry either of them; they would not have driven him into an insane, semi-hysterical, break-this-thing-up experience in a boathouse with a red-haired cousin. He had known even then Linda was an echo person.

"Until this moment," said Linda quietly, "I have never been conscious of the lengths to which you would go, Jim. I am glad we have had this lunch, because it has truly liberated me once and for all from your merciless and inhuman tyranny. Let me say this. I was raised and conditioned by a misguided woman who knew absolutely nothing about human nature and human needs—my grandmother. She scarred me for life and made me vulnerable to such a man as you. Gram was a product of an era of repression, the worst ever known in human history. The suffering caused by the denial of love in the Victorian era is beyond reckoning. I say this with an especial feeling of irony because you yourself have so often derisively parroted these ideas, in order subtly to mock them and compel me to take the other side—against all my common sense and intuition of the truth. But to answer your ruthless and morally filthy questions. I am not afraid to answer. A *real* man has come into my life and I am not afraid of you any more, even if you are cleverer than I am. I have truth on my side."

"Okay, you don't remember how many other men you've slept with in the past two months," said Jim wearily. "Forget it, Linda, it doesn't matter. The only thing that matters is what we're going to do about the children."

"*You . . . horrible . . . son of a bitch!*" said Linda in a low, choked voice of unadulterated rage. "Don't you *dare* speak to me like that! Don't you *dare!*"

"What will you do," asked Jim, "cut me off without a dime?"

For a moment Jim felt she would throw her half-filled glass of sherry into his face, but in the midst of her rage a thought seemed to occur to her. With a blink of her beautiful blue eyes, she opened her purse and took out her gold cigarette case. As she extracted a cigarette and lighted it for herself, ignoring Jim's proffered match, she said calmly:

"Except for goodbye, I have two more things to say to you. First, my private life is none of your business. I am ashamed of nothing I have done but I have no intention of losing my human dignity by giving you the kind of morbid titillation you used to enjoy so much. The day when I come home and confess my 'sins' to you is over. You will have to find someone else to provide you with unhealthy homosexual thrills—I'll never convince you, but you did get a morbid pleasure out of my going with other men."

"I got no pleasure out of it, morbid or otherwise," said Jim. "It was the torment of my life, the cause of my own promiscuity, the cause of my enslavement to Hob, and the cause of my financial madness. I couldn't stand it any more, Linda, and that's why I forced you to leave me."

Linda smiled. "You didn't force me to leave you, I left of my own free will. How far can self-deception go, Jim? You cried like a child and begged me not to leave you."

"I also was relieved when I walked back to the house," said Jim. "I knew what you were, honey, but I loved you and needed you and I couldn't face it."

"You needed me the way Rasputin needed Alexandra," said Linda calmly. "This was the relationship we had, Jim, not Svengali and Trilby, and I'm glad to give credit to Billy for this insight. It was Rasputin and Alexandra, the fanatical peasant and the bewildered empress. Do you know what you *did* to me? You fixed Rasputin eyes on me and told me love is evil and I believed you. You are cleverer than I am, I could never hold my own in arguments with you—the sarcasm, the irony, the little hints, the withering remarks! You made me feel guilty all the time! I was hypnotized, mesmerized—I was under your Rasputin wing. Don't you see what an *awful* thing you did? You used love to destroy love. Love is evil, said Rasputin. Well, love is *not* evil. I won't throw my dignity in the mud by answering your morally filthy questions about other men than Billy, but I'll say this and I assure you, Billy himself is in full agreement with it. Jim, the world has left you behind. I have finished my childbearing period and there is no reason on earth I shouldn't fulfill myself emotionally just as men do."

"Maybe you're right, Linda," said Jim quietly. "Maybe I'm out of step with things."

"I am absolutely faithful to Billy, and he is absolutely faithful to me, in the true sense of faith. Real love is not possessive, Jim, and I hope for your sake someday you will find that out."

"I hope I find it out too, Linda."

Linda paused. Her anger seemed to have vanished. It was a thing Jim had long ago noted, the swiftness with which her emotion came and went. A man would attract her and she'd be madly infatuated with him for a week, then poof!—he'd be out of her mind and forgotten. A pet dog would be run over and she'd weep bitterly for five minutes, then poof!—she'd calmly call the vet and tell him to come get the body. She'd be in a rage, then poof!—an impulse would come upon her and she'd want to make love. There was no depth to her feelings, no passion, no fire. At the moment she seemed to feel rather sad, as if something touched her.

"There's one more thing I want to say, Jim. Believe it or not, I bear no rancor toward you. You can't help your unconscious fears and you can't help behaving as you do. You're a victim of an irrational value system. I have no rancor. I spent important years of my life with you and I loved you. You gave me two beautiful children, you were my husband. I have nothing but contempt for women who divorce their husbands and then speak of them as if they were monsters. Rasputin is only a metaphor, you are not a monster, Jim; you are an extremely clever man with many fine qualities. I loved you when we were together and, believe it or not, I still feel a human love for you."

Jim was tempted to ask her how much Walter and Billy had advised her to offer him for the children; it was obvious she was building up to this. He resisted the temptation, however. A trace of tears was in Linda's eyes. In her way, poor thing, she did love him, she was telling the truth. The fact that her love had no depth, no power, no understanding, no compassion was beyond her comprehension.

"I want to say I have taken care of all the bills and debts we incurred while we were living together. All the mortgages and things have been paid off and the house in Cherry Dale is gone along with its horrible furniture—your clothes and personal things, I'm afraid, are gone too."

"That doesn't matter," said Jim.

"I have even paid personal debts of yours when they were brought to me and there were quite a few of them. We thought you were dead and I felt I should take care of it."

"I'll reimburse you," said Jim.

"No, I won't take it. You made those debts living with me. Now, there's something important I want to say. Jim, I *don't* want an ugly, horrible, unspeakable struggle over the children, I don't even want to think of searing their lives with the memory of such horror and I'm sure you don't either. I know I would be thankful and grateful to you if we can avoid that. Now, Jim, I'm their mother and I must have complete custody. Walter will work out with you liberal visitation rights. I'm imploring you not to fight with me over Debbie and Sandy. And I will be grateful for that."

"Um-hmm," said Jim. Almost from the beginning of the lunchless luncheon, he had been trying to think what he could do to get the children from her and Billy. Now he really put his mind on it as he listened with half an ear to the proposition of Walter and Billy.

"Furthermore, I am grateful to you for having given me the children and for having given me twelve years of your life. I have no rancor, Jim. Therefore, if you will be cooperative about the divorce and not make emotional footballs of our children, I will make a generous settlement with you. Jim, the Numerex stock was to have been a tenth wedding anniversary present to us both. The stock is in my name and legally I don't have to give you any of it, but I want you to have half of that stock. This would give you after all taxes and expenses are paid a sum in the neighborhood of two hundred and ninety thousand dollars. It isn't a bribe in any sense, Jim. It's best for the children that they be with their mother. I'm giving you the money because I did love you and I still do in a human way and I want you to have it."

"Well . . ." said Jim. There was only one thing to do, unpleasant as it would be. The children had to be taken away from her and Billy. It would be difficult and ugly, but it could be done. Linda cared nothing about Debbie and Sandy, she'd stuck them off in boarding school to get rid of them; she wanted the children because she thought it was expected of her to want them, and Billy and Walter were merely going along with her. In reality, Linda and Billy would be relieved and delighted to get rid of the girls. But there was only one way to do it. He would have to hire detectives—and good ones, expensive ones, experts—and send them down to Nassau and get the real dope on her and Billy. Bugging devices, electronic listening instruments, hidden cameras, records of comings and goings. Within a month he could get overwhelming and indisputable proof of her adulterous relations with Billy and with three, four, five other men or boys as well. It was an ugly, sickening kind of thing to do, but abandoning Debbie and Sandy to the tender mercies of Billy McCade was unthinkable.

"I knew you'd agree," said Linda with a little smile of relief, "and it really gives me pleasure to see you have that stock, Jim."

"But I don't agree," said Jim. "I want custody of the girls myself. Now, hear me out before you get excited and throw a fit. It isn't fair to *Billy* for him to have this responsibility for another man's children. I can't ask him to take that responsibility."

"But he wants the girls," said Linda.

"Then why are they in boarding school in Connecticut? I don't want to argue, I'll just say this and I'll make it emphatic so you'll believe I mean it. Because I *do* mean it, Linda. I will see both you and Billy McCade in hell before I'll let you have my children. You think he's gentle—okay, I can't change your mind. But I *don't* think he's gentle and I'm not going to have my daughters at his mercy. You can have a divorce but I want complete custody of the children."

"But they should be with their mother. I can't believe it. After the generous gesture I just made, you can act like this?"

"I don't want your money, Linda, I want my children."

"You will never get them. Aside from the fact I am wealthy and can hire all kinds of legal help, no court is going to take those children away from their mother."

Jim calmly returned her irritated stare. It would be an error to be too emphatic or passionate about it; this, of course, would alert Billy to the possibility of detectives. It was true, under normal circumstances, no court would take the children away from their mother, but it wouldn't even get into court. Billy McCade was a sexual satyr, a heavy drinker, and had little control over his sadistic impulses; it was very probable he had already introduced Linda to the fine art of mate-swapping; in fact, it was practically a dead certainty he had done so. A tape recording of two couples on twin beds copulating in unison and then switching partners and copulating in unison again might not be admissible in court but it would have a horrifying effect on both Linda and Walter McCade and even on Billy. And testimony by detectives of assignations with various men and of her adulterous life with Billy *would* be admissible. They would give him custody of the children without going into court and in actuality would be relieved to do so, but in the meantime it was necessary to throw them off by making Billy think he was bargaining for more money.

"Maybe not," said Jim, "but I can make it very difficult for you, Linda. I can delay the divorce quite a while. And as you say, it would be very distressing for the children."

"I'm not going to give you any more money than that," said Linda as she closed her purse with a snap and began to put on her new nine-thousand-dollar coat. "It's a very generous settlement, Jim. That's almost three hundred thousand dollars."

"Yeah, I figured that would be about the amount Billy would suggest," said Jim. "But he's a cheapskate, Linda. Good grief, you're worth fourteen million and I gave you the best years of my life."

Linda nodded. She wasn't even irritated any more—poof! Billy and the lawyers would work it out, what was the difference. "Yes, you did, that's true. We'll see what the lawyers say."

Jim beckoned to a waiter and paid the bill. As he did, Linda looked at herself in a compact mirror.

"Big date on tonight, Linda?"

The serene blue eyes looked up at him and Jim almost started with surprise. What was the thought in her mind and what was behind this little solemn stare? "Well, no," said Linda in an extracasual tone, "I don't have anything planned. I'd thought I might take a plane on back to Nassau but it's kind of late to make it now."

Jim smiled and said: "Let me ask you something just for fun. It's all over now and believe me this is just idle curiosity. It's a personal question, do you mind?"

"What is it?" asked Linda. She still had the little solemn, meditative look in her beautiful blue eyes.

"You remember the first time we slept together, a few months before we were married?"

"Yes. Of course I remember."

Jim smiled amiably. "This is *pure* idle curiosity. You said you were a virgin and it was painful to you. But I happen to have slept with a *real* virgin recently." Jim made his amiable grin even more amiable. "Come on, 'fess up, Linda. You weren't a virgin, were you?"

Linda hesitated, then returned his smile. "No, I wasn't. But I knew you thought I was and I felt I had to pretend."

Jim continued to smile. "Just out of curiosity, how many were there before me?"

As she paused, the little solemn look still in her eyes, Jim thought she would try to count up the number and tell him, but then she shook her head and replied: "A lady has her secrets."

Yes, indeed, thought Jim, a lady has her secrets. His marriage and Linda herself had been a lie from the very beginning. And he had known it. He himself was the worst liar of all, because he had lied to himself.

As they walked out of the Edwardian Room past the newsstand, Linda said: "You know, it's funny. As angry as I got at you at lunch, and as glad as I am, so help me, that this thing is finally settled and over, do you know, Jim, I still find you a very attractive man?"

Jim returned her smile as they strolled on around the corner toward the Palm Court. "I still find you a very beautiful woman, Linda."

They walked on in silence for a half-dozen steps, then Linda asked, "I wonder if there's time for me to make a plane or if I should stay over tonight and go back tomorrow morning. What time is it?"

Jim stopped to look at his watch. "Oh, it's . . . almost two-thirty."

"Mmm," said Linda. "I gave up my room at the Regency and the town is jammed. You have a room here, you're staying here?"

"Yes, I have a suite upstairs."

Linda was slightly pale. The little solemn look in her eyes had become even more solemn. She moistened her beautiful lips with the tip of her tongue and said, "I have to go to the bathroom. Would you mind if I borrowed yours?"

It was then that the pain and the sorrow hit Jim Kittering. Until that moment, the shock itself had numbed him and carried him through. A dismay filled his soul as he realized he had lost Linda forever, he had lost her as he'd known he would because he never had had her in the first place. Jim stared in grief at the child-woman who had been his wife and the mother of his children.

It was an awful mystery. How could any person be so beautiful and at the same time be such an empty little bitch? There was not the slightest indication of her character in her face. The golden hair, the serene blue eyes, the perfect smile gave no clue. She looked literally like an angel; St. Peter would have opened the celestial gates and let her in. Hers was a beauty that had about it something heartbreaking.

And she wasn't really a bitch, or at least not in a vicious sense; there was no malice or deliberate cruelty in her; she was empty, that was all. *La Jolie*—very pretty, very lovely, very beautiful, a nice thing to have, an object of art, and her soon-to-be-ex-husband's pride. *La Jolie*—who had burned her mink coat and got a better one. *La Jolie*—who had just rid herself of the most revolting man she'd ever known and now wanted to go up to his suite and borrow his bathroom.

Jim was tempted. The thought of kissing once again those beautiful lips and holding that lovely body in his arms filled him with painful longing. It would be a moving experience to take off the beautiful green dress, pull off her slip and underwear, and see again that golden body with the perfect breasts, curving slender waist, and silken blondish pubic V. It would also be tremendously sexy; Linda was wonderful in bed. And she was excited, stirred up, in the mood—the emotion of the lunch had gone to her loins.

"No, I wouldn't mind," said Jim, "but there's no need. There's a powder room right around the corner."

"You're getting dense in your old age, Jim," said Linda with a smile. "What I'm saying is . . . I'll stay with you tonight. I don't have any rancor and I want to prove it to you. I'll take a plane in the morning."

Jim was very tempted. Why not? They could make love all afternoon, go out and have a wonderful dinner, come back and make love for hours in the night. He would not be left quite so soon with nothing at all, he could put it off, he wouldn't have to face the emptiness of his life until tomorrow.

"Well," said Jim in a hollow voice, "I guess maybe we owe ourselves that."

"We do," answered Linda with a smile as she put her small gloved hand in his. "I'm a little surprised, myself, but Billy predicted it and he was right."

"Billy predicted it," said Jim.

"Yes, but it's all right, he doesn't mind. We really don't have a possessive relationship, Jim."

Upon Jim's face came a slow wince of pain. Why put it off? Why add one more piece of foolishness to his years of error? And why let Billy McCade smile at the thought of him in bed with Linda? *La Jolie*—goodbye!

"I don't think so," said Jim. "Forget it, Linda, take a plane and go to Billy and God help you. Come on, I'll walk you to the powder room."

Linda was too flabbergasted to speak until he had walked her all the way to the door of the powder room. Her stunned astonishment provided Jim a penultimate insight into her—she was utterly spoiled, she lived in a world where her whim was law. How could he refuse to go to bed with her if she wanted to do it? There'd been more truth than poetry in his tirade that clear September morning, as filled with agonized confusion and tormented self-deception as the tirade was. He'd said it all about her and hadn't realized it.

Linda was a spoiled, beautiful child, that was her real trouble. The curse of surface beauty in a world of power had destroyed her. Billy McCade would merely give her the *coup de grâce* while in the process of drinking himself to death and scattering her millions with power-mad hysteria into the air. Linda had been ruined long, long ago and not merely by her domineering-indulging grandmother; there'd been character and integrity in Gram, snobbish old fool that she was. The thing that had ruined Linda was her golden ringlets and her beautiful child's blue eyes, her fair and perfect form that gave her prizes she'd never earned and a treasure she'd never bought and paid for. What could one say of a civilization that made a commodity of outer beauty and placed no value on beauty inside—that it had no soul? What was really sadder than *La Jolie?* Very pretty, very lovely, very beautiful, a nice thing to have. Linda was a victim of the beastly values of a beastly civilization that denied the essence of humanity itself. What could one say of such a civilization—give it the hydrogen bomb, let it pass?

"Here we are," said Jim. "I'll wait for you, then get you a taxi."

"Never mind," said Linda. "I don't have to, let's go."

Outside the Palm Court she had bitten her lip and put on a mild abstracted frown that was a perfect simulation of the feminine urge to piss, but this too was a lie. Everything about Linda-schminda was a lie. And a brilliant lie at that; the verisimilitude with which she had echoed him during his years with her was damned near past belief. She had *almost* been the "Linda" of his imagination. If she'd just been able to remember to wear her panties to parties. Careless of her. But not idiotic; she'd understood what she was doing, really, and he had not. He'd spent twelve years with her in the dark and he himself needed an atom bomb on the head.

As Jim took Linda by the crook of her mink-coated elbow and assisted her into a taxi at the eastern entrance of the Plaza, she smiled over her shoulder at him and said: "Well, you really *are* a revolting man. I'm not accustomed to being rejected, you know." In the cab, still smiling, not unfriendly, she said: "What *happened* to you down on that island, anyway? Did you fall in love with one of those women? Has true love come to Jim Kittering after all these years?"

An unborn person was somewhere in Linda. This was the ultimate insight for Jim into *La Jolie*. Maybe, just maybe, if she could survive until her beauty faded, that person could be born. Once again—he himself would never expire from want of lachcrymal capability—tears welled in Jim's eyes. He reached into the taxi and took her gloved hand.

"Linda—for God's sake, for your sake, for the sake of your life and your heart and your soul, don't let Billy get hold of all your money.

It's the last thing I'll ask of you. The children I want, but it's the last thing I'll ask of *you.* Linda, I *did* give you twelve years of my life, for better or for worse. Please do this for me. Put two million of your fourteen in trust where Billy can't touch it. Will you do that, darling, will you please do that for me and for yourself?"

Linda stared at him through the open window of the taxi with a little frown. Was there a dim comprehension in her? Maybe. "I think you *do* love the children," she said. "You're thinking, of course, of Debbie and Sandy. A trust fund for them, a million each. All right, I will. I'll do that for you, Jim."

"Where *you* get the income while you're alive, but the principal *cannot* be touched."

"All right," said Linda with a smile, "even if you've just rejected me when I'm in a . . . nostalgic mood."

She still wanted to go upstairs and borrow his bathroom. "And *not* Walter McCade, have a *bank* draw it up. A *big* bank. Please, Linda, it could save your life."

Linda frowned in annoyance. "I said I would. Goodbye, Jim."

"Goodbye, darling. Goodbye," said Jim, as life-preserving tears again welled in his eyes. Through a blur he watched beautiful Linda ride out of his life forever.

It was a thing he could legitimately insist on as a part of the divorce: iron-clad trust funds for the children, trust funds that would protect the children and also with luck might protect Linda too. As long as she had money, Billy would have to restrain himself. And in time, who could tell, miracles still sometimes happened; as her beauty on the outside faded and disappeared, a beauty in her heart and soul might be born. Maybe he had not been such an absolute fool, after all; he had always felt there was a person in Linda somewhere. He would have the best lawyers possible check those trust funds and maybe, after Billy drank himself to death, Linda-schminda, her beauty gone, would find herself a third husband and enter the kingdom of God.

Under the marquee of the eastern entrance of the Plaza, his favorite hotel, Jim stood beneath the red heat lights and comtemplated eternity. His life was over. Nothing remained. There wasn't enough dignity in the collapse of his efforts for him to bother to get drunk. It was another cup he had to drink. Why numb the final abject misery? No, he would drink it full and drink it deep, the cup of truth he never before had had the courage even to look at, much less drink.

Jim had no thought of suicide. He didn't want to live but he had no thought of ending his life. The fifty-two cards of the weeks of his year did not contain a combination that would permit self-destruction. He would lie groaning with cancer for nine years, if need be, and not swallow the bottle of proffered pills. An angel might come and save him. Flying saucers might arrive with a cure. Live, live, live! As long as breath was in his lungs, he would stumble out of bed in the morning and somehow put on his shoes and tie them to meet the day.

Besides, his life was not over, there were the girls, his beautiful little girls who had written him such wonderful things on the back of the Polaroid snapshots. Their messages to him—"Love to my dear beloved Father" and "Love to my dear Daddy"—might once have struck him as mawkish, but no more. Those words, scrawled by childish hands and dictated by childish hearts that did not know how to be clever, were written in gold. He could not have endured the lunchless luncheon without them. Everything was not gone; he had the girls. Somehow, despite all his misery, he had given something of himself to Debbie and Sandy and as long as they were alive in the world he himself could not be dead.

No, everything was not gone. He had lost Melody, he had lost Florence, and he had lost Linda, but he had won Debbie and Sandy and his trip to the blue sea had not been in vain.

This realization would have been the end of Jim Kittering's adventure on Providence Island but for an odd little bit of knowledge buried deep in the mysterious machine of his mind, a thing someone had said to him recently that was wrong—wrong as Linda's new mink coat was wrong. Was it Hob or Linda herself who had made the remark?

He could not face the white gold suite at the Plaza. Aesthetically pleasing surroundings? Maybe a little. But even more, panoply and display, success and money, power, power, power. The minute he returned to civilization, where did he go? The Plaza. To what restaurant had he taken Florence? La Jolie. The heat lights shone down on Jim's coatless shoulders in the cold, clear January air.

Indifferent to the cold, Jim walked down the steps out from under the red lights of the Plaza marquee. Without any purpose of which he was aware, he walked across the sidewalk and across the street toward the frozen fountain and on beyond slowly toward Fifth Avenue. "When will they ever learn?"—Marlene Dietrich had sung those words in St. Moritz at the Hotel Palace on New Year's Eve six years ago, as he sat beside a smiling Linda who appreciated the show.

"When will they ever learn?" Hadn't she been very interested in the young Swiss-German ski instructor? As he lay with broken ankle on the veranda and stared at white wedding-cake mountains in the Alpine air, where was beautiful Linda? Where have you gone, darling, what strange thing do you do? St. Moritz, with rime on the windows of the Zurich train and squeaky snow under foot—*everyone* goes to the Palace in St. Moritz on New Year's Eve, it was an honor to get in there and very difficult, black tie, elegant, a thing so old-fashioned it was "in," or at least it was six years ago.

And so was Otto "in," poor Otto whose sad little embarrassed smile the next day told the whole story of Linda's long afternoon. Jim had wanted to hobble off on his crutches into the white wedding-cake mountains and die. It was probably the horrible and haunting memory of that boy's pained smile that made him finally decide *anything* was better than total deception. Otto was a harmless young boy who wouldn't even crush an edelweiss with his skillful skis—no, not even a woolly-leaved edelweiss, much less the lovely wife of the rich American who smiled in misery and gave him a big tip for being kind to her. "She's learned a lot, Otto, she skis much better."

But they weren't all harmless, some would hurt her, cause her unhappiness, threaten and endanger her. He'd finally decided it was better to know. And better on his own account too. If he had some "control," the pain was not so awful. Besides, had not a great liberating revolution occurred in the area of morality? His wife did not love him and wanted pretty boys in her arms, but wasn't he in favor of a single standard? Thus webs are woven, not out of whole cloth but out of half-truth. Let women be free, let men be free, but a man with a broken ankle on a hard-earned vacation wants his wife by his side and not off in the arms of a handsome boy.

But *La Jolie* was too fragile a flower to resist either innocent or cruel skis. She could not see in clear Alpine air a broken ankle, much less the pain and humiliation of a man who loved her. *La Jolie*—very pretty, very lovely, very beautiful, but blind as edelweiss and not too dependable a comfort to the broken ankles that occur along life's rocky road. The most painful thing was his memory of the night that followed her afternoon with the boy.

Yes, the night was the most painful thing. Her infidelities—if he did not "know" of them and she did not have to feel guilty about them—always aroused her; it seemed to give her a wicked thrill to come home and make love to him, after having just been unfaithful to him. On that night, the broken ankle was a problem. He was in pain, a cast was on his leg. "I'll get on you," said Linda. "You won't have to move." The enforced passivity seemed to add an extra horror. He had lain there on the bed in the Palace and watched Linda sit upon him as if she were riding a horse in the park. Helpless, he had watched and felt her grind her body down upon him for half an hour, her teeth clenched and her eyes narrowed in a sensual delight. Although Linda ordinarily was refined and ladylike in her language, she could turn the air blue in moments of passion. "Oh, I *love* to fuck!" she said. "I'm going to come. I'm going to—Jim, I'm coming! Right *now!* I'm coming! Oh, I'm coming, I'm coming!" Later, an arm tenderly around him, she said: "That can be a great way to do it sometimes. I came beautifully." Had she, Jim wondered, said the same thing to the boy that afternoon? Probably, or something like it.

Jim hesitated at the corner of Fifth Avenue and Fifty-eighth Street, then, for no reason of which he was aware, turned to the right and walked toward Fifty-seventh Street. Oblivious of the cold, he walked on down Fifth Avenue. He paused for a moment at the Doubleday bookstore beyond Fifty-seventh Street, almost went into it, then walked on. People glanced at him with an uninterested doubtfulness, as if to say, "Fool without coat." Jim did not feel the January cold; the frost inside him was much greater.

When he reached Rockefeller Center, Jim walked over to the skating rink and stood watching the skaters, in particular a young blonde girl who skated very well and reminded him of a seventeen-year-old Linda. Not quite so beautiful as Linda, but pretty. She reminded him more of the girl on the plane than she did of Linda. Was it the little blonde on the plane who'd made the odd and "wrong" remark that kept nagging in the back of his mind? Maybe. He had certainly been very foolish in his reaction to the girl.

Very foolish indeed, thought Jim. He smiled as he stared at the blonde skater. Debbie in another five years would be like that, with a little round cute behind and pretty breasts. The girl on the plane was dead right to give him a cold shoulder. If the cup of truth be drunk, he might as well admit he *had* wanted to take that girl out and had hinted at a dinner invitation. He'd been afraid neither Florence nor Linda would see him and afraid if they did he would get nowhere with them.

It had turned out exactly that way, his fears on the plane were not without basis. And his flirtation with the pretty little girl in the seat beside him was not wholly innocent, even though he had felt human and friendly toward her; she was such a sweet little thing with her child-beautiful smile, her soft voice, tiny feminine hands folded in her lap, little hanging girl breasts in her bra beneath the chic dress—he *loved* her, he really did, and he wouldn't hurt her, he'd be tender and kind to her, the little darling. But not wholly innocent. He'd decided to impress her, make witty remarks, bedazzle her and invite her out to dinner; with his far superior intelligence and force and knowledge of the world he would overwhelm her, then take her by her sweet little hand up the elevator in the Plaza, remove her chic clothes, and make love to her pretty body with an almost religious devotion, even as the misguided children of Israel had worshiped a golden calf.

"When the hell *will* they ever learn?" whispered Jim aloud to himself in the icy air as he watched the girl skater. When will they learn? —not Linda, not *La Jolie*, but those like himself who planted, nurtured, and perpetuated such hothouse flowers. He was as much to blame as Linda. Easily so. His marriage to her, in reality, was a Goblin crime, just as his flirtation with the little blonde on the plane was an attempted Goblin trick.

The terrible truth began to creep upon Jim Kittering. There was more Hob in him than he'd ever dreamed. Was there any difference at all between Hob and himself? Maybe in degree, but was there a difference in kind? Fundamentally, for all practical purposes, down in the marrow of the bone, there was not; a Goblin was in him.

The horror of his reflections was so overwhelming Jim could not stand on his feet any longer and had to turn from the little blonde skater and hobble to a cold bench and sit down. Empty, gray, stricken, he sat bowed and stared into the dreadful pit of his own soul. It was true. A Goblin was in him and that had been the source of Hob's real power over him and the source of Linda's power too.

Of course Hob was a diabolically clever man, far cleverer than he had seemed the other day; the man had deceived and dominated hundreds of people, and he would deceive and dominate many more before he was through. And Linda was even more brilliantly deceptive than Hob. He had not fooled himself about her without inspired assistance. She was a masterly liar, the best he had ever encountered in his lifetime. Again and again she had looked him in the eye with an expression of perfect honesty and given him plausible and reasonable explanations that would have convinced almost anyone she could not possibly be lying. She was a great actress and could play any part and deliver her lines with a superlative conviction that went far beyond mere mendacity—in fact, it *wasn't* mere mendacity; an echo person, especially a brilliant one, *believed* in the echo. She'd thought she was the "Linda" of his imagination; she hadn't liked it, it had interfered with her fun something awful, but she'd thought she was that person and in a sense she had *been* that person, until he had freed her and allowed her to become the echo person of Billy McCade.

But he had known. Neither Hob nor Linda really had fooled him; he had known what they were and gone on being a slave to them both because he himself was no better. He wanted to take the little girl on the plane up to his suite in the Plaza and play with her pretty breasts and use her body for his pleasure. How was this different from Linda and Otto in St. Moritz? Hob wanted power, sure, but so did he—hadn't he married Linda in part for her money? Of course he had, Walter McCade was not all wrong. What right did he have to condemn power, power, power, when the basic decisions of his own life had been determined by it? There wasn't the slightest bit of doubt about it—a Goblin was in him.

Enough of illusions, enough of this business of thinking he was "a nice guy." He was not a nice guy, he was a Goblin and perhaps those fifty-two cards of the weeks of his year *did* contain a suicidal combination. Why live, how *could* he live with such terrible knowledge of himself? Why not go *now* to the Brooklyn Bridge and rid himself of his burden and spare decent people the horror of a Goblin among them? Or better yet, why not go into a subway and hurl himself with unmitigated violence beneath the wheels of a train, why not destroy the monster the way he should be destroyed, why not reduce him to a bundle of blood, guts, and bone?

Jim Kittering believed he had experienced real fear on previous occasions in his lifetime, but the terror he felt on that cold bench was infinitely beyond any fear he had ever known. He was so frightened he felt his heart would stop beating, that he would literally die. On an impulse, with the thought of saving himself from death on the bench, he stood up on shaking legs and walked back to the wall and looked down at the skating rink.

Where was the little blonde skater? Jim looked all over the rink. The girl was gone—no, there she was, hands on hips at the edge of the rink talking to an older woman who perhaps was her mother. The woman had freckles and a cigarette in her mouth and reminded him vaguely of Florence. "Oh, God," he whispered aloud.

He had not thought it was possible to suffer worse, but now pain was added to his fear. *Florence.* This had been his greatest mistake, the most terrible error he had ever made in his life or ever would make. What an absolute and total fool he had been to sit there in that restaurant and let her go away and marry another man. And it was his own Goblin letter to her that had precipitated it. Of course he'd intended to make her his mistress and she would have been a "half-assed" mistress too.

Florence was dead right and she'd run from him for her life. She saw the Goblin in him very clearly. Who could blame her for running from a man who could think of using her in such a way? There was no question of what he'd intended to do, it was obvious. He'd meant to coax her into writing television shows for him just as Hob had tried to coax him into producing such shows; the only difference was that Hob had offered money and he had offered a little bit of sex to a lonely woman.

Well, Florence had had the perception to see through his Goblin plan and thank God for that. A little bit of sex, a bone to a dog—yes, a "dog." But he hadn't really offered her as much as that. She was not "pretty" enough for him, she was homely and unattractive, there was a "vulgar and coarse" streak in her, it embarrassed him to sit beside her in a fashionable restaurant.

What an absolute and utter fool. The Goblin in him was not only vicious but stupid beyond measure. The tragic thing was that he loved Florence, really loved her, and he'd let her go. Worse, he had driven her into the arms of another man. The letter he had written her had frightened her; she loved him and was tempted to accept his Goblin deal, and for this reason she had rushed, as she said, into marrying another man. If he had not sent that Goblin letter he would not have lost Florence.

The irony, the dreadful and unbearable irony, was that he had held in his hand a treasure greater than anything Sir Henry Morgan had ever known and he'd let it go. His love for Florence and her love for him were worth more than all the gold in Panama, and he'd let it go. She would have been an ideal and perfect wife for him. Her wit, her sensitivity, her honesty, her love—what a contrast she was to Linda!

Could two women be more different? Linda's beauty was all on the outside, Florence's beauty was in her heart and soul.

In this moment, in the realization of his loss, Jim Kittering died, something in him gave up the ghost and died.

Jim took one last look at the little blonde skater and the freckled woman with the cigarette, then turned and walked like an old man back toward Fifth Avenue. He would not kill himself under a subway train, he was dead already. It was too agonizing to think of Florence, he would think of something else. What had that little girl said to him on the plane that had stuck in his mind? He couldn't remember, something about "beautiful" or "beautifully," something that started him thinking of *La Jolie*. But how could that be "wrong," as Linda's new mink coat was wrong? Jim stopped and racked his brain to recall what it was, then for no reason of which he was aware turned and walked to the right, a little farther down Fifth Avenue.

On Jim went through the cold until his feet took him to Brentano's bookstore. He had paused outside the Doubleday shop but that pause had been a bit premature; now he walked inside. Hands clasped behind him, he strolled down the aisle looking at the various books. He looked at the reproductions of ancient and modern statues—Brentano's sold all kinds of things these days—and glanced idly at the stairs to the paperbound section in the basement below.

The statues were kind of nice. He'd bought a couple of blue Chinese fu dogs at Brentano's once, but of course the fu dogs were gone. All his personal possessions, Linda had said, were gone. She had probably given his suits to the Salvation Army. And his books, too. He'd had quite a few books, among them Florence's little book. It was a pity to lose Florence's little book; it was out of print in hard cover. But of course it had been reprinted in paperbound.

Hands clasped behind him, Jim walked down the stairs into the paperbound department. He strolled to the shelves where the fiction was kept, looked on the shelf marked "C," moved a folding metal chair to one side, and found it—*The Dragon Dies*, by Florence Carr. Jim's hands began to tremble as he looked at the tiny picture of Florence on the back and read the brief biographical statement concerning her.

"*. . . war child born shortly after Hitler's boots marched in the Sudetenland.*"

What was this? If Florence had been born *after* Hitler invaded the

Sudetenland, then she was *not* thirty-nine. And this could be no mistake, it was no misprint of a date. The thing said plainly, "*born shortly after.*" Florence was not thirty-nine, she was twenty-nine. For some neurotic reason she'd added ten years to her age.

A stabbing pain struck Jim's heart. Florence at thirty-nine would be well worth having, but at twenty-nine she was a young woman. She could have not just one child, but two, three, or four. And he'd known it all the time; the same statement had been on the jacket of the hard-cover edition. He'd looked at her in the light of the kerosene lantern in Morgan's Second Treasure Cave and seen plainly that she had the body of a girl. Why had he accepted her fib as the truth when he knew better? Could it be he had not wanted to regard her as a young woman who would make him an ideal wife? Yes. It was also for this reason he had pretended at first to believe in her Lesbianism, when he knew perfectly well she was not a Lesbian at all. Was there no limit to the lie after lie he had told himself?

Jim's knees became so weak with dismay he had to sit down on the metal folding chair. Tears once again welled in his eyes. What a boundless fool he had been! Twenty-nine years old, a young woman; a real second chance had been given to him and he had thrown it away. Jim took out a handkerchief and wiped his eyes; luckily there were not many people in the big paperbound department to witness his despair, and the clerks could not see him over the tops of the shelves.

It was too painful, too painful and unbearable even to think about Florence . . . but he did want to take a look at certain passages in her book, especially a passage dealing with a Dragon the lonely girl on Cape Cod had thought was in her. The Dragon of the girl reminded him a bit of his own Goblin. He remembered being very moved by that passage when he'd read it before. It was at the very end of the book, an excerpt from the girl's diary or journal, a thing she wrote when she came back from the Cape after her unhappy experience there.

Jim opened the thin little paperbound book and thumbed through it. He found a passage describing a walk the girl took on the Cape. This was the scene in which she realized she loved Pedro, the ugly Portuguese fisherman with whom she'd had a number of rather weird and far-out conversations. The fisherman seemed to be a satanic figure of some kind, frightening and dangerous, but there were several odd little scenes that contradicted such an interpretation; he was very kind to a child and to an injured animal, and very kind in a casual way to the lonely girl herself.

Jim took his reading glasses from his breast pocket and skimmed through the scene. Yes, this was the scene where the girl decided her fears of the fisherman had no basis in reality and that she loved him.

". . . it had to be the end of her imprisonment. What did it matter if he returned her love or not, what difference did it make if he did not even know of her existence? Love at last had bloomed in her Dragon heart, she would not die alone. It was the thing she had feared the most, to fall into eternity all alone. But this would not happen because she no longer lived alone, love for another human being, love for a man had bloomed in her Dragon heart."

Jim closed the book, keeping his place with his finger. Live alone, die alone. These were his reflections in Bonaventure Cemetery, but they had not been original with him. It was soon after these reflections that he had gone to the *Lorna Loone* and "recognized" Melody as Hera, queen of heaven. Had love been born in his Goblin heart? Was that what had happened? If so, the inspiration had come from Florence.

The book seemed to have had more influence upon him than he'd realized. Was there more? Jim opened the book again and turned the pages. There was another passage a little later where the girl was alone in her rented bedroom on the Cape. She had come in after her walk among the dunes and taken off her clothes and looked at her thin body in the mirror and cried. Love had bloomed in her heart but how could any man ever want her? She had imagined herself to be not plain half-Irish Mary with freckles but *Maria. . . .*

". . . an olive-skinned, lovely South American aristocrat with ruby lips and dark flashing eyes, an elegant and beautiful creature of the kind men want and love, Maria, beautiful Maria with pale olive breasts and slender golden thighs."

It was fantastic, incredible. Jim sat erect in the chair as goose flesh appeared all over him. He himself had once imagined an olive-skinned, beautiful *Maria,* he had dreamed she would be aboard the *Lorna Loone.* Florence had also provided the inspiration for his *déjà vu* illusion. From where else had "Maria Concepción" come?

Jim sat lost in thought. Florence's little book had obviously made an impression on him. It was true he'd called her five times after reading it; he had called her again and again and had used all his persuasive powers to talk her into coming down to the office. She had told him she didn't want to write for television, but he'd kept after her, begged her, implored her, told her funny stories, exerted every bit of so-called charm he had.

Yes, the book had made an impression on him. There was something touching about the unattractive girl dreaming she was beautiful. This had been moving to him, the loneliness and heartache of a girl who wanted so badly to love and be loved. Her love for the Portuguese fisherman was pathetic and the scene where she'd finally confessed her love had been so touching Jim had wept when he read it. The fisherman, who hardly knew of her existence, had smiled at her and gone back to his nets and the girl had stood there in tears, unable to move until he finally told her not to worry, to keep looking, she would find a boy friend someday.

But the girl on her final walk among the dunes had not thought so. The fisherman was wrong, she would never find herself a "boy friend," she was too ugly. *Maria* could find love, but not Mary. It was on this walk among the breast-shaped dunes that the girl wept over a dead sea gull and stared out at the slate-colored sea, which seemed to be a symbol for both life and death. It was also on this walk the imaginary "Maria" died.

Jim nodded slowly to himself. Florence's arty little book, as he had called it during the course of his Goblin proposition, had had an impact. The heartbreak of the girl had been affecting and so was the business about the Dragon she thought was in her. It was not clear exactly what the Dragon was—it seemed to be not so much a symbol of evil as of fear. When the girl became frightened, the Dragon would stir. But it was wicked, too, and blew smoke and did evil things.

Jim again opened the little book and read a passage of description of the Cape. The passage was both vivid and precise; he could see the sand of the dunes blowing in the wind, the pale blue sky, the ruffled gray feathers of the dead sea gull and its half-opened beak, the "dark iron shine" of the slate-colored sea. He himself had never particularly dug this type of fancy writing and he wondered why writers bothered with it, but Florence did it well.

Yes, she was a book writer just as she'd said and it was not surprising her books got good reviews. Of course they didn't sell and despite high praise quoted on the cover this particular book hadn't sold many copies. The book did present difficulties to the general reader. There wasn't much of a narrative, as Florence herself admitted; the story was rudimentary—an unattractive girl goes for a vacation to Cape Cod and suffers terribly from loneliness there; she wanders on the dunes in a kind of spiritual crisis, then falls madly in love with a fisherman whom she'd feared until then; she is rejected in a more or less kindly way by the fisherman and goes back to New York somehow encouraged by the experience.

That was perhaps the most interesting thing about the book, the conclusion of it, the fact that it ended on a hopeful note despite everything. Jim thumbed through the pages to the end and read the final words:

"Mary, however, plain Mary not Maria who had died on the Cape, was unafraid. The Dragon would live a little longer, but someday he would die. What did it matter if Pedro loved her or not? She had loved Pedro and had told him so. The Dragon had almost died then and there; she had inflicted upon the beast a mortal injury. Mary was not afraid any more. As she wrote in a journal she occasionally kept:

" 'The Dragon and I are back again trapped in my little dark and gloomy apartment. But I am not afraid, it has a garden outside and all the ugliness of the city cannot conquer my little garden. The Dragon fears it. I put little flowers out there and they look so beautiful in the middle of the ugliness I could cry and often do. The town is grim and gray and a deformity of fair America, but it's possible to look beneath the surface of the drab and ugly city and find a little garden with flowers growing in the sooty air. Someday, someone will come and see my flowers. As my flowers grow, the Dragon sighs, the Dragon cries, the Dragon dies.' "

Jim slowly closed the book. He had found the little thing, he had remembered the remark someone recently had made to him that was "wrong," wrong in the way Linda's mink coat was wrong, wrong in a way that revealed hidden truth. How could Florence *possibly* write such a passage as that and tell him she "came beautifully" with Rufus in a Barnstable motel?

Goose flesh again appeared all over Jim Kittering and he sat forward so suddenly on the chair he almost fell off in the aisle of the fiction section of Brentano's paperbound department. Florence was lying, she had never been in a Wild Turkey Inn with Rufus.

Jim looked down at the little book in his hands. There could be no doubt of it. He had found the "wrong" thing someone had said to him recently. It was not Hob who'd said it and it was not the little girl on the plane, it was Florence. Florence was vulgar, yes, but she was not nasty—and "came beautifully" was nasty. Of course she'd amended it later toward the end of lunch, she'd "confessed" the sex with Rufus hadn't been all that great; but this could be merely a shrewd awareness she'd made a little error in her design of her emotional Rube Goldberg machine—she'd gone back and tightened a loose bolt and squirted a little oil to make it run better, that was all.

"Came beautifully." If Florence had really been to bed with Rufus, she could no more say such a thing than she could grow wings and fly to heaven. Linda, yes. It was Linda's remark in Switzerland and he'd had it right there but he couldn't connect it with Florence, perhaps because the remark had distressed him so. There was no doubt of it. Linda was not vulgar and coarse, but she was nasty. Florence *was* vulgar and coarse, but she was *not* nasty.

Jim groaned aloud as he remembered the diamond ring. Rufus was real after all and he and Florence were on a plane to Nassau at this moment. And the ring wasn't all. She'd been packing her books and clothes. And the details, the many details—the sister in Hyannis, Rufus' boy who had exams and couldn't get out of school. How could she make all of that up? And why? For what motive?

Well, the motive was imaginable. Florence loved him but she had believed he was going back to Linda and that she herself could never be anything but a half-assed mistress to him. Florence also knew that in his Goblin way he loved her, he would keep after her, tempt her, torment her, until finally she would give up. This was what she feared. She probably also had some notion in her head of "doing the best thing" for him, of "giving him up," of freeing him of "guilt"—she'd said something like that. Romantic soul that she was, she undoubtedly had felt she was doing a brave thing by letting him go back free to Linda. If he was right, she *had* done a brave thing. And out of love for him.

A motive could be found. But the *ring*—what about that fifty-thousand-dollar ring, where could Florence put her freckled hands on such a ring? She might invent all the numerous convincing details of the wedding to Rufus—after all, Florence was a writer and lived by her imagination. But that ring, that expensive diamond ring. Or *was* it an expensive diamond ring? She had not been wearing it and she had not given him a good look at it either. The light in La Jolie was dim.

She'd taken the ring out and showed it to him briefly, then put it right back in her purse. The little nut had gone out and bought a phony ring just to fool him! She'd also packed five cartons of books and put half her clothes in a trunk for the same purpose!

Jim jumped to his feet, hurried down the aisle, threw a couple of dollars down on the counter for the book, and ran up the stairs. As he walked rapidly past the reproductions of the statues, he looked in the paperbound book and found the name of the publisher who'd brought out Florence's novel in hard cover. It was a well-known publishing house located up Madison Avenue a few blocks away.

Five minutes later, Jim half walked and half ran through the courtyard of the huge old mansion where Florence's publisher had offices. He hurried to the heavy glass front door, opened it, went inside, and walked over to a receptionist seated at a desk.

"Excuse me," said Jim. "I'd like to see Mr. Rufus Turnbull, please."

"Do you have an appointment?" asked the girl.

"No, but it's urgent. My name is James Kittering."

"Just a moment," said the girl. In terrible anxiety, Jim waited as the girl plugged in a switchboard. He could not believe he was wrong, but it was so fantastic he could not believe he was right either. "Mr. James Kittering to see Mr. Turnbull." A pause. Jim could not breathe. The girl looked around at him. "I'm sorry, Mr. Turnbull isn't here, he's in Hyannis."

"Thank you," said Jim. Demolished, he moved slowly toward the heavy glass door. It had been a Rube Goldberg machine of his own. Men, too, sometimes invented them. But how could Florence have said that nasty thing? She hadn't! She'd said it, but it wasn't true! She'd never been in that Turkey place with Rufus and she hadn't married him either! Jim looked back at the receptionist. "Tell me, do you *know* Mr. Turnbull?"

"Of course, sir, I see him every day."

"This is going to sound a little crazy, but is he a man of forty-three who looks about thirty-five, with no gray in his hair? Could he be singles tennis champion of Hyannis? I mean, how *old* is he?"

The receptionist answered: "Well, I don't know Mr. Turnbull's age, but I'd say he's around seventy-five."

Despite a real effort to control himself, tears of joy came into Jim's eyes. "Honey," he said, "you've just saved my life."

Ten minutes later Jim pressed the bell under CARR in the foyer of

Florence's apartment building. No answer. He waited thirty seconds and pressed the bell again. Finally, ten seconds later, Florence's voice came over the little speaker behind the brass grill.

"Yes, who is it?"

Jim thought rapidly. She might refuse to push the buzzer that would release the lock on the front door. He put a hand over his mouth and said: "Telegram."

The door buzzed and Jim pushed the front door open and went down the dark hall. The door to Florence's apartment was shut. He pressed the button and heard a ding-dong inside, then Florence's voice:

"Slip it under the door."

A problem. Jim again put his hand over his mouth and said: "Collect."

"Oh, hell." Jim heard a rattle of the safety chain on the door, the click of a bolt, then the door opened and Florence stood before him in a white bathrobe with a white lather of shampoo in her hair. For about three seconds she did not move but stood there and stared at him. Then two things happened in rapid succession: first, her mouth opened in horror and the hands that held the white bathrobe together fell limply at her sides and Jim caught a glimpse of her naked body; second, with a gasp she raised her hands and lunged forward against the door in an effort to shut it in his face. Jim just managed to prevent her from shutting the door; he stopped it at about the last inch and managed then by exerting his strength to push it half open despite her frantic effort to prevent him from doing so.

"Florence, wait a minute! I want to talk to you!"

"Go away! Go away, Jim! Please!"

"But wait a second . . . come on now, don't be silly, I want to speak to you."

Florence was not strong and Jim pushed the door on open and stepped inside, at which point she gave up, dropped her head, and began to cry. The white bathrobe hung open, he could see her navel and pubic hair.

"Oh, God . . . oh, God," she said. "Jim, why have you come?"

"Because I want to see you. Now here, tie up your bathrobe, honey, and don't cry. Everything's all right."

Florence allowed him to tie the cord around her waist, then rubbed her eyes with her sleeve. "Jesus Christ in heaven," she said wearily. "I never could fool you. Never. You're always ahead of me and I tried so hard this time. But it's hopeless, just hopeless, that's all."

"It's not as hopeless as you think," said Jim, "and you fooled me pretty good."

"Did I," said Florence gloomily.

"Believe me, honey, if I didn't love you, I never would have figured it out."

Florence gave a little discouraged shrug. "Well, I was in the middle of a shower and shampoo when this . . . godawful telegram arrived. I've got to wash the shampoo out of my hair, it'll take me a minute. Fix yourself a drink if you want one, there's Scotch in the kitchenette."

Jim poured himself a Scotch on ice cubes, then sat in one of the overstuffed chairs and looked around the apartment while Florence finished her shower. It was not an apartment in which Linda would feel at home, but it was not as bad as he'd thought. The various prints on the walls were in good taste and the many books gave the room warmth, a feeling of love for and respect for things of the spirit. The overstuffed furniture was very comfortable and the cages of canaries and parakeets were a cheerful note. The "birdies" made a rather pleasant little twittering sound. And Jim could well imagine that the little garden, although rather drab now in the winter, would be appealing in the summertime with pots of flowers. The apartment was certainly more than adequate for the time being. They'd need a larger place, but Florence's apartment would be fine until they could get a bigger one.

After about five minutes she returned, the bathrobe tied around her, a towel on her head and her eyes pink from weeping. She sat down on the sofa across from Jim and said:

"I tried but the cat's out of the bag. I love you too much to say no, Jim. You can do whatever you want with me."

Jim stared thoughtfully at her. "You're a real nut," he said. "Where'd you get the ring?"

"Place on Forty-second Street," said Florence. "Thirty bucks down the drain."

"A real nut. But not as big a nut as *me*. Do you want to hear the story of my life?"

"Sure."

"I married a bitch. That's the story of my life, Florence."

"What?"

"I married a bitch. Not a bitch in a vicious way exactly, but a bitch."

Florence's arms were hugged around her and she had a look of disbelief on her face. "Are you talking about Linda?"

"I sure am."

"You saw her?"

"Yes, I had lunch with her today."

"And you aren't going back to her? You don't want her?"

"She doesn't want *me*," said Jim. "And I'll have to admit, I don't want her either."

Florence seemed more disappointed than anything else. "What about the children?"

"I'll have to fight her for the children. It'll be ugly and difficult but I'll get them. She doesn't really want them."

"I never expected this," said Florence. "You loved her, I don't understand it. What happened?"

"It's a long story," said Jim, "and I'll tell it to you sometime. At the moment, do you know who I'm thinking of? Can you guess? By the way, do you want a drink?"

"Oh, I don't believe so, it's too early. Who're you thinking of?"

"Melody," said Jim. "I really can't quite understand how Melody got into all of this."

"I don't know exactly what you mean," said Florence.

"I'm talking about our love affair. It's funny how Melody wandered into it in that pale gray dress of hers. I think she was an accident, but also a kind of catalyst for us both. You were tied in awful knots and so was I. The weird thing is I thought of her as Hera, queen of heaven, the goddess of women and marriage. That's exactly what she proved to be and I wonder if it could have happened without her."

"You mean . . . our sleeping together? Well, I don't know. But as I told you at lunch the other day, I'll always love her."

"So will I," said Jim. "Not the way I do you, but I'll always love Melody."

"Huh," said Florence, a hand on her chin. "Maybe I don't understand what you're saying. You think you love me more than Melody?"

"Comparisons are odious," answered Jim, "but yes—I love you more. And I'll tell you something else. You're a bigger liar than Melody. Florence, why did you tell that silly lie about being thirty-nine when you're really twenty-nine?"

Florence smiled. "How'd you find that out?"

"Never mind. Why'd you tell that fib?"

"Oh, I guess to try to make you feel sorry for me, being thirty-nine and never having had a man. Or to make you think I'm ugly because I'm old, something like that. When you asked me if I was a Lesbian, I just had an impulse and added ten years."

Jim smiled and slowly shook his head. "You're a nut. But it's great news, honey. We can have a real family now."

Florence stared emptily at him. "A what?"

"We can have three or four children—and one of them is almost bound to be a boy. I've always wanted a son . . . and a son of yours, he'd be something."

The blood drained from Florence's face and her freckles once again looked like measles and chicken pox combined. "What do you mean?" she asked. "What are you talking about? Do you mean . . . you want to marry me?"

"Of course I want to marry you," said Jim.

"But I . . . I'm not the kind of woman. Jim, you don't *want* me, I'm buck-toothed . . . you don't want me."

"Listen, if it bothers you," said Jim, "a dentist can cap your teeth, that's no problem. And I'll help you get some attractive clothes, we'll take you to a good hairdresser. You'll be a handsome woman, honey, when I get through with you, but that doesn't matter. It's you I love, not the way you look."

Florence stared at him for several seconds, then said: "I think I *will* have that drink."

Jim smiled, amused by her dry tone. "I'll make it a good stiff one."

"Yes, you'd better," said Florence. "It isn't every day my dreams come true."

Jim put ice cubes in a glass and poured Scotch on them. Her self-control was admirable, there was real character in Florence—or, as Al Ingerman might say, "the girl's got class." However, when Jim handed her her drink, Florence lost her self-control for a little while. Her lip began to tremble, the glass fell unheeded from her hand, and she put her head on his shoulder and began to cry. Jim put his arms around her slender, girlish body and lost his own self-control for a while. As life-sustaining tears came from them both, a Goblin expired and a Dragon died.

So ends a seashell tale.

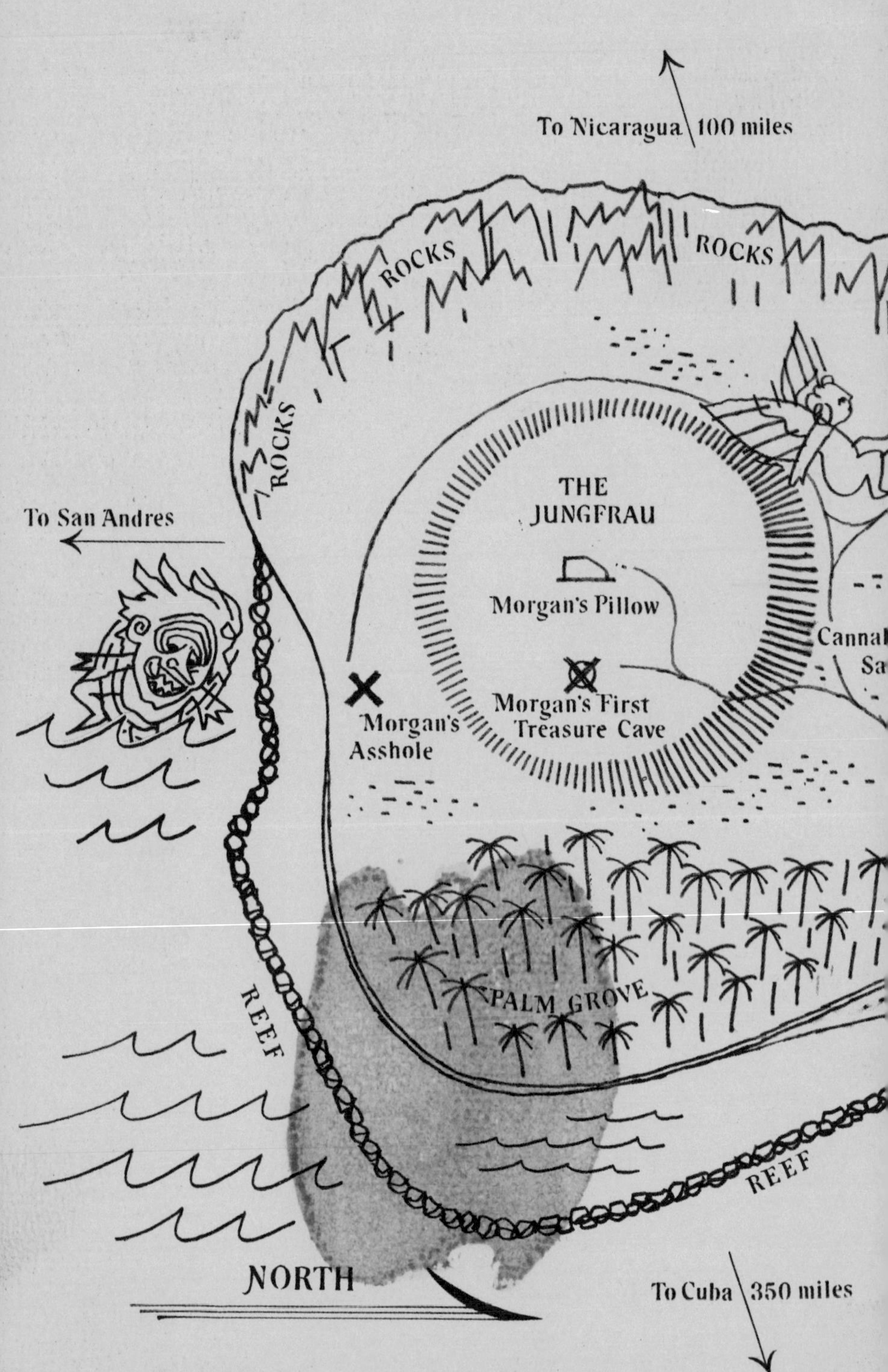
To Nicaragua 100 miles
ROCKS
ROCKS
ROCKS
THE
JUNGFRAU
Morgan's Pillow
Morgan's First
Treasure Cave
Morgan's
Asshole
To San Andres
Canna
Sa
PALM GROVE
REEF
REEF
NORTH
To Cuba 350 miles